The Wonder Book of Stories and Poems

The Wonder Book of Stories and Poems

A Treasury of Poetry and Prose for Young Readers
Edited by Eric Duthie

Hamlyn
London · New York · Sydney · Toronto

Advisory Editors:

J. A. Lauwerys D.Lit., D.Sc., F.R.I.C.

Jack Longland M.A.

J. R. Peddie C.B.E., M.A., D.Litt., LL.D.,
    F.R.S.E., F.E.I.S.

Andrew Scotland M.A., Ph.D.

Mary Stocks B.Sc. (Econ), LL.D., Litt.D.

R. R. Tomlinson O.B.E., A.R.C.A., R.B.A.,
    P.R.D.S.

The selections reprinted in this anthology, which
was first published in 1961 as Book Seven of
The Modern Children's Library of Knowledge, are
used by permission of and special arrangement with
the proprietors of their respective copyrights.

This revised edition first published 1977 by
The Hamlyn Publishing Group Limited
London · New York · Sydney · Toronto
Astronaut House, Feltham, Middlesex, England
© Copyright Waverley Educational Limited 1964
© Copyright new illustrations in this edition
The Hamlyn Publishing Group Limited 1977.
Reprinted 1978

ISBN 0 600 31938 5

Printed and bound in Great Britain

Introduction

Stories, of course, give us pleasure. They are read for enjoyment and while we read them, we enter into other people's lives and learn about the thoughts and feelings and adventures of people who are often very different from ourselves. Sometimes we read about people who lived in a different century from our own – often, too, in a different country. In this way reading can help to make us wiser about other human beings and tell us about places, times and circumstances that we have never experienced ourselves.

The Wonder Book of Stories and Poems is a splendid introduction to the work of writers, artists and poets who have held the imagination of generations of young readers. The extracts which comprise this anthology have been chosen with great care and show why these authors are held in such high regard. The illustrators, too, have been chosen from among the best artists that are working today. We have also retained some of the original illustrations that were used when the books were first published, so that young readers can recognise and appreciate the work of some of the greatest illustrators of children's books.

At the beginning of each story you will find a short introductory note which tells you about the author and the book from which the extract is taken. There is much information in these notes that will interest you and add to your general knowledge.

Contents

page

11 **A House for Eeyore**
A. A. Milne
Illustrated by Ernest Shepard

17 **The Elves and the Shoemaker**
The Brothers Grimm
Illustrated by John Patience

18 **The Cow**
Robert Louis Stevenson

19 **The Prominent Man**
Laura Richards
Illustrated by James Hunt

20 **A Stormy Day**
Anna Sewell
Illustrated by Victor G. Ambrus

22 **Four Ducks on a Pond**
William Allingham

23 **Peter Pan meets Wendy**
Re-told by Daniel O'Connor
from the play by J. M. Barrie
Illustrated by Shirley Tourret

25 **How the Trolls became Giants**
J. B. Morton
Illustrated by John Patience

28 **Written in March**
William Wordsworth

29 **But that's not the end of the Story**
Margaret Baker
Illustrated by Mary Baker

34 **Sea-Fever**
John Masefield

35 **The Ogre Courting**
Juliana Horatia Ewing
Illustrated by John Patience

39 **Cradle Song at Bethlehem**
E. J. Falconer

39 **Carol**
Author unknown

40 **Becky's Christmas**
Louisa May Alcott
*Illustrated by Brenda Seymour
and Victor G. Ambrus*

44 **The Rarest Animal of All**
Hugh Lofting
Illustrated by the Author

47 **The Tiger**
William Blake

48 **The Great Bullfight**
Hugh Lofting
Illustrated by the Author

54 **Boy on a Horse**
R. D. Blackmore
Illustrated by T. S. La-Fontaine

57 **A Mad Tea-Party**
Lewis Carroll
*Illustrated by Charles Mortimer
and John Patience*

63 **Into the Unknown**
Mary Norton
Illustrated by Shirley Tourret

67 **A Narrow Escape**
Felix Salten
*Illustrated by Kurt Wiese
and Val Biro*

70 **The Year**
Coventry Patmore

71 **My First Gun**
Will James
Illustrated by Shirley Hughes

75 **Erich plays Detective**
Erich Kästner
Illustrated by Horst Lemke

78 **Washing Day**
Theodora Roscoe

79 **The Emperor's New Clothes**
Hans Andersen
Illustrated by Rex Whistler

83 **I Stood Tiptoe upon a Little Hill**
John Keats

84 **The Pied Piper of Hamelin**
Robert Browning
*Illustrated by Ru Van Rossem and
John Speirs*

90 **Thomas dines in France**
Enid Bagnold
Illustrated by Richard Kennedy

96 **Sharing the Secret Garden**
Frances Hodgson Burnett
Illustrated by Shirley Hughes

101 **The Autumn Robin**
John Clare

102 **The Birth of Pinocchio**
Carlo Collodi
Illustrated by Val Biro

105 **Dick Whittington**
Author unknown
Illustrated by Arthur Rackham and
John Speirs

111 **Death of My Aunt**
Author unknown

112 **The Storming of Toad Hall**
Kenneth Grahame
Illustrated by Ernest Shepard and Val Biro

118 **Forefathers**
Edmund Blunden

118 **Written in a Country Churchyard**
Thomas Gray

119 **Susan goes to School**
Alison Uttley
Illustrated by Brenda Seymour

124 **Child of Nature**
William Wordsworth

125 **What the Old Man does is always Right**
Hans Andersen
Illustrated by Arthur Rackham

129 **Apple-Time**
Eleanor Farjeon

130 **Robin Hood and the Potter**
Rosemary Sutcliff
Illustrated by Robert Geary and
John Berry

137 **The Deliverers of their Country**
E. Nesbit
Illustrated by Ronald Searle

147 **The Story of Daedalus and Icarus**
Thomas Bulfinch
Illustrated by William Reeves and
Victor G. Ambrus

148 **To The Cuckoo**
William Wordsworth

149 **The Parkhurst Paper Chase**
Talbot Baines Reed
Illustrated by Shirley Hughes

154 **Kangaroos**
Eric Linklater
Illustrated by Nicolas Bentley

158 **The Glass Peacock**
Eleanor Farjeon
Illustrated by Val Biro

163 **The Pool in the Forest**
"B. B."

167 **Salt: An Old Peter's Russian Tale**
Arthur Ransome
Illustrated by Robert Geary

177 **The Dark Child**
Richard Hughes
Illustrated by John Patience

180 **A Lesson in Tickling Trout**
Arthur Ransome
Illustrated by Shirley Hughes

184 **A Boy's Song**
James Hogg

186 **A Day with the Goats**
Johanna Spyri
Illustrated by Shirley Tourret

195 **The Englishman**
Walter de la Mare

196 **The Cat that walked by Himself**
Rudyard Kipling
Illustrated by the Author and Shirley Tourret

203 **When Cats run Home**
Alfred, Lord Tennyson

204 **Father William**
Lewis Carroll
Illustrated by Victor G. Ambrus

205 **My Encounter with Israel Hands**
Robert Louis Stevenson
Illustrated by Victor G. Ambrus

211 **The Mermaid of Zennor**
Eileen Molony
Illustrated by Ronald Reeves

215 **Little Trotty Wagtail**
John Clare

216 **The Man in the Sack**
Alexandre Dumas
Illustrated by Michael Jackson
and Mike Codd

page

222 **The Raider**
Grey Owl
Illustrated by Stuart Tresilian

228 **The Story of Cholmondely**
Gerald Durrell
*Illustrated by Ralph Thompson
and Val Biro*

232 **O For a Booke**
Author unknown

233 **Dinner at the Inn**
Charles Dickens
Illustrated by "Phiz" and Will Nickless

237 **Mr. Nobody**
Author unknown

238 **"Seek 'em Out, Crusoe"**
R. M. Ballantyne
*Illustrated by Robert Geary
and John Berry*

243 **Bonnie George Campbell**
Author unknown

244 **Theseus and the Minotaur**
Re-told by Rex Warner
Illustrated by A. R. Whitear

247 **His First Flight**
Liam O'Flaherty
Illustrated by A. J. Joyce

249 **A Feather for My Cap**
Ivy O. Eastwick

250 **Lily Rose and the Green Silk Petticoat**
Eve Garnett
Illustrated by the Author

255 **Tom Paints the Fence**
Mark Twain
Illustrated by Victor G. Ambrus

259 **The Three Magic Gifts**
Re-told by Harcourt Williams
Illustrated by Biman Mullick

267 **Welcome back, Mary Poppins!**
P. L. Travers
*Illustrated by Mary Shepard
and John Speirs*

273 **Don Quixote and the Windmills**
Miguel de Cervantes
Illustrated by Victor G. Ambrus

276 **The Castaway**
Daniel Defoe
*Illustrated by W. G. Morden
and Thomas Stothard*

284 **Thomas the Rhymer**
Author unknown

285 **The White Magicians**
Sir H. Rider Haggard
Illustrated by Robert Geary

290 **Under the Greenwood Tree**
William Shakespeare

291 **Jeremy at the Fair**
Hugh Walpole
Illustrated by Michael Jackson

295 **From a Railway Carriage**
Robert Louis Stevenson

296 **Fables from Aesop**
Translated by V. S. Vernon Jones
Illustrated by Arthur Rackham

300 **His Treasures**
Robert Herrick

301 **Exploring the Lost World**
Sir Arthur Conan Doyle
Illustrated by Michael Jackson and Mike Codd

307 **The Attack on the Stockade**
Captain Marryat
Illustrated by Robert Geary

315 **Poor Tom Bowling**
Charles Dibdin

316 **Lost in the Bushveld**
Sir Percy Fitzpatrick
Illustrated by Michael Jackson

319 **Lord Ullin's Daughter**
Thomas Campbell

321 **The Piebald Rat**
Eden Phillpotts
Illustrated by Robert Geary

329 **The Prize-giving**
Patricia Lynch
*Illustrated by Shirley Tourret
and Shirley Hughes*

334 **The Escape from the Mill**
Charles Reade
Illustrated by Robert Geary

338 **To Any Reader**
Robert Louis Stevenson

339 **The Lure of the Spanish Main**
Charles Kingsley
*Illustrated by Will Nickless
and John Berry*

344 **When All the World is Young**
Charles Kingsley

345 **Rip Van Winkle**
Washington Irving
*Illustrated by Robert Geary
and John Speirs*

350 **Tu-Whit! Tu-Who!**
William Shakespeare

351 **Skating at Night**
William Wordsworth

351 **A Song**
Percy Bysshe Shelley

352 **The Bargain**
Oliver Goldsmith
Illustrated by Trevor Parkin

355 **Lost in the Corridors of the Earth**
Jules Verne
*Illustrated by Michael Jackson
and Mike Codd*

359 **The Wonderful Tar Baby**
Joel Chandler Harris
Illustrated by Harry Rowntree

363 **The Rum Tum Tugger**
T. S. Eliot

364 **Heroes**
Aubrey de Selincourt
Illustrated by Trevor Parkin

370 **Poem**
Allan Cunningham

371 **Tom Brown at Rugby**
Thomas Hughes
Illustrated by Edmund J. Sullivan

376 **Exploring the Island**
Johann Wyss
Illustrated by Stuart Tresilian

381 **Morte d'Arthur**
Alfred, Lord Tennyson
*Illustrated by Robert Geary
and John Berry*

387 **Some Adventures of Gulliver**
Jonathan Swift
*Illustrated by Robin Jacques
and John Patience*

395 **The Great Pickwick Controversy**
Charles Dickens
Illustrated by Will Nickless

399 **The Solitude of Alexander Selkirk**
William Cowper

400 **Acknowledgements**

Colour Illustrations

*facing
page*

16 *"Now we're boys so fine and neat,
Why cobble more for others' feet?"*
Illustrated by John Patience

17 *"That was a very near touch," said my
master "What's to be done now?"*
Illustrated by Victor G. Ambrus

48 *The fire was burning splendidly, the kettle
simmering, and in a row upon the hearth
stood, not only Aunt Sally's old slippers,
but those of master and mistress also.*
Illustrated by Victor G. Ambrus

49 *"The Dormouse is asleep again," said
the Hatter, and he poured a little hot
tea upon its nose.*
Illustrated by John Patience

64 *"Here we are," Bambi heard the old stag saying.
He walked along the beech trunk and Bambi
walked beside him.*
Illustrated by Val Biro

65 *And nobody could enough admire
The tall man and his quaint attire.*
Illustrated by John Speirs

96 *"It's this," she said. "It's a secret
garden, and I'm the only one in the world
who wants it to be alive."*
Illustrated by Shirley Hughes

97 *"Turn again, Whittington,
Thrice Lord Mayor of London."*
Illustrated by John Speirs

112 *"Look here, Toady! Don't you chatter
so much as usual, or you'll be sent back, as sure
as fate!"*
Illustrated by Val Biro

113 *"Indeed, you're but a poor weapon," sighed
he. "But since there is no better to be had, I
must do the best I can with you."*
Illustrated by John Berry

144 *He fluttered with his arms, but no feathers remained
to hold the air.*
Illustrated by Victor G. Ambrus

145 *In another thirty seconds we are swinging
along at a good pace down the slope of
the warren, in the direction of Colvin meadows,
and the hunt has begun.*
Illustrated by Shirley Hughes

160 *It was quite a little tree, but
such a radiant little tree!*
Illustrated by Val Biro

161 *The other two, who could look over the
parapet without having to lie on the top of
it, stood on each side of Jacky, watching
the water flowing away from under the
arch.*
Illustrated by Shirley Hughes

192 *"Oh, see, see!" cried Heidi in great excitement;
"all the mountains are turning rosy-red! Look
at the one with the snow, and that one with
the high, pointed cliffs!"*
Illustrated by Shirley Tourret

193 *"And yet you incessantly stand on your head –
Do you think, at your age, it is right?"*
Illustrated by Victor G. Ambrus

208 *"One more step, Mr. Hands," said I,
"and I'll blow your brains out!"*
Illustrated by Victor G. Ambrus

209 *Behind him, blacker than the sea, blacker
than the sky, rose like a phantom a giant
of granite, whose projecting crags seemed
like arms extended to seize their prey.*
Illustrated by Mike Codd

240 *Cholmondely had picked up another
stone and was swinging it backwards and forwards
like a professional cricketer, taking better aim.*
Illustrated by Val Biro

241 *"Joe Blunt!" exclaimed Dick in a voice of intense
amazement, while Crusoe snuffed round the
heap of leaves and whined with excitement.*
Illustrated by John Berry

256 *In order to make a man or a boy covert
a thing, it is only necessary to make the
thing difficult to attain.*
Illustrated by Victor G. Ambrus

257 *The curious figure was drifting now
to the tops of the naked trees.*
Illustrated by John Speirs

288 *He rode straight on, never doubting for one
moment that this was the road which held
many adventures in store for him.*
Illustrated by Victor G. Ambrus

289 *"Make for the wood and keep together," cried
Lord John, clubbing his rifle. "The brutes mean
mischief."*
Illustrated by Mike Codd

304 *When I went up to take my prizes Mr. Driscoll
and Chris stamped as well as clapped and I
had to feel happy.*
Illustrated by Shirley Hughes

305 *"Fifteen? If I had half-a-dozen
such lads as you, I would make
knights of them before I died. Eh, Yeo?"*
Illustrated by John Berry

352 *He reiterated his visits to the flagon so
often that at length his senses were overpowered,*

353 *his eyes swam in his head, his head gradually
declined, and he fell into a deep sleep.*
Illustrated by John Speirs

353 *"Besides," I thought, "I have a sure guide in
this labyrinth, a thread which cannot break,
the faithful stream."*
Illustrated by Mike Codd

368 *"We shall never more, at any future time,
Delight our souls with talk of knightly deeds."*
Illustrated by John Berry

369 *The Queen became so fond of my company
that she could not dine without me.*
Illustrated by John Patience

A House for Eeyore

A. A. Milne

Illustrated by Ernest Shepard

Few authors are better known to children than Alan Alexander Milne (1882–1956). After leaving Cambridge, he first became known as a journalist and writer of humorous pieces for "Punch". During the First World War, he began to write plays and soon after the end of the war he achieved considerable success with his light and amusing comedies. In 1923, Rose Fyleman, a fellow contributor on "Punch", invited him to write some verses for a new magazine she was starting for children. These verses grew into "When We Were Very Young" and was followed by "Now We Are Six", two of the most popular books of verse ever written for young children. Soon afterwards "Winnie-the-Pooh" and "The House at Pooh Corner" appeared. These stories were based on bedtime stories told to his son, Christopher Robin, about his own toy animals. Today, the original Pooh, Piglet, Eeyore, Tigger and Kanga live in a glass case in an American publishing company in New York. Our story comes, not from "Winnie-the-Pooh", but from its equally delightful successor, "The House at Pooh Corner".

O NE DAY when Pooh Bear had nothing else to do, he thought he would do something, so he went round to Piglet's house to see what Piglet was doing. It was still snowing as he stumped over the white forest track, and he expected to find Piglet warming his toes in front of his fire, but to his surprise he saw that the door was open, and the more he looked inside the more Piglet wasn't there.

"He's out," said Pooh sadly. "That's what it is. He's not in. I shall have to go a fast Thinking Walk by myself. Bother!"

But first he thought that he would knock very loudly just to make *quite* sure . . . and while he waited for Piglet not to answer, he jumped up and down to keep warm, and a hum came suddenly into his head, which seemed to him a Good Hum, such as is Hummed Hopefully to Others.

> *The more it snows*
> > *(Tiddely pom),*
> *The more it goes*
> > *(Tiddely pom),*
> *The more it goes*
> > *(Tiddely pom)*
> > *On snowing.*
> *And nobody knows*
> > *(Tiddely pom),*
> *How cold my toes*
> > *(Tiddely pom),*
> *How cold my toes*
> > *(Tiddely pom),*
> > *Are growing.*

11

now fluttered gently down until it found a place on which to rest, and sometimes the place was Pooh's nose and sometimes it wasn't, and in a little while Piglet was wearing a white muffler round his neck and feeling more snowy behind the ears than he had ever felt before.

"Pooh," he said at last, and a little timidly, because he didn't want Pooh to think he was Giving In, "I was just wondering. How would it be if we went home now and *practised* your song, and then sang it to Eeyore tomorrow—or—or the next day, when we happen to see him?"

"That's a very good idea, Piglet," said Pooh. "We'll practise it now as we go along. But it's no good going home to practise it, because it's a special Outdoor Song which Has To Be Sung In The Snow."

"Are you sure?" asked Piglet anxiously.

"Well, you'll see, Piglet, when you listen. Because this is how it begins. *The more it snows, tiddely pom—*"

"Tiddely what?" said Piglet.

"Pom," said Pooh. "I put that in to make it more hummy. *The more it goes, tiddely pom, the more—*"

"Didn't you say snows?"

"Yes, but that was *before*."

"Before the tiddely pom?"

"It was a *different* tiddely pom," said Pooh, feeling rather muddled now. "I'll sing it to you properly and then you'll see."

So he sang it again.

"So what I'll do," said Pooh, "is I'll do this. I'll just go home first and see what the time is, and perhaps I'll put a muffler round my neck, and then I'll go and see Eeyore and sing it to him."

He hurried back to his own house; and his mind was so busy on the way with the hum that he was getting ready for Eeyore that, when he suddenly saw Piglet sitting in his best armchair, he could only stand there rubbing his head and wondering whose house he was in.

"Hallo, Piglet," he said. "I thought you were out."

"No," said Piglet, "it's you who were out, Pooh."

"So it was," said Pooh. "I knew one of us was."

He looked up at his clock, which had stopped at five minutes to eleven some weeks ago.

"Nearly eleven o'clock," said Pooh happily. "You're just in time for a little snackerel of something," and he put his head into the cupboard. "And then we'll go out, Piglet, and sing my song to Eeyore."

"Which song, Pooh?"

"The one we're going to sing to Eeyore," explained Pooh.

The clock was still saying five minutes to eleven when Pooh and Piglet set out on their way half an hour later. The wind had stopped, and the snow, tired of rushing round in circles trying to catch itself up,

12

The more it
SNOWS—*tiddely-pom,*
The more it
GOES—*tiddely-pom*
The more it
GOES—*tiddely-pom*
On
Snowing.

And nobody
KNOWS—*tiddely-pom,*
How cold my
TOES—*tiddely-pom*
How cold my
TOES—*tiddely-pom*
Are
Growing.

He sang it like that, which is much the best way of singing it, and when he had finished, he waited for Piglet to say that, of all the Outdoor Hums for Snowy Weather he had ever heard, this was the best. And, after thinking the matter out carefully, Piglet said:

"Pooh," he said solemnly, "it isn't the *toes* so much as the *ears.*"

By the time they were getting near Eeyore's Gloomy Place, which was where he lived, and as it was still very snowy behind Piglet's ears, and he was getting tired of it, they turned into a little pine-wood, and sat down on the gate which led into it. They were out of the snow now, but it was very cold, and to keep themselves warm they sang Pooh's song right through six times, Piglet doing the tiddely-poms and Pooh doing the rest of it, and

both of them thumping on the top of the gate with pieces of stick at the proper places.

And in a little while they felt much warmer, and were able to talk again.

"I've been thinking," said Pooh, "and what I've been thinking is this. I've been thinking about Eeyore."

"What about Eeyore?"

"Well, poor Eeyore has nowhere to live."

"Nor he has," said Piglet.

"*You* have a house, Piglet, and I have a house, and they are very good houses. And Christopher Robin has a house, and Owl and Kanga and Rabbit have houses, and even Rabbit's friends and relations have houses or somethings, but poor Eeyore has nothing. So what I've been thinking is: Let's build him a house."

"That," said Piglet, "is a Grand Idea. Where shall we build it?"

"We will build it here," said Pooh, "just by this wood, out of the wind, because this is where I thought of it. And we will call this Pooh Corner. And we will build an Eeyore House with sticks at Pooh Corner for Eeyore."

"There was a heap of sticks on the other side of the wood," said Piglet. "I saw them. Lots and lots. All piled up."

"Thank you, Piglet," said Pooh. "What you have just said will be a Great Help to us, and because of it I could call this place Poohanpiglet Corner if Pooh Corner didn't sound better, which it does, being smaller and more like a corner. Come along."

So they got down off the gate and went round to the other side of the wood to fetch sticks.

Christopher Robin had spent the morning indoors going to Africa and back, and he had just got off the boat and was wondering what it was like outside, when who should come knocking at the door but Eeyore.

"Hallo, Eeyore," said Christopher Robin, as he opened the door and came out. "How are *you*?"

"It's snowing still," said Eeyore gloomily.

"So it is."

"*And* freezing."

"Is it?"

"Yes," said Eeyore. "However," he said, brightening up a little, "we haven't had an earthquake lately."

"What's the matter, Eeyore?"

"Nothing, Christopher Robin. Nothing important. I suppose you haven't seen a house or what-not anywhere about?"

"What sort of a house?"

"Just a house."

"Who lives there?"

"I do. At least I thought I did. But I suppose I don't. After all, we can't all have houses."

"But, Eeyore, I didn't know—I always thought—"

"I don't know how it is, Christopher Robin, but what with all this snow and one thing and another, not to mention icicles and such-like, it isn't so Hot in my field about three o'clock in the morning as some people think it is.

"It isn't Close, if you know what I mean—not so as to be uncomfortable. It isn't Stuffy. In fact, Christopher Robin," he went on in a loud whisper, "quite-between-ourselves-and-don't-tell-any-body, it's Cold."

"Oh, Eeyore!"

"And I said to myself: The others will be sorry if I'm getting myself all cold. They haven't got Brains, any of them, only grey fluff that's blown into their heads by mistake, and they don't Think, but if it goes on snowing for another six weeks or so, one of them will begin to say to himself: 'Eeyore can't be so very much too Hot about three o'clock in the morning.' And then it will Get About. And they'll be Sorry."

"Oh, Eeyore!" said Christopher Robin, feeling very sorry already.

"I don't mean you, Christopher Robin. You're different. So what it all comes to is that I built myself a house down by my little wood."

"Did you really? How exciting!"

"The really exciting part," said Eeyore in his most melancholy voice, "is that when I left it this morning it was there, and when I came back it wasn't. Not at all, very natural, and it was only Eeyore's house. But still I just wondered."

Christopher Robin didn't stop to

wonder. He was already back in *his* house, putting on his waterproof hat, his waterproof boots and his waterproof macintosh as fast as he could. "We'll go and look for it at once," he called out to Eeyore.

They came round the corner and there was Eeyore's house.

"Sometimes," said Eeyore, "when people have quite finished taking a person's house, there are one or two bits which they don't want and are rather glad for the person to take back, if you know what I mean. So I thought if we just went—"

"Come on," said Christopher Robin, and off they hurried, and in a very little time they got to the corner of the field by the side of the pine-wood, where Eeyore's house wasn't any longer.

"There!" said Eeyore. "Not a stick of it left! Of course, I've still got all this snow to do what I like with. One mustn't complain."

But Christopher Robin wasn't listening to Eeyore, he was listening to something else.

"Can you hear it?" he asked.

"What is it? Somebody laughing?"

"Listen."

They both listened . . . and they heard a deep gruff voice saying in a singing voice that the more it snowed the more it went on snowing, and a small high voice tiddely-pomming in between.

"It's Pooh," said Christopher Robin excitedly. . . .

"Possibly," said Eeyore.

"*And* Piglet!" said Christopher Robin excitedly.

"Probably," said Eeyore. "What we *want* is a Trained Bloodhound."

The words of the song changed suddenly: "*We've finished our* HOUSE!" sang the gruff voice.

"*Tiddely pom!*" sang the squeaky one.

"*It's a beautiful* HOUSE . . .*"

"*Tiddely pom . . .*"

"*I wish it were* MINE . . .*"

"*Tiddely pom . . .*"

"Pooh!" shouted Christopher Robin. . . .

The singers on the gate stopped suddenly.

"It's Christopher Robin!" said Pooh eagerly.

"He's round by the place where we got all those sticks from," said Piglet.

"Come on," said Pooh.

They climbed down their gate and hurried round the corner of the wood, Pooh making welcoming noises all the way.

"Why, here *is* Eeyore," said Pooh, when he had finished hugging Christopher Robin, and he nudged Piglet, and Piglet nudged him, and they thought to themselves what a lovely surprise they had got ready. "Hallo, Eeyore."

15

"Same to you, Pooh Bear, and twice on Thursdays," said Eeyore gloomily.

Before Pooh could say: "Why Thursdays?" Christopher Robin began to explain the sad story of Eeyore's Lost House. And Pooh and Piglet listened, and their eyes seemed to get bigger and bigger.

"*Where* do you say it was?" asked Pooh.

"Just here," said Eeyore.

"Made of sticks?"

"Yes."

"Oh!" said Piglet.

"What?" said Eeyore.

"I just said 'Oh!'" said Piglet nervously. And so as to seem quite at ease he hummed Tiddley-pom once or twice in a what-shall-we-do-now kind of way.

"You're sure it *was* a house?" said Pooh. "I mean, you're sure the house was just here?"

"Of course I am," said Eeyore. And he murmured to himself, "No brain at all, some of them."

"Why, what's the matter, Pooh?" asked Christopher Robin.

"Well," said Pooh. . . . "The fact *is*," said Pooh. . . . "Well, the fact *is*," said Pooh. . . . "You see," said Pooh. . . . "It's like this," said Pooh, and something seemed to tell him that he wasn't explaining very well, and he nudged Piglet again.

"It's like this," said Piglet quickly. . . . "Only warmer," he added after deep thought.

"What's warmer?"

"The other side of the wood, where Eeyore's house is."

"*My* house?" said Eeyore. "My house was here."

"No," said Piglet firmly. "The other side of the wood."

"Because of being warmer," said Pooh. "But I ought to *know*—"

"Come and look," said Piglet simply, and he led the way.

"There wouldn't be *two* houses," said Pooh. "Not so close together."

They came round the corner, and there was Eeyore's house, looking as comfy as anything.

"There you are," said Piglet.

"Inside as well as outside," said Pooh proudly.

Eeyore went inside . . . and came out again.

"It's a remarkable thing," he said. "It *is* my house, and I built it where I said I did, so the wind must have blown it here. And the wind blew it right over the wood, and blew it down here, and here it is as good as ever. In fact, better in places."

"Much better," said Pooh and Piglet together.

"It just shows what can be done by taking a little trouble," said Eeyore. "Do you see, Pooh? Do you see, Piglet? Brains first and then Hard Work. Look at it! *That's* the way to build a house," said Eeyore proudly.

So they left him in it; and Christopher Robin went back to lunch with his friends Pooh and Piglet, and on the way they told him of the Awful Mistake they had made. And when he had finished laughing, they all sang the Outdoor Song for Snowy Weather the rest of the way home, Piglet, who was still not quite sure of his voice, putting in the tiddely-poms again.

"And I know it *seems* easy," said Piglet to himself, "but it isn't *every one* who could do it."

"Now we're boys so fine and neat, why cobble more for others' feet."
From "The Elves and the Shoemaker"

"That was a very near touch," said my master. *"What's to be done now?"*
From "A Stormy Day"

The Elves and the Shoemaker

The Brothers Grimm

Illustrated by John Patience

How strange that two 19th-century German professors of the University of Berlin —Jacob Grimm (1785–1863) and Wilhelm Grimm (1786–1859), both of them world-famous students of languages, and Jacob, the discoverer of certain ways in which language changes through the ages—should become known to every child in millions of homes throughout Europe as the authors of Grimm's Fairy Tales. Actually they did not invent the stories. They made a study of folklore, and wandered about collecting stories ·that had been handed down from father to son through many generations in simple peasant homes—folk tales never before written down. The Grimm Brothers re-told what they picked up in simple words and without adornment. The result was a huge collection of tales about peasants and princes, witches and warriors, elves and enchantments—often ferocious but always satisfying. Their book has held spellbound the children of many lands. Most of these stories you may have read already, but here is one of them—just to remind you:

THERE was once a shoemaker who through no fault of his own had become so poor that at last he had only leather enough left for one pair of shoes. At evening he cut out the shoes which he intended to begin upon the next morning, and since he had a good conscience, he lay down quietly, said his prayers, and fell asleep.

In the morning, when he had said his prayers and was preparing to sit down to work, he found the pair of shoes standing finished on his table. He was amazed and could not understand it in the least.

He took the shoes in his hand to examine them more closely. They were so neatly sewn that not a stitch was out of place, and were as good as the work of a master hand.

Soon afterwards a purchaser came in and, as he was much pleased with the shoes, he paid more than the ordinary price for them, so that the shoemaker was able to buy leather for two pairs of shoes with the money.

He cut them out in the evening, and the next day with fresh courage was about to go to work. But he had no need to, for when he got up the shoes were finished, and buyers were not lacking. These gave him so much money that he was able to buy leather for four pairs of shoes.

Early next morning he found the four pairs finished, and so it went on. What he cut out at evening was finished in the morning, so that he was soon again in comfortable circumstances and became a well-to-do man.

Now it happened one evening not long before Christmas, when he had cut out some shoes as usual, that he said to his wife, "How would it be if we were to sit up tonight to see who it is that lends us such a helping hand?"

The wife agreed and lighted a candle and they hid themselves in the corner of the room behind the clothes which were hanging there.

At midnight came two little naked men who sat down at the shoemaker's table, took up the pieces of leather shaped in readiness for sewing, and began with their tiny fingers to stitch, sew, and hammer so neatly and quickly that the shoemaker could not believe his eyes. They did not stop till everything was quite finished and stood complete on the table. Then they ran swiftly away.

The next day the wife said, "The little men have made us rich, and we ought to show our gratitude. They were running about with nothing on, and must freeze with cold. Now I will make them little shirts, coats, waistcoats, and hose, and will even knit them a pair of stockings. And you shall make them each a pair of shoes."

The husband agreed. And at evening, when they had everything ready, they laid out the presents on the table and hid themselves to see how the little men would behave.

At midnight they came skipping in and were about to set to work. But instead of the leather ready cut out, they found the charming little clothes.

At first they were surprised, then excessively delighted. With the greatest speed they put on and smoothed down the pretty clothes, singing:

"Now we're boys so fine and neat,
    Why cobble more for others' feet?"

Then they hopped and danced about, and leapt over chairs and tables and out the door. Henceforward they came back no more, but the shoemaker fared well as long as he lived, and had good luck in all his undertakings.

The Cow

The friendly cow, all red and white,
    I love with all my heart:
She gives me cream with all her might,
    To eat with apple-tart.

She wanders lowing here and there,
    And yet she cannot stray,
All in the pleasant open air
    The pleasant light of day,

And blown by all the winds that pass
    And wet with all the showers,
She walks among the meadow grass
    And eats the meadow flowers.

ROBERT LOUIS STEVENSON

The Prominent Man

Laura Richards

Illustrated by James Hunt

Laura Richards (1850–1943) is best remembered for the small book of fables for the young called "The Golden Windows", from which The Prominent Man is taken. You can compare this modern fable with the old fables of Aesop. Though not about animals, the little tales of Laura Richards have just as sharp a moral.

ONCE a prominent man was hurrying to his business; and as he hurried along the street, he slipped on a piece of ice, and fell and broke his leg. He was carried home on a stretcher, and lay on his bed in pain of body and distress of mind.

"What will become of everything?" he cried. "By now I should have been at the committee-meeting, where they can do nothing without me. This afternoon there is a directors' meeting, where I was to be chairman, and this evening I am engaged to lecture on a subject of vital importance. This means disaster to the State, and it may be to the whole country. It is terrible!"

Just then came in the Angel-who-attends-to-things.

"How are you feeling?" asked the Angel.

"Oh, I am in a dreadful condition!" said the man. "I slipped on a piece of ice this morning, and broke my leg."

"Yes," said the Angel; "I saw you fall."

"But," said the man, "my pain, which by the way is very severe" (for he did not think the Angel looked sympathetic enough), "is the smallest part of it. I should by now be at a committee-meeting, where they can do nothing without me. This afternoon there is a directors' meeting, where I was to be chairman; and this evening I was engaged to lecture on a subject of vital interest. This means

disaster to the State, and it may be to the whole country." And he groaned aloud.

"Oh, well," said the Angel, "I would not worry about all that, if I were you."

"Not worry!" said the prominent man.

"No," said the Angel. "The truth is, I put that piece of ice there myself. I wanted to get rid of you."

"Get rid of—" said the prominent man; and the rest was gasps.

"Yes," said the Angel. "You see, I didn't want you at the committee-meeting. There is a new man ready to come forward who knows much more than you, and if you had been there he would have been too modest to speak. Then, the directors are going to take action this afternoon on that important case, and if you were there they would vote the wrong way. As to the lecture, it would do more harm than good just now; but when the crisis is passed, you may deliver it without doing any serious damage. So you see!"

"Good heavens!" cried the prominent man. "Am I awake, or is this a dream?"

"It is what you call Life," said the Angel.

"But—but—but—" cried the man, "this is terrible! You don't know anything about business."

"My dear soul," said the Angel, "what do you take me for?" and he went away, and told the nurse to give her patient a composing draught.

19

A Stormy Day

Anna Sewell

Illustrated by Victor G. Ambrus

There are many instances of inherited writing talent and Anna Sewell (1820–1878) is one of them. Her mother was an early Victorian versifier who wrote long moralizing poems in a simple ballad form that sold enormously. Anna injured both ankles when very young and was a semi-invalid for most of her life. Her odd but excellent idea of writing "the autobiography of a horse" was inspired by her wish to make people kinder to their horses. In those days, of course, horses were everywhere, for they were made to do the work that motor cars and tractors do now. "Black Beauty" was a great success in France, Italy and Germany as well as in Britain, and the Royal Society for the Prevention of Cruelty to Animals praised it highly — an unusual recommendation for a book. Here Black Beauty recounts the tale of an exciting night:

ONE day late in the autumn, my master had a long journey to go on business. I was put into the dog-cart, and John went with his master. I always liked to go in the dog-cart; it was so light, and the high wheels ran along so pleasantly. There had been a great deal of rain, and now the wind was very high and blew the dry leaves across the road in a shower. We went along merrily till we came to the toll-bar and the low wooden bridge. The river banks were rather high, and the bridge, instead of rising, went across just level, so that in the middle, if the river was full, the water be nearly up to the wood-work and planks; but as there were good substantial rails on each side, people did not mind it.

The man at the gate said the river was rising fast, and he feared it would be a bad night. Many of the meadows were under water, and in one low part of the road the water was halfway up to my knees; the bottom was good, and master drove gently, so it was no matter.

When we got to the town, of course, I had a good feed, but as the master's business engaged him a long time, we did not start for home till rather late in the afternoon. The wind was then much higher, and I heard the master say to John he had never been out in such a storm; and so I thought, as we went along the skirts of a wood, where great branches were swaying about like twigs, and the rushing sound was terrible.

"I wish we were well out of this wood," said my master.

"Yes, sir," said John, "it would be rather awkward if one of these branches came down upon us." The words were scarcely out of his mouth, when there was a groan, and a crack and a splitting sound, and tear-

20

ing, crashing down amongst the other trees, came an oak, torn up by the roots, and it fell right across the road just before us. I will never say I was not frightened, for I was. I stopped still, and I believe I trembled; of course I did not turn round or run away; I was not brought up to that. John jumped out and was in a moment at my head.

"That was a very near touch," said my master. "What's to be done now?" "Well, sir, we can't drive over that tree nor yet round it; there will be nothing for it but to go back to the four crossways, and that will be a good six miles before we get round to the wooden bridge again; it will make us late, but the horse is fresh." So back we went, and round by the crossroads; but by the time we got to the bridge, it was very nearly dark and we could just see that the water was over the middle of it; but as that happened sometimes when the floods were out, master did not stop. We were going along at a good pace, but the moment my feet touched the first part of the bridge I felt sure there was something wrong. I dare not go forward and I made a dead stop. "Go on, Beauty," said my master and he gave me a touch with the whip, but I dare not stir; he gave me a sharp cut, I jumped, but I dare not go forward.

"There's something wrong, sir," said John, and he sprang out of the dog-cart, and came to my head and looked all about. He tried to lead me forward, "Come on, Beauty, what's the matter?" Of course I could not tell him, but I knew very well that the bridge was not safe.

Just then the man at the toll-gate on the

"There's something wrong, sir," said John, and he sprang out of the dogcart.

other side ran out of the house, tossing a torch about like one mad. "Hoy, hoy, hoy, halloo, stop!" he cried. "What's the matter?" shouted my master.

"The bridge is broken in the middle and part of it is carried away; if you come on you'll be into the river."

"Thank God!" said my master. "You Beauty!" said John, and took the bridle and gently turned me round to the right-hand road by the river-side. The sun had set some time, the wind seemed to have lulled off after that furious blast which tore up the tree. It grew darker and darker, stiller and stiller. I trotted quietly along, the wheels hardly making a sound on the soft road. For a good while neither master nor John spoke, and then master began in a serious voice. I could not understand much of what they said, but I found they thought, if I had gone on as the master wanted me, most likely the bridge would have given way under us, and horse, chaise, master, and man would have fallen into the river; and as the current was flowing very strongly, and there was no light and no help at hand, it was more than likely we should all have been drowned. Master said God had given men reason by which they could find out things for themselves, but He had given animals knowledge which did not depend on reason, and which was much more prompt and perfect in its way, and by which they had often saved the lives of men. John had many stories to tell of dogs and horses, and the wonderful things they had done; he thought people did not value their animals half enough, nor make friends of them as they ought to do. I am sure he makes friends of them if ever a man did.

At last we came to the Park gates, and found the gardener looking out for us. He said that mistress had been in a dreadful way ever since dark, fearing some accident had happened, and that she had sent James off on Justice, the roan cob, to make inquiry after us.

We saw a light at the hall door and at the upper windows, and as we came up, mistress ran out, saying, "Are you really safe, my dear? Oh! I have been so anxious, fancying all sorts of things. Have you had no accident?"

"No, my dear; but if your Black Beauty had not been wiser than we were, we should all have been carried down the river at the wooden bridge." I heard no more, as they went into the house, and John took me to the stable. Oh! what a good supper he gave me that night: a good bran mash and some crushed beans with my oats, and such a thick bed of straw, and I was glad of it, for I was tired.

Four Ducks on a Pond

Four ducks on a pond,
A grass-bank beyond,
A blue sky of spring,
White clouds on the wing;
What a little thing
To remember for years—
To remember with tears!

WILLIAM ALLINGHAM

Peter Pan meets Wendy

Re-told by
Daniel O'Connor
from the play
by J. M. Barrie

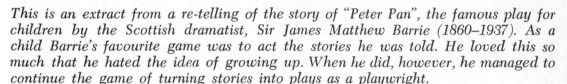

Illustrated by Shirley Tourret

This is an extract from a re-telling of the story of "Peter Pan", the famous play for children by the Scottish dramatist, Sir James Matthew Barrie (1860–1937). As a child Barrie's favourite game was to act the stories he was told. He loved this so much that he hated the idea of growing up. When he did, however, he managed to continue the game of turning stories into plays as a playwright.

So perhaps it was natural that he should hit on the idea of writing a play for children about a boy who never grows up. Peter Pan is a boy like that. He lived with the fairies in Kensington Gardens, and so became half-fairy himself. The play tells about how he meets the Darling family who are quite like other families except that they have a Nanny who is a big St. Bernard dog, and Peter Pan lures the children away from home into a magical Never-Never land where children can fly and dangerous pirates are swallowed by crocodiles. It is said that the first producer to whom the author showed his play thought Barrie had gone mad! But when at last the many difficulties of production were overcome, including the need for child actors to fly back and forth on the stage (with the help of invisible wires), the story proved an enchantment to generations of children.

This extract shows you what happens when Peter, who had lost his shadow through the sudden closing of a window, returns to the Darling nursery to find it and, when he gets it, tries to stick it on with soap:

SITTING on the rug, he soaped his feet and then he soaped his shadow. But his feet and the shadow would not stick together. It is of no use to have a shadow if it will not stick to you. After trying and trying in vain, the poor little fellow put his face in his hands, and sobbed aloud.

It was then that Wendy awoke, and she sat right up in bed. Not at all afraid, she said, "Little boy, why are you crying?"

The boy sprang to his feet, and taking off his cap, bowed very low. Wendy bowed in return, though she found it a hard thing to do in bed.

"What's your name?" asked the little boy.

"Wendy Darling. What's yours?"

"Peter Pan."

"Where do you live?"

"Second turning to the right, and then keep on till morning."

This seemed to Wendy a very funny way of going home, but she was so sorry when she heard that Peter had no mother. But Peter was not crying for that.

Peter was crying because he could not get his shadow to stick on. This made Wendy smile, and she said firmly that soap was no good. The shadow must be sewn on.

"Shall I do it for you?" she asked, and jumped out of bed to get her work-box.

Then she set to work, and though it hurts a good deal to have a shadow sewn on to your feet, Peter bore it very bravely.

It was the right thing to do, for the shadow held on so well. Peter *was* pleased, and he danced up and down the room with delight. He saw the shadow dance on the floor as he flung his arms and legs about.

"Oh, how clever I am!" cried Peter, full of joy, and he crowed, for all the world just as a cock would crow.

"You are vain," said Wendy in a vexed tone, "of course *I* did nothing!"

"Oh, you did a little!"

"A little! If I am no use I can at least withdraw," she said, and she jumped back into bed and put her head under the bed-clothes.

"Oh, Wendy, please don't withdraw," Peter cried sadly. "I can't help crowing when I'm pleased with myself. One girl is of more use than twenty boys."

This was rather clever of Peter, and at these words, Wendy got up again. She even said she would give Peter a kiss if he liked, but Peter did not know what she meant. Then, seeing the thimble on Wendy's finger, he thought she meant to give him that, and held out his hand for it.

Now Wendy saw at once that the poor boy did not even know what a kiss was. Being a nice little girl, she did not hurt his feelings by laughing at him, but just put the thimble on his finger.

Peter liked the thimble very much.

"Shall I give you a kiss?" he asked, and pulling a button off his coat, gave it to her with a grave face.

Wendy at once put it on a chain which she wore round her neck, and then she forgot that he did not know what a kiss was, and again asked him for one. At once he gave back the thimble.

"Oh, I didn't mean a *kiss,* I meant a thimble!" said Wendy.

"What's that?" he asked.

"It's like this," replied Wendy, and gently kissed his cheek.

"Oh," cried Peter, "how nice!" and he began to give her *thimbles* in return, and ever after he called a kiss a thimble, and a thimble a kiss.

How the Trolls became Giants

J. B. Morton

Illustrated by John Patience

John Bingham Morton (born 1893) has written about fifty books, most of them humorous; some verse; a few, serious lives of famous Frenchmen; and one delightful book of humorous fairy tales, from which we take "How the Trolls Became Giants". For fifty-two years he turned the everyday adult world topsy-turvy in a series of little pieces written for a national newspaper under the pen-name of "Beachcomber". In this vein he was a knockabout humorist—a caricaturist in words of the world around us.

IT was a very cold winter, and the trolls who lived in the pine-forest on the side of the mountain were driven down to the plains to keep themselves warm. And the place they chose was an enormous castle belonging to a famous giant called Hum. He was called this because of his habit of saying "Hum" whenever he was surprised or angry. It was quite easy for the trolls to get into the castle, because they were so small, and the giants on guard at the gate were so large. The little fellows took advantage of a gust of wind which blew a cloud of dead leaves through the open gate and into the main courtyard. Nobody suspected that a troll was riding on every leaf.

They scuttled about the courtyard, finding chinks in doors and windows, and cracks in walls, and soon they were all over the castle, and glad to be out of the bitter weather. They could smell roasted meat, and they followed their twitching noses until they came to the giant's feasting-hall. There sat the giant himself. Before him was a pewter dish filled with meat. It was so large that they could not even climb up the rim of it. And by the side of it was an enormous tankard filled with mead. The tankard was as big as a house. The table on which the meal was served was as large as a two-acre field, and as for Hum himself, when they peered up at him it was like gazing up at a mountain. When he drew a breath it was as though one of the Winds had got into the hall.

Of course the giant did not notice the trolls. He sat there pompously, while other giants waited on him. But you could see from the serious look on his face, that he was very vain, and that the only fear he had was the fear of being made to look ridiculous. The trolls, who knew a bit about giants, guessed this, and it was not long before they were planning to play some fine tricks. There was an old cobbler among them, and he took his awl, and very patiently bored a hole in the tankard, so that the mead began to run out. The giant went on eating for a long time, and then seized his tankard for a deep draught. But when he noticed that there was very little mead in it, he grew purple in the face with rage.

"Hum! Hum!" he roared. "What is this?"

The smaller giants who waited on him ran into the hall, but they could not explain what had happened. There was no sign of the mead, for as it ran out through the hole, the trolls held their little caps to it, and filled them, and had a good drink.

Away went the smaller giants, and brought back the tankard again, full to the brim. But the giant was eating once more, and so the mead flowed out, and a second time he looked down and saw only a small amount of mead.

"Hum! Hum!" he roared, louder than before. "What is this?"

And he ordered the giants who had served him at table to be thrown into the dungeons. Then he went and filled the tankard himself, and sat down once more and went on eating. And when, for the third time, he saw that only the bottom of the tankard was covered, he rose in a fury, and hurled the tankard against the wall, where it made a dent as large as a quarry. And he strode about the room with a noise like thunder, while the trolls hid in a corner. When he had got to the far end of the hall and was beating his fists against it, and bellowing, the trolls ran to the table and swarmed up the legs. Standing on each other's shoulders they were able to reach the dish and drag the meat from it. But Hum turned and came back, and they had to leave the meat under the table.

Hum sat down again, exhausted by his anger, and when he saw the empty dish before him, he stared until his great red eyes nearly popped out of his head.

"Hum!" he roared, and banged his fist down on the huge table, and broke it in two. And after roaring and bellowing until he had tired himself out he went to bed in a great tower at the top of the palace. He covered himself with skins of more than a thousand wild beasts, all stitched together to make a coverlet for his mattress, and he put on his head a night-cap of rich fur. But as soon as he was asleep the trolls crept up to his room in the great tower, and threw open all the windows, so that the snow came whirling in and settled over everything. And when Hum awoke in the morning his teeth were chattering, and he had to shout for the giants to come with spades and dig him out. But they could not come, as he had locked them in the dungeons below the castle. However, by heaving and struggling he at last got himself out, and without waiting for his breakfast he went striding off to see a witch he knew who lived near by.

"Good-day, Hum," said the witch.

"It's not a good day, old hag," replied Hum.

"What has happened?" she asked.

"My castle is haunted," said Hum. "My meat and drink are stolen before my eyes, and my windows are opened by night."

"Aren't you the great fool of the world?" hissed the witch. "Why do you come wasting my precious time? Isn't it your own servants that rob you and make a fool of you?"

"It is not," said Hum. "They are locked in my dungeons."

Then the old hag took a very ancient mirror from the wall, and turned it this way and that, and as she gazed into it she could see reflected all the places in the world, and everything that was going on. And when Hum's castle was reflected in the mirror she held it very still and bent over it. And she could see distinctly the trolls, who were dancing all over the castle and having a high time.

"It's a pity you're so big and foolish," said the witch.

"What do you mean?" shouted Hum.

"If you were smaller and cleverer you'd be able to notice small things—and perhaps small people."

"What small people?" asked Hum.

"Perhaps, who knows, it may be the trolls of the pine-forest."

"Hum," roared the giant, and looked so surprised that the witch rocked herself to and fro with laughter. "But how could

first will make you shrink to the size of the trolls. The second will make you big again, so that you can lock them up in your dungeons."

So back went Hum carrying the two

It was a most surprising situation for Hum.

these little midgets get past my sentries?" said Hum.

"You're all too big in that castle," said the witch. "Why, if a million trolls ran between your legs you wouldn't see them. You must make yourself and your servants small, and then these trolls will be friendly with you. Now take these two flasks. The

flasks, one of green liquid to make him small, and one of blue liquid to make him big again. When he got to the gates he gave some of the green liquid to the sentries, and immediately they shrank to the size of trolls. Then he went to the dungeons, and told his plan to his serving-men, and they too drank some of the green liquid and became small. Hum put the flask containing the blue liquid on a shelf above the hearth in the hall, but he forgot that when he had taken the green liquid he would be too small to reach it. He then drank, and became small like the others.

The trolls were surprised when they saw what had happened to the giants, but they were suspicious, and not too ready to be friendly. And presently they noticed that Hum kept on looking anxiously up at the shelf. For he was wondering how to get at the flask. And they could see that he looked at them with fury.

"Welcome to my humble castle," said the giant. "I hope you will invite me to your forest in the summer."

While he spoke he moved nearer to the shelf, which was many, many yards above his head. And he looked up at it so often that the trolls began to guess that they had been tricked. So while some of them surrounded him, others built themselves up like a wall, one standing on another's shoulders, until they could reach the flask.

"What is this blue liquid?" asked one troll. "And see that you tell no lie."

"Don't touch it," cried Hum, whose voice was now very faint. "It will send you to sleep for a thousand years."

"Oh, joy!" cried the laziest of the trolls, "I must have some of it in that case."

Several of them tilted the bottle, and spilt some of the liquid on the shelf. The lazy fellow lapped it up, but instead of going to sleep, he began to swell and swell, until he was as big as Hum had been. Then all the trolls understood the trick which Hum had tried to play. They all lapped up the liquid, and all grew into giants in less than a minute. And there was Hum, feeling ridiculous again, and nearly suffocated with rage. The new giants took no notice of him, but swept out of the castle, waking echoes for miles around with their laughter and singing. And when they had gone Hum found one drop of the precious blue liquid on the floor. He licked it up, and grew to be the size of you or me, and was much happier that way.

His servants remained as small as trolls, and the trolls who had become giants left their pine-forest, and lived high up in the mountains, among the remote glaciers.

The witch, who had watched everything in her mirror, rocked herself to and fro with laughter, and laughed so long that even her sulky old cat joined in.

Written in March
while resting on the Bridge at the
Foot of Brother's Water

The cock is crowing,
The stream is flowing,
The small birds twitter,
The lake doth glitter,
The green field sleeps in the sun;
The oldest and youngest
Are at work with the strongest;
The cattle are grazing,
Their heads never raising;
There are forty feeding like one!

Like an army defeated
The snow hath retreated,
And now doth fare ill
On the top of the bare hill;
The ploughboy is whooping—anon—anon:
There's joy in the mountains;
There's life in the fountains;
Small clouds are sailing,
Blue sky prevailing;
The rain is over and gone!

WILLIAM WORDSWORTH

But that's not the end of the Story

Margaret Baker

Illustrated by Mary Baker

Miss Margaret Baker (born 1890) has been writing for children since she could write at all—"long before I could spell", she says. She is a Quaker; her two brothers are professors, and her sister, Mary, is the artist who illustrated this story. It comes from "A Book of Happy Tales". A spare-time gardener and traveller, Miss Baker lives in a small village near Banbury, Oxfordshire.

ONCE upon a time there was a boy called Bengy and he was discontented.

"I wish I'd even half the chances that come to other folk," he said fretfully. "What sort of a life have I, 'prenticed to a sweep and doing nothing all day except getting blacker and blacker?"

"But think of all the fine houses you go into," said his mother; "the Vicarage and the Hall and Mr. Tape the draper's. If you learn your trade well enough, there's no telling but you may be sent for to sweep the Palace chimneys away up in London Town. Many a one would give a good deal to see what you see every day."

"Which shows how little they know about it," said Bengy sulkily. "It doesn't matter whether it's the Vicarage, or the Hall, or anywhere else, everything's smothered in dust-sheets and newspapers; and it would be no different if I went to the Palace, except that the dust-sheets might be a bit grander and the newspapers a bit more up-to-date. I wish I was a sailor, that I do!"

"But think of the waves rolling up and down and the gales a-blowing!" exclaimed his mother, "and the sharks and the whales and the pirates!"

"What of them?" asked Bengy. "At least I shouldn't smell of soot if I went to sea, for you can't sweep chimneys on board ship."

"But supposing you met a mermaid, or a sea-serpent?"

"I only wish I could! That would be an adventure worth having! I've half a mind to go for a sailor right away; I'd be happy as the day was long and never want for anything different."

"Oh, dear! Oh, dear!" sighed his mother. "Why can't you settle down at home and be thankful for a feather-bed and a good fire, and a tasty supper all hot for you when you get back from work? If you're not contented here, you'll not be contented wherever you go. I'm sure I don't know what will become of you unless you mend your ways!"

But Bengy was not to be persuaded to be thankful for anything he had already, and when one fine day he fell in with a sailor home on leave, nothing would do but that he must go back with him to his ship.

His mother said good-bye with many doleful tears and headshakes, but Bengy was so excited he could hardly keep from throwing his cap in the air and capering down the village street. And when they came to the port and he went aboard the *Saucy Sue*, he was more excited still. He sniffed the tarry, salty, fishy smell with as much delight as if it had been the finest

perfume; he declared a hammock twenty times more comfortable than a bed, and salt beef and ship's biscuits much to be preferred to anything his mother had ever set before him; and when they put off to sea and sailed out of sight of land, he was better pleased still.

"I did well to turn sailor!" he cried.

—*But that's not the end of the story.* They had not been at sea more than a few days before Bengy began to grumble. If he was set to help the cook in the galley, he wished he was climbing the rigging; and if he was sent up aloft, he wished himself in the fo'c'sle. Whatever hour of day or night it came his turn to keep a look-out, it was always the time he disliked most; and if he was told to swab the decks, he would mutter something about the luck of those who were polishing the brass-work.

"What sort of a sailor do you think you'll make if you don't put your mind to it better than this?" shouted the bos'n.

"It's no use putting my mind to it," said Bengy sourly. "It's nothing but doing the same old thing day after day—rubbing the same old handles, and washing up the same old plates and pots and pans, and scrubbing the same old planks. It's worse than sweeping chimneys, for I did have a different chimney to climb every time."

"It's to be hoped you swept chimneys better than you scrub," said the bos'n; "the deck looks worse after you've finished than when you began."

"That's no matter as far as I can see," growled Bengy. "Smears or no smears, I'll be sent to do it all over again to-morrow and the next day and every day that comes. I didn't ship aboard the *Saucy Sue* to be a charwoman."

"Some folk don't know when they're fortunate," said the bos'n.

"I know when I'm not," grunted Bengy. "I'm sent here and sent there till I'm ready to drop; and if I so much as stop to get my breath, someone shouts to me to stir my stumps and look lively or I'll get a taste of the rope's end. I wish there were not so many people to order me about, and I had a chance to do what I want."

He wished it over and over again with every day that came; he wished it aloud when there was anyone near, and to himself when he was alone.

"Shiver my timbers!" shouted the captain. "Do you never stop grumbling?"

"I'd stop soon enough if I had a bit of my own way," said Bengy.

"We'll see about that!" said the captain. "There's a desert island over yonder where you can do as you like from year's end to year's end and no one to say you yes or no."

And with that he picked him up and dropped him overboard.

The *Saucy Sue* sailed away with a stiff breeze behind her and Bengy was left to splash and gasp his way to land as best he could. He was more dead than alive by the time he reached the sandy beach, but when he had energy enough to look around he found the island was not too bad a place. There were coconut palms and bread-fruit trees and a spring of water, and what more could be expected? And from one end to the other, and that was no great distance, there was not a soul to be seen.

He gave a sigh of relief. "I'm in luck now and no mistake," said he; "I'll be able to do exactly as I please for the first time in my life."

—*But that's not the end of the story.*

Before his clothes had time to dry in the sun, he was finding fault with things just as usual. The coconuts took too much chewing and the bread-fruit was going to be uninteresting eating if there was neither butter nor jam to go with it. "And fancy only water to drink and me so fond of a good, strong cup of tea!" he said crossly.

Worst of all, he soon realized that if there was no one to order him about, there was also no one to hear his complaints, and it is little comfort one gets from grumbling to oneself all the time.

"If only there was somebody to listen to me when I want to talk!" he whined. "I wouldn't mind who it was. I'd be able to put up with the coconuts and the bread-fruit and no tea so much better if I could tell someone what I thought about it all. I wish I weren't all by myself."

He wished it again and again and again and then one afternoon he wakened from a nap to find a horde of savages landing on the beach. Before he had time to rub his eyes and make sure he was not dreaming, they were crowding round him, pointing and chattering and pushing for the best places. Bengy's heart turned somersaults inside him and his tongue stuck to the roof of his mouth with terror at sight of their spears and painted faces. He was sure every minute was going to be his last, but nothing happened except that the pointing and chattering and pushing grew more excited, and presently his courage began to come back, and with his courage his voice.

"What do you take me for?" he shouted. "A wild beast show? I'm not half so funny looking as you are, anyway!"

"Oh—ee! Oh-ee!" cried the savages in delight, and they carried him off to their canoe and rowed him to the mainland and put him in a grass hut with a guard of warriors surrounding it. The chief sat in the doorway and charged two coconuts a head to look at the white-faced monster and listen to the noise it made when it was poked, and he rubbed his hands with satisfaction to see how quickly the coconuts accumulated; indeed, he had never gathered so much wealth with so little trouble in all his life.

Bengy should have been perfectly content, for now there were dozens of people

always ready to listen to whatever he chose to say.

—*But that's not the end of the story.*

Although he had his wish, he was far from pleased and he grumbled louder and more often than he had ever done before. The savages did not mind that in the least, for it made him much more interesting to look at, and the chief raised the entrance money to the hut from two coconuts to three.

"I wish I was safely out of it all!" groaned Bengy. "I'd be content wherever I was, if only it wasn't here. I'm sure no one ever had so much trouble as I am having."

His chance of escape, however, was so very small that it might almost be said he had no chance at all. It was not to be supposed the savage chief would run any risk of losing so profitable a curiosity, and Bengy might have languished in the grass hut till his dying day if news of the enormous pile of coconuts he had brought

his owner had not spread far and wide. Before very long another chief arrived to ask for the loan of the monster for a week or two. The arguing and bargaining and quarrelling that followed proved an even greater attraction than Bengy himself; and while everyone was crowding round to get the best view of the new entertainment, Bengy made a hole in the back of the hut and took to his heels.

He was soon out of sight of the savages and also out of breath, and he was just beginning to wonder what to do next when he stumbled over something half buried in the ground. It was an iron ring with a rope tied to it, and in case it might lead to something, he gave it a pull.

"If it isn't an anchor!" he cried. "Now what can an anchor be doing so far from shore? And what in the world is it fastened to? It seems to go straight up into the sky!"

He threw back his head to see better and in that instant the anchor suddenly dragged free and whisked into the air, spinning and swinging and getting rapidly further and further from the ground, with Bengy clinging to it as best he might.

By and by the anchor began to behave more steadily, and Bengy's brain ceased to turn round in his head and he was able to see he was hanging underneath a balloon and being slowly hauled aboard.

The balloon man was vastly astonished when he saw a face appear over the edge of the basket.

"So that's how I come to be cast adrift, is it?" said he with a prodigious frown. "What do you mean by interfering with my anchor?"

"I didn't know it was yours," said Bengy.

"You knew it wasn't your own, I suppose. And there was I just going to climb down and gather some sticks to make a fire and cook my dinner, and because of your meddling I'm out over the sea again and who's to say how long I'll have to wait before I can get a bite of anything better than biscuits and dried beef?"

"I shan't mind biscuits and dried beef," said Bengy, his mouth watering at the very thought of them. "I shan't mind anything now I've left those horrible savages behind."

—But that's not the end of the story.

Before the first day was over, he had begun to lose his cheerfulness; and before the second had gone, he was grumbling just as usual. "There's not room to swing a mouse, let alone a cat, in a balloon basket," he said discontentedly; "and it makes me go all goose-flesh to look over the side, and there's no change of company and never a thing to see except clouds. I wish I was back home again."

"I'm sure I wish you were," growled the balloon man.

They sailed along for a week or more and neither uttered a word that was not a complaint, and then one fine morning they looked over the edge of the basket and saw fields and roads and houses far below them, and people like little black flies walking about.

"Just look at all that down there and me stuck up in the sky!" wailed Bengy. "I never was so tired of anything in my life as being cooped up in this basket. If only I was safe on the ground again, there isn't a thing I'd have to grumble about. I'd sweep chimneys from year's end to year's end and never wish for anything better. Oh, why can't I get down?"

"You'll get down before you know where you are, unless you mind what you're doing!" cried the balloon man, and, even as he spoke, Bengy leaned too far over the edge in his eagerness and fell out.

"Well, he's got what he wanted," said the balloon man as he watched him tumbling head over heels and heels over head; "but I don't suppose he'll be satisfied."

Bengy landed with a bounce in the middle of a half-finished haystack. The

men who were working on it were very much surprised, and so was Bengy, and he was more surprised still when he found the stack was in the field behind his own house. He slid to the ground without waiting to go down by the ladder and raced for the back door.

"Mother! Mother!" he shouted. "Here I am home again, for it's more to my taste than all the rest of the world put together. You'll not find me grumbling now about soot and dirt and dust-sheets."

He hugged his mother till she had to cry out for mercy, and capered round the kitchen till he set everything on the dresser jumping and rattling, and the cat clawed her way up the curtains and sat on the top of the grandfather's clock to keep her tail from being trodden on.

—BUT THAT'S NOT THE END OF THE STORY!

Before his mother's ribs had well recovered from the squeezing they had had, and before the cat had ceased to take shelter whenever he came in, Bengy was beginning to have misgivings about his liking for chimney-sweeping, and very soon he was grumbling and finding fault with everything, just as if he had never left home at all. "It's always the same old thing over and over again," he complained. "What sort of a life have I, 'prenticed to a sweep and doing nothing all day but getting blacker and——"

But here we are at the beginning of the story again! It can't have an end at all.

Sea-Fever

I must down to the seas again, to the lonely sea and the sky,
And all I ask is a tall ship and a star to steer her by,
And the wheel's kick and the wind's song and the white sail's shaking,
And a grey mist on the sea's face and a grey dawn breaking.

I must down to the seas again, for the call of the running tide
Is a wild call and a clear call that may not be denied;
And all I ask is a windy day with the white clouds flying,
And the flung spray and the blown spume, and the seagulls crying.

I must down to the seas again to the vagrant gypsy life.
To the gull's way and the whale's way where the wind's like a whetted knife;
And all I ask is a merry yarn from a laughing fellow-rover,
And quiet sleep and a sweet dream when the long trick's over.

JOHN MASEFIELD

The Ogre Courting

Juliana Horatia Ewing

Illustrated by John Patience

Daughter of a mid-Victorian lady who was herself a writer and magazine editor, Juliana Horatia Ewing (1841–1885) grew up in a literary family, and soon herself became the nursery story-teller, a practice that led by degrees to writing and publishing her own tales for children. Although she rather dominated the family, Juliana was loved by her brothers and sisters for her sweet and generous nature, and, in the way she tells her stories, you can feel a warm and lively person who seems much nearer to us than nearly a hundred years away. Perhaps her most famous book is "The Brownies and Other Tales" which first appeared in book form in 1870. But she also made up fairy tales—a very different thing from re-telling old ones, and one of these we give here as an instance of a comparatively modern fairy tale.

IN DAYS when ogres were still the terror of certain districts, there was one who had long kept a whole neighbourhood in fear without anyone daring to dispute his tyranny.

By thefts and exactions, by heavy ransoms from merchants too old and tough to be eaten, in one way and another, the Ogre had become very rich; and although those who knew could tell of huge cellars full of gold and jewels, and yards and barns groaning with the weight of stolen goods, the richer he grew the more anxious and covetous he became. Moreover, day by day, he added to his stores; for though (like most ogres) he was as stupid as he was strong, no one had ever been found, by force or fraud, to get the better of him.

What he took from the people was not their heaviest grievance. Even to be killed and eaten by him was not the chance they thought of most. A man can die but once; and, if he is a sailor, a shark may eat him, which is not so much better than being devoured by an ogre. No, that was not the worst. The worst was this—he would keep getting married. And, as he liked little wives, all the short women lived in fear and dread. And as his wives always died very soon, he was constantly courting fresh ones.

Some said he ate his wives; some said he tormented, and others, that he only worked them to death. Everybody knew it was not a desirable match, and yet there was not a father who dare refuse his daughter if she were asked for. The Ogre only cared for two things in a woman—he liked her to be little, and a good housewife.

Now it was when the Ogre had just lost his twenty-fourth wife (within the memory of man) that these two qualities were eminently united in the person of the smallest and most notable woman of the district, the daughter of a certain poor farmer. He was so poor that he could not afford properly to dower his daughter, who

35

had in consequence remained single beyond her first youth. Everybody felt sure that Managing Molly must now be married to the Ogre. The tall girls stretched themselves till they looked like maypoles and said: "Poor thing!" The slatterns gossiped from house to house, the heels of their shoes clacking as they went, and cried that this was what came of being too thrifty.

And sure enough, in due time, the giant widower came to the farmer as he was in the field looking over his crops, and proposed for Molly there and then. The farmer was so much put out that he did not know what he said in reply, either when he was saying it, or afterwards, when his friends asked about it. But he remembered that the Ogre had invited himself to sup at the farm that day week.

Managing Molly did not distress herself at the news.

"Do what I bid you, and say as I say," said she to her father; "and if the Ogre does not change his mind, at any rate you shall not come empty-handed out of the business."

By his daughter's desire the farmer now procured a large number of hares, and a barrel of white wine, which expenses completely emptied his slender stocking. Molly herself went round to all her neighbours, and borrowed a lot of new household linen, with which she filled the kitchen shelves. On the day of the Ogre's visit, she made a delicious and savoury stew with the hares in the biggest pickling tub, and the wine-barrel was set on a bench near the table.

When the Ogre came, Molly served up the stew, and the Ogre sat down to sup, his head just touching the kitchen rafters. The stew was perfect, and there was plenty of it. For what Molly and her father ate was hardly to be counted in the tub-full. The Ogre was very much pleased, and said politely:

"I'm afraid, my dear, that you have been put to great trouble and expense on my account. I have a large appetite, and like to sup well."

"Don't mention it, sir," said Molly. "The fewer rats the more corn. How do *you* cook them?"

"Not one of all the extravagant hussies I have had as wives ever cooked them at all," said the Ogre; and he thought to himself: Such a stew out of rats! What frugality! What a housewife! "I suppose you spin?" he inquired.

Molly held out her hand, in which was a linen towel made from the last month's spinnings, and said: "All that came off my wheel last month."

But, as her hand was towards the shelves, the Ogre thought that all the linen he saw there was from thread of her spinning; and his admiration grew every moment.

When he broached the wine, he was no less pleased, for it was of the best.

"This, at any rate, must have cost you a great deal, neighbour," said he, drinking the farmer's health as Molly left the room.

"I don't know that rotten apples could be better used," said the farmer; "but I leave all that to Molly. Do you brew at home?"

"We give *our* rotten apples to the pigs," growled the Ogre. "But things will be better ordered when she is my wife."

The Ogre was now in great haste to conclude the match, and asked what dowry the farmer would give his daughter.

"I should never dream of giving a dowry with Molly," said the farmer boldly. "Whoever gets her gets dowry enough. On the contrary, I shall expect a good round sum from the man who deprives me of her. Our wealthiest farmer is just widowed, and therefore sure to be in a hurry for marriage. He has an eye to the main chance, and would not grudge to pay well for such a wife, I'll warrant."

"I'm no churl myself," said the Ogre, who was anxious to secure his thrifty bride at any price; and he named a large sum of money, thinking: We shall live on rats

"I have a large appetite," said the Ogre, "and like to sup well."

henceforward, and the beef and mutton will soon cover the dowry.

"Double that, and we'll see," said the farmer stoutly. But the Ogre became angry, and cried: "What are you thinking of, man? Who is to hinder my carrying your lass off, without 'with your leave' or 'by your leave,' dowry or none?"

"How little you know her!" said the farmer. "She is so firm that she would be cut to pieces sooner than give you any benefit of her thrift, unless you dealt fairly in the matter."

"Well, well," said the Ogre, "let us meet each other." And he named a sum larger than he at first proposed, and less than the

farmer had asked. This the farmer agreed to, as it was enough to make him prosperous for life.

"Bring it in a sack to-morrow morning," said he to the Ogre, "and then you can speak to Molly; she's gone to bed now."

The next morning, accordingly, the Ogre appeared, carrying the dowry in a sack, and Molly came to meet him.

"There are two things," said she, "I would ask of any lover of mine: a new farmhouse, built as I should direct, with a view to economy; and a feather-bed of fresh goose feathers, filled when the old woman plucks her geese. If I don't sleep well, I cannot work well."

That is better than asking for finery, thought the Ogre; and, after all, the house will be my own. So to save the expense of labour he built it himself, and worked hard, day after day, under Molly's orders, till winter came. Then it was finished.

"Now for the feather-bed," said Molly. "I'll make the ticking, and when the old woman plucks her geese, I'll let you know."

When it snows, they say the old woman up yonder is plucking her geese, and so at the first snowstorm Molly sent for the Ogre. "Now you see the feathers falling," said she, "so fill the bed."

"How am I to catch them?" cried the Ogre.

"Stupid! don't you see them lying there in a heap?" cried Molly; "get a shovel, and set to work."

The Ogre accordingly carried in shovelfuls of snow to the bed, but as it melted as fast as he put it in, his labour never seemed done. Towards night the room got so cold that the snow would not melt, and now the bed was soon filled.

Molly hastily covered it with sheets and blankets, and said:

"Pray rest here to-night, and tell me if the bed is not comfort itself. To-morrow we will be married."

So the tired Ogre lay down on the bed he had filled, but do what he would, he could not get warm.

"The sheets must be damp," said he, and in the morning he woke with such horrible pains in his bones that he could hardly move, and half the bed had melted away. "It's no use," he groaned, "she's a very managing woman, but to sleep on such a bed would be the death of me."

And he went off home as quickly as he could, before Managing Molly could call upon him to be married; for she was so managing, that he was more than half afraid of her already.

When Molly found that he had gone, she sent the farmer after him.

"What does he want?" cried the Ogre, when they told him the farmer was at the door.

"He says the bride is waiting for you," was the reply.

"Tell him I'm too ill to be married," said the Ogre.

But the messenger soon returned·

"He says she wants to know what you will give her to make up for the disappointment."

"She's got the dowry, and the farm, and the feather-bed," groaned the Ogre; "what more does she want?"

But again the messenger returned: "She says you've pressed the feather-bed flat, and she wants some more goose feathers."

"There are geese enough in the yard," yelled the Ogre. "Let him drive them home, and if he has another word to say, put him down to roast."

The farmer, who overheard this order, lost no time in taking his leave, and as he passed through the yard he drove home as fine a flock of geese as you will see on a common.

It is said that the Ogre never recovered from the effects of sleeping on the old woman's feathers, and was less powerful than before.

As for Managing Molly, being now well dowered, she had no lack of offers of marriage, and was soon mated to her mind.

Cradle Song at Bethlehem

Oh! hush Thee, oh! hush Thee, my Baby so small,
The ass hath her crib and the ox hath his stall,
They shelter Thee, Baby, from Heaven above,
Oh! hush Thee, oh! hush Thee, my Baby, my love.

Oh! hush Thee, oh! hush Thee, my Baby so small,
Dim is the light from the lamp on the wall,
Bright in the night sky shineth a star,
Leading the Kings who come from afar.

Oh! hush Thee, oh! hush Thee, my Baby so small,
Joseph is spreading the straw in the stall,
Soon wilt Thou sleep in the nook of my arm
Safe from all trouble and danger and harm.

E. J. FALCONER.

Carol

I sing of a maiden
That is makeles;
King of all kings
To her son she ches.

He came al so still   *He came al so still*
There his mother was,   *There his mother lay,*
As dew in April   *As dew in April*
That falleth on the grass.   *That falleth on the spray.*

He came al so still   *Mother and maiden*
To his mother's bour,   *Was never none but she;*
As dew in April   *Well may such a lady*
That falleth on the flour.   *Goddes mother be.*

makeles = matchless   ches = chose

39

Becky's Christmas

Louisa May Alcott

*Illustrated by Brenda Seymour
and Victor G. Ambrus*

*An American writer, Louisa May Alcott
(1832–1888), was one of the first to write
realistic stories of family life for young
people. Her "Little Women" and "Little
Men" give a lively and interesting picture
of what it was like to grow up in 19th-
century America and they are still read
with enjoyment to-day. She also wrote
many short stories and sketches, of which
this is one that can be appreciated by
younger readers.*

ALL alone, by the kitchen fire, sat little
Becky, for every one else had gone
away to keep Christmas, and left her to
take care of the house. Nobody had
thought to give her any presents, or take
her to any merry-making, or remembered
that Christmas should be made a happy
time to every child, whether poor or rich.
She was only twelve years old—this little
girl from the poorhouse, who was bound
to work for the farmer's wife till she was
eighteen. She had no father or mother, no
friends or home but this, and as she sat
alone by the fire her little heart ached for
someone to love and cherish her.

Becky was a shy, quiet child, with a thin
face and wistful eyes that always seemed
trying to find something which she wanted
very much. She worked away, day after
day, so patiently and silently that no one
ever guessed what curious thoughts filled
the little cropped head, or what a tender
child's heart was hidden under the blue
checked pinafore.

To-night she was wishing that there
were fairies in the world, who would whisk
down the chimney and give her quantities
of pretty things, as they did in the delightful fairy tales.

"I'm sure I am as poor and lonely as
Cinderella, and need a kind godmother to
help me as much as ever she did," said
Becky to herself, as she sat on her little
stool staring at the fire, which didn't burn
very well, for she felt too much out of sorts
to care whether things looked cheerful or
not.

There is an old belief that all dumb
things can speak for one hour on Christmas
Eve. Now, Becky knew nothing of this
story, and no one can say whether what
happened was true, or whether she fell
asleep and dreamed it all. But certain it is,
when Becky compared herself to
Cinderella, she was amazed to hear a small
voice reply:

"Well, my dear, if you want advice, I
shall be very glad to give you some, for
I've had much experience in this trying
world."

Becky stared about her, but all she saw
was the old grey cat, blinking at the fire.

40

"Did you speak, Tabby?" said the child, at last.

"Of course I did. If you wish a godmother, here I am."

Becky laughed at the idea; but Puss, with her silver-grey suit, white handkerchief crossed on her bosom, kind, motherly old face, and cosy purr, did make a very good, Quakerish little godmother after all.

"Well, ma'am, I'm ready to listen," said Becky, respectfully.

"First, my child, what do you want most?" asked the godmother, quite in the fairy-book style.

"To be loved by everybody," answered Becky.

"Good!" said the cat. "I'm pleased with that answer; it's sensible; and I'll tell you how to get your wish. Learn to make people love you by loving them."

"I don't know how," sighed Becky.

"No more did I, in the beginning," returned Puss. "When I first came here, a shy young kitten, I thought only of keeping out of everybody's way, for I was afraid of everyone. I hid under the barn, and only came out when no one was near. I wasn't happy, for I wanted to be petted, but didn't know how to begin.

"One day I heard Aunt Sally say to the master: 'James, that wild kitten ain't no use at all; you'd better drown her, and get a nice tame one to amuse the children and clear the house of mice.'

"'The poor thing has been abused, I guess; so we'll give her another trial, and maybe she'll come to trust us after a while,' said the good master.

"I thought over these things as I lay under the barn and resolved to do my best, for I didn't wish to be drowned. It was hard at first; but I began by coming out when little Jane called me, and letting her play with me. Then I ventured into the house, and finding a welcome at my first visit, I went again and took a mouse with me, to show that I wasn't idle.

"No one hurt or frightened me, and soon I was the household pet. For several years I have led a happy life here."

Becky listened intently, and when Puss ended, she said, timidly, "Do you think if I try not to be afraid, but to show that I want to be affectionate, the people will let me and will like it?"

"Very sure. I heard the mistress say you were a good, handy little thing. Do as I did, my dear, and you will find that there is plenty of love in the world."

"I will; thank you, dear old Puss, for your advice."

Puss came to rub her soft cheek against Becky's hand, and then settled herself in a cosy hunch in Becky's lap. Presently another voice spoke—a queer monotonous voice, high above her.

"Tick, tick; wish again, little Becky, and I'll tell you how to find your wish."

It was the old moon-faced clock behind the door, which had struck twelve just before Tabby first spoke.

"Dear me," said Becky, "how queerly things do act to-night!" She thought a moment, then said, soberly, "I wish I liked my work better; but washing dishes, picking chips, and hemming towels is such tiresome work, I don't see how I can go on doing it for six more years."

"Just what I used to feel," said the clock. "I couldn't bear to think that I had got to stand here and do nothing but tick year after year. I flatly said I wouldn't, and I stopped a dozen times a day. Bless me, what a fuss I made, until I was put in this corner to stand idle for several months. At first I rejoiced; then I got tired of doing nothing, and began to reflect that as I was born a clock, it would be wiser to do my duty and get some satisfaction out of it if I could."

"And so you went to going again—please teach me to be faithful, and to love my duty," cried Becky.

"I will," and the old clock grandly struck the half hour, with a smile on its round face as it ticked steadily on and on.

Here the fire blazed up, and the tea-kettle, hanging on the crane, began to sing.

"How cheerful that is!" said Becky, as the whole kitchen brightened with the ruddy glow. "If I could have a third wish, I'd wish to be as cheerful as the fire."

"Have your wish if you choose; but you must work for it, as I do," cried the fire, as its flames embraced the old kettle till it gurgled with pleasure.

Becky thought she heard a queer voice humming these words:

"I'm an old black kettle,
With a very crooked nose,
But I can't help being gay
When the jolly fire glows."

"I shouldn't wonder a mite if that little no-good had been up to mischief to-night, rummaged all over the house, ate herself sick, or stole something and run away with it," croaked Aunt Sally, as the family went jingling home in the big sleigh about one o'clock from the Christmas party.

"Tut, tut, Aunty, I wouldn't think evil of the thing. If I'd had my way, she'd have gone with us and had a good time. She don't look as if she'd seen many. I've a notion it's what she needs," said the farmer kindly.

"The thought of her alone at home has worried me all the evening; but she didn't seem to mind, and I haven't had time to get a decent dress ready for her, so I let it go," added the farmer's wife, as she cuddled little Jane under the cloaks and shawls, with a regretful memory of Becky knocking at her heart.

"I've got some popcorn and a bouncing big apple for her," said Billy, the red-faced lad perched up by his father playing driver.

"And I'll give her one of my dolls. She said she never had one—wasn't that dreadful?" put in little Jane, popping out her head like a bird from its nest.

"Better see what she has been about fust," advised Aunt Sally. "But if she hasn't done no mischief, and has remembered to have the kettle bilin' so I can have a warm cup of tea after my ride, and if she's kep the fire up, and het my slippers, I don't know but I'll give her the red mittens I knit."

They found poor Becky lying on the bare floor, her head pillowed on the stool, and old Tabby in her arms with a corner of the blue pinafore spread over her. The fire was burning splendidly, the kettle simmering, and in a row upon the hearth stood, not only Aunt Sally's old slippers, but those of master and mistress also, and over a chair hung two little nightgowns, warming for the children.

"Well, now, if that don't beat all for thoughtfulness and sense! Becky *shall* have them mittens, and I'll knit her a couple of pair of stockin's as sure as she's livin'," said Aunt Sally, completely won by this unusual proof of "forehandedness" in a servant.

So Aunt Sally laid the gay mittens close to the little rough hand that worked so busily all day. Billy set his big red apple and bag of popcorn just where she would see them when she woke. Jane laid the doll in Becky's arms, and Tabby smelt of it approvingly, to the children's delight. The farmer had no present ready, but he stroked the little cropped head with a fatherly touch that made Becky smile in her sleep, as he said within himself, "I'll do by this forlorn child as I'd wish any one to do by my Janey if she was left alone." But the mother gave the best gift of all, for she stooped down and kissed Becky as only mothers can kiss, for the good woman's heart reproached her for neglect of the child who had no mother.

That unusual touch waked Becky at once, and looking about her with astonished eyes, she saw such a wonderful change in all the faces that her own lost its pathetic sadness as she clapped her hands and cried with a child's happy laugh——

"My dream's come true! O, my dream's come true!"

43

JOHN DOLITTLE
FRIEND OF
ANIMALS

The Rarest Animal of All

Hugh Lofting

Illustrated by the Author

Hugh Lofting (1886–1947) was of English-Irish parentage, and, when a young man, chose civil engineering as the path of adventure. This led him to railway-building in Africa and Canada. But it was in the trenches of the First World War that he started writing for children. His readers were his own children, and it was in his letters home that he invented Dr. Dolittle to amuse them. These were shown to a publisher when peace came, and became the first book, "The Story of Dr. Dolittle", from which we take the story of "The Rarest Animal of All," the pushmi-pullyu.

This delightful animal-doctor is certainly one of the outstanding characters of modern literature. His love of animals and his understanding of them which extends even to their language, combined with his simplicity and old-world courtesy and John Bull-ish ability to stand up to anything, make him a remarkable man. And he never looks down on animals, but always treats them kindly and politely, if not quite as his equals, certainly as his friends. And how they appreciate it and love him back. Children liked Dr. Dolittle so enormously that Hugh Lofting had to go on writing books about him for the rest of his life; and they are all good, so following this you get a second extract—the story of "The Great Bull Fight" from "The Voyages of Dr. Dolittle".

PUSHMI-PULLYUS are now extinct. That means, there aren't any more. But long ago, when Doctor Dolittle was alive, there were some of them still left in the deepest jungles of Africa; and even then they were very, very scarce. They had no tail, but a head at each end, and sharp horns on each head. They were very shy and terribly hard to catch. The black men get most of their animals by sneaking up behind them while they are not looking. But you could not do this with the pushmi-pullyu—because, no matter which way you came towards him, he was always facing you. And besides, only one half of him slept at a time. The other head was always awake—and watching. This was why they were never caught and never seen in zoos. Though many of the greatest huntsmen and the cleverest menagerie-keepers spent years of their lives searching through the jungles in all weathers for pushmi-pullyus, not a single one had ever been caught. Even then, years ago, he was the only animal in the world with two heads.

Well, the monkeys set out hunting for this animal through the forest. And after they had gone a good many miles, one of them found peculiar footprints near the edge of a river; and they knew that a pushmi-pullyu must be very near that spot.

Then they went along the bank of the river a little way and they saw a place where the grass was high and thick; and they guessed that he was in there.

So they all joined hands and made a great circle round the high grass. The pushmi-pullyu heard them coming, and he tried hard to break through the ring of monkeys. But he couldn't do it. When he saw that it was no use trying to escape, he sat down and waited to see what they wanted.

They asked him if he would go with Doctor Dolittle and be put on show in the Land of the White Men.

But he shook both his heads hard and said, "Certainly not!"

They explained to him that he would not be shut up in a menagerie but would just be looked at. They told him that the Doctor was a very kind man but hadn't any money; and people would pay to see a two-headed animal and the Doctor would get rich and could pay for the boat he had borrowed to come to Africa in.

But he answered: "No. You know how shy I am—I hate being stared at." And he almost began to cry.

Then for three days they tried to persuade him.

And at the end of the third day he said he would come with them and see what kind of a man the Doctor was, first.

So the monkeys travelled back with the pushmi-pullyu. And when they came to where the Doctor's little house of grass was, they knocked on the door.

Dab-Dab, the duck, who was packing the trunk, said: "Come in!"

And Chee-Chee very proudly took the animal inside and showed him to the Doctor.

"What in the world is it?" asked John Dolittle, gazing at the strange creature.

"Lord save us!" cried the duck. "How does it make up its mind?"

"It doesn't look to me as though it had any," said Jip the dog.

"This, Doctor," said Chee-Chee, "is the pushmi-pullyu—the rarest animal of the Africa jungles, the only two-headed beast in the world! Take him home with you and your fortune's made. People will pay any money to see him."

"But I don't want any money," said the Doctor.

"Yes, you do," said Dab-Dab, the duck. "Don't you remember how we had to pinch and scrape to pay the butcher's bill in Puddleby? And how are you going to get the sailor the new boat you spoke of— unless we have the money to buy it?"

"I was going to make him one," said the Doctor.

"Oh, do be sensible!" cried Dab-Dab. "Where would you get all the wood and the nails to make one with? And besides, what are we going to live on? We shall be poorer than ever when we get back. Chee-Chee's perfectly right: take the funny-looking thing along, do!"

"Well, perhaps there is something in what you say," murmured the Doctor. "It certainly would make a nice new kind of pet. But does the er—what-do-you-call-it really want to go abroad?"

"Yes, I'll go," said the pushmi-pullyu, who saw at once, from the Doctor's face, that he was a man to be trusted. "You have been so kind to the animals here—and the monkeys tell me that I am the only one who will do. But you must promise me that if I do not like it in the Land of the White Men you will send me back."

"What in the world is it?" asked John Dolittle, gazing at the strange creature.

"Why, certainly—of course, of course," said the Doctor. "Excuse me, surely you are related to the Deer Family, are you not?"

"Yes," said the pushmi-pullyu—"to the Abyssinian Gazelles and the Asiatic Chamois—on my mother's side. My father's great-grandfather was the last of the Unicorns."

"Most interesting!" murmured the Doctor; and he took a book out of the trunk which Dab-Dab was packing and began turning the pages. "Let us see if Buffon says anything——"

"I notice," said the duck, "that you only talk with one of your mouths. Can't the other head talk as well?"

"Oh yes," said the pushmi-pullyu. "But I keep the other mouth for eating—mostly. In that way I can talk while I am eating without being rude. Our people have always been very polite."

When the packing was finished and everything was ready to start, the monkeys gave a grand party for the Doctor and all the animals of the jungle came. And they had pineapples and mangoes and honey and all sorts of good things to eat and drink.

After they had all finished eating, the Doctor got up and said:

"My friends: I am not clever at speaking long words after dinner like some men; and I have just eaten many fruits and much honey. But I wish to tell you that I am very sad at leaving your beautiful country. Because I have things to do in the Land of the White Men, I must go. After I have gone, remember never to let the flies settle on your food before you eat it; and do not sleep on the ground when the rains are coming. I—er—er—I hope you will all live happily ever after."

When the Doctor stopped speaking and sat down, all the monkeys clapped their hands a long time and said to one another, "Let it be remembered always among our people that he sat and ate with us, here,

46

under the trees. For surely he is the Greatest of Men!"

And the Grand Gorilla, who had the strength of seven horses in his hairy arms, rolled a great rock up to the head of the table and said: "This stone for all time shall mark the spot."

And even to this day, in the heart of the jungle, that stone still is there. And monkey-mothers, passing through the forest with their families, still point down at it from the branches and whisper to their children: "Sh! There it is—look where the Good White Man sat and ate food with us in the Year of the Great Sickness!"

Then, when the party was over, the Doctor and his pets started out to go back to the seashore. And all the monkeys went with him as far as the edge of their country, carrying his trunk and bags, to see him off.

The Tiger

Tiger! Tiger! burning bright
In the forests of the night,
What immortal hand or eye
Could frame thy fearful symmetry?

In what distant deeps or skies
Burnt the fire of thine eyes?
On what wings dare he aspire?
What the hand dare seize the fire?

And what shoulder, and what art
Could twist the sinews of thy heart?
And, when thy heart began to beat,
What dread hand forged thy dread feet?

What the hammer? what the chain?
In what furnace was thy brain?
What the anvil? what dread grasp
Dare its deadly terrors clasp?

When the stars threw down their spears,
And watered heaven with their tears,
Did he smile his work to see?
Did he who made the Lamb make thee?

Tiger! Tiger! burning bright
In the forests of the night,
What immortal hand or eye
Dare frame thy fearful symmetry?

WILLIAM BLAKE

47

The Great Bullfight

Hugh Lofting

Illustrated by the Author

Not only is Dr. Dolittle an animal-doctor—he is an animal champion as well. He has many parts to play in his remarkable life, but none more unexpected and bewildering than that of bullfighter. It is said that those who actually saw the good Doctor in the Spanish bull-ring (as described by Hugh Lofting in his delightful "Voyages of Dr. Dolittle") have never been the same men since!

NEXT morning we were awakened by a great racket. There was a procession coming down the street, a number of men in very gay clothes followed by a large crowd of admiring ladies and cheering children. I asked the Doctor who they were.

"They are the bullfighters," he said. "There is to be a bullfight to-morrow."

"What is a bullfight?" I asked.

To my great surprise the Doctor got red in the face with anger. It reminded me of the time when he had spoken of the lions and tigers in his private zoo.

"A bullfight is a stupid, cruel, disgusting business," said he. "These Spanish people are most lovable and hospitable folk. How they can enjoy these wretched bullfights is a thing I could never understand."

Then the Doctor went on to explain to me how a bull was first made very angry by teasing and then allowed to run into a circus where men came out with red cloaks, waved them at him, and ran away. Next the bull was allowed to tire himself out by tossing and killing a lot of poor, old, broken-down horses who couldn't defend themselves. Then, when the bull was thoroughly out of breath and wearied by this, a man came out with a sword and killed the bull.

"Every Sunday," said the Doctor, "in almost every big town in Spain there are six bulls killed like that and as many horses."

"But aren't the men ever killed by the bull?" I asked.

"Unfortunately, very seldom," said he. "A bull is not nearly as dangerous as he looks, even when he's angry, if you are only quick on your feet and don't lose your head. These bullfighters are very clever and nimble. And the people, especially the Spanish ladies, think no end of them. A famous bullfighter (or matador, as they call them) is a more important man in Spain than a king. Here comes another crowd of them round the corner, look. See the girls throwing kisses to them. Ridiculous business!"

At that moment our friend the bed-maker came out to see the procession go past. And while he was wishing us good morning and inquiring how we had slept, a friend of his walked up and joined us. The bed-maker introduced this friend to us as Don Enrique Cardenas.

Don Enrique, when he heard where we

The fire was burning splendidly, the kettle simmering, and in a row upon the hearth stood, not only Aunt Sally's old slippers, but those of master and mistress also.
From "Becky's Christmas"

"The Dormouse is asleep again," said the Hatter, and he poured a little hot tea
upon its nose.
From "A Mad Tea-Party"

were from, spoke to us in English. He appeared to be a well-educated, gentlemanly sort of person.

"And you go to see the bullfight to-morrow, yes?" he asked the Doctor pleasantly.

"Certainly not," said John Dolittle firmly. "I don't like bullfights—cruel, cowardly shows."

Don Enrique nearly exploded. I never saw a man get so excited. He told the Doctor that he didn't know what he was talking about. He said bullfighting was a noble sport and that the matadors were the bravest men in the world.

"Oh, rubbish!" said the Doctor. "You never give the poor bull a chance. It is only when he is all tired and dazed that your precious matadors dare to try and kill him."

I thought the Spaniard was going to strike the Doctor he got so angry. While he was still spluttering to find words, the bed-maker came between them and took the Doctor aside. He explained to John Dolittle in a whisper that this Don Enrique Cardenas was a very important person; that he it was who supplied the bulls—a special, strong black kind—from his own farm for all the bullfights in the Capa Blancas. He was a very rich man, the bed-maker said, a most important personage. He mustn't be allowed to take offence on any account.

I watched the Doctor's face as the bed-maker finished, and I saw a flash of boyish mischief come into his eyes as though an idea had struck him. He turned to the angry Spaniard.

"Don Enrique," he said, "you tell me your bullfighters are very brave men and skilful. It seems I have offended you by saying that bullfighting is a poor sport. What is the name of the best matador you have for to-morrow's show?"

"Pepito de Malaga," said Don Enrique, "one of the greatest names, one of the bravest men, in all Spain."

"Very well," said the Doctor, "I have a proposal to make to you. I have never fought a bull in my life. Now supposing I were to go into the ring to-morrow with Pepito de Malaga and any other matador you choose; and if I can do more tricks with a bull than they can, would you promise to do something for me?"

Don Enrique threw back his head and laughed.

"Man," he said, "you must be mad! You would be killed at once. One has to be trained for years to become a proper bull-fighter."

"Supposing I were willing to take the risk of that. You are not afraid, I take it, to accept my offer?"

The Spaniard frowned.

"Afraid!" he cried, "Sir, if you can beat Pepito de Malaga in the bull-ring I'll promise you anything it is possible for me to grant."

"Very good," said the Doctor, "now I understand that you are quite a powerful man in these islands. If you wished to stop all bullfighting here after to-morrow, you could do it, couldn't you?"

"Yes," said Don Enrique proudly—"I could."

"Well, that is what I ask of you—if I win my wager," said John Dolittle. "If I can do more with angry bulls than can Pepito de Malaga, you are to promise me that there shall never be another bullfight in the Capa Blancas so long as you are alive to stop it. Is it a bargain?"

The Spaniard held out his hand.

"It is a bargain," he said, "I promise. But I must warn you that you are merely throwing your life away, for you will certainly be killed. However, that is no more than you deserve for saying that bullfighting is an unworthy sport. I will meet you here to-morrow morning if you should wish to arrange any particulars. Good day, sir."

As the Spaniard turned and walked into the shop, Polynesia, the parrot, who had been listening as usual, flew up on to my shoulder and whispered in my ear:

"I have a plan. Get hold of Bumpo and come some place where the Doctor can't hear us. I want to talk to you."

I nudged Bumpo's elbow and we crossed the street and pretended to look into a jeweller's window; while the Doctor sat down upon his bed to lace up his boots, the only part of his clothing he had taken off for the night.

"Listen," said Polynesia, "I've been breaking my head trying to think up some way we can get money to buy those stores with; and at last I've got it."

"The money?" said Bumpo.

"No, stupid. The idea—to make the money with. Listen; the Doctor is simply bound to win this game to-morrow, sure as you're alive. Now all we have to do is to make a side bet with these Spaniards—they're great on gambling—and the trick's done."

"What's a side bet?" I asked.

"Oh, I know what that is," said Bumpo proudly, "We used to have lots of them at Oxford when boat-racing was on. I go to Don Enrique and say, 'I bet you a hundred pounds the Doctor wins.' Then if he does win, Don Enrique pays me a hundred pounds; and if he doesn't, I have to pay Don Enrique."

"That's the idea," said Polynesia. "Only don't say a hundred pounds: say two-thousand five-hundred pesetas. Now come and find old Don Ricky-ticky and try to look rich."

So we crossed the street again and slipped into the bed-maker's shop while the Doctor was still busy with his boots.

"Don Enrique," said Bumpo, "allow me to introduce myself. I am the Crown Prince of Jolliginki. Would you care to have a small bet with me on to-morrow's bull-fight?"

Don Enrique bowed.

"Why, certainly," he said, "I shall be delighted. But I must warn you that you are bound to lose. How much?"

"Oh, a mere truffle," said Bumpo—"just for the fun of the thing, you know. What do you say to three-thousand pesetas?"

"I agree," said the Spaniard, bowing once more. "I will meet you after the bull-fight to-morrow."

"So that's all right," said Polynesia as we came out to join the Doctor. "I feel as though quite a load had been taken off my mind."

The next day was a great day in Monteverde. All the streets were hung with flags; and everywhere gaily dressed crowds were to be seen flocking towards the bull-ring, as the big circus was called where the fights took place.

The news of the Doctor's challenge had gone round the town and, it seemed, had caused much amusement to the islanders. The very idea of a mere foreigner daring to match himself against the great Pepito de Malaga!—Serve him right if he got killed!

The Doctor had borrowed a bullfighter's suit from Don Enrique; and very gay and wonderful he looked in it, though Bumpo and I had hard work getting the waistcoat to close in front and even then the buttons kept bursting off in all directions.

When we set out from the harbour to walk to the bull-ring, crowds of small boys ran after us making fun of the Doctor's fatness, calling out, *Juan Hagapoco, el grueso matador!* which is the Spanish for, "John Dolittle, the fat bullfighter."

As soon as we arrived the Doctor said he would like to take a look at the bulls before the fight began; and we were at once led to the bull pen where, behind a high railing, six enormous black bulls were tramping around wildly.

In a few hurried words and signs the Doctor told the bulls what he was going to do and gave them careful instructions for their part of the show. The poor creatures were tremendously glad when they heard that there was a chance of bullfighting being stopped; and they promised to do exactly as they were told.

Of course the man who took us in there didn't understand what we were doing. He merely thought the fat Englishman was crazy when he saw the Doctor making signs and talking in ox tongue.

From there the Doctor went to the matadors' dressing-rooms, while Bumpo and I with Polynesia made our way into the bull-ring and took our seats in the great open-air theatre.

It was a very gay sight. Thousands of ladies and gentlemen were there, all dressed in their smartest clothes; and everybody seemed very happy and cheerful.

Right at the beginning Don Enrique got up and explained to the people that the first item on the programme was to be a match between the English Doctor and Pepito de Malaga. He told them what he had promised if the Doctor should win. But the people did not seem to think there there was much chance of that. A roar of laughter went up at the very mention of such a thing.

When Pepito came into the ring, everybody cheered, the ladies blew kisses and the men clapped and waved their hats.

Presently a large door on the other side of the ring was rolled back and in galloped one of the bulls; then the door was closed again. At once the matador became very much on the alert. He waved his red cloak and the bull rushed at him. Pepito stepped nimbly aside and the people cheered again.

This game was repeated several times. But I noticed that whenever Pepito got into a tight place and seemed to be in real danger from the bull, an assistant of his, who always hung around somewhere near, drew the bull's attention upon himself by waving another red cloak. Then the bull would chase the assistant and Pepito was left in safety. Most often, as soon as he had drawn the bull off, this assistant ran for the high fence and vaulted out of the ring to save himself. They evidently had it all arranged, these matadors; and it didn't

seem to me that they were in any very great danger from the poor clumsy bull so long as they didn't slip and fall.

After about ten minutes of this kind of thing the small door into the matadors' dressing-room opened and the Doctor strolled into the ring. As soon as his fat figure, dressed in sky-blue velvet, appeared, the crowd rocked in their seats with laughter.

Juan Hagapoco, as they had called him, walked out into the centre of the ring and bowed ceremoniously to the ladies in the boxes. Then he bowed to the bull. Then he bowed to Pepito. While he was bowing to Pepito's assistant the bull started to rush at him from behind.

"Look out! Look out! The bull! You will be killed!" yelled the crowd.

But the Doctor calmly finished his bow. Then turning round he folded his arms, fixed the on-rushing bull with his eye and frowned a terrible frown.

Presently a curious thing happened: the bull's speed got slower and slower. It almost looked as though he were afraid of that frown. Soon he stopped altogether. The Doctor shook his finger at him. He began to tremble. At last, tucking his tail between his legs, the bull turned round and ran away.

The crowd gasped. The Doctor ran after him. Round and round the ring they went both of them puffing and blowing like grampuses. Excited whispers began to break out among the people. This was something new in bullfighting, to have the bull running away from the man, instead of the man away from the bull. At last in the tenth lap, with a final burst of speed, Juan Hagapoco, the English matador, caught the poor bull by the tail.

Then leading the now timid creature into the middle of the ring, the Doctor made him do all manner of tricks; standing on the hind legs, standing on the front legs, dancing, hopping, rolling over. He finished up by making the bull kneel down; then he got on to his back and did hand springs

51

and other acrobatics on the beast's horns.

Pepito and his assistant had their noses sadly out of joint. The crowd had forgotten them entirely. They were standing together by the fence not far from where I sat, muttering to one another and slowly growing green with jealousy.

Finally the Doctor turned towards Don Enrique's seat, and bowing said in a loud voice, "This bull is no good any more. He's

At this a cry of horror burst from the people. They had been used to seeing matadors escaping from one bull at a time. But *five*! That must mean certain death.

Pepito sprang forward and called to Don Enrique not to allow it, saying it was against all the rules of bullfighting. ("Ha!" Polynesia chuckled into my ear. "It's like the Doctor's navigation: he breaks all the rules; but he gets there. If they'll only let

terrified and out of breath. Take him away, please."

"Does the caballero wish for a fresh bull?" asked Don Enrique.

"No," said the Doctor, "I want five fresh bulls. And I would like them all in the ring at once, please."

him, he'll give them the best show for their money they ever saw.") A great argument began. Half the people seemed to be on Pepito's side and half on the Doctor's side. At last the Doctor turned to Pepito and made another very grand bow which burst the last button off his waistcoat.

52

"Well, of course, if the caballero is afraid——" he began with a bland smile.

"Afraid!" screamed Pepito. "I am afraid of nothing on earth. I am the greatest matador in Spain. With this right hand I have killed nine hundred and fifty-seven bulls."

"All right then," said the Doctor, "let us see if you can kill five more. Let the bulls in!" he shouted. "Pepito de Malaga is not afraid."

A dreadful silence hung over the great theatre as the heavy door into the bull pen was rolled back. Then with a roar the five big bulls bounded into the ring.

"Look fierce," I heard the Doctor call to them in cattle language. "Don't scatter. Keep close. Get ready for a rush. Take Pepito, the one in purple, first. But for Heaven's sake don't kill him. Just chase him out of the ring. Now then, all together, go for him!"

The bulls put down their heads and all in line, like a squadron of cavalry, charged across the ring straight for poor Pepito.

For one moment the Spaniard tried his hardest to look brave. But the sight of the five pairs of horns coming at him at full gallop was too much. He turned white to the lips, ran for the fence, vaulted it and disappeared.

"Now the other one," the Doctor hissed. And in two seconds the gallant assistant was nowhere to be seen. Juan Hagapoco, the fat matador, was left alone in the ring with five rampaging bulls.

The rest of the show was really well worth seeing. First, all five bulls went raging round the ring, butting at the fence with their horns, pawing up the sand, hunting for something to kill. Then each one in turn would pretend to catch sight of the Doctor for the first time and giving a bellow of rage, would lower his wicked-looking horns and shoot like an arrow across the ring as though he meant to toss him to the sky.

It was really frightfully exciting. And even I, who knew it was all arranged beforehand, held my breath in terror for the Doctor's life when I saw how near they came to sticking him. But just at the last moment, when the horns' points were two inches from the sky-blue waistcoat, the Doctor would spring nimbly to one side and the great brutes would go thundering harmlessly by, missing him by no more than a hair.

Then all five of them went for him together, completely surrounding him, slashing at him with their horns and bellowing with fury. How he escaped alive I don't know. For several minutes his round figure could hardly be seen at all in that scrimmage of tossing heads, stamping hoofs and waving tails. It was, as Polynesia had prophesied, the greatest bullfight ever seen.

One woman in the crowd got quite hysterical and screamed up to Don Enrique:

"Stop the fight! Stop the fight! He is too brave a man to be killed. This is the most wonderful matador in the world. Let him live! Stop the fight!"

But presently the Doctor was seen to break loose from the mob of animals that surrounded him. Then catching each of them by the horns, one after another, he would give their heads a sudden twist and throw them down flat on the sand. The great fellows acted their parts extremely well. I have never seen trained animals in a circus do better. They lay there panting on the ground where the Doctor threw them as if they were exhausted and completely beaten.

Then with a final bow to the ladies John Dolittle took a cigar from his pocket, lit it and strolled out of the ring.

Boy on a Horse

R. D. Blackmore

Illustrated by T. S. La-Fontaine

Richard Doddridge Blackmore (1825–1900) is a writer who is best known today for his book, "Lorna Doone", the romantic story of a young Exmoor farmer's feud with the Doones, a nest of savage rascals and outlaws in the days of Charles II. Although written for adults it is a book that begins with its hero's boyhood, for John Ridd was still at school when he learned that his father had been murdered by the Doones; and many a young reader has been held by this tale.

In this episode the boy is trying his muscles, so to speak. He thinks he can ride Tom Faggus's famous mare if Tom will let him try. Has he attempted more than he can manage? "Boy on a Horse" provides the answer.

THE gentleman turned round to us, with a pleasant smile on his face, as if he were lightly amused with himself; and we came up and looked at him. He was rather short, about John Fry's height, or may be a little taller, but very strongly built and springy, as his gait at every step showed plainly, although his legs were bowed with much riding, and he looked as if he lived on horseback. To a boy like me he seemed very old, being over twenty, and well-found in beard; but he was not more than four-and-twenty, fresh and ruddy-looking, with a short nose, and keen blue eyes, and a merry waggish jerk about him, as if the world were not in earnest. Yet he had a sharp stern way, like the crack of a pistol, if anything misliked him; and we knew (for children see such things) that it was safer to tickle than tackle him.

"Well, young uns, what be gaping at?" He gave pretty Annie a chuck on the chin, and took me all in without winking.

"Your mare," said I, standing stoutly up, being a tall boy now; "I never saw such a beauty, sir. Will you let me have a ride of her?"

"Think thou couldst ride her, lad? She will have no burden but mine. Thou couldst never ride her. Tut! I would be loath to kill thee."

"Ride her!" I cried with the bravest scorn, for she looked so kind and gentle; "there never was horse upon Exmoor foaled, but I could tackle in half-an-hour. Only I never ride upon saddle. Take them leathers off of her."

He looked at me, with a dry little whistle, and thrust his hands into his breeches-pockets, and so grinned that I could not stand it. And Annie laid hold of me, in such a way, that I was almost mad with her. And he laughed, and approved her for doing so. And the worst of all was —he said nothing.

"Get away, Annie, will you? Do you think I am a fool, good sir? Only trust me with her, and I will not over-ride her."

"For that I will go bail, my son. She is liker to over-ride thee. But the ground is soft to fall upon, after all this rain. Now come out into the yard, young man, for the sake of your mother's cabbages. And the mellow straw-bed will be softer for thee, since pride must have its fall. I am thy mother's cousin, boy, and am going up to house. Tom Faggus is my name, as everybody knows; and this is my young mare, Winnie."

What a fool I must have been not to know it at once! Tom Faggus, the great highwayman, and his young bloodmare, the strawberry! Already her fame was noised abroad, nearly as much as her master's; and my longing to ride her grew tenfold, but fear came at the back of it. Not that I had the smallest fear of what the mare could do to me, by fair play and horse-trickery; but that the glory of sitting upon her seemed to be too great for me; especially as there were rumours abroad that she was not a mare after all, but a witch. However, she looked like a filly all over, and wonderfully beautiful, with her supple stride, and soft slope of shoulder, and glossy coat beaded with water, and prominent eyes, full of love or of fire. Whether this came from her Eastern blood of the Arabs newly imported, and whether the cream-colour, mixed with our bay, led to that bright strawberry tint, is certainly more than I can decide, being chiefly acquainted with farm horses.

Mr. Faggus gave his mare a wink, and she walked demurely after him, a bright young thing, flowing over with life, yet dropping her soul to a higher one, and led by love to anything; as the manner is of females, when they know what is the best for them. Then Winnie trod lightly upon the straw, because it had soft muck under it, and her delicate feet came back again.

"Up for it still, boy, be ye?" Tom Faggus stopped, and the mare stopped there; and they looked at me provokingly.

"Is she able to leap, sir? There is good take-off on this side of the brook."

Mr. Faggus laughed very quietly, turning round to Winnie, so that she might enter into it. And she, for her part, seemed to know exactly where the joke was.

"Good tumble-off, you mean, my boy. Well there can be small harm to thee. I am akin to thy family, and know the substance of their skulls."

"Let me get up," said I, waxing wroth, for reasons I cannot tell you, because they are too manifold, "take off your saddlebag things. I will try not to squeeze her ribs in, unless she plays nonsense with me."

Then Mr. Faggus was up on his mettle, at this proud speech of mine; and John Fry was running up all the while, and Bill Dadds, and a half a dozen. Tom Faggus gave one glance around, and then dropped all regard for me. The high repute of his mare was at stake, and what was my life compared to it? Through my defiance, and stupid ways, here was I in a duello, and my legs not come to their strength yet, and my arms as limp as a herring.

Something of this occurred to him, even in his wrath with me, for he spoke very softly to the filly, who now could scarce subdue herself; but she drew in her nostrils, and breathed to his breath, and did all she could to answer him.

"Not too hard, my dear," he said; "let him gently down on the mixen. That will be quite enough." Then he turned the saddle off, and I was up in a moment. She began at first so easily, and pricked her ears so lovingly, and minced about as if pleased to find so light a weight on her, that I thought she knew I could ride a little, and feared to show any capers. "Gee wugg, Polly!" cried I, for all the men were now looking on, being then at the leaving-off time; "Gee wugg, Polly, and show what thou be'est made of." With that I plugged my heels into her, and Billy Dadds flung his hat up.

Nevertheless, she outraged not, though her eyes were frightening Annie, and John Fry took a pick to keep him safe; but she curbed to and fro, with her strong forearms rising, like springs ingathered, waiting and quivering grievously, and beginning to sweat about it. Then her master gave a shrill clear whistle, when her ears were bent towards him, and I felt her form beneath me gathering up like whalebone, and her hind-legs coming under her, and I knew that I was in for it.

First she reared upright in the air, and struck me full on the nose with her comb, till I bled worse than Robin Snell made me; and then down with her fore-feet deep in the straw, and her hind-feet going to heaven. Finding me stick to her still like wax (for my mettle was up as hers was), away she flew with me, swifter than ever I went before, or since, I trow. She drove full-head at the cobwall—"oh, Jack, slip off," screamed Annie—then she turned like light, when I thought to crush her, and ground my left knee against it. "Mux me," I cried, for my breeches were broken, and short words went the furthest—"if you kill me, you shall die with me." Then she took the court-yard gate at a leap, knocking my words between my teeth, and then right over a quickset hedge, as if the sky were a breath to her; and away for the water-meadows, while I lay on her neck like a child at the breast, and wished I had never been born. Straight away, all in the front of the wind, and scattering clouds around her, all I knew of the speed we made was the frightful flash of her shoulders, and her mane like trees in a tempest. I felt the earth under us rushing away, and the air left far behind us, and my breath came and went, and I prayed to God, and was sorry to be so late of it.

All the long swift while, without power of thought, I clung to her crest and shoulders, and dug my nails into her creases, and my toes into her flank-part, and was proud of holding on so long, though sure of being beaten. Then in her fury at feeling me still, she rushed at another device for it, and leaped the wide water-trough sideways across, to and fro, till no breath was left in me. The hazel-boughs took me too hard in the face, and the tall dog-briars got hold of me, and the

ache of my back was like crimping a fish; till I longed to give up, and lay thoroughly beaten, and lie there and die in the cresses. But there came a shrill whistle from up the home-hill, where the people had hurried to watch us; and the mare stopped as if with a bullet; then set off for home with the speed of a swallow, and going as smoothly and silently. I never had dreamed of such delicate motion, fluent, and graceful, and ambient, soft as the breeze flitting over the flowers, but swift as the summer lightning. I sat up again, but my strength was all spent, and no time left to recover it; and at last, as she rose at our gate like a bird, I tumbled off into the mixen.

"Well done, lad," Mr. Faggus said, good naturedly; for all were now gathered round me, as I rose from the ground somewhat tottering, and miry, and crestfallen, but otherwise none the worse (having fallen upon my head, which is of uncommon substance); nevertheless John Fry was laughing, so that I longed to clout his ears for him; "Not at all bad work, my boy; we may teach you to ride by and by, I see; I thought not to see you stick on so long"——

"I should have stuck on much longer, sir, if her sides had not been wet. She was so slippery"——

"Boy, thou art right. She hath given many the slip. Ha, ha! Vex not, Jack, that I laugh at thee. She is like a sweetheart to me, and better than any of them be. It would have gone to my heart, if thou hadst conquered. None but I can ride my Winnie mare."

A Mad Tea-Party

Lewis Carroll

Illustrated by Charles Mortimer and John Patience

Lewis Carroll (1832–1898) whose real name was Charles Lutwidge Dodgson, son of a clergyman, was a lecturer in mathematics at Oxford University and the author of several learned books. He was a quiet man, rather lonely and very much the Professor. But he was fond of children, and, being unmarried himself, found many young friends among the families of his colleagues. His sense of fun both in speech and in letters chimed in with theirs, and he was much in demand as a story-teller. Among his friends was a real Alice, Henry Liddell's small daughter; and to amuse her and her two sisters, he started a series of adventures for Alice by sending her down a rabbit hole. As a gift for the child he wrote out the story of "Alice's Adventures Underground"—the first draft of "Alice's Adventures in Wonderland". Many would place this book as first among the best half-dozen books ever written for children. Perhaps one should say for British children—and University Professors. (But if you happen not to care for Alice at all, you can claim to be in a rather distinguished though very small minority).

THERE was a table set out under a tree in front of the house, and the March Hare and the Hatter were having tea at it: a Dormouse was sitting between them, fast asleep, and the other two were resting their elbows on it, and talking over its head. "Very uncomfortable for the Dormouse," thought Alice; "only, as it's asleep, I suppose it doesn't mind."

The table was a large one, but the three were all crowded together at one corner of it. "No room! No room!" they cried out when they saw Alice coming. "There's *plenty* of room!" said Alice indignantly, and she sat down in a large arm-chair at one end of the table.

"Have some wine," the March Hare said in an encouraging tone.

Alice looked all round the table, but there was nothing on it but tea. "I don't see any wine," she remarked.

"There isn't any," said the March Hare.

"Then it wasn't very civil of you to offer it," said Alice angrily.

"It wasn't very civil of you to sit down without being invited," said the March Hare.

"I didn't know it was *your* table," said Alice; "it's laid for a great many more than three."

"Your hair wants cutting," said the Hatter. He had been looking at Alice for some time with great curiosity, and this was his first speech.

"You shouldn't make personal remarks," Alice said with some severity; "it's very rude."

The Hatter opened his eyes very wide

on hearing this; but all he *said* was: "Why is a raven like a writing desk?"

"Come, we shall have some fun now!" thought Alice.

"I'm glad they've begun asking riddles. I believe I can guess that," she added aloud.

"Do you mean that you think you can find out the answer to it?" said the March Hare.

"Exactly so," said Alice.

"Then you should say what you mean," the March Hare went on.

"I do," Alice hastily replied; "at least—at least I mean what I say—that's the same thing, you know."

"Not the same thing a bit!" said the Hatter. "You might just as well say that 'I see what I eat' is the same thing as 'I eat what I see'."

"You might just as well say," added the Dormouse, who seemed to be talking in his sleep, "that 'I breathe when I sleep' is the same thing as 'I sleep when I breathe'."

"It *is* the same thing with you," said the Hatter, and here the conversation dropped, and the party sat silent for a minute, while Alice thought over all she could remember about ravens and writing-desks, which wasn't much.

The Hatter was the first to break the silence. "What day of the month is it?" he said, turning to Alice: he had taken his watch out of his pocket, and was looking at it uneasily, shaking it now and then, and holding it to his ear.

Alice considered a little, and then said, "The fourth."

"Two days wrong!" sighed the Hatter. "I told you butter wouldn't suit the works!" he added, looking angrily at the March Hare.

"It was the *best* butter," the March Hare meekly replied.

"Yes, but some crumbs must have got in as well," the Hatter grumbled; "you shouldn't have put it in with the bread-knife."

The March Hare took the watch and looked at it gloomily: then he dipped it it into his cup of tea, and looked at it again: but he could think of nothing better to say than his first remark, "It was the *best* butter, you know."

Alice had been looking over his shoulder with some curiosity. "What a funny watch!" she remarked. "It tells the day of the month, and doesn't tell what o'clock it is!"

"Why should it?" muttered the Hatter. "Does *your* watch tell you what year it is?"

"Of course not," Alice replied very readily; "but that's because it stays the same year for such a long time together."

"Which is just the case with *mine*," said the Hatter.

Alice felt dreadfully puzzled. The Hatter's remark seemed to have no meaning in it, and yet it was certainly English. "I don't quite understand," she said, as politely as she could.

"The Dormouse is asleep again," said

the Hatter, and he poured a little hot tea upon its nose.

The Dormouse shook its head impatiently and said, without opening its eyes: "Of course, of course; just what I was going to remark myself."

"Have you guessed the riddle yet?" the Hatter said, turning to Alice again.

"No, I give it up," Alice replied. "What's the answer?"

"I haven't the slightest idea," said the Hatter.

"Nor I," said the March Hare.

Alice sighed wearily. "I think you might do something better with the time," she said, "than waste it asking riddles with no answers."

"If you knew Time as well as I do," said the Hatter, "you wouldn't talk about wasting *it*. It's *him*."

"I don't know what you mean," said Alice.

"Of course you don't" the Hatter said, tossing his head contemptuously. "I dare say you never even spoke to Time!"

"Perhaps not," Alice cautiously replied; "but I know I have to beat time when I learn music."

"Ah! That accounts for it," said the Hatter. "He won't stand beating. Now, if you only kept on good terms with him, he'd do almost anything you liked with the clock. For instance, suppose it were nine o'clock in the morning, just time to begin lessons: you'd only have to whisper a hint to Time, and round goes the clock in a twinkling! Half-past one, time for dinner!"

("I only wish it was," the March Hare said to itself in a whisper.)

"That would be grand, certainly," said Alice thoughtfully; "but then—I shouldn't be hungry for it, you know."

"Not at first, perhaps," said the Hatter, "but you could keep it to half-past one as long as you liked."

"Is that the way *you* manage?" Alice asked.

The Hatter shook his head mournfully. "Not I!" he replied. "We quarrelled last March—just before *he* went mad, you know (pointing with his teaspoon at the March Hare), "it was at the great concert given by the Queen of Hearts, and I had to sing:

Twinkle, twinkle, little bat!
How I wonder what you're at!

You know the song, perhaps?"

"I've heard something like it," said Alice.

"It goes on, you know," the Hatter continued, "in this way:

Up above the world you fly,
Like a tea-tray in the sky.
Twinkle, twinkle—

"Well, I'd hardly finished the first verse," said the Hatter, "when the Queen jumped up and bawled out, 'He's murdering the time! Off with his head!'"

"How dreadfully savage!" exclaimed Alice.

"And ever since that," the Hatter went on in a mournful tone, "he won't do a thing I ask! It's always six o'clock now."

A bright idea came into Alice's head. "Is that the reason so many tea-things are put out here?" she asked.

"Yes, that's it," said the Hatter with a sigh. "It's always tea-time, and we've no time to wash things in between."

"Then you keep moving round, I suppose?" said Alice.

"Exactly so," said the Hatter. "As things get used up."

"But what happens when you come to the beginning again?" Alice ventured to ask.

"Suppose we change the subject," the March Hare interrupted, yawning. "I'm getting tired of this. I vote the young lady tells us a story."

"I'm afraid I don't know one," said Alice, rather alarmed at the proposal.

"Then the Dormouse shall!" they both cried. "Wake up, Dormouse!" And they pinched it on both sides at once.

The Dormouse slowly opened his eyes. "I wasn't asleep," he said in a hoarse, feeble voice. "I heard every word you fellows were saying."

"Tell us a story!" said the March Hare.

"Yes, please do!" pleaded Alice.

"And be quick about it," added the Hatter, "or you'll be asleep again before it's done."

"Once upon a time there were three

The Queen jumped up: "He's murdering the time! Off with his head!"

little sisters," the Dormouse began in a great hurry, "and their names were Elsie, Lacie and Tillie; and they lived at the bottom of a well——"

"What did they live on?" said Alice, who always took a great interest in questions of eating and drinking.

"They lived on treacles," said the Dormouse, after thinking a minute or two.

"They couldn't have done that, you know," Alice gently remarked; "they'd have been ill."

"So they were," said the Dormouse. "*Very* ill."

Alice tried to fancy to herself what such an extraordinary way of living would be like, but it puzzled her too much, so she went on: "But why did they live at the bottom of a well?"

"Take some more tea," the March Hare said to Alice, very earnestly.

"I've had nothing yet," Alice replied in an offended tone, "so I can't take more."

"You mean you can't take *less*," said the Hatter. "It's very easy to take *more* than nothing."

"Nobody asked *your* opinion."

"Who's making personal remarks now?" the Hatter asked triumphantly.

Alice did not quite know what to say to this; so she helped herself to some tea and bread-and-butter, and then turned to the Dormouse, and repeated her question. "Why did they live at the bottom of a well?"

The Dormouse again took a minute or two to think about it, and then said: "It was a treacle-well."

"There's no such thing!" Alice was beginning very angrily, but the Hatter and the March Hare went "Sh! sh!" and the Dormouse sulkily remarked: "If you can't be civil, you'd better finish the story for yourself."

"No, please go on!" Alice said. "I won't interrupt again. I dare say there may be *one*."

"One, indeed!" said the Dormouse, indignantly. However, he consented to go on. "And so these three little sisters—they were learning to draw, you know——"

"What did they draw?" said Alice, quite forgetting her promise.

"Treacle," said the Dormouse, without considering at all this time.

"I want a clean cup," interrupted the Hatter. "Let's all move one place on."

He moved on as he spoke, and the Dormouse followed him: the March Hare moved into the Dormouse's place, and Alice rather unwillingly took the place of the March Hare. The Hatter was the only one who got any advantage from the change; and Alice was a good deal worse off, as the March Hare had just upset the milk-jug into his plate.

Alice did not wish to offend the Dormouse again, so she began very cautiously: "But I don't understand. Where did they draw the treacle from?"

"You can draw water out of a water-well," said the Hatter, "so I should think you could draw treacle out of a treacle-well—eh, stupid?"

"But they were in the well," Alice said to the Dormouse, not choosing to notice this last remark.

"Of course they were," said the Dormouse; "—well in."

This answer so confused poor Alice, that she let the Dormouse go on for some time without interrupting it.

"They were learning to draw," the Dormouse went on, yawning and rubbing its eyes, for it was getting very sleepy; "and they drew all manner of things—everything that begins with an M——"

"Why with an M?" said Alice.

"Why not?" said the March Hare.

The Dormouse had closed its eyes by this time, and was going off into a doze; but, on being pinched by the Hatter, it woke up again with a little shriek, and went on: "—that begins with an M, such as mouse-traps, and the moon, and memory, and muchness—you know you say things are 'much of a muchness'—did you ever see such a thing as a drawing of a muchness?"

"Really, now you ask me," said Alice, very much confused, "I don't think——"

"Then you shouldn't talk," said the Hatter.

This piece of rudeness was more than Alice could bear; she got up in great disgust, and walked off; the Dormouse fell asleep instantly, and neither of the others took the least notice of her going, though she looked back once or twice, half hoping that they would call after her; the last time she saw them they were trying to put the Dormouse into the teapot.

"At any rate I'll never go *there* again!" said Alice as she picked her way through the wood. "It's the stupidest tea-party I ever was at!"

Into the Unknown

Mary Norton

Illustrated by Shirley Tourret

Many of you will have heard of "The Borrowers" (a Carnegie Medal book) which established its author, Mary Norton, as one of the foremost children's writers of her generation. The "borrowers" are little people, four or five inches high, who live in old houses behind the wainscots or in any odd corner where one would expect to find nothing but mice; and they "borrow" such things as safety-pins and wrist-watches or the odd potato and leftovers from human beings who, they think, exist to provide them with borrowings. When you have lost your pocket handkerchief or paste brooch, it's probably been taken by a "borrower"!

We are concerned with a little family, Arrietty and her father and mother, Pod and Homily. In this extract from the sequel, "The Borrowers Afield", they have had to flee from their comfortable home beneath the kitchen floor and have set out on a desperate journey to try to find relations who have last been heard of living in a deserted badger's set. For all three there is danger a-plenty, but for Arrietty—oh, the joy of the open air and the never-before-explored out-of-doors.

"KEEP your eyes skinned," Pod went on, as they all moved off along the path. "If you see anything, do as I do—and sharp, mind. We don't want no running every which way. We don't want no screaming."

"I know," said Arrietty irritably, adjusting her pack. She moved ahead as though trying to get out of earshot.

"You *think* you know," called Pod after her. "But you don't know nothing really; you don't know nothing about cover; nor does your mother: cover's a trained job, an art like——"

. . . There was a rushing clatter and a dropped shadow and a hoarse, harsh cry; and, suddenly, there was Pod—alone on the path—face to face with a large, black crow.

The bird stared, wickedly, but a little distrustfully, his cramped toes turned in slightly, his great beak just open. Frozen to stillness Pod stared back—something growing in the path, that's what he looked like—a rather peculiar kind of chunky toadstool. The great bird, very curious, turned his head sideways and tried Pod with his other eye. Pod, motionless, stared back. The crow made a murmur in its throat—a tiny bleat—and, puzzled, it moved forward. Pod let it come, a couple of sideways steps, and then—out of a still face—he spoke: "Get back to where you was," he said evenly, almost conversationally, and the bird seemed to hesitate. "We don't want no nonsense from you," Pod went on steadily, "pigeon-toed, that's what you are! Crows is pigeon-toed, first time it struck me. Staring away like that, with one eye, and your head turned sideways . . . think it pretty, no doubt"—Pod spoke quite pleasantly—"but it ain't, not with *that* kind of beak. . . ."

The bird became still, its expression no longer curious: there was stark amazement in every line of its rigid body and, in its eye, a kind of ghastly disbelief. "Go on! Get off with you!" shouted Pod suddenly, moving towards it. "Shoo . . . !" And, with a distraught glance and panic-stricken croak, the great bird flapped away. Pod wiped his brow with his sleeve as Homily, white-faced and still trembling, crawled out from under a foxglove leaf. "Oh, Pod," she gasped, "you were brave—you were wonderful!"

"It's nothing," said Pod, "it's a question of keeping your nerve."

"But the size of it!" said Homily. "You'd never think seeing them flying they was that size!"

"Size is nothing," said Pod, "it's the talk that gets them."

[It begins to rain and they have to seek shelter for the night. Pod finds an old boot.]

"Here it is," said Pod. "Get in here."

The boot lay on its side; they had to crouch to enter. "Oh, my goodness,"

Homily kept saying. "Oh, my goodness me . . ." and would glance fearfully about the darkness inside. "I wonder whoever wore it."

"Go on," said Pod, "get further down; it's all right."

"No, no," said Homily, "I'm not going in no further: there might be something in the toe."

"It's all right," said Pod, "I've looked: there's nothing but a hole in the toe." He stacked the borrowing-bags against the inner side. "Something to lean against," he said.

"I wish I knew who'd wore this boot," Homily went on, peering about uncomfortably, wiping her wet face on her wetter apron.

"What good would that do you?" Pod said, untying the strings of the largest bag.

"Whether he was clean or dirty or what," said Homily, "and what he died of. Suppose he died of something infectious?"

"Why suppose he died?" said Pod. "Why shouldn't he be hale and hearty, and just had a nice wash and be sitting down to a good tea this very minute."

"Tea?" said Homily, her face brightening. "Where's the candle, Pod?"

"It's here," said Pod. "Give me a wax-vesta, Arrietty, and a medium-sized aspirin lid. We got to go careful with the tea, you know; we got to go careful with everything."

Homily put out a finger and touched the worn leather. "I'll give this boot a good clean out in the morning," she said.

"It's not bad," said Pod, taking out the half nail-scissor. "If you ask me, we been lucky to find a boot like this. There ain't nothing to worry about: it's disinfected, all right—what with the sun and the wind and the rain, year after year of it." He stuck the blade of the nail-scissor through an eyelet hole and lashed it firm with a bit of old bootlace.

"What are you doing that for, Papa?" asked Arrietty.

"To stand the lid on, of course," said

"*Here we are,*" *Bambi heard the old stag saying. He walked along the beech-trunk and Bambi walked beside him.*
From "A Narrow Escape"

And nobody could enough admire the tall man and his quaint attire.
From "The Pied Piper of Hamelin"

Pod, "a kind of bracket over the candle; we haven't got no tripod. Now you go and fill it with water, there's a good girl—there's plenty outside. . . ."

There was plenty outside: it was coming down in torrents; but the mouth of the boot faced out of the wind and there was a little dry patch before it. Arrietty filled the tin lid quite easily by tipping a large pointed foxglove leaf towards it so the rain ran off and down the point. All about her was the steady sound of rain, and the lighted candle within the boot made the dusk seem darker: there was a smell of wildness, of space, of leaves and grasses and, as she turned away with the filled tin-lid, another smell—winy, fragrant, spicy. Arrietty took note of it to remember it for morning—it was the smell of wild strawberries.

After they had drunk their hot tea and eaten a good half of sweet, crumbly digestive biscuit, they took off their wet outer clothes and hung them out along the handle of the nail-scissor above the candle. With the old woollen sock about their three shoulders, they talked a little. ". . . Funny," Arrietty remarked, "to be wrapped in a sock and inside a boot." But Pod, watching the candle flame, was worried about wastage and, when the clothes had steamed a little, he doused the flame. Tired out, they lay down at last among the borrowing-bags, cuddled together for warmth. The last sound Arrietty heard as she fell asleep was the steady drumming of the rain on the hollow leather of the boot.

Arrietty was the first to wake. "Where am I!" she wondered. She felt warm—too warm, lying there between her mother and father—and when slightly she turned her head she saw three little golden suns, floating in the darkness; it was a second or two before she realized what they were, and with this knowledge memory flooded back—all that happened yesterday: the escape, the frenzied scramble across the orchard, the weary climb, the rain—

the little golden suns, she realized, were the lace-holes of the boot!

Stealthily Arrietty sat up; a balmy freshness stole in upon her and, framed in the neck of the boot, she saw the bright day: grasses, softly stirring, tenderly sunlit: some were broken, where yesterday they had pushed through them dragging the borrowing-bags; there was a yellow buttercup, sticky and gleaming, it looked—like wet paint; on a tawny stalk of sorrel she saw an aphis—of a green so delicate that, against the sunlight, it looked transparent. "Ants milk them," Arrietty remembered, "perhaps we could."

She slid out from between her sleeping parents and, just as she was, with bare feet and in her vest and petticoat, she ventured out of doors.

It was a glorious day, sunlit and rain-washed—the earth breathing out its scents. "This," Arrietty thought, "is what I have longed for; what I have imagined; what I knew existed—what I knew we'd have!"

She pushed through the grasses and soft drops fell on her benignly, warmed by the sun. Downhill a little way she went, towards the hedge, out of the jungle of higher grass, into the shallow ditch where, last night, the rain and darkness had combined to scare her.

There was warm mud here, between the

shorter grass blades, fast-drying now in the sun; a bank rose between her and the hedge: a glorious bank, it was, filled with roots; with grasses; with tiny ferns; with small sandy holes; with violet leaves and with pale scarlet pimpernel and, here and there, a globe of deeper crimson—wild strawberries!

She climbed the bank—leisurely and happily, feeling the warm sun through her vest, her bare feet picking their way more delicately than clumsy human feet. She gathered three strawberries, heavy with juice, and ate them luxuriously, lying full-length on a sandy terrace before a mouse-hole. From this bank she could see across the field, but today it looked different—as large as ever; as oddly tilted; but alight and alive with the early sunshine: now all the shadows ran a different way, dewy—they seemed—on the gleaming golden grass. She saw in the distance the lonely group of trees: they still seemed to float on a grassy ocean. She thought of her mother's fear of open spaces. "But I could cross this field," she thought, "I could go any-where. . . ." Was this, perhaps, what Eggle-tina had thought? Eggletina—Uncle Hendreary's child—who, they said, had been eaten by the cat. Did enterprise, Arrietty wondered, always meet with disaster? Was it really better, as her parents had always taught her, to live in secret darkness underneath the floor?

The ants were out, she saw, and busy about their business—flurried, eager, weaving their anxious routes among the

grass stems; every now and again, Arrietty noticed, waving its antennae, an ant would run up a grass stem and look around. A great contentment filled Arrietty: yes—here they were, for better or worse—there could be no going back!

Refreshed by the strawberries, she went on up the bank and into the shade of the hedge: here was sunflecked greenness and a hollowness above her. Up and up as far as she could see there were layers and storeys of green chambers, crossed and recrossed with springing branches: cathe-dral-like, the hedge seemed from the inside.

Arrietty put her foot on a lower branch and swung herself up into the green shadows: quite easy, it was, with branches to her hand on all sides—easier than climbing a ladder; a ladder as high as this would mean a feat of endurance, and a ladder at best was a dull thing, whereas here was variety, a changing of direction, exploration of heights unknown. Some twigs were dry and rigid, shedding curls of dusty bark; others were lissom and alive with sap: on these she would swing a little (as so often she had dreamed of swinging in that other lifetime under the floor!). "I will come here when it is windy," she told herself, "when the whole hedge is alive and swaying in the wind. . . ."

Up and up she went. She found an old bird's-nest, the moss inside was straw-dry. She climbed into it and lay for a while leaning over the edge.

She saw the roof of Aunt Sophy's house and the kitchen chimney smoking. On the turn of a distant road, as it wound between the hedges, she saw a milk-cart: the sun-light flashed on the metal churn and she heard the faint fairy-like tinkle of the harness brasses. What a world—mile upon mile, thing after thing, layer upon layer of unimagined richness—and she might never have seen it! She might have lived and died as so many of her relations had done, in dusty twilight—hidden behind a wainscot.

A Narrow Escape

Felix Salten

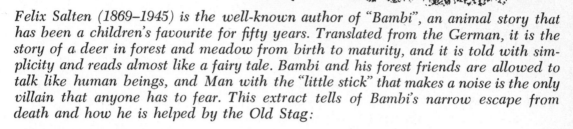

Illustrated by Kurt Wiese and Val Biro

Felix Salten (1869–1945) is the well-known author of "Bambi", an animal story that has been a children's favourite for fifty years. Translated from the German, it is the story of a deer in forest and meadow from birth to maturity, and it is told with simplicity and reads almost like a fairy tale. Bambi and his forest friends are allowed to talk like human beings, and Man with the "little stick" that makes a noise is the only villain that anyone has to fear. This extract tells of Bambi's narrow escape from death and how he is helped by the Old Stag:

ONE morning Bambi came to grief.

The pale grey dawn was just creeping through the forest. A milky-white mist was rising from the meadow and the stillness that precedes the coming of light was everywhere. The crows were not awake yet, nor the magpies. The jays were asleep. . . .

Bambi stood under the great oak at the meadow's edge and peered out cautiously drinking in the pure and odourless morning air. It was moist and fresh from the earth, the dew, the grass and the wet woods. He breathed in great gulps of it. All at once his spirit felt freer than for a long time. He walked happily on to the mist-covered meadow.

Then a sound like thunder crashed.

Bambi felt a fearful blow that made him stagger.

Mad with terror, he sprang back into the thicket and kept running. He did not understand what had happened. He could not grasp a single idea. He could only keep running on and on. Fear gripped his heart so that his breath failed as he rushed blindly on. Then a killing pain shot through him, so that he felt that he could not bear it. He felt something hot running over his left shoulder. It was like a thin burning thread coming from where the pain shot through him. Bambi had to stop running. He was forced to walk slower. Then he saw that he was limping. He sank down.

It was comfortable just to lie there and rest.

"Up, Bambi! Get up!" the old stag was standing beside him and nudging his shoulder gently.

Bambi wanted to answer, "I can't," but the old stag repeated, "Up! Up!" And there was such compulsion in his voice and such tenderness that Bambi kept silent. Even the pain that shot through him stopped for a minute.

Then the old stag said hurriedly and anxiously, "Get up! You must get away, my son." My son! The words seemed to have escaped him. In a flash Bambi was on his feet.

"Good," said the old stag, breathing deeply and speaking emphatically, "come with me now and keep close beside me."

He walked swiftly ahead. Bambi followed him, but he felt a burning desire to let himself drop to the ground, to lie still and rest.

The old stag seemed to guess it and talked to him without stopping. "Now you'll have to bear every pain. You can't think of lying down now. You mustn't think of it even for a moment. That's enough to tire you in itself. You must save yourself; do you understand me, Bambi? Save yourself; or else you are lost. Just remember that He is behind you; do you understand, Bambi? And He will kill you without mercy. Come on. Keep close to me. You'll soon be all right. You must be all right."

Bambi had no strength left to think with. The pain shot through him at every step he took. It took away his breath and his consciousness. The hot trickle, burning his shoulder, seared him like some deep heartfelt trouble.

The old stag made a wide circle. It took a long time. Through his veil of pain and weakness, Bambi was amazed to see that they were passing the great oak again.

The old stag stopped and snuffed the ground. "He's still here," he whispered. "It's He. And that's His dog. Come along. Faster!" They ran.

Suddenly the old stag stopped again. "Look," he said, "that's where you lay on the ground."

Bambi saw the crushed grasses where a wide pool of his own blood was soaking into the earth.

The old stag snuffed warily around the spot. "They were here, He and His dog," he said. "Come along!" He went ahead slowly, snuffing again and again.

Bambi saw the red drops gleaming on the leaves of the bushes and the grass stems. "We passed here before," he thought. But he couldn't speak.

"Aha!" said the old stag, and seemed almost joyful, "we're behind them now."

He continued for a while on the same path. Then he doubled unexpectedly and began a new circle. Bambi staggered after him. They came to the oak again but on the opposite side. For the second time they passed the place where Bambi had fallen down. Then the old stag went in still another direction.

"Eat that," he commanded suddenly, stopping and pushing aside the grasses. He pointed to a pair of short dark-green leaves growing close together near the ground.

Bambi obeyed. They tasted terribly bitter and smelt sickeningly.

"How do you feel now?" the stag asked after a while.

"Better," Bambi answered quickly. He was suddenly able to speak again. His senses had cleared and his fatigue grew less.

"Let's move on again," the old stag commanded after another pause. After Bambi had been following him for a long time he said, "At last!" They stopped.

"The bleeding has stopped," said the old stag, "the blood's stopped flowing from your wound. It isn't emptying your veins now. And it can't betray you any more either. It can't show Him and His dog where to find you and kill you."

The old stag looked worried and tired but his voice sounded joyful. "Come along," he went on, "now you can rest."

They reached a wide ditch which Bambi had never crossed. The old stag climbed down and Bambi tried to follow him. But it cost him a great effort to climb the steep slope on the farther side. The pain began to shoot violently through him again. He stumbled, regained his feet, and stumbled again, breathing hard.

"I can't help you," said the old stag, "you'll have to get up yourself." Bambi reached the top. He felt the hot trickle on his shoulder again. He felt his strength ebbing for the second time.

"You're bleeding again," said the old stag. "I thought you would, but it's only a little," he added in a whisper, "and it doesn't make any difference now."

They walked very slowly through a grove of lofty beeches. The ground was soft and level. They walked easily on it. Bambi felt a longing to lie down there, to stretch out and never move his limbs again. He couldn't go any farther. His head ached. There was a humming in his ears. His nerves were quivering, and fever began to rack him. There was a darkness before his eyes. He felt nothing but a desire for rest and a detached amazement at finding his life so changed and shattered. He remembered how he had walked whole and uninjured through the woods that morning. It was barely an hour

ago, and it seemed to him like some memory out of a distant, long-vanished past.

They passed through a scrub-oak and dogwood thicket. A huge, hollow beech-trunk, thickly entangled with the bushes, lay right in front of them, barring the way.

"Here we are," Bambi heard the old stag saying. He walked along the beech-trunk and Bambi walked beside him. He nearly fell into a hollow that lay in front of him.

"Here it is," said the old stag at the moment; "you can lie down here."

Bambi sank down and did not move again.

The hollow was still deeper under the beech-trunk and formed a little chamber. The bushes closed thickly across the top so that whoever was within lay hidden.

"You'll be safe here," said the old stag.

Days passed.

Bambi lay on the warm earth with the mouldering bark of the fallen tree above him. He felt his pain intensify and then grow less and less until it died away more and more gently.

Sometimes he would creep out and stand swaying weakly on his unsteady legs. He would take a few stiff steps to look for food. He ate plants now that he had never noticed before. Now they appealed to his taste and attracted him by their strange enticing acrid smell. Everything that he had disdained before and would spit out if it got accidentally into his mouth, seemed appetizing to him. He still disliked many of the little leaves and short, coarse shoots; but he ate them anyway as though he were compelled to, and his wound healed faster. He felt his strength returning.

He was cured, but he didn't leave the hollow yet. He walked around a little at night, but lay quietly on his bed by day. Not until the fever had entirely left his body did Bambi begin to think over all that had happened to him. Then a great terror awoke in him, and a profound tremor passed through his heart. He could not shake himself free of it. He could not get up and run about as before. He lay still and troubled. He felt terrified, ashamed, amazed and troubled by turns. Sometimes he was full of despair, at others of joy.

The old stag was always with him. At first he stayed day and night at Bambi's side. Then he left him alone at times, especially when he saw Bambi deep in thought. But he always kept close at hand.

One night there was thunder and lightning and a downpour of rain, although the sky was clear and the setting sun was streaming down. The blackbirds sang loudly in all the neighbouring tree-tops, the finches warbled, the field-mice chirped in the bushes. Among the grasses or from under the bushes, the metallic, throaty cackling of the pheasants sounded at intervals. The woodpecker laughed exultantly and the doves cooed their fervid love.

Bambi crept out of the hollow. Life was beautiful. The old stag was standing there as though he expected Bambi. They sauntered on together. And Bambi did not return to the hollow again.

The Year

The crocus, while the days are dark,
  Unfolds its saffron sheen;
At April's touch, the crudest bark
  Discovers gems of green.

Then sleep the seasons, full of might;
  While slowly swells the pod
And rounds the peach, and in the night
  The mushroom bursts the sod.

The winter comes: the frozen rut
  Is bound with silver bars;
The snow-drift heaps against the hut;
  And night is pierced with stars.

COVENTRY PATMORE

My First Gun

Will James

Illustrated by Shirley Hughes

Born out West in an American covered wagon, Will James (1892–1942) lost his parents when very young and was adopted by a French-Canadian trapper who took him into the far North. There for winters at a time the child saw no other human being but his friend, "Bopy". His adventure with a bear is described in this story from his auto-biography, "Lone Cowboy".

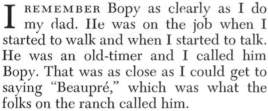

Later he lived as a cowboy, wandering from job to job in the western states of America, loving horses, and both writing about them and drawing them. His "Smoky" is a classic which horse-loving girls and boys should read.

I REMEMBER Bopy as clearly as I do my dad. He was on the job when I started to walk and when I started to talk. He was an old-timer and I called him Bopy. That was as close as I could get to saying "Beaupré," which was what the folks on the ranch called him.

Jean Beaupré was his name, or one of his names, as I found out years later. My dad called him Trapper Jean. That's what he was, a trapper during winters, and he'd try prospecting for gold during the summers. He was a French Canadian from way up in the far north-west country. He could talk many Indian languages and sign talk, all mixed with French. He could talk very little English.

Sometimes the old-timer would bring me a chipmunk in a cage he'd made, or a squirrel. He always kept me supplied with horned toads, young woodchucks, young beavers, and even young porcupines. The young porcupines didn't stay long; as soon as the quills began to show they somehow or other disappeared. Most of the young animals I had made good pets and a few of them stayed around the ranch even after they were full grown.

It was when I was about nine years, going on ten, that Bopy found an extra gun of his. It was one he'd had in the camp for use in case anything happened to the gun he always carried. The old gun, being wrapped in canvas, was still in good shape, and after oiling it, Bopy started to show me how to handle it.

It was a muzzle-loader and about two feet taller than I was. Bopy took a lot of pains showing me how to load it. First a little powder was poured down the barrel from the powder horn. Bopy made sure I understood that there should be very little powder, too much would knock me over and maybe hurt me, he said. After the powder a little piece of paper was tamped in with the long stick that was carried under the barrel. Then about a dozen bird-shot were poured in, another wad of paper, and the whole thing tamped again. The only thing to do after that was to pull back the hammer and slip a little copper cap on that little thing that stuck up under it.

Bopy told me it was best not to put the cap on till I was ready to shoot.

With a lot of instructions and advice and repeatings of all about a gun and the dangerous end of it, I was finally tried out many times, and at last I was told to go ahead and bring home the bacon. "But don't forget what I told you," Bopy said, as a last word.

I remember I was pretty excited when I saw the first thing to shoot at. It was a duck. I missed that first one, I couldn't hold that long rifle barrel steady enough and there was no tree near the pond for me to rest it on. The next time or so I had better luck. There was the crotch of a tree for me to use, and I got my duck, but I came near toppling over backwards as I did. I had put in too much powder in reloading. I was more careful from then on.

I had a lot of fun with that gun, even if I didn't see so much that was worth shooting at. About all I could find were big white rabbits and ducks and things like that. I saw a bear twice, but Bopy had warned me never to shoot big animals, to save them for him because I might spoil the fur and so on. Anyway, he had a lot of reasons to give so I wouldn't even try to get the big ones. His main reason, as I found out afterwards, was that so long as I didn't bother the big ones they wouldn't bother me. He knew what might happen if I stirred up a big, healthy bear or moose with a load of my little bird-shot, and he wanted to make sure I wouldn't rile 'em up that way.

The winter was different from any winter I'd passed before. We were farther north, and the daylight hours were very few. Of course, the "Northern Lights" made things pretty bright during the night, but not bright enough so as to make the greased-paper window of much use in lighting up the dugout.

The short days and light nights made the winter sort of strange for me. The only place I felt at home was inside. When I did go out it would always have to be in snowshoes. The snow was from four to eight feet deep and I soon lost interest in hoofing it through timber and more timber. I missed open country. I wanted to

see distances and get away from that closed-in feeling. What I missed most was going down to some corral and stables. I missed my horses, touching their hides and saddling them up and going some place with bridle reins in one hand and a rope in another. So that's why I didn't stay out so much that winter. I'd get homesick. And that's why I stuck pretty well by the dugout; I felt all right there.

I think I drew more horses during the few winters I was in that northern country than I ever did. It seemed like drawing 'em brought 'em nearer to me. If I drew a man on horseback throwing a rope, or doing anything, I'd imagine myself in that picture and doing whatever was put down there. I drew lots of saddles, too, and boots and spurs. I'd often draw cattle and 'most everything that goes with the life of a range rider.

Bopy wasn't with me much that winter, another thing that made the winter different. He'd be gone three days at a time while covering his trap line. When he was gone I'd draw and read and write. There'd be the cooking, too. I was getting to be quite a cook by then, and I used to mix up what I thought to be some great baits. The only drawback was that I had to be mighty saving with everything excepting meat: bear and moose. Flour, and things that were heavy to pack, was scarce and not to play with. I was told I could use a certain amount a day and no more. Then there were dried fruit and potatoes. I was pretty careful with the dried potatoes and one a day was all I'd cook. Our grub pile was made up of flour, soda, a side of salt pork, dried potatoes and apples, and salt and pepper to season with. That was all. Whatever game we killed was our fresh meat and we never were short of that.

I'd feel pretty tickled when I'd manage to cook up something that turned out real good, specially on the evenings of every third day, when Bopy would come in all frozen up with icicles hanging all the way down from his fur cap to his waist. And when he'd rush near the fire to warm up and smell at the pan of food that was on the coals all ready for him and then grin at me and slap me on the shoulder, why, I felt that what little I'd done had sure turned out big.

'Most every day, while Bopy was gone, and during the daylight hours, I'd strap my snowshoes on my moccasins, take my long gun and go hunting; not that I liked to hunt so much, but I wanted to have some reason to be out, and I'd be wanting a change from moose meat. Once in a while I'd get a big, white snowshoe rabbit. The bears had all hibernated. I hadn't seen a sign of any, *only once*.

It was after a warm spell, a spell that broke that one bear's sleep, and he'd gone out hunting. There was a snowbank alongside the lean-to where we kept the meat and he'd climbed up on that snowbank on top of the cabin. I heard him sniff and paw up there for a long spell. He was sure heavy because even through that thick roof I could tell just where he planted a paw. Then he must have got a whiff of the meat that was in the lean-to because he kept hanging around there, climbing up and down and clawing. He'd circle around and sniff, and I got to thinking of the window. I hadn't closed the shutter on it and all he'd have to do would be to stick his nose to the paper and it'd fall apart. I knew he'd come in then, so as to get to that meat, and I waited for him.

As I waited I reached for my gun, not at all realizing that the bird-shot it was loaded with would only make him mad if I hit him at long distance. Anyway, I waited a spell, hoping he would stick his nose through that window. But he didn't. Instead, he quit his circling and went to tearing at the lean-to as if he sure meant to get that meat. He made plenty of noise and I got to thinking he wasn't doing the house any good, so I ups and slips on my moccasins. I was all dressed but hat, and I opened the door and went out. But I couldn't see the bear and all I could get of his whereabouts were sniffs and grunts. The snow was pretty deep and I couldn't get around very fast, but when I got around the cabin I met him. He looked like a mountain.

I don't think the barrel of my gun was over a foot from his nose when I pulled the trigger. Bopy had often told me always to stick the barrel away ahead and be ready for work when I really wanted to use it. It was ahead that night, and I pulled the trigger at just a good time....

When Bopy came back two days later and I told him about the bear, he grinned at me sort of proud-like, and said words that made me feel good, on how I'd held down the camp and saved the grub. He said that bears "was awful pests." But if Bopy was surprised and pleased at me getting up in the middle of the night and chasing the bear away, he was more than surprised when he began to track him the next day. He hadn't gone over half a mile from camp when he found the bear stretched out and frozen stiff. That little bird-shot at close range had nearly punctured his head through.

Bopy had never thought that I had killed the bear and neither did I. But there

he was, and when I came up to answer Bopy's holler, and saw that hairy elephant stretched out on the snow I didn't know what to think or say.

Bopy said something about a mighty lucky shot and advised me never to try that again with one of those big fellers. He didn't say why right there. But there's one thing Bopy didn't know and that was I'd got to know the old gun pretty well and I was using twice the amount of birdshot I'd started out with, and three times the amount of powder. The powder alone would have burned a hole through him at that close range.

That bear hide would have covered the whole floor of our cabin. It sure was a nice colour, too.

When I got around the cabin I met him. He looked like a mountain.

Erich plays Detective

Erich Kästner

Illustrated by Horst Lemke

Erich Kästner (1899–1974) is a German writer who is known to young people in many lands as the author of the "Emil" books, the first of which, "Emil and the Detectives", you may have read. In 1959 Erich Kästner wrote his own story, "When I was a Little Boy". Shall we have a look at this small boy who lived in pre-1914 Dresden and became an author? Erich tells us that his parents were poor and had to work hard. His mother was a ladies' hairdresser. She worked long hours and often went to customers' houses by appointment. Weddings brought her good business, for they meant visiting the bride's home and dressing the hair of the mother and aunts and bridesmaids as well as the bride's. One day an odd thing happened that caused his mother a sad loss of time and money—we shall see in a minute what it was—but we shall also see how it turned the young Erich into a detective with a mystery to solve and how he solved it. And here is a thought! If this had never happened, would Erich Kästner ever have thought of writing what was to become such a famous book? Would he ever have written about a boy detective? Here, then, is what actually happened:

THE strangest wedding I ever remember became graven in my memory because it did not take place at all. And that was not because the bridegroom had said "No" before the altar or fled from the church. It was because there wasn't any bridegroom at all. The best thing will be to tell the story right from the beginning.

One day an oldish spinster named Fräulein Strempel came and told us that she was going to be married the following Saturday in St. Paul's Church. And she made an appointment with my mother for eight o'clock on that morning. No. 27 Oppel Strasse, two flights up, the left-hand flat. Ten heads of hair were to be done. The bridal carriage and five cabs had been ordered. The Hotel Bellevue was undertaking the catering, with iced soufflé for dessert and a waiter in a dinner jacket. Fräulein Strempel's eyes shone with joy as she chattered on eagerly like a young girl. We congratulated her on her good fortune, and when she was gone we congratulated ourselves on ours. But we did so too soon.

When I came home from school on the Saturday my mother was sitting in the kitchen utterly cast down and red-eyed. She had reached No. 27 Oppel Strasse at eight o'clock sharp, rung the bell on the left-hand door two storeys up, but had been greeted with astonished stares, and angrily sent away. No Fräulein Strempel

75

lived there and there was no one being married at twelve o'clock in St. Paul's Church!

Had my mother taken down the house number incorrectly? She inquired in the shops round about. She asked in the neighbouring houses. She rang at all the doors. She turned the whole of Oppel Strasse upside down. No one knew Fräulein Strempel, and there was no one waiting to have her hair done or going to be married at midday. Some of the people she asked were very nice and polite to her, but not one of them was as obliging as all that!

So now we sat in the kitchen and just wondered. We realized that we had been duped, but why—why on earth had this woman humbugged us? She had injured my mother. But what good had it done her?

A few weeks later I saw her again. I was coming out of school with Gustav Kiessling; and she passed us by without recognizing me. She seemed to be in a hurry, so there was no time to lose. It was now or never. I quickly slipped my satchel off my back, gave it to my friend and whispered, "Here, take this home and tell Mother I'll be home later." And off I ran after the woman. Gustav stared after me, then went on, and dutifully brought home my satchel. "Erich is coming later," he reported. "Why's that?" asked my mother. "No idea!" answered Gustav.

Meanwhile I was playing detective. Since Fräulein Strempel (whose name was probably not Strempel at all) had not recognized me, the matter was simple enough. I did not have to hide nor put on a beard, so why should I be in such a hurry to tackle her? I had only to keep on her heels. Even that was not quite simple, however. For Fräulein Strempel (or not-Strempel) was in a great hurry and had long legs. We made good headway.

Albert Platz, Haupt Strasse, Neustadt Markt, Augustus Brücke, Schloss Platz, the Georgentor, Schloss Strasse—the journey seemed endless. But quite suddenly it came to an end. The lady turned left into the Altmarkt and disappeared behind the glass swing doors of Schlesinger & Co., a high-class ladies' fashion shop. I plucked up courage and followed her. How it was all going to end, I did not know, and I felt painfully embarrassed when the manager, the lady supervisors and the salesladies all fixed their eyes on me. But what was I to do? She walked across the ground floor, the ladies' coats department. So did I. She went up the stairs, passed the first storey, the costumes department, and climbed the next flight. So did I. She entered the department on the second floor, summer frocks and junior miss department, went up to a wall mirror, pushed it aside—and disappeared! The mirror swung back to its old spot behind her. It was like something out of *The Arabian Nights*.

I was now standing in the midst of counters, mirrors, movable wardrobes and leisurely salesladies, and felt rooted to the spot by my fright and my sense of duty. If only there had been some lady customers there trying on or buying things. But it was midday, and the ladies were at home, not at Schlesingers. The shop assistants began giggling. One of them came up to me and asked playfully, "What about a smart little frock for the young gentleman? We have some charming models in stock. Wouldn't you like to come into a cubicle and try some on?" The other girls laughed and held their hands to their mouths. Silly creatures! How was it that Fräulein Strempel (or not-Strempel) had disappeared behind this mirror? And where was she now? I felt as though I was standing on hot coals. A minute can be very long.

But here was another of these vile females coming up to me. She took a brightly coloured gown from a stand, held it under my chin, squinting as if examining it, and said, "The cut shows off her wonderful figure to the best advantage!" The

Where had she gone? I felt rooted to the spot by my fright and my sense of duty.

other girls nearly split their sides laughing. I got red in the face and furious, but at that moment an elderly lady appeared on the scene and a dead silence fell on the whole department. "What are you doing here?" she asked me sternly. As I could think of nothing else to say, I answered, "I'm looking for my mother." "Not one of us, duck!" one of the girls cried, and the laughter broke out again. Even the elderly lady almost smiled.

At this moment the wall mirror moved noiselessly aside and Fräulein not-Strempel walked out of it, without her hat and coat. She smoothed down her hair, said to the others, "It seems to be lunchtime still in here," and went behind one of the counters. So she was a saleslady at Schlesingers, on the second floor. But I was already on the stairs; I had decided to go straight down again and find the manager. This called for a man-to-man discussion!

Having listened to my story the manager told me to wait a few minutes. Then he went up to the second floor and returned, after five minutes, with Fräulein not-Strempel. She had her hat and coat on again, and she looked through me as though I were made of glass. "Now listen to me," said the manager. "Fräulein Nitzche will go back home with you and come to an arrangement with your mother to compensate her in instalment payments. Here's a card with Fräulein Nitzche's address. Put it away safely and give it to your mother. Tell her she may call to see me any time if it's necessary. Goodbye."

The glass doors swung open and shut again. Fräulein Nitzche alias Strempel and I were out in the Altmarkt. Without deigning to look at me she turned into Schloss Strasse and I followed her. It was a frightful march. I had won and yet I was utterly wretched about it. I felt like one of those armed soldiers who walked behind the military prisoners on the Heller. I was proud and ashamed at the same time. That can happen. Schloss Strasse, Schloss Platz, Augustus Brücke, Neustadt Markt, Haupt Strasse, Albert Platz, Königsbrücker Strasse—on she went, straight as an arrow, in front of me. I followed, keeping five paces behind all the time, even up the stairs. At the door of our flat she turned towards the wall. I rang three times. My mother came rushing to the door, wrenched it open, and cried, "Now I want to know at last why you . . .!" Then she noticed that I was not alone and saw whom I had brought. "Please come in, Fräulein Strempel," she said. "Fräulein Nitzche," I corrected her.

They came to an arrangement for three monthly instalments, and Fräulein Nitzche still completely impassive, went back to Schlesinger & Co. with a confirmation from my mother in her handbag. The loss was made good—nevertheless it was a catastrophe, as we found out in the course of time. Creditors turned up on all sides. The hotel, the wine merchants, the cab owner with the wedding carriages, the flower shop, the laundry—all alleged that they had incurred loss and all demanded that part of the loss be made good by instalment payments. And Fräulein Nitzche went on paying it off, for months and months.

Luckily she kept her job at Schlesingers, for she was a capable saleslady and the manager had understood what I could not understand as yet. An ageing spinster who had not found a husband and would have liked to marry had invented a wedding when her wish had not come true. It was a costly dream and a fruitless one; and when she woke up from it she started paying for it in instalments. And with every month's instalments she grew a year older. We often met in the street but we did not look at one another. We had both done right and wrong, but I had come out of it the better. For she was paying for a dream which was at an end, but I was still a little boy.

Washing Day

The washing hangs upon the line,
Between the prunus and the arch
(Where tender leaves of rambler thrust),
On this gay day in middle March.

The washing bellies in the breeze,
Across the clothes blue shadows go,
Above the house the lark sings high,
Before me, see, two aprons blow.

To watch the patterns move criss-cross,
Cast from the branches of the pear;
For symphony the song of birds,
And daffodils beside my chair—

These are the simple joys of life;
With rippling clothes put out to dry,
Reflecting cleanliness and light
Beneath a wide and changing sky.

THEODORA ROSCOE

The Emperor's New Clothes

Hans Andersen

Illustrated by Rex Whistler

The shoemaker's son of Odense in Denmark, the boy who loved making puppets and writing plays to perform in his puppet theatre and who ran away at fourteen to try his hand first as an actor and then as a singer—this was Hans Christian Andersen (1805–1875), the poverty-stricken lad on whom a King of Denmark took pity, for the king heard of the boy and had him educated himself. What a romantic start in life!

Andersen became a writer of plays and novels, but it is his fairy tales for children that are best remembered. Like the Brothers Grimm he was interested in folk tales and often made them the basis of his stories. But whereas the Brothers Grimm remained faithful to the folk originals and became writers for children only by accident, Hans Andersen invents a great deal himself, and pours into his stories all the humour and sympathy and sadness and joy that he feels in life. You think you are too old for fairy tales? Nobody is too old for this famous story!

MANY years ago, there was an Emperor, who was so excessively fond of new clothes that he spent all his money in dress. He did not trouble himself in the least about his soldiers; nor did he care to go either to the theatre or the chase, except for the opportunities they afforded him for displaying his new clothes. He had a different suit for each hour of the day; and as of any other king or emperor one is accustomed to say, "He is sitting in council," it was always said of him, "The Emperor is sitting in his wardrobe."

Time passed away merrily in the large town which was his capital; strangers arrived every day at the court. One day two rogues, calling themselves weavers, made their appearance. They gave out that they knew how to weave stuffs of the most beautiful colours and elaborate patterns, the clothes manufactured from which should have the wonderful property of remaining invisible to every one who was unfit for the office he held, or who was extraordinarily simple in character.

"These must, indeed, be splendid clothes!" thought the Emperor. "Had I such a suit, I might at once find out what men in my realm are unfit for their office, and also be able to distinguish the wise from the foolish! This stuff must be woven for me immediately." And he caused large sums of money to be given to both the weavers, in order that they might begin their work directly.

So the two pretended weavers set up two looms, and affected to work very busily, though in reality they did nothing at all. They asked for the most delicate silk and the purest gold thread; put both into their own knapsacks; and then continued their pretended work at the empty looms until late at night.

"I should like to know how the weavers

are getting on with my cloth," said the Emperor to himself, after some little time had elapsed; he was, however, rather embarrassed when he remembered that a simpleton, or one unfit for his office, would be unable to see the manufacture. "To be sure," he thought, "he had nothing to risk in his own person; but yet he would prefer sending somebody else to bring him intelligence about the weavers, and their work, before he troubled himself in the affair." All the people throughout the city had heard of the wonderful property the cloth was to possess; and all were anxious to learn how wise, or how ignorant, their neighbours might prove to be.

"I will send my faithful old Minister to the weavers," said the Emperor at last, after some deliberation; "he will be best able to see how the cloth looks; for he is a man of sense, and no one can be more suitable for his office than he is."

So the honest old Minister went into the hall, where the knaves were working with all their might at their empty looms. "What can be the meaning of this?" thought the old man, opening his eyes very wide; "I cannot discover the least bit of thread on the looms!" However, he did not express his thoughts aloud.

The impostors requested him very courteously to be so good as to come nearer their looms; and then asked him whether the design pleased him, and whether the colours were not very beautiful; at the same time pointing to the empty frames. The poor old Minister looked and looked; he could not discover anything on the looms, for a very good reason, viz. there was nothing there. "What!" thought he again, "is it possible that I am a simpleton? I have never thought so myself; and, at any rate, if I am so, no one must know it. Can it be that I am unfit for my office? No, that must not be said either. I will never confess that I could not see the stuff."

"Well, Sir Minister!" said one of the knaves, still pretending to work, "you do not say whether the stuff pleases you."

"Oh, it is admirable!" replied the old Minister, looking at the loom through his spectacles. "This pattern, and the colours —yes, I will tell the Emperor without delay how very beautiful I think them."

"We shall be much obliged to you," said the imposters, and then they named the different colours and described the patterns of the pretended stuff. The old Minister listened attentively to their words, in order that he might repeat them to the Emperor; and then the knaves asked for more silk and gold, saying that it was necessary to complete what they had begun. However, they put all that was given them into their knapsacks, and continued to work with as much apparent diligence as before at their empty looms.

The Emperor now sent another officer of his court to see how the men were getting on, and to ascertain whether the cloth would soon be ready. It was just the same with this gentleman as with the Minister; he surveyed the looms on all sides, but could see nothing at all but the empty frames.

"Does not the stuff appear as beautiful to you as it did to my Lord the Minister?" asked the imposters of the Emperor's second ambassador; at the same time making the same gestures as before, and talking of the design and colours which were not there.

"I certainly am not stupid!" thought the messenger. "It must be that I am not fit for my good, profitable office! That is very odd; however, no one shall know anything about it." And accordingly he praised the stuff he could not see, and declared that he was delighted with both colours and patterns. "Indeed, please your Imperial Majesty," said he to his sovereign, when he returned, "the cloth which the weavers are preparing is extraordinarily magnificent."

The whole city was talking of the splendid cloth which the Emperor had ordered to be woven at his own expense.

And now the Emperor himself wished to see the costly manufacture, whilst it was still on the loom. Accompanied by a small number of officers of the court, among whom were the two honest men who had already admired the cloth, he went to the crafty imposters, who, as soon as they were aware of the Emperor's approach, went on working more diligently than ever; although they still did not pass a single thread through the looms.

"Is not the work absolutely magnificent?" said the two officers of the crown already mentioned. "If your Majesty will only be pleased to look at it! What a splendid design! What glorious colours!" and at the same time they pointed to the empty frames, for they imagined that everyone but themselves could see the exquisite piece of workmanship.

"How is this?" said the Emperor to himself; "I can see nothing! This is, indeed, a terrible affair! Am I a simpleton, or am I unfit to be an Emperor? that would be the worst thing that could happen. Oh, the cloth is charming!" said he aloud, "it has my entire approbation." And he smiled most graciously, and looked at the empty looms; for on no account would he say that he could not see what two of the officers of his court had praised so much. All his retinue now strained their eyes, hoping to discover something on the looms, but they could see no more than the others; nevertheless, they all exclaimed, "Oh! How beautiful!" and advised his Majesty to have some new clothes made from this splendid material for the approaching procession. "Magnificent! Charming! Excellent!" resounded on all sides; and every one was uncommonly gay. The Emperor shared in the general satisfaction, and presented the imposters with the riband of an order of knighthood to be worn in their buttonholes, and the title of "Gentlemen Weavers."

The rogues sat up the whole of the night before the day on which the procession was to take place, and had sixteen lights burning, so that everyone might see how anxious they were to finish the Emperor's new suit. They pretended to roll the cloth on the looms; cut the air with their scissors; and sewed with needles without any thread in them. "See!" cried they at last, "the Emperor's new clothes are ready!"

And now the Emperor, with all the grandees of his court, came to the weavers; and the rogues raised their arms, as if in the act of holding something up, saying, "Here are your Majesty's trousers! Here is the scarf! Here is the mantle! The whole suit is as light as a cobweb; one might fancy one has nothing at all on, when dressed in it; that, however, is the great virtue of this delicate cloth."

"Yes, indeed!" said all the courtiers, although not one of them could see anything of this exquisite manufacture.

"If your Imperial Majesty will be graciously pleased to take off your clothes, we will fit on the new suit, in front of the looking-glass."

The Emperor was accordingly undressed, and the rogues pretended to array him in his new suit; the Emperor turning round, from side to side, before the looking-glass.

"How splendid his Majesty looks in his new clothes! and how well they fit!" everyone cried out. "What a design! What colours! These are, indeed, royal robes!"

"The canopy which is to be borne over your Majesty, in the procession, is waiting," announced the Chief Master of the Ceremonies.

"I am quite ready," answered the Emperor. "Do my new clothes fit well?" asked he, turning himself round again before the looking-glass, in order that he might appear to be examining his handsome suit.

The lords of the bedchamber, who were to carry his Majesty's train, felt about on the ground, as if they were lifting up the ends of the mantle, and pretended to be carrying something; for they would by no means betray anything like simplicity, or unfitness for their office.

So now the Emperor walked under his

The Emperor walked under his high canopy in the midst of the procession.

high canopy in the midst of the procession, through the streets of his capital; and all the people standing by, and those at the windows, cried out, "Oh! how beautiful are our Emperor's new clothes! What a magnificent train there is to the mantle! And how gracefully the scarf hangs!" In short, no one would allow that he could not see these much-admired clothes, because, in doing so, he would have declared himself either a simpleton or unfit for his office. Certainly, none of the Emperor's various suits had ever excited so much admiration as this.

"But the Emperor has nothing at all on!" said a little child. "Listen to the voice of innocence!" exclaimed his father; and what the child had said was whispered from one to another.

"But he has nothing at all on!" at last cried out all the people.

The Emperor was vexed, for he knew that the people were right; but he thought "the procession must go on now!" And the lords of the bed-chamber took greater pains than ever to appear holding up a train, although, in reality, there was no train to hold.

I Stood Tiptoe upon a Little Hill

The clouds were pure and white as flocks new-shorn,
And fresh from the clear brook; sweetly they slept
On the blue fields of heaven, and then there crept
A little noiseless noise among the leaves,
Born of the very sigh that silence heaves.

. . . . .

Here are sweet peas, on tiptoe for a flight
With wings of gentle flush o'er delicate white
And taper fingers catching at all things,
To bind them all about with tiny rings.

. . . . .

How silent comes the water round that bend!
Not the minutest whisper does it send
To the o'erhanging sallows: blades of grass
Slowly across the chequer'd shadows pass

. . . . .

Where swarms of minnows show their little heads,
Staying their wavy bodies 'gainst the streams,
To taste the luxury of sunny beams
Temper'd with coolness. How they ever wrestle
With their own sweet delight, and ever nestle
Their silver bellies on the pebbly sand!
If you but scantily hold out the hand,
That very instant not one will remain;
But turn your eye, and they are there again. . . .

JOHN KEATS

The Pied Piper of Hamelin

Robert Browning

*Illustrated by Ru Van Rossem
and John Speirs*

Hamelin Town's in Brunswick,
By famous Hanover City;
  The river Weser, deep and wide,
  Washes its wall on the southern side;
  A pleasanter spot you never spied;
But, when begins my ditty,
  Almost five hundred years ago,
  To see the townsfolk suffer so
From vermin was a pity.

    Rats!
They fought the dogs, and killed the cats,
  And bit the babies in the cradles,
And ate the cheeses out of the vats,
  And licked the soup from the cook's own
      ladles,
Split open the kegs of salted sprats,
Made nests inside men's Sunday hats,
And even spoiled the women's chats,
  By drowning their speaking
  With shrieking and squeaking
In fifty different sharps and flats.

At last the people in a body
  To the Town Hall came flocking:
"'Tis clear," cried they, "our Mayor's a
      noddy;
  And as for our Corporation—shocking
To think we buy gowns lined with ermine
For dolts that can't or won't determine
What's best to rid us of our vermin!
You hope, because you're old and obese,
To find in the furry civic robe ease?
Rouse up, Sirs! Give your brains a racking
To find the remedy we're lacking,

Or, sure as fate, we'll send you packing!"
At this the Mayor and Corporation
Quaked with a mighty consternation.

An hour they sate in council,
    At length the Mayor broke silence:
    "For a guilder I'd my ermine gown sell!
    I wish I were a mile hence!
It's easy to bid one rack one's brain—
I'm sure my poor head aches again
I've scratched it so, and all in vain.
Oh for a trap, a trap, a trap!"
Just as he said this, what should hap
At the chamber door but a gentle tap?
"Bless us," cried the Mayor, "what's that?"
(With the Corporation as he sat,
Looking little though wondrous fat;
Nor brighter was his eye, nor moister,
Than a too-long-opened oyster,
Save when at noon his paunch grew
    mutinous
For a plate of turtle green and glutinous),
"Only a scraping of shoes on the mat?
Anything like the sound of a rat
Makes my heart go pit-a-pat!"

"Come in!"—the Mayor cried, looking
    bigger:
And in did come the strangest figure.
His queer long coat from heel to head
Was half of yellow and half of red;
And he himself was tall and thin,
With sharp blue eyes, each like a pin,
And light, loose hair, yet swarthy skin,
No tuft on cheek nor beard on chin,
But lips where smiles went out and in;
There was no guessing his kith and kin:
And nobody could enough admire
The tall man and his quaint attire.
Quoth one: "It's as my great grandsire,
Starting up at the Trump of Doom's tone,
Had walked this way from his painted
    tombstone!"

He advanced to the council-table;
And "Please your honours," said he, "I'm
    able,
By means of a secret charm, to draw
All creatures living beneath the sun,
That creep or swim or fly or run,
After me so as you never saw!
And I chiefly use my charm
On creatures that do people harm,
The mole and toad and newt and viper;
And people call me the Pied Piper."
(And here they noticed round his neck
    A scarf of red and yellow stripe,
To match with his coat of the selfsame
    cheque;
    And at the scarf's end hung a pipe;
And his fingers, they noticed, were ever
    straying
As if impatient to be playing
Upon this pipe, as low it dangled
Over his vesture so old-fangled.)
"Yet," said he, "poor piper as I am,
In Tartary I freed the Cham,
    Last June, from his huge swarms of
    gnats;
I eased in Asia the Nizam
    Of a monstrous brood of vampire bats:
And as for what your brain bewilders,

If I can rid your town of rats,
Will you give me a thousand guilders?"
"One? Fifty thousand!" was the
    exclamation
Of the astonished Mayor and Corporation.

Into the street the Piper stept,
    Smiling first a little smile,
As if he knew what magic slept
    In his quiet pipe the while;
Then, like a musical adept,
To blow the pipe his lips he wrinkled,
And green and blue his sharp eyes
    twinkled
Like a candle flame where salt is sprinkled;
And ere three shrill notes the pipe uttered,
You heard as if an army muttered;
And the muttering grew to a grumbling;
And the grumbling grew to a mighty
    rumbling;
And out of the house the rats came
    tumbling.
Great rats, small rats, lean rats, brawny
    rats,
Brown rats, black rats, grey rats, tawny
    rats.
Grave old plodders, gay young friskers,
    Fathers, mothers, uncles, cousins,
Cocking tails and pricking whiskers,
    Families by tens and dozens,

Brothers, sisters, husbands, wives—
Followed the Piper for their lives.
From street to street he piped advancing,
And step by step they followed dancing,
Until they came to the river Weser
Wherein all plunged and perished
—Save one, who, stout as Julius Caesar,
Swam across and lived to carry
(As he the manuscript he cherished)
To Rat-land home his commentary
Which was, "At the first shrill notes of the
    pipe,
I heard a sound as of scraping tripe,
And putting apples, wondrous ripe,
Into a cider-press's gripe:
And a moving away of pickle-tub boards,
And a leaving ajar of conserve cupboards,
And a drawing the corks of train-oil-flasks,
And a breaking the hoops of butter-casks:
And it seemed as if a voice
    (Sweeter far than by harp or by psaltery
Is breathed) called out, 'Oh rats, rejoice!
    The world is grown to one vast dry-
        saltery!
So munch on, crunch on, take your
    nuncheon,
Breakfast, supper, dinner, luncheon!'
And just as a bulky sugar-puncheon

All ready staved, like a great sun shone
Glorious scarce an inch before me,
Just as me thought it said, 'Come, bore
   me!'
——I found the Weser rolling o'er me."

You should have heard the Hamelin people
Ringing the bells till they rocked the
   steeple
"Go," cried the Mayor, "and get long
   poles!
Poke out the nests and block up the holes!
   Consult with carpenters and builders,
And leave in our town not even a trace
Of the rats!"—when suddenly, up the face
Of the piper perked in the market-place,
   With a, "First, if you please, my
      thousand guilders!"

A thousand guilders! The Mayor looked
   blue;
So did the Corporation, too.
For Council dinners made rare havoc
With Claret, Moselle, Vin-de-Grave,
   Hock;
And half the money would replenish
Their cellar's biggest butt with Rhenish.
To pay this sum to a wandering fellow
With a gipsy coat of red and yellow!
"Beside," quoth the Mayor with a knowing
   wink,
"Our business was done at the river's
   brink;
We saw with our eyes the vermin sink,
And what's dead can't come to life, I think.
So, friend, we're not the folks to shrink
From the duty of giving you something for
   drink,
And a matter of money to put in your poke;
But as for the guilders, what we spoke
Of them, as you very well know, was in
   joke;
Beside, our losses have made us thrifty:
A thousand guilders! Come, take fifty!"

The Piper's face fell, and he cried,
"No trifling! I can't wait. Beside,
I've promised to visit by dinner time
Bagdad, and accept the prime

Of the Head Cook's pottage, all he's rich
   in,
For having left in the Caliph's kitchen,
Of a nest of scorpions no survivor:
With him I proved no bargain-driver,
With you, don't think I'll bate a stiver!
And folks who put me in a passion
May find me pipe to another fashion."

"How?" cried the Mayor, "d'ye think I'll
   brook
Being worse treated than a Cook?
Insulted by a lazy ribald
With idle pipe and vesture piebald?
You threaten us, fellow? Do your worst,
Blow your pipe there till you burst!"

Once more he stept into the street;
   And to his lips again
   Laid his long pipe of smooth, straight
      cane;
And ere he blew three notes (such sweet
Soft notes as yet musician's cunning
   Never gave the enraptured air),
There was a rustling, that seemed like a
   bustling
Of merry crowds justling at pitching and
   hustling,
Small feet were pattering, wooden shoes
   clattering,
Little hands clapping and little tongues
   chattering,
And, like fowls in a farmyard when barley
   is scattering,
Out came the children running,
All the little boys and girls,
With rosy cheeks and flaxen curls
And sparkling eyes and teeth like pearls,
Tripping and skipping, ran merrily after
The wonderful music with shouting and
   laughter.

The Mayor was dumb, and the Council
   stood
As if they were changed into blocks of
   wood,
Unable to move a step, or cry
To the children merrily skipping by,
And could only follow with the eye

That joyous crowd at the Piper's back.
But how the Mayor was on the rack,
And the wretched Council's bosoms beat,
As the Piper turned from the High Street
To where the Weser rolled its waters
Right in the way of their sons and
    daughters!
However he turned from South to West,
And to Koppelberg Hill his steps
    addressed,
And after him the children pressed;
Great was the joy in every breast.
"He never can cross that mighty top!
He's forced to let the piping drop,
And we shall see our children stop!"
When, lo, as they reached the mountain's
    side,
A wondrous portal opened wide,
As if a cavern were suddenly hollowed;
And the Piper advanced and the children
    followed.
And when all were in to the very last,
The door in the mountain side shut fast.
Did I say, all? No! One was lame,

And could not dance the whole of the way;
And in after years, if you would blame
    His sadness, he was used to say,—
"It's dull in our town since my playmates left;
I can't forget that I'm bereft
Of all the pleasant sights they see,
Which the Piper also promised me;
For he led us, he said, to a joyous land,
Joining the town and just at hand,
Where waters gushed and fruit-trees grew,
And flowers put forth a fairer hue,
And everything was strange and new;
The sparrows were brighter than peacocks here,
And their dogs outran our fallow deer,
And honey-bees had lost their stings;
And horses were born with eagles' wings;
And just as I became assured
My lame foot would be speedily cured,
The music stopped, and I stood still
And found myself outside the Hill,
Left alone against my will,
To go now limping as before,
And never hear of that country more!"

Alas, alas, for Hamelin!
    There came into many a burgher's pate
    A text which says, that Heaven's Gate
    Opes to the Rich at as easy rate
As the needle's eye takes a camel in!
The Mayor sent East, West, North and South,
To offer the Piper by word of mouth,
    Wherever it was men's lot to find him,
Silver and gold to his heart's content,
If he'd only return the way he went,
    And bring the children all behind him.
But when they saw 'twas a lost endeavour,

And Piper and dancers were gone for ever,
They made a decree that lawyers never
    Should think their records date duly
If, after the day of the month and year,
These words did not as well appear,
"And so long after what happened here
    On the twenty-second of July,
Thirteen hundred and seventy-six:"
And the better in memory to fix
The place of the Children's last retreat,
They called it the Pied Piper's Street
Where anyone playing on pipe or tabor
Was sure for the future to lose his labour.
Nor suffered they hostelry or tavern
    To shock with mirth a street so solemn,
But opposite the place of the cavern
    They wrote the story on a column,
And on the great Church Window painted
The same to make the world acquainted
How their children were stolen away,
And there it stands to this very day.
And I must not omit to say
That in Transylvania there's a tribe
Of alien people that ascribe
The outlandish ways and dress,
On which their neighbours lay such a stress,
To their fathers and mothers having risen
Out of some subterraneous prison,
Into which they were trepanned
Long time ago in a mighty band
Out of Hamelin town in Brunswick land,
But how or why, they don't understand.

So, Willy, let me and you be wipers
Of scores out with all men—especially pipers;
And, whether they pipe us free from rats or from mice,
If we've promised them aught, let us keep our promise.

Thomas dines in France

Enid Bagnold

Illustrated by Richard Kennedy

Enid Bagnold (born 1889) is a well-known novelist and playwright. Her "National Velvet", though not written for children, is a favourite with all those who love horses. But her undoubted children's classic (published in 1930) is "Alice and Thomas and Jane"—one of those much-loved books about the adventures of a family; not this time on a desert island, but simply at home in England. At least they were at home until Thomas, who is very young and sometimes does things a little beyond his years, slips on board a Channel steamer and finds himself in France. And what happens then? With some money a lady has given him he has two jugs of hot chocolate and cakes in a pavement café. Then he walks around Dieppe harbour buying presents for his family. He sees a pet-shop and buys three tortoises to take home to his sisters. Of course, you know that he cannot take them back to Britain! By seven o'clock he is really hungry and gets interested in a sailor's restaurant with a fascinating window full of snails in curly shells:

THE black and green snails were shining under the gas-jet, and beyond them he saw some sailors sitting at a wooden table. Then he saw other tables with rough red-checked cloths spread on them, and he knew by the look and the smell that this was where he wanted to have his grown-up dinner.

He went in and at once all the sailors looked up. There were three of them, and they were playing cards and had glasses of red wine before them. The place was warm, and full of smoke, and the sailors shouted something at him, so he stood still and smiled. The sailors laughed and made remarks, then left him alone and he went and put all his parcels on a wooden seat with a high back, and sat down.

Nobody came near him. Nobody asked him what he wanted to eat. There didn't

seem to be anybody about to ask him. He decided that the people who looked after the shop were like the young woman next door, cooking the dinner.

So he fingered his parcels and waited. And presently he took a peep at the tortoises, and they seemed calm and happy too. He meant to give them some of his evening dinner, but he didn't know whether they would eat it.

In a few minutes one of the sailors got up, the biggest, the blackest, and the one with the reddest tie. He came over to Thomas and put his hands on his hips and looked down at him. Then he asked him something, and Thomas had to look up and smile.

It seemed a hopeless fix. The sailor asked again, and Thomas could reply nothing. There is nothing to reply when you don't know what the question is. All he could do was to take off the tortoise lid and show him the tortoises. Whereupon the sailor laughed and said something so funny that the other sailors laughed too, and turned round in their chairs. Thomas laughed too, because he was sure the big sailor would like it.

At that moment a woman appeared in the doorway leading from a back room. She was carrying a clean red cloth and a big tray, and on the tray was a sort of iron tin with holes all over it. And in the holes were snails, all steaming hot. The sailors rammed their chairs back with their legs to give her room to spread the table. The biggest, the dark sailor, left Thomas and crossed the room to take the snail tray from her. She spread the clean red cloth and laid saucers and plates on the table, bread, a tooth-bottle of red wine, and at last the hot dish with the snail tin on it. Thomas felt so excited he had to stand up to look. It was like things out of a history book to see French sailors eating snails.

Now he knew what the smell was that was creeping all over the town as the evening fell and the lamps were lit. Behind all the little doorways and down all the little alleys women were cooking snails for the households to eat.

The room, which had smelt of onions before, now grew hot and thick with the smell.

The men pulled long pins out of their coat collars and picked up the shells delicately with their fingers, for the snails were hot. Then they put in a pin, gave the snail a twirl and out came a green coil like a little root.

First each sailor ate his root, and chumped it as though it were delicious leather, biting and working with his teeth and making happy sucking noises with his tongue. Then, when the creature itself was swallowed, the sailor would lift the empty shell, and tipping his head back, drink some water that was inside and wipe his mouth with the tips of his fingers, at last even sucking the fingers in case some should be lost. Then he would break a little bit of bread and swab up the hollow where the snail shell had lain in case a little of the juice should be spilled.

While Thomas was standing up behind his table watching this with his breath

held, the fat woman came up to him, and it seemed she asked him the same question that the sailor had asked. It had the same shape, and coming from her, it seemed to mean, "What do you want to eat?"

Then Thomas somehow knew that the fat woman and the big man were husband and wife, and that they were both the shopmen of this shop. So he pointed to his mouth and opened and shut his teeth very savagely, meaning that he dreadfully wanted to bite something up. The woman laughed, and shook gently with her fat when she laughed. She said something nice and warm to him, and going to a cupboard she got a fresh checked cloth out and laid his table all ready for him too. Plates she put down, with little cocks painted in the middle of them, and a glass like a heavy toothglass, made of pale green glass.

Off she went to the kitchen and Thomas sat waiting for his dinner. He was so entranced watching the sailors eat that he did not even wonder what she was going to bring him. The big sailor had joined them, and they all took as long as they could over their snails. They filled up their glasses with the red wine from the tooth-bottle, and they had other little glasses with brown wine as well. And they had huge toothpicks with which they hunted most carefully all over their mouths for lost bits of snail. The onion smell seemed even to make the tortoises hungry, and they tapped on their cardboard box with their stretched-out heads.

So Thomas took out one to see if it could catch flies for itself on the table. But he couldn't see how such a slow thing could catch flies any better than he could, unless it had some special way, like the toy magnet that he had at home, which picked up tin-tacks.

But as soon as the tortoise saw the queerness of the shining glass and the gas-jet, it stuck in all its bits and lay like a brown, careful hump, so that it shouldn't get hurt by things it didn't know. And the flies walked over its back with as much daring as if they were playing "Last across."

The heat and the brightness and the clouds of smoke nearly sent Thomas to sleep. His head was dropping sharply forward when out of the tail of his closing eye he saw the fat woman coming with a tray.

Well, what could one do if one was Thomas, and wanting to do the right thing before the sailors, and a very kind woman looking as though she thought you would be pleased, put a big dish down in front of you with a tin of twelve snails upon it?

First of all he hadn't a pin. But as a sailor was looking at him he pretended to hunt his collar for a pin, as though he expected to find one there.

And all the time his heart was almost hammering at the dreadfulness of the thing that had happened to him. If he had had a pin, perhaps he could have twirled the snails out of the shells and slipped them into the box with the tortoises. But then perhaps that was all the dinner he was going to get?

He thought of cannibals, who eat explorers. And of Chinese, who eat dogs. And he made up his mind that a boy was not a man unless he could eat snails and. . . . At least snails.

After all, between explorers and dogs and snails, snails were the easiest. And then he thought how dazzled Jane and Alice would be, and how he could explain even to mother, that the proper way to eat snails, the real sailor's way, was to twirl them out ever so easily, out of their shells with a pin.

But he hadn't a pin.

He looked down at the floor at his feet. But he hadn't much hope, for these pins were evidently special things that you carried tucked in your collar, and sailors

Alone in Dieppe—what a story to tell Jane and Alice when he got home!

wouldn't be likely to leave them about on the floor. In England it was so easy. There were always pins on the floor. Especially in mother's room.

"Mais commencez!" said the fat woman beaming over him. And he knew that meant "commence." He looked up at her and spread his hands open, then took up a hot snail and picked at it with his nail. At once she hauled a pin like a dagger out of her bodice. But he didn't want to be looked at while he was trying the twirl, so he put his hand to his mouth and made a drinking noise, hoping she would fetch him some water.

Off she went, smiling, and he started on his first snail.

He picked, but the snail stuck. Then he watched the sailors again, and this time he dug his pin down deeper. Up came the snail in the most satisfactory way, and as it came up he twisted the shell in his left hand just as they did, and there was the steaming little grey-green root sticking on his pin in his right hand. He drew his hand up to his mouth, but something inside him wouldn't let the snail come any nearer. Still by shutting his eyes tight and making

his mind think it was a chicken's liver, he got the snail between his teeth.

He chumped. But the thing was like indiarubber. He couldn't bring himself to chump twice, so he swallowed it whole, and as it went down, it gave him a pain like swallowing a stone. When it was well down and the pain had gone off, he opened his eyes, and lifting up the shell he drank down the water. The water was good. In the water lay the taste of onions. That was the home of the smell that was wandering about Dieppe.

Then back came the woman and set down on his table, not water, but a tooth-bottle of red wine. He thanked her and nothing surprised him any more. It seemed that boys of eight in this country were treated as men. What glorious things he had to tell Jane and Alice.

After that he sat down to his meal, and worked at it, for he saw his way clearly now. He poured out his wine and drank a little, and very soon he felt that though he couldn't eat the snails he could enjoy the snail-water. He twirled out his snails, slipped them gently in among the tortoises, drank the snail water, smacked

93

his lips, swabbed out the hollow in the tin with his bread, and then washed it down with a sip from his glass of red wine.

Before he had done this for twenty minutes, he was fast asleep on the bench with his head on the back of the shut-up tortoise on the table.

It was the tortoise crawling from under his head that woke him up.

He looked round, and the sailors were standing up putting on their coats. He felt very queer, and his inside was heaving. If he looked hard at the dark corners of the room, he could just keep his mind still, but if he looked at the broken jumps of the gas-jet, his mind went whirling round the room as though it was a stone on a string.

He wanted only one thing. He wanted to pay and get away. But would he ever do it in time?"

Seizing his bread knife he knocked it against his glass. The sailors laughed, but he only heard the laugh break against his ears like water on a wall a long way off. He clanked his glass again, and the woman came hurrying.

He put down a paper sheet of money, and the woman shook her head. He put down another one, and went on putting them down till she smiled.

Then, seizing his parcels and forgetting the careful tortoise, he made for the door. The woman hurried after him and put the tortoise under his arm. He nodded, far beyond smiling, and began to run. It was only a minute down to the quay, but the pavement seemed so narrow he had to run in the road, and when he got to the low parapet that kept the road from the water, the parapet got to him first, and hit him in the middle.

Down went the tortoises and the parcels in the shadow of the wall, and Thomas laid his elbows on the cool of the stone, and was as sick and as sick and as comforted as any boy could be. When he stood up again he was glad to think he hadn't got a snail in his inside. But he was glad too

to think it had been there, because it showed that he could do it.

The churches all over Dieppe rang out that it was nine o'clock, and Thomas straightened up his head and gathered up his presents. After his experience in the snail shop he began to be afraid that he might go to sleep anywhere and sleep the night through without ever meeting Mother. It was only the snail in his inside that had wakened him up this time.

"If I go to sleep again I had better go to sleep in the station," he thought, and he started to walk along beside the wall. He could easily find his way back to the station, for across the corner of the harbour he could see one of the Channel steamers tied up and sleeping peacefully with only one light at her stern. The light was heaving gently up and down, and it made Thomas sleepy to look at it.

The station when he got to it was fast asleep too. There was darkness and peace all over it, and a slight smell of oniony snails there also. Thomas walked quietly all round the sheds and the rooms on the platform to find somewhere where he could lie down and have a sleep. But he wanted somewhere where he could be sure his sleep would be disturbed by the steamer that came in bringing Mother.

In a very dark corner beside a shed he found the gangway that they ran up against the ship for the passengers to walk off by. He had come on board by a gang-way like that at Newhaven, so that he knew what it was when he saw it. It had two sides, a little like a bed, and he thought it would do very well. There was an old overcoat hanging on a peg near by, and he wanted very badly to take it down and lie on it, but he was afraid that someone would be looking for it before the steamer came in, and he would be turned off his bed.

Putting his parcels very carefully in a dark corner, he started to look round the station to see what he could find to sleep on. There was another coat hanging farther on, but he was against coats. Beyond this coat low voices spoke from a little shed, and as he passed the open door, he saw that there were men in their shirt-sleeves cooking inside. The smell made him very hungry again, especially as when he sniffed a second time, he found that it wasn't the snaily smell at all, but a new smell like potatoes frying.

He passed the shed and found a heap of fish-netting at the end of the station yard next the harbour, black fish-netting spread out to dry, with corks on it. This he dragged in the dust to his gangway, and he had hardly arranged it in a soft mass and laid himself down upon it before he was asleep.

Whether the sleeping steamer moored beside him woke and slipped quietly away, he did not know, but he sat up to the sound of a siren calling like an owl in the harbour, and saw another steamer, glittering with lights, slide gently in.

"Mother!" he thought, and got staggering to his feet. Then crept sideways into the nearby darkness when two men came towards him to prepare for the mooring.

In she came, the only shine in the harbour, and in another minute she was churning and back-paddling and elbowing her sides up to the land. Thomas heard a cry and saw a black coil of rope thrown, and then, grunting and straining, the steamer settled against the quay.

Out rolled the gangway on its little wheels, and the men who rolled it cleared the net away from it with exclamations.

Thomas hovered near the foot of it and shivered from his sleep; and there at the top stood Mother.

"Oh, Thomas!" she cried out to him. "Oh, Thomas . . ." and ran down the gang-way. . . .

Sharing the Secret Garden

Frances Hodgson Burnett

Illustrated by Shirley Hughes

Frances Hodgson Burnett (1849–1924) wrote many children's books including "Little Lord Faunterleroy", "A Little Princess" and "The Secret Garden". She is best remembered for "The Secret Garden" which was published in 1910. Mary Lennox is not a likeable girl or at least to begin with. After her parents' death in India, she is sent to live in her uncle's house on a Yorkshire moor. Lonely and neglected, she finds a small, deserted garden which has been locked for many years. Together with a young country boy named Dickon the children make the garden bloom once again, at the same time, and without realising it, coming themselves to grow and bloom, too. Then she finds that her young cousin Colin, a supposed invalid, also lives in the house, and Mary, Dickon and the garden between them restore him to a happy and healthy life. In the incident we have chosen, you will read how Mary decides to share her secret and how the magic of the garden is not lost.

THERE was a laurel-hedged walk which curved round the secret garden and ended at a gate which opened into a wood, in the park. She thought she would skip round this walk and look into the wood and see if there were any rabbits hopping about. She enjoyed the skipping very much and when she reached the little gate she opened it and went through because she heard a low, peculiar whistling sound and wanted to find out what it was.

It was a very strange thing indeed. She quite caught her breath as she stopped to look at it. A boy was sitting under a tree, with his back against it, playing on a rough wooden pipe. He was a funny looking boy about twelve. He looked very clean and his nose turned up and his cheeks were as red as poppies and never had Mistress Mary seen such round and such blue eyes in any boy's face. And on the trunk of the tree he leaned against, a brown squirrel was clinging and watching him, and from behind a bush near by a cock pheasant was

"It's this," she said. "It's a secret garden, and I'm the only one in the world who wants it to be alive."

From "Sharing the Secret Garden"

"Turn again, Whittington, thrice Lord Mayor of London."
From "Dick Whittington"

delicately stretching his neck to peep out, and quite near him were two rabbits sitting up and sniffing with tremulous noses—and actually it appeared as if they were all drawing near to watch him and listen to the strange low little call his pipe seemed to make.

When he saw Mary he held up his hand and spoke to her in a voice almost as low as and rather like his piping.

"Don't tha' move," he said. "It'd flight 'em."

Mary remained motionless. He stopped playing his pipe and began to rise from the ground. He moved so slowly that it scarcely seemed as though he were moving at all, but at last he stood on his feet and then the squirrel scampered back up into the branches of his tree, the pheasant withdrew his head and the rabbits dropped on all fours and began to hop away, though not at all as if they were frightened.

"I'm Dickon," the boy said. "I know tha'rt Miss Mary."

Then Mary realized that somehow she had known at first that he was Dickon. Who else could have been charming rabbits and pheasants as the natives charm snakes in India? He had a wide, red, curving mouth and his smile spread all over his face.

"I got up slow," he explained, "because if tha' makes a quick move it startles 'em. A body 'as to move gentle an' speak low when wild things is about."

He did not speak low to her as if they had never seen each other before but as if he knew her quite well. Mary knew nothing about boys and she spoke to him a little stiffly because she felt rather shy.

"Did you get Martha's letter?" she asked.

He nodded his curly, rust-coloured head.

"That's why I come."

He stooped to pick up something which had been lying on the ground beside him when he piped.

"I've got th' garden tools. There's a little spade an' rake an' a fork an' hoe. Eh! they are good 'uns. There's a trowel, too. An' th' woman in the shop threw in a packet o' white poppy an' one o' blue larkspur when I bought th' other seeds."

"Will you show the seeds to me?" Mary said.

She wished she could talk as he did. His speech was so quick and easy. It sounded as if he liked her and was not the least afraid she would not like him, though he was only a common moor boy, in patched clothes and with a funny face and a rough, rusty-red head. As she came closer to him she noticed that there was a clean fresh scent of heather and grass and leaves about him, almost as if he were made of them. She liked it very much and when she looked into his funny face with the red cheeks and round blue eyes she forgot that she had felt shy.

"Let us sit down on this log and look at them," she said.

They sat down and he took a clumsy little brown paper package out of his coat pocket. He untied the string and inside there were ever so many neater and smaller packages with a picture of a flower on each one.

"There's a lot o' mignonette an' poppies," he said. "Mignonette's th' sweetest smellin'

thing as grows, an' it'll grow wherever you cast it, same as poppies will. Them as'll come up an' bloom if you just whistle to 'em, them's th' nicest of all." He stopped and turned his head quickly, his poppy-cheeked face lighting up. "Where's that robin as is callin' us?" he said.

The chirp came from a thick holly bush, bright with scarlet berries, and Mary thought she knew whose it was.

"Is it really calling us?" she asked.

"Aye," said Dickon, as if it was the most natural thing in the world, "he's callin' some one he's friends with. That's same as sayin' 'Here I am. Look at me. I wants a bit of a chat.' There he is in the bush. Whose is he?"

"He's Ben Weatherstaff's, but I think he knows me a little," answered Mary.

"Aye, he knows thee," said Dickon in his low voice again. "An' he likes thee. He's took thee on. He'll tell me all about thee in a minute."

He moved quite close to the bush with the slow movement Mary had noticed before, and then he made a sound almost like the robin's own twitter. The robin listened a few seconds, intently, and then answered quite as if he were replying to a question.

"Aye, he's a friend o' yours," chuckled Dickon.

"Do you think he is?" cried Mary eagerly. She did so want to know. "Do you think he really likes me?"

"He wouldn't come near thee if he didn't," answered Dickon. "Birds is rare choosers an' a robin can flout a body worse than a man. See, he's making up to thee now. 'Cannot tha' see a chap?' he's sayin'." And it really seemed as if it must be true. He so sidled and twittered and tilted as he hopped on his bush.

"Do you understand everything birds say?" said Mary.

Dickon's grin spread until he seemed all wide, red, curving mouth, and he rubbed his rough head.

"I think I do, and they think I do," he said "I've lived on th' moor with 'em so long. I've watched 'em break shell an' come out an' fledge an' learn to fly an' begin to sing, till I think I'm one of 'em. Sometimes I think p'raps I'm a bird, or a fox, or a rabbit, or a squirrel, or even a beetle, an' I don't know it."

He laughed and came back to the log and began to talk about the flower seeds again. He told her what they looked like when they were flowers; he told her how to plant them, and watch them, and feed and water them.

"See here," he said suddenly, turning round to look at her. "I'll plant them for thee myself. Where is tha' garden?"

Mary's thin hands clutched each other as they lay on her lap. She did not know what to say, so for a whole minute she said nothing. She had never thought of this. She felt miserable. And she felt as if she went red and then pale.

"Tha's got a bit o' garden, hasn't tha'?" Dickon said.

It was true that she had turned red and then pale. Dickon saw her do it, and as she still said nothing, he began to be puzzled.

"Wouldn't they give thee a bit?" he asked. "Hasn't tha' got any yet?"

She held her hands even tighter and turned her eyes toward him.

"I don't know anything about boys," she said slowly. "Could you keep a secret, if I told you one? It's a great secret. I don't know what I should do if any one found it out. I believe I should die!" She said the last sentence quite fiercely.

Dickon looked more puzzled than ever and even rubbed his hand over his rough head again, but he answered quite good-humouredly.

"I'm keepin' secrets all th' time," he said. "If I couldn't keep secrets from th' other lads, secrets about foxes' cubs, an' birds' nests, an' wild things' holes, there'd be naught safe on th' moor. Aye, I can keep secrets."

Mistress Mary did not mean to put out her hand and clutch his sleeve, but she did it.

"I've stolen a garden," she said very fast. "It isn't mine. It isn't anybody's. Nobody wants it, nobody cares for it, nobody ever goes into it. Perhaps everything is dead in it already; I don't know."

She began to feel as hot and as contrary as she had ever felt in her life. . . .

"Where is it?" asked Dickon in a dropped voice.

"Come with me and I'll show you," she said.

She led him round the laurel path and to the walk where the ivy grew so thickly. Dickon followed her with a queer, almost pitying, look on his face. He felt as if he were being led to look at some strange bird's nest and must move softly.

When she stepped to the wall and lifted the hanging ivy he started. There was a door and Mary pushed it slowly open and they passed in together, and then Mary stood and waved her hand round defiantly.

"It's this," she said. "It's a secret garden, and I'm the only one in the world who wants it to be alive."

Dickon looked round and round about it, and round and round again.

"Eh!" he almost whispered, "it is a queer, pretty place! It's like as if a body was in a dream."

For two or three minutes he stood looking round him, while Mary watched him, and then he began to walk about softly, even more lightly than Mary had walked the first time she had found herself inside the four walls. His eyes seemed to be taking in everything—the grey trees with the grey creepers climbing over them and hanging from their branches, the tangle on the walls and among the grass, the evergreen alcoves with the stone seats and tall flower urns standing in them.

"I never thought I'd see this place," he said at last in a whisper.

"Did you know about it?" asked Mary.

She had spoken aloud and he made a sign to her.

"We must talk low," he said, "or some one'll hear us an' wonder what's to do in here."

"Oh! I forgot!" said Mary, feeling frightened and putting her hand quickly against her mouth. "Did you know about the garden?" she asked again when she had recovered herself.

Dickon nodded.

"Martha told me there was one as no one ever went inside," he answered. "Us used to wonder what it was like."

He stopped and looked round at the lovely grey tangle about him, and his round eyes looked queerly happy.

"Eh! the nests as'll be here come springtime," he said. "It'd be th' safest nestin' place in England. No one never comin' near an' tangles o' trees an' roses to build in. I wonder all th' birds on th' moor don't build here."

Mistress Mary put her hand on his arm again without knowing it.

"Will there be roses?" she whispered. "Can you tell? I thought perhaps they were all dead."

"Eh! No! Not them—not all of 'em!" he answered. "Look here!"

He stepped over to the nearest tree—an old, old one with grey lichen all over its bark, but upholding a curtain of tangled sprays and branches. He took a thick knife out of his pocket and opened one of its blades.

"There's lots o' dead wood as ought to be cut out," he said. "An' there's a lot o' old wood, but it made some new last year. This here's a new bit," and he touched a shoot which looked brownish green instead of hard, dry grey.

Mary touched it herself in an eager, reverent way.

"That one?" she said. "Is that one quite alive—quite?"

Dickon curved his wide smiling mouth.

"It's as wick as you or me," he said; and Mary remembered that Martha had told her that "wick" meant "alive" or "lively."

"I'm glad it's wick!" she cried out in her whisper. "I want them all to be wick. Let us go round the garden and count how many wick ones there are."

She quite panted with eagerness, and Dickon was as eager as she was. They went from tree to tree and from bush to bush. Dickon carried his knife in his hand and showed her things which she thought wonderful.

"They've run wild," he said, "but th' strongest ones has fair thrived on it. The delicatest ones has died out, but th' others has growed an' growed, an' spread and spread, till they's a wonder. See here!" and he pulled down a thick grey, dry-looking branch. "A body might think this was dead wood, but I don't believe it is—down to th' root. I'll cut it low down an' see."

He knelt and with his knife cut the lifeless-looking branch through, not far above the earth.

"There!" he said exultantly. "I told thee so. There's green in that wood yet. Look at it."

Mary was down on her knees before he spoke, gazing with all her might.

"When it looks a bit greenish an' juicy like that, it's wick," he explained. "When th' inside is dry an' breaks easy, like this here piece I've cut off, it's done for. There's a big root here as all this live wood sprung out of, an' if th' old wood's cut off an' it's dug round, an' took care of there'll be—" he stopped and lifted his face to look up at the climbing and hanging sprays above him—"there'll be a fountain o' roses here this summer."

They went from bush to bush and from tree to tree. He was very strong and clever with his knife and knew how to cut the dry and dead wood away, and could tell when an unpromising bough or twig had still green life in it. In the course of half an hour Mary thought she could tell too, and when he cut through a lifeless-looking branch she would cry out joyfully under her breath when she caught sight of the least shade of moist green. The spade, and hoe, and fork were very useful. He showed her how to use the fork while he dug about roots with the spade and stirred the earth and let the air in.

They were working industriously round one of the biggest standard roses when he caught sight of something which made him utter an exclamation of surprise.

"Why!" he cried, pointing to the grass a few feet away. "Who did that there?"

It was one of Mary's own little clearings round the pale green points.

"I did it," said Mary.

"Why, I thought tha' didn't know nothin' about gardenin'," he exclaimed.

"I don't," she answered, "but they were so little, and the grass was so thick and strong, and they looked as if they had no room to breathe. So I made a place for them. I don't even know what they are."

Dickon went and knelt down by them, smiling his wide smile.

"Tha' was right," he said. "A gardener couldn't have told thee better. They'll grow now like Jack's bean-stalk. They're crocuses an' snowdrops, an' these here is narcissuses," turning to another patch, "an' here's daffydowndillys. Eh! they will be a sight."

He ran from one clearing to another.

"Tha' has done a lot o' work for such a little wench," he said, looking her over....

He was working all the time he was talking and Mary was following him and helping him with her fork or the trowel....

"Will you come again and help me to do it?" Mary begged. "I'm sure I can help, too. I can dig and pull up weeds, and do whatever you tell me. Oh! do come, Dickon!"

"I'll come every day if tha' wants me, rain or shine," he answered stoutly. "It's th' best fun I ever had in my life—shut in here an' wakenin' up a garden."

"If you will come," said Mary, "if you will help me to make it alive I'll—I don't know what I'll do," she ended helplessly. What could you do for a boy like that?

And then they began to work harder than ever and more joyfully. Mary was startled and sorry when she heard the big clock in the courtyard strike the hour of her midday dinner.

"I shall have to go," she said mournfully. "And you will have to go too, won't you?"

Dickon grinned.

"My dinner's easy to carry about with me," he said. "Mother always lets me put a bit o' somethin' in my pocket."

He picked up his coat from the grass and brought out of a pocket a lumpy little bundle tied up in a quite clean, coarse, blue and white handkerchief. It held two thick pieces of bread with a slice of something laid between them.

"It's oftenest naught but bread," he said, "but I've got a fine slice o' fat bacon with it today."

Mary thought it looked a queer dinner, but he seemed ready to enjoy it.

"Run on an' get thy victuals," he said. "I'll be done with mine first. I'll get some more work done before I start back home."

He sat down with his back against a tree.

"I'll call th' robin up," he said, "and give him th' rind o' th' bacon to peck at. They likes a bit o' fat wonderful."

Mary could scarcely bear to leave him. Suddenly it seemed as if he might be a sort of wood fairy who might be gone when she came into the garden again. He seemed too good to be true. She went slowly halfway to the door in the wall and then she stopped and went back.

"Whatever happens, you—you never would tell?" she said.

His poppy-coloured cheeks were distended with his first big bite of bread and bacon, but he managed to smile encouragingly.

"If tha' was a missel thrush an' showed me where thy nest was, does tha' think I'd tell any one? Not me," he said. "Tha' art as safe as a missel thrush."

And she was quite sure she was.

The Autumn Robin

Sweet little bird in russet coat,
*   The livery of the closing year,*
I love thy lonely plaintive note
*   And tiny whispering song to hear,*
While on the stile or garden seat
*   I sit to watch the falling leaves,*
The song thy little joys repeat
*   My loneliness relieves.*

JOHN CLARE

The Birth of Pinocchio

Carlo Collodi

Illustrated by Val Biro

The story of "Pinocchio", from which this extract comes, is that of a talking puppet, made of wood but endowed with life. No creature was ever more headstrong, more mischievous, more determined to have its own way in everything. In fact, Pinocchio behaves very badly, and "learns better" only by hard experience. After many adventures, each more trying than the last, he begins to gain commonsense, if not wisdom; and, as a reward, is turned into a human child. This is perhaps the best of all Italian books for children, and was written in 1881 by Carlo Lorenzini, whose pen-name was Collodi. Here we have the very beginning of Pinocchio's adventures, and, as you might expect, he gets off to a quick start:

GEPPETTO lived in a small ground-floor room that was only lighted from the staircase. The furniture could not have been simpler—a bad chair, a poor bed, and a broken-down table. At the end of the room there was a fireplace with a lighted fire; but the fire was painted, and by the fire was a painted saucepan that was boiling cheerfully, and sending out a cloud of smoke that looked exactly like real smoke.

As soon as he reached home Geppetto took his tools and set to work to cut out and model his puppet.

"What name shall I give him?" he said to himself. "I think I will call him Pinocchio. It is a name that will bring him luck. I once knew a whole family so called. There was Pinocchio the father, Pinocchia the mother, and Pinocchi the children, and all of them did well. The richest of them was a beggar."

Having found a name for his puppet he began to work in good earnest, and he first made his hair, then his forehead, and then his eyes.

The eyes being finished, imagine his astonishment when he perceived that they moved and looked fixedly at him.

Geppetto, seeing himself stared at by those two wooden eyes, took it almost in bad part, and said in an angry voice:

"Wicked wooden eyes, why do you look at me?"

No one answered.

He then proceeded to carve the nose; but no sooner had he made it than it began to grow. And it grew, and grew, and grew, until in a few minutes it had become an immense nose that seemed as if it would never end.

Poor Geppetto tired himself out with cutting it off; but the more he cut and shortened it, the longer did that impertinent nose become!

The mouth was not even completed

when it began to laugh and deride him.

"Stop laughing!" said Geppetto, provoked; but he might as well have spoken to the wall.

"Stop laughing, I say!" he roared in a threatening tone.

The mouth then ceased laughing, but put out its tongue as far as it would go.

Geppetto, not to spoil his handiwork, pretended not to see, and continued his labours. After the mouth he fashioned the chin, then the throat, then the shoulders, the stomach, the arms and the hands.

The hands were scarcely finished when Geppetto felt his wig snatched from his head. He turned round, and what did he see? He saw his yellow wig in the puppet's hand.

"Pinocchio! Give me back my wig instantly!"

But Pinocchio, instead of returning it, put it on his own head, and was in consequence nearly smothered.

Geppetto at this insolent and derisive behaviour felt sadder and more melancholy than he had ever been in his life before; and turning to Pinocchio he said to him:

"You young rascal! You are not yet completed, and you are already beginning to show want of respect to your father! That is bad, my boy, very bad!"

And he dried a tear.

The legs and the feet remained to be done.

When Geppetto had finished the feet he received a kick on the point of his nose.

"I deserve it!" he said to himself. "I should have thought of it sooner! Now it is too late!"

He then took the puppet under the arms and placed him on the floor to teach him to walk.

Pinocchio's legs were stiff and he could not move, but Geppetto led him by the hand and showed him how to put one foot before the other.

When his legs became flexible Pinocchio began to walk by himself and to run about the room; until, having gone out of the house door, he jumped into the street and escaped.

Poor Geppetto rushed after him but was not able to overtake him, for that rascal Pinocchio leapt in front of him like a hare, and knocking his wooden feet together against the pavement made as much clatter as twenty pairs of peasants' clogs.

"Stop him! Stop him!" shouted Geppetto; but the people in the street, seeing a wooden puppet running like a race horse, stood still in astonishment to look at it, and laughed, and laughed, and laughed, until it beats description.

At last, as good luck would have it, a carabineer arrived who, hearing the uproar, imagined that a colt had escaped from his master. Planting himself courageously with legs apart in the middle of the road, he waited with the determined purpose of stopping him, and thus preventing the chance of worse disasters.

When Pinocchio, still at some distance, saw the carabineer barricading the whole street, he endeavoured to take him by surprise and to pass between his legs. But he failed sadly.

The carabineer without disturbing himself in the least caught him cleverly by the nose—it was an immense nose of ridiculous proportions that seemed made on purpose to be laid hold of by carabineers—and consigned him to Geppetto. Wishing to punish him, Geppetto intended to pull his ears at once. But imagine his feelings when he could not succeed in finding them. And do you know the reason? It was that, in his hurry to model him, he had forgotten to make them.

He then took him by the collar, and as he was leading him away he said to him, shaking his head threateningly:

"We will go home at once, and as soon as we arrive we will regulate our accounts, never doubt it."

At this announcement Pinocchio threw himself on the ground and would not take another step. In the meanwhile a crowd of idlers and inquisitive people began to assemble and to make a ring around them.

Some of them said one thing, some another.

"Poor puppet," said several, "he is right not to wish to return home! Who knows how Geppetto, that bad old man, will beat him!"

And the others added maliciously:

"Geppetto seems a good man, but with boys he is a regular tyrant! If that poor puppet is left in his hands he is quite capable of tearing him in pieces!"

It ended in so much being said and done that the carabineer at last set Pinocchio at liberty and conducted Geppetto to prison. The poor man, not being ready with words to defend himself, cried like a calf, and as he was being led away to prison sobbed out:

"Wretched boy! And to think how I have laboured to make him a well-conducted puppet! But it serves me right! I should have thought of it sooner!"

Dick Whittington

An Old Tale

*Illustrated by Arthur Rackham
and John Speirs*

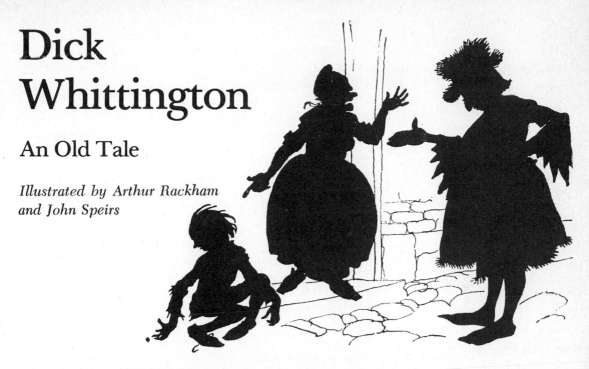

IN THE reign of the famous King Edward III, there was a little boy called Dick Whittington, whose father and mother died when he was very young. As poor Dick was not old enough to work, he was very badly off; he got but little for his dinner, and sometimes nothing at all for his breakfast; for the people who lived in the village were very poor indeed, and could not spare him much more than the parings of potatoes, and now and then a hard crust of bread.

Now Dick had heard many, many very strange things about the great city called London; for the country people at that time thought that folks in London were all fine gentlemen and ladies; and that there was singing and music there all day long; and that the streets were all paved with gold.

One day a large wagon and eight horses, all with bells at their heads, drove through the village while Dick was standing by the sign-post. He thought this wagon must be going to the fine town of London; so he took courage, and asked the wagoner to let him walk with him by the side of the wagon. When the wagoner heard that poor Dick had no father or mother, and saw by his ragged clothes that he could not be worse off than he was, he told him he might go if he would, so off they set together.

Dick got safe to London, and was in such a hurry to see the fine streets paved all over with gold, that he did not even stay to thank the kind wagoner; but ran off as fast as his legs would carry him, through many of the streets, thinking every moment to come to those that were paved with gold. Dick had seen a guinea three times in his own little village, and remembered what a deal of money it brought in change; so he thought he had nothing to do but to take up some little bits of the pavement, and he should then have as much money as he could wish for.

Poor Dick ran till he was tired, and had quite forgotten his friend the wagoner; but at last, when it grew dark, and he found that every way he turned there was nothing but dirt instead of gold, he sat down in a dark corner and cried himself to sleep.

He was all night in the streets; and next

morning, being very hungry, he got up and walked about. He asked everybody he met to give him a halfpenny to keep him from starving; but nobody stayed to answer him, and only two or three gave him a halfpenny; so that the poor boy was quite weak and faint for the want of food.

In his distress he asked charity of several people and one of them said crossly: "Go to work, you idle rogue!"

"That I will," said Dick, "I will go to work for you, if you will let me." But the man only cursed at him and went on.

At last a good-natured looking gentleman saw how hungry he looked. "Why don't you go to work, my lad?" said he to Dick. "That I would, but I do not know how to get any," answered Dick. "If you are willing, come along with me," said the gentleman, and took him to a hay-field, where Dick worked briskly, and lived merrily till the hay was made.

After this he found himself as badly off as before; and being almost starved again, he laid himself down at the door of Mr. Fitzwarren, a rich merchant. Here he was soon seen by the cook-maid, who was an ill-tempered creature, and happened just then to be very busy dressing dinner for her master and mistress; so she called out to poor Dick: "What business have you there, you lazy rogue? There is nothing else but beggars; if you do not take yourself away, we will see how you will like a

sousing of some dish-water; I have some here hot enough to make you jump."

Just at that time Mr. Fitzwarren himself came home to dinner; and when he saw a dirty ragged boy lying at the door, he said to him: "Why do you lie there, my boy? You seem old enough to work; I am afraid you are inclined to be lazy."

"No, indeed, sir," said Dick to him, "that is not the case, for I would work with all my heart, but I do not know anybody, and I believe I am very sick for the want of food." "Poor fellow, get up; let me see what ails you."

Dick now tried to rise, but was obliged to lie down again, being too weak to stand, for he had not eaten any food for three days, and was no longer able to run about and beg a halfpenny of people in the street. So the kind merchant ordered him to be taken into the house, and have a good dinner given him, and be kept to do what work he was able to do for the cook.

Little Dick would have lived very happily in this good family if it had not been for the ill-natured cook. She used to say: "You are under me, so look sharp; clean the spit and the dripping-pan, make the fires, wind up the jack, and do all the scullery work nimbly, or—" and she would shake the ladle at him. Besides, she was so fond of basting, that when she had no meat to baste, she would baste poor Dick's head and shoulders with a broom, or anything else that happened to fall in her way. At last her ill-usage of him was told to Alice, Mr. Fitzwarren's daughter, who told the cook she should be turned away if she did not treat him kinder.

The behaviour of the cook was now a little better; but besides this, Dick had another hardship to get over. His bed stood in a garret, where there were so many holes in the floor and the walls that every night he was tormented with rats and mice. A gentleman having given Dick a penny for cleaning his shoes, he thought he would buy a cat with it. The next day, he saw a girl with a cat, and asked her,

"Will you let me have that cat for a penny?" The girl said: "Yes, that I will, master, though she is an excellent mouser."

Dick hid his cat in the garret, and always took care to carry a part of his dinner for her; and in a short time he had no more trouble with the rats and mice, but slept quite sound every night.

"I have nothing but a cat which I bought for a penny some time since of a little girl."

"Fetch your cat then, my lad," said Mr. Fitzwarren, "and let her go."

Dick went upstairs and brought down poor puss, with tears in his eyes, and gave her to the captain; "For," he said, "I shall

Dick listens to the bells of Bow Church.

Soon after this, his master had a ship ready to sail; and as it was the custom that all his servants should have some chance for good fortune as well as himself, he called them all into the parlour and asked them what they would send out.

They all had something that they were willing to venture except poor Dick, who had neither money nor goods, and therefore could send nothing. For this reason he did not come into the parlour with the rest; but Miss Alice guessed what was the matter, and ordered him to be called in. She then said: "I will lay down some money for him, from my own purse," but her father told her: "This will not do, for it must be something of his own."

When poor Dick heard this, he said:

now be kept awake all night by the rats and mice." All the company laughed at Dick's odd venture; and Miss Alice, who felt pity for him, gave him some money to buy another cat.

This, and many other marks of kindness shown him by Miss Alice, made the ill-tempered cook jealous of poor Dick, and she began to use him more cruelly than ever, and always made game of him for sending his cat to sea. She asked him: "Do you think your cat will sell for as much money as would buy a stick to beat you?"

At last poor Dick could not bear this usage any longer, and he thought he would run away from his place; so he packed up his few things, and started very early in the morning, on Allhallows Day, the first of November. He walked as far as Holloway; and there sat down on a stone, which to this day is called Whittington's Stone, and began to think to himself which road he should take.

While he was thinking what he should do, the Bells of Bow Church, which at that time were only six, began to ring, and at their sound seemed to say to him:

"Turn again, Whittington,
Thrice Lord Mayor of London."

"Lord Mayor of London!" said he to himself. "Why to be sure, I would put up with almost anything now, to be Lord Mayor of London, and ride in a fine coach, when I grow to be a man! Well, I will go back, and think nothing of the cuffing and scolding of the old cook, if I am to be Lord Mayor of London at last."

Dick went back, and was lucky to get into the house, and set about his work, before the old cook came downstairs.

We must now follow Miss Puss to the coast of Africa. The ship with the cat on board was a long time at sea; and was at last driven by the winds on a part of the coast of Barbary, where the only people were the Moors, unknown to the English. The people came in great numbers to see the sailors, because they were of different colour to themselves, and treated them civilly; and, when they became better acquainted, were very eager to buy the fine things that the ship was loaded with.

When the captain saw this, he sent patterns of the best things he had to the king of the country; who was so much pleased with them, that he sent for the captain to the palace. Here they were placed, as it is the custom of the country, on rich carpets flowered with gold and silver. The king and queen were seated at the upper end of the room; and a number of dishes were brought in for dinner. They had not sat long, when a vast number of rats and mice rushed in, and devoured all the meat in an instant. The captain

wondered at this, and asked if these vermin were not unpleasant.

"Oh yes," said they, "very offensive; and the king would give half his treasure to be freed of them, for they not only destroy his dinner, as you see, but they assault him in his chamber, and even in bed, so that he is obliged to be watched while he is sleeping, for fear of them."

The captain jumped for joy; he remembered poor Whittington and his cat, and told the king he had a creature on board the ship that would despatch all these vermin immediately. The king jumped so high at the joy which the news gave him, that his turban dropped off his head. "Bring this creature to me," says he; "vermin are dreadful in a court, and if she will perform what you say, I will load your ship with gold and jewels in exchange for her."

The captain, who knew his business, took this opportunity to set forth the merits of Miss Puss. He told his majesty: "It is not very convenient to part with her, as, when she is gone, the rats and mice may destroy the goods in the ship—but to oblige your majesty, I will fetch her."

"Run, run!" said the queen; "I am impatient to see the dear creature."

Away went the captain to the ship, while another dinner was got ready. He put Puss under his arm, and arrived at the place just in time to see the table full of rats. When the cat saw them, she did not wait for bidding, but jumped out of the captain's arms, and in a few minutes laid almost all the rats and mice dead at her feet. The rest of them in their fright scampered away to their holes.

The king was quite charmed to get rid so easily of such plagues, and the queen desired that the creature who had done them so great a kindness might be brought to her, that she might look at her. Upon which the captain called: "Pussy, pussy, pussy!" and she came to him. He then presented her to the queen, who started back, and was afraid to touch a creature

When the cat saw them, she did not wait for bidding.

who had made such a havoc among the rats and mice. However, when the captain stroked the cat and called: "Pussy, pussy," the queen also touched her and cried: "Putty, putty," for she had not learned English. He then put her down on the queen's lap, where she purred and played with her majesty's hand, and then purred herself to sleep.

The king, having seen the exploits of Miss Puss, and being informed that her kittens would stock the whole country, and keep it free from rats, bargained with the captain for the whole ship's cargo, and then gave him ten times as much for the cat as all the rest amounted to.

The captain then took leave of the royal party, and set sail with a fair wind for England, and after a happy voyage arrived safe in London.

One morning, early, Mr. Fitzwarren had just come to his counting-house and seated himself at the desk, to count over the cash, and settle the business for the day, when somebody came tap, tap, at the door. "Who's there?" said Mr. Fitzwarren. "A friend," answered the other; "I come to bring you good news of your ship *Unicorn*." The merchant, bustling up in such a hurry that he forgot his gout, opened the door, and who should he see waiting but the captain and factor, with a cabinet of jewels and a bill of lading; when he looked at this the merchant lifted up his eyes and thanked Heaven for sending him such a prosperous voyage.

They then told the story of the cat, and showed the rich present that the king and queen had sent for her to poor Dick. As soon as the merchant heard this, he called out to his servants:

"Go send him in, and tell him of his fame:
Pray call him Mr. Whittington by name."

Mr. Fitzwarren now showed himself to be a good man; for when some of his servants said so great a treasure was too much for him, he answered: "God forbid I should deprive him of the value of a single penny; it is his own, and he shall have it to a farthing."

He then sent for Dick, who at that time was scouring pots for the cook, and was quite dirty. He would have excused himself from coming into the counting-house, saying, "The room is swept, and my shoes are dirty and full of hob-nails." But the merchant ordered him to come in.

Mr. Fitzwarren ordered a chair to be set for him, and so he began to think they were making game of him, and at the same time said to them: "Do not play tricks with a poor simple boy, but let me go down again, if you please, to my work."

"Indeed, Mr. Whittington," said the merchant, "we are all quite in earnest with you, and I most heartily rejoice in the news that these gentlemen have brought you; for the captain has sold your cat to the King of Barbary, and brought you in return for her more riches than I possess in the whole world; and I wish you may long enjoy them!"

Mr. Fitzwarren then told the men to open the great treasure they had brought with them, and said: "Mr. Whittington has nothing to do but to put it in some place of safety."

Poor Dick hardly knew how to behave himself for joy. He begged his master to take what part of it he pleased, since he owed it all to his kindness. "No, no," answered Mr. Fitzwarren, "this is all your own; and I have no doubt but you will use it well."

Dick next asked his mistress, and then Miss Alice, to accept a part of his good fortune; but they would not, and at the same time told him they felt great joy at his good success. But he was too kind-hearted to keep it all to himself; so he made a present to the captain, the mate, and the rest of Mr. Fitzwarren's servants; and even to the ill-natured old cook.

After this Mr. Fitzwarren advised him to send for a proper tailor, and get himself dressed like a gentleman; and told him he

110

was welcome to live in his house till he could provide himself with a better.

When Whittington's face was washed, his hair curled, his hat cocked, and he was dressed in a nice suit of clothes he was as handsome and genteel as any young man who visited at Mr. Fitzwarren's; so that Miss Alice, who had once been so kind to him, and thought of him with pity, now looked upon him as fit to be her sweetheart; and the more so, no doubt, because Whittington was now always thinking what he could do to oblige her, and making her the prettiest presents that could be.

Mr. Fitzwarren soon saw their love for each other, and proposed to join them in marriage; and to this they both readily agreed. A day for the wedding was soon fixed; and they were attended to church by the Lord Mayor, the court of aldermen, the sheriffs, and a great number of the richest merchants in London, whom they afterwards treated to a very rich feast.

History tells us that Mr. Whittington and his lady lived in great splendour, and were very happy. They had several children. He was Sheriff of London, thrice Lord Mayor, and received the honour of knighthood by Henry V.

He entertained the king and his queen at dinner, after his conquest of France, so grandly, that the king said: "Never had prince such a subject"; when Sir Richard heard this, he said: "Never had subject such a prince."

The figure of Sir Richard Whittington with his cat in his arms, carved in stone, was to be seen till the year 1780 over the archway of the old prison at Newgate, which he built for criminals.

Death of My Aunt

My aunt she died a month ago,
  And left me all her riches,
A feather-bed and a wooden leg,
  And a pair of calico breeches;
A coffee pot without a spout,
  A mug without a handle,
A baccy box without a lid,
  And half a farthing candle.

UNKNOWN

The Storming of Toad Hall

Kenneth Grahame

Illustrated by Ernest Shepard

Colour illustration by Val Biro based on Ernest Shepard's characters

Kenneth Grahame (1859–1932) was born in Edinburgh. His mother died when he was five years old and he went to live with his grandmother at Cookham Dene in Berkshire. The house was large and rambling with the River Thames running through part of the grounds. Kenneth loved the place and spent many happy hours exploring the river bank and the surrounding countryside. In 1878 he joined the staff of the Bank of England as a clerk and rose over the years to become Secretary in 1898 He started writing essays and articles and his first work was published about 1888. He married in 1899 and his son Alistair, "Mouse" as he was called, was born in 1900. On Mouse's fourth birthday his father began to tell him a bedtime story about a mole and a rat which expanded over the next three years to include a badger and a toad among others. When Mouse went on a long holiday by the sea at the age of seven the story had to be continued in letters! A family friend saw these letters and persuaded Kenneth Grahame to write it all down. The book was called "The Wind in the Willows".

In the part that we have chosen, we join the four friends, Toad, Water Rat, Mole and Badger in a time of crisis. Toad, who is a terrible boaster with a passion for driving expensive cars very fast and very badly, has survived some trying adventures only to find that his mansion, Toad Hall, has been taken over by the stoats and the weasels of the wild wood. Badger, who is a tower of strength in time of trouble, knows of an underground passage from the river bank right into Toad Hall and the friends are determined to win back Toad's ancestral home. They mean to attack at nightfall:

B Y THE time Toad got down he found that the other animals had finished their breakfast some time before. The Mole had slipped off somewhere by himself, without telling anyone where he was going. The Badger sat in the armchair, reading the paper, and not concerning himself in the slightest about what was going to happen that very evening. The Rat, on the other hand, was running round the room busily, with his arms full of weapons of every kind, distributing them in four little heaps on the floor, and saying excitedly under his breath, as he ran, "Here's-a-sword-for-the-Rat, here's-a- sword-for-the-Mole, here's-a-sword-for-the-Toad, here's-a-sword-for-the-Badger! Here's-a-pistol-for-the-Rat, here's-a-pistol-for-the-Mole, here's-a-pistol-for-the-Toad, here's-a-pistol-for-the-Badger!" And so on, in a regular, rhythmical way, while the four little heaps gradually grew and grew.

"That's all very well, Rat," said the Badger presently, looking at the busy little animal over the edge of his newspaper: "I'm not blaming you. But just let us once get past the stoats, with those detestable guns of theirs, and I assure you we shan't want any swords or pistols. We four, with our sticks, once we're inside the dining-

"Look here, Toady! Don't you chatter so much as usual, or you'll be sent back, as sure as fate!"
From "The Storming of Toad Hall"

"Indeed, you're but a poor weapon," sighed he. *"But since there is no better to be had, I must
do the best I can with you."*
From "Robin Hood and the Potter"

hall, why, we shall clear the floor of all the lot of them in five minutes. I'd have done the whole thing by myself, only I didn't want to deprive you fellows of the fun!"

"It's as well to be on the safe side," said the Rat, reflectively, polishing a pistol barrel on his sleeve and looking along it.

The Toad, having finished his breakfast, picked up a stout stick and swung it vigorously, belabouring imaginary animals! "I'll learn 'em to steal my house!" he cried. "I'll learn 'em!"

"Don't say 'learn 'em', Toad," said the Rat, greatly shocked. "It's not good English."

"What are you always nagging at Toad for?" inquired the Badger rather peevishly. "What's the matter with his English? It's the same what I use myself, and if it's good enough for me, it ought to be good enough for you!"

"I'm very sorry," said the Rat humbly. "Only I *think* it ought to be 'teach 'em', not 'learn 'em'."

"But we don't *want* to teach 'em," replied the Badger. "We want to *learn* 'em —learn 'em, learn 'em! And what's more, we're going to *do* it, too!"

"Oh, very well, have it your own way,"

said the Rat. He was getting rather muddled about it himself, and presently he retired into a corner, where he could be heard muttering, "Learn 'em, teach 'em, teach 'em, learn 'em!" till the Badger told him rather sharply to leave off. . . .

When it began to grow dark, the Rat, with an air of excitement and mystery, summoned them back into the parlour, stood each of them up alongside of his little heap, and proceeded to dress them up for the coming expedition. He was very earnest and thoroughgoing about it, and the affair took quite a long time. First, there was a belt to go round each animal, and then a sword to be stuck into each belt, and then a cutlass on the other side to balance it. Then a pair of pistols, a policeman's truncheon, several sets of handcuffs, some bandages and sticking-plaster, and a flask and a sandwich-case. The Badger laughed good-humouredly and said, "All right, Ratty! It amuses you and it doesn't hurt me. I'm going to do all I've got to do with this here stick." But the Rat only said, *"Please* Badger! You know I shouldn't like you to blame me afterwards and say I had forgotten *anything!*"

"But we don't want *to teach 'em,"* replied the Badger. *"We want to* learn *'em!"*

113

When all was quite ready, the Badger took a dark lantern in one paw, grasped his great stick with the other, and said, "Now then, follow me! Mole first, 'cos I'm very pleased with him; Rat next; Toad last. And look here, Toady! Don't you chatter so much as usual, or you'll be sent back, as sure as fate!"

The Toad was so anxious not to be left out that he took up the inferior position assigned to him without a murmur, and the animals set off. The Badger led them along by the river for a little way, and then suddenly swung himself over the edge into a hole in the river bank, a little above the water. The Mole and the Rat followed silently, swinging themselves successfully into the hole as they had seen the Badger do; but when it came to Toad's turn, of course, he managed to slip and fall into the water with a loud splash and a squeal of alarm. He was hauled out by his friends, rubbed down and wrung out hastily, comforted, and set on his legs; but the Badger was seriously angry, and told him the very next time he made a fool of himself he would most certainly be left behind.

So at last they were in the secret passage, and the cutting-out expedition had really begun!

It was cold, and dark, and damp, and low, and narrow, and poor Toad began to shiver, partly from dread of what might be before him, partly because he was wet through. The lantern was far ahead, and he could not help lagging behind a little in the darkness. Then he heard the Rat call out warningly, "*Come* on, Toad!" and a terror seized him of being left behind, alone in the darkness, and he came on with such a rush that he upset the Rat into the Mole and the Mole into the Badger, and for a moment all was confusion. The Badger thought they were being attacked from behind, and, as there was no room to use a stick or a cutlass, drew a pistol, and was on the point of putting a bullet into Toad. When he found out what had really happened he was very angry indeed, and said, "Now, this time that tiresome Toad *shall* be left behind!"

But Toad whimpered, and the other two promised that they would be answerable for his good conduct, and at last the Badger was pacified, and the procession moved on; only this time the Rat brought up the rear, with a firm grip on the shoulder of Toad.

So they groped and shuffled along, with their ears pricked up and their paws on their pistols, till at last the Badger said, "We ought by now to be pretty nearly under the Hall."

Then suddenly they heard, far away as it might be, and yet apparently nearly over their heads, a confused murmur of sound, as if people were shouting and cheering and stamping on the floor and hammering on tables. The Toad's nervous terrors all returned, but the Badger only remarked placidly, "They *are* going it, the weasels!"

The passage now began to slope upwards; they groped onward a little further, and then the noise broke out again, quite distinct this time, and very close above them. "Oo-ray-oo-ray-oo-ray-ooray!" they heard, and the stamping of little feet on the floor, and the clinking of glasses as little fists pounded on the table. "*What* a time they're having!" said the Badger. "Come on!" They hurried along the passage till it came to a full stop, and they found themselves standing under the trap-door that led up into the butler's pantry.

Such a tremendous noise was going on in the banqueting-hall that there was little danger of their being overheard. The Badger said, "Now, boys, all together!" and the four of them put their shoulders to the trap-door and heaved it back. Hoisting each other up, they found themselves standing in the pantry, with only a door between them and the banqueting-hall, where their unconscious enemies were carousing.

The noise, as they emerged from the passage, was simply deafening. At last, as the cheering and hammering slowly subsided, a voice could be made out saying, "Well, I do not propose to detain you much longer"—(great applause)—"but before I resume my seat"—(renewed cheering)—"I should like to say one word about our kind host, Mr. Toad. We all know Toad!"—(great laughter)—"*Good* Toad, *modest* Toad, *honest* Toad!" (shrieks of merriment).

"Only just let me get at him!" muttered Toad, grinding his teeth.

"Hold hard a minute!" said the Badger, restraining him with difficulty. "Get ready, all of you!"

"—Let me sing you a little song," went on the voice, "which I have composed on the subject of Toad"—(prolonged applause).

Then the Chief Weasel—for it was he—began in a high, squeaky voice—

"Toad he went a-pleasuring
Gaily down the street—"

The Badger drew himself up, took a firm grip of his stick with both paws, glanced round at his comrades, and cried—

"The hour is come! Follow me!"

And flung the door wide open.

My!

What a squealing and a squeaking and a screeching filled the air!

Well might the terrified weasels dive under the tables and spring madly up at the windows! Well might the ferrets rush wildly for the fireplace and get hopelessly jammed in the chimney! Well might tables and chairs be upset, and glass and china be sent crashing on the floor, in the panic of that terrible moment when the four Heroes strode wrathfully into the room! The mighty Badger, his whiskers bristling, his great cudgel whistling through the air; Mole, black and grim, brandishing his stick and shouting his awful war-cry, "A Mole! A Mole!" Rat, desperate and determined, his belt bulging with weapons of every age and every variety; Toad, frenzied with excitement and injured pride, swollen to twice his ordinary size, leaping into the air and emitting Toad-whoops that chilled them to the marrow! "Toad he went a-pleasuring!" he yelled. "I'll pleasure 'em!" and he went straight for the Chief Weasel. They were but four in all, but to the panic-stricken weasels the hall seemed full of monstrous animals, grey, black, brown, and yellow, whooping and flourishing enormous cudgels; and they broke and fled with squeals of terror and dismay, this way and that, through the windows, up the chimney, anywhere to get out of reach of those terrible sticks.

The affair was soon over. Up and down, the whole length of the hall, strode the four Friends, whacking with their sticks at every head that showed itself; and in five minutes the room was cleared. Through the broken windows the shrieks of terrified weasels escaping across the lawn were borne faintly to their ears; on the floor lay prostrate some dozen or so of the enemy, on whom the Mole was busily engaged in fitting handcuffs. The Badger, resting from his labours, leant on his stick and wiped his honest brow.

"Mole," he said, "you're the best of fellows! Just cut along outside and look after those stoat-sentries of yours, and see what they're doing. I've an idea that, thanks to you, we shan't have much trouble from *them* tonight!"

The Mole vanished promptly through a window; and the Badger bade the other two set a table on its legs again, pick up knives and forks and plates and glasses from the *débris* on the floor, and see if they could find materials for a supper. "I want some grub, I do," he said, in that rather common way he had of speaking. "Stir your stumps, Toad, and look lively! We've got your house back for you, and you don't offer us so much as a sandwich."

Toad felt rather hurt that the Badger didn't say pleasant things to him, as he had to the Mole, and tell him what a fine fellow he was, and how splendidly he had fought; for he was rather particularly pleased with himself and the way he had gone for the Chief Weasel and sent him flying across the table with one blow of his stick. But he bustled about, and so did the Rat, and soon they found some guava jelly in a glass dish, and a cold chicken, a tongue that had hardly been touched, some trifle, and quite a lot of lobster salad; and in the pantry they came upon a basketful of French rolls and any quantity of cheese, butter, and celery. They were just about to sit down when the Mole clambered in through the window, chuckling, with an armful of rifles.

"It's all over," he reported. "From what I can make out, as soon as the stoats, who were very nervous and jumpy already, heard the shrieks and the yells and the uproar inside the hall, some of them threw down their rifles and fled. The others stood fast for a bit, but when the weasels came rushing out upon them they thought they were betrayed; and the stoats grappled with the weasels, and the weasels fought to get away, and they wrestled and wriggled and punched each other, and rolled over and over, till most of 'em rolled into the river! They've all disappeared by now, one way or another; and I've got their rifles. So *that's* all right!"

"Excellent and deserving animal!" said the Badger, his mouth full of chicken and trifle. "Now, there's just one more thing I want you to do, Mole, before you sit down to your supper along of us; and I wouldn't trouble you only I know I can trust you to see a thing done, and I wish I could say the same of everyone I know. I'd send Rat, if he wasn't a poet. I want you to take those

What a squealing and a squeaking and a screeching filled the air!

116

fellows on the floor there upstairs with you, and have some bedrooms cleaned out and tidied up and made really comfortable. See that they sweep *under* the beds, and put clean sheets and pillow-cases on, and turn down one corner of the bed-clothes, just as you know it ought to be done; and have a can of hot water, and clean towels, and fresh cakes of soap, put in each room. And then you can give them a licking apiece, if it's any satisfaction to you, and put them out by the back door, and we shan't see any more of *them*, I fancy. And then come along and have some of this cold tongue. It's first-rate. I'm very pleased with you, Mole!"

The good-natured Mole picked up a stick, formed his prisoners up in a line on the floor, gave them the order "Quick march!" and led his squad off to the upper floor. After a time, he appeared again, smiling, and said that every room was ready, and as clean as a new pin. "And I didn't have to lick them, either," he added. "I thought, on the whole, they had had licking enough for one night, and the weasels, when I put the point to them, quite agreed with me, and said they wouldn't think of troubling me. They were very penitent, and said they were extremely sorry for what they had done, but it was all the fault of the Chief Weasel and the stoats, and if ever they could do anything for us at any time to make up we had only got to mention it. So I gave them a roll apiece, and let them out at the back, and off they ran, as hard as they could!"

Then the Mole pulled his chair up to the table, and pitched into the cold tongue; and Toad, like the gentleman he was, put all his jealousy from him, and said heartily, "Thank you kindly, dear Mole, for all your pains and trouble tonight, and especially for your cleverness this morning!" The Badger was pleased at that, and said, "There spoke my brave Toad!" So they finished their supper in great joy and contentment, and presently retired to rest between clean sheets, safe in Toad's ancestral home, won back by matchless valour, consummate strategy, and a proper handling of sticks.

Forefathers

Here they went with smock and crook,
 Toiled in the sun, lolled in the shade,
Here they mudded out the brook,
 And here their hatchet cleared the glade.
Harvest-supper woke their wit,
Huntsman's moon their wooings lit.

From this church they led their brides,
 From this church themselves were led
Shoulder-high; on these waysides
 Sat to take their beer and bread.
Names are gone—what men they were
These their cottages declare.

Names are vanished, save the few
 In the old brown Bible scrawled;
These were men of pith and thew,
 Whom the city never called;
Scarce could read or hold a quill,
Built the barn, the forge, the mill.

On the green they watched their sons
 Playing till too dark to see,
As their fathers watched them once,
 As my father once watched me;
While the bat and beetle flew
On the warm air webbed with dew.

Unrecorded, unrenowned,
 Men from whom my ways begin,
Here I know you by your ground
 But I know you not within—
All is mist, and there survives
Not a moment of your lives.

Like the bee that now is blown
 Honey-heavy on my hand,
From the toppling tansy-throne
 In the green tempestuous land,—
I'm in clover now, nor know
Who made honey long ago.

EDMUND BLUNDEN

Written in a Country Churchyard

For them no more the blazing hearth shall
 burn,
 Or busy housewife ply her evening care:
No children run to lisp their sire's return,
 Or climb his knees the envied kiss to
 share . . .

Let not Ambition mock their useful toil,
 Their homely joys, and destiny obscure;
Nor Grandeur hear with a disdainful smile,
 The short and simple annals of the poor . . .

Full many a gem of purest ray serene,
 The dark unfathomed caves of ocean bear:
Full many a flower is born to blush unseen,
 And waste its sweetness on the desert air.

Some village Hampden, that with dauntless
 breast
 The little tyrant of his fields withstood;
Some mute inglorious Milton here may rest,
 Some Cromwell guiltless of his country's
 blood . . .

Far from the madding crowd's ignoble strife,
 Their sober wishes never learned to stray;
Along the cool sequestered vale of life
 They kept the noiseless tenor of their
 way . . .

THOMAS GRAY

Susan goes to School

Alison Uttley

Illustrated by Brenda Seymour

Well-known to younger children for her tales of Sam Pig, Tim Rabbit and Brock the Badger, Alison Uttley (1885–1976) is a delightful writer who wrote books for adults out of her childhood memories of life on the farm. These memoirs, such as "Ambush of Young Days" and "The Farm on the Hill", are most enjoyable and full of anecdotes from her own childhood. And what a wonderful memory Alison Uttley had, and what a gift that is to any writer! The extract is chosen from "The Country Child", and although it is about a girl called Susan the author would not mind our saying that the experiences of Susan and the memories of Alison have much in common.

WHEN Susan Garland was seven years old her mother sent her to the village school near Dangle, four miles away, for education was a serious problem in the out-of-the-way farms. It was a long way for the child to go alone, but Mrs. Garland prayed long and earnestly for protection, and then left Susan in God's charge.

Susan was delighted, for she knew no children; the farm was too remote from others, except beautiful Oak Meadow Farm where old Mr. and Mrs. Wolff lived with their middle-aged daughter, Mary. So Susan had never a friend except the farm men and Becky. Margaret was glad she would mix with others, for the child was fanciful, and too fond of talking to herself and imaginary people. Her mind was full of fairies, goblins, and grown-up religious talk which she had overheard in the kitchen at home.

She had been taught to read, she was familiar with the Bible, and had read *Pilgrim's Progress*, the unabridged *Robinson Crusoe* complete with the sermons, *Æsop's Fables*, and many religious stories and poems with morals attached. She was quick at figures, and she had already made a sampler with cross-stitch men and trees. Susan looked forward to being someone of importance, when her mother took her to see the headmistress, but her hopes were soon dashed to the ground. Mrs. Garland had found in an oak chest a dress which had belonged to a girl of a bygone age. It lay among blue silk-fringed crinolines and soft coloured Paisley shawls: a brown checked woollen frock with *ruches* of cut material trimming the tight bodice, and edging the high neck and the flounced skirt. It was buttoned from chin to foot with large cream bone buttons with steel centres. It was a godsend to Mrs. Garland, warm as a blanket, strong as a horse-cloth, and thick. With a little alteration it made a dress for Susan. She protested in vain, she wept, she hated its ugliness and the horrible buttons. So, a quaint old-fashioned little figure, her feet peeping out of the bottom frill which

pointed at her. "What's your name?" they shouted.

"Susanna Catherine Mary Garland," replied Susan, with her dark eyes wide and startled.

"What's your father?" they sang, sway-

went nearly to her ankles, her chin almost lost in the top, she went for her first day at school.

Her hair was strained back from her forehead and threaded through a round black comb which encircled her head like a coronet.

She kept near her mother whilst she explained her hopes and fears for Susan to the sharp-eyed, thin-faced headmistress, and watched with alarm the horde of children playing round the big door. Then Mrs. Garland smiled benignly at all the little ruffians, kissed Susan "God bless you, child," and left her.

The village children laughed and

ing and swinging in a row, and pushing against her.

"I don't know," said Susan, hesitating. It was the first time she had thought of this. In her little world there were no trades.

"Where do you come from?" they jeered, louder and louder, as they rocked with laughter at her simplicity.

Susan was on safe ground now. Had she not written it on the milk tickets each morning?

"From Windystone Hall, near Mellow," she replied with a shy pride, as she thought of her domain, the wide fields and woods, the rambling house and buildings, and compared it with the tiny rose-filled gardens and thatched cottages of the village.

"Windy stone, rain stone, who went down the lane alone?" mocked a wit, and the children shook back their hair and yelled with glee.

"Aye. What a figure of fun. Where did you get that frock?" they gibed.

She had loathed her dress, but now she held it tightly with one hand. It came from her own home, and was part of her. She had been called "a figure of fun." She stood with her back against the wall and a crowd of jeering girls jostled her. One pulled her hair with a mischievous tug, one opened her satchel and looked at her sandwiches, and one, the most shameless, put her tongue out at her. A little boy her own age ran up rudely and kissed her. He rushed away screaming with laughter, and Susan took out her handkerchief and rubbed her cheek as the cries and jibes rose higher. She stood like a frightened rabbit, her face white, her eyes big with horror. "Mother," she whispered to her heart, and the school bell rang.

The rabble dropped away and lined up in the playground. Susan went to the end of the row and followed them into a large room with pictures on the painted wall of Daniel in the lion's den, and a cocoa tree in flower. The lessons passed over her head. She could neither understand the strange accent and high voice of the town-bred teacher, nor grasp why she had to thread coloured strips through paper mats, with care and precision, and then pull them all out again. It was all working for nothing.

The sums were too easy, and the children round copied off her slate.

Books were given out for reading, and Susan's eye flitted rapidly down the pages. She was told not to turn over, so she sat dull and tired, waiting whilst the infants stumbled and fell over the little words. She was called on to read, and she read with expression, as her mother had taught her.

The children all turned round and stared, tittering and nudging one another. Susan's white cheeks became scarlet, her only wish was to be unnoticed. Covered with confusion she sat down, and her hair was sharply pulled from behind. She gave a short stifled cry, and Miss Hilda turned to her.

"What's the matter, Susan?" she asked kindly.

Susan whispered, "Some one pulled my hair."

Miss Hilda sent the naughty boy to a corner, but as he passed he hissed :

> "Tell Tale Tit,
> Your tongue shall be slit
> And every dog in England
> Shall have a little bit."

Susan sat half stifled. Dan had once told her that he slit a starnel's tongue to make it talk. The story had sickened her, and now her tongue was to be slit. She determined to fight to the death before they should get it from her.

Other children read in a monotonous sing-song, and so the weary time dragged on.

At playtime she went out with the others as a lamb to the slaughter. There were more questions and laughter, but Susan noticed some nice little girls whom she hadn't seen before standing in a group and smiling shyly at her. The horrible little boy came up. Susan stood, with lips firmly shut and her tongue safe inside her red mouth, ready for the struggle, but he only punched her arm and ran off crying, "Tell tale tit."

Then one of the girls asked Susan if she would like a drink, and took her to a tap in the wall with an iron mug hanging by a chain. The water was strange and flat, it was the first tap water Susan had ever tasted, but she was grateful.

"Take no notice of them," said her new friend. "They don't mean anything," and Susan was comforted. A weight was lifted off her heart, and as she walked into school again she felt she had been there for years. She could raise her head now and look at Elijah ascending into heaven in the chariot of fire, drawn by two prancing ponies, and the picture of a peacock hanging ready for a lesson, and the strange black stove which stood all alone in the middle of the floor with a pipe going out of its head. It was the strangest thing she had ever seen.

She was moved up, and took her place in the grammar class. Grammar was a nice-sounding word, she thought, like Mother, or Hammer, a comfortably homely word, but the lesson was incomprehensible. It was all about owls. Miss Dahlia, who came from London, and was treated with great respect as if she had come from heaven itself, Miss Dahlia began by informing the class that an owl was the name of anything.

"A table is an owl," said Miss Dahlia, and nobody disagreed. Indeed nobody ever disputed anything Miss Dahlia said. The children vied with one another in calling everything an owl—chairs, horses, desks, and elephants. They had heard it all before, and joined in when she told them of common and proper owls.

Now Susan, too, knew about owls. Her mind left the close stuffy room, with the smell of dust and children, and the high-pitched voice of Miss Dahlia. She saw the great tawny barn-owl which called over the house roof and hunted in the stackyard and among the barns and cowsheds. At evening, when the stars first appeared in the green sky, he sat in the fir tree at the corner of the garden. Susan had watched his dark shape against the starry sky. He sat on a branch just below Orion's belt, and cried to the great hunter in the sky. Then he spread his wings and flew noiselessly to the sycamore tree.

She lay in the attic with the moonlight pouring in at the uncurtained window, making a pattern of elm leaves on the beamed ceiling, whilst the owls hunted overhead crying like babies, and the mice cowered in their holes.

Once one flew through the window of the parlour bedroom which had been left open and forgotten. He broke a blue Wedgwood jug and swept a white patterned bowl off the mantelpiece. Her father caught him the next morning as he sat sulkily on the old lavender wash-hand jug, his eyes blinking and his funny eyebrows upraised. What a mercy he had not broken that, her mother said, holding up her hands in consternation at the mess.

They put him in the summer-house. That was an exciting day for Susan, she felt as if he were a captive Golden Eagle who could carry off a lamb, when she looked at him through the little panes of glass, and he stared back at her.

They took him bread and milk, and a dead mouse in the mouse trap. But at night she heard his call, Too-whoo-oo-oo, and his mate answered from the wood. The calls grew more frequent, nearer, and she sat up in bed, listening, excited. She won-

dered if the wife had her round eyes glued to the window. Then the cries became faint and ceased, but the next morning there was no owl, only broken panes of glass.

Still she heard him cry Too-whoo-oo when an arm shook her, and a voice cried in her ear, "Susan Garland. What did I say? Wake up, you naughty little girl."

Susan awoke in a fright. Strange faces were round her, people were laughing, she wasn't in her own bed.

"Stand on the form," said Miss Dahlia sternly, and Susan climbed up, disgraced utterly on her first day. She was tired, bewildered, and confused when the afternoon ended.

The mistress held up a pin. "I must hear this pin drop before any one goes home." Everybody held their breath, and the shuffles of little heavy boots ceased. The pin dramatically dropped with a tiny tinkle. School was surprisingly over and Susan was free.

Her gloves were taken from her and her hat thrown in the road. She picked it up and dusted it, overwhelmed by the manners of rude little boys. If they came to her house she would set the dog on them, she comforted herself. Her mother met her in the wood, but Susan was years older, secretive, puzzled by life, determined to escape from school at all costs.

The next day she played truant. She stayed in the wood, hiding, and crept home after a few hours with a tale of a holiday. She pretended to be ill, and was kept at home and dosed with camomile and wormwood tea. She doubled back when she got beyond the orchard and slipped upstairs to her bedroom, where the sympathetic Becky fed her like a fugitive

Royalist. She hid in a barn all day, braving the rats and darkness, sitting on a stone step with her skirts drawn tightly round her, a little ghost with no friend. They began to watch her enter the Dark Wood, but still she eluded them. Her desire was to find a hollow oak in which she could live during school hours, but although she searched and searched the big trees, like a woodpecker seeking a home, she never found a hole large enough to shelter her.

But gradually she became used to school life. She made friends among the little girls, and adored Miss Jessie, as the custom was. The brown dress got shorter as she shot up, and at last it wore out with the rough treatment it received, and she was promoted to last year's Sunday frock. . . .

Every day she became happier, every season brought its games: whips and tops, and marbles, blood-alleys and alley-taws, skipping-ropes, shuttlecocks and battle-dores, five stones, hopscotch, and hoops, but every night she had the same anxious walk among bogles and ghosties and giants and dwarfs.

So her school education went on, but her true learning was at home, in the fields and woods, or in the kitchen after tea, when her mother recited "The Wind and the Sun" and ballads of Robin Hood and Dick Turpin, and Susan read her four-fold library.

One evening she went out into the fields with her rope. The sun had dipped behind the far-away hill and it was too late to run up the fields to catch another glimpse of him. How often she had caught another minute of his red light and then another by racing up the steep hills after he had set, and finding him again. So she had climbed till she could go no higher, and watched his face slowly move below Boar Ridge. Then down she ran, long legs leaping, arms outstretched, and the cold air filled her blood and blew through her body to the wraith inside.

But now indigo shadows had crept up the valley from the river, up past the little hills, past the crag on which the farm stood, to the highest peaks, and the mysterious warm dusk filled the vast cup. From the fir trees came the cries of owls, and late rooks flapped across the pale green sky.

Susan skipped slowly across the broad field path, smooth and worn by the constant passing of men to the far barns. The rope dropped from her fingers and dragged through the grass. She stood very still, with her head thrown back, searching the pale sky for the first star.

She could feel the earth moving, a great majestic motion, the fields and farm, the woods and hills were sailing away through that limpid sky. She held her breath in wonder, she felt as if she floated up and up into that silvery dome above her. Then she saw her first star, a pin-point deep in that sea of space. She lost it and found it again. Then another came out, and another, from nowhere. She stared at the roof of the world, and behold, a star appeared. She began to count. They were all round her, the green sky had become radiantly, darkly blue, the trees were black, the earth flew like a great bird.

She counted till she was mazed, and a beam of light shone across the field from the house. It was the lamp in the kitchen. She turned and walked home.

In bed she lay counting, hundreds and hundreds, every night more hundreds till she slept. Each day she went on, more and more, but the numbers never ended. They were more than the stars. So she got her first glimpse of infinity.

Child of Nature

Three years she grew in sun and shower;
Then Nature said, "A lovelier flower
On earth was never sown:
This Child I to myself will take;
She shall be mine, and I will make
A lady of my own.

"She shall be sportive as the fawn
That wild with glee across the lawn
Or up the mountain springs;
And hers shall be the breathing balm,
And hers the silence and the calm
Of mute insensate things . . .

"The stars of midnight shall be dear
To her; and she shall lean her ear
In many a secret place
Where rivulets dance their wayward round,
And beauty born of murmuring sound
Shall pass into her face . . ."

WILLIAM WORDSWORTH

What the Old Man does is always Right

Hans Andersen

Illustrated by Arthur Rackham

Here is another Hans Andersen tale, one which you are unlikely to have met before. But it is worth remembering, for it probably holds the secret of a happy life!

I WILL tell you the story which I heard when I was a little boy. Every time I thought of the story it seemed to me to become more and more charming, for it is with stories as it is with many people— they become better and better the older they grow; and that is so delightful.

You have been in the country, of course. Well, then, you must have seen a very old farmhouse with a thatched roof, and mosses and weeds growing wild upon it. There is a stork's nest on the ridge of the roof, for we can't do without the stork. The walls of the house are aslant, and the windows low, and only one of the latter is made so that it will open. The baking-oven sticks out of the wall like a little fat body. The elder-tree hangs over the paling, and beneath its branches, at the foot of the paling, is a little pond with a duck and some ducklings under a knotted old willow-tree. There is a yard dog too, who barks at every passer-by.

Well, there was just such a farmhouse out in the country, and in it dwelt an old couple—a peasant and his wife. Small as was their property, there was one of their possessions that they could do without—a horse, which managed to live on the grass it found in the ditch by the side of the high-road. The old peasant rode it to town, and often his neighbours borrowed it, and

rendered the old couple some service in return for the loan. But still they thought it would be best if they sold the horse or exchanged it for something that might be more useful to them. But what was it to be?

"You'll know that best, old man," said the wife. "It is fair-day to-day; so ride to town and get rid of the horse for money, or make a good exchange—whatever you do will be right to me. Ride off to the fair."

And she tied his neckerchief for him, for she could do that better than he could; and she tied it in a double bow, and made him look quite smart. Then she brushed his hat round and round with the palm of her hand and gave him a kiss. So he rode away upon the horse that was to be sold or exchanged for something else. Yes, the old man knew what he was about.

The sun shone hot, and there was not a cloud in the sky. The road was very dusty, for many people who were all bound for the fair were driving, or riding, or walking upon it. There was no shade anywhere from the burning sun.

Among the rest a man was going along driving a cow to the fair. The cow was as pretty as a cow could be.

"She gives good milk, I'm sure," thought the peasant. "That would be a very good exchange—the cow for the horse."

Yes, the old man knew what he was about!

"Hallo, you there with the cow!" he said. "Let's have a word together. I fancy a horse costs more than a cow, but I don't mind that; a cow would be more useful to me. If you like we'll exchange."

"To be sure I will," said the man with the cow. And so they exchanged.

So that was settled, and the peasant might just as well have turned back, for he had done the business he came to do, but as he had once made up his mind to go to the fair he thought he'd go all the same, if only to have a look at it; and so he went on to the town with his cow.

Leading the cow, he strode on briskly, and after a short time he overtook a man who was driving a sheep. It was a fine fat sheep, well covered with wool.

"I should like to have that," said our peasant to himself. "It would find plenty of grass by our fence, and in winter we could have it in the room with us. Perhaps it would be more practical to have a sheep instead of a cow. Shall we change?"

The man with the sheep was quite ready, and the exchange was made. So our peasant went on along the highroad with his sheep.

Soon he saw another man, who came into the road from a field, carrying a big goose under his arm.

"That's a heavy bird you have there. It has plenty of feathers and plenty of fat, and would look well tied by a string in our pond at home. That would be something for my old woman to save up her scraps for. How often she has said, 'If only we had a goose!' Now, perhaps, she can have one; and, if possible it shall be hers. Shall we exchange? I'll give you my sheep for your goose, and say 'Thank you' into the bargain."

The other man had no objection, and so they exchanged, and our peasant got the goose.

By this time he was very near the town. The crowd on the highroad became greater and greater; there was quite a crush of men and cattle. They walked in the road and close by the palings, and at the toll-gate they even went into the toll-keeper's potato-field, where his only hen was strutting about with a string to her leg, lest she should take fright at the crowd and run away and get lost. She had short feathers on her tail, and winked with one eye, and looked very cunning. "Cluck, cluck!" said the hen. What she meant by it I cannot tell you; but directly our good man saw her he thought, "That's the finest hen I've ever seen in my life! Why, she's finer than our parson's brood hen. Upon my word, I should like to have that hen. A fowl can always find a grain or two; she can almost keep herself. I think it would be a good exchange if I could get that for my goose."

"Shall we exchange?" he asked the toll-keeper.

"Exchange!" said the man. "Well, that wouldn't be a bad thing." And so they exchanged, and the tollkeeper got the goose and the peasant got the hen.

Now he had done a good deal of business on his way to town, and he was hot and tired. He must have a drop of brandy and a bit to eat, and soon he was in front of the inn.

He was just about to go in when the ostler came out, and they met in the doorway. The ostler was carrying a sackful of something on his back.

"What have you there?" said the peasant.

"Rotten apples," answered the ostler. "A whole sackful of them—enough to feed the pigs with."

"Why, that's terrible waste! I wish my old woman at home could see that lot.

Last year the old tree by the turf-stack only bore a single apple, and we kept it in the cupboard till it was quite rotten and spoiled. 'It's something, anyhow,' my old woman said; but here she could see any quantity—a whole sackful. Yes, I should be glad to show her that."

"What will you give me for the sackful?" asked the ostler. "What'll I give? I'll give you my hen in exchange."

And so he gave him the hen and got the apples, which he carried into the bar parlour. He stood the sack carefully by the stove, and then went to the table. But the stove was hot; he had not thought of that. There were many strangers in the room—horse-dealers, drovers, and two Englishmen, and the two Englishmen were so rich that their pockets were bursting with gold, and they were making bets—just as they are always supposed to.

Hiss-s-s! hiss-s-s! What was that by the stove? The apples were beginning to roast.

"What's that?"

"Why, do you know——" said our peasant.

And he told the whole story of the horse that he had changed for a cow, and all the rest of it, right down to the apples.

"Well, your old woman will give it you well when you get home!" said the Englishman. "There'll be a pretty row!"

"What? She'll give me what?" said the peasant. "She will kiss me, and say, 'What the old man does is always right.'"

"Shall we have a bet?" said the Englishman. "We'll wager gold by the ton—a hundred pounds to the hundredweight!"

"A bushel will be enough," said the peasant. "I can only set the bushel of apples against it; and I'll throw in myself and my old woman into the bargain—and that's piling up the measure, I should say."

"Done!"

And so the bet was made. The inn-keeper's cart was brought out, and the Englishmen got in, and the peasant got in, and the rotten apples, and away they went, and soon they reached the peasant's little farm.

"Good evening, old woman!"

"Good evening, old man!"

"Well, I've made the exchange!"

"Yes, you know what you're about," said the woman, and she put her arms round him, paying no attention to the strangers, nor did she notice the sack.

"I got a cow in exchange for the horse," said he. "Heaven be thanked!" said she. "What lovely milk we shall have now, and butter and cheese on the table! That was a most capital exchange!"

"Yes, but I changed the cow for a sheep."

"Why, that's better still!" said the old woman. "You always think of everything. We have just grass enough for a sheep. Ewe's milk and cheese, and woollen stockings, and even woollen jackets too! The cow cannot give those, and her hairs will only come off. How you think of everything!"

"But I gave away the sheep for a goose."

"Then this year we shall really have roast goose to eat, my dear old man. You are always thinking of something to give me pleasure. How lovely that is! We can let the goose walk about with a string to her leg, and she'll grow fatter still before Michaelmas."

"But then I exchanged the goose for a hen," said the man.

"A hen? That *was* a good exchange!" replied the woman. "The hen will lay eggs and hatch them, and we shall have chickens; we shall have a whole poultry-yard! Oh, that's just what I was wishing for."

"Yes, but then I exchanged the hen for a sack of rotten apples."

"Well! Now I must really kiss you for that," exclaimed the wife. "My dear, good husband! Now I'll tell you something. Do you know, you had hardly left me this morning before I began thinking how I could give you something very nice this evening. I thought it should be pancakes with savoury herbs. I had eggs, and bacon too; but I wanted herbs. So I went over to the schoolmaster's—they have herbs there, I know—but his wife is a mean woman, though she looks so sweet. I begged her to lend me a handful of herbs. 'Lend!' she answered. 'Nothing at all grows in our garden, not even a rotten apple. I could not even lend you a rotten apple.' But now I can lend *her* ten—a whole sackful even. That I'm very glad of; that makes me laugh!" And with that she gave him a good smacking kiss.

"I like that!" said both the Englishmen together. "Always going downhill, and always happy; that's easily worth the money." So they paid a bushel of gold to the peasant, who had not been cuffed but kissed.

Yes, it always pays when the wife always sees and says that her husband is the wisest, and that whatever he does is right.

You see, that's my story. I heard it when I was a child, and now you've heard it too, and know that "What the old man does is always right."

Apple-Time

Your time is come, you apple-trees,
  Your labours weigh upon the bough,
Your heavy branches ask for ease
  And here we come to ease them now.
In April's hour of bridal bliss
You bloomed for this, you bloomed for this.

All day the lengthy ladders lean
  Their stairs against the twisty trunk;
We mount on them to chambers green,
  And before twilight falls are drunk
As bees upon the heady scent
In which the golden day was spent.

The baskets bear away the yield:
  Dull Russet, glossy Quarrenden,
Green Wellington, and scarlet-peeled
  Pearmain; the arms of girls and men
Ache with the streaked and yellow bales
Of Pippins and small Curlytails.

And some must to the cider-press
  Their juices in the crush to spill,
Some to the larder, some to dress
  The table, some must barrels fill,
And some must to the apple-loft
Whence greedy hands shall steal them oft.

The ruddy apple of the sun,
  The golden apple of the night,
Shall watch our toil till all is done,
  And we grow tired as you grow light.
You apple-trees, give up your sun,
Your time is come, your time is come.

ELEANOR FARJEON

Robin Hood and the Potter

Rosemary Sutcliff

Illustrated by Robert Geary and John Berry

The daughter of a naval officer, Rosemary Sutcliff became very ill as a small child and was unable to attend school until she was nine years old. Up to then she was taught by her mother who read her Dickens, Thackeray and Trollope, Greek and Roman legends, fairy tales and stories by Kipling, Whyte-Melville and Kenneth Grahame. A period at a little Dame school at Chatham was followed by years of painting at the Bideford Art School, after which she specialized in miniature painting and was made a member of the Royal Society of Miniature Painters. In 1950 her first book, "The Queen Elizabeth Story", was published and she started to write the historical novels for children that have made her name. The story we give here comes from "The Chronicles of Robin Hood".

ONCE again the forest was a place of rustling leaves, and dancing sun-splashes on turf and tree-bole. The haw-thorn trees were in bloom, and in the open parts of the forest the gorse flamed golden as though all the furze was afire.

Three months had passed since Marian came to the Greenwood. At first the out-laws had been shy of her, and shy of having a woman among them—"And her a fine lady, too!" as Hob-o'-the-Hoar-Oak said to Much-the-Miller's-Son. But Marian had shown herself a worthy comrade. When Roger Lightfoot had cut his hand half off she had neither shrieked nor swooned but held the edges of the gash together while Robin stitched it. She had not been afraid when there was an alarm of an attack, but had calmly strung her bow and taken her place beside Robin. She had not com-plained when the nights were cold. She took her turn at cooking and cleaning, and her place among the younger outlaws at the daily target-practice. Above all, she was friendly: laughing with them, sharing their joys and sorrows; and so, little by little, they grew to accept her as one of themselves, especially Friar Tuck's dogs, who loved her dearly.

On this particular morning she had gone up with Robin to visit the pickets watch-ing the Nottingham road for a rich merchant who they had heard was to pass that day. She stood looking away down the road: tall and slender as a birch tree in her long green gown, with her russet hair bound closely round her head. Her gown was of the same Lincoln cloth as the tunics of the wood-rangers, and the skirt was caught up through her belt so that it should not get in her way; under it she wore men's long hose and rawhide shoes. There were four clothyard shafts in her belt, and she carried a bow which Will Scarlet had built for her. It was a light bow with a pull of thirty pounds—very differ-ent from the great bows with their lateral pull of a hundred pounds which none but

130

Robin and Little John could bend—but already she could use it well.

It was very pleasant among the nut trees by the wayside, and very quiet, so that they heard the trit-trot of pony's hooves and the trundling of cart wheels while they were yet a long way off.

"Now, who comes here?" said Robin softly, as the outlaws rose and moved back into the deeper shadows of the trees.

Little John remained where he was, gazing northward through a little opening between the nut trees. Then, as the trit-trot and the trundling drew nearer he laughed, and stepped back.

"It is the proud Potter of Wentbridge. I know him of old—a stiff-necked creature, and he has never, to my knowledge, paid any toll for passing through the forest."

"Has he not?" replied Robin. "By the powers, he shall do so now!"

A moment later he parted the nut bushes and stepped out into the road. A fat little pony was coming along the Nottingham road at a fast trot, drawing behind him a neat, small cart. Seated in the cart, among a pile of gaily coloured earthenware pots, was a large, burly man with a brown smock, a red face, and a jaunty pheasant's feather in his slouch hat.

Robin stood waiting at the side of the road, and caught the pony's bridle as it drew level with him. The fat little creature came to a docile halt at once, and Robin laughed up into the indignant face of the potter above him.

"Come, Master Potter," said he. "Why such a surly visage? All I ask is that you pay me my just toll of silver; then you may go on your way unmolested."

The potter's usually pleasant face grew dark with rage. "Not a piece of my good silver do you see!" he cried; and then, leaning down to look more closely at the tall man in green, demanded with a sudden suspicion: "What might *your* name be?"

"Men call me—Robin Hood," answered Robin, warily watching the potter's face.

"*Do* they?" asked the man. "Do they indeed?" And he leapt down from his little cart and hurled himself upon the outlaw.

Robin was ready for him, and the two came together in the middle of the road. The potter was a powerful man and, though he was a little shorter than Robin, he had a grip like the hug of a brown bear, and a face which did not seem to feel the blows which the other planted on it.

For a while they reeled to and fro, sometimes locked together, sometimes smiting joyously at arm's length. At last Robin got in a strong left to the point of the jaw. The potter sagged for a moment, and then bore heavily forward. As Robin stepped back he caught his heel against a half-buried stone, and next instant lay flat on his back with his antagonist on top of him. He had hit his head in falling, and was half-stunned, so that for a moment the potter had him at his mercy. Then the outlaws, who had been watching delightedly all this while, broke from cover and flung themselves upon the potter.

Little John was the first to reach him, Peterkin was the second, and then came all the rest of the picket, including Marian. They hauled the potter off his victim, rapped his head sharply on the hard road to mend his manners for him, and sat him up against the wheel of his own cart.

Robin was by this time also sitting up, and the two surveyed each other dizzily, rubbing their heads. Then they smiled, and getting slowly to his knees, Robin held out his hand in token of friendship. Still sitting against the wheel of his cart, the potter returned his grip warmly, and nodded.

"Wolfshead you may be," he said; "but you're a good man to fight!"

"So are you," answered Robin, "though you *are* only a potter!"

"*Only* a potter?" cried the other. "*Only* a potter? Now by the saints in Heaven, I am minded to give you the trouncing you deserve, for you are an insolent puppy if ever there was one!"

Robin shook his head. "No, no, friend Potter, for my bones are still sore from the last one. But I see you have a bow in your cart—come and beat me at the butts instead."

Now it was the potter's turn to shake his head. "I am not such a fool as to pit myself for marksmanship against the best marksman in all the North Country. If you wish to show off your shooting, go to Nottingham, good lad. The sheriff is holding an archery contest this afternoon for his men-at-arms and any other folk who like to try their skill. Go and win the forty shillings he is offering as the prize."

"An archery contest, eh?" said Robin thoughtfully; and then he laughed. "Yes, I will go to Nottingham. I will go at once. Friend Potter, will you lend me your clothes and cart?"

"And what of my pots, may I ask?"

"I will sell your pots for you—as well as even *you* could do yourself, I'll warrant!"

Marian did not like him to run into needless danger, and looking at Little John's gloomy face, she knew that he liked it no better than she did; but they knew better than to try talking Robin out of anything on which he had once set his mind. So Robin changed clothes with the potter and climbed into the little cart. The little pony, which had stood placidly all this time, started at once when he shook the reins, and broke into a trot. So pony, cart, pots and make-believe potter disappeared round the corner of the road, and the trit-trot of hooves and the trundling of wheels grew quickly fainter in the distance.

The real potter, the outlaws, and Marian looked at one another. "The lad's mad!" exclaimed the potter.

Meanwhile, Robin was bowling gaily along the road in the sunshine, whistling to himself and the pony as blithely as a blackbird on a hawthorn branch.

It was yet early when he reached Nottingham, and, after leaving the pony and cart at an inn in Chandler's Lane, he made his way to the market, carrying his wares with him in two great baskets. There he took up his pitch, arranging the pots round him, and began to cry his wares.

Soon he had attracted a large crowd, and the housewives of the town began to press forward handling the pots and admiring their shapes and the gay colours of the glaze. Robin sold cheaply, charging only threepence for five pots, and did such a roaring trade that by noon he had only five pots left. These he gathered into one of the baskets, and set out along the narrow cobbled streets towards the house of Ralf Murdoch, the sheriff.

The sheriff's house was a fine building: heavily timbered, and gay with painted carvings above the door and windows. Robin mounted the milk-white steps to the door and beat upon the timbers with his clenched fist. When a servant came in answer to his summons, he gave her the pots, bidding her take them to her mistress as a gift from the Potter of Wentbridge.

The girl disappeared and Robin remained where he was, admiring the carved and painted garlands above the door, until a few moments later the sheriff's wife came herself to thank him very prettily for his gift. "Such fine pots I never did see," she said. "Next time you come to Nottingham, Master Potter, bring me some more, and I will buy as many as you will sell me—especially if they are popinjay blue, like the largest of those you have given me, for I do dearly love popinjay blue."

Robin bowed pompously and pretended to turn away; then he hesitated, sniffing loudly at the savoury smell of cooking which was beginning to steal out through the doorway. The sheriff's wife was an hospitable soul, and she said at once: "Will you not stay and dine with us, Master Potter? You will be very welcome, both for the sake of your pots and yourself."

Robin bowed again. "I shall be very glad to dine with you," said he, "and I thank you for your hospitality, madam."

And doffing his hat he followed her into the house.

The sheriff was in a bad temper, having just been worsted in a business deal; but surly as he was by nature, even he could not turn away a guest simply because of his own ill humour, for such churlish conduct would not look well in the Sheriff of Nottingham. So he grunted out a half-hearted welcome and, turning on his heel, left his wife and Robin to follow him into his hall, where the long trestle tables were already set for dinner.

Being only a potter, Robin did not sit among the sheriff's friends at the high table, but among the men-at-arms and poorer folk farther down the hall. Little he cared, for the men-at-arms were better company than the fat merchants; and so he made a very merry meal and ate heartily of the sheriff's roast beef and crusty bread, washing it down with draughts of ale out of a horn mug.

When the meal was over the diners got up, pulled each a forelock to the sheriff's lady, and drifted out in ones and twos and little groups towards the archery-butts outside the town walls. Presently, the sheriff joined them with his lady, and Robin found himself standing quite close to them, with the rough walls of Nottingham behind him and a long space of smooth turf in front, blocked at either end by the hundred-paces-distant straw targets. Many of the townsfolk had gathered there to watch, some had brought their bows, meaning to compete for the forty shillings.

The first man-at-arms stepped out to shoot, and Robin watched him closely as he nocked his arrow and loosed; but the arrow sped down the range and missed its target altogether. Another man came forward and again Robin watched; but as the afternoon wore on, and men-at-arms shot against townsmen, and townsmen against men-at-arms, he began to lose interest, for the marksmanship was poor, and not a single shaft struck within an arrow-length of the mark.

"It seems to me, Master Sheriff, that

these men of yours have little skill with the bow," said he at last.

"Perhaps *you* could do better?" grunted the sheriff, peevishly.

Robin nodded. "I could—easily."

Sheriff Murdoch stared at him scornfully for a moment, and then, turning to a yeoman standing near, bade him bring two or three bows for the potter to choose from. When the bows were brought Robin tested them, and at once laid two of them aside; the third he tested again, shaking his head gloomily.

"Indeed, you're but a poor weapon," sighed he. "But since there is no better to be had, I must do the best that I can with you."

A little, merry-faced man brought him a quiver, from which he chose the best arrow. Then he stepped out into the open, ignoring the good-natured jeers of the onlookers, and bending the borrowed bow, nocked his arrow to the string, and loosed well above the target to allow for the bow being a much less powerful one than he was wont to use. The shaft soared away like a giant bee in the sunshine, and everybody heard the clear "thwack" as it struck the straw target scarcely a hand-breadth from the central peg. A ragged cheer went up from the onlookers, and Robin strolled down to the target, and plucking out his arrow, turned about to shoot back. There was no jeering this time, and a

moment later a yell broke from yeomen and men-at-arms alike, as the arrow thudded into the second target. It had split the peg in three!

There was no more shooting after that, for no one could hope to equal the potter's marksmanship; and so he was adjudged the winner, and hustled along to where the sheriff's wife waited to give him the prize. Doffing his hat, with its jaunty pheasant's feather, he bowed low to her as she put the little jingling bag into his hand, and she smiled and said: "Never did I see a potter the like of you!"

"Humph!" said the sheriff gruffly, as though it hurt him to give praise. "How did you learn to shoot like that, my man?"

"Why, my father was a forester, and I have handled a bow since I was scarce as tall as a clothyard shaft is long," replied Robin. "And indeed I have shot with Robin Hood himself, before now, respectable potter though I am."

When the sheriff heard this his eyes glistened in his fat, ruddy face, for he had long wished to have the hanging of the famous outlaw; and he said: "Robin Hood, that rascally wolfshead? And do you know where Robin Hood is now?"

"Aye," answered Robin. "He is in Clumber Forest, not a dozen miles from here, and but ten of his band with him, for the rest have gone north to their summer quarters."

Sheriff Murdoch began to fairly tremble with eagerness, and putting a hand on Robin's shoulder, he said: "Good Master Potter, will you lead me to the lair of this wolfshead?"

Robin pretended to consider deeply. At last he said: "I do not like to betray a man whom I have shot with, and yet—I seem to have heard of a reward on his head?"

"One hundred golden nobles," said Murdoch; and added unwillingly: "If you help me to take him you shall have twenty for your trouble."

"Twenty-five," said Robin briefly, in the manner of a tradesman closing a bargain.

Murdoch swallowed, and grew purple in the face. "Twenty-five," he agreed at last; so the matter was settled.

Robin slept in the sheriff's house that night; and next morning took a courteous farewell of Mistress Murdoch, and, fetching the pony and cart from the inn where he had left them, drove blithely away. With him went the sheriff riding a bay horse, and twenty of the men-at-arms trudging in the dust behind.

Out through the north gate they went, and took the Doncaster road; but soon after the road ran into the forest Robin got down from his cart, and leaving it and the pony in charge of one of the men-at-arms, struck off down a bridle-path, followed by the rest. Soon he left the path also and took to the forest, leading the sheriff's horse by the bridle.

They went on and on, through tangled thickets, down long glades, across boggy clearings, by narrow deer-paths so faint that none but the trained eye of a forester could follow them, deeper and deeper into the heart of the forest. Sometimes a jay screamed harshly overhead; once a red shadow slunk away into the undergrowth at their approach, and a little farther on a late-hunting owl swept across their path, making the sheriff's horse snort and whinny with terror.

By now they had come to the oldest part of the forest. Here the trees were hoary with age and crowded in upon each other, grey with lichen and twisted into uncanny shapes, seeming, in the half-light, to stretch out clutching hands; and the little band of men-at-arms began to mutter together and glance uneasily over their shoulders into the crowding shadows behind them. None of them had ever been as deep as this into the forest, and they liked it not at all.

Sheriff Murdoch did not like it either, and at last he spoke uneasily: "This is a strange, uncanny place that you have brought us to, Master Potter!"

"Would you expect a wolfshead to have his lair on the high-road for any chance comer to find?" asked Robin grumpily; and they went on again in silence.

The forest began to open out again, becoming greener and more friendly, so that the sheriff and his men breathed more freely and glanced less often behind them.

At last they came to the head of a long glade, and here Robin halted them. He seemed to be listening for something, and when the harsh honking of a carrion-crow sounded three times from a nearby thicket, the men-at-arms could not have known that it was made by Little John and that it meant: "Who goes there?" Nor could they know, when the potter gave an odd, shrill whistle in reply, that it meant: "It is I, Robin." But they did think he was behaving very oddly, and suspicion began to dawn on them that they had walked into a trap.

Robin turned to face them, laughing, and taking his horn from under his cloak wound a gay call, "Tan-tan tar-tran-tan," and under the horrified eyes of the sheriff and his followers, seemed to melt into the forest. In terror they turned to fly, but it was too late; before they had stumbled twenty paces, before the sheriff had even managed to turn his terrified horse, they were surrounded by tall, green-clad men who suddenly appeared between the trees, and closed in on them.

Robin's voice sang out cheerfully from

some distance ahead of them. "Take their weapons away, lads, but don't hurt them overmuch."

The twenty men-at-arms stood no chance against four-score forest-rangers. In a few moments they had been disarmed and taken prisoner. Then Robin turned to the sheriff, who had been pulled from his horse and now stood fuming between Will Scarlet and grim old Watkin, with his arms twisted behind his back.

"You'll not see your hundred gold nobles *this* time, Master Sheriff!" said Robin. "And indeed you may think yourself lucky if you go home with your head still fixed to your fat shoulders!"

The sheriff was purple with rage, but to do him justice, he was no coward.

"You—you tricked me!" he spluttered.

"Yes," Robin nodded, "I tricked you very prettily. Now I shall have you stripped of those fine clothes of yours, and any money you have in your wallet, and perhaps the memory of your loss may make you more cautious another time!"

The sheriff looked at his men-at-arms, as though hoping they would rescue him; but they were as helpless as he, each man in the grip of two burly forest-rangers. And seeing no help for it, Sheriff Murdoch stood still while Little John took from him his wallet and the gold chain from his neck and the gold ring from his finger, then stripped him of his rich furred gown and velvet cap. When it was done he stood miserably in nothing but his shirt and hose.

Robin cast one scornful, laughing glance at him, and turned to Little John, saying: "Take away the horse, John; it is too fine a steed for such a sorry rider; and bring in its place the white palfrey we took last week."

When Little John came back with the palfrey, Robin himself aided the raging and shirt-clad sheriff to mount. "Ah! rage away, Master Sheriff," said he. "Maybe it will keep you warm on your homeward ride! Give the palfrey to your lady wife, with all thanks for her hospitality, from Robin Hood." Then, turning to his tall lieutenant: "Take them up to the Nottingham road by the shortest way, John, and two score of the lads with you, to make sure they do not miss their way and wander back."

"You shall pay for this!" shouted the sheriff. "I will have you hanged, drawn, and quartered! I will appeal to the king! I will——"

Little John caught his bridle and turned the palfrey's head towards the forest glooms; and so, still spluttering, swearing, and vowing vengeance, the sheriff was hustled off on his homeward way.

When he and his men-at-arms, together with the outlaw escort, had all disappeared among the trees, Robin sent Much, Peterkin, and George-a-Green to reclaim the pony and cart; then, followed by the rest, he walked down the long glade, parted a mass of hazel and dogwood at the farther end, and came out into the open ride below Dunwold Scar.

Marian was standing beside the cooking fire, with the large iron stew-spoon still in her hand. "Robin!" she called. "What has happened? We heard your horn, and the lads ran; but I could not leave the stew. Why did you sound your horn? And what was the meaning of the shouting and laughter I heard afterwards?"

Meanwhile, the potter, who had been sitting on a log beside the fire, had got up and was demanding: "What of my pony? What of my cart? What of my pots?"

Robin did his best to answer both of them at once, and at last, opening the sheriff's wallet, counted out five gold nobles. "Will this cover the cost of your pots?" he asked, smiling.

The potter took the money without a word, looking very hard at Robin the while. "Folks call you a robber," said he at last; "but *I* think you are an honest man and a generous one, and so, after I have changed clothes with you, and before I take to the road, I should like to shake your hand again."

"And so you shall," said Robin.

The Deliverers of their Country

E. Nesbit

Illustrated by Ronald Searle

Edith Nesbit (1858–1924) was born in Kennington, London, the youngest of a family of six. In 1880 she married Hubert Bland and unfortunately the marriage got off to a bad start with her husband losing all his money in an ill-fated business venture and then becoming seriously ill. Edith Nesbit turned to writing in order to make some money, and for fifteen years she produced short stories, romantic novels, verses and a few children's stories. In 1896 she was asked to contribute to "Girl's Own Paper" and she enjoyed her work so much it gave her the idea for a children's book, and at Christmas 1899 "The Treasure Seekers" was published. Edith Nesbit had found her true metier as a superlative writer of children's books. In the naturalness of her boys and girls and especially of the Bastable family who people "The Treasure Seekers" and "The Would-Be-Goods", she was the Arthur Ransome of her day. We have chosen one of her more startling stories. It comes, as you can see, from "The Book of Dragons".

IT ALL began with Effie's getting something in her eye. It hurt very much indeed, and it felt something like a red-hot spark—only it seemed to have legs as well, and wings like a fly. Effie rubbed and cried—not real crying, but the kind your eye does all by itself without your being miserable inside your mind—and then she went to her father to have the thing in her eye taken out. Effie's father was a doctor, so of course he knew how to take things out of eyes—he did it very cleverly with a soft paintbrush dipped in castor oil. When he had got the thing out he said : "This is very curious."

Effie had often got things in her eye before, and her father had always seemed to think it was natural—rather tiresome and naughty perhaps, but still natural. He had never before thought it curious. She stood holding her handkerchief to her eye, and said : "I don't believe it's out."

People always say this when they have had something in their eyes.

137

"Oh, yes—it's *out,*" said the doctor. "Here it is on the brush. This is very interesting."

Effie had never heard her father say that about anything that she had any share in. She said: *"What?"*

The doctor carried the brush very carefully across the room and held the point of it under his microscope, and looked through the top with one eye.

"Dear me," he said. "Dear, *dear* me! Four well-developed limbs; a long caudal appendage; five toes, unequal in length, almost like one of the Lacertidae, yet there are traces of wings." The creature under his eye wriggled a little in the castor oil, and he went on: "Yes; a bat-like wing. A new specimen, undoubtedly. Effie, run round to the professor and ask him to be kind enough to step in for a few minutes.

"You might give me sixpence, Daddy," said Effie, "because I did bring you the new specimen. I took great care of it inside my eye; and my eye *does* hurt."

The doctor was so pleased with the new specimen that he gave Effie a shilling, and presently the professor stepped round. He stayed to lunch, and he and the doctor quarrelled very happily all the afternoon about the name and the family of the thing that had come out of Effie's eye.

But at teatime another thing happened. Effie's brother Harry fished something out of his tea, which he thought at first was an earwig. He was just getting ready to drop it on the floor and end its life in the usual

way, when it shook itself in the spoon—spread two wet wings, and flopped on to the table-cloth. There it sat stroking itself with its feet and stretching its wings, and Harry said: "Why, it's a tiny newt!"

The professor leaned forward before the doctor could say a word.

"I'll give you half a crown for it, Harry, my lad," he said, speaking very fast; and then he picked it up very carefully on his handkerchief.

"It's a new specimen," he said. "And finer than yours, Doctor." It was a tiny lizard, about half an inch long—with scales and wings.

So now the doctor and the professor each had a specimen, and they were both very pleased. But before long these specimens began to seem less valuable. For the next morning, when the knife-boy was cleaning the doctor's boots, he suddenly dropped the brushes and the boots and the blacking and screamed out that he was burnt.

And from inside the boot came crawling a lizard as big as a kitten, with large, shiny wings.

"Why," Effie said, "I know what it is. It is a dragon like St. George killed."

And Effie was right. That afternoon Towser was bitten in the garden by a dragon about the size of a rabbit, which he had tried to chase, and next morning all the papers were full of the wonderful "winged lizards" that were appearing all over the country. The papers would not call them dragons, because, of course, no one believes in dragons nowadays—and, at

any rate, the papers were not going to be so silly as to believe in fairy stories. At first there were only a few, but in a week or two the country was simply running alive with dragons of all sizes, and in the air you could sometimes see them as thick as a swarm of bees. They all looked alike except as to size. They were green, with scales, and they had four legs and a long tail and great wings like bats' wings, only the wings were a pale, half-transparent yellow, like the gear cases on bicycles.

And they breathed fire and smoke, as all proper dragons must, but still the newspapers went on pretending they were lizards, until the editor of the *Standard* was picked up and carried away by a very large one, and then the other newspaper people had not anyone left to tell them what they ought not to believe. So that when the largest elephant in the Zoo was carried off by a dragon, the papers gave up pretending—and put "ALARMING PLAGUE OF DRAGONS" at the top of the paper.

And you have no idea how alarming it was, and at the same time how aggravating. The large-size dragons were terrible certainly, but when once you had found out that the dragons always went to bed early because they were afraid of the chill night air, you had only to stay indoors all day and you were pretty safe from the big ones. But the smaller ones were a perfect nuisance. The ones as big as earwigs got in the soup and they got in the butter. The ones as big as dogs got in the bath, and the fire and smoke inside them made them steam like anything when the cold-water tap was turned on, so that careless people were often scalded quite severely. The ones that were as large as pigeons would get into work-baskets or corner drawers, and bite you when you were in a hurry to get a needle or a handkerchief. The ones as big as sheep were easier to avoid, because you could see them coming; but when they flew in at the windows and curled up under your eiderdown, and you did not find them until you went to bed, it was always a

shock. The ones this size did not eat people, only lettuces, but they always scorched the sheets and pillow-cases dreadfully.

Of course, the County Council and the police did everything that could be done; it was no use offering the hand of the Princess to anyone who killed a dragon. This way was all very well in olden times—when there was only one dragon and one princess; but now there were far more dragons than princesses—although the Royal Family was a large one. And besides, it would have been mere waste of princesses to offer rewards for killing dragons, because everybody killed as many dragons as they could, quite out of their own heads and without rewards at all, just to get the nasty things out of the way. The County Council undertook to cremate all dragons delivered at their offices between the hours of ten and two, and whole wagon-loads and cart-loads and truck-loads of dead dragons could be seen any day of the week standing in a long line in the street where the County Council lived. Boys brought barrow-loads of dead dragons, and children home from morning school would call in to leave the handful or two of little dragons they had brought in their satchels, or carried in their knotted pocket-handkerchiefs. And yet there seemed to be as many dragons as ever. Then the police stuck up great wood and canvas towers covered with patent glue. When the dragons flew against these towers they stuck fast, as flies and wasps do on the sticky papers in the

kitchen; and when the towers were covered all over with dragons the police inspector used to set light to the towers, and burnt them and dragons and all.

And yet there seemed to be more dragons than ever. The shops were full of patent dragon poison and anti-dragon soap, and dragon-proof curtains for the windows; and, indeed, everything that could be done was done.

And yet there seemed to be more dragons than ever.

It was not very easy to know with what you would poison a dragon, because you see they ate such different things. The largest ate elephants as long as there were any, and then went on with horses and cows. Another size ate only lilies-of-the-valley, and a third size ate only Prime Ministers if they were to be had and, if not, would feed freely on boys in buttons. Another size lived on bricks, and three of them ate two-thirds of the South Lambeth Infirmary in one afternoon.

But the size Effie was most afraid of was about as big as your dining-room, and that size ate *little girls and boys.*

At first Effie and her brother were quite pleased with the change in their lives. It was so amusing to sit up all night instead of going to sleep, and to play in the garden lighted by electric lamps. And it was funny to hear Mother say, when they were going to bed:

"Good night, my darlings, sleep sound all day and don't get up too soon. You must not get up before it's *quite* dark. You

wouldn't like the nasty dragons to catch you."

But after a time they got very tired of it all; they wanted to see the flowers and trees growing in the fields, and to see the pretty sunshine out-of-doors, and not just through glass windows and patent dragon-proof curtains. And they wanted to play on the grass, which they were not allowed to do in the electric-lamp-lighted garden because of the night dew.

And they wanted so much to get out, just for once, in the beautiful, bright, dangerous daylight, that they began to try to think of some reason why they *ought* to go out. Only they did not like to disobey their mother.

But one morning their mother was busy preparing some new dragon poison to lay down in the cellar, and their father was bandaging the hand of the boot-boy, which had been scratched by one of the dragons who liked to eat Prime Ministers when they were to be had, so nobody remembered to say to the children: "Don't get up till it is quite dark!"

"So now," said Harry; "it would not be disobedient to go. And I know what exactly we ought to do, but I don't know how we ought to do it."

"What ought we to do?" said Effie.

"We ought to wake St. George, of course," said Harry. "He was the only person in this town who knew how to manage dragons; the people in the fairy tales don't count. But St. George is a real person, and he is only asleep, and he is waiting to be waked up. Only nobody believes in St. George now. I heard Father say so."

"*We* do," said Effie.

"Of course we do. And don't you see, Ef, that's the very reason why we could wake him? You can't wake people if you don't believe in them, can you?"

Effie said no, but where could they find St. George?

"We must go and look," said Harry boldly. "You shall wear a dragon-proof frock, made of stuff like the curtains. And I shall smear myself all over with the best dragon poison, and . . ."

Effie clasped her hands and skipped with joy, and cried: "Oh, Harry! I know where we can find St. George! In St. George's Church, of course."

"Um," said Harry, wishing he had thought of it for himself. "You have a little sense sometimes, for a girl."

So the next afternoon quite early, long before the beams of sunset announced the coming night, the two children got out of bed. Effie wrapped herself in a shawl of dragon-proof muslin—there was no time to make the frock—and Harry made a horrid mess of himself with the patent dragon poison. It was warranted harmless to infants and invalids, so he felt quite safe.

Then they took hands and set out to walk to St. George's Church. As you know, there are many St. George's churches, but fortunately they took the turning that leads to the right one, and went along in the bright sunshine, feeling very brave and adventurous.

There was no one about in the streets except dragons, and the place was simply swarming with them. Fortunately, none of the dragons was just the right size for eating little boys and girls, or perhaps this story might have had to end here. There were dragons on the pavements, and dragons on the roadway, dragons backing on the front-door steps of public buildings, and dragons preening their wings on the roofs in the hot afternoon sun. The town was quite green with them. Even when the children had got out of the towns and were walking in the lanes, they noticed that the fields on each side were greener than usual with the scaly legs and tails; and some of the smaller sizes had made themselves asbestos nests in the flowering hawthorn hedges.

Effie held her brother's hand very tight, and once, when a fat dragon flopped against her ear, she screamed out, and a whole flight of green dragons rose from the field at the sound and sprawled away across the sky. The children could hear the rattle of their wings as they flew.

"Oh, I want to go home," said Effie.

"Don't be silly," said Harry. "People who are going to be their country's deliverers never scream and say they want to go home."

"And are we?" asked Effie. "Deliverers, I mean."

"You'll see," said her brother, and on they went.

When they came to St. George's Church they found the door open, and they walked right in—but St. George was not there, so they walked round the churchyard outside, and presently they found the great stone tomb of St. George, with the figure of him carved in marble outside, in his armour and helmet, and with his hands folded on his breast.

"However can we wake him?" they said.

Then Harry spoke to St. George—but he

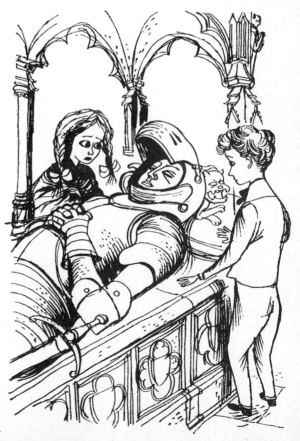

141

would not answer; and he called, but St. George did not seem to hear; and then he actually tried to waken the great dragon-slayer by shaking his marble shoulders. But St. George took no notice.

Then Effie began to cry, and she put her arms round St. George's neck as well as she could for the marble, which was very much in the way at the back, and she kissed the marble face, and she said: "Oh dear, good, kind St. George, please wake up and help us."

And at that St. George opened his eyes sleepily, and stretched himself and said: "What's the matter, little girl?"

So the children told him all about it. He turned over in his marble and leaned on one elbow to listen. But when he heard that there were so many dragons he shook his head.

"It's no good," he said. "They would be one too many for poor old George. You should have waked me before. I was always for a fair fight—one man one dragon, was my motto."

Just then a flight of dragons passed overhead, and St. George half-drew his sword. But he shook his head again, and pushed the sword back as the flight of dragons grew small in the distance.

"I can't do anything," he said. "Things have changed since my time. St. Andrew told me about it. They woke him up over the engineers' strike, and he came to talk to me. He says everything is done by machinery now. There must be some way of settling these dragons. By the way, what sort of weather have you been having lately?"

This seemed so careless and unkind that Harry would not answer, but Effie said, patiently: "It has been very fine. Father says it is the hottest weather there has ever been in this country."

"Ah, I guessed as much," said the Champion, thoughtfully. "Well, the only thing would be . . . dragons can't stand wet and cold, that's the only thing. If you could find the taps."

St. George was beginning to settle down again on his marble slab.

"Good night. Very sorry I can't help you," he said, yawning behind his marble hand.

"Oh, but you can," cried Effie. "Tell us—what taps?"

"Oh, like in the bathroom," said St. George, still more sleepily, "and there's a looking-glass, too; shows you all the world and what's going on. St. Denis told me about it; said it was a very pretty thing. I'm sorry I can't—good night."

And he fell back into his marble and was fast asleep again in a moment.

"We shall never find the taps," said Harry. "I say, wouldn't it be awful if St. George woke up when there was a dragon near, the size that eats Champions?"

Effie pulled off her dragon-proof veil. "We didn't meet any the size of the dining-room as we came along," she said; "I daresay we shall be quite safe."

So she covered St. George with the veil, and Harry rubbed off as much as he could of the dragon poison on to St. George's armour, so as to make everything quite safe for him.

"We might hide in the church till it is dark," he said, "and then. . . ."

But at that moment a dark shadow fell on them, and they saw that it was a dragon exactly the size of the dining-room at home.

So then they knew that all was lost. The dragon swooped down and caught the two children in his claws. He caught Effie by her green silk sash, and Harry by the little point at the back of his Eton jacket—and then, spreading his great yellow wings, he rose into the air, rattling like a third-class carriage when the brake is hard on.

"Oh, Harry," said Effie, "I wonder when he will eat us!"

The dragon was flying across woods and fields with great flaps of his wings that carried him a quarter of a mile at each flap.

Harry and Effie could see the country below, hedges and rivers and churches and

"Oh, Harry," said Effie, "I wonder when he will eat us!"

farmhouses flowing away from under them, much faster than you see them running away from the sides of the fastest express train.

And still the dragon flew on. The children saw other dragons in the air as they went, but the dragon who was as big as the dining-room never stopped to speak to any of them, but just flew on quite steadily. "He knows where he wants to go," said Harry. "Oh, if he would only drop us before he gets there!"

But the dragon held on tight, and he flew and flew and flew until at last, when the children were quite giddy, he settled down, with a rattling of all his scales, on the top of a mountain. And he lay there on his great, green scaly side, panting and very much out of breath, because he had come such a long way. But his claws were fast in Effie's sash and the little point at the back of Harry's Eton jacket.

Then Effie took out the knife Harry had given her on her birthday. It only cost sixpence to begin with, and she had had it a month, and it never could sharpen anything but slate-pencils; but somehow she managed to make that knife cut her sash in front, and crept out of it, leaving the dragon with only a green silk bow in one of his claws. That knife would never have cut Harry's jacket-tail off though, and when Effie had tried for some time she saw that this was so and gave it up. But with her help Harry managed to wriggle quietly out of his sleeves, so that the dragon had only an Eton jacket in his other claw. Then the children crept on tiptoe to a crack in the rocks and got in. It was much too narrow for the dragon to get in also, so they stayed in there and waited to make faces at the dragon when he felt rested enough to sit and begin to think about eating them. He was very angry indeed

143

when they made faces at him, and he blew out fire and smoke at them, but they ran farther into the cave so that he could not reach them, and when he was tired of blowing he went away.

But they were afraid to come out of the cave, so they went farther in, and presently the cave opened out and grew bigger, and the floor was soft sand, and when they had come to the very end of the cave there was a door, and on it was written: *"Universal Taproom. Private. No one allowed inside."*

So they opened the door at once just to peep in, and then they remembered what St. George had said.

"We can't be worse off than we are," said Harry, "with a dragon waiting for us outside. Let's go in."

So they went boldly into the taproom, and shut the door behind them.

And now they were in a sort of room cut out of the solid rock, and all along one side of the room were taps, and all the taps were labelled with china labels like those you see on baths. And as they could read words of two syllables, or even three sometimes, they understood at once that they had got to the place where the weather is turned on from. There were six big taps labelled "Sunshine," "Wind," "Rain," "Snow," "Hail," "Ice," and a lot of little ones labelled "Fair to Moderate," "Showery," "South Breeze," "Nice Growing Weather for the Crops," "Skating," "Good Open Weather," "South Wind," "East Wind," and so on. And the big tap labelled "Sunshine" was turned full on. They could not see any sunshine—the cave was lighted by a skylight of blue glass—so they supposed the sunlight was pouring out by some other way, as it does with the tap that washes out the underneath parts of patent sinks in kitchens.

Then they saw that one side of the room was just a big looking-glass, and when you looked in it you could see everything that was going on in the world—and all at once, too, which is not like most looking-glasses. They saw the carts delivering the dead dragons at the County Council offices, and they saw St. George asleep under the dragon-proof veil. And they saw their mother crying at home because her children had gone out in the dreadful, dangerous daylight, and she was afraid a dragon had eaten them. And they saw the whole of England, like a great puzzle-map —green in the field parts and brown in the towns, and black in the places where they make coal, and crockery, and cutlery, and chemicals. And all over it, on the black parts, and on the brown, and on the green, there was a network of green dragons. And they could see that it was still broad daylight, and no dragons had gone to bed yet.

So Effie said: "Dragons do not like cold." And she tried to turn off the sunshine, but the tap was out of order, and that was why there had been so much hot weather, and why the dragons had been able to be hatched. So they left the sunshine-tap alone, and they turned on the snow and left the tap full on while they went to look in the glass. There they saw the dragons running all sorts of ways like ants if you are cruel enough to pour water into an ant-heap, which, of course, you never are. And the snow fell more and more.

Then Effie turned the rain-tap full on, and presently the dragons began to wriggle less, and by and by some of them lay quite still, so the children knew the water had put out the fires inside them and they were dead.

So then they turned on the hail—only half on, for fear of breaking people's windows—and after a while there were no more dragons to be seen moving.

Then the children knew that they were the deliverers of their country.

"They will put up a monument to us," said Harry, "as high as Nelson's! All the dragons are dead."

"I hope the one that was waiting outside for us is dead!" said Effie. "And about the monument, Harry, I'm not so sure. What can they do with such a lot of dead

He fluttered with his arms, but no feathers remained to hold the air.
From "The Story of Daedalus and Icarus"

In another thirty seconds we are swinging along at a good pace down the slope of the warren,
in the direction of Colvin meadows, and the hunt has begun.
From "The Parkhurst Paper Chase"

dragons? It would take years and years to bury them, and they could never be burnt now they are so soaking wet. I wish the rain would wash them off into the sea."

But this did not happen, and the children began to feel that they had not been so frightfully clever after all.

"I wonder what this old thing's for," said Harry. He had found a rusty old tap, which then ran to the mirror to see what happened.

Already a great, round, black hole had opened in the very middle of the map of England, and the sides of the map were tilting themselves up, so that the rain ran down towards the hole.

"Oh, hurrah, hurrah, hurrah!" cried Effie, and she hurried back to the taps and

Thanks to Harry and Effie there was not a single dragon left alive.

seemed as though it had not been used for ages. Its china label was quite coated over with dirt and cobwebs. When Effie had cleaned it with a bit of her skirt—for, curiously enough, both children had come out without pocket-handkerchiefs—she found that the label said *Waste.*

"Let's turn it on," she said; "it might carry off all the dragons."

The tap was very stiff from not having been used for such a long time, but together they managed to turn it on, and turned on everything that seemed wet. "Showery," "Good Open Weather," "Nice Growing Weather for the Crops," and even "South" and "South-West" because she had heard her father say that those winds brought rain.

And now the floods of rain were pouring down on the country, and great sheets of water flowed towards the centre of the map, and cataracts of water poured into the great round hole in the middle of the map, and the dragons were being washed away and disappearing down the waste-pipe in great green masses and scattered green shoals—single dragons and dragons by the dozen; of all sizes from the ones that carry off elephants down to the ones that get in your tea.

And presently there was not a dragon left. So then they turned off the tap named "Waste," and they half-turned off the one labelled "Sunshine"—it was broken, so that they could not turn it off altogether—and they turned on "Fair to Moderate" and "Showery," and both taps stuck, so that they could not be turned off, which accounts for the changes in our climate.

How did they get home again? By the Snowdon railway—of course.

And was the nation grateful? Well—the nation was very wet. And by the time the nation had got dry again it was interested in the new invention for toasting muffins by electricity, and all the dragons were almost forgotten. Dragons do not seem so important when they are dead and gone,

and, you know, there never was a reward offered.

And what did Father and Mother say when they got home?

My dear, that is the sort of silly question you children always will ask. However, just for this once I don't mind telling you.

Mother said: "Oh, my darlings, my darlings, you're safe—you're safe! You naughty children—how could you be so disobedient? Go to bed at once!"

And their father, the doctor, said: "I wish I had known what you were going to do! I should have liked to preserve a specimen. I threw away the one I got out of Effie's eye. I intended to get a more perfect specimen. I did not anticipate this immediate extinction of the species."

The professor said nothing, but he rubbed his hands. He had kept his specimen—the one the size of an earwig that he gave Harry half a crown for—and he has it to this day.

You must get him to show it to you!

The Story of Daedalus and Icarus

Thomas Bulfinch

Illustrated by William Reeves and Victor G. Ambrus

Thomas Bulfinch (1796–1867) was born in Boston in the United States and spent his life there in the service of a bank. He was no great novelist or poet, but he undertook the valuable task of re-telling in simple English the stories and fables of bygone civilizations; the legends of the Middle Ages and of chivalry and particularly the myths of ancient Greece and Rome. Here is the legendary tale of the first men to fly, extracted from his best-known work, "The Age of Fable":

THE labyrinth from which Theseus escaped by means of the clue of Ariadne was built by Dædalus, a most skilful artificer. It was an edifice with numberless winding passages and turnings opening into one another, and seeming to have neither beginning nor end, like the river Mæander, which returns on itself, and flows now onward, now backward, in its course to the sea. Dædalus built the labyrinth for King Minos, but afterwards lost the favour of the king, and was shut up in a tower. He contrived to make his escape from his prison, but could not leave the island by sea, as the king kept strict watch on all the vessels, and permitted none to sail without being carefully searched. "Minos may control the land and sea," said Dædalus, "but not the regions of the air. I will try that way." So he set to work to fabricate wings for himself and his young son Icarus. He wrought feathers together, beginning with the smallest and adding larger, so as to form an increasing surface. The larger ones he secured with thread and the smaller with wax, and gave the whole a gentle curvature like the wings of a bird. Icarus, the boy, stood and looked on, sometimes running to gather up the feathers which the wind had blown away, and then handling the wax and working it over with his fingers, by his play impeding his father in his labours. When at last the work was done, the artist, waving his wings, found himself buoyed upward, and hung suspended, poising himself on the beaten air. He next equipped his son in the same manner and taught him how to fly, as a bird tempts her young ones from the lofty nest into the air. When all was prepared for flight he said, "Icarus, my son, I charge you to keep at a moderate height, for if you fly too low the damp will clog your wings, and if too high the heat will melt them. Keep near me and you will be safe." While he gave him these instructions and fitted the wings to his shoulders, the face of the father was wet with tears, and his hands trembled. He kissed the boy, not knowing that it was for the last time. Then rising on his wings, he flew off, encouraging him to follow, and looked back from his own flight to see how his son managed his wings. As they flew the ploughman stopped his work to gaze, and the shepherd leaned on his staff and watched them, astonished at the sight, and thinking they were gods who could thus cleave the air.

They passed Samos and Delos on the left and Lebynthos on the right, when the boy, exulting in his career, began to leave the guidance of his companion and soar upward as if to reach heaven. The nearness of the blazing sun softened the wax which held the feathers together, and they came off. He fluttered with his arms, but no feathers remained to hold the air. While his mouth uttered cries to his father it was submerged in the blue waters of the sea, which thenceforth was called by his name. His father cried, "Icarus, Icarus, where are you?" At last he saw the feathers floating on the water, and bitterly lamenting his own arts, he buried the body and called the land Icaria in memory of his child.

Dædalus arrived safe in Sicily, where he built a temple to Apollo, and hung up his wings, an offering to the god.

To The Cuckoo

O blithe new-comer! I have heard,
I hear thee and rejoice:
O Cuckoo! shall I call thee Bird,
Or but a wandering Voice?

While I am lying on the grass
Thy twofold shout I hear;
From hill to hill it seems to pass,
At once far off and near.

Though babbling only to the vale
Of sunshine and of flowers,
Thou bringest unto me a tale
Of visionary hours.

Thrice welcome, darling of the Spring!
Even yet thou art to me
No bird, but an invisible thing,
A voice, a mystery;

The same whom in my school-boy days
I listen'd to; that Cry
Which made me look a thousand ways
In bush, and tree, and sky.

To seek thee did I often rove
Through woods and on the green;
And thou wert still a hope, a love;
Still long'd for, never seen!

And I can listen to thee yet;
Can lie upon the plain
And listen, till I do beget
That golden time again.

O blessèd Bird! the earth we pace
Again appears to be
An unsubstantial, faery place,
That is fit home for thee!

WILLIAM WORDSWORTH

The Parkhurst Paper Chase

Talbot Baines Reed

Illustrated by Shirley Hughes

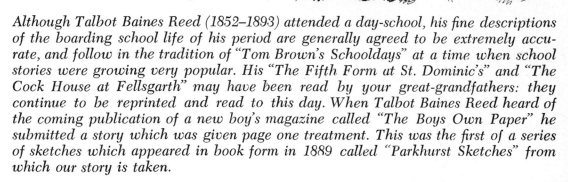

Although Talbot Baines Reed (1852–1893) attended a day-school, his fine descriptions of the boarding school life of his period are generally agreed to be extremely accurate, and follow in the tradition of "Tom Brown's Schooldays" at a time when school stories were growing very popular. His "The Fifth Form at St. Dominic's" and "The Cock House at Fellsgarth" may have been read by your great-grandfathers: they continue to be reprinted and read to this day. When Talbot Baines Reed heard of the coming publication of a new boy's magazine called "The Boys Own Paper" he submitted a story which was given page one treatment. This was the first of a series of sketches which appeared in book form in 1889 called "Parkhurst Sketches" from which our story is taken.

"THE meet is to be at one o'clock, sharp, in the Dean's Warren—don't forget!"

So said Forwood, the "whipper-in" of the Parkhurst Hare and Hounds Club, to me, one March morning in the year 18—.

I had no need to be reminded of the appointment; for this was the day of the "great hunt" of the year, always held by the running set at Parkhurst School to yield in interest to no other fixture of the athletic calendar.

In fine weather, and over good country, a paper-chase is one of the grandest sports ever indulged in—at least, so we thought when we were boys—and the "great hunt" was, of course, the grandest run of the year, and looked forward to, consequently, with the utmost eagerness by all lovers of running in our school.

This year, too, I had a special interest in the event, for it was my turn to run hare —in other words, to be, with another fellow, the object of the united pursuit of some twenty or thirty of my school-fellows, who would glory in running me down not a whit less than I should glory in escaping them.

For some weeks previously we had been taking short trial runs, to test our pace and powers of endurance; and Birch (my fellow hare) and I had more than once surveyed the course we proposed to take on the occasion of the great hunt, making ourselves, as far as possible, acquainted with the bearings of several streams, ploughed fields, and high walls to be avoided, and the whereabouts of certain gaps, woods, and hollows to be desired.

I can't say if the Parkhurst method of conducting our hunts was the orthodox one; I know *we* considered it was, as our rules were our own making, or rather a legacy left to us by a former generation of runners at the school.

We were to take, in all, a twelve miles' course, of nearly an oval shape, six miles out and six miles home. Any amount of dodging or doubling was to be allowed to us hares, except crossing our own path. We were to get five minutes' clear start, and, of course, were expected to drop our paper scent wherever we went.

Luckily for me, Birch was an old hand at running hare, and up to all sorts of dodges, so that I knew all it was needful for me to do was to husband my wind,

and run evenly with him, leaving him to shape our course and regulate our pace.

It was a lively scene at the Dean's Warren, when we reached it a few minutes before the appointed time that afternoon. The pack—that is, the twenty or thirty fellows who were to run as hounds—were fast assembling, and divesting themselves of everything but their light flannels. The whipper-in, conspicuous by the little bugle slung across his shoulders, and the light flag in his hand, was there in all the importance of his office; and, as usual, the doctor and a party of visitors, ladies and gentlemen, had turned out to witness the start.

"Five minutes, hares!" shouts Forwood, as Birch and I came on the spot.

We use the interval in stripping off all unnecessary apparel, and girding ourselves with our bags of scent, or scraps of torn-up paper, which we are to drop as we run. Then we sit and wait for the moment for starting. The turf is crisp under our feet; the sun is just warm enough to keep us from shivering as we sit, and the wind just strong enough to be fresh. Altogether it is to be doubted if a real meet of real hounds to hunt real hares—a cruel and not very manly sport, after all—could be much more exciting than this is.

"Half a minute!" sings out the whipper-in, as we spring to our feet.

In another thirty seconds we are swinging along at a good pace down the slope of the warren, in the direction of Colvin meadows, and the hunt has begun.

As long as we were in sight of the pack we kept up a good hard pace, but on reaching cover we settled down at once to a somewhat more sober jog-trot, in anticipation of the long chase before us.

We made good use of our five minutes' start, for by the time a distant bugle note announced that the hounds were let loose on our track we had covered a good piece of ground, and put several wide fields and ditches and ugly hedges between us and our pursuers.

Now it was that Birch's experiences served us in good stead. I never knew a fellow more thoroughly cunning; he might have been a fox instead of a hare. Sometimes he made me run behind him and drop my scent on the top of his, and sometimes keep a good distance off, and let the wind scatter it as much as it could. When we came to a gap, instead of starting straight across the next field he would turn suddenly at right angles, and keep close up under the hedge half-way round before striking off into the open. Among trees and bushes he zigzagged and doubled to an alarming extent, so that it seemed as if we were losing ground every moment. So we should have been if the chase had been by sight instead of by *scent*; but that would have been against all rules.

If the hounds were to see the hares twenty yards in front of them, and the scent lay half-a-mile round, they would be bound, according to our rules, to go the half-mile, however tempting the short cut.

It was after a very wide circuit, ending up on the top of a moderate rise, that we first caught sight of our pursuers. As they were a full six minutes behind us, we agreed to sit down under cover for a minute and watch them.

At that moment they had evidently lost the scent, and were ferreting about among some low trees and bushes in search of it. We saw the flag of the whipper-in marking the spot where it was last visible, and round this, on all sides, the hounds were exploring busily in search of the new departure.

Then presently, came a cry of "Forward!" and off they all started in our direction; and as the scent after that seemed to lie pretty clear we considered it high time for us to resume our flight.

So we made off again, and being refreshed by our brief halt, made over a couple of ploughed fields, which Birch suggested "would make a few of the hounds look foolish"; and so on till we reached the first water we had encountered since the start. This was a trout-stream, well known to some of us who were fond of fishing—nowhere more than half a foot deep, and in some places easily passable, dry shod, on stepping-stones. Birch, however, avoided these, and boldly splashing into the stream over his ankles, bade me follow.

"We'll soon dry up," he said, "and this will gain us a minute or two."

Instead of going straight across, the wily hare began to paddle up the middle of the stream for twenty or thirty yards, and, of course, in so doing our scent was soon drifted away down the current. So we flattered ourselves, when we at last did make the opposite bank, that our pursuers would be puzzled for a minute or two to know what had become of us.

After a further quarter of a mile we thought we might venture to take another brief halt on the strength of this last manoeuvre. We were unable to do so where we could command a view of the hounds, but as we reckoned we had at least gained three minutes, we felt we could quite afford to take it easy for that length of time.

Fancy, then, our horror when, after about a couple of minutes, we heard a cry

of "Forward!" close to us, and evidently on this side of the stream.

Off we dashed like mad, in a regular panic, and never checked our pace till we had put three ploughed fields and a couple of wide ditches to our credit. We did not discover till it was all over how it was our cunning scheme to perplex the hounds had thus miscarried. Then we were told that some of the scent, instead of dropping into the water, as we intended, had lodged on top of some stones in mid-stream, and this had at once betrayed our dodge to the practised eyes of the foremost hounds. It was a caution to be more careful another time. . . .

Half a mile farther brought us to Wincot village, down the main street of which we sped, greatly to the admiration of the inhabitants, who turned out in force to see the sport.

By this time we had fairly got our second winds, and began to realize the benefit of the steady training of the past fortnight. At an ordinary pace, with the second wind well laid on, we felt we ought to be able to hold out for the run home, unless some very unexpected accident should intervene.

Past the village, we rattled on till we

Next moment came the splash of a double header and the shouts of astonished onlookers.

came to the railway embankment, across which we trespassed, not without some difficulty, as it was steep and railed off on either side by high palisades. Once over this, we turned at right angles, and ran for half a mile close alongside the line, and past Wincot station. Here it was necessary to recross the line (down a cutting this time), and as we were doing so we caught sight, on our left, of the leading hounds scrambling to the top of the embankment, which we had passed only a minute or two before.

But Birch and I were determined it should not be our fault if the great hunt of this year ended in a victory for the hounds. So we spurted for nearly a mile, jumping most of the narrow ditches and low hedges that crossed our path, and making as straight a course as the hilly ground allowed of. But, despite all our efforts, the occasional glimpses which we caught of our pursuers showed us that we

were unable to shake off four or five of the leading hounds.

This would never do. . . . So the cunning Birch had once again to resort to his dodges to gain time.

Suddenly altering our track, and leaving the fields, he struck a dusty lane, which wound in and out out in the direction of Parkhurst. Now, this was a very dusty and a very chalky lane. . . . Our white scraps of paper, falling on the white road, and being fallen on by the white dust, had a good chance of escaping detection, unless looked after very carefully; and to make matters more secure, we dodged off into the fields, and back again into the lane, pretty often, leaving our pursuers a ditch to jump each time.

This manoeuvre answered fairly well, for the next time we saw the hounds they were searching about by the side of a ditch for our track, a good way to the rear.

We had now to face the hardest bit of

work of the afternoon. The last two miles home were over a perfectly flat bit of country—so flat that the hounds would have us in view nearly all the way, and, consequently, to dodge or double would be simply useless. Our only course was a straight hard run for it, trusting to our legs and our wind to pull us through. So we settled down to the task with a will. Scarcely had we emerged into the open ground for a couple of minutes, when we saw a figure dash out of the lane in full cry after us.

It was Forwood, the whipper-in, a terrible scud across country, and he was only fifty yards or so ahead of three others, also celebrated for their pace. So we hares had our work cut out for us, and no mistake!

For a mile we ran as hard as we well could, turning neither to right nor left, and halting neither at ditch nor dike. Parkhurst Towers rose before us in the distance, and more than one boy was strolling out in our direction to witness the finish.

How we wished we were as fresh as they!

"Put it on, hares!" shouted the first who met us, "you'll do it yet."

"Hounds are gaining!" cried the next we passed—a young urchin sitting on a bank and eating toffee.

And now there met us not single spectators only, but groups, who cheered loudly, backing, some the hares and some the hounds, till we hardly knew where we were. Some even began to run along with us, at a respectful distance, in order to be in at the death.

The playground wall was now visible only half a mile away, on the other side of the Gravelshire Canal, which had to be crossed by a bridge which we were fast approaching.

I gave a rapid look back. Forwood was now only a hundred yards behind us, with lots of running still in him. He would certainly run us down in the next half-mile.

"Birch," I said, as I ran beside him, "are you good for a swim?"

"Rather!" he exclaimed; "if you are. Quick!"

We swerved suddenly in our course, and, to the amazement of all spectators, left the bridge on our left. In another minute we were on the margin of the canal, and the next moment the splash of a double header, and the shouts of the assembled onlookers, proclaimed that we had made a plunge for it. The canal was only about thirty feet wide, and we were across it in a twinkling, our light flannel clothes scarcely interfering with our swimming, and certainly not adding much to the weight we carried after being soaked.

Three hundred yards now! Ah! that cheer behind means that Forwood has followed our plunge. What are they laughing at, though? Can he have foundered? No! Another shout! That means he is safe over, and hard at our heels.

For the last three hundred yards we run a regular steeplechase. The meadows are intersected with lines of hurdles, and these we take one after another in our run, as hard as we can.

Only one more, and then we are safe!

Suddenly I find myself on my face on the grass! I have tripped on the last hurdle, and come to grief!

Birch in an instant hauls me to my feet, just as Forwood rises to the leap. Then for a hundred yards it is a race for very life. What a shouting there is! And what a rushing of boys and waving of caps pass before our eyes! On comes Forwood, the gallant hound, at our heels; we can hear him behind us distinctly!

"Now you have them!" shouts one.

"One spurt more, hares!" cries another, "and you are safe!"

On we bound, and on comes the pursuer, not ten yards behind—not *ten*, but more than *five*. And that five he never makes up till Birch and I are safe inside the school-gates, winners by a neck—and a neck only—of that famous hunt.

Kangaroos

Eric Linklater

Illustrated by Nicolas Bentley

Son of a sea captain of Orkney, Eric Linklater (1899–1974) liked to remember that his ancestry goes back to the time of the Vikings. As a boy of sixteen, he joined the Gordon Highlanders in the First World War, but was sent back to school . . . Time remedied that, and he joined The Black Watch and was severely wounded. Afterwards, he had a distinguished and most varied life—as journalist on "The Times of India", as Commonwealth scholar in American universities, as the writer of brilliantly amusing novels, as fortress commander in Orkney in the Second World War, as Rector of his old university of Aberdeen, and as historian of the war in Korea. A witty talker and debater, Eric Linklater had a bold fancifulness and delight in absurdities which he turned to account in his books for young readers. All are distinguished, and "The Wind on the Moon" (from which this comes) is a Carnegie Medal book.

Dinah and Dorinda have been playing at being kangaroos, but it is not 'till they get an old lady to give them a witch's brew that things really happen.

DORINDA had been the first to wake that morning. She had dreamt that she was already a kangaroo, and she was disappointed to find herself still in human shape. She began to imagine, or try to imagine, what it would feel like to be enclosed in a furry hide, and to lean backwards, as if in a chair, against the support of a long strong tail. And from that position she would also be able to leap the length of quite a long room. Kangaroos were very lucky in some ways.

She slipped out of bed to practise a jumping position, and at that moment Dinah got quietly out of her bed with the same idea in her head. For she too, as soon as she woke, had started to think about the new experiences that were awaiting her. So she and Dorinda both began to practise kangaroo jumps on the bedroom floor, but found it difficult without tails to help them. They had to wait, it seemed, a very long time before breakfast was ready.

Then, as soon as they could get away, they left the house and ran without stopping to the nearest part of the Forest of Weal. That, they had decided, was the best place in which to drink the magic draught, because they did not want, of course, to turn into kangaroos in the nursery, where they might frighten their mother. And it might be difficult, added Dinah, to get downstairs. She did not think that kangaroos were very good on stairs.

So they hurried to the Forest, carrying the little box of plaited grass with Mrs. Grimble's medicine in it, and two small bundles that held all the things they wanted to take with them. When they came to a suitable place, they stopped and looked all around to make sure there was no one within sight. Then they opened the grass box, and read the directions on the bottle. This is what Mrs. Grimble had written on the label:

Directions for Turning Yourself into Anything You Want to Be

1. Shake the Bottle.
2. Undress Yourself.
3. Fold your Clothes Neatly and Put in Safe Place.
4. Turn Three Times against the Sun and say: I Want to Be Whatever You do Want to Be.
5. Shake the Bottle again.
6. Drink one Dose.
7. Replace the Cork.
8. Go for a Little Walk.

(*Signed*)
MRS. GRIMBLE

"This is a solemn moment," said Dinah as she began to take off her shoes.

"Very solemn," said Dorinda. "I'm glad it's a warm day."

"There's a hole in that oak-tree," said Dinah. "We can put our clothes away there."

They packed their clothes into the hole in the oak-tree, and shook the bottle for the second time.

There were just four doses in it, and Dinah had remembered to bring a table-spoon.

She gave Dorinda the first dose, and quickly took her own.

"Oh!" cried Dorinda, turning quite pale.

"I have never in all my life tasted anything so horrible," said Dinah. But she put the cork back in the bottle, and in a firm voice said to Dorinda, "Now we must take a little walk. You go that way, and I'll go this."

She wanted to be alone, because she thought she was going to be sick. But in a little while she felt much better, and curiously strong. She felt far stronger than she had ever been, or ever dreamt of being, and never, she thought, had all the leaves and the grass looked so nice. She put a few leaves in her mouth and chewed them, and to her surprise they tasted rather like bread-and-honey. Then, seeing a bush in front of her, she jumped over it, and thought: Well, I've never been able to jump as high as that before! But then she got a terrible fright, because a few yards away she saw a wild animal. A tall grey kangaroo!

Her heart nearly stopped beating for she had never expected to meet a real kangaroo, and she was just going to turn and run away as fast as she could when she remembered Dorinda. She must warn Dorinda.

So as loud as she could she shouted, "Dorinda, Dorinda! Take care, there's a kangaroo in the Forest!"

Her voice sounded curiously unlike anything she had heard before, but that, she supposed, was due to the fright she had had.

The kangaroo, it seemed, had also been on the point of running away. But it stopped when it heard Dinah, and then

155

Dinah heard Dorinda's voice. At least, she supposed it was Dorinda's voice, though it wasn't like her ordinary voice, because it said: "Dinah, Dinah! Take care, I can see a kangaroo!"

And the voice, which was Dorinda's, came from the kangaroo of which Dinah had been frightened. The kangaroo *was* Dorinda!

And Dinah, feeling rather hot and quite embarrassed, looked down at her own great legs, and over her shoulder at her long powerful tail, and realized that she too had become a kangaroo, and that she had made Dorinda equally frightened. The medicine had worked!

"Oh, Dorinda!" she exclaimed.

"Oh, Dinah!" said Dorinda.

"I got such a fright when I saw you," said Dinah.

"So did I when I saw you," said Dorinda.

"We certainly look exactly like real kangaroos," said Dinah.

"Mrs. Grimble must be a very good sort of witch," said Dorinda.

"I think it will be nice when we get used to it," said Dinah. "I've done one or two marvellous jumps already."

"But it does feel strange to begin with," said Dorinda.

In a few minutes, however, they felt perfectly at home in their new shape, and greatly pleased with themselves. They practised long jumping and standing on their tails, and found that their arms, though quite small in comparison with their great legs, were very useful. Almost as useful, indeed, as human arms and hands.

After practising running for about half an hour, they decided to go to the village. But first of all they returned to the place where they had drunk the magic draught, and carefully packed in their pouches the things they had brought from home.

Dinah had taken a note-book and a pencil and a rubber; two pocket-handkerchiefs and a toothbrush; the key of the back door and a slab of chocolate. She put them all into her pouch, and also the bottle of medicine and the tablespoon.

Dorinda had taken some milk chocolate and her new watch; a toothbrush and a comb and a pencil-sharpener and a book called *Wild Life in Borneo,* which she thought might be useful, but it was too big to go into her pouch, and had to be left behind. She had forgotten to bring a handkerchief, but Dinah said she would lend her one if she needed it.

Then they set off for the village.

"Now for revenge!" said Dinah.

"Revenge!" said Dorinda, and jumped across a hedge and back again.

In the outer streets of the village they saw no one at all. The streets were deserted because everyone was waiting outside the Police Court to hear the result of the trial of Mrs. Taper. Not a soul was to be seen till they came into Elm Lane, and there, approaching them, was a great procession of people. All the people, indeed, who were escorting the Members of the Jury to Midmeddlecum Gaol. They were singing a very fine French song which the Vicar had taught them only a few weeks before. It was called *Avec mes Sabots.*

Seeing so many people all at once, and hearing such a great noise of singing, Dinah and Dorinda became slightly nervous, and stopped for a moment. It needed, they felt, a lot of courage to charge the whole population of Midmeddlecum. They had not expected to see them all together like this.

But the people of Midmeddlecum, seeing two tall grey kangaroos coming towards them, were far more frightened than Dinah and Dorinda. They also stopped, and their fine song died away.

Then Dinah said, "Father is a soldier. He would never flinch from the enemy. Charge, Dorinda, charge!"

Bounding and waving their arms, they advanced at top speed. Never before had such a sight been seen in Elm Lane.

The villagers turned and ran in all directions, but the prisoners, who were handcuffed two by two, were rather at a disadvantage, and some of them were left in the lurch. Only one man tried to defend the village, and that was Constable Drum. He stood very bravely in the middle of the lane, and shouted to the kangaroos, "Halt, in the King's name! Halt, and be arrested!"

But Dinah, with a kick as she passed, knocked him head over heels. She did this as gently as she could, because she was quite fond of Constable Drum who was a good man, but her great kangaroo legs were so strong that even a gentle kick made him turn two complete somersaults. Then she caught Tom Leathercow the butcher's son, and kicked him into a ditch. And Dorinda caught Robin and Robina Wax, who were trying to climb a tree, but the tree was already full of people, so there was no room for them, and Dorinda kicked them both into a convenient garden.

All the trees in Elm Lane were crowded with people who had climbed into their branches to get away from the kangaroos.

But a great many villagers, including the prisoners who were handcuffed and therefore could not climb trees, were running towards the Square, and Dinah and Dorinda chased them across Elm Street, and up Tulip Street, and round the statue of Queen Victoria. As they passed the door of the Police Court, Mr. Justice Rumple came out to see what all the noise was about. His shirt-sleeves were still rolled up, and he was smoking a cigar. When he saw the kangaroos he retreated very quickly into the Police Court, and slammed the door behind him, and bolted it and locked it. Then he went to the telephone, and telephoned to Sir Lankester Lemon.

Dinah and Dorinda chased the people three times round the statue of Queen Victoria. The Vicar, who was good at climbing, was sitting on her lap with Mrs. Fullalove, and the Vicar was saying, "I wish I had my camera! Oh, I *wish* I had my camera!" But everybody else had only one wish in the world, and that was not to be kicked by the kangaroos.

She knocked him head over heels as gently as she could.

157

The Glass Peacock

Eleanor Farjeon

Illustrated by Val Biro

The daughter of a novelist father and an actress mother, Eleanor Farjeon (1881–1965) was to become one of the best-known writers and editors for children in England this century. Her publications include long stories (of which "Martin Pippin in the Apple Orchard" is one of the best); many poems and many short stories.

As a child Eleanor had the run of her father's library which held thousands of books. What a paradise in which to roam! She, at least, found it so. This delightful tale is taken from her collection of stories called "The Little Bookroom"—so named in memory of that delectable library. This collection received the Carnegie Medal award for the best children's book of 1955. Her last story, "Mr. Garden" appeared in 1966, and the same year saw "The Eleanor Farjeon Book", an anthology of stories and poems published as a special tribute a few months after her death.

ANNAR-MARIAR lived in a queer old alley in one of the queerest and oldest parts of London. Once this part had been a real village all by itself, looking down from its hill upon the fields and lanes that divided it from the town. Then gradually the town had climbed the hill, the fields were eaten up by houses, and the lanes suffered that change which turned them into streets. But the hill was so steep, and the ways were so twisty, that even the town couldn't swallow the village when it got to the top. It was too much trouble to make broad roads of all the funny little narrow turnings, so some of them were left much as they were, and one of these was the alley where Annar-Mariar lived. It ran across from one broad road to another, a way for walkers, but not for carts and cars. The two big roads met at a point a little farther on, so there was no need to turn Annar-Mariar's alley into a thoroughfare for traffic, and it remained a paved court, with poor, irregular dwellings and a few humble shops on each side. Being paved, and out of the way of the motors, it became a natural playground for the children who lived in it; and even from the other alleys nearby children came to play in Mellin's Court. The organ-grinder, making his way from one big road to another, sometimes made it across Mellin's Court. One day, as he was passing, a group of children were clustered round the little sweetstuff shop that sold bright sweets in ha'porths, or even farthings-worths. The shop had an old bow window nearly touching the pavement—it came down about as far as a little girl's skirt and went up about as high as a man's collar. To enter the shop, you went down three steps into a dim little room. None of the children had any farthings that day except Annar-Mariar, and *she* had a whole penny. Her little brother Willyum was clinging to the hand that held the penny, and telling her all the things he liked best in the jars in the window. He knew his Annar-Mariar, and so did the other children who were not her brothers and sisters.

"I like the lickerish shoe strings," said Willyum.

"*I* like the comfits with motters on," said Mabel Baker.

"And I like the pink and white mouses," said Willyum.

"Them bulls' eyes is scrumpchous," observed Doris Goodenough.

"And the chocklit mouses," continued Willyum, "and I like them long stripey sticks, and them chocklit cream bars with pink inside."

"Peardrops," murmured Kitty Farmer.

"And white inside, too," said Willyum.

While Annar-Mariar was puzzling and puzzling how to make her penny go round she saw the organ-grinder, and cried, "Oo! an orgin!" The other children turned. "Ply us a chune, mister!" they cried. "Ply us a chune!" The organ-grinder shook his head. "No time today," he said. Annar-Mariar saw the way out of her problem. She went up to the organ-grinder and smiled at him, plucking his coat.

"Do ply 'em a chune to dance to," she said, and held out her penny. It was Annar-Mariar's nice smile, and not her penny, that won the day. Annar-Mariar was quite an ordinary-looking little girl until she smiled. Then you felt you would do anything for her. This was because Annar-

Mariar would always do anything for anybody. It came out in her smile, and got back at her, so to speak, by winning her her own way. All day long Mellin's Court was calling her name. "Annar-Mariar! Johnny's bin and hurted hisself." "Annar-Mariar! Come quick! Bobby and Joan is fighting somethink orful!" "Annar-Mariar, boo-boo! I've broke my dolly!" Or it might be an older voice. "Annar-Mariar! jest keep an eye on baby for me while I go round the corner." Yes, everybody knew that Annar-Mariar would always be ready to heal the hurt, and soothe the quarrel, and mend the doll, and mind the baby. She would not only be ready to, but she could *do* it; because everybody did what she wanted them to.

So the organ-grinder refused her penny, and stopped and played three tunes for her smile; and the children got a jolly dance for nothing, and Willyum got a pair of liquorice shoe-strings for a farthing. The rest of Annar-Mariar's penny went in hundreds and thousands, and every child licked its finger and had a dip. There wasn't a fingerful over for Annar-Mariar, so she tore open the tiny bag and licked it off with her tongue.

After that the organ-grinder made a point of cutting across Mellin's Court on his rounds, stopping outside the rat-catcher's, where it was at its broadest, to play his tunes; and the children gathered there and danced, and sometimes he got a copper for his kindness, but whether he did or not made no difference. He always came once a week.

Christmas drew near, and the little shops in Mellin's Court began to look happy. The sweetstuff shop had a fairy doll in white muslin and tinsel in the middle of the window, and some paper festoons and cheap toys appeared among the glass bottles. At the greengrocer's, a sort of glorified open stall which overflowed into the courtyard, evergreens and pineapples appeared, and one magic morning Christmas-trees. The grocery windows at

The organ grinder stopped in Mellin's Court and the children gathered there and danced.

the corner had already blossomed into dates and figs and candied fruits, and blue-and-white jars of ginger; and the big confectioner's in the High Street, as well as puddings in basins, had a Christmas cake in the window a yard square—a great flat frosted "set piece," covered with robins, windmills, snow babies, and a scarlet Santa Claus with a sled full of tiny toys. This cake would presently be cut up and sold by the pound, and you got the attractions on top "as you came"—oh, lucky, lucky buyer-to-be of the Santa Claus sled!

The children of Mellin's Court were already choosing their favourite toys and cakes and fruits from the rich windows, and Annar-Mariar and Willyum chose like all the rest. Of course, they never *thought* they could have the fairy queen, the Christmas-tree, the big box of sugary fruits, or the marvellous cake—but how they *dreamed* they could! As Christmas drew nearer, smaller hopes of what it would actually bring began to take shape in the different homes. Bobby's mother had *told* him he'd better hang his stocking up Christmas Eve "and see." That meant something. And the Goodenoughs were

going to be sent a hamper. And Mabel Baker was going to be taken to the panto-mime, and the Jacksons were all going to their Granny's in Lambeth for a party. And this child and that had so much, or so little, in the sweet club.

And as Christmas drew nearer, it became plainer and plainer to Annar-Mariar that this year, for one reason or another, Christmas wasn't going to bring her and Willyum anything. And it didn't. Up to the last they got *their* treat from the shop-windows, and did all their shopping there. Annar-Mariar never stinted her Christmas shopping.

"What'll *you* 'ave, Willyum? I'll 'ave the fairy queen, I think. Would you like them trains?"

"Ss!" said Willyum. "And I'd like the fairy queen."

"Orl right. You 'ave her. I'll 'ave that music box."

At the confectioners'. "Shall we 'ave a big puddin' for us both, or a little puddin' each, Willyum?"

"A big puddin' each," said Willyum.

"Orl right. And them red crackers with the gold balls on, and I'll tell 'em to send the big cake too, shall I?"

It was quite a little tree, but such a radiant little tree!
From "The Glass Peacock"

The other two, who could look over the parapet without having to lie on the top of it, stood on each side of Jacky, watching the water flowing away from under the arch.
From "A Lesson in Tickling Trout"

"Ss!" said Willyum, "and I'll 'ave the Farver Chrismuss."

"Orl right, ducks. You can."

And at the grocer's, Willyum had the biggest box of candied fruits, and at the greengrocer's the biggest pineapple. He agreed, however, to a single tree—the biggest—between them, and under Annar-Mariar's lavish disregard of money there was plenty of everything for them both, and for anybody who cared to "drop in" on Christmas Day.

It came and passed. The windows began to be emptied of their attractions for another year. Mabel Baker went to the pantomime, and told them all about it. Annar-Mariar dreamed of it for nights; she thought she was a very lucky girl to have a friend who went to the panto.

Life went on. The New Year rang itself in. At dusk, on twelfth night, Annar-Mariar knelt on the paving-stones in Mellin's Court and renewed a chalk game that had suffered during the day. She happened to be the only child about, a rare occurrence there.

She heard footsteps go by her, but did not look up at once; only, as they passed, she became aware of a tiny tinkling accompaniment to the footsteps. Then she did look up. A lady was going slowly along the alley with something astonishing in her hands.

"Oo!" gasped Annar-Mariar.

The lady stopped. What she was carrying was a Christmas-tree, quite a little tree, the eighteenpenny size, but such a radiant little tree! It was glittering and tinkling with all the prettiest fantasies in glass that the mind of Christmas had been able to invent, little glass lamps and candlesticks, shining balls of every colour, a scarlet-and-silver Father Christmas, also in glass, chains and festoons of gold and silver beads, stars, and flowers, and long clear drops like icicles; birds, too, in glass, blue and yellow birds, seeming to fly, and one, proudest and loveliest of all, a peacock, shimmering in blue and green and gold,

with a crest and long, long tail of fine spun glass.

"Oo!" gasped Annar-Mariar. "A Chrismuss-tree!"

The lady did an undreamed-of thing. She came straight up to Annar-Mariar and said, "Would you like it?"

Annar-Mariar gazed at her, and very slowly smiled. The lady put the tinkling, twinkling tree into her hands.

"This," she said, "was for the first little girl that said 'Oo!' and you're the little girl."

Annar-Mariar began to giggle—she simply *couldn't* say "Thank you"; she could only giggle and giggle. Her smile, however, turned her giggling into the loveliest laughter, and seemed to be saying "Thank you" on top of it. The lady laughed, and disappeared from Mellin's Court.

Willyum appeared in her place. "Wot's that?"

"'Ts a Chrismuss-tree. A lidy give it to me."

Willyum scampered screaming down the alley. "Annar-Mariar's gotter Crismuss-tree wot a lidy give 'er!"

The crowd collected. They gathered round the tree, looking, touching, admiring, and the "Oos!" came thick and fast.

"Oo! see ol' Farver Crismuss!"

"Oo! see them birds, like flying, ain't they?"

"Do the lamps really light, Annar-Mariar?"

"Oo! ain't that flower loverly!"

"Watcher goin' to do wiv it, Annar?"

"I shall keep it by my bed ternight," said Annar-Mariar, "and termorrer I shall give a party."

Longing glances flew about her.

"Can I come, Annar-Mariar?"

"Can I?"

"Can I?"

"Let *me* come, won't yer, Annar?"

"You can all come," said Annar-Mariar.

That night, that one blissful night, the little tree in all its gleaming beauty shone upon Annar-Mariar's dreams—waking dreams, for she hardly slept at all. She kept looking at it, and feeling it when she couldn't see it, running her finger along the glassy chains, outlining the fragile flowers and stars, stroking the silken tail of the miraculous peacock. To-morrow night, she knew, her tree would be harvested, but she thought her own particular fruit might be the peacock. If so, he could sit on the tree beside her bed for ever, and every night she could stroke his spun-glass tail.

The morrow came. The party was held after tea. Every child in Mellin's Court took home a treasure. Willyum wanted the Father Christmas, and had him. The other children did not ask for the peacock. Some-how they knew how *much* Annar-Mariar wanted it, and recognized that off *her* tree she should have what she prized most. Little Lily Kensil *did* murmur, when her turn came, "I'd like the peack——" But her big brother clapped his hand over her mouth, and said firmly, "Lil'd like the rose, Annar-Mariar. Look, Lil, it's got a diamond in the middle."

"Oo!" said Lil greedily.

So when the party was over, and the little empty tree was dropping its dried needles on the table, Annar-Mariar was left in possession of the magical bird whose tail she had touched in her dreams.

When she came to put Willyum to bed, he was sobbing bitterly.

"Wot's the matter, ducks?"

"I broke my Farver Crismuss."

"Oh, Willyum . . . you never."

"Yus, I did." Willyum was inconsolable.

"Don't cry, ducks."

"I want your peacock."

"Orl right. You can. Don't cry."

Annar-Mariar gave Willyum her peacock. He sobbed himself to sleep, clutching it, and in the night he dropped it out of bed. Annar-Mariar heard it "go" as she lay beside her little empty tree. All night long its pungent scent was in her nostrils, and the tiny crickle of its dropping needles in her ears.

And in the room of every other child in Mellin's Court some lovely thing was set above its dreams, a bird, or flower, or star of coloured glass; to last perhaps a day, a week, a few months, or a year—or even many years.

The Pool in the Forest

"B.B."

Here is an author with two names and, you could say, two professions.

Under the modest nom-de-plume of "B.B." this author has written books that have delighted children for years. His real name, however, is D. J. Watkins-Pitchford, and this he uses for his no less distinguished work as artist and illustrator. For fifteen years he taught art at Rugby School (so if we count teaching he has a third profession) and now devotes all his time to writing and illustrating his own books. One of these, "The Little Grey Men", was a Carnegie Medal winner in 1942 for the best children's book of that year.

If you have read his stories you will not be surprised to learn that he loves looking at nature, fishing, shooting and camping; for, whether he is writing or drawing, nature and wild life are always revealed in his work—revealed and enjoyed. This passage from his "Brendon Chase" will show you what we mean.

AT LAST Robin came to an open space in the forest where the bracken was up to his shoulders. The air was perfectly windless and heavy with the scent of summer. And at that spot the little brooklet had carved out for itself a fairy pool some ten yards long. It looked quite deep. He could see the spotted shingle on the bottom where some thick hazels overhung it, and knew it was no more than a foot or two. Tiny fish darted about. They were sticklebacks. Robin lay on his stomach and drew himself close up to the margin of the pool, his face hidden in the lush sweet-smelling bracken. Pink "mild-maid" flowers dropped over him and his back was partly shielded from the sun by the chequered shade of the leaves overhead.

What a beautiful spot, could anything be nearer Paradise? The wood pigeons were cooing all about him in the trees, the whole forest was murmuring with their drowsy voices.

Robin was a strange boy, at least to many people he would have appeared strange. He loved best to be by himself in the woods, he liked to hunt on his wild lone and wander just like this, for a whole day, in some leafy secret place where nobody bothered to come. It was his idea of Heaven. When, as now, he would come upon something which took his fancy and then time would cease to be for him; he would be lost in a kind of ecstatic stupor.

As he lay looking down into this miniature pool his sharp eyes took in every detail, even the minute shadows of the sticklebacks were noted. Each fish had a shadow beneath it on the sandy floor. After a while, as he kept very still, they became bold and emerged from the shaded water under the hazel leaves and went about their business in their own watery kingdom.

He could see their minute fins trembling, and what perfect fins! These fishes in miniature were truly fascinating. The Creator must have had eyes like a watchmaker, thought Robin, to have made such delicate fishes, and he smiled to himself.

The cock fish were very pretty with their bright blue backs and red throats.

They did not glide along in the water, they seemed to progress in jerks. Sometimes a cock stickleback would chase another away and then it moved with great speed, like an arrow, coming to a sudden full stop, opening and shutting its mouth, puffing out its lips.

On this same pool were water skaters or fiddlers. When Robin had come up to the pool these insects had all darted into the grass and ferns at the edge but as he lay quiet they emerged again and began skating about the surface. He saw the tiny dimple made in the water by their feet. They seemed to run about with as much ease as if they were on hard ground.

After a while a fly fell off the hazel leaves, a greenfly. It landed close to the edge but in a minute quite half a dozen water skaters had seized it and the largest bore it away in its jaws with all the others jumping after him.

Then a buzzing sounded in Robin's ear. It was a wild honey bee. He knocked it with his hand and it too, fell into the water in front of him where it buzzed round making a circular fan of minute ripples. Several fiddlers immediately came skating up. They seemed at first rather afraid of the bee, but one, bolder than his fellows, darted in a rapier thrust. The bee's struggles grew weaker and finally its attacker began to run off with it wedged across his jaws. Robin never realized what savage little insects they were, they reminded him of a pack of hounds.

The bee vainly tried to sting its captor but it was held fast. As Robin watched these fierce little creatures he noticed some were fighting, now and again one would fall over on to its back and show its silver underside, they skipped about each other like crickets.

It was delicious lying there among the cool bracken but the water seemed more inviting still. So he stripped off his shirt and his trousers and rolled off the bank.

The pool only just covered his body when he lay down full length; it was a natural bath.

The water was warm in the full sun's glare, but when he sidled under the nut leaves it was quite chill. What a fairy-like little pool it was! Then he turned over on to his stomach facing upstream and watched the ripples hurrying round the bend towards him. He stretched out his arms—they looked blue under the water —and raised his fingers so that streams of silver bubbles came past his ears and nostrils.

He scrabbled the stones on the streambed and the water clouded for a second, but it soon ran clear again so that he could see his fingers showing bluish-white against the pied stones and silver sand.

Overhead a dragonfly passed to and fro, a bright blue dragonfly with dark spots on the ends of its wings like those he had seen by the Willow Pool at Cherry Walden. It settled on a reed in the full sun with its wings cocked high above its back. There were mayflies on the wing too, dancing up and down with their long graceful tails cocked up behind. When Robin was smaller he used to be rather afraid of them, he thought those long thread-like tails were stings.

It was so dreamy and cool and summery in that miniature paradise that Robin felt he could stay there for ever, and ever. But at last he had to get out and lie on the warm bracken to let the sun dry him. The green fronds felt quite hot against his body after the cold embrace of the limpid water.

When he had dressed again he suddenly felt terribly hungry. You may have noticed that after a swim one often has a good appetite. And he had brought nothing with him to eat. They only had two meals a day, breakfast and supper. It was all they wanted and they were invariably ravenous for either.

It was quite an effort to tear himself away from this little fairy glade with its amber pool, but soon he was pushing down the streamside again, his body still tingling and delightful after the bathe. It had not been a *real* swim, he would have liked to strike out into deep water and oar himself along like a very fat carp and nose among green water plants. Perhaps he could do this when he found the Blind Pool, if there *was* such a place.

Then, quite miraculously, the trees thinned and he saw the object of his search. It was a long narrow pool, dark and very still, with beds of white water-lilies growing near the banks. High oaks surrounded it on three sides, on the fourth were some tall and very gloomy pines whose tops were lit by the late afternoon sun so that their red branches seemed to be artificial, almost painted, or stained with blood.

At the far end, backed by the dark trees, stood a heron, its head sunk in its shoulders. It was standing on a mossy log which was protruding from the water. The pool was so still that a faithful reflection of the bird was visible, perfect in every detail.

Robin crawled through the bracken right up to the edge of the water and stared down into the depths. It was deep, so deep that he could see no bottom, and the water was a very, very dark green. By staring hard he could at last make out the steeply shelving sides diving down into the gloom. Robin saw his own reflection, curiously dark, so that his eyes were almost invisible and behind his head an indigo sky such as one sees in an old Umbrian painting with the few white clouds which were passing slowly overhead, mirrored very soft and dim. It was like looking at a richly-coloured picture through a smoked glass.

As he lay screened by the reeds and fern, staring down, down, into the green depths, a dim movement attracted his attention below and a grave procession of massive bronze fish passed silently by, some five feet down. In weight and girth they were larger than any freshwater fish he had ever seen, with the exception of a pike. They were tench.

Robin was enthralled—bewitched! This place was even more magical than the tiny pool he had discovered away back down the trail! He lifted his eyes again and saw the heron had come to life and was walking rather awkwardly down the mossy log, clasping it with its long green claws and bobbing its head. It had not seen him, so well was he hidden in the reeds.

Several moorhens, which have the sharpest eyes of any wild bird, were feeding on a little grassy bank on the shore opposite to where he lay in hiding. They quested about like chickens, flirting their white tails. Moorhens are good to eat and so far Robin had shot nothing for the pot all day.

So he raised his rifle and took a steady sight on the nearest bird through the 'scope. It was not an easy shot for the moorhen was moving slowly forward, pecking as it went.

But Robin chose his own time and at the right instant the finger obeyed the brain and the crack was followed by the welcome thud of the bullet going home. The bird rolled over, flapped a wing once, twice, and lay still.

At the report of the rifle, muffled as it was, the heron sprang vertically into the air as if stung and came down again on the log. A moment before it had been hunched, now it was like a long slender grey reed and even from where Robin lay he could see its circular eye staring about it in the most comical manner. It had heard the muffled crack of the rifle but did not know from which direction it had come. Then it launched itself into the air and flapped away over the trees on wide cupped wings. One moment it was a grey bird against a wall of dark foliage, the next it was soaring into the sunlight and had vanished over the tops of the oaks.

All the other moorhens had run for cover when Robin had fired and now the pool was deserted, not a movement anywhere save some ripples on the water where a moorhen had dived. These came wheeling out towards him, breaking up the dark green shadow reflections.

He did not retrieve his bird at once. He still lay hidden among the thick reeds watching and listening. On the far green bank he could see the dark sooty spot of the dead moorhen. It would be delicious roast. Robin was so hungry he almost felt he could eat it raw with the greatest of gusto!

After a while he was aware of another bird moving among the sturdy reed swords at the far end of the pond, close to the sunken green log where the heron had stood. For some time Robin was puzzled as to what it could be and after a while he tried to see through the telescope of the rifle. At last he made out what it was, a mallard duck. Close behind her swam a lot of cheeping striped babies. She was threading her way in between the reed pallisades. What a heavenly place! How the others would love it! The white water-lilies so perfect and waxy, looked as though they were artificial. And those fascinating flat circular leaves, strange fleshy leaves like dishes, how they seemed the very spirit of the water itself! There was a very faint smell of wild thyme and heated pond water. Earlier in the day the sun must have been shining full on the pool for when Robin dipped a finger in it was quite warm. Another time they must come here and swim and fish. Alas! Robin Hood's day was nearly over. Why did the sun sink so soon? He had a long weary march back to camp. He must be starting. But as the sun dipped lower and lower behind the trees the powerful magic of the scene held him all the more. This place was surely far more lovely than Thoreau's pond he talked so much about. There was something mysterious, almost a little sinister about it. Why should it be set away in the heart of this ancient forest? The deer drank here perhaps, and all the woodland

creatures, foxes, badgers, stoats, and the like, pheasants, too, and all the wild forest birds. When Robin looked again in his magic mirror he saw no white clouds sailing, he saw a sky of rarest aquamarine and, as he watched, against that background a bird swam into view, a wide-winged bird, which wheeled and wheeled in vast circles.

Robin looked up at the sky above and saw the whole scene, only more distinctly now and in clearer and more vivid colours. The bird was wheeling like a buzzard, the sunlight shining on the spread fingers of the wide-extended rigid wings. Could it be a honey buzzard? If so, perhaps it had a nest somewhere in the forest!

At last it soared from view behind the oak tops and was gone. He knew what he wanted to complete the picture of this dark green lake, set among the trees, starred with ivory lilies. Why, of course, it wanted this one thing, a moose, a huge black moose, pulling at the water-lilies! He could imagine it so clearly, the loose pendulous lips dribbling sparkling drops, its echoing sloshings, as it moved about in the shallow water of that remote and silent place.

Sadly Robin turned back upon his trail, the moorhen safely in his pocket. He took one last look at the Blind Pool. It was the loveliest thing he had so far seen in the forest, and he had enjoyed this day more than any other they had had so far.

He did not know then that years afterwards he would remember that picture; the dark pool set among the trees, so still, so calm, starred with those wax-like lilies, and the grey heron sitting on the log. Some things we see pass out of the mind, or, at least, are forgotten; others, little things, little glimpses such as this never depart. And the memory of that first view of the Blind Pool would still be in his mind forty years afterwards, rather faded, perhaps, like an old photograph in an album, but still there, an imperishable masterpiece.

Salt
An Old Peter's Russian Tale

Arthur Ransome

Illustrated by Robert Geary

Although Arthur Ransome is best known for his novels for boys and girls (from which we have a piece on page 180 of this book), his "Old Peter's Russian Tales" has long been a favourite with younger children. These stories are based on Russian fairy tales which Arthur Ransome grew to love during his years in Russia as a newspaper correspondent. "Salt" is one of the best of them.

ONE evening, when they were sitting round the table after their supper, old Peter asked the children what story they they would like to hear. Vanya asked whether there were any stories left which they had not already heard.

"Why," said old Peter, "you have heard scarcely any of the stories, for there is a story to be told about everything in the world."

"About everything, grandfather?" asked Vanya.

"About everything," said old Peter.

"About the sky, and the thunder, and the dogs, and the flies, and the birds, and the trees, and the milk?"

"There is a story about every one of those things."

"I know something there isn't a story about," said Vanya.

"And what's that?" asked old Peter, smiling in his beard.

"Salt," said Vanya. "There can't be a story about salt." He put the tip of his finger into the little box of salt on the table and then he touched his tongue with his finger to taste.

"But of course there is a story about salt," said old Peter.

"Tell it us," said Maroosia, and presently, when his pipe had been lit twice and gone out, old Peter began.

Once upon a time there were three brothers, and their father was a great merchant who sent his ships far over the sea, and traded here and there in countries the names of which I, being an old man, can never rightly call to mind. Well, the names of the two elder brothers do not matter, but the youngest was called Ivan the Ninny, because he was always playing and never working; and if there was a silly thing to do, why, off he went and did it. And so, when the brothers grew up, the father sent the two elder ones off, each in a fine ship laden with gold and jewels, and rings and bracelets, and laces and silks, and sticks with little bits of silver hammered into their handles, and spoons with patterns of blue and red, and everything else you can think of that costs too much to buy. But he made Ivan the Ninny stay at home, and did not give him a ship at all.

167

Ivan saw his brothers go sailing off over the sea on a summer morning, to make their fortunes and come back rich men; and then, for the first time in his life, he wanted to work and do something useful. He went to his father and kissed his hand, and he kissed the hand of his little old mother, and he begged his father to give him a ship so that he could try his fortune like his brothers.

"But you have never done a wise thing in your life, and no one could count all the silly things you've done if he spent a hundred days in counting," said his father.

"True," said Ivan, "but now I am going to be wise, and sail the sea and come back with something in my pockets to show that I am not a ninny any longer. Give me just a little ship, father mine—just a little ship for myself."

"Give him a little ship," said the mother. "He may not be a ninny after all."

"Very well," said his father. "I will give him a little ship, but I am not going to waste good roubles by giving him a rich cargo."

"Give me any cargo you like," said Ivan.

So his father gave him a little ship, a little old ship, and a cargo of rags and scraps and things that were not fit for anything but to be thrown away. And he gave him a crew of ancient old sailormen who were past work; and Ivan went on board and sailed away at sunset, like the ninny he was. And the feeble, ancient old sailormen pulled up the ragged, dirty sails, and away they went over the sea to learn what fortune, good or bad, God had in mind for a crew of old men with a ninny for a master.

The fourth day after they set sail, there came a great wind over the sea. The feeble old men did the best they could with the ship, but the old, torn sails tore from the masts, and the wind did what it pleased and threw the little ship on an unknown island away in the middle of the sea. Then the wind dropped, and left the little ship on the beach, and Ivan the Ninny and his ancient old men, like good Russians, praising God that they were still alive.

"Well, children," said Ivan, for he knew how to talk to sailors, "do you stay here and mend the sails, and make new ones out of the rags we carry as cargo, while I go inland and see if there is anything that could be of use to us."

So the ancient old sailormen sat on deck, with their legs crossed, and made sails out of rags, of torn scraps of old brocades, of soiled embroidered shawls, of all the rubbish that they had with them for a cargo. You never saw such sails. The tide came up and floated the ship, and they threw out anchors at bow and stern, and sat there in the sunlight, making sails and patching them and talking of the days when they were young. All this while Ivan the Ninny went walking off into the island.

Now in the middle of that island was a mountain; a high mountain it was, and so white that, when he came near it, Ivan the Ninny began thinking of sheepskin coats, although it was midsummer and the sun was hot in the sky. The trees were green round about, but there was nothing growing on the mountain at all. It was just a great white mountain piled up into the sky in the middle of a green island. Ivan walked a little way up the white slopes of the mountain, and then, because he felt thirsty, he thought he would let a little snow melt in his mouth. He took some in his fingers and stuffed it in. Quickly enough it came out again, I can tell you, for the mountain was not made of snow but of good Russian salt. And if you want to try what a mouthful of salt is like, you may.

"No, thank you, grandfather," the children said hurriedly together.

Old Peter went on with his tale.

Ivan the Ninny did not stop to think twice. The salt was so clean and shone so brightly in the sunlight. He just turned round and ran back to the shore, and called out to his ancient old sailormen and told them to empty everything they had on board over into the sea. Over it all went, rags and tags and rotten timbers, till the little ship was as empty as a soup bowl after supper. And then those ancient old men were set to work carrying salt from the mountain and taking it on board the little ship, and stowing it away below deck till there was not room for another grain. Ivan the Ninny would have liked to take the whole mountain but there was not room in the little ship. And for that the ancient old sailormen thanked God, because their backs ached and their old legs were weak, and they said they would have died if they had had to carry any more.

Then they hoisted up the new sails they had patched together out of the rags and scraps of shawls and old brocades, and they sailed away once more over the blue sea. And the wind stood fair, and they sailed before it, and the ancient old sailors rested their backs, and told old tales, and took turn and turn about at the tiller.

And after many days' sailing they came to a town, with towers and churches and painted roofs, all set on the side of a hill that sloped down into the sea. At the foot of the hill was a quiet harbour, and they sailed in there and moored the ship and hauled down their patchwork sails.

Ivan the Ninny went ashore, and took with him a little bag of clean, white salt to show what kind of goods he had for sale, and he asked his way to the palace of the tsar of that town. He came to the palace, and went in and bowed to the ground before the tsar.

"Who are you?" says the tsar.

"I, great lord, am a Russian merchant, and here in a bag is some of my merchandise, and I beg your leave to trade with your subjects in this town."

"Let me see what is in the bag," says the tsar.

Ivan the Ninny took a handful from the bag and showed it to the tsar.

"What is it?" says the tsar.

"Good Russian salt," says Ivan the Ninny.

Now in that country they had never heard of salt, and the tsar looked at the salt, and he looked at Ivan and he laughed.

"Why, this," says he, "is nothing but white dust, and that we can pick up for nothing. The men of my town have no need to trade with you. You must be a ninny."

Ivan grew very red, for he knew what his father used to call him. He was ashamed to say anything, so he bowed to the ground and went away out of the palace.

But when he was outside he thought to himself, "I wonder what sort of salt they use in these parts if they do not know good Russian salt when they see it. I will go to the kitchen."

So he went round to the back door of the palace, and put his head into the kitchen, and said "I am very tired. May I sit down here and rest a little while?"

"Come in," says one of the cooks. "But you must sit just there, and not put even your little finger in the way of us, for we

are the tsar's cooks and we are in the middle of making ready his dinner." And the cook put a stool in a corner out of the way, and Ivan slipped in round the door and sat down in the corner and looked about him. There were seven cooks at least, boiling and baking, and stewing and toasting, and roasting and frying. And as for scullions, they were as thick as cockroaches, dozens of them, running to and fro, tumbling over each other, and helping the cooks.

Ivan the Ninny sat on his stool, with his legs tucked under him and the bag of salt on his knees. He watched the cooks and the scullions, but he did not see them put anything in the dishes which he thought could take the place of salt. No, the meat was without salt, the *kasha* (porridge) was without salt, and there was no salt in the potatoes. Ivan nearly turned sick at the thought of the tastelessness of all that food.

There came the moment when all the cooks and scullions ran out of the kitchen to fetch the silver platters on which to lay the dishes. Ivan slipped down from his

stool and, running from stove to stove, from saucepan to frying pan, he dropped a pinch of salt, just what was wanted, no more no less, in every one of the dishes. Then he ran back to the stool in the corner, and sat there and watched the dishes being put on the silver platters and carried off in gold-embroidered napkins to be the dinner of the tsar.

The tsar sat at table and took his first spoonful of soup.

"The soup is very good today," says he, and he finishes the soup to the last drop.

"I've never known the soup so good," says the tsaritsa, and she finishes hers.

"This is the best soup I ever tasted," says the princess, and down goes hers, and she, you know, was the prettiest princess who ever had dinner in this world.

It was the same with the *kasha* and the same with the meat. The tsar and the tsaritsa and the princess wondered why they had never had so good a dinner in all their lives before.

"Call the cooks," says the tsar. And they called the cooks, and the cooks all came in, and bowed to the ground, and stood in a row before the tsar.

"What did you put in the dishes today that you never put before?" says the tsar.

"We put nothing unusual, your greatness," says the cooks, and bowed to the ground again..

"Then why do the dishes taste better?"

"We do not know, your greatness," say the cooks.

"Call the scullions," says the tsar. And the scullions were called, and they, too, bowed to the ground, and stood in a row before the tsar.

"What was done in the kitchen today that has not been done there before?" says the tsar.

"Nothing, your greatness," say all the scullions except one.

And that one scullion bowed again, and kept on bowing, and then he said, "Please, your greatness, please, great lord, there is usually none in the kitchen but ourselves, but today there was a young Russian merchant, who sat on a stool in the corner and said he was tired."

"Call the merchant," says the tsar.

So they brought in Ivan the Ninny, and he bowed before the tsar, and stood there with his little bag of salt in his hand.

"Did you do anything to my dinner?" says the tsar.

"I did, your greatness," says Ivan.

"What did you do?"

"I put a pinch of Russian salt in every dish."

"That white dust?" says the tsar.

"Nothing but that."

"Have you got any more of it?"

"I have a little ship in the harbour laden with nothing else," says Ivan.

"It is the most wonderful dust in the world," says the tsar, "and I will buy every grain of it you have. What do you want for it?"

Ivan the Ninny scratched his head and thought. He thought that if the tsar liked it as much as all that it must be worth a fair price, so he said, "We will put the salt into bags, and for every bag of salt you must give me three bags of the same weight— one of gold, one of silver, and one of precious stones. Cheaper than that, your greatness, I could not possibly sell."

"Agreed," says the tsar. "And a cheap price, too, for a dust so full of magic that it makes dull dishes tasty, and tasty dishes so good that there is no looking away from them."

So all day long, and far into the night, the ancient old sailormen bent their backs under sacks of salt, and bent them again under sacks of gold and silver and precious stones. When all the salt had been put in the tsar's treasury—yes, with twenty soldiers guarding it with great swords shining in the moonlight—and when the little ship was loaded with riches, so that even the deck was piled high with precious stones, the ancient old men lay down among the jewels and slept till morning, when Ivan the Ninny went to bid goodbye to the tsar.

"And whither shall you sail now?" asked the tsar.

"I shall sail away to Russia in my little ship," says Ivan.

And the princess, who was very beautiful, said, "A little Russian ship?"

"Yes," says Ivan.

"I have never seen a Russian ship," says the princess, and she begs her father to let her go to the harbour with her nurses and maids to see the little Russian ship before Ivan set sail.

She came with Ivan to the harbour, and the ancient old sailormen took them on board.

She ran all over the ship, looking now at this and now at that, and Ivan told her the names of everything—deck, mast and rudder.

"May I see the sails?" she asked.

And the ancient old men hoisted the ragged sails, and the wind filled the sails and tugged.

"Why doesn't the ship move when the sails are up?" asked the princess.

"The anchor holds her," said Ivan.

"Please let me see the anchor," says the princess.

"Haul up the anchor, my children, and show it to the princess," says Ivan to the ancient old sailormen.

And the old men hauled up the anchor, and showed it to the princess, and she said it was a very good little anchor. But, of course, as soon as the anchor was up the ship began to move. One of the ancient old men bent over the tiller, and, with a fair wind behind her, the little ship slipped out of the harbour and away to the blue sea. When the princess looked round thinking it was time to go home, the little ship was far from land, and away in the distance she could only see the gold towers of her father's palace, glittering like pin-points in the sunlight. Her nurses and maids wrung their hands and made an outcry, and the

tent, and agreed to have a marriage feast as soon as the little ship should bring them to the home of Ivan's father. Merry was that voyage. All day long Ivan and the princess sat on deck and said sweet things to each other, and at twilight they sang songs and drank tea, and told stories. As for the nurses and maids, the princess told them to be glad, and so they danced and clapped their hands and ran about the ship, and teased the ancient old sailormen.

When they had been sailing many days, the princess was looking out over the sea, and she cried out to Ivan, "See, over there, far away, are two big ships with white sails, not like our sails of brocade and bits of silk."

Ivan looked, shading his eyes with his hands.

"Why, those are the ships of my elder

The little ship slipped out of the harbour and away to sea.

princess sat down on a heap of jewels, and put a handkerchief to her eyes, and cried and cried and cried.

Ivan the Ninny took her hands and comforted her, and told her of the wonders of the sea that he would show her, and the wonders of the land. And she looked up at him while he talked, and his eyes were kind and hers were sweet, and the end of it was that they were both very well con-

brothers," said he. "We shall all sail home together."

And he made the ancient old sailormen give a hail in their cracked old voices. And the brothers heard them, and came on board to greet Ivan and his bride. And when they saw that she was a tsar's daughter, and that the very decks were heaped with precious stones, because there was no room below, they said one thing to Ivan and something else to each other.

To Ivan they said, "Thanks be to God, He has given you good trading."

But to each other, "How can this be?" says one. "Ivan the Ninny bringing back such a cargo, while we in our fine ships have only a bag or two of gold."

"And what is Ivan the Ninny doing with a princess?" says the other.

And they ground their teeth, and waited their time, and came up suddenly, when Ivan was alone in the twilight, and picked him up by his head and his heels, and hove him overboard into the dark blue sea.

Not one of the old men had seen them, and the princess was not on deck. In the morning they said that Ivan the Ninny must have walked overboard in his sleep. And they drew lots. The eldest brother took the princess, and the second brother took the little ship laden with gold and silver and precious stones. And so the brothers sailed home very well content. But the princess sat and wept all day long, looking down into the blue water. The eldest brother could not comfort her, and the second brother did not try. And the ancient old sailormen muttered in their beards, and were sorry, and prayed to God to give rest to Ivan's soul, for, although he had been a ninny and although he had made them carry a lot of salt and other things, yet they loved him, because he knew how to talk to ancient old sailormen.

But Ivan was not dead. As soon as he splashed into the water, he crammed his fur hat a little tighter on his head and began swimming in the sea. He swam about until the sun rose, and then, not far away, he saw a floating timber log, and he swam to the log and got astride of it, and thanked God. And he sat there on the log in the middle of the sea, twiddling his thumbs for want of something to do.

There was a strong current in the sea that carried him along, and at last, after floating for many days without ever a bite for his teeth or a drop for his gullet, his

He stood looking down at Ivan.

feet touched land. Now that was at night, and he left the log and walked up out of the sea and lay down on the shore and waited for morning.

When the sun rose he stood up, and saw that he was on a bare island, and he saw nothing at all on the island except a huge house as big as a mountain; and as he was looking at the house the great door creaked with a noise like that of a hurricane among the pine forests, and opened; and a giant came walking out and came to the shore, and stood there looking down at Ivan.

173

"What are you doing here, little one?" says the giant.

Ivan told him the whole story, just as I have told it to you.

The giant listened to the very end, pulling at his monstrous whiskers. Then he said, "Listen, little one. I know more of the story than you, for I can tell you that tomorrow morning your eldest brother is going to marry your princess. But there is no need for you to take on about it. If you want to be there, I will carry you and set you down before the house in time for the wedding. And a fine wedding it is likely to be, for your father thinks well of those brothers of yours bringing back all those precious stones, and silver and gold enough to buy a kingdom."

And with that he picked up Ivan the Ninny and set him on his great shoulders, and set off, striding through the sea.

He went so fast that the wind of his going blew off Ivan's hat.

"Stop a moment," shouts Ivan, "my hat has blown off."

"We can't turn back for that," says the giant, "we have already left your hat five hundred versts behind us." And he rushed on, splashing through the sea. The sea was up to his armpits. He rushed on, and the sea was up to his waist. He rushed on, and before the sun had climbed to the top of the blue sky he was splashing up out of the sea with the water about his ankles. He lifted Ivan from his shoulders and set him on the ground.

"Now," says he, "little man, off you run, and you'll be in time for the feast. But don't you dare to boast about riding on my shoulders. If you open your mouth about that you'll smart for it, if I have to come ten thousand versts."

Ivan the Ninny thanked the giant for carrying him through the sea, promised that he would not boast, and then ran off to his father's house. Long before he got there he heard the musicians in the courtyard playing as if they wanted to wear out their instruments before night. The wedding feast had begun, and when Ivan ran in, there, at the high board, was sitting the princess, and beside her his eldest brother. And there were his father and mother, his second brother and all the guests. And every one of them was as merry as could be, except the princess, and she was as white as the salt he had sold to her father.

Suddenly the blood flushed up into her cheeks. She saw Ivan in the doorway. Up she jumped at the high board, and cried out, "There, there is my true love, and not this man who sits beside me at the table."

"What is this?" says Ivan's father, and in a few minutes knew the whole story.

He turned the two elder brothers out of doors, gave their ships to Ivan, married him to the princess, and made him his heir. And the wedding feast began again, and they sent for the ancient old sailormen to take part in it. And the ancient old sailormen wept with joy when they saw Ivan and the princess, like two sweet pigeons, sitting side by side. Yes, and they lifted their flagons with their old, shaking hands, and cheered with their old, cracked voices, and poured the wine down their dry old throats.

There was wine enough and to spare; beer, too, and mead—enough to drown a herd of cattle. And as the guests drank and grew merry and proud, they set to boasting. This one bragged of his riches, that one of his wife. Another boasted of his cunning, another of his new house, another of his strength, and this one was angry because they would not let him show how he could lift the table on one hand. They all drank Ivan's health, and he drank theirs, and in the end he could not bear to listen to their proud boasts.

"That's all very well," says he, "but I am the only man in the world who rode on the shoulders of a giant to come to his wedding feast."

The words were scarcely out of his mouth before there was a tremendous trampling and a roar of a great wind. The house shook with the footsteps of the giant

174

as he strode up. The giant bent down over the courtyard and looked in at the feast.

"Little man, little man," says he, "you promised not to boast of me. I told you what would come if you did, and here you are and have boasted already."

smaller. "Try the taste of that," says Ivan the Ninny.

Well, the giant did not wait to be asked twice. He lifted the barrel of wine as if it had been a little glass, and emptied it down his throat. He lifted the barrel of

"Forgive me," says Ivan. "It was the drink that boasted, not I."

"What sort of drink is it that knows how to boast?" says the giant.

"You shall taste it," says Ivan.

And he made his ancient old sailormen roll a great barrel of wine into the yard, more than enough for a hundred men, and after that a barrel of beer that was as big, and then a barrel of mead that was no

beer as if it had been an acorn, and emptied it after the wine. Then he lifted the barrel of mead as if it had been a very small pea, and swallowed every drop of mead that was in it. And after that he began stamping about and breaking things. Houses fell to pieces this way and that, and trees were swept flat like grass. Every step the giant took was followed by the crash of breaking timbers. Then suddenly he fell flat on his back and slept. For three days and nights he slept without waking. At last he opened his eyes.

"Just look about," says Ivan, "and see the damage that you've done."

"And did that little drop of drink make me do all that?" says the giant. "Well, well, I can well understand that a drink like that can do a bit of bragging. And after that," says he, looking at the wrecks of houses and all the broken things scattered about —"after that," says he, "you can boast of me for a thousand years, and I'll have nothing against you."

And he tugged at his great whiskers, and wrinkled his eyes, and went striding off into the sea.

That is the story about salt, and how it made a rich man of Ivan the Ninny, and, besides, gave him the prettiest wife in the world, and she a tsar's daughter.

The Dark Child

Richard Hughes

Illustrated by John Patience

Richard Hughes (1900–1976) was educated at Charterhouse School and Oxford University, and was a Doctor of Letters of the University of Wales. He wrote some most unusual stories and plays. Among his books of imaginative tales for children is "The Spider's Palace", from which this story is taken.

In a big house at one end of a village there used to live a very large family. There were so many children that it was lucky it was a big house. Now the curious thing was that all these children were fair as fair could be, except one; and he wasn't just dark, he was black.

He wasn't just black like a Negro either, he was much blacker than that; he was black in the same way the night is; in fact, he was so black that anyone anywhere near him could hardly see anything. Just as a lamp gives out light, he gave out dark —and his name was Joey.

One morning poor Joey came into the nursery where all his brothers and sisters were playing.

"Oh, Joey dear, *please* go away. We can't see to play," they all said together.

So, very sad, poor Joey went downstairs and into the library, where his father sat reading his paper.

"Hallo!" said his father without looking up. "Dark morning, what? Hardly see to read!"

Then he looked round and saw Joey.

"That you, my boy? Run away now, like a good little chap. Father's busy."

So, sadder still, Joey went out into the garden. It was a lovely sunny morning, and he wandered down to the fruit garden and stopped to think. Presently he heard the gardener's voice: "Now then, Master Joey, how do you think my peaches is ever going to ripen if you stand there keeping the sun off them?"

Poor Joey began to cry quietly to himself. "The only thing to do," he thought, "is to run away; I see that."

So he ran away, all down the village. But before he got to the far end, a nice brown spaniel came out of a garden to see why it was so dark outside; and just then, too, a motor came along. When he got into Joey's dark the driver couldn't see the dog, and ran over it; but he didn't kill it, he only hurt one of its legs.

When the motor had gone on, Joey went out and picked up the dog and carried it to its house. "That was *my* fault," he thought, "for making the dark."

Someone opened the door and, very surprised, took the dog in, and Joey went away. But while this was happening, a little girl who lived in the house looked out of the window. She was astonished to see that it was almost night in the garden below, but she could just see something black moving about in the middle of it.

"I must go and see what that is," she

"How do you know who I am?" he asked. "I have never been down the village before, because I didn't want people to know about me."

The little girl tried to answer "I don't know," but what she actually said was: "Of course I know!"

"Then can you help me?" asked Joey. "Can you tell me what to do so as not to be so dark?"

The little girl tried to say "I'm afraid I can't," but what she *did* say was: "Of course I can! Try standing on your hands instead of your feet."

said, "and I mustn't forget my magic grain of rice."

So she took a very secret matchbox that she kept hidden behind the clock, and opened it; and inside there was nothing but a single grain of rice. This she took out and put in her mouth, just inside her underlip, between that and her teeth, so that anything she said would have to come out over the magic grain of rice. The advantage of this was that whatever the little girl tried to say, only the truth could come out over the grain of rice; and that happened even if it was something the little girl didn't herself know. If you asked her a question about something she had never heard of even, if she had the grain of rice inside her lip she always gave the right answer.

She had often found it useful in school. So she followed Joey down the road (though keeping outside his dark herself) and into a field. There he stopped, and she spoke to him.

What she tried to say was: "Who are you, black boy, that makes such a dark? I *am* frightened of you"; but what came out (because of the grain of rice) was: "*Poor Joey! I am sorry for you!*"

When he heard himself spoken to like that, of course he was ever so pleased.

"I don't know how," said Joey. So she helped him stand on his hands against a haystack. The change was sudden and wonderful; for no sooner did he stand on his hands than he shone as bright as a motor lamp, but when he stood on his feet again he gave out as much dark as before.

"I don't know that this is going to be much better," said Joey; "but at least it's a change. I *wish* I could be just ordinary!"

"You can't be that just yet," said the little girl. "Well, thank you very much for the change, anyway," said Joey.

She stayed and talked to him in the field all day, while he practised standing on his hands, until by the evening he could walk about on them quite as easily as on his feet.

"I think I'll try going home again now," he said, and said goodbye.

You may imagine how surprised all the village were to look out of their windows and see a little boy walking up the street on his hands, and shining so brightly he lit up the whole place. When he got back home his father and mother were even more surprised than the villagers had been and very glad to see him.

But poor Joey's life wasn't any happier. Before, everyone had told him to go away. Now, everyone called to him to come. In fact, the electric light had gone wrong and they found him very useful.

"Joey, dear," said his mother, "just walk upstairs in front of me on your hands, will you? I want to fetch a book." And so it went on until grown-up dinner-time, when, instead of sending him to bed as usual, they said: "Joey, dear, *would* you mind standing in the middle of the table on your hands all dinner-time? You will light it up so nicely."

At that Joey got very cross, and rushed out of the house on his feet darkly.

When he got to the street, *"This* is a new idea!" he said to himself, and started turn-

ing cartwheels up the street. Certainly the effect was surprising, for when he was one way up in his cartwheel he was dark, and when he was the other way up he was bright, so he went flashing along the road and flashing through the village, and flashing past the village policeman (who nearly fell down with astonishment), and flashing up to the little girl's house, and flashing into the kitchen. He went on turning cartwheels three times round the kitchen even. Meanwhile the cook was mixing a Christmas pudding, and being, like many other cooks, a very sensible woman, she saw at once what was needed. She fetched a fresh basin, a very big one, and then she seized Joey, while he was still cartwheeling, and popped him in it. Immediately she began to stir with a big wooden spoon; and she mixed the dark and the light so thoroughly together that presently he got out of the bowl just ordinary.

The little girl had already gone to bed; but anyhow I don't suppose she would have been interested in him any more now he was ordinary. In fact, he never in all his life saw her again.

But his parents were; and when he went home, and his father and mother and brothers and sisters found he was now quite ordinary, and there was nothing by which you could possibly tell him from any other child, they were pleased as pleased as pleased; and often used to tell each other how clever of him it was.

179

A Lesson in Tickling Trout

Arthur Ransome

Illustrated by Shirley Hughes

Few British children will need to be told about Arthur Ransome, for most will have read some of his dozen or so true-to-life novels for boys and girls with their realistic backgrounds of the English Lake District or the Norfolk and Suffolk Broads, and their wonderful holiday atmosphere. Almost all of them "Swallows and Amazons", "Pigeon Post", "The Picts and the Martyrs", and "Secret Water", "The Coot Club", "The Big Six"—relate such adventures as might really happen to families of boys and girls, provided they have pluck, enterprise and a lively imagination.

Arthur Ransome (1884–1967) went to Rugby School and, after his schooldays, to Russia. In 1913 he published some delightful Russian folk tales, "Old Peter's Russian Tales" (one of which you will find on page 167 of this book). He stayed in Russia to report Russian affairs for British newspapers during the First World War and remained in Russia throughout the Revolution. He travelled widely and wrote books on his great hobbies—sailing and fishing. He was a scholar, a Doctor of Letters, and in 1953 was made a Commander of the British Empire. Here is a piece from "The Picts and the Martyrs" in which a country-bred youngster shows Dick and Dorothea how to catch trout with their hands. Don't let a gamekeeper catch you at it or you will be arrested as a poacher!

THEY climbed over a stile into the road and stood on the bridge looking at the river. There could be no doubt about the trout now. Dick counted seven, three in the smooth water close under the bridge, one behind a stone in midstream, another in front of the stone, another in a smooth patch a few yards higher up, and another in some rippled water. This one he could see only when it splashed up after a floating fly. Every now and then the splash came in the same place, and, by keeping his eyes on that place, he saw the trout itself, a head, a flash of silver, and then nothing but rippling water as before. . . .

"Hey!"

They looked up and saw the small boy, Jacky, hurrying towards them with an old rusty tin in his hand.

"Thought you said you couldn't come today," he said as he joined them on the bridge.

"We were going to do something else," said Dorothea, "but it's been put off."

"Lucky I happen to see you coming up

180

t'beck." Jacky crossed to the other side of the bridge and hove himself up so that he lay with his stomach on the parapet.

"There's a big yin down yonder."

The other two, who could look over the parapet without having to lie on the top of it, stood on each side of Jacky, watching the water flowing away from under the arch. They saw a sudden ring of ripples that drifted with the stream and was gone.

"That's him," said Jacky. He was scratching at the moss between the stones, and they saw him reach out a hand and let something slip from between his fingers.

"You'll see him now . . . now. . . . Nay, it's passed him. . . . See him get ut. . . ." There was a swirl in the water and they had all seen the flash as the big trout turned.

"What did you drop?" asked Dick.

"Wingy ant. . . . Here's another."

Again the big trout rose. Dick, too, began hunting.

"Will any insect do?"

"Ay. But ants is best or flies. Bracken clock's best of all when you can get 'em."

"What's a bracken clock?"

"June beetle," said Jacky. "Here's an ant. You take ut. You mun drop ut in t'reet spot."

The ant floated away a bit to the side of the place where the big trout was lying. It was taken by a much smaller one farther down the river.

"I don't see how you can catch them without a fishing rod," said Dick.

"We'll not catch yon," said Jacky. "You come wi' me. I'll show you."

He wriggled down from the parapet and led the way from the bridge along a cart track above the river. They passed a gate where the cart track turned through trees towards the white farm house. They kept on by a footpath close to the water and came to a place where a smaller stream came hurrying down from Kanchenjunga to join the bigger one.

Jacky stopped. He dropped on his stomach and wriggled to the edge of the stream. He pulled up his sleeve and, as it slipped down again, took his coat off and rolled up the sleeves of his shirt.

"You aren't going to catch them in your hands!" said Dick.

"Whisht!" said Jacky, and Dick and Dorothea, Picts with everything to learn, watched in silence.

With his head close to the ground, Jacky was dipping his arm under water. He wriggled a little nearer. His arm went in to the elbow. They saw one of his feet that had been moving stop as if it had been suddenly frozen. Half a minute went by like half an hour. Suddenly Jacky rolled sideways. His arm shot up out of the water and something flew through the air over the heads of the watchers. The next moment Jacky was on his feet searching the brambles where it had fallen. They saw his white arm plunge. They saw him bang something on a stone. He came back to them grinning with a small trout in his hand, and blood trickling from a scratch on his forearm.

"Get 'em away from t'water quick's you can," he said. "Or you'll lose 'em sure."

"But how did you catch it?" said Dick, looking at the trout.

"You've scratched your arm," said Dorothea.

"That's nowt," said Jacky, licked the scratch and began to explain how the thing was done.

"Easy," he said. "You've nobbut to guddle 'em."

"But how?" said Dick.

"Why don't they just swim away?" said Dorothea.

Jacky held the dead trout in his left hand as if it was swimming. He brought his right hand towards it, with all his fingers gently moving.

"You mun do it artful," he murmured. He looked away, as if to show that he could not see the trout that he was holding. The fingers of his right hand were never still for a moment, like weeds stirring in a stream. He shut his eyes. Dick and Doro-

181

thea saw the moving fingers coming nearer and nearer to the trout. They touched, but still kept moving till the tips of them had worked up from underneath and round the body of the trout. Suddenly the fingers closed. Jacky's left hand was empty. His right hand held the trout. He opened his eyes, looked at it as if surprised to see what he had caught, and grinned happily at his pupils.

"Got him!" he said.

"But why doesn't the trout just bolt?" said Dick.

"Nay," squeaked Jacky. "Put your hand in below him. You don't want to give him your fist to smell. Aye. Yon's t'place. . . . Is owt there? . . . Can you feel him?"

One of Dick's feet waved in the air.

"He's found one," said Dorothea.

"Keep guddling," urged Jacky. "Get your fingers round the thick of him. . . . Eh, but you lost a good yin there."

Dick's arm had plunged to the shoulder. A sharp V of ripples shot across the pool.

"I'm awfully sorry," said Dick.

"I'll catch another," said Jacky. "There's

"It's the guddling," said Jacky. "If you go for to take him he's gone. You mun keep guddling and guddling till you've your fingers round the middle of him. He'll lig quiet. But you mun keep guddling. And you mun keep clear of his tail or he's off. Let's see you get yin. There's aye a good yin under yon stone."

He put the dead trout in his tin, and warily moved back towards the beck, pointing out the stone he meant.

Dick rolled up his shirt sleeves and crawled to the edge of the stream.

plenty more fish in t'beck." He pushed his tin at Dorothea, and went quickly up the stream, stooping as he went.

"You've got your shirt wet," said Dorothea.

"Never mind," said Dick. "I felt him. I felt his fins waving and then I wasn't sure. I must have let my fingers stop. Come on. Let's see him catch another."

Jacky was already down on his stomach, clinging to a tree with his right hand, while his left reached down into the water that ran under it. He had lain there hardly more than a few seconds before he was scrambling to his feet with a small trout.

"Easy, that yin," he said.

He banged its head on a stone, dropped it into the tin that Dorothea was holding, and darted off to another favourite place. He changed his mind. "Nay, you get this yin," he said. "Right under t'bank."

"How do you know?" asked Dorothea.

"I've had many a trout from yon spot," said Jacky. "Catch yin today and there'll be another in t'same spot in t'morning."

This time he did not wait to watch, but hurried on up the side of the stream.

"I'm going to get this one," said Dick, and he did.

"Oh, well done," cried Dorothea, and Jacky came running back, to bang the trout on the head and put it with the others.

"I felt his fins tickling my hand. At least it wasn't his fins. It was the stir they made in the water. It's quite easy if only you can keep your fingers moving all the time."

"Plenty more likely spots along here," said Jacky. "I'm going higher up. See who can catch most."

Dick chose what he thought was a good place, but there was no trout in it. He tried again and after long careful tickling caught a small stick that he had made sure was a fish. Then he had two failures with trout that darted away before he had made up his mind that he had worked his fingers into position.

"Go on, Dot. You try. We've simply got to learn."

Dorothea, after several tries in places where there were no trout, caught one to her own surprise. "Jacky," she shouted, and got an answer from much further up the beck. Dick had failed again and yet again, and they hurried along to find Jacky, who was sitting by the stream with a row of seven small trout on the mossy bank beside him.

"Bang ut on t'neb," said Jacky jumping up when he saw that Dorothea had something leaping in her cupped hands. "You'll lose ut in t'beck if you don't look sharp. I

telled you," he added as the little fish fell on the bank, flapped its tail, and, before she could pick it up, had dropped with a splash into the water and was gone.

"Never mind," said Dorothea. "I say, you have got a lot."

"Nay, we want more nor that," said Jacky.

Tickling trout takes longer than telling about it and it was late in the day when they came back to the place where the small beck ran into the Amazon river, and laid out the catch. There were thirteen. "Lisle yins," said Jacky, "but them's the sweetest." Jacky himself had caught all but five, Dick had caught three, and Dorothea two.

"It isn't only the tickling," said Dick. "It's knowing the right places."

"Nay, you've done none so bad for a first asking," said Jacky. "It's a gey good supper, but they won't look so big when you've fried 'em."

Dorothea did not think they looked very big even before frying, but she did not say so.

Jacky began separating them into two lots, but he changed his mind and put them all together.

"I can get plenty more," he said. "You put 'em in my fry pan wi' a dollop of butter. Have you got any butter?"

"Yes."

"Swizzle it round the fry pan," said Jacky. "Real hot. Lay 'em in and turn 'em after. Turn 'em over when they start curling. Eat 'em as hot as you can lay your tongue to."

"Put them in just as they are?" asked Dorothea.

"Gut 'em," said Jacky. "I'll show you." He pulled out the huge pocket knife they had found when cleaning out the hut. One by one, he ripped up the little fish and scraped their insides out over the beck. "My mother rolls 'em in flour," he said. "But there's no need. Or you can make do wi' breadcrumbs."

"Jacky! JACKEE!"

"That'll be my supper," said Jacky. "And hens to feed and cows to milk and what all." He jumped up after putting the last of the little fish into the tin where they were packed like sardines, and gave the tin to Dorothea.

"Thanks most awfully," said Dorothea.

"Thank you very much," said Dick.

"Nay, I can do better for you nor that," said Jacky. "And happen I will before morning." And he bolted off towards the farmhouse.

A Boy's Song

Where the pools are bright and deep,
Where the grey trout lies asleep,
Up the river and o'er the lea—
That's the way for Billy and me.

Where the blackbird sings the latest,
Where the hawthorn blooms the sweetest,
Where the nestlings chirp and flee—
That's the way for Billy and me.

Where the mowers mow the cleanest,
Where the hay lies thick and greenest,
There to trace the homeward bee—
That's the way for Billy and me.

Where the hazel bank is steepest,
Where the shadow falls the deepest,
Where the clustering nuts fall free—
That's the way for Billy and me.

There let us walk, there let us play,
Through the meadows, among the hay.
Up the water, and o'er the lea—
That's the way for Billy and me.

JAMES HOGG

Where the shadow falls the deepest. . . .

185

A Day with the Goats

Johanna Spyri

Illustrated by Shirley Tourret

Johanna Spyri (1829–1901) was born in a village near Zurich, Switzerland. She began writing in order to earn money to help wounded refugees arriving in Zurich from the Franco-Prussian War (1870), and in 1880 "Heidi" was first published. It was an immediate success and has maintained its place in the affections of young readers ever since. An orphan, little Heidi is taken right up into the Alps to live in a cabin with her poor, but dignified, old grandfather. Just glance at the picture to see the real wonderland in which she finds herself, and then go on to share her first experience of life in the mountains.

HEIDI was awakened early by a shrill whistle. The yellow sun was shining through the window, full on her bed and on the hay beside it, turning it all to shimmering gold. Heidi looked about her in surprise, and wondered where she was.

Soon, she heard her grandfather's deep voice outside, and then she remembered. Now she was going to live with her grandfather up on the Alm, and not with old Ursel who was almost deaf as a post, and was always chilly. That was why she liked to sit by the kitchen hearth, or beside the stove in the other room, and, since she could not hear Heidi and liked to keep her in sight, the child had to stay with her, although the little room often stifled her and she longed to be outdoors. Heidi was very glad when she awoke in her new home and thought of everythng—all the new things she had seen yesterday, and what she would see again today, especially the goats, Swanli and Bearli.

Heidi jumped quickly out of bed and was soon dressed. She climbed down the ladder and ran out through the open door. There stood Peter, the goatherd, with his goats. Her grandfather was just opening the stable door to let Swanli and Bearli out to join the others. Heidi ran toward the old man to say good morning to him and the goats.

"Would you like to go with them up to the pasture?" he asked. There was nothing that Heidi would have liked better, and she danced up and down for joy at the very thought.

"Come here, commander of goats, and bring your haversack with you," grandfather called to Peter.

In great surprise, Peter followed him into the house and held out the little bag in which he carried his meagre dinner.

"Open it," was the old man's next order. He then put into it a huge slice of bread and an equally large piece of cheese. Peter looked on in round-eyed wonder, for the two pieces were each half again as large as those which had been put in for his dinner.

"There now, the bowl must go in," said the grandfather, "for the child cannot drink as you do, right from the goats themselves; she doesn't know how. You are to fill the bowl twice for her dinner, for she is going with you and will stay until you come back. Take good care of her, and don't let her fall over the cliffs; do you hear?"

Heidi now came running up and away they went, up the mountain, as merry as could be. The wind that had blown so hard all night had not left a cloud in the sky. From the deep blue overhead, the glorious sun poured its warmth and light down the mountain side until all the blue and yellow flowers opened wide their cups and smiled back at it in gratitude. Heidi ran hither and thither, shouting for joy; for here were whole troops of delicate pink primroses, and beyond them the ground was blue with gentians, while everywhere were nodding yellow rock roses dancing in the golden sunshine. So delighted was Heidi with all these nodding and shining blossoms that she quite forgot the goats, and even Peter himself. She ran far ahead, and then off to one side, for here she saw a sheen of red, and yonder a glimmer of yellow which she could not resist. And wherever she went she gathered great bunches of the gay blossoms and stowed them away in her apron, for she meant to take them home with her and set them all round in the hay up in her loft so that the place where she slept might be as beautiful as it was here.

Poor Peter had to look in every direction at once today, and those round eyes of his, that were never very quick, had more to do than they could well manage, for the goats followed Heidi's example. They ran hither and thither, and he had to whistle and call and swing his long stick to get all the truants into line again.

"Where have you gone now, Heidi?" he shouted rather angrily.

"Here," came the answer from somewhere out of sight, for Heidi was sitting on the ground behind a little knoll that was quite covered with blossoming prunelles. The air was filled with their sweet odour and as Heidi sat among the flowers drinking in their perfume in deep breaths, she thought she had never before smelled anything half so delightful.

"Come on," cried Peter again. "Remember, you are not to fall down over the cliffs; your grandfather forbade it."

"Where are the cliffs?" asked Heidi without, however, showing any intention of rising, for the sweet fragrance of the flowers seemed more delicious to her with every breath she drew.

"Up yonder, away up yonder. But we have still a long way before us, so come on. Up there on the highest cliff of all the old eagle sits and screams."

That brought Heidi to her feet, and she ran after Peter as fast as she could, with her apron full of flowers.

"You have enough now," said he as the two were again clambering upward together; "else you'll be stopping all along the way, and besides, if you take them all today there'll be none left for tomorrow."

The last reason appealed to Heidi. Moreover, her apron was already so full of flowers there was little room for more, and tomorrow she would come again to see them. So she trudged along at Peter's side : and the goats, too, were more tractable, for they sniffed from afar the tempting fragrance of the herbs that awaited them on the upper pastures and so climbed on without delay.

The grazing place where Peter usually made a halt with his goats, and set up his quarters for the day, lay at the foot of great cliffs, whose base was green with bushes and scrub-pines, but whose jagged peaks towered bare and bleak into the heavens. On one side the pasture lands fell away in sheer precipices to the valley below, and the grandfather's warning with regard to them was not without reason.

When Peter reached this place he laid

aside his bag and stowed it carefully away in a little hollow where the wind, which often came in rude and sudden gusts up here, could not carry it off; for he had no wish to see his precious bag go rolling down the mountain. Then he stretched himself out on the warm and sunny ground, for he felt the need of rest after the morning's climb.

Meanwhile Heidi had untied her apron and, with all the flowers it contained, rolled it into a neat, tight little bundle, and tucked it away for safekeeping next the lunch bag. Then she sat down beside the prostrate Peter and looked about her. Far below lay the valley bathed in the glorious morning sunshine; opposite her a great, wide snowfield stretched upward, rising higher and higher until it seemed to touch the dark blue sky beyond; to the left of it towered a gigantic mass of rocks, on either side of which stood a great rocky pillar whose bare and jagged peaks pierced the blue above, and seemed to Heidi to be looking down at her, gravely and solemnly. The child sat as still as a mouse, gazing about her; there was a deep silence all around, only the wind whispered very gently among the shimmering rock roses and delicate bluebells that everywhere nodded gaily on their slender stems. Peter had fallen asleep after his exertions, and the goats were climbing about among the bushes farther up. As she drank in the golden sunshine, the pure fresh air and the delicate perfume of the flowers, she wished for nothing better than to stay where she was forever, for she had never been so happy in all her life before.

In this way a long time passed and Heidi looked so long and steadily at the high mountain peaks, that at length they seemed all to have faces and to be looking back at her like good old friends.

Suddenly she heard loud, shrill cries above her in the air, and looking up beheld the largest bird she had ever seen, poised above her on wide outstretched wings; then it soared about in great circles, returning again and again to a point just over her head.

"Peter, Peter, wake up!" cried Heidi as

loud as she could. "See, the eagle has come! See, there, there!"

Peter roused himself at her cry of alarm, and the two children watched the bird as it rose higher and higher into the blue dome above and finally vanished behind the grey cliffs.

"Where has he gone?" asked Heidi, whose eyes had followed the bird with the deepest interest.

"Home, to his nest," was Peter's answer.

"Is his home away up yonder? Oh, how lovely to live so high up. Why does he scream so?" Heidi continued.

"Because he must," was Peter's explanation.

"Let us climb up there and see where he lives," proposed Heidi.

"Oh, oh, oh," Peter broke forth, each exclamation marked by a tone of greater disapproval. "Why, even the goats can't get up there, and your grandfather said you were not to fall over the cliffs."

And now Peter set up such a tremendous shouting and whistling that Heidi wondered what was going to happen. But the goats must have understood it well enough, for they came jumping and running down the mountain side, one after the other, until the whole flock was assembled on the green pasture, some nibbling away at the juicy stalks, others skipping hither and thither, while still others tried their horns on one another in playful combat.

Heidi had jumped to her feet and was soon in the midst of them, for to her it was a new and highly amusing sight to see the little creatures skip about and carry on their merry antics. She ran from one to the other, getting personally acquainted with each in turn, for no two were alike, each one having its own peculiar appearance and ways.

Meanwhile Peter had fetched his bag and taken out the two slices of bread and two pieces of cheese, and laid them in a neat square on the grass, the two larger pieces on Heidi's side, the small ones on his

own; for he knew very well to whom each one belonged. Then, taking the bowl, he milked it full of sweet, fresh milk from Swanli, and set it in the middle of the square. Then he called Heidi, but she did

not obey his call as promptly as had the goats, for she was so delighted and amused by the varied antics of her new playfellows that she could see and hear nothing else.

But Peter knew how to make himself heard; he shouted until the cliffs resounded, and presently Heidi appeared and was so pleased with the inviting-looking table that she danced up and down with glee.

"Stop your jumping; it is time to eat," said Peter. "Sit down, and begin."

Heidi sat down.

"Is the milk for me?" she asked with another glance of undisguised admiration at the beautiful square with its central point of interest.

"Yes," answered Peter; "and the two big pieces are yours too; and when you have emptied your bowl, I am to fill it again for you from Swanli, and then it will be my turn."

"And from which goat will you get your milk?" Heidi now wanted to know.

"From my own goat, Snaili. Now do begin to eat," urged Peter again.

Heidi began with the milk, and no sooner had she set down the empty bowl than Peter got up and filled it a second time. In the meantime Heidi had broken off a part of her bread, and now handed Peter all that was left; and even this was a much larger slice than his own which, together with his cheese, was fast disappearing. Putting the whole of her large piece of cheese with the bread, she said, "You can have that; I have had enough."

Peter started and stared at her in speechless amazement. Never in his life had he had enough to eat and something left over to give away. He hesitated a momont, for he could not believe that Heidi was in earnest; but she did not withdraw her hand, and when Peter did not take what she offered, she laid it on his knee. Then he saw that she meant what she said, and seizing the welcome gift, he nodded his thanks and approval as he fell to upon the heartiest meal he had ever had in his whole career as goatherd. Meanwhile Heidi watched the goats.

"What are all their names, Peter?" she asked.

Now this was something that Peter knew very well, and perhaps it was easier for him to carry it in his head because there was little else there to crowd it out. So he began and, without hesitating once, named them all, one after the other, and pointed them out as he did so. Heidi paid close attention, and before long she knew each goat from its fellows and could call it by name; for each one had its own peculiarities, easily remembered by anyone who looked at the little creatures carefully, and this Heidi did.

There was big Turk with his strong horns which he was always so ready to use against the others, so that most of them ran away at his approach, and would have nothing to do with their rough comrade. The only one that never retreated before him was the valiant little Goldfinch, a slender, nimble fellow who often ran at him three or four times, one after the other, and with such speed and energy that the big Turk stopped short in astonishment

and forgot to renew his attack; for there stood Goldfinch ready to return it with his sharp little horns.

There was little white Snowhopli, who was always bleating so plaintively that Heidi had to run to the little creature a number of times attempting to comfort it by taking its head in her arms. Now the child was again at the little goat's side, for she could not resist the tender young voice. Putting her arms around the little animal's neck, she asked very sympathetically, "What is the matter, Snowhopli? Why are you always crying so pitifully?"

The goat nestled confidingly against the child and ceased complaining.

From his seat on the grass Peter called out in a voice somewhat choked at times, for he still had much to chew and swallow, "Snowhopli cries so because the old one

doesn't come up with us any more; she was sold to someone in Mayenfeld day before yesterday, and since then she doesn't come to the pasture with us."

"Who is the old one?" called Heidi in return.

"Pooh! The mother, to be sure," was Peter's scornful reply.

"Where is the grandmother?" Heidi called again.

"Hasn't any."

"Where is the grandfather?"

"Hasn't any."

"Oh, you poor little Snowhopli," cried Heidi as she hugged the little creature close to her; "but you needn't cry any more, for I am coming up with you every day now, and then you will not be so lonely, and when something troubles you, you can run to me."

Snowhopli rubbed her head contentedly against Heidi's shoulder and did not bleat any more. Peter had finished his dinner by this time and now joined his flock and

was full length on the ground again, "Peter, the prettiest of them all are Swanli and Bearli."

"I know that well enough," was the reply; "the Alm-Uncle washes and brushes them, and gives them salt, and they have the best stable."

Suddenly Peter sprang to his feet and

Heidi, who was again earnestly watching the goats.

Of all the flock, the two prettiest and best-kept by far were Swanli and Bearli. They had a superior air, too, and kept to themselves most of the time, especially avoiding the big Turk, whom they treated with great scorn.

The goats were climbing upward again to the bushes they liked best, each one in his own peculiar way—some running on, heedless of everything; others prudently searching for all that was good along the way, while the big Turk tried his horns on one or the other of his companions. Swanli and Bearli climbed gracefully and lightly, and were quick to find the best bushes, from which they then nibbled the leaves in a skilful and dainty fashion. With her hands clasped behind her, Heidi stood watching all this.

"Peter," said she to her companion, who

ran leaping after the goats, Heidi following him at top speed, for she knew that something must be happening and she wanted to be in on it. Peter rushed through the flock toward the side where the pasture land ended abruptly in a high and rocky precipice over which a heedless goat, venturing too near the edge, might easily fall and break its legs. Peter had seen bold little Goldfinch running merrily toward this dangerous point, and the boy reached him none too soon, for the little fellow was about to leap toward the edge of the precipice. Peter was just about to seize him, when he tripped and fell to the ground, but managed to catch the animal's leg. Goldfinch did not like to be held by the leg. He bleated with anger and surprise at this rude interruption of his merry little excursion and he struggled stubbornly to get loose. Peter screamed for Heidi to come and help him, for he could not get up, and was in danger of pulling the poor animal's leg off. Heidi instantly understood the peril that threatened. As quick as a flash she pulled a handful of tempting herbs and held them under the goat's nose, saying coaxingly, "Come, come, Goldfinch, you must be sensible. Don't you see that you might fall down there and break your leg, and that would hurt dreadfully."

The little creature turned at once and very contentedly began to nibble the herbs that the child held out to him. Meanwhile Peter got on his feet again, and slipped his hand through the cord that Goldfinch wore round his neck, and on which hung his little bell. Heidi caught hold of it from the other side, and in this way the two children led the runaway back to where his companions were peacefully grazing.

When Peter had him safely back, he raised his long stick to punish him with a sound whipping. Goldfinch drew back timidly, for he knew what was coming. But Heidi cried out, "No, no, Peter! You must not strike him! See how frightened he is."

"He deserves it," snarled Peter angrily, and was just going to strike, when Heidi caught him by the arm and cried indignantly, "You shall not strike him; it will hurt him! Let him go!"

Peter looked with astonishment at the imperious little girl, with her black flashing eyes and involuntarily dropped his stick.

"Well then, he may go if you will give me some of your cheese again tomorrow," said Peter, yielding, but at the same time trying to get something to make up to him for the fright he had suffered.

"You may have it all—the whole piece—tomorrow and every day; I do not need it," was Heidi's ready assent. "And I will give you some of my bread, too; a piece as big as the one today; but then you must promise never to strike Goldfinch, never; nor Snowhopli, nor any of the goats."

"It's all one to me," was the reply, which was Peter's way of giving his promise. Then he let the little culprit go, and away

went Goldfinch, leaping back to the flock with many a merry caper.

Thus the day slipped by unnoticed, and already the sun was nearing the tops of the western mountains. Heidi was sitting very quietly on the ground looking at the bluebells and tender rock roses glistening in the golden evening sunshine; even the grass had caught the golden light, and the cliffs above were beginning to gleam and glow, when suddenly the child sprang to her feet, crying, "Peter! See! The fire, the fire, Peter! All the mountains are in flames, and the big snowfield yonder is burning, and the sky! Oh, look, look! The great rocks are all red! Oh, the beautiful burning snow! Peter, get up! See, the fire has reached the eagle's nest! Oh, do look at the rocks! Look at the pine trees! Everything, everything is on fire!"

"It is always so," said Peter quite unmoved as he whittled away at his stick; "but it's no fire."

"What is it, then?" asked Heidi eagerly, and ran hither and thither to look in every direction, for she could not see enough, it was so beautiful on every side.

"What is it, then, Peter? What is it?" she asked again.

"Oh, it just comes so of itself," was Peter's explanation.

"Oh, see, see!" cried Heidi in great excitement; "all the mountains are turning rosy-red! Look at the one with the snow, and that one with the high, pointed cliffs! What are their names, Peter? What are their names?"

"Mountains have no names," was the reply.

"Oh, how beautiful! Look at the pink snow!

"And oh, see all the many, many roses up yonder on the rocks! Oh, now they are turning grey! Oh, oh! Now it is all fading out! Now it is all gone, Peter!" And Heidi sat down on the grass looking as disconsolate as though the world were coming to an end.

"Tomorrow it will be so again," said

"Oh, see, see!" cried Heidi in great excitement; "all the mountains are turning rosy-red!
Look at the one with the snow, and that one with the high, pointed cliffs!"
From "A Day with the Goats"

"And yet you incessantly stand on your head – do you think, at your age, it is right?"
From "Father William"

Down she ran to tell her grandfather all about her wonderful day.

Peter. "Come, get up; we must go home now." The boy shouted and whistled for his goats, and then the whole company started homeward.

"Will it be so every day, every day that we come up here?" asked Heidi in eager hope of an assuring answer as she trudged along at Peter's side.

"Usually," was the answer.

"But tomorrow? Are you sure it will be so tomorrow?" she wanted to know.

"Yes, yes; tomorrow, of course!" Peter assured her, whereupon Heidi's good spirits returned.

But she had seen so much that was new, and had so many things to think about, that she was quite silent all the way down to her grandfather's hut. There they saw the old man sitting near his cabin-door where he had set a bench so that it faced the side of the mountain down which the goats usually came. Heidi ran toward him, with Swanli and Bearli close behind her, for the goats knew their master and their stable well.

As Peter went on with his goats he called back to Heidi, "Good night! Come again tomorrow," for he had good reason for wanting her to go again.

Heidi ran after him and gave him her hand in assurance that she would certainly go with him in the morning. Then she darted into the midst of the departing flock and throwing her arms around Snowhopli's neck, said tenderly, "Sleep well, Snowhopli, and remember that I am going with you tomorrow, and that you must never bleat so sadly again."

Snowhopli looked gratefully at the little girl, and then ran merrily after the other goats.

Heidi ran back to her grandfather, and could not wait until she had reached him to call out, "Oh, grandfather, it was so beautiful! The fire, and the roses on the rocks, and all the blue and yellow flowers! And see what I have brought you!" She undid her tightly folded apron and emptied her whole store of flowers on the ground at her grandfather's feet.

But how the poor little things looked! Heidi hardly recognized them, for they were as dry as hay, and not one little cup was open.

"Oh, grandfather! What ails them?" cried Heidi, very much shocked. "They weren't so when I picked them. What makes them look so now?"

"They were made to live out in the sunshine, and not to be folded up in a little girl's apron," said her grandfather.

"Oh, what a pity! I will never bring any

193

more home with me. But grandfather, why does the eagle scream so?" was Heidi's next eager question.

"Now you must get into the tub while I go to the stable to get some milk, and then we will go in and have our supper, and while we are eating I will tell you."

When all this was done, and Heidi was sitting on her high stool beside her grandfather, her bowl of milk before her, she asked her question again. "Why does the eagle scream down at us so, grandfather?"

"He jeers at the people down below because they live crowded together in villages and vex one another. He cries out at them scornfully: 'If you would leave one another, and each one go his own way and live high upon a mountain top, as I do, you would be happier!'"

Her grandfather said this in so loud and fierce a tone that Heidi seemed to hear the eagle's wild scream once more.

"Why do the mountains have no names, grandfather?" was her next question.

"They have names," was the reply; "and if you will describe one so that I can recognize it, I will tell you what it is called."

Heidi now described the rocky peak with the towering cliffs on either side, at which her grandfather nodded approvingly, and said, "I know that one; its name is Falkniss. Did you see any other?"

Heidi then described the mountain with the great snowfield that had suddenly glowed like fire, then turned rosy-red, and at last had grown pale and grey.

"I recognize that one, too," said her grandfather; "it is Casaplana. So you like to go up to the pasture, do you?"

Heidi now told him all that had happened during the day—how beautiful it had been, especially the fire in the evening, and she wanted her grandfather to tell her where it had come from, for Peter had not known.

"It is the sun that does that," explained her grandfather. "You see, when he says good night to the mountains he sends them his brightest rays to remember him by until he comes again in the morning."

This pleased Heidi, and she could hardly wait for the coming of another day when she could go up to the pasture again and watch the sun say good night to the mountains.

The Englishman

I met a sailor in the woods,
  A silver ring wore he,
His hair hung black, his eyes shone blue,
  And thus he said to me:

"What country, say, of this round earth,
  What shore of what salt sea,
Be this, my son, I wander in,
  And looks so strange to me?"

Says I, "O foreign sailorman,
  In England now you be,
This is her wood, and there her sky,
  And that her roaring sea."

He lifts his voice yet louder,
  "What smell be this," says he,
"My nose on the sharp morning air
  Snuffs up so greedily?"

Says I, "It is wild roses
  Do smell so winsomely,
And winy briar, too," says I,
  "That in these thickets be."

"And oh!" says he, "what leetle bird
  Is singing in yon high tree,
So every shrill and long-drawn note
  Like bubbles breaks in me?"

Says I, "It is the mavis
  That perches in the tree,
And sings so shrill, and sings so sweet,
  When dawn comes up the sea."

At which he fell a-musing,
  And fixed his eye on me,
As one alone 'twixt light and dark
  A spirit thinks to see.

"England!" he whispers soft and harsh,
  "England!" repeated he,
"And briar, and rose, and mavis,
  A-singing in yon high tree.

"Ye speak me true, my leetle son,
  So—so, it came to me,
A-drifting landwards on a spar,
  And grey dawn on the sea.

"Ay, ay, I could not be mistook;
  I knew them leafy trees,
I knew that land so witchery sweet,
  And that old noise of seas.

"Though here I've sailed a score of years,
  And heard 'em, dream or wake,
Lap small and hollow 'gainst my cheek,
  On sand and coral break;

" 'Yet now,' my leetle son, says I,
  A-drifting on the wave,
'That land I see so safe and green
  Is England, I believe.

" 'And that there wood is English wood,
  And this here cruel sea,
The selfsame old blue ocean
  Years gone remembers me,

" 'A-sitting with my bread and butter
  Down behind yon chitterin' mill;
And this same Marinere'—(that's me),
  'Is that same leetle Will!—

" 'That very same wee leetle Will
  Eating his bread and butter there,
A-looking on the broad blue sea
  Betwixt his yaller hair!'

"And here be I, my son, throwed up
  Like corpses from the sea,
Ships, stars, winds, tempests, pirates past,
  Yet leetle Will I be!"

He said no more, that sailorman,
  But in a reverie
Stared like the figure of a ship
  With painted eyes to sea.

WALTER DE LA MARE

The Cat
that walked by Himself
Rudyard Kipling

Illustrated by the Author and Shirley Tourret

Born in Bombay, the son of the Principal of the newly founded British School of Art, Rudyard Kipling (1865–1936) was educated at an unconventional boarding school in Devon (which gave him the themes and background for his school stories, "Stalky and Co."). He returned to India to work as a journalist on a newspaper, and began to write the collections of short stories, including "Plain Tales from the Hill", that brought him fame, about the life of the British in India which he had come to know so well.

Another side of Kipling, however, was his fondness for children and his ability to tell them stories. His two "Jungle Books", containing the Mowgli stories, are among the very best of animal stories, while his even more fanciful "Just So Stories" (from which comes "The Cat that Walked by Himself") has some very funny explanations about how certain things happened in the early history of the world. Believe it or not, they happened "just so"!

Hear and attend and listen; for this befell and behappened and became and was, O my Best Beloved, when the Tame animals were wild. The Dog was wild, and the Horse was wild, and the Cow was wild, and the Sheep was wild, and the Pig was wild—as wild as wild could be—and they walked in the Wet Wild Woods by their wild lones. But the wildest of all the wild animals was the Cat. He walked by himself, and all places were alike to him.

Of course the Man was wild too. He was dreadfully wild. He didn't even begin to be tame till he met the Woman, and she told him that she did not like living in his wild ways. She picked out a nice dry Cave, instead of a heap of wet leaves, to lie down in; and she strewed clean sand on the floor; and she lit a nice fire of wood at the back of the Cave; and she hung a dried wild-horse skin, tail-down, across the opening of the Cave; and she said, "Wipe your feet, dear, when you come in, and now we'll keep house."

That night, Best Beloved, they ate wild sheep roasted on the hot stones, and flavoured with wild garlic and wild pepper; and wild duck stuffed with wild rice and wild fenugreek and wild coriander; and marrow-bones of wild oxen; and wild cherries, and wild grenadillas. Then the Man went to sleep in front of the fire ever so happy; but the Woman sat up, combing her hair. She took the bone of the shoulder of mutton—the big flat blade-bone—and she looked at the wonderful marks on it, and she threw more wood on the fire, and she made a Magic. She made the First Singing Magic in the world.

Out in the Wet Wild Woods all the wild animals gathered together where they could see the light of the fire a long way off, and they wondered what it meant.

Then Wild Horse stamped with his wild foot and said, "O my Friends and O my Enemies, why have the Man and the Woman made that great light in that great Cave, and what harm will it do us?"

Wild Dog lifted up his wild nose and smelled the smell of the roast mutton, and said, Cave. But when he had gone a little way the Cat said to himself, "All places are alike to me. Why should I not go too and see and look and come away at my own liking?" So he slipped after Wild Dog softly, very softly, and hid himself where he could hear everything.

"I am the cat who walks by himself, and all places are alike to me. I will not come."

said, "I will go up and see and look, and say; for I think it is good. Cat, come with me."

"Nenni!" said the Cat. "I am the Cat who walks by himself, and all places are alike to me. I will not come."

"Then we can never be friends again," said Wild Dog, and he trotted off to the When Wild Dog reached the mouth of the Cave he lifted up the dried horse-skin with his nose and sniffed the beautiful smell of the roast mutton, and the Woman, looking at the blade-bone, heard him, and laughed, and said, "Here comes the first. Wild Thing out of the Wild Woods, what do you want?"

Wild Dog said, "O my Enemy and Wife of my Enemy, what is this that smells so good in the Wild Woods?"

Then the Woman picked up a roasted mutton-bone and threw it to Wild Dog, and said, "Wild Thing out of the Wild Woods, taste and try." Wild Dog gnawed the bone, and it was more delicious than anything he had ever tasted, and he said,

"O my Enemy and Wife of my Enemy, give me another."

The Woman said, "Wild Thing out of the Wild Woods, help my Man to hunt through the day and guard this Cave at night, and I will give you as many roast bones as you need."

"Ah!" said the Cat, listening. "This is a very wise Woman, but she is not so wise as I am."

Wild Dog crawled into the Cave and laid his head on the Woman's lap, and said, "O my Friend and Wife of my Friend, I will help your Man to hunt through the day, and at night I will guard your Cave."

"Ah!" said the Cat, listening. "That is a very foolish Dog." And he went back through the Wet Wild Woods waving his wild tail, and walking by his wild lone. But he never told anybody.

When the Man waked up he said, "What is Wild Dog doing here?" And the Woman said, "His name is not Wild Dog any more, but the First Friend, because he will be our friend for always and always and always. Take him with you when you go hunting."

Next night the Woman cut great green armfuls of fresh grass from the water-meadows, and dried it before the fire, so that it smelt like new-mown hay, and she sat at the mouth of the Cave and plaited a halter out of horse-hide, and she looked at the shoulder-of-mutton bone—at the big broad blade-bone—and she made a Magic. She made the Second Singing Magic in the world.

Out in the Wild Woods all the wild animals wondered what had happened to Wild Dog, and at last Wild Horse stamped with his foot and said, "I will go and see and say why Wild Dog has not returned. Cat, come with me."

"Nenni," said the Cat. "I am the Cat who walks by himself, and all places are alike to me. I will not come." But all the same he followed Wild Horse softly, very softly, and hid himself where he could hear everything.

When the Woman heard Wild Horse tripping and stumbling on his long mane, she laughed and said, "Here comes the second. Wild Thing out of the Wild Woods, what do you want?"

Wild Horse said, "O my Enemy and Wife of my Enemy, where is Wild Dog?"

The Woman laughed, and picked up the blade-bone and looked at it, and said, "Wild Thing out of the Wild Woods, you did not come here for Wild Dog, but for the sake of this good grass."

And Wild Horse, tripping and stumbling on his long mane, said, "That is true; give it me to eat."

The Woman said, "Wild Thing out of the Wild Woods, bend your wild head and wear what I give you, and you shall eat the wonderful grass three times a day."

"Ah!" said the Cat, listening. "This is a clever Woman, but she is not so clever as I am."

Wild Horse bent his wild head, and the Woman slipped the plaited-hide halter over it, and Wild Horse breathed on the Woman's feet and said, "O my Mistress, and Wife of my Master, I will be your servant for the sake of the wonderful grass."

"Ah!" said the Cat, listening. "That is a very foolish Horse." And he went back through the Wet Wild Woods, waving his wild tail and walking by his wild lone. But he never told anybody.

When the Man and the Dog came back from the hunting, the Man said, "What is Wild Horse doing here?" And the Woman

said, "His name is not Wild Horse any more, but the First Servant, because he will carry us from place to place for always and always and always. Ride on his back when you go hunting."

Next day, holding her wild head high that her wild horns should not catch in the wild trees, Wild Cow came up to the Cave, and the Cat followed, and hid himself just the same as before; and everything happened just the same as before; and the cat said the same things as before; and when Wild Cow had promised to give her milk to the Woman every day in exchange for the wonderful grass, the Cat went back through the Wet Wild

Woods waving his wild tail and walking by his wild lone, just the same as before. But he never told anybody. And when the Man and the Horse and the Dog came home from hunting and asked the same questions same as before, the Woman said, "Her name is not Wild Cow any more, but the Giver of Good Food. She will give us the warm white milk for always and always and always, and I will take care

of her while you and the First Friend and the First Servant go hunting."

Next day the Cat waited to see if any other Wild Thing would go up to the Cave, but no one moved in the Wet Wild Woods, so the Cat walked there by himself; and he saw the Woman milking the Cow, and he saw the light of the fire in the Cave, and he smelt the smell of the warm white milk.

Cat said, "O my Enemy and Wife of my Enemy, where did Wild Cow go?"

The Woman laughed and said, "Wild Thing out of the Wild Woods, go back to the Woods again, for I have braided up my hair, and I have put away the magic blade-bone, and we have no more need of either friends or servants in our Cave."

Cat said, "I am not a friend, and I am not a servant. I am the Cat who walks by himself, and I wish to come into your Cave."

Woman said, "Then why did you not come with First Friend on the first night?" Cat grew very angry and said, "Has Wild Dog told tales of me?"

Then the Woman laughed and said, "You are the Cat who walks by himself, and all places are alike to you. You are neither a friend nor a servant. You have said it yourself. Go away and walk by yourself in all places alike."

Then Cat pretended to be sorry and said, "Must I never come into the Cave? Must I never sit by the warm fire? Must I never drink the warm white-milk? You are very wise and very beautiful. You should not be cruel even to a Cat."

Woman said, "I knew I was wise, but I did not know I was beautiful. So I will make a bargain with you. If ever I say one word in your praise, you may come into the Cave."

"And if you say two words in my praise?" said the Cat.

"I never shall," said the Woman, "but if I say two words in your praise, you may sit by the fire in the Cave."

"And if you say three words?" said the Cat.

"I never shall," said the Woman, "but if I say three words in your praise, you may drink the warm white milk three times a day for always and always and always."

Then the Cat arched his back and said, "Now let the Curtain at the mouth of the Cave, and the Fire at the back of the Cave, and the Milk-pots that stand beside the Fire, remember what my Enemy and the Wife of my Enemy has said." And he went away through the Wet Wild Woods waving his wild tail and walking by his wild lone.

That night when the Man and the Horse and the Dog came home from hunting, the Woman did not tell them of the bargain that she had made with the Cat, because she was afraid that they might not like it.

Cat went far and far away and hid himself in the Wet Wild Woods by his wild lone for a long time till the Woman forgot all about him. Only the Bat—the little upside-down Bat—that hung inside the Cave knew where Cat hid; and every evening Bat would fly to Cat with news of what was happening.

One evening Bat said, "There is a Baby in the Cave. He is new and pink and fat and small, and the Woman is very fond of him."

"Ah," said the Cat, listening, "but what is the Baby fond of?"

"He is fond of things that are soft and tickle," said the Bat. "He is fond of warm things to hold in his arms when he goes to sleep. He is fond of being played with. He is fond of all those things."

"Ah," said the Cat, listening, "then my time has come."

Next night Cat walked through the Wet Wild Woods and hid very near the Cave till morning-time, and Man and Dog and Horse went hunting. The Woman was busy cooking that morning, and the Baby cried and interrupted. So she carried him outside the Cave and gave him a handful of pebbles to play with. But still the Baby cried.

Then the Cat put out his paddy paw and patted the Baby on the cheek, and it cooed; and the Cat rubbed against its fat knees and tickled it under its fat chin with his tail. And the Baby laughed; and the Woman heard him and smiled.

Then the Bat—the little upside-down Bat—that hung in the mouth of the Cave said, "O my Hostess and Wife of my Host and Mother of my Host's Son, a Wild Thing from the Wild Woods is most beautifully playing with your Baby."

"A blessing on that Wild Thing whoever

he may be," said the Woman, straightening her back, "for I was a busy woman this morning and he has done me a service."

That very minute and second, Best Beloved, the dried horse-skin Curtain that was stretched tail-down at the mouth of the Cave fell down—*woosh!*—because it remembered the bargain she had made with the Cat; and when the Woman went to pick it up—lo and behold!—the Cat was sitting quite comfy inside the Cave.

"O my Enemy and Wife of my Enemy and Mother of my Enemy," said the Cat, "it is I: for you have spoken a word in my praise, and now I can sit within the Cave for always and always and always. But still I am the Cat who walks by himself, and all places are alike to me."

The Woman was very angry, and shut her lips tight and took up her spinning-wheel and began to spin.

But the Baby cried because the Cat had gone away, and the Woman could not hush it, for it struggled and kicked and grew black in the face.

"O my Enemy and Wife of my Enemy and Mother of my Enemy," said the Cat,

"take a strand of the thread that you are spinning and tie it to your spindle-whorl and drag it along the floor, and I will show you a Magic that shall make your Baby laugh as loudly as he is now crying."

"I will do so," said the Woman, "because I am at my wits' end; but I will not thank you for it."

She tied the thread to the little clay spindle-whorl and drew it across the floor, and the Cat ran after it and patted it with his paws and rolled head over heels, and tossed it backward over his shoulder and chased it between his hind-legs and pretended to lose it, and pounced down upon it again, till the Baby laughed as loudly as it had been crying, and scrambled after the Cat and frolicked all over the Cave till it grew tired and settled down to sleep with the Cat in its arms.

"Now," said Cat, "I will sing the Baby a song that shall keep him asleep for an hour." And he began to purr, loud and low, low and loud, till the Baby fell fast asleep. The Woman smiled as she looked down upon the two of them, and said, "That was wonderfully done. No question but you are very clever, O Cat."

That very minute and second, Best Beloved, the smoke of the Fire at the back of the Cave came down in clouds from the roof—*puff!*—because it remembered the bargain she had made with the Cat; and when it had cleared away—lo and behold!—the Cat was sitting quite comfy close to the fire.

"O my Enemy and Wife of my Enemy and Mother of my Enemy," said the Cat, "it is I: for you have spoken a second word in my praise, and now I can sit by the warm fire at the back of the Cave for always and always and always. But still I am the Cat who walks by himself, and all places are alike to me."

Then the Woman was very very angry, and let down her hair and put more wood on the fire and brought out the broad blade-bone of the shoulder of mutton and began to make a Magic that should prevent her from saying a third word in praise of the Cat. It was not a Singing Magic, Best Beloved, it was a Still Magic; and by and by the Cave grew so still that a little wee-wee mouse crept out of a corner and ran across the floor.

"O my Enemy and Wife of my Enemy

and Mother of my Enemy," said the Cat, "is that little mouse part of your Magic?"

"Ouh! Chee! No indeed!" said the Woman, and she dropped the blade-bone and jumped upon the footstool in front of the fire and braided up her hair very quick for fear that the mouse should run up it.

"Ah," said the Cat, watching, "then the mouse will do me no harm if I eat it?"

"No," said the Woman, braiding up her hair, "eat it quickly and I will ever be grateful to you."

Cat made one jump and caught the little mouse, and the Woman said, "A hundred thanks. Even the First Friend is not quick enough to catch little mice as you have done. You must be very wise."

That very moment and second, O Best Beloved, the Milk-pot that stood by the fire cracked in two pieces—*ffft!*—because it remembered the bargain she had made with the Cat; and when the Woman jumped down from the footstool—lo and behold!—the Cat was lapping up the warm white milk that lay in one of the broken pieces.

"O my Enemy and Wife of my Enemy and Mother of my Enemy," said the Cat, "it is I: for you have spoken three words in my praise, and now I can drink the warm white milk three times a day for always and always and always. But *still* I am the Cat who walks by himself, and all places are alike to me."

Then the Woman laughed and set the Cat a bowl of the warm white milk and said, "O Cat, you are as clever as a man, but remember that your bargain was not made with the Man or the Dog, and I do not know what they will do when they come home."

"What is that to me?" said the Cat. "If I have my place in the Cave by the fire and my warm white milk three times a day I do not care what the Man or the Dog can do."

That evening when the Man and the Dog came into the Cave, the Woman told them all the story of the bargain, while the Cat sat by the fire and smiled. Then the Man said, "Yes, but he has not made a bargain, with *me* or with all proper Men after me." Then he took off his two leather boots and he took up his little stone axe (that makes three) and he fetched a piece of wood and a hatchet (that is five altogether), and he set them out in a row and he said, "Now we will make *our* bargain. If you do not catch mice when you are in the Cave for always and always and always, I will throw these five things at you whenever I see you, and so shall all proper Men do after me."

"Ah," said the Woman, listening, "this is a very clever Cat, but he is not so clever as my Man."

The Cat counted the five things (and they looked very knobby) and he said, "I will catch mice when I am in the Cave for always and always and always; but *still* I am the Cat who walks by himself, and all places are alike to me."

"Not when I am near," said the Man. "If you had not said that last I would have put all these things away for always and always and always; but now I am going to throw my two boots and my little stone axe (that makes three) at you whenever I meet you. And so shall all proper Men do after me!"

Then the Dog said, "Wait a minute. He has not made a bargain with *me* or with all proper Dogs after me." And he showed his teeth and said "If you are not kind to the Baby while I am in the Cave for always and always and always, I will hunt you till I catch you, and when I catch you I will

you had not said that last I would have shut my mouth for always and always and always; but *now* I am going to hunt you up a tree whenever I meet you. And so shall all proper Dogs do after me."

Then the Man threw his two boots and his little stone axe (that makes three) at the Cat, and the Cat ran out of the Cave and the Dog chased him up a tree; and from that day to this, Best Beloved, three proper Men out of five will always throw things at a Cat whenever they meet him, and all proper Dogs will chase him up a tree. But the Cat keeps his side of the bargain too. He will kill mice, and he will be kind to Babies when he is in the house, just as long as they do not pull his tail too hard. But when he has done that, and between times, and when the moon gets up and night comes, he is the Cat that walks by himself, and all places are alike to him. Then he goes out to the Wet Wild Woods or up the Wet Wild Trees or on the Wet Wild Roofs, waving his wild tail and walking by his wild lone.

bite you. And so shall all proper Dogs do after me."

"Ah," said the Woman, listening, "this is a very clever Cat, but he is not so clever as the Dog."

Cat counted the Dog's teeth (and they looked very pointed) and he said, "I will be kind to the Baby while I am in the Cave, as long as he does not pull my tail too hard, for always and always and always. But *still* I am the Cat that walks by himself, and all places are alike to me."

"Not when I am near," said the Dog. "If

When Cats run Home

When cats run home and light is come,
  And dew is cold upon the ground,
And the far-off stream is dumb,
  And the whirring sail goes round,
  And the whirring sail goes round;
    Alone and warming his five wits,
    The white owl in the belfry sits.

When merry milkmaids click the latch,
  And rarely smells the new-mown hay,
And the cock hath sung beneath the thatch
  Twice or thrice his roundelay,
  Twice or thrice his roundelay;
    Alone and warming his five wits,
    The white owl in the belfry sits.

ALFRED, LORD TENNYSON

Father William
(From 'Alice's Adventures
in Wonderland')

"You are old, Father William," the young man said,
  "And your hair has become very white;
And yet you incessantly stand on your head—
  Do you think, at your age, it is right?"

"In my youth," Father William replied to his son,
  "I feared it might injure the brain;
But now that I'm perfectly sure I have none,
  Why, I do it again and again."

"You are old," said the youth, "as I mentioned before,
  And have grown most uncommonly fat;
Yet you turned a back somersault in at the door—
  Pray, what is the reason of that?"

"In my youth," said the sage, as he shook his grey locks,
  "I kept all my limbs very supple.
By the use of this ointment—one shilling the box—
  Allow me to sell you a couple?"

"You are old," said the youth, "and your jaws are too weak
  For anything tougher than suet;
Yet you finished the goose, with the bones and the beak—
  Pray, how did you manage to do it?"

"In my youth," said his father, "I took to the law,
  And argued each case with my wife;
And the muscular strength which it gave to my jaw,
  Has lasted the rest of my life."

"You are old," said the youth, "one would hardly suppose
  That your eye was as steady as ever;
Yet you balanced an eel on the end of your nose—
  What made you so awfully clever?"

"I have answered three questions, and that is enough,"
  Said his father. "Don't give yourself airs!
Do you think I can listen all day to such stuff!
  Be off, or I'll kick you downstairs!"

LEWIS CARROLL

My Encounter with Israel Hands

Robert Louis Stevenson

Illustrated by Victor G. Ambrus

Son of a civil engineer, Robert Louis Stevenson (1850–1894) disappointed his father (as sons so rightly do) by following his own bent, which was writing stories, instead of becoming the engineer or lawyer his father wanted him to be. A delicate boy, he was harried by illness throughout his life. Yet, short though it was, it was a full and busy one. He travelled in quest of health on two continents—and wrote books of travel. He wrote essays, short stories and poems for children. When too ill to be up, he wrote in bed. Best of all he wrote historical romances full of adventure, pre-eminent being "The Master of Ballantrae", "Kidnapped" and "Catriona". All of them can be relished by young readers. But his first novel, "Treasure Island", was a boys' book by intention. It started as an entertainment for his twelve year-old stepson during a wet holiday at Braemar, and ever since it has remained the lord and prince of treasure-hunting tales. Stevenson's quest for health led him ultimately to the South Sea Island of Samoa, where he set up home and where, after a few years, he died, a romantic and valiant figure to the end.

In the chapter we include, young Jim Hawkins, the cabin-boy hero, tells of his terrifying battle with that most guileful of mutinous mariners, Israel Hands. They are alone on the drifting "Hispaniola". The rest of the mutinous crew—prepared for murder, and seeking only to gain the treasure for themselves—are ashore, as are the members of the expedition, now in peril. Such a tale could be written only by one who was young in spirit: "It's awful fun, boys' stories," wrote Stevenson when he had finished. "You just indulge the pleasure of your heart, that's all."

THE wind, serving us to a desire, now hauled into the west. We could run so much the easier from the north-east corner of the island to the mouth of the North Inlet. Only, as we had no power to anchor, and dared not beach her till the tide had flowed a good deal farther, time hung on our hands. The coxswain told me how to lay the ship to; after a good many trials I succeeded, and we both sat in silence, over another meal.

"Cap'n," said he, at length, with that same uncomfortable smile, "here's my old shipmate, O'Brien; s'pose you was to heave him overboard. I ain't partic'lar as a rule, and I don't take no blame for settling his hash; but I don't reckon him ornamental, now, do you?"

"I'm not strong enough, and I don't like the job; and there he lies, for me," said I.

"This here's an unlucky ship—this *Hispaniola*, Jim," he went on, blinking. "There's a power of men been killed in this *Hispaniola*—a sight o' poor seamen dead and gone since you and me took ship to Bristol. I never seen sich dirty luck, not I. There was this here O'Brien, now—he's dead, ain't he? Well, now, I'm no scholar, and you're a lad as can read and figure; and to put it straight, do you take it as a dead man is dead for good, or do he come alive again?"

"You can kill the body, Mr. Hands, but not the spirit; you must know that already," I replied. "O'Brien there is in another world, and maybe watching us."

"Ah!" says he. "Well, that's unfort'nate —appears as if killing parties was a waste of time. Howsomever, sperrits don't reckon for much, by what I've seen. I'll chance it with the sperrits, Jim. And now, you've spoke up free, and I'll take it kind if you'd step down into that there cabin and get me a—well, a—shiver my timbers! I can't hit the name on't; well, you get me a bottle of wine, Jim—this here brandy's too strong for my head."

Now, the coxswain's hesitation seemed to be unnatural; and as for the notion of his preferring wine to brandy, I entirely disbelieved it. The whole story was a pretext. He wanted me to leave the deck—so much was plain; but with what purpose I could in no way imagine. His eyes never met mine; they kept wandering to and fro, up and down, now with a look to the sky, now with a flitting glance upon the dead O'Brien. All the time he kept smiling, and putting his tongue out in the most guilty,

embarrassed manner, so that a child could have told that he was bent on some deception. I was prompt with my answer, however, for I saw where my advantage lay; and that with a fellow so densely stupid I could easily conceal my suspicions to the end.

"Some wine?" I said. "Far better. Will you have white or red?"

"Well, I reckon it's about the blessed same to me, shipmate," he replied; "so it's strong, and plenty of it, what's the odds?"

"All right," I answered. "I'll bring you port, Mr. Hands. But I'll have to dig for it."

With that I scuttled down the companion with all the noise I could, slipped off my shoes, ran quietly along the sparred gallery, mounted the forecastle ladder, and popped my head out of the fore companion. I knew he would not expect to see me there; yet I took every precaution possible; and certainly the worst of my suspicions proved too true.

He had risen from his position to his hands and knees; and, though his leg obviously hurt him pretty sharply when he moved—for I could hear him stifle a groan —yet it was at a good, rattling rate that he trailed himself across the deck. In half a minute he had reached the port scuppers, and picked, out of a coil of rope, a long knife, or rather a short dirk, discoloured to the hilt with blood. He looked upon it for a moment, thrusting forth his under jaw, tried the point upon his hand, and then, hastily concealing it in the bosom of his jacket, trundled back again into his old place against the bulwark.

This was all that I required to know. Israel could move about; he was now armed; and if he had been at so much trouble to get rid of me, it was plain that I was meant to be the victim. What he would do afterwards—whether he would try to crawl right across the island from North Inlet to the camp among the swamps, or whether he would fire Long Tom, trusting that his own comrades might come first to help him, was, of course, more than I could say.

Yet I felt sure that I could trust him in one point, since in that our interests jumped together, and that was in the disposition of the schooner. We both desired to have her stranded safe enough, in a sheltered place, and so that, when the time came, she could be got off again with as little labour and danger as might be; and until that was done I considered that my life would certainly be spared.

While I was thus turning the business over in my mind, I had not been idle with my body. I had stolen back to the cabin, slipped once more into my shoes, and laid my hand at random on a bottle of wine, and now, with this for an excuse, I made my re-appearance on the deck.

Hands lay as I had left him, all fallen together in a bundle, and with his eyelids lowered, as though he were too weak to bear the light. He looked up, however, at my coming, knocked the neck off the bottle, like a man who had done the same thing often, and took a good swig, with his favourite toast of "Here's luck!" Then he lay quiet for a little, and then, pulling out a stick of tobacco, begged me to cut him a quid.

"Cut me a junk o' that," says he, "for I haven't no knife, and hardly strength enough so be as I had. Ah, Jim, Jim, I reckon I've missed stays! Cut me a quid, as 'll likely be the last, lad; for I'm for my long home, and no mistake."

"Well," said I, "I'll cut you some tobacco; but if I was you and thought myself so badly, I would go to my prayers, like a Christian man."

"Why?" said he. "Now, you tell me why."

"Why?" I cried. "You were asking me just now about the dead. You've broken your trust; you've lived in sin and lies and blood; there's a man you killed lying at your feet this moment; and you ask me why! For God's mercy, Mr. Hands, that's why."

I spoke with a little heat, thinking of the bloody dirk he had hidden in his pocket, and designed, in his ill thoughts, to end me with. He, for his part, took a great draught of the wine, and spoke with the most unusual solemnity.

"For thirty years," he said, "I've sailed the seas, and seen good and bad, better and worse, fair weather and foul, provisions running out, knives going, and what not. Well, now I tell you, I never seen good come o' goodness yet. Him as strikes first is my fancy; dead men don't bite; them's my views—amen, so be it. And now, you look here," he added, suddenly changing his tone, "we've had about enough of this foolery. The tide's made good enough by now. You just take my orders, Cap'n Hawkins, and we'll sail slap in and be done with it."

All told, we had scarce two miles to run; but the navigation was delicate, the entrance to this northern anchorage was not only narrow and shoal, but lay east and west, so that the schooner must be nicely handled to be got in. I think I was a good, prompt subaltern, and I am very sure that Hands was an excellent pilot; for we went about and about, and dodged in, shaving the banks, with a certainty and a neatness that were a pleasure to behold.

Scarcely had we passed the heads before the land closed around us. The shores of North Inlet were as thickly wooded as those of the southern anchorage; but the space was longer and narrower, and more like, what in truth it was, the estuary of a river. Right before us, at the southern end we saw the wreck of a ship in the last stages of dilapidation. It had been a great vessel of three masts, but had lain so long exposed to the injuries of the weather, that it was hung about with great webs of dripping seaweed, and on the deck of it shore bushes had taken root, and now flourished thick with flowers. It was a sad sight, but it showed us that the anchorage was calm.

"Now," said Hands, "look there; there's

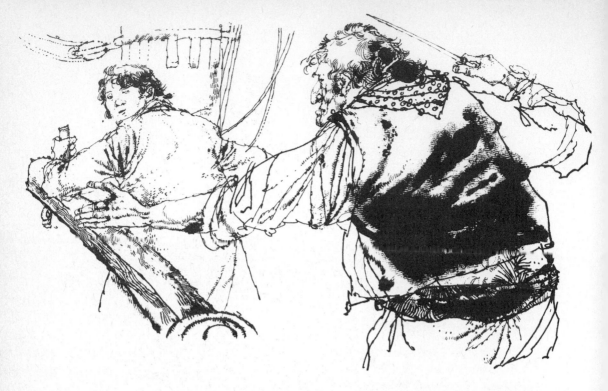

There was Hands already half-way towards me with the dirk in his right hand.

a pet bit for to beach a ship on. Fine flat sand, never a catspaw, trees all around of it, and flowers a-blowing like a garding on that old ship."

"And once beached," I inquired, "how shall we get her off again?"

"Why so," he replied; "you take a line ashore there on the other side at low water: take a turn about one o' them big pines; bring it back, take a turn around the capstan, and lie-to for the tide. Come high water, all hands take a pull upon the line, and off she comes as sweet as natur'. And now, boy, you stand by. We're near the bit now, and she's too much way on her. Starboard a little—so—steady—starboard —larboard a little—steady—steady!"

So he issued his commands, which I breathlessly obeyed; till, all of a sudden, he cried, "Now, my hearty, luff!" And I put the helm hard up, and the *Hispaniola* swung round rapidly, and ran stem on for the low wooded shore.

The excitement of these last manoeuvres

had somewhat interfered with the watch I had kept hitherto, sharply enough, upon the coxswain. Even then I was still so much interested, waiting for the ship to touch, that I had quite forgot the peril that hung over my head, and stood craning over the starboard bulwarks and watching the ripples spreading wide before the bows. I might have fallen without a struggle for my life, had not a sudden disquietude seized upon me, and made me turn my head. Perhaps I had heard a creak, or seen his shadow moving with the tail of my eye; perhaps it was an instinct like a cat's; but, sure enough, when I looked round, there was Hands, already half-way towards me, with the dirk in his right hand.

We must both have cried out aloud when our eyes met; but while mine was the shrill cry of terror, his was a roar of fury like a charging bull's. At the same instant he threw himself forward, and I leapt sideways towards the bows. As I did so, I left

"One more step, Mr. Hands," said I, "and I'll blow your brains out!"
From "My Encounter with Israel Hands"

Behind him, blacker than the sea, blacker than the sky, rose like a phantom a giant of granite, whose projecting crags seemed like arms extended to seize their prey.
From "The Man in the Sack"

hold of the tiller, which sprang sharp to leeward; and I think this saved my life, for it struck Hands across the chest, and stopped him, for the moment, dead.

Before he could recover, I was safe out of the corner where he had me trapped, with all the deck to dodge about. Just forward of the mainmast I stopped, drew a pistol from my pocket, took a cool aim, though he had already turned and was once more coming directly after me, and drew the trigger. The hammer fell, but there followed neither flash nor sound; the priming was useless with sea water. I cursed myself for my neglect. Why had not I, long before, reprimed and reloaded my only weapons? Then I should not have been, as now, a mere fleeing sheep before this butcher.

Wounded as he was, it was wonderful how fast he could move, his grizzled hair tumbling over his face, and his face itself as red as a red ensign with his haste and fury. I had no time to try my other pistol, nor, indeed, much inclination, for I was sure it would be useless. One thing I saw plainly: I must not simply retreat before him, or he would speedily hold me boxed into the bows, as a moment since he had so nearly boxed me in the stern. Once so caught, and nine or ten inches of the blood-stained dirk would be my last experience on this side of eternity. I placed my palms against the mainmast, which was of a goodish bigness, and waited, every nerve upon the stretch.

Seeing that I meant to dodge, he also paused; and a moment or two passed in feints on his part, and corresponding movements upon mine. It was such a game as I had often played at home about the rocks of Black Hill Cove; but never before, you may be sure, with such a wildly beating heart as now. Still, as I say, it was a boy's game, and I thought I could hold my own at it, against an elderly seaman with a wounded thigh. Indeed, my courage had begun to rise so high, that I allowed myself a few darting thoughts on what would be the end of the affair, and while I saw certainly that I could spin it out for long, I saw no hope of any ultimate escape.

Well, while things stood thus, suddenly the *Hispaniola* struck, staggered, ground for an instant in the sand, and then swift as a blow, canted over to the port side till the deck stood at an angle of forty-five degrees, and about a puncheon of water splashed into the scupper holes, and lay, in a pool, between the deck and bulwark.

We were both of us capsized in a second, and both of us rolled, almost together, into the scuppers; the dead redcap, with his arms still spread out, tumbling stiffly after us. So near were we, indeed, that my head came against the coxswain's foot with a crack that made my teeth rattle. Blow and all, I was the first afoot again; for Hands had got involved with the dead body. The sudden canting of the ship had made the deck no place for running on; I had to find some new way of escape, and that upon the instant, for my foe was almost touching me. Quick as thought I sprang into the mizzen shrouds, rattled up hand over hand, and did not draw a breath till I was seated on the crosstrees.

I had been saved by being prompt; the dirk had struck not half a foot below me, as I pursued my upward flight; and there stood Israel Hands, with his mouth open and his face upturned to mine, a perfect statue of surprise and disappointment.

Now that I had a moment to myself, I lost no time in changing the priming of my pistol, and then, having one ready for service, and to make assurance doubly sure, I proceeded to draw the load of the other, and recharge it afresh from the beginning.

My new employment struck Hands all of a heap; he began to see the dice going against him; and after an obvious hesitation, he also hauled himself heavily into the shrouds, and with the dirk in his teeth, began slowly and painfully to mount. It cost him no end of time and groans to haul his wounded leg behind him; and I had quietly finished my arrangements before he was much more than a third of the way up. Then, with a pistol in either hand, I addressed him.

"One more step, Mr. Hands," said I, "and I'll blow your brains out! Dead men don't bite, you know," I added, with a chuckle.

He stopped instantly. I could see by the working of his face that he was trying to think, and the process was so slow and laborious that, in my new-found security, I laughed aloud. At last, with a swallow or two, he spoke, his face still wearing the same expression of extreme perplexity. In order to speak he had to take the dagger from his mouth, but, in all else, he remained unmoved.

"Jim," says he, "I reckon we're fouled, you and me, and w'll have to sign articles.

I'd have had you but for that there lurch; but I don't have no luck, not I; and I reckon I'll have to strike, which comes hard, you see, for a master mariner to a ship's younker like you, Jim."

I was drinking in his words and smiling away, as conceited as a cock upon a wall, when, all in a breath, back went his right hand over his shoulder. Something sang like an arrow through the air; I felt a blow and then a sharp pang, and there I was pinned by the shoulder to the mast. In the horrid pain and surprise of the moment—I scarce can say it was by my own volition, and I am sure it was without a conscious aim—both my pistols went off, and both escaped out of my hands.

They did not fall alone; with a choked cry, the coxswain loosed his grasp upon the shrouds, and plunged head first into the water.

The Mermaid of Zennor

Eileen Molony

Illustrated by
Ronald Reeves

Eileen Molony is the author of "The Mermaid of Zennor", a charming collection of Cornish folk tales from which this story comes.

ZENNOR church stands high up on the Cornish cliffs. If you go there, someone is sure to point out to you the Zennor Merrymaid, carved on one of the old bench ends at the back of the church.

Truth to tell she isn't much cop to look at, but that's because Grandfer Polruan wasn't much cop at carving. All the same, she's there, with her tail, and her hair streaming out behind her, and a comb in her hand the size of a garden rake.

Grandfer Polruan was the church organist and choirmaster, and a brave job he made of it, too. The Zennor boys sang so sweetly they were known in every parish in Cornwall.

But Grandfer didn't spend all his time teaching singing. He was also a fisherman, and he used to make half his living lobster-fishing down to Portzennor Cove.

One day he was out in his boat looking at his lobster pots when something happened which gave him a proper turn and no mistake. One of the lobster pots seemed brave and heavy, but Grandfer Polruan gave an extra bit of a tug and jerked the wicker pot up into the boat.

There wasn't no lobster there, but there was a deal of seaweed, and sticking out of the seaweed the tail of a great fish, unlike any fish Grandfer Polruan had ever seen before.

"My dear life," he said, and gave it a great tug. And there at the bottom of the boat lay not a fish at all, but a merrymaid.

Her eyes were green, and her skin was pale with a greeny bloom on it, like ice on a stormy sea. Her hair was dull gold, and her little waist tapered away into a silver tail, shot, like mackerel's scales, with blue and green and purple, and she twisted and struggled to the side of the boat and tried to slip back into the water.

But Grandfer Polruan

211

spat on the palm of his hand and held tight hold of her tail. He had never seen a merrymaid before and he wasn't going to let her go in a hurry.

By and by she lay quiet, and he asked her questions. She told him how she and her children had followed the warm Gulf Stream south, until they could see the golden Cornish beaches and the sea-pinks on the grassy cliffs. They made their home in a nearby cave, and on Sundays they would come up on the rocks under the cliff edge to hear the choirboys singing in Zennor church. All the children were maidens except the youngest, a boy, who was mute.

"It does seem mortal hard," said the merrymaid, "that when the children of the land can sing like the angels in heaven, my own boy, one of the sea-people, cannot sing at all."

Grandfer Polruan felt sorry for her, and when she asked to be put back in the water he could not refuse her.

"But it's a temptation," he said, "for if I let you go, no one in Cornwall will believe me when I say that once I caught a merry-maid in a lobster pot."

"Yes, they will," she said. "You're a deal too stupid to make up such a tale. But take my comb as well, and if ever you're in trouble and the sea-folk can help you, go out in your boat and comb the foam from off the water. They'll give you what you ask."

Then Grandfer Polruan picked her up in his arms and dropped her back into the water, and as she slid down through the waves he caught sight of a beautiful little boy coming to meet her. But neither spoke a word and they both sank beneath the water.

For a long time after that Grandfer Polruan never made use of the merry-maid's comb. He didn't have many troubles, and what he did have—well, he didn't rightly see how the sea-folk could help him, so he stuck the comb up on his mantelshelf, and there it stayed.

As he grew older, Granfer Polruan began to be troubled with the rheumatics, and round about this time he made friends with Jenny Trebetherick and her little son Philip.

Jenny was a widow woman whose husband had been drowned at sea, and Grandfer Polruan began to take an interest in Philip as soon as he joined the choir.

He was a handsome little boy with a good voice, and Grandfer dearly loved to take him up to the church and play the organ for him to sing "Eternal Father" and "Fierce Raged the Tempest," and suchlike hymns about fisher-folk.

Jenny was some proud, and people would come from miles around to see the little boy standing up before all they scores of people, with his cheeks shining like cherries, and the notes dropping as clean and true as pebbles in a pond.

Jenny thought the world of Grandfer Polruan, and towards autumn, when his rheumatics were bad, she would run in often with a pasty or a piece of saffron cake for the old man.

But the rheumatics grew no better, and so Grandfer Polruan wasn't in church one Sunday when a handsome young woman came in and sat next to Jenny in one of the backmost pews.

She was bravely turned out and no mistake, but there was something very strange about her. Most of our Cornish maids are brown enough from being out and about the seashore in all kinds of weather, and a town-bred lady will always look white beside them. But Jenny had never seen a maid with a paler skin.

She looked like the first snowdrop, when the green bud whitens into flower. Her hair was long and thick and the colour of pale honey. The clothes she wore were so handsome that it didn't seem right to Jenny for her to wear them in church.

Her dress was bright silver, but when the sun streamed in through the stained-glass windows of the church it seemed to be shot with purple and green and gold. It frothed in a train around her ankles so that not even the toes of her shoes peeped out from under it.

But what Jenny disliked about the lady most of all was that when little Philip stood up to sing she sat as still as the grave, and gazed at him so hungrily with her sea-

because of the change in the boy himself.

From being a sunny, trusting little boy, he began to spend long hours sitting by the window watching the sea. He would go for walks by himself along the seashore and bring home the strangest treasures: cuttlefish and seashells, pieces

He would go for walks by himself and bring home the strangest treasures.

green eyes that Jenny's heart turned cold inside her.

Philip saw the lady looking at him, and he in his turn stared back, as well he might, for he had never seen anyone like her in all his life.

The following Sunday the lady was in church again, and so for every Sunday after she would sit and gaze at Philip when he stood up in the choir to sing. Jenny began to grow uneasy, and the more so

of red and white seaweed and green sea-anemones.

"Did you know that young seals are white, Mother?" he would say to her one day. Or: "There's a shoal of whales off the Lizard." And Jenny would marvel how such a little fellow would know so much.

But worst of all, if ever there were a north-east gale blowing and the wind and the rain came beating in from the sea, and the cone from the Godrevy Lighthouse was endways up, then, do what she could to stop him, Philip would slip out. And he would come back drenched to the bone, with salt water and seaweed dripping from his jet-black curls, clutching in his hand a starfish or a piece of wrecked driftwood from the shore.

"I'm some worried," said Jenny to Grandfer Polruan one day. "It's my belief the child's bewitched. I'm feared of my life he'll drown himself," and she told the old man the story.

Grandfer Polruan listened carefully and said little, but he told her to keep Philip indoors for a week or so, and never to let him out of her sight.

One day, soon after that, when his rheumatics had begun to mend, Grandfer Polruan reached up on the mantelshelf and took down the comb.

He gave it a bit of a polish on his cuff, and then he went to the shed at the back of the house and picked the biggest lobster pot he could find and took it down on to the seashore. He clambered slowly and stiffly into his boat and rowed out to sea.

When he had got a fair way out, he leaned over the boat's side, combed the foam from the water with the merrymaid's comb, and lowered the lobster pot into the sea.

When he drew it up again *there was something in it which gleamed silver in the moonlight.*

That evening a tremendous storm blew up, and for fourteen days after the wind blew and the sea raged and tides were higher than any ever known on the Cornish coast.

During all that fortnight Jenny stayed indoors and never took her eyes off Philip. But one evening she thought she would like to look in and see how Granfer Polruan had fared in the terrible storm. So she told Philip to stay in bed and be a good boy, and she slipped out of the back door and locked it behind her.

The night was dark and windswept, but a full moon shone fitfully. Just as Jenny was drawing near Grandfer Polruan's cottage the clouds parted, and she saw a pale figure glide out of the gate.

There was no mistaking the dull gleam of silver. It was the lady who stared at Philip as he sang in the choir.

Jenny turned to follow her, for she thought: "If I follow the strange lady carefully, no harm can come to Philip." But the lady wasn't going towards Jenny's cottage. Instead she turned up the road to the church. Jenny stole after her.

Someone was playing the organ, and the strange lady entered the church by the north door and made straight for the organ loft.

Jenny followed in time to see Grandfer Polruan drop his hand from the stops and turn to face the lady.

"Can I do anything for you, my maidy?"

"I've come for my boy," said the strange lady. "When I promised you the comb should bring you whatever you asked, I little thought you would use it to take away my child."

"I'm main sorry for you, and that's the truth," said Grandfer Polruan, "but whatever made *you* take away a land woman's boy and teach him the ways of the sea, and turn him strange on her?"

An emerald tear formed in the green eye of the merrymaid and glistened in the moonlight.

"He could sing better than any of the sea-people," she said, "and my own boy was dumb. I had hopes he would teach my little one to sing as he did."

"There, there, maidy," said Grandfer Polruan, "supposing someone was to take your own boy and teach him to sing and return him to you, would you leave the land child to his own mother?"

"I'd be main glad," she said.

"Come with me," said Grandfer Polruan. And he led her round to the west end of the church.

Jenny stole along behind the two of them. And what did she see?

There, splashing in the font and singing

214

to himself like a muted nightingale, was a lovely little fairhaired boy with a fish's tail.

"I should have dearly loved to have had him in the choir," said Grandfer Polruan, regretful, "for he knows his litany the same as any Christian child."

But the merrymaid picked up the little sea-child in her arms, like a young dolphin, and even Jenny couldn't find the heart to scold her. "Maybe Grandfer Polruan wouldn't like folk to know that he spent his evenings teaching a mer-child to sing Christian hymns," thought she.

So she stole quietly out of the church, and slipped back to her own cottage, where she found Philip sleeping safe in his cot. And she was the only woman in the parish who could ever make out why Grandfer Polruan spent so much time and trouble in carving the merrymaid for the bench end on the back pew of the church.

Little Trotty Wagtail

Little trotty wagtail, he went in the rain,
And twittering, tottering sideways he ne'er
*   got straight again.*
He stooped to get a worm, and looked up
*   to get a fly,*
And then he flew away ere his feathers they
*   were dry.*

Little trotty wagtail, he waddled in the mud,
And he left his little footmarks, trample
*   where he would.*
He waddled in the water-pudge, and waggle
*   went his tail,*
And chirrupt up his wings to dry upon the
*   garden rail.*

Little trotty wagtail, you nimble all about,
And in the dimpling water-pudge you
*   waddle in and out;*
Your home is nigh at hand, and in the warm
*   pig-stye,*
So little Master Wagtail, I'll bid you a
*   good-bye.*

JOHN CLARE

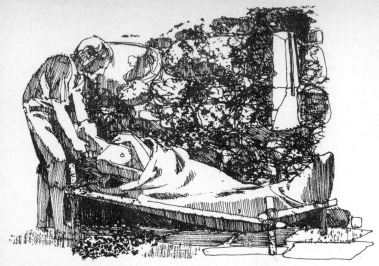

The Man in the Sack

Alexandre Dumas

Illustrated by Michael Jackson and Mike Codd

Few writers could equal the prolific Alexandre Dumas (1802–1870), whose collected works in French fill 227 volumes. Yet, much as he earned by his pen, he spent too lavishly, and died unhappy and in debt. He is one of the world's greatest writers of tales of action and adventure; a much easier author for the young than Walter Scott, for example. Most of his stories, like the one we know best—"The Three Musketeers" —are historical romances, but the no less famous "Count of Monte Cristo" is about the times through which the author himself had lived. The tale that follows comes from that book. It is the story of its hero's escape from the Château d'If, a fortress prison into which he had been flung at the age of nineteen through the plotting of his foes. For fourteen terrible years young Dantès has been a prisoner, his only friend, a fellow-prisoner, the Abbé Faria, with whom he had been able to make contact. Dantès thinks always of escaping if he can, and the sudden death of the old Abbé hints to him a way out—a dreadful way out. Will he dare to take it?

ON the bed, at full length, and faintly lighted by the pale ray that penetrated the window, was a sack of coarse cloth, under the large folds of which was stretched a long and stiffened form; it was Faria's last winding-sheet—a winding-sheet which, as the turnkey said, cost little. All then was completed. A material separation had taken place between Dantès and his old friend—he could no longer see those eyes which had remained open as if to look even beyond death—he could no longer clasp that hand of industry which had lifted for him the veil that had concealed hidden and obscure things. Faria, the usual and the good companion, with whom he was accustomed to live so intimately, no longer breathed. He seated himself on the edge of that terrible bed, and fell into a melancholy and gloomy reverie.

Alone! he was alone again! . . .

No longer to see—no longer to hear the voice of the only human being who attached him to life! Was it not better, like Faria, to seek the presence of his Maker?

Dantès recoiled from the idea of this infamous death, and passed suddenly from despair to an ardent desire for life and liberty.

"Die! oh, no," he exclaimed, "not die now, after having lived and suffered so long and so much! . . . I desire to live, I desire to struggle to the very last, I wish to reconquer the happiness of which I have been deprived. Before I die, I must not forget that I have my executioners to punish, and, perhaps, too, who knows?

some friends to reward. Yet they will forget me here, and I shall die in my dungeon like Faria."

As he said this, he remained motionless, his eyes fixed like a man struck with a sudden idea, but whom this idea fills with amazement. Suddenly he rose, lifted his hand to his brow as if his brain were giddy, paced twice or thrice round his chamber, and then paused abruptly at the bed.

"Ah! ah!" he mutttered, "who inspires me with this thought? Is that Thou, gracious God? Since none but the dead pass freely from this dungeon, let me assume the place of the dead!"

Without giving himself time to reconsider his decision, and, indeed, that he might not allow his thoughts to be distracted from his desperate resolution, he bent over the appalling sack, opened it with the knife which Faria had made, drew the corpse from the sack, and transported it along the gallery to his own chamber, laid it on his couch, passed round its head the rag he wore at night round his own, covered it with his counterpane, once again kissed the ice-cold brow . . . turned the head towards the wall, so that the gaoler might, when he brought his evening meal, believe that he was asleep as was his frequent custom; returned along the gallery, threw the bed against the wall, returned to the other cell, took from the hiding-place the needle and thread, flung off his rags that they might feel naked flesh only beneath the coarse sackcloth, and getting inside the sack, placed himself in the posture in which the dead body had been laid, and sewed up the mouth of the sack from the inside.

The beating of his heart might have been heard, if by any mischance the gaolers had entered at that moment.

Dantès might have waited until the evening visit was over, but he was afraid the governor might change his mind and order the dead body to be removed earlier.

In that case his last hope would have been destroyed.

Now his project was settled, and he hoped thus to carry it into effect.

If during the time he was being conveyed the grave-diggers should discover that they were carrying a live instead of a dead body, Dantès did not intend to give them time to recognize him, but with a sudden cut of the knife, he meant to open the sack from top to bottom, and, profiting by their alarm, escape; if they tried to catch him he would use his knife.

If they conducted him to the cemetery and laid him in the grave, he would allow himself to be covered with earth, and then, as it was night, the grave-diggers could scarcely have turned their backs, ere he would have worked his way through the soft soil and escaped, hoping that the weight would not be too heavy for him to support.

If he was deceived in this and the earth proved too heavy, he would be stifled, and then, so much the better, all would be over.

Dantès had not eaten since the previous evening, but he had not thought of hunger or thirst, nor did he now think of it. His position was too precarious to allow him even time to reflect on any thought but one.

The first risk that Dantès ran was, that the gaoler when he brought him his supper at seven o'clock, might notice the change he had effected; fortunately Dantès had often received his gaoler in bed, and then the man placed his bread and soup on the table, and went away without saying a word.

This time the gaoler might not be as silent as usual, but speak to Dantès, and, receiving no reply, might examine the bed, and thus discover all.

When seven o'clock came, Dantès' agony really commenced. His hand placed on his heart was unable to repress its throbbings, whilst, with the other, he wiped the perspiration from his temples. From time to time shudderings ran through his whole frame and made him feel he was going to die. Yet the hours passed on without any stir in the Château, and Dantès felt he had escaped this first danger: it was a good augury. At length, about the hour the governor had appointed, footsteps were heard on the stairs. Edmond felt that the moment had arrived, and summoning up all his courage, held his breath, happy if at the same time he could have repressed in like manner the pulsing of his arteries.

They stopped at the door—there were two steps, and Dantès guessed it was the two grave diggers who had come to seek him—this idea was soon converted into certainty, when he heard the noise they made in putting down the hand-bier.

The door opened, and a dim light reached Dantès' eyes through the coarse sack that covered him; he saw two shadows approach his bed, a third remaining at the door with a torch in his hand. Each of these two men, approaching the ends of the bed, took the sack by its extremities.

"He's heavy for an old and thin man," said one, as he raised the head.

"They say every year adds half a pound to the weight of the bones," said another, lifting the feet.

"Have you tied the knot?" inquired the first speaker.

"What would be the use of carrying so much more weight?" was the reply; "I can do that when we get there."

"Yes, you're right," replied the companion.

"What's the knot for?" thought Dantès.

They deposited the supposed corpse on the bier. Edmond stiffened himself in order to play his part of a dead man, and then the party, lighted by the man with the torch, who went first, ascended the stairs.

Suddenly he felt the fresh and sharp night air. . . .

The bearers advanced twenty paces, then stopped, putting their bier down on the ground.

One of them went away, and Dantès heard his shoes on the pavement.

"Where am I then?" he asked himself.

"Really, he is by no means a light load!" said the other bearer, sitting on the edge of the hand-barrow.

Dantès' first impulse was to escape, but fortunately he did not attempt it.

"Light me, you sir," said the other bearer, "or I shall not find what I am looking for."

The man with the torch complied, although not asked in the most polite terms.

"What can he be looking for?" thought Edmond. "The spade, perhaps."

An exclamation of satisfaction indicated that the gravedigger had found the object of his search. "Here it is at last," he said, "not without some trouble though."

"Yes," was the answer, "but it has lost nothing by waiting."

As he said this, the man came towards Edmond, who heard a heavy and sounding substance laid down beside him, and at the same moment a cord was fastened round his feet with sudden and painful violence.

"Well, have you tied the knot?" inquired the grave-digger, who was looking on.

"Yes, and pretty tight too, I can tell you," was the answer.

"Move on, then."

And the bier was lifted once more, and they proceeded.

They advanced fifty paces farther, and then stopped to open a door, then went forward again. The noise of the waves dashing against the rocks, on which the Château is built, reached Dantès ear distinctly as they progressed.

"Bad weather!" observed one of the bearers; "not a pleasant night for a dip in the sea."

"Why, yes, the abbé runs a chance of being wet," said the other; and then there was a burst of brutal laughter.

Dantès did not comprehend the jest, but his hair stood erect on his head.

At the same instant Dantès felt himself flung into the air.

"Well, here we are at last," said one of them. "A little farther—a little farther," said the other. "You know very well that the last corpse was dashed on the rocks, and the governor told us next day that we were careless fellows."

They ascended five or six more steps, and then Dantès felt that they took him, one by the head and the other by the heels, and swung him to and fro.

"One!" said the grave-diggers. "Two! Three, and away!"

And at the same instant Dantès felt himself flung into the air like a wounded bird, falling, falling with a rapidity that made his blood curdle. Although drawn downwards by the same heavy weight which hastened his rapid descent, it seemed to him as if the time were a century. At last, with a terrific dash, he entered the ice-cold water, and as he did so he uttered a shrill cry, stifled in a moment by his immersion beneath the waves.

Dantès had been flung into the sea, into whose depths he was dragged by a thirty-six pound cannon ball tied to his feet.

The sea is the cemetery of Château d'If.

Dantès, although giddy and almost suffocated, had yet sufficient presence of mind to hold his breath; and as his right hand (prepared as he was for every chance) held his knife open, he rapidly ripped up the sack, extricated his arm, and then his body; but in spite of all his efforts to free himself from the cannon ball he felt it dragging him down still lower; he then bent his body, and by a desperate effort severed the cord that bound his legs at the moment he was suffocating. With a vigorous spring he rose to the surface of the sea, whilst the heavy ball bore to its depths the sack that had so nearly become his shroud.

Dantès merely paused to breathe, and then dived again in order to avoid being seen.

When he arose a second time he was fifty paces from where he had first sunk.

He saw overhead a black and tempestuous sky, over which the wind was driving the fleeting vapours that occasionally suffered a twinkling star to appear : before him was the vast expanse of waters, sombre and terrible, whose waves foamed and roared as if before the approach of a storm. Behind him, blacker than the sea, blacker than the sky, rose like a phantom a giant of granite, whose projecting crags seemed like arms extended to seize their prey; and on the highest rock was a torch that lighted two figures. He fancied these two forms were looking at the sea; doubtless these strange grave-diggers had heard his cry. Dantès dived again, and remained a long time beneath the water. . . .

When he rose again the light had disappeared.

It was necessary to strike out to sea. Ratonneau and Pomègue are the nearest isles of all those that surround the Château d'If. But Ratonneau and Pomègue are inhabited, together with the islet of Oaume; Tiboulen or Lemaire were the most secure. The isles of Tiboulen and Lemaire are a league from the Château d'If. Dantès, nevertheless, determined to make for them; but how could he find his way in the darkness of the night?

At this moment he saw before him, like a brilliant star, the lighthouse of Planier.

By leaving this light on the right, he kept the isle of Tiboulen a little on the left; by turning to the left, therefore, he would find it. But, as we have said, it was at least a league from the Château d'If to this island.

Often in prison Abbé Faria had said to him when he saw him idle and inactive :

"Dantès, you must not give way to this listlessness; you will be drowned, if you seek to escape; and your strength has not been properly exercised and prepared for exertion."

These words rang in Dantès' ears even beneath the waves : he hastened to cleave his way through them to see if he had not lost his strength; he found with pleasure that his captivity had taken away nothing of his power, and that he was still master of that element on whose bosom he had so often sported as a boy.

Fear, that relentless pursuer, clogged Dantès' efforts; he listened if any noise was audible; each time that he rose over the waves his looks scanned the horizon, and strove to penetrate the darkness; every wave seemed a boat in his pursuit, and he redoubled exertions that increased his distance from the Château, but the repetition of which weakened his strength. He swam on still, and already the terrible Château had disappeared in the darkness. He could not see it, but he *felt* its presence. An hour passed, during which Dantès, excited by the feeling of freedom, continued to cleave the waves.

"Let us see," said he, "I have swum above an hour; but as the wind is against me, that has retarded my speed; however, if I am not mistaken, I must be close to the isle of Tiboulen. But what if I were mistaken?"

A shudder passed over him. He sought to tread water in order to rest himself, but the sea was too violent, and he felt that he could not make use of this means of repose.

"Well," said he, "I will swim on until I am worn out, or the cramp seizes me, and then I shall sink"; and he struck out with the energy of despair.

Suddenly the sky seemed to him to become still darker and more dense, and compact clouds lowered towards him; at the same time he felt a violent pain in his knee. His imagination told him a ball had struck him, and that in a moment he would hear the report; but he heard nothing. Dantès put out his hand and felt resistance; he then extended his leg and felt the land, and in an instant guessed the nature of the object he had taken for a cloud.

Before him rose a mass of strangely formed rocks that resembled nothing so much as a vast fire petrified at the moment of its most fervent combustion. It was the isle of Tiboulen.

Dantès rose, advanced a few steps, and, with a fervent prayer of gratitude, stretched himself on the granite, which seemed to him softer than down. Then, in spite of the wind and rain, he fell into the deep sweet sleep of those worn out by fatigue.

The Raider

Grey Owl

Illustrated by Stuart Tresilian

Grey Owl (1885–1937) was born Archie Belaney in Hastings, England. He was brought up by two aunts there and left at the age of fifteen to seek his fortune in Canada. He became a trapper and grew to know and love the ways of the Indians who lived in the Canadian forests. Eventually, he was adopted by a tribe and he lived with them as an Indian. He was given the name "He who walks by Night" but he called himself "Grey Owl". He served with the Canadian Army during the First World War and was wounded in 1917. He returned to Canada and joined the Ojibway tribe. He married an Indian girl and they had a daughter "Little Dawn".

The death and destruction of the First World War made Grey Owl turn against all form of killing and he gave up his former life as a trapper and began to campaign tirelessly to save the beaver from extinction. He began writing in the late 1920's and his first book "Men of the Last Frontier" was published in 1931. This was followed by "Pilgrims of the Wild" and "The Adventures of Sajo and her Beaver People". He returned to Britain in 1936 and embarked on an enormously successful lecture tour, in fact, it was so successful that he immediately started a second one culminating in a Royal Command to lecture at Buckingham Palace before King George VI and Queen Elizabeth and the young princesses, Elizabeth and Margaret. Grey Owl's last book "Tales of an Empty Cabin" appeared in 1936 and he died suddenly in 1937. The story we have chosen comes from "The Adventures of Sajo and her Beaver People".

THE pond was bright with sunshine; very silent and peaceful it was, back there among the Hills of the Whispering Leaves, and so calm, that the few ducks dozing quietly upon its waters seemed almost to be floating on air, and the slim white poplar trees that stood upon its banks were reflected so plainly on its smooth surface, that it was hard to tell where the water stopped and the trees began. It was very beautiful, like a fairyland, with its silver poplars and May flowers and blue water. And it was very still, for nothing moved there, and it seemed quite lifeless except for the sleeping ducks. Yet, had you watched patiently for a little while, being careful not to move or talk, or even whisper, you would have seen, before very long, a ripple on the water near the shore as a dark brown head, with round ears that showed very plainly, peered cautiously out from the rushes at the water's edge, and watched and listened and sniffed. The head was followed by a furry body, as its owner now came out in full sight and swam rapidly, but without a sound, to another place on the far shore, there to disappear among the reeds. The tall reeds swayed and shook for a minute as he worked there, and then he reappeared, this time holding before him a large bundle of grass, and swam over towards an enormous black mound of earth that we had been wondering about all this time, and dived, bundle and all, right in front of it. He had scarcely disappeared before another head, with another bundle, could be seen swimming from a different direction when—somebody moved, and with no warning at all, a huge flat tail came down on the water with a heavy smack, and with a mighty splash and a plunge the head and its bundle were gone. That great mound, taller than any of us, before which the swimmers had dived, was a beaver house, and the dark brown, furry heads were those of the Beaver People themselves. And they had been very busy.

The lodge had been built up to more than six feet in height, and was a good ten feet across. It had lately been well plastered with wet mud, and heavy billets of wood had been laid on the slopes of it to hold everything firmly in place. It all looked very strong and safe, like a fortress, and even a moose could have walked around on top of it without doing it a bit of harm. Up the side of it there was a wide pathway, on which the building materials were carried, and had you been more patient or careful awhile ago, or perhaps had the wind not played a trick on you and given you away to those keen noses, you might have seen old father beaver dig out a load of earth from the shore, go with it to the house, swimming slowly and carefully so as not to lose any, and then, standing upright like a man, walk to the top of the roof with the load in his arms and there dump it, pushing it into nooks and crannies with his hands, and shoving a good-sized stick in after it to keep it there.

And all this work had been done with a purpose. Inside that queer-looking home, hidden away from the eyes of all the world, were four tiny little kitten beavers. Woolly little fellows they were, perfectly formed, with bright black eyes, big webbed hind feet, little hand-like fore-paws and tiny, flat, rubbery-looking tails. They had marvellous appetites, and their lungs must have been very good too, for they were the noisiest little creatures imaginable, and cried continuously in long, loud wails that were very much like the cries of small human babies: and like any other babies, they needed a great deal of attention —and you may be sure that they were getting a lot of it too.

The living-room, or chamber, inside the lodge, was large enough for a man to have curled up in it with ease, and was very clean and sweet smelling, with its floor of willow bark and bed of scented grasses. The entrance was through a short, slanting tunnel, one end of which, called the plunge-hole, was in the floor, and the other end came out below, near the bottom of the lake. The dam held the pond up to a level nearly even with the floor, keeping the plunge-hole always full, so that the tiny kittens, who were a little wobbly on their legs as yet, could drink there without falling into it; or if they did (which happened rather regularly), they could climb out again quite easily. The whole tunnel and the outer doorway were under water, so that no land animals could enter or even see it, unless they were first-class divers, which most of them are not. But if the dam should break and let the saved-up water out, the beaver would be in grave danger, as not only could their enemies, such as wolves and foxes, find their way into the house, but the beaver would be unable to protect or hide themselves by diving suddenly out of sight.

The father beaver spent much of his time watching the dam and fixing any small leaks that appeared. He had, too, a pretty steady job keeping the outlet clear of rubbish, so that the dammed-up water, when it had reached the height of the outlet, could flow away freely. Otherwise it would become too high, and so flood the house. Always it must be kept at exactly the right level.

Between whiles, both the father and the mother attended to their babies' every want, changing their bedding every so often, bringing in small sprays of tender leaves for them to eat, combing and brushing their wool (you could hardly call it fur), while they made queer, soft sounds of affection and talked to them in that strange beaver language that, at a little distance, sounds almost as though human people were speaking together in low voices. And the shrill wailing cries of the little ones, and their chattering, and their little squawks and squeals, could be heard even through the thick walls of the lodge, so noisy were they when they were hungry or pleased or in some small trouble, which, one way and another, was pretty nearly all the time. And when either their father or their mother returned (they were never away together; one or the other was always on guard) from a trip to the so-important dam, or brought in new bedding of sweet-grass, he or she would give a low, crooning sound of greeting, to be immediately answered by a very bedlam of loud shouts of welcome from the youngsters, that went on long after it was at all necessary. They were never still unless they were asleep, and were continually scrambling around, and tussling together, and clambering over everything, and by the noise they made, seemed to be enjoying themselves immensely. And altogether they were pretty much like any other family, and

were very snug and happy in their home.

The little ones were now old enough to try their hand at swimming in the plunge-hole, though at present this exercise consisted mostly in lying on top of the water, not always right side up, and going round and round in circles, screeching with excitement. And being so very light, and their fluffy coats containing so much air, they could not seem to sink deep enough for their webbed hind feet to get a grip on the water both at the same time, so they swam with first one foot and then the other, rolling from side to side and bobbing up and down, squirming and squealing and wriggling, while their parents passed anxiously around amongst them, giving them encouragement, or perhaps advice, in their deep, strong voices. . . .

But they would soon become tired, and climbing out on to the drying-off place (a little lower than the rest of the floor, so the water would soak away and not run all over the beds), every little beaver carefully squeezed, rubbed and scrubbed the water from his coat on the front, sides, back, every place he could reach, sitting upright and working very industriously, puffing and blowing as most of us do after a swim. Then, when this was all over and everybody was dry, or thought he was (some of them would topple over once in a while and made rather a poor job of it), the call for lunch would go up in a loud chorus, and the new green leaflets and water plants that had been provided ahead of time (with the idea, no doubt, of putting a stop to the uproar as soon as possible), would be divided up, and pretty soon all the busy little jaws would be munching away, and the piercing cries have died down to mumbles and mutterings of contentment. And soon the little voices became quiet and the small black eyes closed, while they lay cuddled together on their sweet-smelling, grassy bed, with their tiny fore-paws, so much like hands, clutched tightly in each other's fur.

This would be their daily programme

until, after perhaps three weeks, would come that glorious day when they would venture down the long, dim tunnel out into the brightness of the great unknown world that was all about them, but which they had never seen. And while they slept the old ones stood watch and guard, turn about, and took turns to inspect the defences of their castle and the dam on which their very lives depended, and kept a weather eye out for enemies, and collected food and bedding for when the babies should awaken, and carried on at the hundred and one jobs that make father and mother beaver a very busy pair of people during the latter part of May, the Month of Flowers.

Our four young heroes, or heroines, or both, had just arrived at that thrilling stage of the proceedings when they could at last dive without bobbing up immediately, tail first, like a rubber ball, and could swim around on the surface for quite a respectable distance without calling loudly for help, when one day at noon the father noticed that the water in the entrance was sinking. He watched it for a moment; the mother heard it too, heard it gurgling and came to look—the water was going down, swirling into the tunnel—was gone!

Someone had broken the dam!

Into the empty plunge-hole, one after another tumbled the two big beaver. There was no time to be lost. They were losing their precious water, the water upon which the lives of their little ones so much depended! Their home was open now to all the world; it might mean the death of all of them. The four kittens, terrified, realizing that something fearful was wrong, but too young to know just what it might be, crept close together, whimpering, while their alarmed parents tore through what was left of the water, towards the dam.

They found a hole, nearly as big as a barrel, right at the deepest part of it, where it would quickly drain the lake to the very bottom. Madly the beaver began to work, pulling down sticks from anywhere, tearing out great armfuls of earth from the marshy shore, slashing off limbs from fallen trees with their razor-sharp teeth, rolling stones into the hole and shoving grass and brush in between them, digging up mud and pushing it before them into the break, where the suction of the now rapidly falling water held it plastered tight against the stick and stones and brush. But the pond had been too small for so big a leak, and water was not coming in from the tiny stream that fed it, nearly as fast as it was going out.

And now that the dam was almost repaired, the pond was empty!

Despair seized on the beaver as they worked (don't let anyone ever tell you that animals cannot feel despair!), but they never gave up until the very last load was in its place, and then, their task at length finished, they turned and plodded wearily and unhappily back towards their four little babies in the house, useless now as a protection—the house they had worked so

225

hard to build, the babies that they loved so very much. Beaver are slow walkers and what had once been a short, easy swim had now become a slow, awkward scramble through slippery mud and over rocks and tangled, fallen water-plants and weeds. Precious minutes would pass before they would have staggered, and crawled, and dragged their way to that dark mound that now seemed so far away.' Anything could

evil head, that crept slowly through the entrance towards them, his teeth bared, hissing like a snake as he came. Negik the Otter, the hungry, the cruel and the sly, having broken the dam and so drained the pond, could now get what he had come for —kitten beaver meat! Now was his time. His snaky body blocked the plunge-hole; there seemed to be no escape. He gathered his legs beneath him, ready to spring. . . .

The otter fought hard, but he had all he could do to defend his own throat.

catch them. If a bear or a wolf should pass and see them they would have no chance; the Beaver People were defenceless now, for they were never made to fight, only to work. . . .

Across the muddy bottom of the empty pond the two big beavers struggled slowly, painfully and pitifully on their short and weary legs towards their unprotected home and babies, while—within the lodge, huddled together, their tiny hands clutched tightly in each other's woolly fur, four helpless little kitten beavers stared in terror at a sleek, black monster with a flat,

But in his eagerness, so greedy he was, he tried to seize them all at once, and the little beavers, quick as so many coiled springs, threw themselves sideways in the way that beaver have, and scattered before him as he came. Aiming at no particular one, he missed them all, nearly stunning himself against the wall of the lodge with the force of his leap. This confused him for a second, and the kittens rushed past him through the entrance, now no longer blocked by his body. The otter, roused to ferocious anger by his failure, and knowing very well that he could catch them one by one outside, was about to turn in pursuit, when the doorway was again darkened. That was all the warning he had. The next moment he was fighting for his life with the two big beavers. They had arrived only just in time; and they, usually so playful and good-natured, would fight to the death in defence of their young ones.

The otter was quicker on his feet and fiercer than they were, and could lock his jaws like a vice once he had bitten in, like a bulldog; but a beaver's hide is tough, and their chisel-shaped teeth, that could hew down big trees and had never before been used to do harm to anyone, now slashed through skin and muscle, inches deep. They held on with their hands, and drove their razor-edged cutting teeth in deeper and deeper. The otter fought hard, for he was no coward, trying for his favourite hold on a beaver's nose and mouth, so as to prevent at least one of them from using his teeth. But he had all he could do to defend his own throat, at which the beavers were aiming.

He twisted and turned like a great hairy lizard, lashing out right and left with his snaky head, hissing, snapping, and snarling. The beaver held on in deadly silence, while he dragged them here and there, and they drove their teeth in again and again. For here was an enemy, the worst one of them all, who must be got rid of somehow—anyhow. Fighting fair with this evil beast was only a waste of time; the matter must be settled once and for all. Over and over they fought and wrestled and rolled, until they rolled right out through the plunge-hole, a squirming, tangled mixture of legs, tails and glistening teeth. . . .

Then with a violent effort the raider broke loose and in one leap was beyond the beavers' reach. They scrambled after the fleeing otter, but the slimy mud that held them back gave the otter just the kind of going that he needed, and he threw himself forward in the slippery ooze and slid twenty feet at one shot, took two or three jumps and another slide, and kept this up until he was at the dam, and over it, and away—for ever.

Everything was all right now, for water was beginning to collect again. A good-sized pool had already formed in the basin of the pond, getting larger all the time, and held there by the dam, which, as you remember, the beavers had repaired.

Never again would Negik, the otter, make war on the Beaver People!

227

The Story of Cholmondely

Gerald Durrell

Illustrated by Ralph Thompson and Val Biro

Gerald Durrell is one of those people who seem to know from their earliest years what they are going to be when they grow up. Youngest brother of a gifted, highly original and harum-scarum family, he spent several youthful years on the island of Corfu, off Greece, and was fascinated by the birds, beasts and insects of the island: the tale is told in "My Family and Other Animals", from which you can see that Gerald was bound to become some sort of naturalist. He has made a profession of collecting wild animals around the world, and—what is surely no less important—telling us all about them in delightful books. The present story comes from "The New Noah", in which he shares with young readers some of his African experiences when collecting beasts for his "ark".

WHEN Cholmondely, the chimpanzee, joined the collection, he immediately became the uncrowned king of it, not only because of his size, but also because he was so remarkably intelligent. Cholmondely had been the pet of a District Officer who, wanting to send the ape to the London zoo, and hearing that I was collecting wild animals in that region and would shortly be returning to England, wrote and asked me if I would mind taking Cholmondely with me and handing him over to the zoo authorities. I wrote back to say that, as I already had a large collection of monkeys, another chimpanzee would not make any difference, so I would gladly escort Cholmondely back to England. I imagined that he would be quite a young chimp, perhaps two years old, and standing about two feet high. When he arrived I got a considerable shock.

A small van drew up outside the camp one morning and in the back of it was an enormous wooden crate. It was big enough, I thought, to house an elephant. I wondered what on earth could be inside, and when the driver told me that it contained Cholmondely I remember thinking how silly his owner was to send such a small chimpanzee in such a huge crate. I opened the door and looked inside and there sat Cholmondely. One glance at him and I realized that this was no baby chimpanzee but a fully grown one about eight or nine years old. Sitting hunched up in the dark crate, he looked as though he were about twice as big as me, and from the expression on his face I gathered that the trip had not been to his liking. Before I could shut the door of the box, however, Cholmondely had extended a long, hairy arm, clasped my hand in his and shaken it warmly. Then he turned round and gathered up a great length of chain (one end of which was fastened to a collar round his neck), draped it carefully over his arm, and stepped down, out of the box. He stood there for a moment and, after surveying me carefully, examined the camp with great interest, whereupon he held out his hand, looking at me inquiringly. I took it in mine and we walked into the marquee together.

Cholmondely immediately went and seated himself on one of the chairs by the camp table, dropped his chain on the floor and sat back and crossed his legs. He gazed round the tent for a few minutes with a rather supercilious expression on his face, and evidently deciding that it would do he turned and looked at me inquiringly again. Obviously, he wanted me to offer him something after his tiring journey. I had been warned before he arrived that he was a hardened tea drinker, and so I called out to the cook and told him to make a pot of tea. Then I went out and had a look in Cholmondely's crate, and in the bottom I found an enormous and very battered tin mug. When I returned to the tent with this, Cholmondely was quite overjoyed and even praised me for my cleverness in finding it, by uttering a few cheerful "hoo hoo" noises.

While we were waiting for the tea to arrive, I sat down opposite Cholmondely and lit a cigarette. To my surprise, he became very excited and held out his hand across the table to me. Wondering what he would do, I handed him the cigarette packet. He opened it, took out a cigarette and put it between his lips. He then reached out his hand again and I gave him the matches; to my astonishment, he took one out of the box, struck it, lit his cigarette and threw the box down on the table. Lying back in his chair he blew out clouds of smoke in the most professional manner. No one had told me that Cholmondely smoked. I wondered rather anxiously what other bad habits he might have which his master had not warned me about.

Just at that moment, the tea was brought in and Cholmondely greeted its appearance with loud and expressive hoots of joy. He watched me carefully while I half-filled his mug with milk and then added the tea. I had been told that he had a very sweet tooth, so I put in six large spoons of sugar, an action which he greeted with grunts of satisfaction. He placed his cigarette on the table and seized the mug with both hands; then he stuck out his lower lip very carefully and dipped it into the tea to make sure it was not too hot. As it was a trifle warm, he sat there blowing on it vigorously until it was cool enough, and then he drank it all down without stopping once. When he had drained the last drops, he peered into the mug and scooped out all the sugar he could with his forefinger. After that, he tipped the mug up on his nose and sat with it like that for about five minutes until the very last of the sugar had trickled down into his mouth.

I had Cholmondely's big box placed some distance away from the marquee, and fixed the end of his chain to a large tree stump. He was too far away, I thought, to make a nuisance of himself but near enough to be able to watch everything that went on and to conduct long conversations with me in his "hoo hoo" language. But on the day of his arrival he caused trouble almost as soon as I had fixed him to his tree stump. Outside the marquee was a lot of small tame monkeys tied on long strings attached to stakes driven into the ground. They were about ten in number, and over them I had constructed a palm leaf roof as a shelter from the sun. As Cholmondely was examining his surroundings, he noticed these monkeys, some eating fruit and others lying asleep in the sun, and decided he would have a little under-arm bowling practice. I was working inside the marquee when all at once I heard the most terrific uproar going on outside. The monkeys were screaming and chattering with rage, and I rushed out to see what had happened. Cholmondely, apparently, had picked up a rock the size of a cabbage and hurled it at the smaller monkeys, luckily missing them all, but frightening them out of their wits. If one of them had been hit by such a big rock, it would have been killed instantly.

Just as I arrived on the scene, no impression on him at all, for his back was as broad and as hard as a table.

I gave him two sharp cuts with this silly little twig and followed it up with a serious scolding. He sat there picking bits of leaf off his fur and looking very guilty. With

No one had told me that Cholmondely smoked. . . .

Cholmondely had picked up another stone and was swinging it backwards and forwards like a professional cricketer, taking better aim. He was annoyed at having missed all the monkeys with his first shot. I grabbed a stick and hurried towards him, shouting, and, to my surprise Cholmondely dropped the rock and put his arms over his head, and started to roll on the ground and scream. In my haste, I had picked up a very small twig and this made

the aid of the Africans, I set to work and cleared away all the rocks and stones near his box, and, giving him another scolding, went back to my work. I hoped that this telling-off might have some effect on him, but when I looked out of the marquee some time later, I saw him digging in the earth, presumably in search of more ammunition.

Not long after his arrival at the camp, Cholmondely, to my alarm, fell ill. For

230

nearly two weeks he went off his food, refusing even the most tempting fruit and other delicacies, and even rejecting his daily ration of tea, a most unheard-of occurrence. All he had was a few sips of water every day, and gradually he grew thinner and thinner, his eyes sank into their sockets, and I really thought he was going to die. He lost all interest in life and sat hunched up in his box all day, with his eyes closed. It was very bad for him to spend all day moping in this fashion, so in the evenings, just before the sun went down, when it was cool, I used to make him come out for walks with me. These walks were only short, and we had to rest every few yards, for Cholmondely was weak with lack of food.

One evening, just before I took him out for a walk, I filled my pockets with a special kind of biscuit that he had been very fond of. We went slowly up to the top of a small hill just beyond the camp and then sat there to admire the view. As we rested, I took a biscuit out of my pocket and ate it, smacking my lips with enjoyment, but not offering any to Cholmondely. He looked very surprised, for he knew that I always shared my food with him when we were out together. I ate a second biscuit and he watched me

closely to see if I enjoyed it as much as the first. When he saw that I did, he dipped his hand into my pocket, pulled out a biscuit, smelled it suspiciously, and then, to my delight, ate it up and started looking for another. I knew then that he was going to get better. The next morning he drank a mugful of sweet tea and ate seventeen biscuits, and for three days lived entirely on this diet. After this his appetite returned with a rush, and for the next fortnight he ate twice as much as he had ever done before, and cost me a small fortune in bananas.

There were only two things that Cholmondely disliked. One of them was the Africans and the other, snakes. I think that when he was a baby some Africans must have teased him. Whatever the reason, however, he certainly got his own back on more than one occasion. He would hide inside the box and wait until an African passed close by and then he would rush out with all his hair standing on end, swinging his long arms and screaming in the most terrifying manner. Many a fat African woman carrying a basket of fruit on her head would chance to pass too closely to Cholmondely's box, and would have to drop her basket, pick up her skirts and run for dear life, while Cholmondely

She would have to drop her basket, pick up her skirts and run for dear life.

231

danced victoriously at the end of his chain, hooting and showing all his teeth in a grin of delight.

With snakes, of course, he was not nearly so brave. If he saw me handling one, he would get very agitated, wringing his hands and moaning with fear, and if I put the reptile on the ground and it started to crawl towards him, he would run to the very end of his chain and scream loudly for help, throwing bits of stick and grass at the snake to try and stop it coming any closer.

One night, I went to shut him up in his box, as usual, and, to my surprise, he flatly refused to go into it. His bed of banana leaves was nicely made, and so I thought he was simply being naughty, but when I started to scold him, he took me by the hand, led me up to his box and left me there while he retreated to the safety of the end of his chain, and stood watching me anxiously. I realized there must be something inside, of which he was frightened, and when I cautiously investigated I found a very small snake coiled up in the centre of his bed. After I had captured it, I found that it was a harmless type; Cholmondely, of course, could not tell the difference, and he was taking no chances.

Cholmondely was so quick at learning tricks and so willing to show off that when he returned to England, he became quite famous and even made several appearances on television, delighting the audiences by sitting on a chair, with a hat on, taking a cigarette and lighting it for himself; pouring out and drinking a glass of beer and many other things. I think he must have become rather swollen-headed with his success, for not long after this he managed to escape from the zoo and went wandering off by himself through Regent's Park, much to the horror of everyone he met. On reaching the main road, he found a bus standing there and promptly climbed aboard, for he loved being taken for a ride. The passengers, however, decided they would rather not travel by that particular bus if Cholmondely was going to use it as well, and they were all struggling to get out when some keepers arrived from the zoo and took Cholmondely in charge. He was marched back to his cage in disgrace, but if I know Cholmondely, he must have thought it worth any amount of scoldings just for the sight of all those people trying to get off the bus together, and getting stuck in the door. Cholmondely had a great sense of humour.

O For a Booke

O for a Booke and a shadie nooke,
  eyther in-a-doore or out;
With the grene leaves whispering overhede,
  or the Streete cryes all about.
Where I maie Reade all at my ease,
  both of the Newe and Olde;
For a jollie goode Booke whereon to looke,
  is better to me than Golde.

UNKNOWN POET—PROBABLY 16TH-CENTURY

Dinner at the Inn

Charles Dickens

Illustrated by "Phiz"
and Will Nickless

Charles Dickens (1812–70) was born near Portsmouth where his father was a clerk in the Navy Pay Office. His parents were very poor and his father was imprisoned for debt. As a result, Charles Dickens had an unhappy childhood and received little education. However, he became a newspaper reporter in spite of his early difficulties and by the age of twenty-four he was a well-known and successful writer. Today, his fame is based, of course, on his series of colourful novels. He wrote very little for children although generations have enjoyed his books, especially the early chapters of "David Copperfield", "Great Expectations", "Oliver Twist" and "Nicholas Nickleby". Another great favourite is "A Christmas Carol". His books are marvellously atmospheric and peopled with a fascinating gallery of characters. Who can forget Mr. Micawber, Betsy Trotwood, Miss Havisham, Bill Sykes, Wackford Squeers and the dreadful Mr. Scrooge?

Here is an extract from "David Copperfield". If you read this book, you will find many of Dicken's unhappy childhood experiences related there. In the piece we have chosen, Mr. Murdstone, David's cruel and domineering stepfather, has decided that David should go to boarding-school, and for the first time in his life, David is on his own. This is what happens on his journey:

THE coach was in the yard, shining very much all over, but without any horses to it as yet; and it looked in that state as if nothing was more unlikely than its ever going to London. I was thinking this, and wondering what would ultimately become of my box, which Mr. Barkis had put down on the yard-pavement by the pole (he having driven up the yard to turn his cart), and also what would ultimately become of me, when a lady looked out of a bow-window where some fowls and joints of meat were hanging up, and said: "Is that the little gentleman from Blunderstone?"

"Yes, ma'am," I said.

"What name?" inquired the lady.

"Copperfield, ma'am," I said.

"That won't do," returned the lady, "nobody's dinner is paid for here, in that name."

"Is it Murdstone, ma'am?" I said.

"If you're Master Murdstone," said the lady, "why do you go and give another name first?"

I explained to the lady how it was, who then rang a bell, and called out, "William! Show the coffee-room!" upon which a waiter came running out of a kitchen on the opposite side of the yard to show it, and seemed a good deal surprised when he was only to show it to me.

It was a large long room with some large maps in it. I doubt if I could have felt much stranger if the maps had been real foreign countries, and I cast away in the middle of them. I felt it was taking a liberty to sit down, with my cap in my hand, on the corner of the chair nearest the door; and when the waiter laid a cloth on purpose for me, and put a set of casters on it, I think I must have turned red all over with modesty.

He brought me some chops, and vegetables, and took the covers off in such a bouncing manner that I was afraid I must have given him some offence. But he greatly relieved my mind by putting a chair for me at the table, and saying very affably:

"Now, six-foot! Come on!"

I thanked him, and took my seat at the board; but found it extremely difficult to handle my knife and fork with anything like dexterity, or to avoid splashing myself with the gravy, while he was standing opposite, staring so hard, and making me blush in the most dreadful manner every time I caught his eye. After watching me into the second chop, he said:

"There's half a pint of ale for you. Will you have it now?"

I thanked him and said "Yes." Upon which he poured it out of a jug into a large tumbler, and held it up against the light, and made it look beautiful.

"My eye!" he said. "It seems a good deal, don't it?"

"It does seem a good deal," I answered with a smile. For it was quite delightful to me to find him so pleasant. He was a twinkling-eyed pimple-faced man, with his hair standing upright all over his head; and as he stood with one arm akimbo, holding up the glass to the light with the other hand, he looked quite friendly.

"There was a gentleman here yesterday," he said—"a stout gentleman, by the name of Topsawyer—perhaps you know him?"

"No," I said, "I don't think——"

"In breeches, and gaiters, broad-brimmed hat, grey coat, speckled choker," said the waiter.

"No," I said bashfully, "I haven't the pleasure——"

"He came in here," said the waiter, looking at the light through the tumbler, "ordered a glass of this ale—*would* order it—I told him not—drank it, and fell dead. It was too old for him. It oughtn't to be drawn; that's the fact."

I was very much shocked to hear of this melancholy accident, and said I thought I had better have some water.

"Why you see," said the waiter, still looking at the light through the tumbler, with one of his eyes shut up, "our people don't like things being ordered and left. It offends 'em. But I'll drink it, if you like. I'm used to it, and use is everything. I don't think it'll hurt me, if I throw my head back, and take it off quick. Shall I?"

I replied that he would much oblige me by drinking it, if he thought he could do it safely, but by no means otherwise. When he did throw his head back, and take it off quick, I had a horrible fear, I confess, of seeing him meet the fate of the lamented Mr. Topsawyer, and fall lifeless on the carpet. But it didn't hurt him. On the contrary, I thought he seemed the fresher for it.

"What have we got here?" he said, putting a fork into my dish. "Not chops?"

"Chops," I said.

"Lord bless my soul!" he exclaimed. "I didn't know they were chops. Why a chop's the very thing to take off the bad effects of that beer! Ain't it lucky?"

So he took a chop by the bone in one hand, and a potato in the other, and ate away with a very good appetite, to my extreme satisfaction. He afterwards took another chop, and another potato; and after that another chop and another potato. When he had done, he brought me a pudding, and having set it before me, seemed to become absent in his mind for some moments.

"How's the pie?" he said, rousing himself.

"It's a pudding," I made answer.

"Pudding!" he exclaimed. "Why bless me, so it is! What!" looking at it nearer.

"I don't think it'll hurt me if I take it off quick."

"You don't mean to say it's a batter-pudding?"

"Yes, it is indeed."

"Why a batter-pudding," he said, taking up a tablespoon, "is my favourite pudding! Ain't that lucky? Come on, little 'un, and let's see who'll get most."

The waiter certainly got most. He entreated me more than once to come in and win, but what with his tablespoon to my teaspoon, his dispatch to my dispatch, and his appetite to my appetite, I was left far behind at the first mouthful, and had no chance with him. I never saw anyone enjoy a pudding so much, I think; and he laughed, when it was all gone, as if his enjoyment of it lasted still.

Finding him so very friendly and companionable, it was then that I asked for the pen and ink and paper, to write to Peggotty. He not only brought it immediately, but was good enough to look over me while I wrote the letter. When I had finished it, he asked me where I was going to school.

I said: "Near London," which was all I knew.

"Oh! my eye!" he said, looking very low-spirited, "I am sorry for that!"

"Why?" I asked him.

"Oh, Lord!" he said, shaking his head, "that's the school where they broke the boy's ribs—two ribs—a little boy he was. I should say he was—let me see—how old are you, about?"

I told him between eight and nine.

"That's just his age," he said. "He was eight years and six months old when they broke his first rib; eight years and eight months old when they broke his second, and did for him."

I could not disguise from myself, or from the waiter, that this was an uncomfortable coincidence, and inquired how it was done. His answer was not cheering to my spirits, for it consisted of two dismal words, "With whopping."

The blowing of the coach-horn in the yard was a seasonable diversion, which made me get up and hesitatingly inquire, in the mingled pride and diffidence of having a purse (which I took out of my pocket), if there were anything to pay.

"There's a sheet of letter-paper," he returned, "Did you ever buy a sheet of letter-paper?"

I could not remember that I ever had.

"It's dear," he said, "on account of duty. Threepence. That's the way we're taxed in this country. There's nothing else, except the waiter. Never mind the ink. I lose by that."

"What should you—what should I—how much ought I to—what would it be right to pay the waiter, if you please?" I stammered, blushing.

"If I hadn't a family, and that family hadn't the cowpock," said the waiter, "I wouldn't take a sixpence. If I didn't support a aged parent, and a lovely sister,"—

here the waiter was greatly agitated—"I wouldn't take a farthing. If I had a good place, and was treated well here, I should beg acceptance of a trifle, instead of taking it. But I live on broken wittles—and I sleep on the coals"—here the waiter burst into tears.

I was very much concerned for his misfortunes, and felt that any recognition short of ninepence would be mere brutality and hardness of heart. Therefore I gave him one of my three bright shillings, which he received with much humility and veneration, and spun up with his thumb, directly afterwards, to try the goodness of

It was a little disconcerting to me, to find, when I was being helped up behind the coach, that I was supposed to have eaten all the dinner without any assistance. I discovered this, from overhearing the lady in the bow-window say to the guard, "Take care of that child, George, or he'll burst," and from observing that the women-servants who were about the place came out to look and giggle at me as a young phenomenon. My unfortunate friend the waiter, who had quite recovered his spirits, did not appear to be disturbed by this, but joined in the general admiration without being at all confused. If I had any doubt of him, I suppose this half-awakened it; but I am inclined to believe that with the simple confidence of a child, and the natural reliance of a child upon superior years (qualities I am very sorry any children should prematurely change for worldly wisdom), I had no serious mistrust of him on the whole, even then.

I felt it rather hard, I must own, to be made, without deserving it, the subject of jokes between the coachman and guard as to the coach drawing heavy behind, on account of my sitting there, and as to the greater expediency of my travelling by wagon. The story of my supposed appetite getting wind among the outside passengers, they were merry upon it likewise; and asked me whether I was going to be paid for, at school, as two brothers or three, and whether I was contracted for, or went upon the regular terms; with other pleasant questions. But the worst of it was, that I knew I should be ashamed to eat anything, when an opportunity offered, and that, after a rather light dinner, I should remain hungry all night—for I had left my cakes behind, at the hotel, in my hurry. My apprehensions were realized. When we stopped for supper I couldn't muster courage to take any, though I should have liked it very much, but sat by the fire and said I didn't want anything. This did not save me from more jokes either; for a husky-voiced gentleman with a rough face, who had been eating out of a sandwich-box nearly all the way, except when he had been drinking out of a bottle, said I was like a boa constrictor, who took enough at one meal to last him a long time; after which he actually brought a rash out upon himself with boiled beef.

Mr Nobody

I know a funny little man,
   As quiet as a mouse,
Who does the mischief that is done
   In everybody's house!
There's no one ever sees his face,
   And yet we all agree
That every plate we break was cracked
   By Mr. Nobody.

'Tis he who always tears our books,
   Who leaves the door ajar,
He pulls the buttons from our shirts,
   And scatters pins afar;
That squeaking door will always squeak
   For, prithee, don't you see,
We leave the oiling to be done
   By Mr. Nobody.

He puts damp wood upon the fire,
   That kettles cannot boil;
His are the feet that bring in mud,
   And all the carpets soil.
The papers always are mislaid,
Who had them last but he?
There's not one tosses them about
   But Mr. Nobody.

The finger-marks upon the door
   By none of us are made;
We never leave the blinds unclosed,
   To let the curtains fade;
The ink we never spill; the boots
   That lying round you see
Are not our boots; they all belong
   To Mr. Nobody.

UNKNOWN

"Seek 'em Out, Crusoe"

R. M. Ballantyne

Illustrated by Robert Geary and John Berry

Born in Edinburgh, Robert Michael Ballantyne (1825–1894) joined the Hudson Bay Company as a clerk and spent six years in Canada fur-trading with the Indians. This gave him his background for "The Young Fur Traders" and "The Dog Crusoe" (from which our story comes). Ballantyne produced over a hundred books and was doubtless the most popular boys' writer of his century. Always adventurous, he is never far-fetched; his tales are straightforward, his characters lively, and his stories have an air of simple truth. There are few writers for boys who remain in demand a hundred years after their books were published; but this is true of Ballantyne, and "The Coral Island", "The Gorilla Hunters" and "Martin Rattler" are among those still enjoyed. Here, Dick Varley, owner of the splendid dog, Crusoe, believes that his two companions have been captured by Indians. He meets a band of white trappers, and together they search for the lost men:

A RUN of twenty miles brought the travellers to a rugged defile in the mountains, from which they had a view of a beautiful valley of considerable extent. During the last two days a steady thaw had been rapidly melting away the snow, so that it appeared only here and there in the landscape in dazzling patches. At the distance of about half-a-mile from where they halted to breathe the horses before commencing the descent into this vale, several thin wreaths of smoke were seen rising above the trees.

"Is that your camp?" inquired Cameron, riding up to the Indian runners, who stood in a group in front, looking as fresh after their twenty miles' run as though they had only had a short walk.

To this they answered in the affirmative, adding that there were about two hundred Peigans there.

It might have been thought that thirty men would have hesitated to venture to attack so large a number as two hundred; but it had always been found in the experience of Indian life that a few resolute white men well armed were more than a match for ten times their number of Indians. And this arose not so much from the superior strength or agility of the Whites over their red foes, as from that bull-dog courage and utter recklessness of their lives in combat—qualities which the crafty savage can neither imitate nor understand. The information was received with perfect indifference by most of the trappers, and with contemptuous laughter by some; for a large number of Cameron's men were wild, evil-disposed fellows, who would have as gladly taken the life of an Indian as that of a buffalo.

Just as the word was given to resume the march Dick Varley rode up to Cameron and said in a somewhat anxious tone—

"D've obsarve, sir, that one o' the Redskins has gone off ahead o' his comrades?"

"I see that, Master Dick; and it was a mistake of mine not to have stopped him, but he was gone too far before I observed it, and I thought it better to appear unconcerned. We must push on, though, and give him as short time as possible to talk with his comrades in the camp."

The trappers pressed forward accordingly at a gallop, and were soon in front of the clump of trees amongst which the Peigans were encamped. Their approach had evidently spread great alarm among them, for there was a good deal of bustle and running to and fro; but by the time the trappers had dismounted and advanced in a body on foot, the savages had resumed their usual quiet dignity of appearance, and were seated calmly round their fires with their bows and arrows beside them. There were no tents, no women or children, and the general aspect of the men showed Cameron conclusively that his surmise about their being a war party was correct.

A council was immediately called. The trappers ranged themselves on one side of the council fire and the Indians on the other. Meanwhile, our friend Crusoe had been displaying considerable irritability against the Indians, and he would certainly have attacked the whole two hundred single-handed if he had not been ordered by his master to lie still; but never in his life before had Crusoe obeyed with such a bad grace. He bristled and whined in a low tremulous tone, and looked imploringly at Dick as if for permission to fly at them.

"The Pale-face traders are glad to meet with Peigans," began Cameron, who determined to make no allusion to his knowledge that they were a war party, "for they wish to be friends with all the children of the woods and prairies. They wish to trade with them—to exchange blankets, and guns, and beads, and other goods which the Peigans require, for furs of animals which the Pale-faces require."

"Ho! ho!" exclaimed the Indians, which expression might be translated, "Hear, hear!"

"But," continued Cameron, "we wish to have no war. We wish to see the hatchet buried, and to see all the Red-men and the White-men smoking the pipe of peace and hunting like brothers." The "Ho—ho—ing" at this was very emphatic.

"Now," resumed the trader, "the Peigans have got two prisoners—two Pale-faces—in their camp, and as we cannot be on good terms while our brothers are detained, we have come to ask for them, and to *present some gifts* to the Peigans."

To this there was no "Ho" at all, but a prolonged silence, which was at length interrupted by a tall chief stepping forward to address the trappers.

"What the Pale-face chief has said is good," began the Indian. "His words are wise, and his heart is not double. The Red-men are willing to smoke the pipe of peace, and to hunt with all men as brothers, but they cannot do it while many of their scalps are hanging in the lodges of their enemies and fringing the robes of the warriors. The Peigans must have vengeance; then they will make peace."

After a short pause he continued—

"The chief is wrong when he says there are Pale-faces in the Peigan camp. The Peigans are not at war with the Pale-faces; neither have they seen any on their march. The camp is open. Let the Pale-faces look round and see that what we say is true."

The chief waved his hand towards his warriors as he concluded, as if to say, "Search amongst them. There are no Pale-faces there."

Cameron now spoke to Dick in a low tone. "They speak confidently," he said, "and I fear greatly that your poor comrades have either been killed or conveyed away from the camp and hidden among the mountains, in which case, even though they should not be far off, it would be next to impossible to find them, especially when such a band of rascals is near, compelling us to keep together. But I'll try what a little tempting them with goods will do. At any rate, we shan't give in without a scuffle."

It now, for the first time, flashed across Dick Varley that there was something more than he imagined in Crusoe's restless anxiety, which had not in the least abated, and the idea of making use of him now occurred to his mind.

"I've a notion that I'll settle this matter in a shorter time than you think," he said hurriedly, "if you'll agree to try what *threatening* will do."

The trader looked grave and undecided. "I never resort to that except as a last hope," he answered; "but I've a good deal of confidence in your prudence. What would you advise?"

Dick and the trader whispered a few minutes together, while some of the men, in order to show the Indians how perfectly unconcerned they were, and how ready for *anything*, took out their pipes and began to smoke. Both parties were seated on the ground, and during this interval the Indians also held eager discussion.

At length Cameron stood up, and said to his men in a quiet tone, "Be ready, lads, for instant action. When I give the word 'Up', spring to your feet and cock your guns; but *don't fire a shot till you get the word*." He then stepped forward and said—

"The Peigan warriors are double-tongued; they know that they have hid the Pale-face prisoners. We do not wish to quarrel, but if they are not delivered up at once the Pale-faces and the Peigans will not be friends."

Upon this the Indian chief again stood forward and said, "The Peigans are *not* double-tongued. They have not seen Pale-faces till to-day. They can say no more."

Without moving hand or foot, Cameron then said in a firm tone, "The first Peigan that moves shall die! Up, lads, and ready!"

In the twinkling of an eye the trappers sprang to their feet, and cocking their rifles stood perfectly motionless, scowling at the savages, who were completely taken by surprise at the unusual suddenness and informality of such a declaration of war. Not a man moved, for, unlike white men,

they seldom risk their lives in open fight; and as they looked at the formidable row of muzzles that waited but a word to send instant death into their midst, they felt that discretion was at that time the better part of valour.

"Now," said Cameron, while Dick Varley and Crusoe stepped up beside him, "my young warrior will search for the Pale-face prisoners. If they are found, we will take them and go away. If they are not found, we will ask the Peigans to forgive us, and will give them gifts. But in the meantime, if a Peigan moves from the spot where he sits, or lifts a bow, my young men shall fire, and the Peigans know that the rifle of the Pale-face always kills."

Without waiting for an answer, Dick immediately said, "Seek 'em out, pup," and Crusoe bounded away.

For a few minutes he sprang hither and thither through the camp, quite regardless of the Indians, and snuffed the air several times, whining in an excited tone, as if to relieve his feelings. Then he put his nose to the ground and ran straight forward into the woods. Dick immediately bounded after him like a deer, while the trappers kept silent guard over the savages.

For some time Crusoe ran straight forward. Then he came to a spot where there was a good deal of drifted snow on the ground. Here he seemed to lose the trail for a little, and ran about in all directions, whining in a most piteous tone.

"Seek 'em out, pup," repeated Dick encouragingly, while his own breast heaved with excitement and expectation.

In a few seconds the dog resumed its onward course, and led the way into a wild, dark spot, which was so overshadowed by trees and precipitous cliffs that the light of the sun scarce found entrance. There were many huge masses of rock scattered over the ground, which had fallen from the cliffs. Behind one of these lay a mound of dried leaves, towards which Crusoe darted and commenced scraping violently.

Cholmondely had picked up another stone and was swinging it backwards and forwards like a professional cricketer, taking better aim.
From "The Story of Cholmondely"

*"Joe Blunt!" exclaimed Dick in a voice of intense amazement, while Crusoe snuffed round
the heap of leaves and whined with excitement.*
From "Seek 'em Out, Crusoe"

In a moment Dick's knife was out and cords were severed.

Trembling with dread that he should find this to be the grave of his murdered companions, Dick rushed forward and hastily cleared away the leaves. The first handful thrown off revealed part of the figure of a man. Dick's heart beat audibly as he cleared the leaves from the face, and he uttered a suppressed cry on beholding the well-known features of Joe Blunt. But they were not those of a dead man. Joe's eyes met his with a scowl of anger, which instantly gave place to one of intense surprise.

"Joe Blunt!" exclaimed Dick in a voice of intense amazement, while Crusoe snuffed round the heap of leaves and whined with excitement. But Joe did not move, neither did he speak a word in reply —for the very good reason that his mouth was tightly bound with a band of leather, his hands and feet were tied, and his whole body was secured in a rigid, immovable position by being bound to a pole of about his own length. In a moment Dick's knife was out, bands and cords were severed, and Joe Blunt was free.

"Thank God!" exclaimed Joe with a deep, earnest sigh, the instant his lips were loosened, "and thanks to *you,* lad!" he added, endeavouring to rise; but his limbs had become so benumbed in consequence of the cords by which they had been com-pressed that for some time he could not move.

"I'll rub ye, Joe; I'll soon rub ye into a right state," said Dick, going down on his knees.

"No, no, lad, look sharp and dig up Henri. He's just beside me here."

Dick immediately rose, and pushing aside the heap of leaves, found Henri securely bound in the same fashion. But he could scarce refrain from laughing at the expression of that worthy's face. Hearing the voices of Joe and Dick Varley in con-versation, though unable to see their persons, he was filled with such un-bounded amazement that his eyes, when uncovered, were found to be at their largest possible stretch, and as for the eye-brows they were gone, utterly lost among the roots of his voluminous hair.

"Henri, friend, I knew I should find ye," said Dick, cutting the thongs that bound him. "Get up if ye can; we haven't much time to lose, an' mayhap we'll have to fight afore we're done wi' the Red-skins. Can ye rise?"

Henri could do nothing but lie on his back and gasp, "Eh! possible! mon frère! Oh, non, non, *not* possible. Oui! my broder Deek!"

Here he attempted to rise, but being unable fell back again, and the whole thing came so suddenly, and made so deep an impression on his impulsive mind, that he incontinently burst into tears; then he burst into a long laugh. Suddenly he paused, and scrambling up to a sitting posture, looked earnestly into Dick's face through his tearful eyes.

"Oh, non, non!" he exclaimed, stretching himself out at full length again, and closing his eyes; "it are too goot to be true. I am dream. I vill vait till I am avake."

Dick roused him out of his resolute sleep, however, somewhat roughly. Meanwhile Joe had rubbed and kicked himself into a state of animation, exclaiming that he felt as if he was walkin' on a thousand needles and pins, and in a few minutes they were ready to accompany their over-joyed deliverer back to the Peigan camp. Crusoe testified his delight in various elephantine gambols round the persons of his old friends, who were not slow to acknowledge his services.

"They haven't treated us overly well," remarked Joe Blunt, as they strode through the underwood.

"Non, ze rascale, vraiment, zey are villains. Oui! How zey have talk, too, 'bout —oh-o-oo-ooo-wah!—roastin' us alive, an' puttin' ze scalp in ze vigvam for ze poo-poose to play vis!"

"Well, niver mind, Henri, we'll be quits wi' them now," said Joe, as they came in sight of the two bands, who remained in precisely the same position in which they had been left, except that one or two of the more reckless of the trappers had lit their pipes and taken to smoking, without, however, laying down their rifles or taking their eyes off the savages.

A loud cheer greeted the arrival of the prisoners, and looks of considerable discomfort began to be evinced by the Indians.

"Glad to see you, friends," said Cameron, as they came up.

"Ve is 'appy ov ze same," replied Henri, swaggering up in the joviality of his heart, and seizing the trader's hand in his own enormous fist. "Shall ve go to vork an' slay zem all at vounce, or von at a time?"

"We'll consider that afterwards, my lad. Meantime, go you to the rear and get a weapon of some sort."

"Oui. Ah! c'est charmant," he cried, going with an immense flounder into the midst of the amused trappers, and slapping those next to him on the back. "Give me veapon, do, mes amis—gun, pistol, anyting —cannon, if you have von."

Meanwhile Cameron and Joe spoke together for a few moments.

"You had goods with you, and horses, I believe, when you were captured," said the former.

"Ay, that we had. Yonder stand the horses, under the pine-tree, along wi' the rest o' the Red-skin troop; an' a hard time they've had o't, as their bones may tell without speakin'. As for the goods," he continued, glancing round the camp, "I don't know where—ah! yes, there they be in the old pack. I see all safe."

Cameron now addressed the Indians.

"The Peigans," he said, "have not done well. Their hearts have not been true to the Pale-faces. Even now I could take your scalps where you sit, but white men do not like war, they do not like revenge. The Peigans may go free."

Considering the fewness of their numbers, this was bold language to use towards the Indians; but the boldest is generally the best policy on such occasions. Moreover, Cameron felt that, being armed with rifles, while the Indians had only bows and arrows, the trappers had a great advantage over them.

The Indian who had spoken before now rose and said he was sorry there should be any cause of difference between them, and added he was sorry for a great many more things besides, but did not say he was sorry for having told a lie.

"But, before you go, you must deliver up the horses and goods belonging to these men," said Cameron, pointing to Joe and Henri.

This was agreed to. The horses were led out, the two little packs containing Joe's goods were strapped upon them, and then the trappers turned to depart. The Indians did not move until they had mounted; then they rose and advanced in a body to the edge of the wood, to see the Pale-faces go away. Meanwhile Joe spoke a few words to Cameron, and the men were ordered to halt, while the former dismounted and led his horse towards the band of savages.

"Peigans," he said, "you know the object for which I came into this country was to make peace between you and the Pale-faces. I have often told you so when you would not listen, and when you told me that I had a double heart and told lies. You were wrong when you said this; but I do not wonder, for you live among nations who do not fear God, and who think it right to lie. I now repeat to you what I said before. It would be good for the Red-men if they would make peace with the Pale-faces, and if they would make peace with each other. I will now convince you that I am in earnest, and have all along been speaking the truth."

Hereupon Joe Blunt opened his bundle of goods, and presented fully one-half of the gaudy and brilliant contents to the astonished Indians, who seemed quite taken aback by such generous treatment. The result of this was that the two parties separated with mutual expressions of esteem and good-will. The Indians then returned to the forest, and the white men galloped back to their camp among the hills.

Bonnie George Campbell

Hie upon Hielands,
  and laigh upon Tay,
Bonnie George Campbell
  rade out on a day.

Saddled and bridled
  and booted rade he;
Toom hame cam' the saddle,
  but never cam' he.

Down cam' his auld mither,
  greetin' fu' sair,
And down cam' his bonny bryde,
  rivin' her hair:

"My meadow lies green,
  and my corn is unshorn,
My barn is to build
  and my babe is unborn."

Saddled and bridled
  and booted rade he;
Toom hame cam' the saddle
  but never cam' he.

UNKNOWN

| Hie = high | rade = rode. | auld = old. | greetin' = weeping. |
| laigh = low. | toom = empty. | mither = mother. | rivin' = tearing. |

243

Theseus and the Minotaur

Re-told by Rex Warner

Illustrated by A. R. Whitear

Rex Warner (born 1905), the son of a clergyman and educated at Oxford University, has the unusual distinction of being equally at home in English and Greek literatures. At first a schoolmaster in Egypt and England, he became a novelist of great originality. But he is also a poet, and a translator of Greek poet-dramatists. He loves Greece and writes about that land and its ancient philosophers. His "Men and Gods", from which comes our tale of Theseus's fight with the Minotaur, is a re-telling of the stories from Greek myth and legend. Theseus, son of Aegeus, King of Athens, has already proved himself a hero by deeds of strength and daring; and this tells how he freed the Athenians from their bond to the King of Crete:

ATHENS was now safe and peaceful within the borders of her own land, but still every year she had to make a cruel sacrifice to a foreign power. At this time Minos, King of Crete, ruled the sea with his fleet of ships. Once he had made war on Athens because his son, a famous wrestler, had been murdered by the Athenians. He refused to make peace except on the condition that every year the Athenians should send him seven young men and seven girls. These, when they arrived in Crete, were to be put inside the famous labyrinth which the great artist Daedalus had built, and then they were to be devoured by the monstrous creature, half man, half bull, which was known as the Minotaur. The Athenians were forced to accept these conditions. Every year the youths and maidens were chosen by lot, and every year amongst the lamentations of the whole people, they set out for Crete in a ship which carried black sails as a sign of mourning.

When Theseus heard of this cruel custom he resolved to be himself one of the seven young men who were handed over to Minos. "Either I shall save my people," he said, "or I shall die with them. In any case I shall have done what I can."

His old father Aegeus was reluctant to let him go, but Theseus insisted on the plan which he had made. "Go then," said his father, "and may the gods preserve you! When the time comes I shall watch every day for your return. If you are successful and come back alive, change the sails of your ship to white, so that I may know at once what has happened."

Theseus promised to do as his father had asked him. Then he and the other thirteen victims, girls and young men, said farewell to their city, their friends, and their relations and embarked in a black ship with black sails which was to take them to Crete.

When they arrived at the great city of King Minos they looked in astonishment at the huge buildings decorated with paintings in all kinds of colours. There were paintings of bull-fights, at which the Cretans were particularly expert, of sea creatures, octopuses, dolphins and twining sea weeds. There were other paintings showing the life of the country—pictures of Cretan officers with their hired negro troops, of priestesses, naked above the waist, with outstretched arms round which coiled sacred serpents. There were high halls and galleries, enormous buildings; and at the sea port thronged the ships of Egypt and of Asia doing trade with the kingdom of Minos.

Theseus and his companions were, according to the custom, entertained for one night at the palace of the king. On the next day they were to be sent into the intricate mazes of the labyrinth. It was known that there was no escape from this place. The most that anyone could hope for was to die of hunger while wandering in the countless passages before meeting the monstrous Minotaur who would devour any human creature whom he met.

Theseus, as he sat at dinner and told King Minos of the exploits which he had already achieved, won not only the attention but also the love of the king's daughter Ariadne. She could not bear the thought that so beautiful and distinguished a young man should perish miserably on the next day and she determined to help him.

When, therefore, the fourteen young Athenians were led to the entrance of the labyrinth, Ariadne took Theseus aside and put into his hands a ball of wool. "Fasten one end of this wool," she said to him, "inside the doors, and, as you go, unwind the rest. Then, if you are successful in killing the monster, you will be able to find your way back again. I shall be waiting for you. In return for helping you I want you to take me back with you to Greece and make me your wife."

Theseus readily agreed to do as she said. As well as the ball of wool she had brought him a sword, and, hiding this underneath his cloak, he went forward into the labyrinth. The girls and the other young men waited for him inside the gates, while he picked his way along passages which turned and twisted and linked up with other passages, winding in and out, turning abruptly, or sweeping in long or short curves. As he went he unwound the ball of wool and listened carefully for any noise that might tell him of the whereabouts of the strange monster with whom he was to fight.

For long he wandered in complete silence and then, as he approached a part of the labyrinth where the walls turned at right angles, he heard the noise of heavy breathing, a noise that might have been made by an animal or might almost have been made by a man. He put down the ball of wool, gripped his sword in his hand, and advanced cautiously to the corner. Looking round it he saw a monstrous shape. Standing, with his head lowered, was the figure of a giant, but, on the massive neck and shoulders was not a human head but the swinging dewlaps, blunt muzzle and huge horns of a bull.

For a moment Theseus and the Minotaur gazed at each other. Then, after pawing the ground with his feet, the monster lowered his head and plunged forward. In the narrow passage Theseus had no room to step aside. With his left hand he seized one of the creature's horns and violently threw the head back while he buried his sword in the thick muscles of its neck. With a roar of pain the Minotaur shook his head and fell backwards. Theseus clung to the beast's throat, avoiding the blows of the great horns, and stabbing with his sword, soon drenched the floors and walls with blood. The struggle was soon over.

Theseus left the great body on the ground and, picking up what was left of the ball of wool, he began to rewind it and so retrace his steps to the place where he had left his companions. Seeing him safe, with the blood upon his hands, they knew that he had been victorious and crowded round him to press his hand and congratulate him upon his victory.

But there was no time to lose. Ariadne was waiting for them and she hid them until nightfall. In the dark they reached their ship, hoisted the sails and escaped.

Never more would Athens have to pay the abominable tribute to the King of Crete.

On their return voyage they stopped for the night at the island of Naxos. Here some god put into the hearts and minds of Theseus and his companions a strange and cruel forgetfulness. They rose at dawn and sailed away, leaving Ariadne asleep on the seashore. When she woke and saw the ship far away on the horizon and realized that she had been deserted, she wept and tore her hair, calling all the gods to witness how treacherously she had been treated by the man whose life she had saved. Alone and miserable she wandered on the rocky shore, frightened of wild beasts, but grieving most of all for the loss of her lover.

Here, in her terror, misery and loneliness, she was saved by the god Bacchus. Tigers and lynxes drew the chariot in which he rode. Behind him came, riding on a mule, his drunken old companion Silenus, with a band of fauns, satyrs and dancing worshippers waving their ivy wands, their loose hair wreathed in ivy or in myrtle. The sand and rocks of the deserted shore grew green with sprouting vines as the procession passed. Ariadne, too, felt the joy of the god's presence. Bacchus loved her and made her his wife. He took the crown that she wore upon her head and set it in the sky as a constellation among the stars.

Meanwhile Theseus sailed on to Athens. The joy and glory of his return was spoiled by another act of forgetfulness. His father Aegeus had told him that, if he returned safe, he was to change the black sails of the ship and hoist white sails as a sign of victory. This Theseus forgot to do, and when his old father, watching from the cliffs, saw a vessel with black sails coming from the south, believing that his son was dead, he threw himself down into the sea. So the day of Theseus's return was a day not only of triumph but of mourning.

On the death of Aegeus Theseus became king of Athens and the surrounding country. His government, both in peace and war, was strong and just, and, though at the end of his life the Athenians showed themselves ungrateful to him, long after his death they gave him the honours due to gods and heroes.

His First Flight

Liam O'Flaherty

Illustrated by A. J. Joyce

Liam O'Flaherty (born 1897) is an Irish novelist and short-story writer in whose work can be found some excellent short tales about animals. These animals do not talk like the beasts in the fables or in Kipling's stories. Nor are they fanciful like Dr. Dolittle's friends. They are just animals described as a sharply observant human eye might see them with lives and problems important to themselves and outside our human world. The story we have chosen is about sea-gulls.

THE young seagull was alone on his ledge. His two brothers and his sister had already flown away the day before. He had been afraid to fly with them. Somehow when he had taken a little run forward to the brink of the ledge and attempted to flap his wings he became afraid. The great expanse of sea stretched down beneath, and it was such a long way down—miles down. He felt certain that his wings would never support him, so he bent his head and ran away back to the little hole under the ledge where he slept at night. Even when each of his brothers and his little sister, whose wings were far shorter than his own, ran to the brink, flapped their wings, and

flew away he failed to muster up courage to take that plunge which appeared to him so desperate. His father and mother had come around calling to him shrilly, upbraiding him, threatening to let him starve on his ledge unless he flew away. But for the life of him he could not move.

That was twenty-four hours ago. Since then nobody had come near him. The day before, all day long, he had watched his parents flying about with his brothers and sister, perfecting them in the art of flight, teaching them how to skim the waves and how to dive for fish. He had, in fact, seen his older brother catch his first herring and devour it, standing on a rock, while his

parents circled around raising a proud cackle. And all the morning the whole family had walked about on the big plateau midway down the opposite cliff, taunting him with his cowardice.

The sun was now ascending the sky, blazing warmly on his ledge that faced the south. He felt the heat because he had not eaten since the previous nightfall. Then he had found a dried piece of mackerel's tail at the far end of his ledge. Now there was not a single scrap of food left. He had searched every inch, rooting among the rough, dirt-caked straw nest where he and his brothers and sister had been hatched. He even gnawed at the dried pieces of spotted eggshell. It was like eating part of himself. He had then trotted back and forth from one end of the ledge to the other, his grey body the colour of the cliff, his long grey legs stepping daintily, trying to find some means of reaching his parents without having to fly. But on each side of him the ledge ended in a sheer fall of precipice, with the sea beneath. And between him and his parents there was a deep, wide chasm. Surely he could reach them without flying if he could only move northwards along the cliff face? But then on what could he walk? There was no ledge, and he was not a fly. And above him he could see nothing. The precipice was sheer, and the

top of it was perhaps farther away than the sea beneath him.

He stepped slowly out to the brink of the ledge, and, standing on one leg, with the other leg hidden under his wing, he closed one eye, then the other, and pretended to be falling asleep. Still they took no notice of him. He saw his two brothers and his sister lying on the plateau dozing, with their heads sunk into their necks. His father was preening the feathers on his white back. Only his mother was looking at him. She was standing on a little high hump on the plateau, her white breast thrust forward. Now and again she tore at a piece of fish that lay at her feet, and then scraped each side of her beak on the rock. The sight of the food maddened him. How he loved to tear food that way, scraping his beak now and again to whet it! He uttered a low cackle. His mother cackled too, and looked over at him.

"Ga, ga, ga," he cried, begging her to bring him over some food. "Gaw-ool-ah," she screamed back derisively. But he kept calling plaintively, and after a minute or so he uttered a joyful scream. His mother had picked up a piece of the fish and was flying across to him with it. He leaned out eagerly, tapping the rock with his feet, trying to get nearer to her as she flew across. But when she was just opposite to him, abreast of the ledge, she halted, her legs hanging limp, her wings motionless, the piece of fish in her beak almost within reach of his beak. He waited a moment in surprise, wondering why she did not come nearer, and then, maddened by hunger, he dived at the fish. With a loud scream he fell outwards and downwards into space. His mother had swooped upwards. As he passed beneath her he heard the swish of her wings. Then a monstrous terror seized him and his heart stood still. He could hear nothing. But it only lasted a moment. The next moment he felt his wings spread outwards. The wind rushed against his breast feathers, then under his stomach and against his wings. He could feel the tips of his wings cutting through the air. He was not falling headlong now. He was soaring gradually downwards and outwards. He was no longer afraid. He just felt a bit dizzy. Then he flapped his wings once and he soared upwards. He uttered a joyous scream and flapped them again. He soared higher. He raised his breast and banked against the wind. "Ga, ga, ga. Ga, ga, ga. Gaw-ool-ah." His mother swooped past him, her wings making a loud noise. He answered her with another scream. Then his father flew over him screaming. Then he saw his two brothers and his sister flying around him, curving and banking and soaring and diving.

Then he completely forgot that he had not always been able to fly, and commenced himself to dive and soar and curvet, shrieking shrilly.

He was near the sea now, flying straight over it, facing straight out over the ocean. He saw a vast green sea beneath him, with little ridges moving over it, and he turned his beak sideways and crowed amusedly. His parents and his brothers and sister had landed on this green floor in front of him. They were beckoning to him, calling shrilly. He dropped his legs to stand on the green sea. His legs sank into it. He screamed with fright and attempted to rise again, flapping his wings. But he was tired and weak with hunger and he could not rise, exhausted by the strange exercise. His feet sank into the green sea, and then his belly touched it and he sank no farther. He was floating on it. And around him his family was screaming, praising him, and their beaks were offering him scraps of dog-fish.

He had made his first flight.

A Feather for My Cap

Seagull flying from the sea,
Drop a feather here for me!
Drop it down into my lap—
I need a feather for my cap!

My satin gown's as white as milk,
My stockings are the finest silk,
My shoes are made of Spanish leather,
But oh! my cap! it lacks a feather!

My girdle is of precious gold,
A bouquet in my hands I hold
Of wild rose buds and lucky heather—
But oh! my cap! it lacks a feather!

What use a gown of satin fine?
What use a grand bouquet—like mine?
What use are shoes of Spanish leather
If caps, or hats, do lack a feather?

IVY O. EASTWICK

Lily Rose and the Green Silk Petticoat

Eve Garnett

Illustrated by the Author

The youngest daughter of an English colonel and an Irish mother, Eve Garnett studied art at the Chelsea Polytechnic and Royal Academy School of Art and has had several exhibitions of her work in London. In 1937 she wrote and illustrated "The Family from One End Street" (from which this story comes) as "a shot in the battle against slums". It won the Carnegie Medal for the best children's book of the year. It is interesting to know that German and French and American and even Japanese children as well as British can understand and enjoy the family at One End Street for the book has been translated seven times.

LILY ROSE, as no one will deny, was Helpful in the Home. She could wash and mangle fairly well, scrub steps, knew how to fry bacon-and-eggs and kippers, and was an expert at blowing the noses and scrubbing the ears of her young brothers and sisters. Her great ambition was to own a laundry too—not a hand affair like her mother's, but a real steam one where she would walk about and tell dozens of girls in white overalls how to work. When she was not doing this, she would be showing visitors round or sitting in an office writing letters to the customers to explain why such a tired-looking handkerchief had been returned in place of their nice linen one with an embroidered initial in the corner. (Lily Rose knew all about this kind of correspondence—her mother did a lot of it.)

One afternoon, a pipe having burst and flooded her class-room, Lily Rose came home early from school. The front door was shut and locked, so evidently her mother and the two youngest children were out. She found the key in its usual place under a broken brick on the second step, and went in.

It was ironing day and piles of ironed and unironed garments lay about. The house linen—sheets and towels and things—seemed to be finished and were piled up in heaps ready to be aired.

So far Lily Rose's ironing activities on customers' washing had been confined to these dull and easy goods, though she had often tried her hand, not always very successfully, on her own and the family's clothes. The brilliant thought occurred to her that it would be an excellent idea and also her good deed for the day (she was a Girl Guide) if she were to finish off the ironing by the time her mother returned. It would be a lovely surprise, and at the same time a way of showing what she could do once she really had a free hand.

The irons were heating on the fire, and Lily Rose, without further hesitation, threw off her hat and coat, rolled up her sleeves, spread out a garment on the ironing blanket and seized one. Forgetting the stand, she put the iron down for a moment on the ironing sheet. Immediately a rich smell of burning blanket filled the room, and Lily Rose was sorry to see a large smouldering hole. She hastily put the iron on the stand and waited patiently for it to cool, testing the heat at intervals by the simple and professional method of spitting on her finger and dabbing it quickly on the iron. After some minutes of this she decided the iron was ready and set to work on a baby's overall. She made quite a good job of this and hung it proudly over a chairback to air, and, encouraged by such success, embarked upon the next garment —a green artificial silk petticoat. Now Lily Rose had heard much talk about the difficulties and dangers of ironing artificial silk, and, although she had never attempted such a thing before, she was not deterred; the great thing, she knew, was not to have too hot an iron. She spread out the petticoat carefully, took what she thought to be the cool iron from the stove and began. She made one long sweep up and down with the iron, and oh! what was happening! The petticoat was shrinking . . . shrinking . . . shrivelling up, running away before her eyes! Smaller and smaller it grew, while Lily Rose gazed fascinated and as if rooted to the spot, her eyes and mouth round "o's" of horror!

At last the shrinking seemed to stop and there it lay, the beautiful green silk petticoat, no bigger than a doll's—too small even for William—had he worn such things!

Poor Lily Rose! The smoking ironholder in her hand soon told her that she had taken the hot iron from the fire by mistake, and, of course, artificial silk——! Lily Rose put the iron back on the fire, sat down on a pile of airing sheets and wept!

Five minutes later the door opened and in came Mrs. Ruggles with William in her arms and Peg hanging on to her skirt. "Goodness gracious, what a smell of burning!" she cried, "something's scorching!" and then, catching sight of the tearful Lily Rose: "What you here so early for—been sent home from school?—In my day we got kept *in* not let *out*." Then, as Lily Rose made no reply, "You're not *hurt*?"

But Lily Rose was past speech; she could only point to the table where the remains of the petticoat lay.

"Whatever *is* the matter?" cried Mrs. Ruggles. "Speak, *do*. I can see you've been and burnt my ironing blanket, anyway, and what's this thing?" she added, going up to the table. "Doll's clothes? *How often have I told you not to touch the irons when I'm out!*"

"It's not doll's clothes," wept Lily Rose, now very tearful indeed. "It's a customer's petticoat; we was all sent home early (sniff) because there was a flood (sniff), and I was trying to help you and do my good deed for the day (sniff) for the Guides (several sniffs)."

Mrs. Ruggles was very angry. Although she lost handkerchiefs and *did* shrink woollens occasionally, she was a good and careful worker, and in all her long career as a laundress had certainly never reduced a garment to one-sixth of its original size!

"That petticoat belongs to Mrs. Beaseley up at The Laurels in Sycamore Road—one of my best customers, I'd have you know," she cried. "Both her children have a clean frock a day each in the summer, and I've given her satisfaction for over three years! It will have to be replaced, and a nice expense *that's* going to be! 'Good deed' *indeed*! Well, it don't look like it to me, and I've no patience with these Guides— seems to me Guiding's about the last thing they do. To-morrow you'll come with me to Mrs. Beaseley's and explain as it was you and not your mother, who's a careful, hard-working, reliable laundress, as spoilt her nice petticoat, and she'll have something to say to you, I shouldn't wonder; and you'll get no jam for tea to-day, and no cake on Sunday neither. Now then, stop that sniffing, put the kettle on and get the tea."

The next morning Lily Rose and her mother set off to return Mrs. Beaseley's laundry.

If only, thought Lily Rose, it hadn't been Saturday! Then she would have been safe at school. But, instead, here she was, help-

The whole Ruggles family, with Lily Rose leaning against the door post.

ing her mother, still very cross with her, to carry the laundry basket with one hand, and clasping the remains of the green silk petticoat done up in a parcel in the other. And what she felt like inside—ough! Sick at the very thought of Mrs. Beaseley and her house and her fat cook who usually opened the back door to them and made silly remarks. What remarks she'd make to-day! And Mrs. Beaseley herself! Probably she would be going to a party on Sunday and want to wear her beautiful petticoat; perhaps she might even say that Mrs. Ruggles must buy her one by this evening, and how awful that would be! Both the twins and Mr. Ruggles had had their boots soled this week, and Mr. Ruggles' auntie had died and they'd sent a wreath which cost a whole 3s. 6d.—the family funds were very low, she knew. Worse still, perhaps Mrs. Beaseley would say Mrs. Ruggles needn't wash for her any more after this. And the silly part of it all was that she, Lily Rose, had meant to be so kind and give Mrs. Ruggles a surprise. Life was a puzzle, she decided.

At last they reached the house, and Lily Rose, wishing she were dead twice over, knocked at the back door. The fat cook opened it.

"Early to-day, Mrs. Ruggles," she said. "Got a helper, I see; come right in and wait a minute, will you?"

Just at that moment Mrs. Beaseley herself came into the kitchen. "Good morning, Mrs. Ruggles," she said, "you're early to-day. Is this one of your large family—I don't think I've seen her before? I expect she'd like a glass of lemonade or some cake, wouldn't she?"

"She'd *like* it all right, thank you," replied Mrs. Ruggles, "but she don't *deserve* it!"

"How's that?" said Mrs. Beaseley, turning to Lily Rose, but with such a twinkle in her eye that that young lady felt better at once.

"You tell Mrs. Beaseley yourself," commanded Mrs. Ruggles.

"Well, come in and have the cake first, and tell me after," said Mrs. Beaseley. "Bertha," she called to the fat cook, "get a cup of tea for Mrs. Ruggles and some cake for the little girl"—she turned to Lily Rose—"I don't know your name?"

"Please, it's Lily Rose," said the child shyly — she *hated* telling her name — people so nearly always laughed. But Mrs. Beaseley didn't laugh. Surprisingly instead, she said; "What a pretty name! I don't think anyone with such a nice name could do anything *very* dreadful, do you!" And she smiled so kindly that Lily Rose nearly began to cry again.

"Silly fool I am," she said to herself, "she's ever so kind."

They went into the kitchen, and while Mrs. Ruggles drank her tea and Lily Rose ate her cake—she took a good slice for she knew she wasn't going to have any next day at home—Mrs. Beaseley asked after Mr. Ruggles and the family, and especially the progress of William.

"Grows fine he does," said Mrs. Ruggles, pleased and smiling again at such interest in her family. "Nurse says he's the best baby at the Welfare Centre—I takes him there once a week to be weighed."

"You'll have to send him to the baby show in July, Mrs. Ruggles," said Mrs. Beaseley.

"Well, *I'd* like to," said Mrs. Ruggles, "but his father don't hold with them. He gets *Ideas* in his Head, Ruggles does," she added.

"I'd like to meet your husband, Mrs. Ruggles," laughed Mrs. Beaseley. "I come across so few people with ideas in their heads!"

Lily Rose stared. This was a new way of looking at things. Her own head was always full of ideas—too many it seemed. Yesterday's trouble had been an idea—if only she could explain that to Mrs. Beaseley perhaps she wouldn't mind quite so much about her petticoat.

Just then the fat cook returned with the empty laundry basket. "I'm afraid there's something missing, Mrs. Ruggles," she said. "There's one green and one pink petticoat on the list, the pink one is here all right—I'm afraid you've forgotten to put in the other."

Mrs. Ruggles looked at Lily Rose, and Lily Rose looked at Mrs. Ruggles, while Mrs. Beaseley looked inquiringly at them both. "Please Miss—Madame I mean," began Lily Rose breathlessly, "It was an idea (gasp)—I mean I had an idea. I ironed your petticoat to surprise Mum and (gasp), because I'm a Guide and have to do a good deed every day. I didn't mean to spoil it (gasp)—truly I didn't—I used the hot iron by mistake and the stuff ran away soon as I touched it (gasp)—and oh, please, *do* you think you could wear the pink one if you go to a party to-morrow and wait till next week for Mum to get you another (gasp)—because you see Dad and the twins all had their boots soled, and Auntie died (gasp) and we sent a wreath and . . ." thrusting the parcel into Mrs. Beaseley's hands, Lily Rose burst into tears.

But when Mrs. Beaseley undid the parcel and saw her petticoat *she* burst out laughing. "I never saw anything so funny!" she cried, "I should *love* to have seen it running away from the iron—it doesn't matter a bit, Mrs. Ruggles. It was a cheap petticoat, and I know artificial silk behaves like that sometimes if the iron is too hot. Cheer up, Lily Rose. Even if your ideas aren't always a success it's a good thing to have them, and I'm sure you meant to do a good deed. I used to be a Guide once," she added, "and I've made lots of mistakes over good deeds in my time. Cheer up now and have some cake and tell me what you're going to do when you leave school?"

There was a long pause. Lily Rose sniffed. "I want to run a laundry," she said shyly at last.

Oh, how Mrs. Ruggles and Mrs. Beaseley laughed, and as to the fat cook, Lily Rose thought she would have a fit! At last she began to giggle herself—did seem a bit of cheek after what she'd done!

"I mean a *steam* laundry," she said, but they only laughed more.

"Never mind, Lily Rose," said Mrs. Beaseley. "It's another Idea, and a very good one, but don't practise on my clothes again, will you? And now how about taking home the remains of that cake for the other children, and some of these biscuits for yourself?"

It was a very different journey home! To begin with, Mrs. Ruggles was no longer cross—she was laughing. "You beat all, you do, you and your ideas and your laundry," she kept saying. And although Lily Rose still held one side of the laundry basket it was empty and light, and instead of the remains of the petticoat in her other hand, she carried the remains of a very good cake and a bag of biscuits. She felt perfectly happy again, and only longing for the evening to tell the story of her good deed and adventures at the weekly Guide meeting. As for the no cake and jam at home, she'd eaten so much she felt she didn't want any more for a week, and anyway, if she did, she'd got the biscuits.

Lily Rose began to sing.

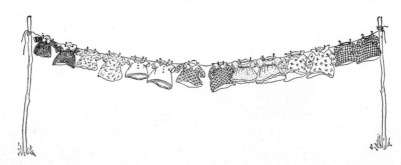

Tom Paints the Fence

Mark Twain

Illustrated by Victor G. Ambrus

Born in Florida, Missouri, a central state of the U.S.A., Mark Twain (1835–1910), whose real name was Samuel Langhorne Clemens, began his career as a printer's apprentice. He started writing, and travelled through various parts of America working as a journeyman printer. He obtained his river pilot's licence on the Mississippi steam-boats but the outbreak of the Civil War forced him to return to journalism. His famous pen-name comes from the well-known call of the man sounding the Mississippi in shallow places. ("Mark Twain" meaning "by the mark two fathoms"). If Dickens had found much to laugh at when he visited America, Mark Twain, in "The Innocents Abroad" and "A Tramp Abroad", kept the New World laughing at the Old. But his best books grew out of his memories of the hard life on the Mississippi—"Tom Sawyer" and "Huckleberry Finn". Not only do these books hold for Americans the life and spirit of a day that is gone, but they keep fresh for both young and old the enterprise and adventures of youth. The extract introduces you to "Tom Sawyer":

Saturday morning was come and all the summer world was bright and fresh, and brimming with life. There was a song in every heart; and if the heart was young the music issued at the lips. There was cheer in every face, and a spring in every step. The locust trees were in bloom, and the fragrance of the blossoms filled the air.

Cardiff Hill, beyond the village and above it, was green with vegetation, and it lay just far enough away to seem a Delectable Land, dreamy, reposeful, and inviting.

Tom appeared on the side-walk with a bucket of whitewash and a long-handled brush. He surveyed the fence, and the gladness went out of nature, and a deep melancholy settled down upon his spirit. Thirty yards of broad fence nine feet high! It seemed to him that life was hollow, and existence but a burden. Sighing he dipped his brush and passed it along the topmost plank; repeated the operation; did it again; compared the insignificant white-washed streak with the far-reaching continent of unwhitewashed fence, and sat down on a tree-box discouraged. Jim came skipping out at the gate with a tin pail, and singing "Buffalo Gals". Bringing water from the town pump had always been hateful work in Tom's eyes before, but now it did not strike him so. He remembered that there was company at the pump. White, mulatto, and Negro boys and girls were always there waiting their turns, resting, trading playthings, quarrelling, fighting, skylarking. And he remembered that although the pump was only a hundred and fifty yards off, Jim never got back with a bucket of water under an hour; and even then somebody generally had to go after him. Tom said:

"Say, Jim; I'll fetch the water if you'll whitewash some."

Jim shook his head, and said:

"Can't, Ma'rs Tom. Ole missis she tole me I got to go an git dis water an' not stop foolin' 'roun wid anybody. She say she spec' Ma'rs Tom gwyne to ax me to white-wash, an' so she tole me go 'long an' 'tend to my own business—she 'lowed *she'd* 'tend to de whitewashin'."

"Oh, never you mind what she said, Jim. That's the way she always talks. Gimme the bucket—I won't be gone only a minute. *She* won't ever know."

"Oh, I dasn't, Ma'rs Tom. Ole missis she'd take an' tar de head off'n me. 'Deed she would."

"*She!* She never licks anybody—whacks 'em over the head with her thimble, and who cares for that, I'd like to know? She talks awful, but talk don't hurt—anyways, it don't if she don't cry. Jim, I'll give you a marble. I'll give you a white alley!"

Jim began to waver.

"White alley, Jim; and it's a bully tow."

"My; dat's a mighty gay marvel, *I* tell you. But, Ma'rs Tom, I's powerful 'fraid ole missis."

But Jim was only human—this attraction was too much for him. He put down his pail, took the white alley. In another minute he was flying down the street with his pail and a tingling rear, Tom was whitewashing with vigour, and Aunt Polly was retiring from the field with a slipper in her hand and triumph in her eye.

But Tom's energy did not last. He began to think of the fun he had planned for this day, and his sorrows multiplied. Soon the free boys would come tripping along on all sorts of delicious expeditions, and they would make a world of fun of him for having to work—the very thought of it burnt him like fire. He got out his worldly wealth and examined it—bits of toys, marbles, and trash; enough to buy an exchange of work maybe, but not enough to buy so much as half-an-hour of pure freedom. So he returned his straitened means to his pocket, and gave up the idea of trying to buy the boys. At this dark and hopeless moment an inspiration burst upon him. Nothing less than a great, magnificent inspiration. He took up his

brush and went tranquilly to work. Ben Rogers hove in sight presently; the very boy of all boys whose ridicule he had been dreading. Ben's gait was the hop, skip, and jump—proof enough that his heart was light and his anticipations high. He was eating an apple, and giving a long, melodious whoop at intervals, followed by a deep-toned ding dong dong, dong dong dong, for he was personating a steamboat. As he drew near he slackened speed, took the middle of the street, leaned far over to starboard, and rounded-to ponderously, and with laborious pomp and circumstance, for he was personating the *Big Missouri*, and considered himself to be drawing nine feet of water. He was a paddle-boat, and captain, and engine-bells combined, so he had to imagine himself standing on his own hurricane-deck giving the orders and executing them.

"Stop her, sir! Ling-a-ling-ling." The headway ran almost out, and he drew up slowly toward the side-walk. "Ship up to back! Ling-a-ling-ling!" His arms straightened and stiffened down his sides. "Set her back on the stabboard! Ling-a-ling-ling! Chow! Ch-chow-wow-chow!" His right hand meantime describing stately circles, for it was representing a forty-foot wheel. "Let her go back on the labboard! Ling-a-ling-ling! Chow-ch-chow-chow!" The left hand began to describe circles.

"Stop the stabboard! Ling-a-ling-ling! Stop the labboard! Come ahead on the stabboard! Stop her! Let your outside turn over slow! Ling-a-ling-ling! Chow-ow-ow! Get out that head-line! Lively, now! Come—out with your spring-line—what're you about there? Take a turn round that stump with the bight of it! Stand by that stage now—let her go! Done with the engines, sir! Ling-a-ling-ling!"

"Sht! s'sht! sht!" (Trying the gauge-cocks.)

Tom went on whitewashing—paid no attention to the steamer. Ben stared a moment, and then said:

In order to make a man or a boy covert a thing, it is only necessary to make the thing difficult to attain.
From "Tom Paints the Fence"

The curious figure was drifting now to the tops of the naked trees.
From "Welcome back, Mary Poppins!"

"Hi-yi! You're up a stump, ain't you!"
No answer. Tom surveyed his last touch with the eye of an artist; then he gave his brush another gentle sweep, and surveyed the result as before. Ben ranged up alongside of him. Tom's mouth watered for the apple, but he stuck to his work. Ben said: "Hallo, old chap! You got to work, hey?"

"Why, it's you, Ben! I warn't noticing."

"Say, I'm going in a-swimming, I am.

oughtn't to like it. Does a boy get a chance to whitewash a fence every day?"

That put the thing in a new light. Ben stopped nibbling his apple. Tom swept his brush daintily back and forth—stepped back to note the effect—added a touch here and there—criticized the effect again, Ben watching every move, and getting more and more interested, more and more absorbed. Presently he said:

"Say, Tom, let me whitewash a little."

Don't you wish you could? But of course you'd druther work, wouldn't you? 'Course you would!"

Tom contemplated the boy a bit, and said: "What do you call work?"

"Why, ain't that work?"

Tom resumed his whitewashing, and answered carelessly:

"Well, maybe it is, and maybe it ain't. All I know is, it suits Tom Sawyer."

"Oh, come now, you don't mean to let on that you like it?"

The brush continued to move.

"Like it? Well, I don't see why I

Tom considered; was about to consent; but he altered his mind: "No, no; I reckon it wouldn't hardly do, Ben. You see, Aunt Polly's awful particular about this fence—right here on the street, you know—but if it was the back fence I wouldn't mind, and she wouldn't. Yes, she's awful particular about this fence; it's got to be done very careful; I reckon there ain't one boy in a thousand, maybe two thousand, that can do it the way it's got to be done."

"No—is that so? Oh, come now; lemme just try, only just a little. I'd let you, if you was me, Tom."

"Ben, I'd like to, honest injun; but Aunt Polly—well, Jim wanted to do it, but she wouldn't let him. Sid wanted to do it, but she wouldn't let Sid. Now, don't you see how I am fixed? If you was to tackle this fence, and anything was to happen to it——"

"Oh, shucks; I'll be just as careful. Now lemme try. Say—I'll give you the core of my apple."

"Well, here. No, Ben; now don't; I'm afeard——"

"I'll give you all of it!"

Tom gave up the brush with reluctance in his face, but alacrity in his heart. And while the late steamer *Big Missouri* worked and sweated in the sun, the retired artist sat on a barrel in the shade close by, dangled his legs, munched his apple, and planned the slaughter of more innocents. There was no lack of material; boys happened along every little while; they came to jeer, but remained to whitewash. By the time Ben was fagged out, Tom had traded the next chance to Billy Fisher for a kite in good repair; and when he played out, Johnny Miller bought in for a dead rat and a string to swing it with; and so on, and so on, hour after hour. And when the middle of the afternoon came, from being a poor poverty-stricken boy in the morning, Tom was literally rolling in wealth. He had, besides the things I have mentioned, twelve marbles, part of a jew's harp, a piece of blue bottle-glass to look through, a spool-cannon, a key that wouldn't unlock anything, a fragment of chalk, a glass stopper of a decanter, a tin soldier, a couple of tadpoles, six firecrackers, a kitten with only one eye, a brass door-knob, a dog-collar—but no dog—the handle of a knife, four pieces of orange-peel, and a dilapidated old window-sash. He had had a nice, good, idle time all the while—plenty of company—and the fence had three coats of whitewash on it! If he hadn't run out of whitewash, he would have bankrupted every boy in the village.

Tom said to himself that it was not such a hollow world after all. He had discovered a great law of human action, without knowing it, namely, that, in order to make a man or a boy covet a thing, it is only necessary to make the thing difficult to attain. If he had been a great and wise philosopher, like the writer of this book, he would now have comprehended that work consists of whatever a body is obliged to do, and that play consists of whatever a body is not obliged to do. And this would help him to understand why constructing artificial flowers, or performing on a tread-mill, is work, whilst rolling nine-pins or climbing Mont Blanc is only amusement. There are wealthy gentlemen in England who drive four-horse passenger-coaches twenty or thirty miles on a daily line, in the summer, because the privilege costs them considerable money; but if they were offered wages for the service, that would turn it into work, and then they would resign.

The Three Magic Gifts

Re-told
by Harcourt Williams

Illustrated by Biman Mullick

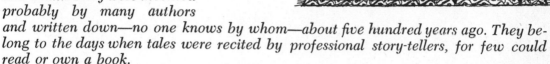

"The Arabian Nights Entertainments", from which this story comes, is a famous collection of old Eastern tales that combine the flavour of fairy tales with the glamour of ancient Arabia, India, Persia and China. They were invented probably by many authors and written down—no one knows by whom—about five hundred years ago. They belong to the days when tales were recited by professional story-tellers, for few could read or own a book.

In their present form these tales are linked together by a Sultan's wife who is under sentence of death. Most cleverly, she always stops her tales at such an exciting point that her husband, the Sultan, has to spare her life for another day—whereupon, before nightfall, she will start another story. We won't leave out the ending of this one!

THERE was once a Sultan of India who had three sons; the eldest was named Houssain, the second Ali, and the youngest Ahmed. There also lived at his Court the Princess Nourounnihar, his niece, who was the daughter of his younger brother. She was not only of unusual beauty but possessed every personal grace, and her uncle, out of brotherly love, had brought her up in the palace with his three sons.

Some years later the Sultan was seriously thinking of finding her a husband when he discovered that all three princes were desperately in love with their fair cousin.

He talked to each of the princes in private, and after remarking that it was impossible for one princess to be married to them all, he used every argument to persuade them either to submit to the choice which the princess might make in favour of one of the three, or to relinquish their pretensions to her hand. But meeting with an unconquerable obstinacy in each of them, he called them all three before him and thus addressed them:

"Oh, my children, since I cannot persuade you to give up the Princess, and as I am not inclined to use my authority in giving her to one in preference to the other two, I think it advisable that you should set out upon your travels, each into a different country, and since, as you know, I take great interest in everything that is curious and rare, I will promise the hand of the Princess Nourounnihar to whichever one shall bring me the most marvellous and rare curiosity. To defray the expenses of travelling, and for the purchase of the curiosity, I will give to each of you a sum suitable to the dignity of your birth."

As the three Princes were always obedient to their father's will, and each flattered himself that fortune would favour him, they all agreed, and that very day they took leave of the Sultan and prepared to set out early the next morning. Disguised as merchants and each with a trusty attendant dressed like a slave, they left by the same gate of the city. They travelled together for the first day until they came to an inn where the road divided into three. There they passed the night and, while supping, they agreed to travel for a year, and then to meet at the same place; and that the first to return should wait for the other two, so that they might all return to their father together. The next morning at daybreak, after having embraced and wished one another an agreeable journey, they mounted their horses and each took a different road.

Prince Houssain, the eldest brother, having often heard of the splendour of the kingdom of Bisnagar, set out towards the Indian Sea; and, having travelled for three months, arrived at the capital of that country. He took up his abode at a khan, appointed for foreign merchants, and the next day visited one of the principal bazaars, where the multitude of shops, stocked with finest Indian linen, silks and brocades from Persia, porcelain from China and Japan, filled him with admiration; but when he came to the goldsmiths' and jewellers' shops he was dazzled by the lustre of the precious stones exposed for sale. Another thing that attracted Prince Houssain was the number of rose-sellers that crowded the streets; indeed, he met no one who did not carry a flower or wear a wreath upon his head. The merchants, too, had flowers in their shops and the whole bazaar was fragrant with their perfume.

After Prince Houssain had walked through every street he felt tired and gladly accepted a merchant's civil invitation to rest in his shop. He had not been seated long before he saw a crier carrying a carpet about six feet square which he offered to put up for auction at forty purses. The Prince called to him and asked to see the carpet. When he had thoroughly examined it he told the crier that he could not understand how so small and poor a carpet could be priced so high. The crier, who took him for a merchant, replied: "O, master, if the price seems to you unreasonable you will be more astonished when I tell you that I am ordered not to let it go for less."

"Then," answered Prince Houssain, "there must be some secret about the carpet that makes it so valuable."

"You have guessed right," said the crier, "and you will understand when I tell you that by merely sitting on this carpet you may be instantly transported to whatever place you wish to visit, without being stopped by any obstacle."

The Prince, remembering that the object of his journey was to procure some rare curiosity for the Sultan, his father, thought that he could not find anything that would please him better, and thus addressed the crier: "If the carpet has the power you say it possesses, I will give you the forty purses and make you a present besides." "O, stranger," replied the crier, "I assure you I have told you the truth and it will be an easy matter to convince you. As you probably have not so much as forty purses upon you, let us go into the room behind the shop and I will spread the carpet; when we have both seated ourselves upon it and you have expressed the wish to be transported into your room at the khan where you lodge, if you are not instantly conveyed thither the bargain shall not stand."

The Prince accepted the conditions and, having obtained the owner's leave, they went into the back of the shop. The crier spread the carpet and they seated themselves upon it, and no sooner had the Prince expressed a wish to be transported to his room at the khan than he found himself there, and as he wanted no further proof of the virtue of the carpet he counted out the forty purses of gold and gave the crier twenty pieces for himself.

Great was Prince Houssain's joy at having thus fortunately become the possessor of such a wonderful carpet, which he had not the least doubt would win him the hand of the Princess Nourounnihar. By sitting on the carpet he might instantly have returned to the inn where the princes had agreed to meet, but as he was obliged to wait for his brothers, and was curious to see the King of Bisnagar and his Court, he resolved to stay longer.

Before the full year was completed he was fully satisfied with what he had seen and, his thoughts being continually with the Princess Nourounnihar, he fancied that he should be happier if he were only nearer to her. He therefore paid the master of the khan for the room he had occupied and, without telling him how he should go, put the key on the outside and shut the door. He then spread the carpet and seated himself thereon with his attendant.

Meditating for a moment, in a very deliberate manner, he wished to be conveyed to the inn where he and his brothers had agreed to meet, and instantly he was there.

Prince Ali, the second brother, after four months' travelling arrived at Schiraz, which was then the capital of Persia, and having on the way made friends with some merchants, lodged in the same khan with them.

The next morning he took a walk in that quarter of the city where they sold precious stones and merchandise of a curious and valuable nature, and among the criers who passed backwards and forwards he was much surprised to see one who held in his hand an ivory tube, about a foot long and an inch thick, which he put up for auction at forty purses. Turning to a merchant who stood at the door of his shop, he inquired whether the man was mad. "Oh, no," answered the merchant, "he is one of our best criers, and if he cries the ivory tube at forty purses it must be worth as much, or more, for some reason

or other which does not appear. He will pass my door in a moment and we will call him; in the meantime sit down on my sofa and rest yourself."

Prince Ali accepted the merchant's obliging offer, and when the crier passed the merchant called him by name. "Tell this stranger," said the merchant, "whether you are in your right senses as, from your putting up that ivory tube at forty purses, he has some doubts on the subject."

"O, my master," replied the crier, addressing himself to Prince Ali, "you are not the only person who takes me for a madman because of this tube, but when I have told you its peculiarity you shall judge for yourself whether I am or not. You will observe that this tube is fitted with a glass at both ends. By looking through one of them you see whatever object you wish to behold."

"If you can prove the truth of this," said the Prince, "I will retract my opinion," and having the tube in his hands he continued: "Show me through which of these ends I must look." The crier showed him and he looked through, wishing at the same time to see his father, the Sultan. At once he beheld him, in perfect health, sitting on his throne in the midst of his council. Then as there was no one in the world so dear to him, after his father, as the Princess Nourounnihar, he desired to see her, and immediately she appeared, surrounded by her women and seemingly in the best of health and spirits.

Prince Ali needed no further proof to persuade him that this tube was the most valuable thing not only in the city of Schiraz, but in all the world. He believed that he would never meet with such another rarity, and he thus addressed the crier: "I am very sorry that I should have thought you were mad, but hope to make amends by buying the tube, so tell me the lowest price the seller has fixed upon it." The crier assured him that he was ordered not to let the tube go for less than forty purses. The Prince then took him to the

apple and tell me what particular excellence it possesses that you should put it up at the extraordinary price of thirty-five purses."

"O, stranger," said the crier, putting the apple into his hands, "if you look at the outside of this apple it appears to be of very little value indeed; but if you consider the great use and benefit it is to mankind, you will confess that it is beyond price. He who possesses it is master of a great treasure. It cures all sick persons of the most mortal diseases, and if the patient is dying it will immediately restore him to perfect health; and this is effected in the easiest possible manner— merely by the sick person smelling the apple."

khan where he lodged and, counting out the money, received the tube.

Prince Ali was overjoyed at his bargain, and persuaded himself that as his brothers would not be able to find anything so rare, the Princess Nourounnihar would become his wife.

He now gave himself no further trouble, but spent his time seeing the wonders of Schiraz without disclosing his real character, until the caravan, with which he travelled thither, returned back to the Indies. This he joined and, without suffering any other inconvenience than the fatigue inseparable from so long a journey, he arrived at the inn, where he found his brother Prince Houssain, and together they awaited impatiently the arrival of Prince Ahmed.

Prince Ahmed, the third son, took the road to Samarkand, and the day after his arrival went into the bazaar. He had hardly entered the place before he saw a crier carrying an artificial apple in his hand which he put up to auction at the price of thirty-five purses. He stopped the crier, saying to him: "Let me see that

262

"If one may believe you," replied Ahmed, "the virtues of this apple are wonderful, and it is indeed valuable. But how can I, who may wish to become the purchaser, be persuaded that there is no deception or exaggeration in what you have told me?"

"O, my master," replied the crier, "the thing is known and can be vouched for by the whole city of Samarkand; but, without going any further, ask any of these merchants here and hear what they say. Several of them would not have been alive today if they had not made use of this excellent remedy. This apple is the result of the work and experience of a celebrated philosopher of this city, who applied himself all his life to the study of plants and minerals, and at last performed such surprising cures as will never be forgotten. He himself died suddenly before he could apply his own sovereign remedy, leaving his wife and several young children but poorly provided for, and to support them the widow has resolved to put it up for sale."

While the crier was telling Prince Ahmed the virtues of the artificial apple, a great many people gathered round them and confirmed what he said; and one among them said that he had a friend who was lying so dangerously ill that his life was despaired of, and would not this be a favourable opportunity of showing the Prince the virtue of the apple? Thereupon Prince Ahmed told the crier that if the smell of the apple cured the sick person he would give him forty purses.

The crier replied: "Let us go and make the experiment and the apple shall be yours."

The experiment succeeded and the Prince counted out forty purses to the crier, who delivered the apple to him. He then waited with the greatest impatience for the first caravan returning to the Indies. In the meantime he explored the city of Samarkand and the neighbouring country. On the arrival of the caravan he

set out and arrived in perfect health at the inn where his brothers were awaiting him.

Prince Ali, who had arrived some time before his brother Ahmed, asked Prince Houssain, who had been the first to arrive, how long he had been waiting. "Three months," answered Prince Houssain. "Then you certainly have not been very far," said Prince Ali.

"I will tell you nothing now," said his brother, "but only assure you that I was more than three months travelling to the place I went to."

"Then you must have made a short stay there," replied Prince Ali.

"You are mistaken, brother," said Houssain. "I stayed there for nearly five months, and might have remained longer."

"Then you must certainly have flown back!" resumed Prince Ali. "Otherwise I cannot understand how you can have been three months here as you would have me believe."

"I am telling you the truth," added Prince Houssain, "but it is a riddle which I shall not explain until our brother Ahmed comes; then I will let you know what curiosity I have brought home from my travels. I know not what you have brought, but believe it to be of small account, as I do not see that your baggage is increased."

"And pray what have you brought?" replied Prince Ali. "For I can see nothing but an ordinary piece of carpet with which you cover your sofa. But as you make a mystery of the gift you have brought, I shall do the same!"

"I consider the rarity I have purchased," replied Prince Houssain, "to excel all others; but we must wait until our brother Ahmed arrives so that we can communicate to each other our good fortune."

Prince Ali, who was fully persuaded that his ivory tube could have no rival, agreed to wait for Prince Ahmed before disclosing their treasures. When Prince Ahmed arrived they embraced and congratulated each other on the happiness of meeting together at the same place.

Then Prince Houssain, as the eldest brother, said: "Brothers, we shall have time enough hereafter to entertain ourselves with the particulars of our travels; let us come to that which is of the greatest importance for us to know. Let us no longer conceal the curiosities which we have brought home, but show them, that we may see to which of us the Sultan, our father, may give preference. To set the example," continued Prince Houssain, "I will tell you that I have brought from the kingdom of Bisnagar this carpet on which I sit. It is not of great beauty, as you see, but when I have told you its virtues you will be struck with admiration and confess that you have never heard of anything like it. Whoever sits on it and wishes to be transported to any place, however distant it may be, is immediately carried thither. I made the experiment myself before I paid for it, and when I had a mind to return from Bisnagar I made use of no other means than this wonderful carpet for myself and my servant, who can tell you both of the experiment whenever you please. I now await to hear what you have brought that can be compared with this carpet."

Here Prince Houssain ended, and Prince Ali said: "I must own, brother, that your carpet is one of the most surprising things imaginable, and I have no doubt of its virtue. But you must allow that there may be other things, I will not say more wonderful than your carpet, but at least as marvellous in another way. And to convince you of it, here is an ivory tube which appears to the eye no more a rarity than your carpet. It cost me as much, and I am as well satisfied with my purchase as you can be with yours. You will own that I have not been cheated when I tell you that by looking through one end of this tube you can see whatever you wish to behold. Take it," cried Prince Ali, "and make trial of it yourself."

Prince Houssain took the ivory tube and clapped it to his eye, desiring to see the Princess Nourounnihar. Prince Ali and Prince Ahmed, keeping their gaze fixed upon him, were surprised to see his countenance suddenly change and express great grief. "Alas, my brothers," cried Houssain, "to what purpose have we undertaken long and arduous journeys? In a few moments our lovely Princess will breathe her last. I saw her in her bed, surrounded by her women and attendants, who were all in tears. Take the tube, and behold for yourselves the pitiable state she is in." Prince Ali took the tube from Prince Houssain's hand and after he had looked presented it to his younger brother.

When Prince Ahmed saw that the Princess Nourounnihar's end was so near, he thus addressed the two Princes:

"Brothers, the Princess Nourounnihar, the object of our vows, is indeed at death's door; but provided we lose no time we may yet save her life." Then he took out the artificial apple and, showing it to his brothers, continued: "This apple which you see here cost as much as either the carpet or the ivory tube. The opportunity now presents itself to show its wonderful virtue. If a sick person smells it, though in the last agonies, it restores him to perfect health immediately. I have made the experiment, and can show you its wonderful effect on the Princess Nourounnihar if we make haste to reach her."

"If that is all," exclaimed Prince Houssain, "we cannot make more haste than transporting ourselves instantly into her room by means of my carpet. Let us then lose no time. Come and seat yourselves by my side, for the carpet is large enough to hold us."

As soon as the three were seated they all wished to be transported to the Princess Nourounnihar's chamber, and instantly they were there.

side to side, looking at those about her, and then rose from her bed just as if she had been awakened out of a sound sleep. Her women informed her with great joy that she was obliged to the three Princes for her sudden recovery. She immediately expressed great joy at seeing them again, and thanked them all.

While the Princess was attiring herself,

The sudden appearance of the three men startled the women. And the attendants, not at first recognizing the Princes, prepared to attack them with their weapons, but soon discovered their error.

Prince Ahmed no sooner found himself in the Princess's presence than he went to the bedside and held the apple beneath her nose. Some moments later the Princess opened her eyes, turned her head from

the Princes went to throw themselves at their father's feet and pay their respects to him. The Sultan received them and, embracing them, was greatly rejoiced at their return and for the wonderful recovery of the Princess, his niece, whom he loved as if she had been his own daughter. Then the Princes each presented the gift which he had brought: Prince Houssain, the carpet; Prince Ali, his ivory tube; and Prince Ahmed, the artificial apple; and begged the Sultan to declare which of them had won the Princess for a wife, according to his promise.

The Sultan of the Indies, having heard all that the Princes had to say, and being well informed of the wonderful way in which Princess Nourounnihar had been cured, remained silent for some time, considering what answer he should make. At last he delivered the following wise words: "I would declare for one of you, my children, with a great deal of pleasure, but can I do so with justice? It is true, Ahmed, the Princess is obliged to your artificial apple for her cure, but let me ask you whether you could have been so serviceable to her had you not known by Ali's ivory tube the danger she was in, and if Houssain's carpet had not brought you to her so soon? Your ivory tube, Ali, informed you and your brothers that you were likely to lose the Princess, and so far she is greatly obliged to you; but you must grant that that knowledge would have been of no service without the artificial apple and the carpet. And for you, Houssain, your carpet would have been of little use if you had not been acquainted with the Princess's illness by Ali's ivory tube and Ahmed had not applied his artificial apple. Therefore, as neither the carpet, the ivory tube nor the artificial apple has the least preference one over the other, but on the contrary there is perfect equality, I cannot grant the Princess to any one of you, and the only fruit you have reaped from your travels is the happiness of having helped equally to restore her again to health.

"If this be true," added the Sultan, "you see that I must have recourse to other means to determine the matter. Go, therefore, and take each of you a bow and arrow, and repair to the great plain outside the city, and I declare that I will give the Princess Nourounnihar to him who shoots farthest. I do not forget to thank you all for the wonderful gifts you have brought me in the carpet, the ivory tube and the artificial apple, which shall not only be preserved carefully, but used to advantage upon all occasions."

The three Princes had nothing to say against the decision of the Sultan. With their bows and arrows they went to the plain appointed, accompanied by a great concourse of people.

Prince Houssain, the eldest, shot first. Prince Ali shot next, and his arrow fell at a little distance beyond that of his brother. Prince Ahmed shot last, but his arrow went out of sight, and no one saw it fall, and in spite of a most diligent search it could not be discovered.

Although it was believed that Prince Ahmed had shot the farthest, it was necessary that his arrow should be found to establish his claim to the Princess's hand. The Sultan, therefore, decided in favour of Prince Ali, and gave orders for preparation to be made for the wedding, which was celebrated a few days afterwards.

Prince Houssain, whose affection for the Princess Nourounnihar was sincere and strong, abandoned the Court, became a Dervish and lived in pious solitude. Prince Ahmed resolved to search for the missing arrow. His wanderings led him away over vast distances until he encountered an unexpected happiness . . . but that is another story.

Welcome back, Mary Poppins!

P. L. Travers

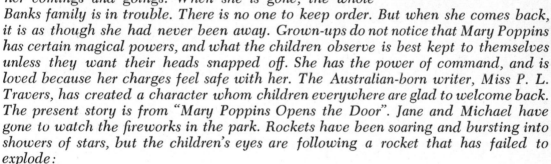

Illustrated by Mary Shepard and John Speirs

No nursemaid was ever more loved by her charges than the prim, unbending, self-assured, dictatorial Mary Poppins, whose extreme matter-of-factness is only equalled by the utter mysteriousness of her comings and goings. When she is gone, the whole Banks family is in trouble. There is no one to keep order. But when she comes back, it is as though she had never been away. Grown-ups do not notice that Mary Poppins has certain magical powers, and what the children observe is best kept to themselves unless they want their heads snapped off. She has the power of command, and is loved because her charges feel safe with her. The Australian-born writer, Miss P. L. Travers, has created a character whom children everywhere are glad to welcome back. The present story is from "Mary Poppins Opens the Door". Jane and Michael have gone to watch the fireworks in the park. Rockets have been soaring and bursting into showers of stars, but the children's eyes are following a rocket that has failed to explode:

"CLOSING TIME! Everyone out of the Park!" cried the Park Keeper importantly.

But Jane and Michael took no notice. They stood there watching, hand in hand. For their hopeful eyes had noticed something that nobody else had seen. Up in the sky a tiny spark hovered and swayed in the darkness. What could it be? Not the rocket, for that must have burnt itself out long ago.

And certainly not a star, they thought, for the little spark was moving.

"Perhaps it's a special kind of rocket, that has only one spark," said Michael.

"Perhaps," Jane answered quietly, as she watched the tiny light.

They stood together, gazing upwards. Even if there was only one spark they would watch till it went out. But, strangely enough, it did not go out. In fact, it was growing larger. . . .

Then suddenly Jane caught her breath. And Michael gave a gasp. Oh, was it possible——? Could it be——? they silently asked each other.

Down came the spark, growing longer and wider. And as it came, it took on a shape that was strange and also familiar. Out of the glowing core of light emerged a curious figure—a figure in a black-straw hat and a blue coat trimmed with silver buttons—a figure that carried in one hand something that looked like a carpet-bag, and in the other—oh, could it be true?—a parrot-headed umbrella.

The curious figure was drifting now to the tops of the naked trees. Its feet touched the highest bough of an oak and stepped down daintily through the branches.

It stood for a moment on the lowest bough and balanced itself neatly.

Jane and Michael began to run and their breath broke from them in a happy shout.

"Mary Poppins! Mary Poppins! Mary Poppins!" Half-laughing, half-weeping, they flung themselves upon her.

"You've c-come b-back at l-last!" stammered Michael excitedly, as he clutched her neatly-shod foot. It was warm and bony and quite real and it smelt of Black Boot-polish.

"We knew you'd come back. We trusted you!" Jane seized Mary Poppins' other foot and dragged at her cotton stockings.

Mary Poppins' mouth crinkled with the ghost of a smile. Then she looked at the children fiercely.

"I'll thank you to let go my shoes!" she snapped. "I am not an object in a Bargain Basement."

She shook them off and stepped down from the tree, as John and Barbara, mewing like kittens, rushed over the grass towards her.

"Hyenas!" she said with an angry glare, as she loosened their clutching fingers. "And what, may I ask, are you all doing—running about in the Park at night and looking like Blackamoors?"

Quickly they pulled out handkerchiefs and began to rub their cheeks. . . .

"But-but! Glog-glog! Er-rumph! Glug-glug!" Speechless with astonishment, the Park Keeper blocked their path.

"Out of my way, please!" said Mary Poppins, haughtily brushing him aside as she pushed the children in front of her.

"You can't do things like this," he gasped. "It's against the Law. And, furthermore, it's all against Nature."

He flung out his hand in a wild gesture and Mary Poppins popped into it a small piece of cardboard.

"Wot's this?" he demanded, turning it over.

"My Return Ticket," she calmly replied.

And Jane and Michael looked at each other and nodded wisely together. . . .

"Where did you come from? 'Ow did you get 'ere? That's what I want to know!"

"Curiosity Killed the Cat!" said Mary Poppins primly. She pushed the Park Keeper to one side and left him staring at the little green ticket as though it were a ghost.

The children danced and leapt about her as they came to the Park Gates.

"Walk quietly, please," she told them crossly. "You are not a School of Porpoises."

Up in the Nursery Annabel was screaming her head off. Mrs. Banks was running along the hall, calling out soothing phrases. As the children opened the Front door, she gave one look at Mary Poppins, and collapsed upon the stairs.

"Can it be you, Mary Poppins?" she gasped.

"It can, ma'am," Mary Poppins said calmly.

"But—where did you spring from?" Mrs. Banks cried.

"She sprang right out of a——" Michael was just about to explain when he felt Mary Poppins' eyes upon him. He knew very well what that look meant. He stammered and was silent.

"I came from the Park, ma'am," said Mary Poppins, with the patient air of a martyr.

"Thank goodness!" breathed Mrs. Banks from her heart. Then she remembered all that had happened since Mary Poppins had left them. I mustn't seem too pleased, she thought. Or she'll be more uppish than ever!

"You left me Without a Word, Mary Poppins," she said with an air of dignity. "I think you might tell me when you're coming and going. I never know where I am."

"Nobody does, ma'am," said Mary Poppins, as she calmly unbuttoned her gloves.

"Don't *you*, Mary Poppins?" asked Mrs. Banks, in a very wistful voice.

"Oh, *she* knows," Michael answered daringly. Mary Poppins gave him an angry glare.

"Well, you're here, now, anyway!" Mrs. Banks cried. She felt extremely relieved. For now she need neither advertise nor send for Miss Andrew.

"Yes, ma'am. Excuse me," said Mary Poppins.

And she neatly stepped past Mrs. Banks and put her carpet-bag on the banisters. It slid up swiftly with a whistling sound and bounced into the Nursery. Then she gave the umbrella a little toss. It spread its black silk wings like a bird and flew up after the carpet-bag with a parrot-like squawk.

The children gave an astonished gasp and turned to see if their Mother had noticed.

But Mrs. Banks had no thought for anything but to get to the telephone.

"The Drawing-room chimney has been cleaned. We are having Lamb Chops and peas for dinner. And Mary Poppins is back!" she cried breathlessly.

"I don't believe it!" crackled Mr. Banks' voice. "I shall come and see for myself!"

Mrs. Banks smiled happily as she hung up the receiver. . . .

Mary Poppins went primly up the stairs and the children tore past her into the Nursery. There on the hearth lay the carpet-bag. And standing in its usual corner was the parrot-headed umbrella. They had a settled, satisfied air as though they had been there for years.

In the cradle, Annabel, blue in the face, was tying herself into knots. She stared in surprise at Mary Poppins, and smiled a toothless smile. Then she put on her Innocent Angel look and began to play tunes on her toes.

"Humph!" said Mary Poppins grimly, as she put her straw hat in its paper bag. She took off her coat and hung it up on the hook behind the door. Then she glanced at herself in the Nursery mirror and stopped to unlock the carpet-bag.

It was quite empty except for a curled-up Tape Measure.

"What's that for, Mary Poppins?" asked Jane.

"To measure you," she replied quickly. "To see how you've grown."

"You needn't bother," Michael informed her confidently. "We've all grown two inches. Daddy measured us."

"Stand straight, please!" Mary Poppins said calmly, ignoring the remark. She measured him from his head to his feet and gave a loud sniff.

"I might have known it!" she said, snorting. "You've grown Worse and Worse."

Michael stared. "Tape Measures don't tell words, they tell inches," he said, protestingly.

"Since when?" she demanded haughtily, as she thrust it under his nose. There on the Tape were the tell-tale words in big blue letters:

W-O-R-S-E A-N-D W-O-R-S-E

"Oh!" he said, in a horrified whisper.

"Head up, please!" said Mary Poppins, stretching the Tape against Jane.

"Jane has grown into a Wilful, Lazy, Selfish child," she read out in triumph.

The tears came pricking into Jane's eyes. "Oh, I haven't, Mary Poppins!" she cried. For, funnily enough, she only remembered the times when she had been good.

Mary Poppins slipped the Tape round the Twins. "Quarrelsome" was their measurement. "Fretful and Spoilt," was Annabel's.

"I thought so!" Mary Poppins said, sniffing. "I've only got to turn my back for you to become a Menagerie!"

She drew the Tape round her own waist; and a satisfied smile spread over her face.

"Better Than Ever, Practically Perfect," her own measurement read.

"No more than I expected," she preened. And added, with a furious glare, "Now, spit-spot into the Bathroom!"

They hurried eagerly to obey her. For now that Mary Poppins was back, everything went with a swing. They undressed and bathed in the wink of an eye. Nobody dawdled over Supper, nobody left a crumb or a drop. They pushed in their chairs, folded their napkins and scrambled into bed.

Up and down the Nursery went Mary Poppins, tucking them all in. They could smell her old familiar smell, a mixture of toast and starchy aprons. They could feel her old familiar shape, solid and real beneath her clothes. They watched her in adoring silence, drinking her in.

Michael, as she passed his bed, peered over the edge and under it. There was nothing there, except dust and slippers. Then he peeped under Jane's bed. Nothing there, either.

"But where are you going to sleep, Mary Poppins?" he inquired curiously.

As he spoke, she touched the door of the clothes cupboard. It burst open noisily and out of it, with a graceful sweep, came the old camp bed. It was made up, ready to be slept in. And upon it, in a neat pile, were Mary Poppins' possessions. There were the Sunlight Soap and the hairpins, the bottle of scent, the folding armchair, the toothbrush and the lozenges. The nightgowns, cotton and flannel as well, were tidily laid on the pillow. And beside them were the boots and the dominoes, and the bathing caps and the postcard album.

The children sat up in a gaping row.

"But how did it get in there?" demanded Michael. "There wasn't a sign of it today. I know, 'cos I hid there from Ellen!"

He dared not go on with his questions, however, for Mary Poppins looked so haughty that the words froze on his lips.

With a sniff, she turned away from him and unfolded a flannel nightgown.

Jane and Michael looked at each other. And their eyes said all that their tongues could not: It's no good expecting her to explain, they told each other silently.

They watched her comical scarecrow movements as she undressed beneath the nightgown. Clip, clip—the buttons flew apart. Off went her petticoat—swish, swish, swish! A peaceful feeling stole into the children. And they knew that it came from Mary Poppins. . . . The thoughts he was thinking rose up in Michael like bubbles in soda water. And before he could stop them, they burst right out.

"Oh, Mary Poppins," he cried eagerly, "it's been just awful without you!"

Her lip quivered. It seemed as though a smile might break out. But it changed its mind and didn't.

"*You've* been awful—that's more like it! This house is nothing but a Bear Garden. I wonder anyone stays in it!"

"But *you* will, won't you?" he said wheedlingly.

"We'll be good as gold, if only you'll stay!" Jane promised solemnly.

She looked from one to the other calmly, seeing right down inside their hearts and understanding everything.

"I'll stay——" she said, after a little pause. . . .

"I'm glad I shook hands with the Sweep," said Michael. "It brought us wonderful luck. Perhaps he'll do the Nursery next and shake hands with *you*, Mary Poppins!"

"Pooh!" she replied, with a toss of her head. "I don't need any luck, thank you!"

"No," he said thoughtfully, "I suppose you don't. Anyone who can come out of a rocket—as you did to-night—must be born lucky. I mean—er—oh, don't look at me!"

He gave a little beseeching cry, for Mary Poppins was glaring at him in a way that made him shudder. Standing there in her flannel nightgown, she seemed to freeze him in his cosy bed.

"I wonder if I heard you correctly?" she inquired in an icy voice. "Did I understand you to mention *Me*—in connection with a Rocket?" She said the word "Rocket" in such a way as to make it seem quite shocking.

In terror, Michael glanced about him. But no help came from the other children. And he knew he would have to go through with it.

"But you did, Mary Poppins!" he protested bravely. "The rocket went pop! and there you were, coming out of it down the sky!"

She seemed to grow larger as she came towards him.

"Pop?" she repeated, furiously. "I popped—and came out of a rocket?"

He shrank back feebly against the pillow. "Well—that's what it looked like —didn't it, Jane?"

"Hush!" whispered Jane, with a shake of her head. She knew it was no good arguing.

"I have to say it, Mary Poppins! We saw you!" Michael wailed. "And if *you* didn't come out of the rocket, what did! There weren't any stars!"

"Pop!" said Mary Poppins again. "Out of a rocket with a pop! You have often insulted me, Michael Banks, but this is the Very Worst. If I hear any more about Pops —or Rockets——" She did not tell him what she would do but he knew it would be dreadful.

"*Wee-twee! Wee-twee!*"

A small voice sounded from the window-sill. An old Starling peered into the Nursery and flapped his wings excitedly.

Mary Poppins bounded to the window.

"Be off, you sparrer!" she said fiercely. And as the Starling darted away she switched out the light and pounced into bed. They heard her angrily muttering "Pop!" as she pulled the blankets up.

Then silence settled over them like a soft comforting cloud. It had almost folded them to sleep when the faintest murmur came from Jane's bed.

"Michael!" she said, in a careful whisper.

He sat up cautiously and looked in the direction of her pointing finger.

From the corner by the fireplace came a little glow of light. And they saw that the folds of the parrot umbrella were full of coloured stars—the kind of stars you expect to see when a rocket breaks in the sky. Their eyes grew wide with astonishment as the parrot's head bent down. Then, one by one, its beak plucked the stars from the silken folds and threw them on the floor. They gleamed for a moment, gold and silver, then faded and went out.

Then the parrot head straightened upon the handle, and Mary Poppins' black umbrella stood stiff and still in its corner.

The children looked at each other and smiled. But they said nothing. They could only wonder and be silent. They knew there were not enough words in the Dictionary for the things that happened to Mary Poppins.

"Tick-tock!" said the clock on the mantelpiece. "Go to sleep, children! Tick, tock, tick!"

Then they closed their eyes on the happy day and the clock kept time with their quiet breathing.

Don Quixote and the Windmills

Miguel de Cervantes

(re-told by Marjorie Hill and Audrey Walton)

Illustrated by Victor G. Ambrus

Miguel de Cervantes (1547–1616) was a Spaniard who lived about the same time as Shakespeare. Few writers can have had such an adventurous life. A young soldier in Italy, he was wounded in a sea battle off Greece, and was later captured and held as a slave for five years by Algerian pirates.

His "Adventures of Don Quixote" is one of the first novels ever written. It is about an elderly Spanish gentleman whose head has been turned by reading too many high-flown romances about knights and their romantic quests and adventures that were still popular at that time. Cervantes makes fun of these romances and the

"Adventures of Don Quixote" is rightly considered to be one of the great masterpieces of European literature. Here is Don Quixote near the beginning of his adventures:

DON QUIXOTE seemed quite happy during the next fortnight, and no one would have guessed that he was making plans for a new venture. Among other things, he still had to find a squire and so he had a quiet talk with one of the peasants who lived nearby, a good, honest sort of man, who was by no means well off. Among the many inducements our hero held out to him was the assurance that it was quite usual for anyone following the noble profession of squire to be made governor of an island. The gullible peasant, whose name was Sancho Panza, was so carried away by this hope that he made up his mind to leave his wife and children and go in search of such a governorship.

Once he had made sure of a squire, Don Quixote began to collect a little money. He sold a piece of land, mortgaged another, in each case getting the worst of the bargain but still amassing quite a reasonable sum of money. He borrowed a shield that was better than his own from one of his friends, mended his helmet once more, packed his bag and arranged with Sancho the day and the hour they would set out on their journey. Above all he advised Sancho to bring a satchel with him. Sancho promised not to forget, and added that as he was not used to much walking he would also like to bring his donkey, who was an excellent animal. The idea of a donkey rather worried Don Quixote. He could not recall any famous squire who had followed his master in this way. But comforting himself with the

273

thought that he would be able to give Sancho the horse belonging to the first knight whom he vanquished, he saw no real objection to Sancho starting out on a donkey.

When all plans had been made, Don Quixote and his squire set out one fine night, without taking leave of anybody, and when dawn broke they had made such good progress that there was little fear of their being overtaken. Good old Sancho rode like a patriarch, seated on his donkey between his satchel and his large water-bottle, bursting with eagerness to find the island he was some day to govern. Don Quixote, full of hope, sat proudly on Rosinante with his head held high. Sancho was longing to talk.

"Good master," he said, "I beg you will not forget what you promised me. You may be sure that that island, however big it is, won't be badly governed."

"Friend Sancho," replied Don Quixote, "knights have always been in the habit of giving their squires islands or kingdoms of which their valour makes them master, and you know that I would never depart from this custom. By the end of the week, if we are spared, I may have conquered a great empire, one of the kingdoms of which will be just the sort of place for you to govern. Do not imagine this is anything difficult or out of the ordinary; in our profession nothing is simpler or more usual."

"If that's so," replied Sancho, "once I'm a king, then my wife would at least be queen and my children would be princes and princesses?"

"Of course, who can doubt it?"

"Ah, but I doubt it—I know my wife and I tell you that if it rained crowns from heaven not a single one of them would sit well on her head. I warn you, she's not at all cut out for a queen; countess—well, I don't say no to that, but more than that, I won't vouch for."

"Don't worry, my friend; leave the matter to Providence. As for yourself, do not be too modest; you must not content yourself with being anything less than a governor."

Just then Don Quixote saw twenty or thirty windmills and, turning to his squire, he said:

"See how fortune favours us. Do you see those terrible giants in the distance? There are over thirty of them. But no matter; I'll fight these fierce enemies of God and man. Then we can begin to enrich ourselves with their spoils."

"What giants?" replied Sancho.

"Those you see there with their huge arms—some as much as two leagues long."

"Oh, take care, sir! They're only wind-mills. Those aren't arms, sir—it's just their sails. . . ."

"Ah, my poor innocent friend—it's easy to see you don't know much about adventures. They are giants. I know what I'm talking about. If you're afraid, you had better keep out of the way and say your prayers, while I undertake this dangerous and unequal combat."

Don Quixote clapped his spurs to his horse, paying no heed to poor Sancho, who still called out desperately that these were no giants but only windmills, nor did he discover his mistake when he drew nearer. He still saw a band of giants with long, threatening arms.

"Hold!" he shouted. "Hold, you cowardly brigands! A knight attacks you —single-handed!"

At that moment a light wind rose and the sails of the windmills began to turn.

"That won't help you," cried Don Quixote, "though you move more arms than the giant Briareus, it will do you no good."

Then, grasping his shield and commending himself to Dulcinea, he rushed with his lance at the sails of the first windmill.

With tremendous force, the knight and Rosinante were swept from the ground, then hurled violently to earth again, where they fell at least twenty paces apart.

Sancho urged on his donkey and reached Don Quixote with all possible speed. His master had fallen so heavily that it was difficult to set him on his feet again.

"Oh, Heaven help us!" cried Sancho. "I've been telling you for the last hour they were windmills. It was just crazy to think they were anything else."

"Peace, peace!" cried our hero. "In a life devoted to fighting one is ever subject to Fortune's changes, especially when one has an enemy like the dreadful sorcerer, Freston, who stole my books. I know now what he has done. He changed the giants into windmills in order to rob me of the glory of victory. But, patience! In the end my sword shall triumph over his wickedness!"

"Heaven grant it may!" said Sancho as he helped his master to his feet and hurried to Rosinante, whose legs were nearly out of joint.

When at last our hero was on his horse once more, he rode straight on, never doubting for one moment that this was the road which held many adventures in store for him. When Sancho asked whether the bruises were hurting him he answered:

"I confess that the reason I am not complaining is that knights are forbidden to complain, even when their stomachs are rent open."

"Oh, my goodness!" answered Sancho, "if squires too are forbidden to complain, it'll be the end of me. The least scratch, and I howl as though I'm flayed alive. . . . But don't you think, sir, it's time for supper?"

Don Quixote said he was not hungry, but that his squire might eat if he wished. So Sancho sat on his donkey, took some food from his satchel, and thought what a pleasant life it was to travel in search of adventures. He worried no more about the promises made him by his master, and

jogged along on his donkey, eating a hearty meal and drinking from his bottle with so much relish that a well-fed drinker of Malaga wine might have envied him. . . . Night fell and our adventurers spent it beneath the trees.

The Castaway

Daniel Defoe

Illustrated by W. G. Morden and Thomas Stothard

Daniel Defoe (1660–1731) was born in Cripplegate, London. He was the son of James Foe, a butcher, (Daniel changed his name about 1703) and he became a most successful businessman. He was a friend of King William III and after some experience of being a merchant adventurer in Spain and Portugal, he decided to take up writing. He wrote many political, religious and social pamphlets and was soon employed as a Government writer. One of his pamphlets got him into trouble with the authorities, and he was fined, imprisoned and put in the pillory. This was followed by more troubles and misunderstandings which led him to decide to leave London and retire to the country where he began writing a novel—"The Life and Strange Surprising Adventures of Robinson Crusoe of York, Mariner". This book, which we know simply as "Robinson Crusoe", was published in 1719 and was an immediate success. Though not originally intended for children, they soon took it to their hearts and it came to be regarded as a children's classic.

The part we have chosen is that in which Robinson Crusoe saves himself and starts to save what he can from the wreck—the beginning—the tremendously important beginning—in which every nail saved is a triumph:

I WAS wet, had no clothes to shift me, nor anything either to eat or drink to comfort me; neither did I see any prospect before me but that of perishing with hunger, or being devoured by wild beasts: and that which was particularly afflicting to me was, that I had no weapon either to hunt and kill any creature for my sustenance, or to defend myself against any other creature that might desire to kill me for theirs: in a word, I had nothing about me but a knife, a tobacco-pipe, and a little tobacco in a box; this was all my provision, and this threw me into terrible agonies of mind, that for a while I ran about like a madman; night coming upon me, I began with a heavy heart to consider what would be my lot if there were any ravenous beasts in that country, seeing at night they always come abroad for their prey.

All the remedy that offered to my thoughts at that time, was, to get up into a thick bushy tree like a fir, but thorny, which grew near me, and where I resolved to sit all night, and consider the next day what death I should die, for as yet I saw no prospect of life. I walked about a furlong from the shore, to see if I could find any fresh water to drink, which I did, to my great joy; and having drank, and put a little tobacco in my mouth to prevent hunger, I went to the tree, and getting up into it, endeavoured to place myself so, as that if I should sleep I might not fall; and

276

having cut me a short stick, like a truncheon, for my defence, I took up my lodging, and having been excessively fatigued, I fell fast asleep, and slept as comfortably as, I believe, few could have done in my condition, and found myself the most refreshed with it that I think I ever was on such an occasion.

When I waked it was broad day, the weather clear, and the storm abated, so that the sea did not rage and swell as before: but that which surprised me most, was, that the ship was lifted off in the night from the sand where she lay, by the swelling of the tide, and was driven up almost as far as the rock which I first mentioned, where I had been so bruised by the dashing me against it; this being within about a mile from the shore where I was, and the ship seeming to stand upright still, I wished myself on board, that, at least, I might save some necessary things for my use.

When I came down from my apartment in the tree, I looked about me again, and the first thing I found was the boat, which lay as the wind and the sea had tossed her, up upon the land, about two miles on my right hand: I walked as far as I could upon the shore to have got to her, but found a neck or inlet of water between me and the boat, which was about half a mile broad; so I came back for the present, being more intent upon getting at the ship, where I hoped to find something for my present subsistence.

A little after noon I found the sea very calm, and the tide ebbed so far out, that I could come within a quarter of a mile of the ship; and here I found a fresh renewing of my grief; for I saw evidently, that if we had kept on board, we had been all safe, that is to say, we had all got safe on shore, and I had not been so miserable as to be left entirely destitute of all comfort and company, as I now was: this forced tears from my eyes again, but as there was little relief in that, I resolved, if possible, to get to the ship; so I pulled off my clothes, for the weather was hot to extremity, and took the water; but when I came to the ship, my difficulty was still greater to know how to get on board, for as she lay a-ground, and high out of the water, there was nothing within my reach to lay hold of. I swam round her twice, and the second time I spied a small piece of a rope, which I wondered I did not see at first, hang down by the fore-chains so low as that with great difficulty I got hold of it, and by the help of that rope got up into the forecastle of the ship: here I found that the ship was bulged, and had a great deal of water in her hold, but that she lay so on the side of a bank of hard sand, or rather earth, and her stern lay lifted up upon the bank, and her head low almost to the water; by this means all her quarter was free, and all that was in that part was dry; for you may be sure my first work was to search and to see what was spoiled and what was free: and first I found that all the ship's provisions were dry, and untouched by the water; and being very well disposed to eat, I went to the bread room and filled my pockets with biscuit, and eat it as I went about other things, for I had no time to lose. I also found some rum in the great cabin, of which I took a large dram, and which I had indeed need enough of to spirit me for what was before me. Now I wanted nothing but a boat to furnish myself with many things which I foresaw would be very necessary to me.

It was in vain to sit still and wish for what was not to be had, and this extremity roused my application. We had several spare yards, and two or three large spars of wood, and a spare top-mast or two in the ship; I resolved to fall to work with these, and flung as many of them overboard as I could manage of their weight, tying every one with a rope that they might not drive away; when this was done I went down the ship's side, and pulling them to me, I tied four of them fast together at both ends, as well as I could, in the form of a raft, and laying two or three short pieces of plank upon them crossways, I found I could walk upon it very well, but that it was not able to bear any great weight, the pieces being too light; so I went to work, and with the carpenter's saw I cut a spare topmast into three lengths, and added them to my raft, with a great deal of labour and pains: but hope of furnishing myself with necessaries, encouraged me to go beyond what I should have been able to have done upon another occasion.

My raft was now strong enough to bear any reasonable weight; my next care was what to load it with, and how to preserve what I laid upon it from the surf of the sea; but I was not long considering this; I first laid all the planks or boards upon it that I could get, and having considered well what I most wanted, I first got three of the seamen's chests, which I had broken open and emptied, and lowered them down upon my raft; the first of these I filled with provisions, viz., bread, rice, three Dutch cheeses, five pieces of dried goat's flesh,

which we lived much upon, and a little remainder of European corn which had been laid by for some fowls which we brought to sea with us, but the fowls were killed; there had been some barley and wheat together, but to my great disappointment, I found afterwards that the rats had eaten or spoiled it all; as for liquors, I found several cases of bottles belonging to our skipper, in which were some cordial waters, and in all above five or six gallons of rack; these I stowed by themselves, there being no need to put them into the chest, nor no room for them. While I was doing this I found the tide began to flow, though very calm; and I had the mortification to see my coat, shirt, and waistcoat, which I had left on shore upon the sand, swim away; as for my breeches, which were only linen, and open-kneed, I swam on board in them and my stockings: however, this put me upon rummaging for clothes, of which I found enough, but took no more than I wanted for present use, for I had other things which my eye was more upon; as, first, tools to work with on shore; and it was after long searching that I found out the carpenter's chest, which was indeed a very useful prize to me, and much more valuable than a ship-loading of gold would have been at that time: I got it down to my raft, even whole as it was, without losing time to look into it, for I knew in general what it contained.

My next care was for some ammunition and arms; there were two very good fowling-pieces in the great cabin, and two pistols; these I secured first, with some powder-horns, and a small bag of shot, and two old rusty swords: I knew there were three barrels of powder in the ship, but knew not where our gunner had stowed them; but with much search I found them, two of them dry and good, the third had taken water: those two I got to my raft, with the arms; and now I thought myself pretty well freighted, and began to think how I should get to shore with them, having neither sail, oar, or rudder, and the least capful of wind would have overset all my navigation.

I had three encouragements: 1. A smooth, calm sea; 2. The tide rising and setting into the shore; 3. What little wind there was blew me towards the land; and thus, having found two or three broken oars belonging to the boat, and besides the tools which were in the chest, I found two saws, an ax and a hammer, and with this cargo I put to sea. For a mile, or there-abouts, my raft went very well, only that I found it drive a little distant from the place where I had landed before, by which I perceived that there was some indraft of the water, and consequently I hoped to find some creek or river there, which I might make use of as a port to get to land with my cargo.

As I imagined, so it was; there appeared before me a little opening of the land, and I found a strong current of the tide set into it, so I guided my raft as well as I could to keep in the middle of the stream: but here I had like to have suffered a second ship-wreck, which, if I had, I think verily would have broke my heart; for knowing nothing of the coast, my raft run a-ground at one end of it upon a shoal, and not being a-ground at the other end, it wanted but a little that all my cargo had slipped off to-wards that end that was afloat, and so fallen into the water. I did my utmost, by setting my back against the chests, to keep them in their places, but could not thrust off the raft with all my strength, neither durst I stir from the posture I was in; but holding up the chests with all my might, stood in that manner near half an hour, in which time the rising of the water brought me a little more upon a level; and a little after, the water still rising, my raft floated again, and I thrust her off with the oar I had, into the channel; and then driving up higher, I at length found myself in the mouth of a little river, with land on both sides, and a strong current or tide running up: I looked on both sides for a proper place to get to shore, for I was not willing to be driven too high up the river, hoping in time to see some ship at sea, and there-fore resolved to place myself as near the coast as I could.

At length I spied a little cove on the right shore of the creek, to which, with great pain and difficulty, I guided my raft, and at last got so near, as that, reaching ground with my oar, I could thrust her directly in; but here I had like to have dipped all my cargo in the sea again; for that shore lying pretty steep, that is to say sloping, there was no place to land, but where one end of the float, if it run on shore, would lie so high, and the other sink lower as before, that it would endanger my cargo again: all that I could do, was to wait till the tide was at the highest, keep-ing the raft with my oar like an anchor to hold the side of it fast to the shore, near a flat piece of ground, which I expected the water would flow over; and so it did. As soon as I found water enough (for my raft drew about a foot of water), I thrust her on upon that flat piece of ground, and there fastened or moored her by sticking my two broken oars into the ground; one on one side near one end; and one on the other side near the other end; and thus I lay till the water ebbed away, and left my raft and all my cargo safe on shore.

My next work was to view the country, and seek a proper place for my habitation, and where to stow my goods, to secure them from whatever might happen; where I was I yet knew not; whether on the continent or on an island, whether in-habited or not inhabited, whether in danger of wild beasts or not: there was a hill not above a mile from me, which rose up very steep and high, and which seemed to over-top some other hills which lay as in a ridge from it northward; I took out one of the fowling-pieces, and one of the pistols, and a horn of powder, and thus armed I travelled for discovery up to the top of that hill, where, after I had with great labour and difficulty got to the top,

I went every day on board and brought away what I could get.

I saw my fate to my great affliction, viz., that I was in an island environed every way with the sea, no land to be seen, except some rocks which lay a great way off, and two small islands less than this, which lay about three leagues to the west.

I found also that the island I was in was barren, and, as I saw good reason to believe, uninhabited, except by wild beasts, of whom however I saw none; yet I saw abundance of fowls, but knew not their kinds, neither when I killed them could I tell what was fit for food, and what not. At my coming back, I shot at a great bird, which I saw sitting upon a tree on the side of a great wood; I believe it was the first gun that had been fired there since the creation of the world. I had no sooner fired, but from all the parts of the wood there arose an innumerable number of fowls of many sorts, making a confused screaming, and crying every one according to his usual note; but not one of them of any kind that I knew: as for the creature I killed, I took it to be a kind of hawk, its colour and beak resembling it, but had no talons or claws more than common; its flesh was carrion, and fit for nothing.

Contented with this discovery, I came back to my raft, and fell to work to bring my cargo on shore, which took me up the rest of that day; and what to do with myself at night I knew not, nor indeed where to rest; for I was afraid to lie down on the ground, not knowing but some wild beast might devour me, though, as I afterwards found, there was really no need for those fears.

However, as well as I could, I barricaded myself round with the chests and boards that I had brought on shore, and made a kind of a hut for that night's lodging: as for food, I yet saw not which way to supply myself, except that I had seen two or three creatures, like hares, run out of the wood where I shot the fowl.

I now began to consider, that I might yet get a great many things out of the ship, which would be useful to me, and particularly some of the rigging and sails, and such other things as might come to land, and I resolved to make another voyage on board the vessel, if possible; and as I knew that the first storm that blew must necessarily break her all in pieces, I resolved to set all other things apart, till I got everything out of the ship that I could get; then I called a council, that is to say, in my thoughts, whether I should take back the raft; but this appeared impracticable; so I resolved to go as before, when the tide was down, and I did so, only that I stripped before I went from my hut, having nothing on but a chequered shirt, and a pair of linen trousers, and a pair of pumps on my feet.

I got on board the ship, as before, and prepared a second raft; and having had experience of the first, I neither made this so unwieldy, nor loaded it so hard; but, yet I brought away several things very useful to me; as first, in the carpenter's stores, I found two or three bags full of nails and spikes, a great screw-jack, a dozen or two of hatchets, and above all, that most useful thing called a grindstone: all these I secured, together with several things belonging to the gunner, particularly two or three iron crows, and two barrels of musket-bullets, seven muskets, and another fowling-piece, with some small quantity of powder more; a large bag full of small shot, and a great roll of sheet lead; but this last was so heavy I could not hoist it up to get it over the ship's side.

Besides these things, I took all the men's clothes that I could find, and a spare fore-top-sail, hammock, and some bedding; and with this I loaded my second raft, and brought them all safe on shore, to my very great comfort.

I was under some apprehensions during my absence from the land, that at least my provisions might be devoured on shore; but when I came back, I found no sign of any visitor, only there sat a creature like a wild cat upon one of the chests, which, when I came towards it, ran away a little distance, and then stood still; she sat very composed, and unconcerned, and looked full in my face, as if she had a mind to be acquainted with me; I presented my gun at her, but as she did not understand it, she was perfectly unconcerned at it, nor did she offer to stir away: upon which I tossed her a bit of biscuit, though by the way I was not very free of it, for my store was not great: however, I spared her a bit, I say, and she went to it, smelled at it, ate it, and looked, as pleased, for more: but I thanked her, and could spare no more; so she marched off.

Having got my second cargo on shore, though I was fain to open the barrels of powder, and bring them by parcels (for they were too heavy, being large casks) I went to work to make me a little tent with the sail and some poles which I cut for that purpose; and into this tent I brought everything that I knew would spoil, either with rain or sun, and I piled all the empty chests and casks up in a circle round the tent, to fortify it from any sudden attempt, either from man or beast.

When I had done this I blocked up the door of the tent with some boards within, and an empty chest set up on-end without: and spreading one of the beds upon the ground, laying my two pistols just at my head, and my gun at length by me, I went to bed for the first time, and slept very quietly all night, for I was very weary and heavy; for the night before I had slept little, and had laboured very hard all day, as well to fetch all those things from the ship, as to get them on shore.

I had the biggest magazine of all kinds now, that ever were laid up, I believe, for one man; but I was not satisfied still; for while the ship sat upright in that posture, I thought I ought to get everything out of her that I could: so every day at low water I went on board, and brought away something or other; but particularly the third time I went, I brought away as much of the rigging as I could, as also all the small ropes and rope twine I could get, with a piece of spare canvas, which was to mend the sails upon occasion, and the barrel of wet gun-powder: in a word I brought away all the sails first and last, only that I was fain to cut them in pieces, and bring as much at a time as I could; for they were no more useful to be sails, but as mere canvas only.

But that which comforted me more still, was, that, last of all, after I had made five or six such voyages as these, and thought I had nothing more to expect from the ship that was worth my meddling with; I say, after all this, I found a great hogshead of bread, and three large runlets of rum or spirits, and a box of sugar and a barrel of fine flour: this was surprising to me, because I had given over expecting any more provisions, except what was spoiled by the water: I soon emptied the hogshead of that bread, and wrapped it up, parcel by parcel, in pieces of the sails, which I cut out; and, in a word, I got all this safe on shore also.

The next day I made another voyage; and now, having plundered the ship of what was portable and fit to hand out, I began with the cables; and cutting the great cable into pieces, such as I could move, I got two cables and a hawser on shore, with all the iron-work I could get; and having cut down the spritsail-yard, and the mizen-yard, and everything I could to make a large raft, I loaded it with all those heavy goods, and came away: but my good luck began now to leave me; for this raft was so unwieldy and so overladen, that after I had entered the little cove, where I had landed the rest of my goods, not being able to guide it so handily as I did the other, it overset, and threw me and all my cargo into the water. As for myself it was no great harm, for I was near the shore; but as to my cargo, it was great part of it lost, especially the iron, which I expected would have been of great use to me: however, when the tide was out, I got most of the pieces of cable ashore; and some of the iron, though with infinite labour; for I was fain to dip for it into the water, a work which fatigued me very much. After this, I went every day on board, and brought away what I could get.

I had been now thirteen days on shore, and had been eleven times on board the ship in which time I had brought away all that one pair of hands could well be supposed capable to bring: though I believe verily, had the calm weather held, I should have brought away the whole ship, piece by piece; but preparing the twelfth time to go on board, I found the wind began to rise; however at low water I went on board, and though I thought I had rummaged the cabin so effectually, as that nothing more could be found, yet I discovered a locker with drawers in it, in one of which I found two or three razors, and one pair of large scissors, with some ten or a dozen of good knives and forks; in another I found about thirty-six pounds value in money, some European coin, some Brazil, some pieces of eight, some gold, some silver.

I smiled to myself at the sight of this money. "O Drug!" said I, aloud, "what art thou good for? thou art not worth to me, no not the taking off of the ground: one of those knives is worth all this heap: I have no manner of use for thee, even remain where thou art and go to the bottom, as a creature whose life is not worth saving." However, upon second thoughts, I took it away, and wrapping all this in a piece of canvas, I began to think of making another raft; but while I was preparing this, I found the sky over-cast, and the wind began to rise, and in a quarter of an hour it blew a fresh gale from the shore: It presently occurred to me, that it was in vain to pretend to make a raft with the wind off-shore, and that it was my business to be gone before the tide of flood began, otherwise I might not be able to reach the shore at all; accordingly I let myself down into the water, and swam across the channel, which lay between the ship and the sands, and even that with difficulty enough, partly with the weight of things I had about me, and partly the roughness of the water; for the wind rose very hastily, and before it was quite high water it blew a storm.

But I was gotten home to my little tent, where I lay with all my wealth about me very secure. It blew very hard all that night; and in the morning when I looked out, behold no more ship was to be seen....

283

Thomas the Rhymer

True Thomas lay o'er yond grassy bank,
   And he beheld a ladie gay,
A ladie that was brisk and bold,
   Come riding o'er the fernie brae.

Her skirt was of the grass-green silk,
   Her mantel of the velvet fine,
At ilka tett of her horse's mane
   Hung fifty silver bells and nine.

True Thomas he took off his hat,
   And bowed him low down till his knee:
"All hail, thou mighty Queen of Heaven!
   For your peer on earth I never did see."

"O no, O no, True Thomas," she says,
   "That name does not belong to me;
I am but the queen of fair Elfland,
   And I'm come here for to visit thee. . . .

"But ye maun go wi' me now, Thomas,
   True Thomas, ye maun go wi' me,
For ye maun serve me seven years,
   Thro' weel or wae as may chance to be.

"Then harp and carp, Thomas," she said,
   "Then harp and carp alang wi' me;
But it will be seven years and a day
   Till ye win back to yere ain countrie."

She turned about her milk-white steed,
   And took True Thomas up behind,
And aye whene'er her bridle rang,
   The steed flew swifter than the wind.

For forty days and forty nights
   He wade thro' red blude to the knee,
And he saw neither sun nor moon,
   But heard the roaring of the sea.

---

fernie = ferny	blude = blood
brae = hillside	rade = rode
ilka tett = each tuft	fairlies = wonders
maun = must	braid = broad
wae = woe	lillie leven = lily
harp and carp = play the	lawn
harp and recite or sing	gae = go
ain = own	gin = if

O they rade on, and further on,
   Until they came to a garden green:
"Light down, light down, ye ladie free,
   Some of that fruit let me pull to thee."

"O no, O no, True Thomas," she says,
   "That fruit maun not be touched by thee,
For a' the plagues that are in hell
   Light on the fruit of this countrie.

"But I have a loaf here in my lap,
   Likewise a bottle of claret wine,
And now ere we go farther on,
   We'll rest a while, and ye may dine."

When he had eaten and drunk his fill:
   "Lay down your head upon my knee,"
The ladie said, "ere we climb yon hill
   And I will show you fairlies three.

"O see not ye yon narrow road,
   So thick beset wi' thorns and briers?
That is the path of righteousness,
   Tho' after it but few enquires.

"And see not ye that braid braid road,
   That lies across yon lillie leven?
That is the path of wickedness,
   Tho' some call it the road to heaven.

"And see not ye that bonny road,
   Which winds about the fernie brae?
That is the road to fair Elfland,
   Where you and I this night maun gae.

"But Thomas, ye maun hold your tongue,
   Whatever you may hear or see,
For gin ae word you should chance to speak,
   You will ne'er get back to your ain countrie."

He has gotten a coate of the even cloth,
   And a pair of shoes of velvet green,
And till seven years were past and gone
   True Thomas on earth was never seen.

A medieval story handed down, and written out possibly in the 18th century.

The White Magicians

Sir H. Rider Haggard

Illustrated by
Robert Geary

Sir Henry Rider Haggard (1856–1925) the eighth child of a Norfolk squire's large family of ten, became an author more by chance than by intention. He went to Africa on the staff of the governor of Natal Province, and his years in government service took him by ox-wagon through the territories of many tribes and chiefs—a background of memories that inspired his books. Following the Boer War he went back to England, studied law and wrote a life of Cetewayo, one of the fiercest and most remarkable of the African chiefs. After an argument about "Treasure Island", at that time a sensational best-seller, Haggard bet his brother a shilling that he could write an adventure story just as good. The bet was accepted, and for the next six weeks, he spent his spare time writing "King Solomon's Mines". Its reception was tremendous from public and critics alike and Haggard won his bet! He then went on to write more romantic and adventurous stories of the African continent, Mexico and Egypt. Among the best of them are those that purport to be written by Alan Quatermain, a professional hunter, whom we gradually discover to be both modest and brave, cautious, reliable and loved, one of whom it can be said, as Kipling said of the author: "He was trusted at sight". You can meet Alan Quatermain in this extract we have chosen from "King Solomon's Mines". Other books that you will find exciting are: "Alan Quatermain", "She", "The Holy Flower", "The Ivory Child", "The Yellow God" and "Queen Sheba's Ring". In this extract Alan and his companions, Captain Good, Sir Henry Curtis and their native friend, Umbopa, are on the brink of a great adventure which will lead them to King Solomon's treasure.

THE brook, of which the banks were clothed with dense masses of a gigantic species of maidenhair fern interspersed with feathery tufts of wild asparagus, sung merrily at our side, the soft air murmured through the leaves of the silver trees, doves cooed around, and bright-winged birds flashed like living gems from bough to bough. It was a Paradise.

The magic of the place combined with an overwhelming sense of dangers left behind, and of the promised land reached at last, seemed to charm us into silence. Sir Henry and Umbopa sat conversing in a mixture of broken English and Kitchen Zulu in a low voice, but earnestly enough, and I lay, with my eyes half shut, upon that fragrant bed of fern and watched them.

Presently I missed Good, and I looked to see what had become of him. Soon I observed him sitting by the bank of the stream, in which he had been bathing. He had nothing on but his flannel shirt, and his natural habits of extreme neatness having reasserted themselves, he was actively employed in making a most elaborate toilet. He had washed his gutta-percha collar, had thoroughly shaken out his trousers, coat and waistcoat, and was now folding them up neatly till he was ready to put them on, shaking his head sadly, as he scanned the numerous rents and tears in them, which naturally had resulted from our frightful journey. Then he took his boots, scrubbed them with a handful of fern, and finally rubbed them over with a piece of fat, which he had carefully saved from the *inco* meat, till they looked, comparatively speaking, respectable. Having inspected them judicially through his eye-glass, he put the boots on and began a fresh operation. From a little bag that he carried he produced a pocket-comb in which was fixed a tiny looking-glass, and in this he surveyed himself. Apparently he was not satisfied, for he proceeded to do his hair with great care. Then came a pause whilst he again contemplated the effect; still it was not satisfactory. He felt his chin, on which the accumulated scrub of a ten days' beard was flourishing.

"Surely," thought I, "he is not going to try to shave." But so it was. Taking the piece of fat with which he had greased his boots, Good washed it thoroughly in the stream. Then diving again into the bag he brought out a little pocket razor with a guard to it, such as are bought by people who are afraid of cutting themselves, or by those about to undertake a sea voyage. Then he rubbed his face and chin vigorously with the fat and began. Evidently it proved a painful process, for he groaned very much over it, and I was convulsed with inward laughter as I watched him struggling with that stubbly beard. It seemed so very odd that a man should take the trouble to shave himself with a piece of fat in such a place and in our circumstances. At last he succeeded in getting the hair off the right side of his face and chin, when suddenly I, who was watching, became conscious of a flash of light that passed just by his head.

Good sprang up with a profane exclamation (if it had not been a safety razor he

would certainly have cut his throat), and so did I, without the exclamation, and this was what I saw. Standing not more than ten paces from where I was, and twenty from Good, were a group of men. They were very tall and copper-coloured, and some of them wore great plumes of black feathers and short cloaks of leopard skins; this was all I noticed at the moment. In front of them stood a youth of about seventeen, his hand still raised and his body bent forward in the attitude of a Grecian statue of a spear-thrower. Evidently the flash of light had been caused by a weapon which he had hurled.

As I looked an old soldier-like man stepped forward out of the group, and catching the youth by the arm said something to him. Then they advanced upon us.

Sir Henry, Good, and Umbopa by this time had seized their rifles and lifted them threateningly. The party of natives still came on. It struck me that they could not know what rifles were, or they would not have treated them with such contempt.

"Put down your guns!" I hallooed to the others, seeing that our only chance of safety lay in conciliation. They obeyed, and walking to the front I addressed the elderly man who had checked the youth.

"Greeting," I said in Zulu, not knowing what language to use. To my surprise I was understood.

"Greeting," answered the man, not, indeed, in the same tongue, but in a dialect so closely allied to it that neither Umbopa nor myself had any difficulty in understanding him. Indeed, as we afterwards found out, the language spoken by this people is an old-fashioned form of the Zulu tongue, bearing about the same relationship to it that the English of Chaucer does to the English of the nineteenth century.

"Whence come you?" he went on, "who are you? and why are the faces of three of you white, and the face of the fourth as the face of our mother's sons?" and he pointed to Umbopa. I looked at Umbopa as he said it, and it flashed across me that he was right. The face of Umbopa was like the faces of the men before me, and so was his great form like their forms. But I had not time to reflect on this coincidence.

"We are strangers, and come in peace," I answered, speaking very slowly, so that he might understand me, "and this man is our servant."

"Ye lie," he answered, "no strangers can cross the mountains where all things perish. But what do your lies matter?—if ye are strangers then ye must die, for no strangers may live in the land of the Kuku-anas. It is the king's law. Prepare then to die, O strangers!"

I was slightly staggered at this, more especially as I saw the hands of some of the men steal down to their sides, where hung on each what looked to me like a large and heavy knife.

"What does that beggar say?" asked Good.

"He says we are going to be killed," I answered grimly.

"Oh, Lord!" groaned Good, and, as was his way when perplexed, he put his hand to his false teeth, dragging the top set down and allowing them to fly back to his jaw with a snap. It was a most fortunate move, for next second the dignified crowd of Kukuanas uttered a simultaneous yell of horror, and bolted back some yards.

"What's up?" said I.

"It's his teeth," whispered Sir Henry excitedly. "He moved them. Take them out, Good, take them out!"

He obeyed, slipping the set into the sleeve of his flannel shirt.

In another second curiosity had overcome fear, and the men advanced slowly. Apparently they had now forgotten their amiable intention of killing us.

"How is it, O strangers," asked the old man solemnly, "that this fat man (pointing to Good, who was clad in nothing but boots and a flannel shirt, and had only half finished his shaving), whose body is clothed, and whose legs are bare, who grows hair on one side of his sickly face and not on the other, and who wears one shining and transparent eye—how is it, I ask, that he has teeth which move of themselves, coming away from the jaws and returning of their own will?"

"Open your mouth," I said to Good, who promptly curled up his lips and grinned at the old gentleman like an angry dog, revealing to his astonished gaze two thin red lines of gum as utterly innocent of ivories as a new-born elephant. The audience gasped.

"Where are his teeth?" they shouted; "with our eyes we saw them."

Turning his head slowly and with a gesture of ineffable contempt, Good swept his hand across his mouth. Then he grinned again, and lo, there were two rows of lovely teeth.

Now the young man who had flung the knife threw himself down on the grass and gave vent to a prolonged howl of terror; and as for the old gentleman, his knees knocked together with fear.

"I see that ye are spirits," he said falter-ingly; "did ever man born of woman have hair on one side of his face and not on the other, or a round and transparent eye, or teeth which moved and melted away and grew again? Pardon us, O my lords."

Here was luck indeed, and, needless to say, I jumped at the chance.

"It is granted," I said with an imperial smile. "Nay, ye shall know the truth. We come from another world, though we are men such as ye; we come," I went on, "from the biggest star that shines at night."

"Oh! oh!" groaned the chorus of astonished aborigines.

"Yes," I went on, "we do, indeed"; and again I smiled benignly, as I uttered that amazing lie. "We come to stay with you a little while, and to bless you by our sojourn. Ye will see, O friends, that I have prepared myself for this visit by the learn-ing of your language."

"It is so, it is so," said the chorus.

"Only, my lord," put in the old gentleman, "thou hast learnt it very badly."

I cast an indignant glance at him, and he quailed.

"Now friends," I continued, "ye might think that after so long a journey we should find it in our hearts to avenge such a reception, mayhap to strike cold in death the impious hand that—that, in short—threw a knife at the head of him whose teeth come and go."

"Spare him, my lords," said the old man in supplication; "he is the king's son, and I am his uncle. If anything befalls him his blood will be required at my hands."

"Yes, that is certainly so," put in the young man with great emphasis.

"Ye may perhaps doubt our power to avenge," I went on, heedless of this by-play. "Stay, I will show you. Here, thou dog and slave (addressing Umbopa in a savage tone), give me the magic tube that speaks"; and I tipped a wink towards my express rifle.

Umbopa rose to the occasion, and with something as nearly resembling a grin as I have ever seen on his dignified face he handed me the gun.

"It is here, O Lord of Lords," he said with a deep obeisance.

Now just before I had asked for the rifle I had perceived a little *klipspringer* antelope standing on a mass of rock about seventy yards away, and determined to risk the shot.

"Ye see that buck," I said, pointing the animal out to the party before me. "Tell me, is it possible for man born of woman to kill it from here with a noise?"

"It is not possible, my lord," answered the old man.

"Yet shall I kill it," I said quietly.

The old man smiled. "That my lord cannot do," he answered.

I raised the rifle and covered the buck. It was a small animal, and one which a man might well be excused for missing, but I knew that it would not do to miss.

I drew a deep breath, and slowly pressed on the trigger. The buck stood still as a stone.

*He rode straight on, never doubting for one moment that this was the road which held many
adventures in store for him.*
From "Don Quixote and the Windmills"

"Make for the wood and keep together," cried Lord John, clubbing his rifle. *"The brutes mean mischief."*
From "Exploring the Lost World"

Bang! thud! The antelope sprang into the air and fell on the rock dead as a door nail.

A groan of simultaneous terror burst from the group before us.

"If you want meat," I remarked coolly, "go fetch that buck."

The old man made a sign, and one of his followers departed, and presently returned bearing the *klipspringer*. I noticed with satisfaction that I had hit it fairly behind the shoulder. They gathered round the poor creature's body, gazing at the bullet-hole in consternation.

"Ye see," I said, "I do not speak empty words." There was no answer.

"If ye yet doubt our power," I went on, "let one of you go stand upon that rock that I may make him as this buck."

None of them seemed at all inclined to take the hint, till at last the king's son spoke.

"It is well said. Do thou, my uncle, go stand upon the rock. It is but a buck that the magic has killed. Surely it cannot kill a man."

The old gentleman did not take the suggestion in good part. Indeed, he seemed hurt.

"No! no!" he ejaculated hastily, "my old eyes have seen enough. These are wizards, indeed. Let us bring them to the king. Yet if any should wish a further proof, let *him* stand upon the rock, that the magic tube may speak with him."

There was a most general and hasty expression of dissent.

"Let not good magic be wasted on our poor bodies," said one; "we are satisfied. All the witchcraft of our people cannot show the like of this."

"It is so," remarked the old gentleman, in a tone of intense relief; "without any doubt it is so. Listen, children of the Stars, children of the shining Eye and the movable Teeth, who roar out in thunder and slay from afar. I am Infadoos, son of Kafa, once king of the Kukuana people. This youth is Scragga."

"He nearly scragged me," murmured Good.

"Scragga, son of Twala, the great king—Twala, husband of a thousand wives, chief and lord paramount of the Kukuanas, keeper of the great Road, terror of his enemies, student of the Black Arts, leader of a hundred thousand warriors, Twala the One-eyed, the Black, the Terrible."

"So," said I superciliously, "lead us then to Twala. We do not talk with low people and underlings."

"It is well, my lords, we will lead you; but the way is long. We are hunting three days' journey from the place of the king. But let my lords have patience, and we will lead them."

"So be it," I said carelessly; "all time is before us, for we do not die. We are ready, lead on. But Infadoos, and thou Scragga, beware! Play us no monkey tricks, set for us no foxes' snares, for before your brains of mud have thought of them we shall know and avenge. The light from the transparent eye of him with the bare legs and the half-haired face shall destroy you, and go through your land; his vanishing teeth shall fix themselves fast in you and eat you up, you and your wives and children; the magic tubes shall argue with you loudly, and make you as sieves. Beware!"

This magnificent address did not fail of its effect; indeed, it might almost have been spared, so deeply were our friends already impressed with our powers.

The old man made a deep obeisance, and murmured the words, "*Koom Koom*," which I afterwards discovered was their royal salute, corresponding to the *Bayete* of the Zulus, and turning, addressed his followers. These at once proceeded to lay hold of all our goods and chattels, in order to bear them for us, excepting only the guns, which they would on no account touch. They even seized Good's clothes, that, as the reader may remember, were neatly folded up beside him.

He saw and made a dive for them, and a loud altercation ensued.

"Let not my lord of the transparent Eye and the melting Teeth touch them," said the old man. "Surely his slave shall carry the things."

"But I want to put 'em on!" roared Good, in nervous English.

Umbopa translated.

"Nay, my lord," answered Infadoos, "would my lord cover up his beautiful white legs (although he is so dark Good has a singularly white skin) from the eyes of his servants? Have we offended my lord that he should do such a thing?"

Here I nearly exploded with laughing; and meanwhile one of the men started on with the garments.

"Damn it!" roared Good, "that black villain has got my trousers."

"Look here, Good," said Sir Henry; "you have appeared in this country in a certain character, and you must live up to it. It will never do for you to put on trousers again. Henceforth you must exist in a flannel shirt, a pair of boots, and an eye-glass."

"Yes," I said, "and with whiskers on one side of your face and not on the other. If you change any of these things the people will think that we are impostors. I am very sorry for you, but seriously, you must. If once they begin to suspect us our lives will not be worth a brass farthing."

"Do you really think so?" said Good gloomily.

"I do, indeed. Your 'beautiful white legs' and your eye-glass are now *the* features of our party, and as Sir Henry says, you must live up to them. Be thankful that you have got your boots on, and that the air is warm."

Good sighed, and said no more, but it took him a fortnight to become accustomed to his new and scant attire.

Under the Greenwood Tree

Under the greenwood tree
Who loves to lie with me,
And turn his merry note
Unto the sweet bird's throat—
Come hither, come hither, come hither!
     Here shall he see
     No enemy
But winter and rough weather.

Who doth ambition shun
And loves to live i' th' sun,
Seeking the food he eats
And pleased with what he gets,
Come hither, come hither, come hither!
     Here shall he see
     No enemy
But winter and rough weather.

WILLIAM SHAKESPEARE

Jeremy at the Fair

Hugh Walpole

Illustrated by Michael Jackson

Born in New Zealand, Sir Hugh Walpole (1884–1941) was the son of a clergyman who later became Bishop of Edinburgh. His Jeremy of the story is a clergyman's son, too, and the three books about Jeremy—"Jeremy", "Jeremy and Hamlet" and "Jeremy at Crale" contain many incidents from the author's own boyhood.

Hugh Walpole wrote over thirty novels for adults and several books of short stories, among them some good ghost stories, and was knighted for his work in furthering reading, writing and book-publishing as well as for his work as author.

Although written for adults rather than for young readers, the Jeremy stories make excellent reading.

"COME along now . . . pay your sixpences . . . pay your sixpences," cried the man. Jeremy was through. He stepped at once into something that had for him all the elements of the most terrifying and enchanting of fairy tales. He was planted, it seemed, in a giant world. At first he could see nothing but the high and thick bodies of the people who moved on every side of him; he peered under shoulders, he was lost amongst legs and arms, he walked suddenly into waistcoat buttons and was flung thence on to walking-sticks.

But it was, if he had known it, the most magical hour of all for him to have chosen. . . .

Lights, even as Jeremy watched, sprang into the air, wavered, faltered, hesitated, then rocked into a steady glow, only shifting a little with the haze. On either side of him were rough, wooden stalls, and these were illuminated with gas, which sizzled and hissed like angry snakes. The stalls were covered with everything invented by man; here a sweet stall, with thick, sticky lumps of white and green and red, glass bottles of bulls' eyes and peppermints, thick slabs of almond toffee and pink coconut icing, boxes of round chocolate creams and sticks of liquorice, lumps of gingerbread, with coloured pictures stuck upon them, saffron buns, plum cakes in

291

glass jars, and chains of little sugary biscuits hanging on long red strings. There was the old-clothes stall with trousers and coats and waistcoats, all shabby and lanky, swinging beneath the gas, and piles of clothes on the boards, all nondescript and unhappy and faded; there was the stall with the farm implements, and the medicine stall, and the flower stall, and the vegetable stall, and many, many another. Each place had its guardian, man or woman, vociferous, red-faced, screaming out the wares, lowering the voice to cajole, raising it again to draw back a retreating customer, carrying on suddenly an intimate conversation with the next-door shopkeeper, laughing, quarrelling, arguing.

To Jeremy it was a world of giant heights and depths. Behind the stalls, beyond the lane down which he moved, was an uncertain glory, a threatening peril. He fancied that strange animals moved there; he thought he heard a lion roar and an elephant bellow. The din of the sellers all about him made it impossible to tell what was happening beyond there; only the lights and bells, shouts and cries, confusing smells, and a great roar of distant voices.

He almost wished that he had not come, he felt so very small and helpless; he wondered whether he could find his way out again, and looking back, he was for a moment terrified to see that the stream of people behind him shut him in so that he could not see the stile, nor the wooden barrier, nor the red-faced man. Pushed forward, he found himself at the end of the lane and standing in a semi-circular space surrounded by strange-looking booths with painted pictures upon them, and in front of them platforms with wooden steps running up to them. Then, so unexpectedly that he gave a little scream, a sudden roar burst out behind him. He turned and, indeed, the world seemed to have gone mad. A moment ago there had been darkness and dim shadow. Now,

suddenly, there was a huge whistling, tossing circle of light and flame, and from the centre of this a banging, brazen, cymbal-clashing scream issued—a scream that, through its strident shrillness, he recognized as a tune that he knew—a tune often whistled by Jim at Cow Farm. Whence the tune came he could not tell; from the very belly of the flaming monster, it seemed; but, as he watched, he saw that the huge circle whirled ever faster and faster, and that up and down on the flame of it coloured horses rose and fell, vanishing from light to darkness, from darkness to light, and seeming of their own free will and motion to dance to the thundering music.

It was the most terrific thing that he had ever seen. The most terrific thing. . . . He stood there, his cap on the back of his head, his legs apart, his mouth open; forgetting utterly the crowd, thinking nothing of time or danger or punishment—he gazed with his whole body.

As his eyes grew more accustomed to the glare of the hissing gas, he saw that in the centre figures were painted standing on the edge of a pillar that revolved without pause. There was a woman with flaming red cheeks, a gold dress and dead white dusty arms, a man with a golden crown and a purple robe, but a broken nose, and a minstrel with a harp. The woman and the king moved stiffly their arms up and down, that they might strike instruments, one a cymbal and the other a drum.

But it was finally the horses that caught Jeremy's heart. Half of them at least were without riders, and the empty ones went round pathetically, envying the more successful ones and dancing to the music as though with an effort. One especially moved Jeremy's sympathy. He was a fine horse, rather fresher than the others, with a coal-black mane and great black bulging eyes; his saddle was of gold and his trappings of red. As he went round he seemed to catch Jeremy's eye and to beg him to come to him. He rode more securely than the rest, rising nobly like a horse of fine breeding, falling again with an implication of restrained force as though he would say: "I have only to let myself go and there, my word, you *would* see where I'd get to." His bold black eyes turned beseechingly to Jeremy—surely it was not only a trick of the waving gas; the boy drew closer and closer, never moving his gaze from the horses who had hitherto been whirling at a bacchanalian pace, but now, as at some sudden secret command, suddenly slackened, hesitated, fell into a gentle jog-trot, then scarcely rose, scarcely fell, were suddenly still. Jeremy saw what it was that you did if you wanted a ride. A stout dirty man came out amongst the horses and, resting his hands on their backs as though they were less than nothing to him, shouted: "Now's your chance, lidies and gents! Now, lidies and gents! Come along hup! Come along hup! The ride of your life now! A 'alfpenny a time! A 'alfpenny a time, and the finest ride of your life!"

People began to mount the steps that led on to the platform where the horses stood. A woman, then a man and a boy, then two men, then two girls giggling together, then a man and a girl.

And the stout fellow shouted: "Come along hup! Come along hup! Now, lidies and gents! A 'alfpenny a ride! Come along hup!"

Jeremy noticed then that the fine horse with the black mane had stopped close beside him. Impossible to say whether the horse had intended it or no!...

"One ride—little gen'elman. 'Ere you are! 'Old on now! Oh, you wants that one, do yer? Right yer are—yer pays yer money and yer takes yer choice." He lifted Jeremy up. "Put yer arms round 'is neck now—'e won't bite yer!"

Bite him indeed! Jeremy felt, as he clutched the cool head and let his hand slide over the stiff black mane, that he knew more about that horse than his owner did. He seemed to feel beneath him the horse's response to his clutching knees, the head seemed to rise for a moment and nod to him and the eyes to say: "It's all right. I'll look after you. I'll give you the best ride of your life!"

He felt, indeed, that the gaze of the whole world was upon him, but he responded to it proudly, staring boldly around him as though he had been seated on merry-go-rounds all his days. Perhaps some in the gaping crowd knew him and were saying: "Why, there's the Rev. Cole's kid——" never mind; he was above scandal. From where he was he could see the Fair lifted up and translated into a fantastic splendour. Nothing was certain, nothing defined—above him a canopy of evening sky, with circles and chains of stars mixed with the rosy haze of the flame of the Fair; opposite him was the Palace of "The Two-Headed Giant from the Caucasus", a huge man as portrayed in the picture hanging on his outer walls, a giant naked, save for a bearskin, with one head black and one yellow, and white protruding teeth in both mouths. Next to him was the Fortune Teller's, and outside this a little man with a hump beat a drum. Then there was "The Theatre of Tragedy and Mirth", with a poster on one side of the door portraying a lady drowning in the swiftest of rivers, but with the prospect of being saved by a stout gentleman who leaned over from the bank and grasped her hair. Then there was the "Chamber of the Fat Lady and the Six Little Dwarfs", and the entry to this was guarded by a dirty sour-looking female who gnashed her teeth at a hesitating public, before whom, with a splendid indifference to appearance, she consumed, out of a piece of newspaper, her evening meal.

All these things were in Jeremy's immediate vision, and beyond them was a haze that his eyes could not penetrate. It held, he knew, wild beasts, because he could hear quite clearly from time to time the lion and the elephant and the tiger; it held music, because from somewhere through all the noise and confusion the tune of a band penetrated; it held buyers and sellers and treasures and riches, and all the inhabitants of the world—surely all the world *must* be here to-night. And then, beyond the haze, there were the silent and mysterious gipsy caravans.

Dark with their little square windows, and their coloured walls, and their round wheels, and the smell of wood fires, and the noise of hissing kettles and horses cropping the grass, and around them the still night world with the thick woods and the dark river.

They were off! He felt his horse quiver under him, he saw the mansions of the Two-Headed Giant and the Fat Lady slip to the right, the light seemed to swing like the skirt of someone's dress, upwards across the floor, and from the heart of the golden woman and the king and the minstrel a scream burst forth as though they were announcing the end of the world. After that he had no clear idea as to what occurred. He was swung into space, and all the life that had been so stationary, the booths, the lights, the men and women, the very stars went swinging with him as though to cheer him on; the horse under him galloped before, and the faster he galloped the wilder was the music and the dizzier the world. He was exultant, omnipotent, supreme. He had long known that this glory was somewhere if it could only be found, all his days he seemed to have been searching for it; he beat his horse's neck, he drove his legs

against its sides. "Go on! Go on! Go on!" he said. "Faster! Faster! Faster!"

The strangest things seemed to rise to his notice and then fall again—a peaked policeman's hat, flowers, a sudden flame of gas, the staring eyes and dead white arms of the golden woman, the flying forms of the horses in front of him. All the world was on horseback, all the world was racing higher and higher, faster and faster. He saw someone near him rise on to his horse's back and stand on it, waving his arms. He would have liked to have done that, but he found that he was part of the horse, as though he had been glued to it. He shouted, he cried aloud, he was so happy that he thought of no one and nothing. . . . The flame danced about him in a circle, he seemed to rise so high that there was a sudden stillness, he was in the very heart of the stars; then came the supreme moment when, as he had always known, that one day he would be, he was master of the world. . . .

Then, like Lucifer, he fell. Slowly the stars receded, the music slackened, people

rocked on to their feet again. . . . The Two-Headed Giant slipped back once more into his place, he saw that sinister lady still devouring her supper, women looking up at him gaped. His horse gave a last little leap and died.

This marvellous experience he repeated four times, and every time with an ecstasy more complete than the last.

quiet and cool, a little below him, but very near:

"Jeremy. . . . Jeremy. Come off that. You've got to go home."

He looked down and saw his Uncle Samuel.

It was all over; he knew at once that it was all over. As he slipped down from his dear horse he gave the glossy dark mane one last pat; then, with a little sigh, he found his feet, stumbled over the wooden steps and was at his uncle's side.

He rushed to a height, he fell, he rushed again, he fell, and at every return to a sober life his one intention was instantly to be off on his steed once more. He was about to start on his fifth journey, he had paid his half-penny, he was sitting forward with his hands on the black mane, his eyes, staring, were filled already with the glory that he knew was coming to him, his cheeks were crimson, his hat on the back of his head, his hair flying. He heard a voice,

From a Railway Carriage

Faster than fairies, faster than witches,
Bridges and houses, hedges and ditches;
And charging along like troops in a battle,
All through the meadows the horses and
*   cattle:*
All of the sights of the hill and the plain
Fly as thick as driving rain;
And ever again, in the wink of an eye,
Painted stations whistle by.

Here is a child who clambers and scrambles,
All by himself and gathering brambles;
Here is a tramp who stands and gazes;
And there is the green for stringing the daisies!
Here is a cart run away in the road
Lumping along with man and load;
And here is a mill, and there is a river:
Each a glimpse and gone for ever!

ROBERT LOUIS STEVENSON

Fables from Aesop

Translated by V. S. Vernon Jones

Illustrated by Arthur Rackham

Little is known about Aesop except that he was a slave of the Greeks and lived four or five centuries before Christ. He was probably a native of Sardis in Asia Minor. His name is associated with many of the best of the world's fables, such as the story of the dog who lost his bone when he attacked his own reflection in the river. But these stories can be found in many of the world's languages, so Aesop certainly did not invent them all.

Fables are little tales, usually but not always, about animals. They are always meant to tell us truths about ourselves. (It seems hard on the animals to make them behave like some human beings!) Not all fables are old, for you will find a modern one called "The Prominent Man" elsewhere in this book.

Here are some of Aesop's fables:

THE FOX AND THE CROW

A CROW was sitting on a branch of a tree with a piece of cheese in her beak when a Fox observed her and set his wits to work to discover some way of getting the cheese. Coming and standing under the tree he looked up and said, "What a noble bird I see above me! Her beauty is without equal, the hue of her plumage exquisite. If only her voice is as sweet as her looks are fair, she ought without doubt to be Queen of the Birds." The Crow was hugely flattered by this, and just to show the Fox that she could sing she gave a loud caw. Down came the cheese, of course, and the Fox, snatching it up, said, "You have a voice, madam, I see: what you want is wits."

THE CAT AND THE COCK

A CAT pounced on a cock, and cast about for some good excuse for making a meal off him, for Cats don't as a rule eat Cocks, and she knew she ought not to. At last she said: "You make a great nuisance of yourself at night by crowing and keeping people awake: so I am going to make an end of you." But the Cock defended himself by saying that he crowed in order that men might wake up and set about the day's work in good time, and that they really couldn't very well do without him. "That may be," said the Cat, "but whether they can or not, I'm not going without my dinner"; and she killed and ate him.

The want of a good excuse never kept a villain from crime.

THE PEACOCK
AND JUNO

THE PEACOCK was greatly discontented because he had not a beautiful voice like the nightingale, and he went and complained to Juno about it. "The nightingale's song," said he, "is the envy of all the birds; but whenever I utter a sound I become a laughing-stock." The goddess tried to console him by saying, "You have not, it is true, the power of song, but then you far excel all the rest in beauty: your neck flashes like the emerald and your splendid tail is a marvel of gorgeous colour." But the Peacock was not appeased. "What is the use," said he, "of being beautiful, with a voice like mine?" Then Juno replied, with a shade of sternness in her tones, "Fate has allotted to all their destined gifts: to yourself beauty, to the eagle strength, to the nightingale song, and so on to all the rest in their degree; but you alone are dissatisfied with your portion. Make, then, no more complaints: for, if your present wish were granted, you would quickly find cause for fresh discontent."

THE OAK AND
THE REEDS

AN OAK that grew on the bank of a river was uprooted by a severe gale of wind, and thrown across the stream. It fell among some Reeds growing by the water, and said to them: "How is it that you, who are so frail and slender, have managed to weather the storm, whereas I, with all my strength, have been torn up by the roots and hurled into the river?" "You were stubborn," came the reply, "and fought against the storm, which proved stronger than you; but we bow and yield to every breeze, and thus the gale passed harmlessly over our heads."

The little reeds are standing,
but the oak has fallen.

THE LION AND
THE MOUSE

A LION asleep in his lair was waked up by a Mouse running over his face. Losing his temper he seized it with his paw and was about to kill it. The Mouse, terrified, piteously entreated him to spare its life. "Please let me go," it cried, "and one day I will repay you for your kindness." The idea of so insignificant a creature ever being able to do anything for him amused the Lion so much that he laughed aloud, and good-humouredly let it go. But the Mouse's chance came, after all. One day the Lion got entangled in a net which had been spread for game by some hunters, and the Mouse heard and recognized his roars of anger and ran to the spot. Without more ado it set to work to gnaw the ropes with its teeth, and succeeded before long in setting the Lion free. "There!" said the Mouse, "you laughed at me when I promised I would repay you: but now you see, even a Mouse can help a Lion."

THE MILLER, HIS SON, AND THEIR ASS

A MILLER, accompanied by his young Son, was driving his Ass to market in hopes of finding a purchaser for him. On the road they met a troop of girls, laughing and talking, who exclaimed, "Did you ever see such a pair of fools? To be trudging along the dusty road when they might be riding!" The Miller thought there was

sense in what they said, so he made his Son mount the Ass, and himself walked at the head. Presently they met some of his

old cronies, who greeted them and said, "You'll spoil that Son of yours, letting him ride while you toil along on foot! Make

him walk, young lazybones! It'll do him all the good in the world." The Miller followed their advice, and took his Son's

place on the back of the Ass while the boy trudged along behind. They had not gone far when they overtook a party of women and children, and the Miller heard them say, "What a selfish old man! He lets his

poor little boy follow as best he can on his own legs!" So he made his Son get up behind him. Farther along the road they met some travellers, who asked the Miller whether the Ass he was riding was his own property, or a beast hired for the occasion. He replied that it was his own, and that he was taking it to market to sell. "Good heavens!" said they, "with a load like that the poor beast will be so exhausted by the time he gets there that no one will look at him. Why, you'd do better to carry him!"

"Anything to please you," said the old man, "we can but try." So they got off, tied the Ass's legs together with a rope and slung him on a pole, and at last reached the town, carrying him between them.

This was so absurd a sight that the people ran out in crowds to laugh at it, and chaffed the Father and Son unmercifully, some even calling them lunatics. They had then got to a bridge over the river, where the Ass, frightened by the noise and his unusual situation, kicked and struggled till he broke the ropes that bound him, and fell into the water and was drowned. Whereupon the unfortunate Miller, vexed and ashamed, made the best of his way home again, convinced that in trying to please all he had pleased none, and had lost his Ass into the bargain.

THE MILKMAID AND HER PAIL

A FARMER's daughter had been out to milk the cows, and was returning to the dairy carrying her pail of milk upon her head. As she walked along, she fell a-musing after this fashion: "The milk in this pail will provide me with cream, which I will make into butter and take to market to sell. With the money I will buy a number of eggs, and these, when hatched, will produce chickens, and by and by I shall have quite a large poultry-yard. Then I shall sell some of my fowls, and with the money which they will bring in I will buy myself a new gown, which I shall wear when I go to the fair; and all the young fellows will admire it, and come and make love to me, but I shall toss my head and have nothing to say to them." Forgetting all about the pail, and suiting the action to the word, she tossed her head. Down went the pail, all the milk was spilled, and all her fine castles in the air vanished in a moment!

Do not count your chickens before they are hatched.

THE FARMER AND THE STORK

A FARMER set some traps in a field which he had lately sown with corn, in order to catch the cranes which came to pick up the seed. When he returned to look at his traps he found several cranes caught, and among them a Stork, which begged to be let go, and said: "You ought not to kill me: I am not a crane, but a Stork, as you can easily see by my feathers, and I am the most honest and harmless of birds." But the Farmer replied: "It's nothing to me what you are: I find you among these cranes, who ruin my crops, and, like them, you shall suffer."

If you choose bad companions no one will believe that you are anything but bad yourself.

THE HARE AND THE TORTOISE

A HARE was one day making fun of a Tortoise for being so slow upon his feet. "Wait a bit," said the Tortoise; "I'll run a race with you and I'll wager that I win." "Oh, well," replied the Hare, who was much amused at the idea, "let's try and see"; and it was soon agreed that the Fox should set a course for them, and be the judge. When the time came both started off together, but the Hare was soon so far ahead that he thought he might as well have a rest: so down he lay and fell fast asleep. Meanwhile the Tortoise kept plodding on, and in time reached the goal. At last the Hare woke up with a start, and dashed on at his fastest, but only to find that the Tortoise had already won the race. *Slow and steady wins the race.*

His Treasures

Though Clock
To tell how night draws hence, I've none,
A Cock,
I have, to sing how day draws on . . .
A Hen
I keep, which creaking day by day,
Tells when
She goes her long white egg to lay.
A Goose
I have, which, with a jealous care,
Lets loose
Her tongue to tell what danger's near.
A Lamb
I keep (tame) with my morsels fed,
Whose Dam
An orphan left him (lately dead).
A Cat
I keep, that plays about my House,
Grown fat
With eating many a miching Mouse
To these
A Trasy I do keep, whereby
I please
The more my rural privacy:
Which are
But toys, to give my heart some ease:
Where care
None is, slight things do lightly please.

ROBERT HERRICK

miching = thieving   Trasy = Spaniel

300

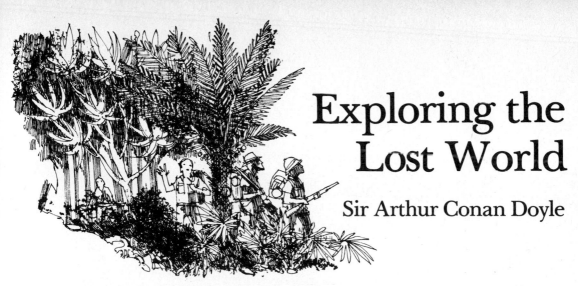

Exploring the Lost World

Sir Arthur Conan Doyle

Illustrated by Michael Jackson and Mike Codd

Born in Edinburgh and educated at its University, Sir Arthur Conan Doyle (1859–1930) began his professional life as a doctor in the south of England, but patients at first were few and he sought to make a little extra money by writing stories.

Conan Doyle wrote no books for children, but his bold and original imagination combines with his plain and simple style to produce stories which are striking and easy to read. His Sherlock Holmes—and the three novels and five books of stories that accompany his doings—are known everywhere. Then, too, his admirable stories of Brigadier Gerard and the Napoleonic Wars, are no less lively. Another turn of his imagination took him into the realm of what is nowadays called science fiction, in which H. G. Wells was the earlier and greater pioneer. Here is an extract from "The Lost World", in which the bull-like, bearded and ferociously quick-tempered Professor Challenger is leading a small expedition to prove the existence of animals, long thought to be extinct, on a plateau he has discovered in South America. The four adventurers are Challenger himself; Professor Summerlee who thinks Challenger is a liar and who is now finding out that he isn't; Lord John Roxton, soldier and sportsman; and the young reporter who is writing the account you are about to read. The adventurers have scaled the cliff-like side of the plateau, and they see that even the plant life is of a kind that was believed to have perished from the earth long ago. As for the animals—well, you will see:

OUR situation, stranded without possibility of escape in such a land, was clearly full of danger, and our reasons endorsed every measure of caution which Lord John's experience could suggest. Yet it was surely impossible that we should halt on the edge of this world of mystery when our very souls were tingling with impatience to push forward and to pluck the heart from it.

Hardly had we started when we came across signs that there were indeed wonders awaiting us. After a few hundred yards of thick forest, containing many trees which were quite unknown to me, but which Summerlee, who was the botanist of the party, recognized as forms of conifera and of cycadaceous plants which have long passed away in the world below, we entered a region where the stream widened out and formed a considerable bog. High reeds of a peculiar type grew thickly before us, which were pronounced to be equisetacea, or mare's-tails, with

All five were sitting up, balancing themselves upon their broad, powerful tails and

tree-ferns scattered amongst them, all of them swaying in a brisk wind. Suddenly Lord John, who was walking first, halted with uplifted hand.

"Look at this!" said he. "By George, this must be the trail of the father of all birds!"

An enormous three-toed track was imprinted in the soft mud before us. The creature, whatever it was, had crossed the swamp and had passed on into the forest. We all stopped to examine that monstrous spoor. If it were indeed a bird—and what animal could leave such a mark?—its foot was so much larger than an ostrich's that its height upon the same scale must be enormous. Lord John looked eagerly round him and slipped two cartridges into his elephant-gun.

"I'll stake my good name as a shikaree," said he, "that the track is a fresh one. The creature has not passed ten minutes. Look how the water is still oozing into that deeper print! By Jove! See, here is the mark of a little one!"

Sure enough, smaller tracks of the same general form were running parallel to the large ones.

"But what do you make of this?" cried Professor Summerlee triumphantly, pointing to what looked like the huge print of a five-fingered human hand appearing among the three-toed marks.

"Wealden!" cried Challenger, in an ecstasy. "I've seen them in the Wealden clay. It is a creature walking erect upon three-toed feet, and occasionally putting one of its five-fingered fore-paws upon the ground. Not a bird, my dear Roxton—not a bird."

"A beast?"

"No; a reptile—a dinosaur. Nothing else could have left such a track. They puzzled

302

heir huge three-toed hind feet.

five were sitting up, balancing themselves upon their broad, powerful tails and their huge three-toed hind feet, while with their small five-fingered front feet they pulled down the branches upon which they browsed. I do not know that I can bring their appearance home to you better than by saying that they looked like monstrous kangaroos, twenty feet in length, and with skins like black crocodiles.

I do not know how long we stayed motionless gazing at this marvellous spectacle. A strong wind blew towards us and we were well concealed, so there was no chance of discovery. From time to time the little ones played round their parents in unwieldy gambols, the great beasts bounding into the air and falling with dull thuds upon the earth. The strength of the parents seemed to be limitless, for one of them, having some difficulty in reaching a bunch of foliage which grew upon a considerable-sized tree, put his forelegs round the trunk and tore it down as if it had been a sapling. The action seemed, as I thought, to show not only the great development of its muscles, but also the small one of its brain, for the whole weight came crashing down upon the top of it, and it uttered a series of shrill yelps to show that, big as it was, there was a limit to what it could endure. The incident made it think, apparently, that the neighbourhood was dangerous, for it slowly lurched off through the wood, followed by its mate and its three enormous infants. We saw the shimmering slaty gleam of their skins between the tree-trunks, and their heads undulating high above the brushwood. Then they vanished from our sight.

I looked at my comrades. Lord John was standing at gaze with his finger on the trigger of his elephant-gun, his eager hunter's soul shining from his fierce eyes. What would he not give for one such head to place between the two crossed oars above the mantelpiece in his snuggery at the Albany! And yet his reason held him in, for all our exploration of the wonders

a worthy Sussex doctor some ninety years ago; but who in the world could have hoped—hoped—to have seen a sight like that?"

His words died away into a whisper, and we all stood motionless in amazement. Following the tracks, we had left the morass and passed through a screen of brushwood and trees. Beyond was an open glade, and in this were five of the most extraordinary creatures that I have ever seen. Crouching down among the bushes, we observed them at our leisure.

There were, as I say, five of them, two being adults and three young ones. In size they were enormous. Even the babies were as big as elephants, while the two large ones were far beyond all creatures I have ever seen. They had slate-coloured skin, which was scaled like a lizard's and shimmered where the sun shone upon it. All of this unknown land depended upon our presence being concealed from its inhabitants. The two Professors were in silent ecstasy. In their excitement they had unconsciously seized each other by the hand, and stood like two children in the presence of a marvel, Challenger's cheeks bunched up into a seraphic smile, and Summerlee's sardonic face softening for the moment into wonder and reverence.

"What will they say in England of this?" he cried at last.

"My dear Summerlee, I will tell you with great confidence exactly what they will say in England," said Challenger. "They will say that you are an infernal liar and a scientific charlatan, exactly as you and others said of me."

"In face of photographs?"

"Faked, Summerlee! Clumsily faked!"

"In the face of specimens?"

"Ah, there we may have them! Malone and his filthy Fleet Street crew may be all yelping our praises yet. August the twenty-eighth—the day we saw five live iguanodons in a glade of Maple White Land. Put it down in your diary, my young friend, and send it to your rag."

"And be ready to get the toe-end of the editorial boot in return," said Lord John. "Things look a bit different from the latitude of London, young fellah my lad. There's many a man who never tells his adventures, for he can't hope to be believed. Who's to blame them? For this will seem a bit of a dream to ourselves in a month or two. *What* did you say they were?"

"Iguanodons," said Summerlee. "You'll find their footmarks all over the Hastings sands, in Kent, and in Sussex. The South of England was alive with them when there was plenty of good lush green-stuff to keep them going. Conditions have changed, and the beasts died. Here it seems that the conditions have not changed, and the beasts have lived."

"If ever we get out of this alive, I must have a head with me," said Lord John.

"Lord, how some of that Somaliland-Uganda crowd would turn a beautiful pea-green if they saw it! I don't know what you chaps think, but it strikes me that we are on mighty thin ice all this time."

I had the same feeling of mystery and danger around us. In the gloom of the trees there seemed a constant menace, and as we looked up into their shadowy foliage vague terrors crept into one's heart. It is true that these monstrous creatures which we had seen were lumbering, inoffensive brutes which were unlikely to hurt anyone, but in this world of wonders what other survivals might there not be—what fierce, active horrors ready to pounce upon us from their lair among the rocks or brushwood? I knew little of prehistoric life, but I had a clear remembrance of one book which I had read in which it spoke of creatures who would live upon our lions and tigers as a cat lives upon mice. What if these also were to be found in the woods of Maple White Land!

It was destined that on this very morning—our first in the new country—we were to find out what strange hazards lay around us. It was a loathsome adventure, and one of which I hate to think. If, as Lord John said, the glade of the iguanodons will remain with us as a dream, then surely the swamp of the pterodactyls will for ever be our nightmare. Let me set down exactly what occurred.

We passed very slowly through the woods, partly because Lord John acted as scout before he would let us advance, and partly because at every second step one or other of our Professors would fall, with a cry of wonder, before some flower or insect which presented him with a new type. We may have travelled two or three miles in all, keeping to the right of the line of the stream, when we came upon a considerable opening in the trees. A belt of brushwood led up to a tangle of rocks—the whole plateau was strewn with boulders. We were walking slowly towards these rocks, among bushes which reached over

When I went up to take my prizes Mr. Driscoll and Chris stamped as well as clapped and I had to feel happy.
From "The Prize-giving"

"Fifteen? If I had half-a-dozen such lads as you, I would make knights of them before I died. Eh, Yeo?"
From "The Lure of the Spanish Main"

our waists, when we became aware of a strange low gabbling and whistling sound, which filled the air with a constant clamour and appeared to come from some spot immediately before us. Lord John held up his hand as a signal for us to stop, and he made his way swiftly, stooping and running, to the line of rocks. We saw him peep over them and give a gesture of amazement. Then he stood staring as if forgetting us, so utterly entranced was he by what he saw. Finally he waved us to come on, holding up his hand as a signal for caution. His whole bearing made me feel that something wonderful but dangerous lay before us.

Creeping to his side, we looked over the rocks. The place into which we gazed was a pit, and may, in the early days, have been one of the smaller volcanic blow-holes of the plateau. It was bowl-shaped, and at the bottom, some hundreds of yards from where we lay, were pools of green-scummed, stagnant water, fringed with bulrushes. It was a weird place in itself, but its occupants made it seem like a scene from the Seven Circles of Dante. The place was a rookery of pterodactyls. There were hundreds of them congregated within view. All the bottom area round the water-edge was alive with their young ones, and with the hideous mothers brooding upon their leathery, yellowish eggs. From this crawling flapping mass of obscene reptilian life came the shocking clamour which filled the air and the mephitic, horrible, musty odour which turned us sick. But above, perched each upon its own stone, tall, grey, and withered, more like dead and dried specimens than actual living creatures, sat the horrible males, absolutely motionless save for the rolling of their red eyes or an occasional snap of their rat-trap beaks as a dragon-fly went past them. Their huge, membranous wings were closed by folding their forearms, so that they sat like gigantic old women, wrapped in hideous web-coloured shawls, and with their

ferocious heads protruding above them. Large and small, not less than a thousand of these filthy creatures lay in the hollow before us.

Our Professors would gladly have stayed there all day, so entranced were they by this opportunity of studying the life of a prehistoric age. They pointed out the fish and dead birds lying about among the rocks as proving the nature of the food of these creatures, and I heard them congratulating each other on having cleared up the point why the bones of this flying dragon are found in such great numbers in certain well-defined areas, as in the Cambridge Green-sand, since it was now seen that, like penguins they lived in gregarious fashion.

Finally, however, Challenger, bent upon proving some point which Summerlee had contested, thrust his head over the rock

305

and nearly brought destruction upon us all. In an instant the nearest male gave a shrill, whistling cry, and flapped its twenty-foot span of leathery wings as it soared up into the air. The females and young ones huddled together beside the water, while the whole circle of sentinels rose one after the other and sailed off into the sky. It was a wonderful sight to see at least a hundred creatures of such enormous size and hideous appearance all swooping like swallows with swift, shearing wing-strokes above us; but soon we realized that it was not one on which we could afford to linger. At first the great brutes flew round in a huge ring, as if to make sure what the exact extent of the danger might be. Then the flight grew lower and the circle narrower, until they were whizzing round and round us, the dry, rustling flap of their huge slate-coloured wings filling the air with a volume of sound that made me think of Hendon aerodrome upon a race day.

"Make for the wood and keep together," cried Lord John, clubbing his rifle. "The brutes mean mischief."

The moment we attempted to retreat the circle closed in upon us, until the tips of the wings of those nearest to us nearly touched our faces. We beat at them with the stocks of our guns, but there was nothing solid or vulnerable to strike. Then suddenly out of the whizzing, slate-coloured circle a long neck shot out, and a fierce beak made a thrust at us. Another and another followed. Summerlee gave a cry and put his hand to his face, from which the blood was streaming. I felt a prod at the back of my neck, and turned dizzy with the shock. Challenger fell, and as I stooped to pick him up I was again struck from behind and dropped on the top of him. At the same instant I heard the crash of Lord John's elephant-gun, and, looking up, saw one of the creatures with a broken wing struggling upon the ground, spitting and gurgling at us with a wide-opened beak and bloodshot, goggled eyes,

like some devil in a medieval picture. Its comrades had flown higher at the sudden sound, and were circling above our heads.

"Now," cried Lord John, "now for our lives!"

We staggered through the brushwood, and even as we reached the trees the harpies were on us again. Summerlee was knocked down, but we bore him up and rushed among the trunks. Once there we were safe, for those huge wings had no space for their sweep beneath the branches. As we limped homewards, sadly mauled and discomfited, we saw them for a long time flying at a great height against the deep blue sky above our heads, soaring round and round, no bigger than wood-pigeons, with their eyes no doubt still following our progress. At last, however, as we reached the thicker woods they gave up the chase, and we saw them no more.

"A most interesting and convincing experience," said Challenger, as we halted beside the brook and he bathed a swollen knee. "We are exceptionally well informed, Summerlee, as to the habits of the enraged pterodactyl."

Summerlee was wiping the blood from a cut in his forehead, while I was tying up a nasty stab in the muscle of the neck. Lord John had the shoulder of his coat torn away, but the creature's teeth had only grazed the flesh.

"It is worth noting," Challenger continued, "that our young friend has received an undoubted stab, while Lord John's coat could only have been torn by a bite. In my own case, I was beaten about the head by their wings, so we have had a remarkable exhibition of their various methods of offence."

"It has been touch and go for our lives," said Lord John gravely, "and I could not think of a more rotten sort of death than to be outed by such filthy vermin. I was sorry to fire my rifle, but, by Jove! there was no great choice."

"We should not be here if you hadn't," said I, with conviction.

The Attack on the Stockade
Captain Marryat

Illustrated by Robert Geary

The works of the sailor-author Captain Frederick Marryat (1792–1848) tell us what seafaring life was like in the first half of the nineteenth century, when Dickens was a young man and Victoria a young queen. His books are full of vigour and those for adults can be read by young people who enjoy adventure yarns. In his later life, however, Marryat was encouraged by his children to write for boys and girls, producing such favourites as "The Children of the New Forest" and "Masterman Ready".

Like Defoe, Marryat gives us plenty of facts and explains exactly how things were done. This gives an air of solid reality to the most adventurous happenings. The story here comes from "Masterman Ready" in which the Seagrave family and their old seaman friend, Ready, are wrecked on a Pacific island and have to fight for their lives. To get in the full account of the attack the piece has been somewhat shortened; but the words are otherwise unchanged.

Mrs. SEAGRAVE had been shown how to load a musket, and Juno was now taught the same.

"Now, sir, we are all prepared," said old Ready, "and madam and Juno can go and look a little after the children, and get breakfast."

"Breakfast all ready. Kettle boil long time," said Juno.

As soon as the children were dressed, Mr. Seagrave called Ready, who was outside, watching the canoes, and they went to their morning devotions, and prayed heartily for succour in this time of need. They then breakfasted in haste; for, as may be supposed, they were almost too anxious to eat. Mrs. Seagrave pressed her children in her arms, but kept up her spirits wonderfully.

"This suspense is worse than all," said she at last. "I wish now that they were come."

The savages evidently had a knowledge of the passages through the reefs, as they had steered right in, and had lowered their sails. Ready and William were on the look-out, but concealed behind the coconut trees.

"I hope they will not stay out too long."

"No fear of that, my dear Selina; but they had better watch their motions to the last minute."

During this conversation between Mr. and Mrs. Seagrave within the stockade, William and Ready were watching the motions of the savages, a large portion of whom had landed out of ten of the canoes, and the others were following their example as fast as they could, forcing their way through the reefs. The savages were all painted, with their war-cloaks and feathers on, and armed with spears and clubs, evidently having come with no peaceable intentions. At first they occupied themselves with beaching the canoes, and as they were very large and heavy, this was a work of some few minutes' employment for the whole of them.

William, who had taken the telescope to examine them more minutely, said to Ready: "What a fierce, cruel set of wretches they appear to be; if they overpower us, they will certainly kill us."

"Of that there is no doubt, Master William; but we must fight hard, and not let them overpower us. Kill us they certainly will, and I am not sure that they may not eat us afterwards, but that is of little consequence."

William shuddered at the idea, and then replied in a determined tone: "I'll fight as long as I have breath in my body."

The loud yells of the savages struck terror into the heart of Mrs. Seagrave; it was well that she had not seen their painted bodies and fierce appearance, or she would have been much more alarmed. Little Albert and Caroline clung round her neck with terror in their faces; they did not cry, but looked round and round to see from whence the horrid noise proceeded, and then clung faster to their mother. Master Tommy was very busy, finishing all the breakfast which had been left, for there was no one to check him as usual; Juno was busy outside, and was very active and courageous. Mr. Seagrave had been employed making the holes between the palisades large enough to admit the barrels of the muskets, so that they could fire at the savages without being exposed; while William and Ready, with their muskets loaded, were on the look-out for their approach.

"They are busy with the old house just now, sir," observed Ready, "but that won't detain them long."

"Here they come," replied William.

"Ah! they have stopped; they did not expect the stockade, that is clear, and it has puzzled them; see how they are all crowding together and talking; they are holding a council of war how to proceed; that tall man must be one of their chiefs. Now, Master William, although I intend to fight as hard as I can, yet I always feel a dislike to begin first; I shall therefore show myself over the palisades, and if they attack me, I shall then fire with a quiet conscience."

"But take care they don't hit you, Ready."

Ready now stood upon the plank within, so as to show himself to the savages, who gave a tremendous yell, and, as they advanced, a dozen spears were thrown at him with so true an aim that, had he not instantly dodged behind the stockade, he must have been killed. Three or four spears remained quivering in the palisades, just below the top; the others went over it, and fell down inside of the stockade, at the further end.

"Now, Master William, take good aim"; but before William could fire, Mr. Seagrave, who had agreed to be stationed at the corner so that he might see if the savages went round to the other side, fired his musket, and the tall chief fell to the ground.

Ready and William also fired, and two more of the savages were seen to drop, amidst the yells of their companions. Juno handed up the other muskets which were ready loaded, and took those discharged, and Mrs. Seagrave, having desired Caroline to take care of her little brother, and Tommy to be very quiet and good, came out and turned the key of the door upon them, and hastened to assist Juno in reloading the muskets.

The spears now rushed through the air, and it was well that they could fire from the stockade without exposing their persons, or they would have had but little chance. The yells increased, and the savages now began to attack on every quarter; the most active, who climbed like cats, actually succeeded in gaining the top of the palisade but, as soon as their heads appeared above, they were fired at with so true an aim that they dropped down dead outside. This combat lasted for more than an hour when the savages, having lost a great many men, drew off from the assault, and the parties within the stockade had time to breathe.

"They have not gained much in this bout, at all events," said Ready; "it was well fought on our side, and Master William, you certainly behaved as if you had been brought up to it; I don't think you ever missed your man once."

"Do you think they will go away now?" said Mrs. Seagrave.

"Oh, no, madam, not yet; they will try us every way before they leave us. You see these are very brave men and it is clear that they know what gunpowder is, or they would have been more astonished. . . . I reckon it is not the first time that they have fought with Europeans."

"Are they all gone, Ready?" said William who had come down from the plank to his mother.

"No, sir; I see them between the trees now; they are sitting round in a circle, and, I suppose, making speeches: it's the custom of these people."

"Well, I'm very thirsty, at all events," said William; "Juno, bring me a little water." Juno went to the water-tub, to comply with William's request, and in a few moments afterwards came back in great consternation.

"Oh, massa! oh, missy! no water; water all gone."

"Water all gone!" cried Ready and all of them in a breath.

"Yes; not one little drop in the cask."

"I filled it up to the top!" exclaimed Ready very gravely; "the tub did not leak, that I am sure of; how can this have happened?"

"Missy, I tink I know now," said Juno; "you remember you send Massa Tommy, the two or three days we wash, to fetch water from well in little bucket. You know how soon he come back, and how you say what good boy he was, and how you tell Massa Seagrave when he come to dinner. Now, missy, I quite certain Massa Tommy no take trouble go to well, but fetch water from tub all the while, and so he empty it."

"I'm afraid you're right, Juno," replied Mrs. Seagrave. "What shall we do?"

"I go speak Massa Tommy," said Juno, running to the house.

"This is a very awkward thing, Mr. Seagrave," observed Ready gravely.

Mr. Seagrave shook his head.

The fact was, that they all perceived the danger of their position: if the savages did not leave the island, they would perish of thirst or have to surrender; and in the latter case, all their lives would most certainly be sacrificed.

Juno now returned: her suspicions were but too true. Tommy, pleased with the praise of being so quick in bringing the water, had taken out the spigot of the cask, and drawn it all off. He was now crying, and promising not to take the water again.

"His promises come too late," observed Mr. Seagrave.

"If I had but a little for the children, I should not care," said Mrs. Seagrave; "but to see those poor things suffer—is there not a drop left, Juno, anywhere?"

Juno shook her head. "All gone, missy; none nowhere."

Mrs. Seagrave said she would go and examine, and went away into the house accompanied by Juno.

"This is a very bad business, Ready," observed Mr. Seagrave. "What would we give for a shower of rain now, that we might catch the falling drops!"

"I wish the savages would come on again," said William; "for the sooner they come, the sooner the affair will be decided."

"I doubt if they will today, sir; at night-time I think it very probable, and I fear the night attack more than the day. We must make preparations for it."

"Why, what can we do, Ready?"

"We must contrive to have a large fire ready for lighting, that we may not have to fight altogether in the dark. We must have plenty of tar in it, to make it burn bright, and we must not, of course, light it until after we are attacked. We shall then see where they are trying for an entrance, and where to aim with our muskets."

"The idea is very good, Ready," said Mr. Seagrave; "if it had not been for this unfortunate want of water, I really should be sanguine of beating them off."

"We may suffer very much, Mr. Seagrave, I have no doubt; but who knows what the morrow may bring forth?"

"True, Ready. Do you see the savages now?"

"No, sir; they have left the spot where they were in consultation, and I do not even hear them; I suppose they are busy with their wounded and their dead."

As Ready had supposed, no further attack was made by the savages on that day. They prepared a large fire in a tar-barrel full of coconut leaves mixed with wood and tar, so as to burn fiercely. Dinner or supper they had none, for there was nothing but salt pork and beef and live turtle, and, by Ready's advice, they did not eat, as it would only increase their desire to drink.

The poor children suffered much; little Albert wailed and cried for "water, water"; Caroline knew that there was none, and was quiet, poor little girl, although she suffered much; as for Tommy, the author of all this misery, he was the most impatient, and roared for some time till William, quite angry at his behaviour, gave him a smart box on the ear.

But the moaning of the children was very soon after dusk drowned by the yells of the savages, who, as Ready had prognosticated, now advanced to the night attack.

Every part of the stockade was at once assailed, and their attempts now made were to climb into it; a few spears were occasionally thrown, but it was evident that the object was to obtain an entrance by dint of numbers. It was well that Ready had taken the precaution of nailing the deal planks above the original stockade, for there is little doubt but that the savages would have gained their object; as it was, before the flames of the fire, which Juno had lighted by Ready's order, gave them sufficient light, three or four savages had climbed up and had been shot by William and Mr. Seagrave, as they were on the top of the stockade.

When the fire burnt brightly, the savages outside were more easily aimed at, and a great many fell in their attempts to get over. The attack continued more than an hour, when at last, satisfied that they could not succeed, the savages once more withdrew, carrying with them, as before, their dead and wounded.

"I trust that they will now re-embark,

and leave the island," said Mr. Seagrave to Ready.

"I only wish they may, sir; it is not at all impossible but there is no saying."

The second day was passed in keeping a look-out upon the savages, and awaiting a fresh attack. They could perceive from the top of the coconut tree that the savages held a council of war in the forenoon, sitting round in a large circle, while one got up in the centre, and made a speech, flourishing his club and spear while he spoke. In the afternoon the council broke up, and the savages were observed to be very busy in all directions, cutting down the coconut trees, and collecting all the brushwood.

Ready watched them for a long while, and at last came down a little before sunset. "Mr. Seagrave," said he, "we shall have, in my opinion, no attack this night, but tomorrow we must expect something very serious; the savages are cutting down the trees, and making large faggots; they do not get on very fast, because their hatchets are made of stone and don't cut very well, but perseverance and numbers will effect everything, and I dare say that they will work all night till they have obtained as many faggots as they want."

"But what do you imagine to be their object, Ready, in cutting down trees, and making the faggots?"

"Either, sir, to pile them up outside the palisades, so large as to be able to walk up upon them, or else to pile them up to set fire to them, and burn us out."

"Do you think they will succeed?"

"Not without very heavy loss; perhaps we may beat them off, but it will be a hard fight; harder than any we have had yet. We must have the women to load the muskets, so that we may fire as fast as we can. I should not think much of their attempts to burn us, if it were not for the smoke. Coconut wood, especially with the bark on, as our palisades have, will char a long while, but not burn easily when standing upright; but the fire, when the faggots are kindled, although it will be fierce, will not last long."

"But suffering as we are now, Ready, for want of water, how can we possibly keep up our strength to meet them in a suffocating smoke and flame. We must drop with sheer exhaustion."

"We must hope for the best, and do our best, Mr. Seagrave," replied Ready; "and recollect that should anything happen to me during the conflict, that if there is any chance of your being overpowered, you must take advantage of the smoke, to escape into the woods."

As soon as Mr. Seagrave had gone into the house, Ready called William, and said: "Master William, water we must have. I cannot bear to see the agony of the poor children, and the state of mind which your poor mother is in; and more, without water we never shall be able to beat off the savages tomorrow. We shall literally die of choking in the smoke, if they use fire. Now, William, I intend to take one of the seven-gallon barricos, and go down to the well for water. I may succeed, and I may not, but attempt it I must, and if I fail it cannot be helped."

"Why not let me go, Ready?" replied William.

"For many reasons, William," said Ready; "and the chief one is that I do not think you would succeed so well as I shall. Now observe, you must let me out of the door, and when I am out, in case of accident, put one of the poles across it inside; that will keep the door fast, if they attack it, until you can secure it with the others. Watch my return, and be all ready to let me in. Do you understand me?"

"Yes, perfectly, Ready; but I am now, I must confess, really frightened; if anything was to happen to you, what a misery it would be."

"There is no help for it, William. Water must, if possible, be procured, and now is a better time to make the attempt than later."

Ready went for the barrico, a little cask, which held six or seven gallons of water.

He put on the head-dress and war-cloak of the savage, and, taking the barrico on his shoulder, and the spear in his hand, the poles which barred the door were softly removed by William, and after ascertaining that no one was concealed beneath the palisades, Ready pressed William's hand, and set off across the cleared space outside of the stockade, and gained the coconut trees. William remained on the watch. He was in an awful state of suspense, listening to the slightest noise, even the slight rustling by the wind of the coconut boughs above him made him start; there he continued for some minutes, his gun ready cocked by his side.

It is time that he returned, thought William; the distance is not a hundred yards, and yet I have heard no noise. At last he thought he heard footsteps coming very softly. Yes, it was so. Ready was returning, and without any accident. William had his hand upon the pole, to slip it on one side, and open the door, when he heard a scuffle and a fall close to the door. He immediately threw down the pole, and opened it just as Ready called him by name. William seized his musket, and sprang out; he found Ready struggling with a savage, who was uppermost, and with his spear at Ready's breast. In a second William levelled and fired, and the savage fell dead by the side of Ready.

"Take the water in quick, William," said Ready in a faint voice. "I will contrive to crawl in, if I can."

William caught up the barrico of water, and took it in; he then hastened to Ready, who was on his knees. Mr. Seagrave, hearing the musket fired, had run out, and finding the stockade door open, followed William, and seeing him endeavouring to support Ready, caught hold of his other arm, and they led him tottering into the stockade; the door was then immediately secured, and they went to his assistance.

"Are you hurt, Ready?" said William.

"Yes, dear boy, yes; hurt to death, I fear: his spear went through my breast. Water, quick, water!"

"Alas! that we had some," said Mr. Seagrave.

"We have, Papa," replied William; "but it has cost us dearly."

William ran for a pannikin, and taking out the bung, poured some water out of the barrico, and gave it to Ready, who drank it with eagerness.

"I am better now," said he in a low voice; "bind up the wound, William; an old man like me has not much blood to spare."

Mr. Seagrave and William then opened his shirt, and examined the wound; the spear had gone deep into the lungs. William threw off his own shirt, tore it up into strips, and then bound up the wound so as to stop the effusion of blood.

Ready, who at first appeared much exhausted with being moved about, gradually recovered so as to be able to speak in a low voice, when Mrs. Seagrave came out of the house.

"Where is that brave, kind man?" cried she, "that I may bless him and thank him."

Mr. Seagrave went to her, and caught her by the arm.

"He is hurt, my dear; I am afraid very much hurt. I did not tell you at the time."

Mr. Seagrave first briefly related what had occurred, and then led her to where old Ready was lying. Mrs. Seagrave knelt by his side, took his hand, and burst into tears.

"Don't weep for me, dear madam," said Ready; "my days have been numbered; I'm only sorry that I cannot any more be useful to you."

"Dear, good old man," said Mrs. Seagrave, after a pause, "whatever may be our fates, and that is for the Almighty to decide for us, as long as I have life, what you have done for me and mine shall never be forgotten."

Mrs. Seagrave then bent over him, and, kissing his forehead, rose from her knees, and retired weeping into the house.

"This is a sad business, William," said Mr. Seagrave.

William shook his head. "He would not let me go," replied he; "I wish he had. I fear that he is much hurt; do you think so, Papa?"

"I should say that he cannot recover, William. We shall miss him tomorrow if they attack us; I fear much for the result."

They carried the barrico of water into the house, and put it in Mrs. Seagrave's charge, that it might not be wasted; and now that their thirst had been appeased, they all felt the calls of hunger. Juno and William went and cut off steaks from the turtle, and fried them; they all made a hearty meal, and perhaps never had they taken one with so much relish in their lives.

It was nearly daylight, when William, who had several times been softly up to Ready to ascertain whether he slept or not, found him with his eyes open.

"How do you find yourself, Ready?" said William.

"I am quiet and easy, William, and without much pain; but I think I am sinking, and shall not last long. Recollect that if you are obliged to escape from the stockade, William, you take no heed of me, but leave me where I am. I cannot live, and were you to move me, I should only die the sooner."

"I had rather die with you, than leave you, Ready."

"No, sir, that is wrong and foolish; you must save your mother, and your brothers and sister; promise me that you will do as I wish."

William squeezed Ready's hand; his heart was too full to speak.

At the dawn of day, William perceived that the savages were at work, that they every one shouldered a faggot, and commenced their advance towards the stockade; William immediately descended from the tree, and called his father, who was talking with Mrs. Seagrave. The muskets were all loaded, and Mrs. Seagrave and Juno took their posts below the planking, to reload them as fast as they were fired.

"We must fire upon them as soon as we are sure of not missing them, William," said Mr. Seagrave, "for the more we check their advance, the better."

When the first savages were within fifty yards, they both fired, and two of the men dropped; and they continued to fire as their assailants came up, with great success for the first ten minutes; after which the savages advanced in a larger body, and took the precaution to hold the faggots in front of them for some protection as they approached. By these means they gained the stockade in safety, and commenced laying their faggots. Mr. Seagrave and William still kept up an incessant fire upon them, but not with so much success as before.

Although many fell, the faggots were gradually heaped up, till they almost reached to the holes between the palisades, through which they pointed their muskets; and as the savages contrived to slope them down from the stockade to the ground, it was evident that they meant to mount up, and take them by escalade. At last, it appeared as if all the faggots had been placed, and the savages retired

farther back, to where the coconut trees were still standing.

"They have gone away, father," said William; "but they will come again, and I fear it is all over with us."

"I fear so too, my noble boy," replied Mr. Seagrave; "they are only retreating, to arrange for a general assault, and they now will be able to gain an entrance. I almost wish that they had fired the faggots; we might have escaped as Ready pointed out to us, but now I fear we have no chance."

"Don't say a word to my mother," said William; "let us defend ourselves to the last, and if we are overpowered it is the will of God."

"Well, God bless you, my boy; we shall all, I trust, meet in heaven."

The whole body of savages were now advancing from the coconut wood in a solid mass; they raised a yell, which struck terror into the hearts of Mrs. Seagrave and Juno, yet they flinched not. The savages were again within fifty yards of them, when the fire was opened upon them; the fire was answered by loud yells, and the savages had already reached the bottom of the sloping pile of faggots, when the yells and the reports of the muskets were drowned by a much louder report, followed by the crackling and breaking of the coconut trees, which made both parties start with surprise; another and another followed, the ground was ploughed up, and the savages fell in numbers.

"It must be the cannon of a ship, father," said William; "we are saved—we are saved!"

"It can be nothing else; we are saved, and by a miracle," replied Mr. Seagrave in utter astonishment.

The savages paused in the advance, quite stupefied; again, again, again, the report of the loud guns boomed through the air, and the round shot and grape came whizzing and tearing through the coconut grove; at this last broadside, the savages turned, and fled towards their canoes: not one was left to be seen.

"We are saved!" cried Mr. Seagrave,

leaping off the plank and embracing his wife, who sank down on her knees, and held up her clasped hands in thankfulness to heaven.

William had hastened up to the lookout on the coconut tree, and now cried out to them below, as the guns were again discharged:

"A large schooner, father; she is firing at the savages, who are at the canoes; they are falling in every direction: some have plunged into the water; there is a boat full of armed men coming on shore; they are close to the beach, by the garden point. Three of the canoes have got off full of men; there go the guns again; two of the canoes are sunk, father; the boat has landed, and the people are coming up this way." William then descended from the lookout as fast as he could.

As soon as he was down, he commenced unbarring the door of the stockade. He pulled out the last pole just as he heard the feet of their deliverers outside. He threw open the door, and a second after, found himself in the arms of Captain Osborn.

Poor Tom Bowling

Here, a sheer hulk, lies poor Tom Bowling,
  The darling of our crew;
No more he'll hear the tempest howling,
  For death has broach'd him to.
His form was of the manliest beauty,
  His heart was kind and soft,
Faithful below he did his duty,
  And now he's gone aloft.

Tom never from his word departed,
  His virtues were so rare,
His friends were many, and true-hearted,
  His Poll was kind and fair:
And then he'd sing so blithe and jolly,
  Ah many's the time and oft!
But mirth is turned to melancholy,
  For Tom is gone aloft.

Yet shall Poor Tom find pleasant weather,
  When he who all commands
Shall give, to call life's crew together,
  The word to pipe all hands.
Thus death, who Kings and Tars dispatches,
  In vain Tom's life has doff'd,
For, though his body's under hatches,
  His soul is gone aloft.

CHARLES DIBDIN

Lost in the Bushveld

Sir Percy Fitzpatrick

Illustrated by Michael Jackson

The eldest son of a Cape Colony judge, Sir Percy Fitzpatrick (1862–1931) was a well-known South African politician in the troubled period that preceded and followed the Boer War, and his activities touched many important fields, including the development of African railways and of the mining industry there. His literary fame is based on "Jock of the Bushveld", a classic among dog stories. But besides the adventures of this remarkable dog there is much of interest in his book about life and sport on the African veld in those pioneering days, as the following shows:

So FAR I had never lost my way out hunting. The experiences of other men and the warnings from the old hands had made me very careful. We were always hearing of men being lost through leaving the road and following up the game while they were excited, without noticing which way they went and how long they had been going. There were no beaten tracks and very few landmarks, so that even experienced hunters went astray sometimes for a few hours or a day or two when the mists or heavy rains came on and nothing could be seen beyond fifty or a hundred yards.

Nearly every one who goes hunting in the Bushveld gets lost some time or other —generally in the beginning before he has learned to notice things. Some have been lost for many days until they blundered on to a track by accident or were found by a search-party; others have been lost and, finding no water or food, have died; others have been killed by lions, and only a boot or a coat—or, as it happened in one case

that I know of, a ring found inside a lion— told what had occurred; others have been lost and nothing more ever heard of them.

The man who loses his head is really lost. He cannot think, remember, reason, or understand; and the strangest thing of all is that he often cannot even *see* properly—he fails to see the very things that he most wants to see, even when they are as large as life before him. Crossing the road without seeing it is not the only or the most extraordinary example of this sort of thing. We were out hunting once in a mounted party, but to spare a tired horse I went on foot and took up my stand in a game run among some thorn trees on the low spur of a hill, while the others made a big circuit to head off a troop of koodoo. Among us there was one who was very nervous, he had been lost once for six or eight hours, and being haunted by the dread of being lost again, his nerve was all gone and he would not go fifty yards without a companion. In the excitement of shooting at and galloping

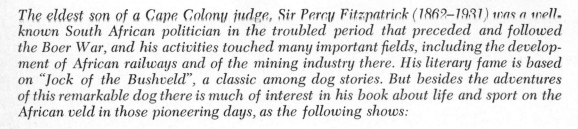

316

after the koodoo probably this dread was forgotten for a moment: he himself could not tell how he became separated, and no one else had noticed him.

The strip of wood along the hills in which I was waiting was four or five miles long but only from one to three hundred yards wide, a mere fringe enclosing the little range of kopjes; and between the stems of the trees I could see our camp and wagons in the open a quarter of a mile away. Ten or twelve shots faintly heard in the distance told me that the others were on to the koodoo, and knowing the preference of those animals for the bush I took cover behind a big stump and waited. For over half an hour, however, nothing came towards me, and believing then that the game had broken off another way, I was about to return to camp when I heard the tapping of galloping feet a long way off. In a few minutes the hard thud and occasional ring on the ground told that it was not the koodoo; and soon afterwards I saw a man on horseback. He was leaning eagerly forward and thumping the exhausted horse with his rifle and his heels to keep up its staggering gallop. I looked about quickly to see what it was he was chasing that could have slipped past me unnoticed, but there was nothing; then thinking there had been an accident and he was coming for help, I stepped out into the open and waited for him to come up. I stood quite still, and he galloped past within ten yards of me—so close that his muttered "Get on, you brute; get on, get on!" as he thumped away at his poor tired horse, was perfectly audible.

"What's up, sportsman?" I asked no louder than you would say it across a tennis-court; but the words brought him up, white-faced and terrified, and he half slid, half tumbled, off the horse gasping out, "I was lost, I was lost!" How he had managed to keep within that strip of bush, without once getting into the open where he would have seen the line of kopjes to which I had told him to stick or could have

seen the wagons and the smoke of the big camp-fire, he could never explain. I turned him round where he stood, and through the trees showed him the white tents of the wagons and the cattle grazing near by, but he was too dazed to understand or explain anything.

Buggins who was with us in the first season was no hunter, but he was a good shot and not a bad fellow. In his case there was no tragedy; there was much laughter and—to me—a wonderful revelation. He showed us, as in a play, how you can be lost; how you can walk for ever in one little circle, as though drawn to a centre by magnetic force, and how you can miss seeing things in the bush if they do not move.

We had outspanned in a flat covered with close grass about two feet high and shady flat-topped thorn trees. The wagons, four in number, were drawn up a few yards off the road, two abreast. The grass was sweet and plentiful; the day was hot and still; and as we had had a very long early morning trek there was not much inclination to move. The cattle soon filled themselves and lay down to sleep; the boys did the same; and we, when breakfast was over, got into the shade of the wagons, some to sleep and others to smoke.

Buggins—that was his pet name—was a passenger returning to "England, Home, and Beauty"—that is to say, literally, to a comfortable home, admiring sisters and a rich indulgent father—after having sought his fortune unsuccessfully on the gold fields for fully four months. Buggins was good-natured, unselfish, and credulous; but he had one fault—he "yapped": he talked until our heads buzzed. He used to sleep contentedly in a rumpled tarpaulin all through the night treks and come up fresh as a daisy and full of accumulated chat at the morning outspan, just when we were wanting to get some sleep.

We knew well enough what to expect, so after breakfast Jimmy, who understood Buggins well, told him pleasantly that he could "sleep, shoot, or shut up." To shut up was impossible, and to sleep again—without a rest—difficult, even for Buggins; so with a good-natured laugh he took the shotgun saying that he "would potter around a bit and give us a treat." Well, he did!

We had outspanned on the edge of an open space in the thorn bush; there are plenty of them to be found in the Bush-veld—spaces a few hundred yards in diameter, like open park land, where not a single tree breaks the expanse of wavy yellow grass. The wagons with their grey-ish tents and buck sails and dusty wood-work stood in the fringe of the trees where this little arena touched the road, and into it sallied Buggins, gently drawn by the benevolent purpose of giving us a treat. What he hoped to find in the open on that sweltering day he only could tell; we knew that no living thing but lizards would be out of the shade just then, but we wanted to find him employment harmless to him and us.

He had been gone for more than half an hour when we heard a shot, and a few minutes later Jimmy's voice roused us.

"What the dickens is Buggins doing?" he asked in a tone so puzzled and interested that we all turned to watch that sportsman. According to Jimmy, he had been walking about in an erratic way for some time on the far side of the open ground—going from the one end to the other and then back again; then disappear-

ing for a few minutes in the bush and reappearing to again manoeuvre in the open in loops and circles, angles and straight lines. Now he was walking about at a smart pace, looking from side to side apparently searching for something. We could see the whole of the arena as clearly as you can see a cricket-field from the rail-ings—for our wagon formed part of the boundary—but we could see nothing to explain Buggins's manoeuvres. Next we saw him face the thorns opposite, raise his gun very deliberately, and fire into the top of the trees.

"Green pigeons," said Jimmy firmly; and we all agreed that Buggins was after specimens for stuffing; but either our guess was wrong or his aim was bad, for after standing dead still for a minute he resumed his vigorous walk. By this time Buggins fairly fascinated us; even the kaffirs had roused each other and were watching him. Away he went at once off to our left, and there he repeated the per-formance, but again made no attempt to pick up anything and showed no further interest in whatever it was he had fired at, but turned right about face and walked across the open ground in our direction until he was only a couple of hundred yards away. There he stopped and began to look about him, and making off some few yards in another direction climbed on to a fair-sized ant-heap five or six feet high, and balancing himself cautiously on this he deliberately fired off both barrels in quick succession. Then the same idea struck us all together, and "Buggins is lost" came from several—all choking with laughter.

Jimmy got up and, stepping out into the open beside the wagon, called, "Say, Buggins, what in thunder *are* you doing?"

To see Buggins slide off the ant-heap and shuffle shamefacedly back to the wagon before a gallery of four white men and a lot of kaffirs, all cracking and crying with laughter, was a sight never to be forgotten.

Lord Ullin's Daughter

A Chieftain to the Highlands bound
Cries "Boatman, do not tarry!
And I'll give thee a silver pound
To row us o'er the ferry!"

"Now who be ye, would cross Lochgyle,
This dark and stormy water?"
"O I'm the chief of Ulva's isle,
And this, Lord Ullin's daughter.

"And fast before her father's men
Three days we've fled together,
For should he find us in the glen,
My blood would stain the heather.

"His horsemen hard behind us ride—
Should they our steps discover,
Then who will cheer my bonny bride,
When they have slain her lover?"

Out spoke the hardy Highland wight,
"I'll go, my chief, I'm ready:
It is not for your silver bright,
But for your winsome lady:—

"And by my word! the bonny bird
In danger shall not tarry;
So though the waves are raging white
I'll row you o'er the ferry."

By this the storm grew loud apace,
The water-wraith was shrieking;
And in the scowl of Heaven each face
Grew dark as they were speaking.

But still, as wilder blew the wind,
And as the night grew drearer,
Adown the glen rode arméd men—
Their tramping sounded nearer.

"O haste thee, haste!" the lady cries,
"Though tempests round us gather;
I'll meet the raging of the skies,
But not an angry father."

The boat has left a stormy land,
A stormy sea before her,
When, oh! too strong for human hand
The tempest gather'd o'er her.

And still they row'd amidst the roar
Of water fast prevailing:
Lord Ullin reach'd that fatal shore—
His wrath was changed to wailing.

For, sore dismay'd, through storm and shade
His child he did discover:
One lovely hand she stretch'd for aid,
And one was round her lover.

"Come back! come back!" he cried in grief,
"Across this stormy water:
And I'll forgive your Highland chief,
My daughter!—Oh, my daughter!"

'Twas vain: the loud waves lash'd the shore,
Return or aid preventing:
The waters wild went o'er his child,
And he was left lamenting.

THOMAS CAMPBELL

The Piebald Rat

Eden Phillpotts

Illustrated by Robert Geary

At the turn of this century the well-loved novelist and playwright Eden Phillpotts (1862–1960) wrote several books of school stories, the first of which was "The Human Boy". These warmly written, authentically observed and beautifully characterised stories told from the boys' angle are set in a small private school presided over by the awesome but often kindly Dr. Dunston. These school stories are among the funniest and most entertaining that have ever been written and were said to have been loosely based on the author's own schooldays in Plymouth.

It was all the result of old Briggs asking the Doctor if he might "instil the lads with a wholesome fondness for natural history." That's how he put it, because I heard him; and the Doctor said it was an admirable notion, and would very probably keep some boys out of mischief on half-holidays. It also kept some boys out of bounds on half-holidays; and after a time I think the Doctor was pretty savage with old Briggs, and wished he'd stuck to his regular work, which was writing and drawing and such-like; because, when one or two of the chaps really got keen about natural history, and even chucked cricket for butterflies and beetles, others, who didn't care a straw about it, pretended they did to gain their own ends. And it was these chaps, if you understand, who finally made the Doctor so unfavourable to natural history generally and old Briggs for starting it.

My chum, West, began the rage for study of "our humble relations," as old Briggs called everything down to wood-lice. He let it be generally known that he had two live lizards in his desk; and, this being the best thing that West had ever thought of, the idea caught on well. I had a dormouse myself, my name being Ashby minor, and Ashby major kept a spider pretty nearly as big as a young bird, which he had poked out of a hole in the playground wall. He caged it in a tin matchbox, and fed it with bluebottles and wasps. At least, he got bluebottles and wasps for it, but the fool wouldn't eat them; and after a week he found it with its legs all tucked up as neatly as anything. Only it was very feeble, and evidently passing out for lack of nourishment, so he let it go where it could find a lot of flies for itself. I thought the matchbox must have been too tight a fit for it, but Ashby major did not. He believed there was something about a tin matchbox which must be rather poisonous for outdoor spiders.

The chaps went on collecting till it got to be swagger to keep big live things in your desk; and the bigger the thing the more swagger it was.

Maine, generally known as "Freckles," had a couple of guinea-pigs in his desk for a week. Then Mannering, the classical master in the Fifth, who must have had a nose like a gimlet, smelt them at prayers, happening to come in late and kneeling down by Freckles at the time. The Doctor didn't make much fuss then, because that was just at the beginning of the business; only he said a desk was not the place for guinea-pigs, and added that a chap in Maine's position in the school ought to have known it. He let the gardener look after them from that time forward. But Freckles naturally lost all interest in them after the gardener had them; because a guinea-pig merely *as* a guinea-pig is nothing. Anyhow, it was rough on him to be landed over it, because, as a matter of fact, guinea-pigs have no scent worth mentioning, and nobody but Mannering would have spotted them. After that Gideon and Brookes caught a blindworm one foot two inches long; and Gideon sold his half for fivepence, so Brookes got it all. But nobody knew what a blindworm likes to eat, unfortunately, so he had to let it go after a time, and got his fivepence refunded. Then there was another scene with my dormouse, which led to tremend-ous things. There's a hole in a desk where

the inkpot goes in, and one day my mouse got out through it, having climbed up two dictionaries and a Greek Testament to do so. It happened old Briggs himself was taking the Lower Fourth, which is my class, and I hoped it would be all right. But he didn't seem friendly over it, and I noticed, when he told us to find the mouse, he put his feet upon the rungs of his chair. It's a rum thing about old Briggs that he doesn't care much for natural history objects while they're alive; he likes them dead and dried, or stuffed and pinned on cards, or in glass cases all labelled and neat. My dormouse gave us a jolly good hunt round, then it finally tripped over a lead-pencil and got its tail and hind legs into West's ink. So we caught it, and I was drying it with a piece of blotting-paper, and old Briggs was just telling us that dormice belong to a genus of rodents called Myoxus, and are allied to mice, though they have a squirrel's habits, which he seemed to think was a pity, when Dunston came in. The Doctor asked particulars, looked as if he could have jolly well killed my mouse, which was shivering rather badly owing to the ink on its hinder parts, and said once for all that he would allow no animals of any kind inside any of the desks, or in school.

Then, unluckily, as an after-thought, he demanded a clearance on the spot; and he was pretty well staggered to find the result.

"I will ask you, Ferrars, as head boy of the class, and one, I am happy to think, above any of this childish folly, to inspect the desks, one by one, and report to me where you find indications of life," said the Doctor.

Ferrars is always right with the Doctor, chiefly because he has a face like a stone angel in church, and a very smooth voice, and a remarkably swagger knowledge of the Scriptures. He is also a tremendous worker, and will go into the Upper Fourth next term as sure as eggs. It was jolly awkward for Ferrars then, because he happened to be one of the keenest natural history chaps of all, and had a piebald rat, which even fellows in the Sixth had offered him half-a-crown and three shillings for, yet he would not part with it. So, though we didn't like him much, we felt almost sorry for the fix he was in now. Of course, we thought that such a demon on Religious Knowledge as Ferrars was would drag out his piebald rat right away, and perhaps even give it to the Doctor, or offer to sell it for the alms-box; but he didn't. He got up, rather white about the gills, and opened the desks one by one; and a jolly happy family it was. Only the Doctor scattered the things to the four winds, till there wasn't an atom of natural history left in the whole classroom except Ferrars's piebald rat snug in his desk.

First Fowle, who goes in for water things, had to empty his jam-jar of tadpoles out into the pond where he got them from; then Freckles was sent off with a young rabbit to the hayfield, and he got caned too, because, strangely enough, the Doctor hadn't forgotten his guinea-pigs; and Morrant's two sparrows were let go, which was no kindness to them, because they had come to depend on Morrant for their meals; and Playfair's mole, which, by the way, had been queer for some time, owing to having no earth to burrow in, was ordered to be sent to the cricket-field. There were a lot of other things, but Corkey minimus scored rather, because his privet hawk-moth laid a hundred and fourteen eggs on Todhunter's *Algebra* a few hours before it was let free. Corkey minimus says a privet hawk-moth's nothing worth mentioning after it's laid eggs, but the eggs turn into fine cater-pillars.

The few things the Doctor didn't know what to do with, and didn't like to have killed, he said must be given to the gardener. He thought it would be better to put my mouse out of its misery, and turned it over on my hand with a gold pencil-case, and said it had probably got a chill to its vital organs and would die; but old Briggs explained that it might live if put in cotton-wool; so the gardener looked to it, and it did live, and I took it home at the end of that term and have it still, though it is getting oldish now, and has lost half its tail. But it's a good mouse yet.

Of course the extraordinary thing was Ferrars. After the Doctor had gone, old Briggs, to whom he had whispered some-thing before he went, gave out that his natural history half-hours would be suspended for the rest of the term; then I got a word with Ferrars. I said:

"However did you have the cheek—you supposed to be such a saint?"

He said:

"I don't know. Something came over me to do it. I've got a jolly peculiar feeling about that rat. It's not an ordinary rat. I'm wrapped up in it. Even my respect for the Doctor couldn't stand against it. I know what you chaps think. I daresay you reckon I'm a hound, but I couldn't help doing what I did. Somehow that rat's a sort of mascot to me. A mascot's a thing that brings luck. All my best luck's hap-pened since I had it."

Of course, when a chap goes on like that, what can you do? I didn't understand Ferrars. He seemed to me to be simply talking rot. So I said:

"Well, it's pretty measly, considering the opinion the Doctor's got of you. I shan't try to score off your rat, because I know it's a jolly fine one but Freckles or somebody will very likely kill it after this."

He looked in a fair funk when the dreadful thought of having his rat killed came to him. Before the end of that day he spoke to every chap in the class separately, and all but three promised and swore not to lay a finger on the rat. But Freckles, Murdoch, and Morrant wouldn't swear. Finally he paid Morrant sixpence and so got him over, and Murdoch he let crib off him in "prep." three times; and Freckles, who was an awfully sportsmanlike chap really, said he was only rotting all the time, and would be the last to do a classy rat like Ferrars's any harm. In fact, he said he'd much sooner kill Ferrars himself.

Mind you, though, of course, it was simply barbarous for Ferrars to think that his piebald rat could have any effect on his work, yet he proved to me that his success in school and his great popularity with the Doctor dated from the coming of the thing. When he first got it, it was a mere cub-rat, so to say; now, though not a year old, it had turned into as fine a rat as you could wish to meet anywhere. In appearance it had pink eyes and a white head, and a fairish amount of white fur about the body, which got thinner on its stomach, so that you could see the pink skin through to some extent. But the piebaldness of the rat was the great feature. It had two big round patches of fur like the common or garden rat, and one small patch at the nape of its neck; and in addition to this it had one large patch of beautiful yellowish fur, such as you chiefly see on guinea-pigs. Its tail was pink and long, and quite hairless.

Ferrars often kept back good things at meals for it, and the bond between them seemed to grow rummer and rummer, till he let the rat get on his mind, and Wilson said he was getting dotty about it. Which I think was true, for one day, going into the classroom to get a knife from my desk, I saw Ferrars with his rat out, talking to it. He was swotting like anything in play-hours for a special Old Testament history

prize, and he had the rat and the Bible and various books of reference all before him. Then, not knowing I was there, he spoke:

"I must win it, Mayne Reid. Stick to me this time, old chap, and see me through."

He called his rat "Mayne Reid" because that was his favourite author.

And Mayne Reid seemed to understand, and he turned his pink eyes on to the open Bible and walked over it. Finding he'd walked over the ninth chapter of the Second Book of Kings, Ferrars got excited, and, seeing me, said "By Jove! then I'll learn that chapter by heart, though it is so long. It's good exciting stuff anyway, and I bet my rat walking over it means that there'll be a question about Jehu and Jezebel."

"You'll go cracked about that rat," I said.

"It's part of my life," he answered. "I know it seems very peculiar, and so it is, and I don't suppose such a thing ever happened before, but something tells me my prosperity and success are bound up in that rat. He's a familiar spirit, in fact, like Saul had. If he died I should never do much more good, and very likely stick in this class for the rest of my days."

"You'd better not think like that," I said, "because rats are short-lived things, owing to the nasty food they eat. Not that Mayne Reid has nasty food; but all pink-eyed animals are delicate, and you'll have to lose him sooner or later."

Ferrars didn't take warning by me, but after he really did win the Old Testament prize, and there really was a question about Jezebel, he made a sort of idol out of the rat, and some chaps declared he said his prayers to it. I know he constantly bought it coconut chips, which it was very fond of. He trained it, too, to live in his breast-pocket, and I often saw him glancing down in class just to get a glimpse of its little eyes looking up at him. That taking the piebald rat into class shows the lengths Ferrars ran. The whole thing was very peculiar. Some chaps said there was a strong likeness growing up between Ferrars and the rat; and certainly his thin, white face had a rattish look sometimes. Other fellows told him his rat was an evil spirit, and would end by doing him a bad turn, but Ferrars turned upon them and jawed them with such frightful language that they never said it again. Meanwhile people we'd never even heard of, and getting a string of dead right answers out of him, would dismiss us all in great good temper, forgetting that he'd only been having a go at one chap.

A day came when the Doctor left us for five minutes in the middle of this class, and while most of us had a hurried dip into the plagues of Egypt, which was the business

the Doctor went on taking to Ferrars more and more, and there seemed every chance of his getting the whole Bible by heart before he left Merivale.

Then came the end of the affair like this. Ferrars was so dependent on his rat now that he wouldn't do a lesson without it, and he lugged it fearlessly into the Doctor's study at those times, fortunately rare, when the Doctor took our class himself in Scripture. But Ferrars was such a flyer that we all got tarred with the same brush; and the Doctor, after questioning Ferrars for half an hour about Bible in hand, Ferrars, who knew as much about the plagues as ever Moses did, just got out his rat and gave it a bit of almond and a short breather of a yard or so along the floor. But, the Doctor coming back suddenly, he had only just time to pop it into his pocket, and even then he put the rat into an unusual pocket which it was not accustomed to, and didn't like, namely, a trouser-pocket. Ferrars also shoved a handkerchief down in the pocket to steady the rat.

Then I saw an awful rum expression come over him, and he grabbed at the pocket and his mouth fell open, and his face got the colour of new putty. At the same time I saw his eyes turn to a big bookshelf with glass doors against the side of the room.

"What's the matter, Ferrars?" said the Doctor. "You appear unwell."

"Nothing, sir; merely a little passing sickness, I think."

"Then withdraw, my boy, and ask the matron to give you a few drops of brandy and water. You need not dine to-day," said the Doctor very kindly.

But Ferrars wouldn't withdraw. He knew Mayne Reid had got through his pocket and down his trouser-leg; he also knew it was now behind the bookshelf, and might reappear at any moment. So he said he was better, and, actually! that it would be a grief to him to miss one of the Doctor's own lessons.

But afterwards, when the rat didn't come out and the class was dismissed,

Ferrars was frightful to see. His hair all got on end somehow, and his eyes swelled and stuck out of his head like glass beads, and his cheeks got hollow. He ran awful risks going into the Doctor's study that day, but the rat wouldn't come out, and Ferrars looked old enough to be a master

when he went to bed, though only eleven and a half really.

"One of two things has happened," he said to me, for we were in the same dormitory; "either it's got wedged in behind the bookshelf and will die if not let out, or else there was a rat-hole there, and it went down and has joined common rats, and became a sort of king rat among them."

"Or been killed," I said.

"No, they would not kill it," he answered. "Anyway, to-morrow after the Doctor's class is over, and everybody has gone, I shall stop and make a clean breast of it, and ask him for the sake of humanity to have the bookshelf moved. But it's all up with me if the rat has lost its feeling towards me and won't come back; only if it was stuck and couldn't come back, that's different."

He didn't sleep much that night, but he said some prayers, which was a thing he didn't often do; and, of course he was praying that the piebald rat might be allowed to return.

But next day, after the Scripture class, in which Ferrars was not nearly so much to the front as usual, and got regularly muddled over a potty question about Jacob, the Doctor saved him the trouble of asking about his rat. He—the Doctor, I mean—had been jolly glum all through class, and when it was ended he did a rum thing, which was awful to see, knowing all we did. He told us to keep our places, then went to the fireplace and picked up the shovel. From the face of it he removed a bit of newspaper, and under the newspaper was Mayne Reid. His pink eyes had gone foggy, and there was a little streak of blood on his mouth. Otherwise his body looked all right.

"Now, here," said the Doctor in an awfully solemn way, "we have a dead piebald rat. There can be no outlet for error concerning such a rat as this. To have seen such a rat is to remember it. Already three classes have been before me to-day, but

"Please, sir, it might be a foreign sort of rat," said Corkey minimus.

nobody knew anything about this animal. That it was a tame rat is evident, its fatness and sleekness come of artificiality. A wild rat in a state of nature is brown or black, as the case may be. This rat, then, had an owner, and that owner brought it into my study—my study—and suffered it to escape here. That I do well to be angry you will the more easily understand when I tell you that the unsavoury creature was upon my desk last night, and has scratched and even gnawed some papers whereon were notes for my next sermon. It was discovered this morning by one of the domestics. She, upon seeing some object moving upon my desk, struck with the broom-handle, and destroyed this rat. Now, let there be no prevarication or evasion of the questions I am going to put to you. First, I wish to know if this rat belongs, or rather belonged, to any among you; and secondly, I desire to learn whether, supposing the rat be not the property of any present, you happen to know whose property it is, or rather was?"

I stole a look at Ferrars, and he appeared so frightful to see, that for some reason I thought I'd try and help him. So, like a fool, I was just going to speak when young Corkey minimus did. He said:

"Please, sir, it might be a foreign sort of rat that came over in that box of pineapples and things that Ashby major had sent him from the West Indies."

"When I desire your aid in the elucidation of this problem I will apply for it, Corkey minimus," answered the Doctor; so Corkey dried up.

Then, in a sort of voice that was strange to us, and seemed to come from his stomach or somewhere new, Ferrars spoke, and I never saw a chap look so ghastly. His eyes were fixed on the rat, and he came forward slowly.

"Please, sir, it was my rat," he said.

"Yours, Ferrars! *You* to disobey! You, of all boys, to set my orders at defiance!"

"It wasn't an ordinary rat, sir."

"I can see what sort of rat it was, sir, for myself," thundered the Doctor. "This it is to consider a boy, to devote thought to him, to particularly commend him for his theological knowledge."

"I don't take any credit for knowing anything now, sir. It was the rat as much as me."

"Robert Ferrars!" said the Doctor, in his caning voice, "you are now adding wicked buffoonery to an act in itself sufficiently disreputable!"

"I can't explain, sir; I don't mean any buffoonery. That rat was more to me than you'd think. It—it *did* help me somehow, and now it's dead it wouldn't be sportsmanlike to it to say not. And if you'll let me b-bury it properly, I'll be very thankful to you."

The Doctor looked at Ferrars awfully close during this speech.

"Either you are lying," he said, "or you suffer from some hysterical and neurotic condition, Robert Ferrars, which I have neither suspected nor discovered until this moment."

Then he told us to go; but Ferrars he kept for half an hour; and when Ferrars came in to dinner I saw he'd been blubbing. He explained to me after we'd gone to bed. He said:

"No, he didn't cane me or anything. He just talked, and told me a lot about several things I didn't know, and said that familiar spirits were specially barred in the Bible. I never thought he'd have even tried to understand me; but he did, and he quite saw my side about the rat. He said kind words over it, too, and was sorry it was dead. And I've got to see Doctor Barnes to-morrow, too, though, of course, it's only having my rat on my mind that's upset me. And he let me have it to b-bury gladly."

"Where shall you arrange the rat?" I said.

"I'm sending it home in a corsets-box that Jane gave me. I've written to my sister where to bury it. Jane it was who killed it. She cried like anything when I told her what Mayne Reid was to me. But he's in the book-post by now, beautifully done up in shavings and fresh geranium leaves. It's no good talking any more. Only I will say that if he was a familiar spirit, he was a jolly good one, very different to the sort barred in the Scriptures. I don't know how I'll get on in the exams now. I wish I was dead, too." Then he sniffed a bit, and went to sleep.

The Prize-giving

Patricia Lynch

Illustrated by Shirley Tourret and Shirley Hughes

No one has made the Irish countryside a more attractive place for children to live in than Patricia Lynch; for in her many stories such as "The Turf-cutter's Donkey" and "The Grey Goose of Kilnevin", there are fine adventures with rogues and tinkers and ballad singers, and the geese and donkeys of Ireland are certainly better than those elsewhere! It is a land where ordinary things are delightful, where the fantastical and the magical look as natural as bread and butter. As a child the author had more than her share of travelling and endured some unhappy separations from her delightful and much-loved mother, whose fanciful stories may well have set her daughter on the story-telling path. You can read about it in "A Story-teller's Childhood", from which we take her memories of her schooldays at a convent school. A girl with the odd nickname of Charlie Pryor has come to the class—Patricia little guessed that she and Charlotte were to become great friends:

CHARLIE PRYOR was dressed so babyishly that some of the girls poked one another and laughed behind their books. She wore a check frock with short puffed sleeves, white socks, and black strap shoes. Her straight dark hair was drawn back from her face with a ribbon, and she looked round at the class as if she felt too sad to care how much we laughed.

"Cassie!" I whispered. "She's Alice in Wonderland!"

"Chatterbox!" snapped Sister Batilda, our new teacher. "Stand up and repeat what you said!"

I stood up. I was too excited to mind a bit.

"I told Cassie Driscoll the new girl is Alice in Wonderland, Sister Batilda!" I answered. "Her picture is in my book!"

Every one in the class had seen my book and now they stared at the new girl, not laughing but envying her. I had *Alice in Wonderland* in my desk and I pulled it out.

"You'd better sit next to Patricia, Charlotte!" said Sister Batilda. "She seems to know you already."

Charlotte sat beside me and under the desk she squeezed my hand.

"Thank you, Patricia," she said.

We walked homeward together, for Charlotte lived farther along the canal. Her mother was dead, so she lived with her grandparents. Because *Alice in Wonderland* had been her mother's favourite book the old people dressed Charlotte like Alice.

"It's a beautiful story," she said seriously. "But everybody hasn't read it

329

"Sit next to Patricia, Charlotte. She seems to know you already."

and—well—you know how the girls laughed!"

She was pleased when we called her Charlie and while she was in school she was happy, but she hated walking along the streets, and we discovered back lanes which no one but ourselves seemed to use. Often she came through the wood yard and took the path by the canal. My mother liked Charlie and talked to her as if she were grown up. She came in to tea and, though her grandmother dressed her like a baby, she let Charlie stay out as late as she liked.

Charlie hadn't been at St. Winifred's many weeks when she discovered my secret—I couldn't tell the time! Patrick Henry had taught me long ago when I was quite small, but he didn't know that I never learned anything but writing from him. Then I was ashamed to tell the nuns. Sister Damien was always sending girls in from the playground to look at the clock

in the refectory, and because Carmel Butterworth loved running messages, she was usually chosen. But now Sister Batilda often asked me. Luckily the refectory was downstairs next to the kitchen and I could ask any lay sister I met in the passages. One day I couldn't find anyone and I couldn't think what to do, when suddenly the angelus rang and I knew it was twelve o'clock. But sooner or later Sister Batilda was sure to find me out.

One day Charlie and I were sitting in my favourite cave, playing Indians with the rag doll. I had many dolls, for I never lost or broke them, but Poosie was the one I loved. Rain was falling; Charlie loved rain, for she had a mackintosh cape which covered her Alice clothes and made her look like an ordinary girl. We had bows and arrows, and Charlie was shooting. Suddenly she dropped her bow.

"I'll teach you to tell the time," she said, "if you like."

"Ch-Charlie!" I stammered, feeling my face go hot and red.

"You'll have to learn some time and I can teach anything I know."

"How did you guess?" I asked.

"You always look bothered when Sister Batilda sends you for the time and you can't do clock sums. I'll teach you all about clocks."

I felt such relief I wasn't the least bit ashamed. Charlie made a heap of sawdust, drew a circle in it with a bit of stick, and marked the hours. She used the stick as the hour hand, and a smaller piece was the minute hand. In ten minutes I understood.

"Charlie! I'll do anything in the world for you!" I declared.

That was the day my mother told me I must take my lunch to school instead of having dinner with Cassie and the others. Many of the girls brought sandwiches and bought milk or cocoa. I was dismayed, not because I was greedy, but taking my lunch meant going among strangers instead of sitting with my friends.

When I had got over the excitement of learning the clock, I told Charlie my new trouble.

"My mother says we haven't any more money to spend," I explained. "And, mebbe, I won't be having extras. But I don't mind them."

"If you're going to take your lunch I'll take mine," said Charlie. "I'll say I don't like the dinners."

When Cassie heard this she insisted on joining us. We sat at tables in the big hall, unwrapped our sandwiches or meat pies, put them on plates, paid our pennies for milk, stuck our elbows on the table, and talked as much as we liked. Mrs. Driscoll gave Cassie a basket every day with fruit and cake as well as her lunch, so that we never regretted the dinners of our grand days.

I did miss the dancing and music, though it was the violin I wanted to learn, not the piano. Because I had fewer lessons to prepare and I worked as hard, I learned better. From being in the first ten of the class I climbed to the first four. My reports pleased my mother, though she didn't give me all the credit.

"Why wouldn't you learn well?" she asked. "Look at the clever father you had, and isn't your grandfather a famous scholar! And where would be the use of sending you to a grand school if you were nothing better than a numskull?"

When I realized that I was to be given three prizes at the Christmas prize-giving as well as a present from the Christmas tree, I thought she would at last be really proud of me. But there was news from Mr. Blanchard, and she and Patrick Henry (my brother) could think of nothing else.

"Will I have a new frock?" I demanded. "Cassie is having a blue one, and even Charlie will have a proper frock. I want buckle shoes!"

"I'm ashamed of you!" cried my mother. "Here's Mr. Blanchard letting us have a share in a gold-mine that may make us rich and all you think about is a new frock! You think too much of clothes!"

"Wear your best frock," said Patrick Henry kindly. "You'll look prettier than any of the other girls. And when they find the gold in the mine you shall have a new dress every Sunday!"

"Me best is too short," I told him. "Sister Batilda says I'm a disgrace and she'll send me back to the babies."

331

But all they would talk about was Mr. Blanchard and his gold-mine.

I had good strong winter boots, but my indoor shoes were coming to pieces and my mother absent-mindedly mended them with white thread, the last ball of thread she had left over from her lace-making.

"I'm having three prizes!" I grumbled. "There isn't another girl with three prizes and I'll be a show. You'll be sorry when you see their lovely frocks!"

Then I found out they weren't even coming to the prize-giving!

"You're only a little girl," said my mother. "Next prize-giving you'll be the best dressed of them all and we'll bring Mr. Blanchard to see you. Mind you win four prizes next time! And don't be fretting. You can bring Charlie Pryor back with you and I'll leave the key under the mat in case we won't be in."

I forgot my shabby frock when I saw the convent all lit up. I thought how Sister Batilda said she was proud of me. But when I came into the cloak-room I remembered my clothes, for it was like fairyland

and the fairies in bright-coloured silks and velvets were my schoolfellows. I opened the door of my locker and hung up my hat and coat; then stood watching, growing more unhappy every moment. Sister Batilda was sending the girls who were dressed out into the corridor to leave room for the others. She saw me standing there and clapped her hands impatiently.

"My dear child! Dress yourself! Where is your frock? I'll help you."

"I haven't a party frock," I told her. "This is me best one."

She looked at the frock, too tight and too short, at my shoes sewn with white cotton.

"I am sorry, Patricia!" she said. "But you can't show yourself like that! I'll have to take your name off the list and give you your prizes upstairs."

She hurried off. The other girls went away and I was left alone in the cloak-room. I sat on the floor and tried to tell myself a story. The door was pushed open and Cassie came running in.

"Tricia! Tricia! Where are you?"

She came over and knelt beside me.

"What's wrong? Why aren't you dressed? Why are you crying?"

I told her.

"It's a shame!" she muttered. "I'll tell mummy! She'll know what to do!"

I loved Cassie for her friendship, but what could Mrs. Driscoll do? If she had known before, she'd have given me a frock, I knew she would. But would my mother let me take it? I was considering this when Mrs. Driscoll swept into the cloak-room, Cassie running behind her. She lifted me to my feet and hugged me.

"Cassie! Take off your shoes. You can wear your school ones. They're new and not too bad. Thanks be I brought an extra pair of stockings in case you made holes in those. Into them, Tricia, quick! Now, off with that frock!"

She wore a wide cream lace scarf. She pulled it off, draped it round me, and fixed the folds with safety-pins. She had Cassie running out of the cloak-room and back again, and presently Sister Batilda arrived with a green silk sash.

"Now!" said Mrs. Driscoll. "Is Tricia going to receive her prizes in the cloakroom or is she to sit in the front row?"

"It'll have to be in the front row," replied Sister Batilda. "And she'll be the best dressed there!"

"There's not many women can beat me with a lace scarf and a packet of pins!" bragged Mrs. Driscoll. "Now, children, run along and be happy!"

I was glad of the lovely lace frock, with its smell of scent, the green sash, and Cassie's buckled shoes, but I wished I had been dressed in them when I came from home. However, when I went up to take my prizes Mr. Driscoll and Chris stamped as well as clapped and I had to feel happy, and when I won the fairy doll from the top of the tree I almost forgot those terrible shoes mended with white thread!

"What are your prizes?" asked Cassie, when we hid ourselves behind one of the big curtains with a plate of cakes and two big glasses of pink lemonade.

I let her take my prizes into her hands.

"They're books!" I told her proudly.

Cassie looked disappointed.

"Oh, Tricia! And I thought they were boxes of chocolates! Do you remember the ones Mary Bernadette's grand-uncle used to give her?"

We were still talking of Mary Bernadette when Charlie, bringing her plate and glass, slipped between the curtains and sat on the window seat beside us. She was dressed in black velvet with a lace collar, and I thought her lovely with her big solemn eyes and straight, dark hair. She carried her one prize for arithmetic —the hardest of all to win—a wooden work-box with spools of coloured cottons, needles, pins, and cards of silk. Proudly I showed mine for composition, history, geography—*Hans Andersen's Fairy Tales, Robinson Crusoe, Arabian Nights.*

"You'll never be able to read through them!" said Cassie admiringly.

She hadn't even one prize. I looked at her buckle shoes which I was wearing.

"Have one of my books," I suggested. "I'll still have two."

Cassie was tempted. Then she shook her head. "No, Tricia! It wouldn't be fair! Anyway, mummy and daddy don't care what *we* do. Your mother expects *you* to win prizes."

Charlie came home with me, and when we pushed open the green gate the little house shone with light and Patrick Henry was coming down the path to meet me. He went on with Charlie, for the night was dark, and I ran in to show my three prizes. My mother hugged me, but when I threw off my coat and she saw the lace frock Mrs. Driscoll had fixed, she wrung her hands.

"What kind of a mother am I at all! Who dressed you, Tricia? I'm ashamed!"

"Mrs. Driscoll. And it isn't really a frock. It's her scarf and Cassie's party shoes, and here's me prizes."

"You poor child!" she cried. "And will you look what came! I wrote to Cousin Kate you were winning three prizes and she sent you this party frock for a Christmas present. I've never seen anything lovelier! Patrick Henry would have taken it to St. Winifred's, only it came too late."

I looked at the cardboard box which lay open on the table. My mother lifted out a frock of old gold silk, with long stockings and shoes to match. I wished it had come in time, but suddenly I knew the lovely frock didn't matter. My mother had cared, so had Cousin Kate, so had Mrs. Driscoll, and I had three prizes!

"You won't want me to be telling you any more stories," said my mother. "Now you'll be reading them to me."

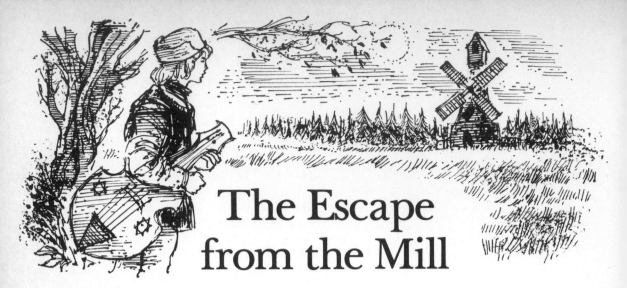

The Escape from the Mill

Charles Reade

Illustrated by Robert Geary

"The Cloister and the Hearth" from which this story comes is a celebrated historical novel, written in the last century. Its author, Charles Reade (1814–1884) took great care to make the details of his novels historically accurate; and here we are shown the adventures of Gerard, a young Dutch artist of the fifteenth century, who has had to flee from his own country and has wandered through Germany and Burgundy to reach Italy. Gerard himself sends this account of his latest adventure to his sweetheart Margaret in Holland. Here, he is seeking a lodging for the night. It proves to be a very exciting night!

I N THE midst of life we are in death. Here I lie in pain and dole, and shall write thee that, which read you it in a romance ye should cry, "Most improbable!" And so still wondering that I am alive to write it, and thanking for it God and the saints, this is what befell thy Gerard. Yestreen I wearied of being shut up in a litter, and of the mule's slow pace, and so went forward; and being, I know not why, strangely full of spirit and hope, as I have heard befall some men when on trouble's brink, seemed to tread on air, and soon distanced them all. Presently I came to two roads, and took the larger; I should have taken the smaller. After travelling a good half-hour, I found my error, and returned; and deeming my company had long passed by, pushed bravely on, but I

could not overtake them. Then I was anxious, and ran, but bare was the road of those I sought; and night came down, and the wild beasts afoot, and I bemoaned my folly; also I was hungered. The moon rose clear and bright exceedingly, and presently a little way off the road I saw a tall windmill. "Come," said I, "mayhap the miller will take ruth on me." Near the mill was a haystack, and scattered about were store of little barrels; but lo! they were not flour-barrels, but tar-barrels, one or two, and the rest of spirits, Brant vein and Schiedam; I knew them momently, having seen the like in Holland. I knocked at the mill-door, but none answered. I lifted the latch, and the door opened inwards. I went in, and gladly, for the night was fine but cold, and a rime on the trees, which

Yestreen = last evening   distanced = outdistanced   mayhap = perhaps   ruth = pity were a kind of lofty sycamores. There was a stove, but black; I lighted it with some of the hay and wood, for there was a great pile of wood outside, and I know not how, I went to sleep. Not long had I slept, I trow, when hearing a noise, I awoke; and there were a dozen men around me with wild faces, and long black hair, and black sparkling eyes.

"I made my excuses in such Italian as I knew, and eking out by signs. They grinned. 'I had lost my company.' They grinned. 'I was an hungered.' Still they grinned, and spoke to one another in a tongue I knew not. At last one gave me a piece of bread and a tin mug of wine, as I thought, but it was spirits neat. I made a wry face, and asked for water: then these wild men laughed a horrible laugh. I thought to fly, but looking towards the door, it was bolted with two enormous bolts of iron, and now first, as I ate my bread, I saw it was all guarded too, and ribbed with iron. My blood curdled within me, and yet I could not tell thee why; but hadst thou seen the faces, wild, stupid, and ruthless. I mumbled my bread, not to let them see I feared them; but oh, it cost me to swallow it and keep it in me. Then it whirled in my brain, was there no way to escape? Said I, 'They will not let me forth by the door; these be smugglers or robbers.' So I feigned drowsiness, and taking out two batzen said, 'Good men, for our Lady's grace let me lie on a bed and sleep, for I am faint with travel.' They nodded and grinned their horrible grin, and bade one light a lanthorn and lead me. He took me up a winding staircase up, up, and I saw no windows, but the wooden walls were pierced like a barbican tower, and methinks for the same purpose, and through these slits I got glimpses of the sky, and thought, 'Shall I e'er see thee again?' He took me to the very top of the mill, and there was a room with a heap of straw in one corner and many empty barrels, and by the wall a truckle bed. He pointed to it, and went downstairs heavily,

taking the light, for in this room was a great window, and the moon came in bright. I looked out to see, and lo, it was so high that even the mill sails at their highest came not up to my window by some feet, but turned very slow and stately underneath, for wind there was scarce a breath; and the trees seemed silver filagree made by angel craftsmen. My hope of flight was gone.

"But now, these wild faces being out of sight, I smiled at my fears: what an if they were ill men, would it profit them to hurt me? Natheless, for caution against surprise, I would put the bed against the door. I went to move it, but could not. It was free at the head, but at the foot fast clamped with iron to the floor. So I flung my psaltery on the bed, but for myself made a layer of straw at the door, so as none could open on me unawares. And I laid my sword ready to my hand. And said my prayers for thee and me, and turned to sleep.

"Below they drank and made merry. And hearing this gave me confidence. Said I, 'Out of sight, out of mind. Another hour and the good Schiedam will make them forget that I am here.' And so I composed myself to sleep. And for some time could

not for the boisterous mirth below. At last I dropped off. How long I slept I know not; but I woke with a start: the noise had ceased below, and the sudden silence woke me. And scarce was I awake, when sudden the truckle bed was gone with a loud clang all but the feet, and the floor yawned, and I heard my psaltery fall and break to atoms deep, deep, below the very floor of the mill. It had fallen into a well. And so had I done, lying where it lay.

"I lay stupefied at first. Then horror fell on me, and I rose but stood rooted there, shaking from head to foot. At last I found myself looking down into that fearsome gap, and my very hair did bristle as I peered. And then, I remember, I turned quite calm, and made up my mind to die sword in hand. For I saw no man must know this their bloody secret and live.

"Presently thinking, all in a whirl, of all that ever passed between us, and taking leave of all those pleasant hours, I called to mind how one day at Sevenbergen thou taughtest me to make a rope of straw. Mindest thou? I woke from my lethargy. I seized on the straw and twisted it eagerly, as thou didst teach me, but my fingers trembled and delayed the task. Whiles I wrought I heard a door open below. That was a terrible moment. Even as I twisted my rope I got to the window and looked down at the great arms of the mill coming slowly up, then passing, then turning less slowly down, as it seemed; and I thought, 'They go not as when there is wind: yet, slow or fast, what man ever rid on such a steed as these, and lived. Yet,' said I, 'better trust to them and God than to ill men.' And I prayed to Him whom even the wind obeyeth.

"I fastened my rope, and let myself gently down, and fixed my eye on that huge arm of the mill, which then was creeping up to me, and went to spring on to it. But my heart failed me at the pinch. And methought it was not near enow. And it passed calm and awful by. I watched for another; they were three. And after a little while one crept up slower than the rest methought. And I with my foot thrust myself in good time somewhat out from the wall, and crying aloud 'Margaret!' did grip with all my soul the wood-work of the sail, and that moment was swimming in the air.

"Motion I felt little; but the stars seemed to go round the sky, and then the grass came up to me nearer and nearer, and when the hoary grass was quite close I was sent rolling along it as if hurled from a catapult, and got up breathless, and every point and tie about me broken. I rose, but fell down again in agony. I had but one leg I could stand on.

"And e'en as I lay groaning, I heard a sound like thunder. It was the assassins running up the stairs. The crazy old mill shook under them. They must have found that I had not fallen into their bloody trap, and were running to despatch me. I felt no fear, for I had now no hope. I could neither run nor hide; so wild was the place; so bright the moon. I struggled up all agony and revenge, more like some wounded wild beast than your Gerard. Leaning on my sword-hilt I hobbled round; and swift as lightning, or vengeance, I heaped a great pile of their hay and wood at the mill door; then drove my dagger into a barrel of their smuggled spirits, and flung it on; then out with my tinder and lighted the pile. 'This will bring true men round my dead body,' said I. 'Aha!' I cried, 'think you that I'll die alone, cowards, assassins! reckless fiends!' and at each word on went a barrel pierced. But oh! the fire fed by the spirits surprised me: it shot up and singed my very hair, it went roaring up the side of the mill, swift as falls the lightning; and I yelled and laughed in my torture and despair, and pierced more barrels and the very tar-barrels, and flung them on. The fire roared like a lion for its prey, and voices answered it inside from the top of the mill, and the feet came thundering down, and I stood as near that awful fire as I could, with uplifted sword

There was naught to do but turn and fight. I wheeled, our swords clashed.

to slay and be slain. The bolt was drawn. A tar-barrel caught fire. The door was opened. What followed? Not the men came out, but the fire rushed in at them like a living death, and the first I thought to fight with was blackened and crumpled on the floor like a leaf. One fearsome yell, and dumb for ever. The feet ran up again, but fewer. I heard them hack with their swords a little way up at the mill's wooden sides; but they had no time to hew their way out: the fire and reek were at their heels, and the smoke burst out at every loophole, and oozed blue in the moonlight through each crevice. I hobbled back, racked with pain and fury. There were white faces up at my window. They saw me. They cursed me. I cursed them back and shook my naked sword: 'Come down the road I came,' I cried. 'But ye must come one by one, and as ye come, ye die upon this steel.' Some cursed at that, but others wailed. For I had them all at deadly vantage. And doubtless, with my smoke-grimed face and fiendish rage I looked like a demon. And now there was a steady roar

inside the mill. The flame was going up it as a furnace up its chimney. The mill caught fire. Fire glimmered through it. Tongues of flame darted through each loophole and shot sparks and fiery flakes into the night. One of the assassins leaped on to the sail as I had done. In his hurry he missed his grasp and fell at my feet, and bounded from the hard ground like a ball, and never spoke, nor moved again. And the rest screamed like women, and with their despair came back to me both ruth for them and hope of life for myself. And the fire gnawed through the mill in places, and shot forth great flat sparks like flakes of fiery snow; and the sails caught fire one after another; and I became a man again, and staggered away terror-stricken, leaning on my sword, from the sight of my revenge, and with great bodily pain crawled back to the road. And, dear Margaret, the rimy trees were now all like pyramids of golden filagree, and lace, cob-web fine, in the red firelight. Oh! most beautiful. . . . The next moment there was a loud crash. The mill fell in on its destroyer, and a million great sparks flew up, and the sails fell over the burning wreck, and at that a million more sparks flew up, and the ground was strewn with burning wood and men. I prayed God forgive me, and kneeling with my back to that fiery shambles, I saw lights on the road; a welcome sight. It was a company coming towards me, and scarce two furlongs off. I hobbled towards them. Ere I had gone far I heard a swift step behind me. I turned. One had escaped; how escaped, who can divine? His sword shone in the moonlight. I feared him. Methought the ghosts of all those dead sat on that glittering glaive. I put my other foot to the ground, maugre the anguish, and fled towards the torches, moaning with pain, and shouting for aid. But what could I do? He gained on me. Behooved me turn and fight. Denys had taught me sword-play in sport. I wheeled, our swords clashed. His clothes they smelled all singed. I cut swiftly upward with supple hand, and his dangled bleeding at the wrist, and his sword fell; it tinkled on the ground. I raised my sword to hew him should he stoop for it. He stood and cursed me. He drew his dagger with his left; I opposed my point and dared him with my eye to close. A great shout arose behind me from true men's throats. He started. He spat at me in his rage, then gnashed his teeth and fled blaspheming. I turned and saw torches close at hand. Lo, they fell to dancing up and down methought, and the next—moment—all—was—dark.

"When I came to myself I was seated in the litter, and my good merchant holding of my hand. I babbled I know not what, and then shuddered awhile in silence. He put a horn of wine to my lips.

"And I told him what had befallen. He would see my leg. It was sprained sore, and swelled at the ankle; and all my points were broken, as I could scarce keep up my hose, and I said, 'Sir, I shall be but a burden to you, I doubt, and can make you no harmony now; my poor psaltery is broken.' And I did grieve over my broken music, companion of so many weary leagues. But he patted me on the cheek, and bade me not fret; also he did put up my leg on a pillow, and tended me like a kind father."

glaive=sword   maugre=in spite of   behooved me=it became needful for me to

To Any Reader

As from the house your mother sees
You playing round the garden trees,
So you may see, if you but look
Through the windows of this book,
Another child, far away,
And in another garden, play.
But do not think you can at all,
By knocking on the window, call
That child to hear you. He intent
Is still on his play-business bent.
He does not hear; he will not look,
Nor yet be lured out of this book.
For long ago, the truth to say,
He has grown up and gone away,
And it is but a child of air
That lingers in the garden there.

ROBERT LOUIS STEVENSON

The Lure of the Spanish Main

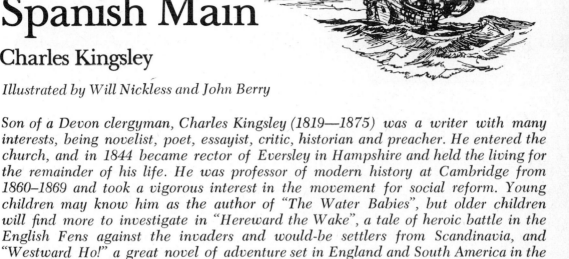

Charles Kingsley

Illustrated by Will Nickless and John Berry

Son of a Devon clergyman, Charles Kingsley (1819—1875) was a writer with many interests, being novelist, poet, essayist, critic, historian and preacher. He entered the church, and in 1844 became rector of Eversley in Hampshire and held the living for the remainder of his life. He was professor of modern history at Cambridge from 1860–1869 and took a vigorous interest in the movement for social reform. Young children may know him as the author of "The Water Babies", but older children will find more to investigate in "Hereward the Wake", a tale of heroic battle in the English Fens against the invaders and would-be settlers from Scandinavia, and "Westward Ho!" a great novel of adventure set in England and South America in the days of Drake, Raleigh and Queen Elizabeth I, when a hit-and-run war was being waged by Devon men against the Dons of Spain for the treasure they were wresting from the natives of South America. The extract from "Westward Ho!" tells how the imagination of the boy-hero is fired by the talk of these mettlesome seamen—the beginning of a long sequence of adventure that ends only with the defeat of the Spanish Armada itself:

O NE bright summer's afternoon, in the year of grace 1575, a tall and fair boy came lingering along Bideford quay, in his scholar's gown, with satchel and slate in hand, watching wistfully the shipping and the sailors till, just after he had passed the bottom of the High Street, he came opposite to one of the many taverns which looked out upon the river. In the open bay window sat merchants and gentlemen, discoursing over their afternoon's draught of sack; and outside the door was gathered a group of sailors, listening earnestly to someone who stood in the midst. The boy, all alive for any sea-news, must needs go up to them, and take his place among the sailor-lads who were peeping and whispering under the elbows of the men; and so came in for the following speech, delivered in a loud bold voice, with a strong Devonshire accent, and a fair sprinkling of oaths.

"If you don't believe me, go and see, or stay here and grow all over blue mould. I tell you, as I am a gentleman, I saw it with these eyes, and so did Salvation Yeo there, through a window in the lower room; and we measured the heap, as I am a christened man, seventy foot long, ten foot broad, and twelve foot high, of silver bars, and each bar between a thirty and forty pound weight. And says Captain Drake: 'There, my lads of Devon, I've brought you to the mouth of the world's treasure-house, and it's your own fault now if you don't sweep it out as empty as a stock-fish.'"

"Why didn't you bring some of they home, then, Mr. Oxenham?"

"Why weren't you there to help to carry them? We would have brought 'em away, safe enough, and young Drake and I had broke the door abroad already, but Captain Drake goes off in a dead faint; and

One hinted that he doubted the Spaniards were too many for them. "Too mar

when we came to look, he had a wound in his leg you might have laid three fingers in, and his boots were full of blood, and had been for an hour or more; but the heart of him was that, that he never knew it till he dropped, and then his brother and I got him away to the boats, he kicking and struggling, and bidding us let him go on with the fight, though every step he took in the sand was in a pool of blood; and so we got off. And tell me, ye sons of shotten herrings, wasn't it worth more to save him than the dirty silver? For silver we can get again, brave boys: there's more fish in the sea than ever came out of it, and more silver in Nombre de Dios than would pave all the streets in the west country: but of such captains as Franky Drake, Heaven

never makes but one at a time, and if we lose him, good-bye to England's luck, say I, and who don't agree, let him choose his weapons, and I'm his man."

He who delivered this harangue was a tall and sturdy personage, with a florid black-bearded face, and bold restless dark eyes, who leaned, with crossed legs and arms akimbo, against the wall of the house; and seemed in the eyes of the schoolboy a very magnifico, some prince or duke at least.

He was dressed (contrary to all sumptuary laws of the time) in a suit of crimson velvet, a little the worse, perhaps, for wear; by his side were a long Spanish rapier and a brace of daggers, gaudy enough about the hilts; his fingers

shotten herrings = herrings that have spawned   magnifico = Spanish noble   sumptuary = relating to expense

How many men did we take Nombre de Dios with? Seventy-three were we!"

sparkled with rings; he had two or three gold chains about his neck, and large earrings in his ears behind one of which a red rose was stuck jauntily enough among the glossy black curls; on his head was a broad velvet Spanish hat, in which instead of a feather was fastened with a great gold clasp a whole Quezal bird, whose gorgeous plumage of fretted golden green shone like one entire precious stone. As he finished his speech, he took off the said hat, and looking at the bird in it—

"Look ye, my lads, did you ever see such a fowl as that before? That's the bird which the old Indian kings of Mexico let no one wear but their own selves; and therefore I wear it—I, John Oxenham of South Tawton, for a sign to all brave lads of Devon, that as the Spaniards are the masters of the Indians, we're the masters of the Spaniards!" and he replaced his hat. A murmur of applause followed: but one hinted that he "doubted the Spaniards were too many for them."

"Too many? How many men did we take Nombre de Dios with? Seventy-three were we, and no more when we sailed out of Plymouth Sound; and before we saw the Spanish Main, half were 'gastados,' used up, as the Dons say, with the scurvy; and in Port Pheasant Captain Rawse of Cows fell in with us, and that gave us some thirty hands more; and with that handful, my lads, only fifty-three in all, we picked the lock of the new world! And whom did we lose but our trumpeter, who stood braying like an ass in the middle of the square, instead of taking care of his neck like a Christian? I tell you those Spaniards are rank cowards, as all bullies are. They pray

to a woman, the idolatrous rascals! And no wonder they fight like women."

"You'm right, captain," sang out a tall gaunt fellow who stood close to him; "one westcountryman can fight two easterlings, and an easterling can beat three Dons any day. Eh! my lads of Devon?
"For O! it's the herrings and the good brown beef,
 And the cider and the cream so white;
O! they are the making of the jolly Devon lads,
 For to play, and eke to fight."

"Come," said Oxenham, "come along! Who lists? Who lists? Who'll make his fortune?
"Oh, who will join, jolly mariners all?
 And who will join, says he, O!
To fill his pockets with the good red goold,
 By sailing on the sea, O!"

"Who'll list?" cried the gaunt man again; "now's your time! We've got forty men to Plymouth now, ready to sail the minute we get back, and we want a dozen out of you Bideford men, and just a boy or two, and then we'm off and away, and make our fortunes, or go to heaven.
"Our bodies in the sea so deep,
 Our souls in heaven to rest!
Where valiant seamen, one and all,
 Here after shall be blest!"

"Now," said Oxenham, "you won't let the Plymouth men say that the Bideford men daren't follow them? North Devon against South, it is. Who'll join? Who'll join? It is but a step of a way, after all, and sailing as smooth as a duck-pond as soon as you're past Cape Finisterre. I'll run a Clovelly herring-boat there and back for a wager of twenty pound, and never ship a bucketful all the way. Who'll join? Don't think you're buying a pig in a poke. I know the road, and Salvation Yeo, here, too, who was gunner's mate, as well as I do the narrow seas, and better. You ask him to show you the chart of it, now, and see if he don't tell you over the ruttier as well as Drake himself."

On which the gaunt man pulled from under his arm a great white buffalo horn covered with rough etchings of land and sea, and held it up to the admiring ring.

"See here, boys all, and behold the picture of the place, dra'ed out so natural as ever was life. I got mun from a Portingal, down to the Azores; and he'd pricked mun out, and pricked mun out, wheresoever he'd sailed, and whatsoever he'd seen. Take mun in your hands now, Simon Evans, take mun in your hands; look mun over, and I'll warrant you'll know the way in five minutes so well as ever a shark in the seas."

And the horn was passed from hand to hand; while Oxenham, who saw that his hearers were becoming moved, called through the open window for a great tankard of sack, and passed that from hand to hand, after the horn.

The schoolboy, who had been devouring with eyes and ears all which passed, and had contrived by this time to edge himself into the inner ring, now stood face to face with the hero of the emerald crest, and got as many peeps as he could at the wonder. But when he saw the sailors, one after another, having turned it over a while, come forward and offer to join Mr. Oxen-

Mun = it   Portingal = Portuguese

342

ham, his soul burned within him for a nearer view of that wondrous horn, as magical in its effects as that of Tristram, or the enchanter's in Ariosto; and when the group had somewhat broken up, and Oxenham was going into the tavern with his recruits, he asked boldly for a nearer sight of the marvel, which was granted at once.

And now to his astonished gaze displayed themselves cities and harbours, dragons and elephants, whales which fought with sharks, plate ships of Spain, islands with apes and palmtrees, each with its name over-written, and here and there, "Here is gold," and again, "Much gold and silver"; inserted most probably, as the words were in English, by the hands of Mr. Oxenham himself. Lingeringly and longingly the boy turned it round and round, and thought the owner of it more fortunate than Khan or Kaiser. Oh, if he could but possess that horn, what needed he on earth beside to make him blest!

"I say, will you sell this?"

"Yea, marry, or my own soul, if I can get the worth of it."

"I want the horn—I do not want your soul; it's somewhat of a stale sole, for aught I know; and there are plenty of fresh ones in the bay."

And therewith, after much fumbling, he pulled out a tester (the only one he had), and asked if that would buy it?

"That! No, nor twenty of them."

The boy thought over what a good knight-errant would do in such case, and then answered, "Tell you what: I'll fight you for it."

"Thank'ee, sir!"

"Break the jackanapes's head for him, Yeo," said Oxenham.

"Call me jackanapes again, and I break yours, sir." And the boy lifted his fist fiercely.

Oxenham looked at him a minute smilingly. "Tut! tut! my man, hit one of your own size, if you will, and spare little folk like me!"

"If I have a boy's age, sir, I have a man's fist. I shall be fifteen years old this month, and know how to answer anyone who insults me!"

"Fifteen, my young cockerel? You look liker twenty," said Oxenham, with an admiring glance at the lad's broad limbs, keen blue eyes, curling golden locks, and round honest face. "Fifteen? If I had half-a-dozen such lads as you, I would make knights of them before I died. Eh, Yeo?"

"He'll do," said Yeo; "he will make a brave gamecock in a year or two, if he dares ruffle up so early at a tough old hen-master like the Captain."

At which there was a general laugh, in which Oxenham joined as loudly as any, and then bade the lad tell him why he was so keen after the horn.

"Because," said he, looking up boldly, "I want to go to sea. I want to see the Indies. I want to fight the Spaniards. Though I am a gentleman's son, I'd a deal liever be a cabin boy on board your ship." And the lad, having hurried out his say fiercely enough, dropped his head again.

"And you shall," cried Oxenham, with a great oath; "and take a galloon, and dine off carbonadoed Dons. Whose son are you, my gallant fellow?"

"Mr. Leigh's of Burrough Court."

"Bless his soul! I know him as well as I do the Eddystone, and his kitchen, too. Who sups with him tonight?"

"Sir Richard Grenvil."

"Dick Grenvil? I did not know he was in town. Go home and tell your father John Oxenham will come and keep him company. There, off with you! I'll make all straight with the good gentleman, and you shall have your venture with me; and as for the horn, let him have the horn, Yeo, and I'll give you a noble for it."

"Not a penny, noble Captain. If young master will take a poor mariner's gift, there

tester = shilling of Henry VIII   liever = rather   galloon = galleon   carbonadoed = charred it is, for the sake of his love to the calling, and Heaven send him luck therein." And the good fellow, with the impulsive generosity of a true sailor, thrust the horn into the boy's hands, and walked away to escape thanks.

"And now," quoth Oxenham, "my merry men all, make up your minds what mannered men you be minded to be before you take your bounties. I want none of your rascally lurching longshore vermin who get five pounds out of this captain, and ten out of that, and let him sail without them after all, while they are stowed away under women's mufflers, and in tavern cellars. If any man is of that humour he had better to cut himself up, and salt himself down in a barrel for pork, before he meets me again; for by this light, let me catch him, be it seven years hence, and if I do not cut his throat upon the streets, it's a pity! But if any man will be true brother to me, true brother to him I'll be, come wreck or prize, storm or calm, salt water or fresh, victuals or none, share and fare alike; and here's my hand upon it, for every man and all! And so—

"*Westward ho! with a rumbelow,*
*   And hurra for the Spanish Main,*
*   O!*"

After which oration Mr. Oxenham swaggered into the tavern, followed by his new men; and the boy took his way homewards, nursing his precious horn, trembling between hope and fear, and blushing with maidenly shame, and a half-sense of wrong-doing at having revealed suddenly to a stranger the darling wish which he had hidden from his father and mother ever since he was ten years old.

When All the World is Young

When all the world is young, lad,
*   And all the trees are green;*
And every goose a swan, lad,
*   And every lass a queen;*
Then hey for boot and horse, lad,
*   And round the world away;*
Young blood must have its course, lad,
*   And every dog his day.*

When all the world is old, lad,
*   And all the trees are brown;*
And all the sport is stale, lad,
*   And all the wheels run down:*
Creep home, and take your place there,
*   The spent and maimed among:*
God grant you find one face there
*   You loved when all was young.*

CHARLES KINGSLEY

Rip Van Winkle

Washington Irving

Illustrated by Robert Geary and John Speirs

Washington Irving (1783–1859) was one of the first American writers to win international acclaim. He travelled extensively in Britain and Europe and in 1842 he was appointed American Ambassador in Spain. He wrote essays and books of travel that are still read with pleasure, but he is known to children all over the world for "Rip Van Winkle", a tale that illuminates the delicious question of what would happen if you went to sleep for twenty years, and then woke up.

WHOEVER has made a voyage up the Hudson must remember the Kaatskill Mountains. At the foot of these fairy mountains the voyager may have descried the light smoke curling up from a village, whose shingle roofs gleam among the trees. In that small village, and in one of these very houses, there lived, many years since, a simple, good-natured fellow, of the name of Rip Van Winkle. He was a simple, good-natured man, a kind neighbour and an obedient, hen-pecked husband. Indeed, to the latter circumstances might be owing that meekness of spirit which gained him such universal popularity; for those men are most apt to be obsequious and conciliating abroad who are under the discipline of shrews at home. Certain it is that he was a great favourite among all the good-wives of the neighbourhood. The children of the village, too, would shout with joy whenever he approached. The great error in Rip's composition was an insuperable aversion to all kinds of profitable labour. It could not be from the want of assiduity or perseverance. He would never refuse to assist a neighbour, even in the roughest

toil, and was a foremost man in all country frolics for husking Indian corn or building stone fences. In a word, Rip was ready to attend to anybody's business but his own; but as to doing family duty and keeping his farm in order, he found it impossible. If left to himself, he would have whistled life away in perfect contentment; but his wife kept continually dinning in his ears about his idleness, his carelessness, and the ruin he was bringing on his family. Morning, noon and night her tongue was incessantly going and everything he said or did was sure to produce a torrent of household eloquence.

Times grew worse and worse with Rip Van Winkle as years of matrimony rolled on. A tart temper never mellows with age, and a sharp tongue is the only edge-tool that grows keener with constant use. For a long while he used to console himself, when driven from home, by frequenting a kind of perpetual club of the sages, philosophers, and other idle personages of the village, which held its session on a bench before a small inn, designated by a rubicund portrait of His Majesty George III. From even this stronghold the unlucky Rip

345

was at length routed by his termagant wife, who would suddenly break in upon the tranquillity of the assemblage and call the members all to naught.

Poor Rip was at last reduced almost to despair, and his only alternative to escape from the labour of the farm and clamour of his wife, was to take gun in hand and stroll away in the woods. In a long ramble of this kind on a fine, autumnal day, he had unconsciously scrambled to one of the highest parts of the Kaatskill Mountains. As he was about to descend, he heard a voice from a distance hallooing, "Rip Van Winkle! Rip Van Winkle!" He looked around, but could see nothing but a crow winging its solitary flight across the mountains. He thought his fancy must have deceived him and turned again to descend when he heard the same cry ring through the still, evening air, "Rip Van Winkle! Rip Van Winkle!" Rip now felt a vague apprehension stealing over him. He looked anxiously in the same direction and perceived a strange figure slowly toiling up the rocks and bending under the weight of something he carried on his back. He was surprised to see any human being in this lonely and unfrequented place, but supposing it to be someone of the neighbourhood in need of his assistance, he hastened down to yield it. He was a short, square-built old fellow, with thick, bushy hair and a grizzled beard. His dress was of the antique Dutch fashion: a cloth jerkin strapped round the waist, several pairs of breeches, the outer one of ample volume, decorated with rows of buttons down the sides and bunches at the knees. He bore on his shoulder a stout keg that seemed full of liquor, and made signs for Rip to approach and assist him with the load. Though rather shy and distrustful of this new acquaintance, Rip complied with his usual alacrity and, mutually relieving each other, they clambered up a narrow gully, the dry bed of a mountain torrent.

Passing through the ravine, they came to a hollow like a small amphitheatre, surrounded by perpendicular precipices, over the brink of which impending trees shot their branches, merely allowing glimpses of the azure sky and the bright evening cloud.

During the whole time, Rip and his companion had laboured on in silence, for there was something strange and incomprehensible about the unknown that inspired awe and checked familiarity. On entering the amphitheatre, new objects of wonder presented themselves. On a level spot in the centre was a company of odd personages playing at nine-pins.

They were dressed in a quaint outlandish fashion: some wore short doublets, others jerkins with long knives in their belts, and most of them had enormous breeches, in similar style with that of the guide's. Their visages, too, were peculiar; one had a large head, broad face, and small, piggish eyes; the face of another seemed entirely to consist of nose, and was surmounted by a white sugar-loaf hat set off with a little, red cock's tail. They all had beards of various shapes and colours. There was one who seemed to be the commander. He was a stout, old gentleman, with a weather-beaten countenance; he wore a laced doublet, broad belt and hanger, high-crowned hat and feather, red stockings, and high-heeled shoes with roses in them.

The group reminded Rip of the figures in an old Flemish painting in the parlour of Dominie Van Schaick, the village parson, which had been brought over from Holland at the time of the settlement. Nothing interrupted the stillness of the scene but the noise of the balls which, whenever they were rolled, echoed along the mountains like rumbling peals of thunder. As Rip and his companion approached them, they suddenly desisted from their play and stared at him with such fixed, statue-like gaze, and such strange, uncouth countenances, that his heart turned within him and his knees smote together.

His companion now emptied the contents of the keg into large flagons and made signs to him to wait upon the company. He obeyed with fear and trembling; they quaffed the liquor in profound silence and then returned to their game. By were overpowered, his eyes swam in his head, his head gradually declined, and he fell into a deep sleep.

On waking, he found himself on the green knoll from which he had first seen the old man of the glen. It was a bright,

degrees Rip's awe and apprehension subsided. He even ventured, when no eye was fixed upon him, to taste the beverage, which he found had much of the flavour of excellent Hollands. He was naturally a thirsty soul and was soon tempted to repeat the draught. One taste provoked another, and he reiterated his visits to the flagon so often that at length his senses sunny morning. The birds were hopping and twittering among the bushes and the eagle was wheeling aloft and breasting the pure, mountain breeze. "Surely," thought Rip, "I have not slept here all night." He recalled the occurrences before he fell asleep—the strange man with a keg of liquor, the mountain ravine, the wild retreat among the rocks, the woebegone party at nine-pins, the flagon. "Oh, that flagon! That wicked flagon!" thought Rip. "What excuse shall I make to Dame Van Winkle?" He looked round for his gun, but in place of the clean, well-oiled fowling-piece he found an old firelock lying by him, the barrel encrusted with rust, the lock falling off, and the stock worm-eaten. He now suspected that the grave roisterers of the mountain had put a trick upon him and, having dosed him with liquor, had robbed him of his gun. Wolf, too, had disappeared, but he might have strayed away after a squirrel or partridge. He whistled after him and shouted his name, but all in vain; the echoes repeated his whistle and shout, but no dog was to be seen.

What was to be done? The morning was passing away, and Rip felt famished. He grieved to give up his dog and gun, he dreaded to meet his wife, but it would not do to starve among the mountains. He shook his head, shouldered the rusty firelock and, with a heart full of trouble and anxiety, turned his steps homeward. As he approached the village he met a number of people, but none whom he knew, which somewhat surprised him.

Their dress was of a different fashion from that to which he was accustomed. They all stared at him with equal marks of surprise, and whenever they cast eyes upon him, invariably stroked their chins. The constant recurrence of this gesture induced Rip, involuntarily, to do the same, when, to his astonishment, he found his beard a foot long!

He had now entered the skirts of the village. A troop of strange children ran at his heels, hooting after him, and pointing at his grey beard. The dogs, too, barked at him as he passed. The very village was altered; it was larger and more populous. There were rows of houses which he had never seen before, and those which had been his familiar haunts had disappeared. It was with some difficulty he found the way to his own house, which he approached with silent awe, expecting every moment to hear the shrill voice of Dame Van Winkle. He found the house gone to decay—the roof fallen in, the windows shattered, and the doors off the hinges. A half-starved dog, that looked like Wolf, was skulking about it. Rip called him by name, but the cur showed his teeth, and passed on.

He entered the house. It was empty, forlorn, and apparently abandoned. He now hurried forth and hastened to the village inn, but it, too, was gone. A large, rickety wooden building stood in its place, with great gaping windows, some of them broken, and over the door was painted, "The Union Hotel, by Jonathan Doolittle." He recognized on the sign, however, the ruby face of King George, under which he had smoked so many a peaceable pipe; but even this was singularly metamorphosed. The red coat was changed for one of blue and buff and a sword was held in the hand instead of a sceptre; the head was decorated with a cocked hat, and underneath was painted in large characters, "General Washington." There was, as usual, a crowd of folk about the door, but none that Rip recollected. The appearance of Rip, with his long, grizzled beard, his rusty fowling-piece, his uncouth dress, and the army of women and children that had gathered at his heels, soon attracted the attention of the tavern politicians. They crowded round him, eyeing him from head to foot with great curiosity.

One orator bustled up to him and, drawing him partly aside, inquired "on which side he voted?" Rip stared in vacant stupidity. Another short but busy little fellow pulled him by the arm and, rising on tiptoe, inquired in his ear, "whether he was a Federal or Democrat?"

"Alas, gentlemen," cried Rip, somewhat dismayed, "I am a poor, quiet man, a native of the place, and a loyal subject of the King, God bless him!"

Here a general shout burst from the bystanders: "A Tory! A Tory! A spy! A refugee! Hustle him! Away with him!"

It was with great difficulty that a self-important man in a cocked hat restored order and, having assumed a tenfold austerity of brow, demanded what he came there for and whom he was seeking.

The poor man humbly assured him that he meant no harm, but merely came there in search of some of his neighbours who used to keep about the tavern.

"Well, who are they? Name them."

Rip bethought himself a moment and inquired, "Where's Nicholas Vedder?"

There was silence for a little while, when an old man replied in a thin, piping voice, "Nicholas Vedder! Why, he's dead and gone these eighteen years."

"Where's Van Bummel, the school-master?"

"He went off to the wars, too; was a great militia general and is now in Congress."

Rip's heart died away at hearing of these sad changes in his home and friends, and finding himself thus alone. He had no courage to ask after any more friends, but cried out in despair, "Does anybody here know Rip Van Winkle?"

"Oh, Rip Van Winkle!" exclaimed two or three. "Oh, to be sure! That's Rip Van Winkle yonder, leaning against the tree."

Rip looked and beheld a precise counterpart of himself as he went up to the mountain, apparently as lazy, and certainly as ragged. The poor fellow was now completely confounded. He doubted his own identity and whether he was himself or another man. In the midst of his bewilderment, the man in the cocked hat demanded who he was and what was his name? "God knows," exclaimed he, at his wits' end. "I'm not myself; I'm somebody else; that's me yonder—no; that's somebody else got into my shoes. I was myself last night, but I fell asleep on the mountain and they've changed my gun and everything's changed, and I'm changed, and I can't tell what's my name, or who I am!"

The bystanders began now to look at each other, nod, wink significantly, and tap their fingers against their foreheads; there was a whisper, also, about securing the gun and keeping the old fellow from doing mischief. At this critical moment, a fresh, comely woman pressed through the throng to get a peep at the grey-bearded man. She had a chubby child in her arms, which, frightened at his looks, began to cry. "Hush, Rip," cried she; "hush, the old man won't hurt you."

The name of the child, the air of the mother, the tone of her voice, all awakened a train of recollections in his mind. "What is your name, my good woman?" asked he. "Judith Gardenier." "And your father's name?" "Ah, poor man, his name was Rip Van Winkle. It's twenty years since he went away with his gun, and never has been heard of since. His dog came home without him, but whether he shot himself or was carried away by the Indians, nobody, nobody can tell. I was then but a little girl."

Rip had but one more question to ask, but he put it with a faltering voice. "Where's your mother?" "Oh, she died but a short time since; she broke a blood vessel in a fit of passion at a New England pedlar." The honest man could contain himself no longer. He caught his daughter

349

and her child in his arms. "I'm your father," cried he. "Young Rip Van Winkle once— old Rip Van Winkle now! Does nobody know poor Rip Van Winkle?" Rip's story was soon told, for the whole twenty years had been to him but as one night. The neighbours stared when they heard it; some were seen to wink at each other and put their tongues in their cheeks. It was determined, however, to take the opinion of old Peter Vanderdonk, who was seen slowly advancing up the road. Peter recollected Rip at once and corroborated his story in the most satisfactory manner. He assured the company that it was a fact, that the Kaatskill Mountains had always been haunted by strange beings; that it was affirmed that the great Hendrick Hudson, the first discoverer of the river and country, kept a kind of vigil there every twenty years, with his crew of the *Half Moon*, being accustomed in this way to revisit the scenes of his enterprise, and keep a guardian eye upon the river and the great city called by his name; that his father had once seen them in their old Dutch dresses, playing at nine-pins in the hollow of the mountain; and that he himself had heard, one summer's afternoon, the sound of their balls, like distant peals of thunder.

Rip soon found many of his former cronies, though all rather the worse for wear, and made friends among the rising generation, with whom he grew into great favour.

Three Winter Scenes

Tu-Whit! Tu-Who!

When icicles hang by the wall
   And Dick the shepherd blows his nail,
And Tom bears logs into the hall,
   And milk comes frozen home in pail;
When blood is nipt, and ways be foul,
Then nightly sings the staring owl
       Tu-whit!
Tu-who! A merry note!
While greasy Joan doth keel the pot.

When all about the wind doth blow,
   And coughing drowns the parson's saw,
And birds sit brooding in the snow,
   And Marian's nose looks red and raw;
When roasted crabs hiss in the bowl—
Then nightly sings the staring owl
       Tu-whit!
Tu-who! A merry note!
While greasy Joan doth keel the pot.

saw = wise saying

WILLIAM SHAKESPEARE

Skating at Night

. . . And in the frosty season, when the sun
Was set, and visible for many a mile
The cottage windows blazed through twi-
    light gloom,
I heeded not their summons: happy time
It was indeed for all of us—for me
It was a time of rapture! Clear and loud
The village clock tolled six—I wheeled
    about,
Proud and exulting like an untired horse
That cares not for his home. All shod with
    steel,
We hissed along the polished ice in games
Confederate, imitative of the chase
And woodland pleasures—the resounding
    horn,
The pack loud chiming, and the hunted hare.
So through the darkness and the cold we
    flew,
And not a voice was idle; with the din
Smitten, the precipices rang aloud;
The leafless trees and every icy crag
Tinkled like iron; while far distant hills
Into the tumult sent an alien sound
Of melancholy, while the stars

Eastward were sparkling clear, and in the
    west
The orange light of evening died away.
Not seldom from the uproar I retired
Into a silent bay, or sportively
Glanced sideway, leaving the tumultuous
    throng,
To cut across the reflex of a star
That fled, and, flying still before me, gleamed
Upon the glassy plain; and oftentimes,
When we had given our bodies to the
    wind,
And all the shadowy banks on either side
Came sweeping through the darkness, spin-
    ning still
The rapid line of motion, then at once
Have I, reclining back upon my heels,
Stopped short; yet still the solitary cliffs
Wheeled by me—even as if the earth had
    rolled
With visible motion her diurnal round!
Behind me did they stretch in solemn train,
Feebler and feebler, and I stood and
    watched
Till all was tranquil as a dreamless sleep . . .

WILLIAM WORDSWORTH

A Song

A widow bird sate mourning for her love
    Upon a wintry bough;
The frozen wind crept on above,
    The freezing stream below.

There was no leaf upon the forest bare,
    No flower upon the ground,
And little motion in the air
    Except the mill-wheel's sound.

PERCY BYSSHE SHELLEY

The Bargain

Oliver Goldsmith

Illustrated by Trevor Parkin

Oliver Goldsmith (1730–1774) was the second son of an Irish clergyman. As a young man he failed to settle in a profession and wandered around France, Italy and Switzerland pleasing himself and studying medicine. He arrived in London in 1756 without money and had great difficulty supporting himself as a physician in Southwark. Sheer necessity forced him to try his hand at writing, and he found his true talent at last. He became poet, essayist, novelist and playwright, as well as the writer of a survey of animal life so large and so full of terrible mistakes that it has been called "the unnatural Natural History".

His single novel, "The Vicar of Wakefield", has great charm. Its plot is far removed from life, for if ever a family was prone to disaster it is that of the good Vicar, who himself tells the tale. Yet, in its episodes and turns and twists, this story seems to mirror human nature very truly. Here is an episode both funny and rueful. The Vicar's wife wants him to sell their old colt. Maybe she has hopes of their getting something better some day—possibly a carriage and pair:

As we were now to hold up our heads a little higher in the world, it would be proper to sell the Colt, which was grown old, at a neighbouring fair, and buy us a horse that would carry a single or double upon an occasion, and make a pretty appearance at church, or upon a visit. This at first I opposed stoutly; but it was stoutly defended. However, as I weakened, my antagonist gained strength, till at last it was resolved to part with him.

As the fair happened on the following day, I had intentions of going myself; but my wife persuaded me that I had got a cold, and nothing could prevail upon her to permit me from home. "No, my dear," said she, "our son Moses is a discreet boy, and can buy and sell to a very good advantage: you know all our great bargains are of his purchasing. He always stands out and higgles, and actually tires them till he gets a bargain."

As I had some opinion of my son's prudence, I was willing enough to entrust him with this commission: and the next morning I perceived his sisters mighty busy in fitting out Moses for the fair; trimming his hair, brushing his buckles, and cocking his hat with pins. The business of the toilet being over, we had at last the satisfaction of seeing him mounted upon the Colt, with a deal box before him to bring home groceries in. He had on a coat made of that cloth they call thunder-and-lightning, which, though grown too short, was much too good to be thrown away. His waistcoat was of a gosling green, and his sisters had tied his hair with a broad black ribbon. We all followed him several paces from the door, bawling after him,

He reiterated his visits to the flagon so often that at length his senses were overpowered, his eyes swam in his head, his head gradually declined, and he fell into a deep sleep.
From "Rip Van Winkle"

"Besides," I thought, *"I have a sure guide in this labyrinth, a thread which cannot break, the faithful stream."*
From "Lost in the Corridors of the Earth"

"Good luck! good luck!" till we could see him no longer.

He was scarce gone, when Mr. Thornhill's butler came to congratulate us upon our good fortune, saying that he overheard his young master mention our names with great commendation.

Good fortune seemed resolved not to come alone. Another footman from the same family followed, with a card for my daughters, importing that the two ladies had received such pleasing accounts from Mr. Thornhill of us all, that after a few previous inquiries they hoped to be perfectly satisfied.

"Ay," cried my wife, "I now see it is no easy matter to get into the families of the great; but when one once gets in, then, as Moses says, one may go to sleep."

To this piece of humour, for she intended it for wit, my daughters assented with a loud laugh of pleasure. In short, such was her satisfaction at this message, that she actually put her hand in her pocket, and gave the messenger sevenpence halfpenny.

This was to be our visiting day. The next that came was Mr. Burchell, who had been at the fair. He brought my little ones a pennyworth of gingerbread each, which my wife undertook to keep for them, and give them by letters at a time. He brought my daughters also a couple of boxes, in which they might keep wafers, snuff, patches, or even money, when they got it. My wife was usually fond of a weasel-skin purse, as being the most lucky; but this by the by. We had still a regard for Mr. Burchell, though his late rude behaviour was in some measure displeasing; nor could we now avoid communicating our happiness to him, and asking his advice: although we seldom followed advice, we were all ready enough to ask it. When he read the note from the two ladies, he shook his head, and observed that an affair of this sort demanded the utmost circumspection.

This air of diffidence highly displeased my wife. "I never doubted, sir," cried she, "your readiness to be against my daughters and me. You have more circumspection than is wanted. However, I fancy when we come to ask advice, we will apply to persons who seem to have made use of it themselves."

I changed the subject, by seeming to wonder what could keep our son so long at the fair, as it was now almost nightfall.

"Never mind our son," cried my wife; "depend upon it he knows what he is about. I'll warrant we'll never see him sell his hen of a rainy day. I have seen him buy such bargains as would amaze one. I'll tell you a good story about that, that will make you split your sides with laughing. But, as I live, yonder comes Moses, without a horse, and the box at his back."

As she spoke, Moses came slowly on foot, and sweating under the deal box, which he had strapt round his shoulders like a pedlar. "Welcome, welcome, Moses! Well, my boy, what have you brought us from the fair?"

"I have brought you myself," cried Moses, with a sly look, and resting the box on the dresser.

"Ay, Moses," cried my wife, "that we know; but where is the horse?"

"I have sold him," cried Moses, "for three pounds five shillings and twopence."

"Well done, my good boy," returned she; "I knew you would touch them off. Between ourselves, three pounds five shil-

lings and twopence is no bad day's work. Come, let us have it then."

"I have brought back no money," cried Moses again. "I have laid it all out in a bargain, and here it is," pulling out a bundle from his breast: "here they are; a gross of green spectacles, with silver rims and shagreen cases."

"A gross of green spectacles!" repeated my wife, in a faint voice. "And you have parted with the Colt, and brought us back nothing but a gross of green paltry spectacles!"

"Dear mother," cried the boy, "why won't you listen to reason? I had them a dead bargain, or I should not have brought them. The silver rims alone will sell for double the money."

"A fig for the silver rims," cried my wife, in a passion. "I dare swear they won't sell for above half the money at the rate of broken silver, five shillings an ounce."

"You need be under no uneasiness," cried I, "about selling the rims, for they are not worth sixpence; for I perceive they are only copper varnished over."

"What!" cried my wife, "not silver! The rims not silver?"

"No," cried I, "no more silver than your sauce-pan."

"And so," returned she, "we have parted with the Colt, and have only got a gross of green spectacles, with copper rims and shagreen cases? A murrain take such trumpery! The blockhead has been imposed upon, and should have known his company better."

"There, my dear," cried I, "you are wrong; he should not have known them at all."

"Marry, hang the idiot!" returned she, "to bring me such stuff: if I had them I would throw them in the fire."

"There again you are wrong, my dear," cried I; "for though they be copper, we will keep them by us; as copper spectacles, you know, are better than nothing."

By this time the unfortunate Moses was undeceived. He now saw that he had been imposed upon by a prowling sharper, who, observing his figure, had marked him for an easy prey. I therefore asked the circumstances of his deception. He sold the horse, it seems, and walked the fair in search of another. A reverend-looking man brought him to a tent, under pretence of having one to sell. "Here," continued Moses, "we met another man, very well dressed, who desired to borrow twenty pounds upon these, saying that he wanted money, and would dispose of them for a third of the value. The first gentleman, who pretended to be my friend, whispered me to buy them, and cautioned me not to let so good an offer pass. I sent for Mr. Flamborough, and they talked him up as finely as they did me; and so at last we were persuaded to buy the two gross between us."

Lost in the Corridors of the Earth

Jules Verne

Illustrated by Michael Jackson and Mike Codd

A native of Nantes, France, Jules Verne (1828–1905) studied to be a lawyer in Paris, but was soon striking out on a most original line as a writer. Great advances in science and invention had roused him to speculate about the future, and he poured his imaginings into tales about explorers in balloons, super-scientists in submarines, and gigantic shells fired to the moon with men in them. Far in advance of his time, he was translated into many languages and serialized in the old "Boys' Own Paper". Painstaking in his research, celebrated scientists used to look forward to the latest Verne book because he was always up to date with their discoveries and frequently improved on them! Today, science has outpaced his inventions, yet in spite of this, we are still thrilled when Jules Verne characters get themselves into tough corners. In this extract from "Journey to the Centre of the Earth", the young narrator has become separated from his explorer-uncle and their Danish man-servant. They have descended a volcano in Iceland and are progressing underground many miles deep on their way to Europe. The modern pot-holer may smile at this fantasy; yet Verne could almost claim to have invented the whole idea of underground exploration:

ON THE 7th of August, our successive descents had taken us to a depth of ninety miles, and we were about six hundred miles from Iceland. That day the slope down was fairly gradual; my uncle had one of the Ruhmkorff lights, and I the other, and I was examining the nature of the granite. Suddenly, on turning round, I found myself alone.

"Well," I thought, "I must have walked too fast, or else my uncle and Hans have stopped somewhere. I must go back and find them. Fortunately it's not steep."

I started back and walked for a quarter of an hour, looking about and seeing nobody, calling aloud and hearing nobody, my voice lost amid cavernous echoes. I began to feel nervous.

"I must be calm," I said aloud to myself. "I am sure to find them—there is only one path, and I was ahead. So I have only to go back."

I did so for half an hour. I listened to hear if anyone was calling, and in that dense atmosphere sound carried marvellously. But an extraordinary silence reigned throughout the great corridor.

"Come," I said to myself "it *must* be

right to go back. The only thing is, when they lost sight of me, they might forget I was in front, and turn back themselves. Even then I should catch them up if I hurried. Of course!"

Then a doubt seized me. Was I *sure* I was ahead? Yes, Hans was next, and then my uncle. I even remembered Hans pausing to adjust the burden on his shoulder.

"Besides," I thought, "I have a sure guide in this labyrinth, a thread which cannot break, the faithful stream. I have only to follow it backwards, and I am sure to find my companions."

This thought cheered me and I blessed the forethought of my uncle, who had prevented Hans from stopping up the hole made for the issue of the water. I thought that before starting back again a wash in it would do me good, and I stooped to plunge my head in the Hansbach.

Judge of my horror when I found nothing but dry and sandy soil! There was no stream at my feet!

I cannot depict my despair, for there is no word for it in any human language. I was buried alive, with the prospect of dying of the tortures of hunger and thirst. My burning hands felt the soil; how utterly dry it seemed!

But how had I left the course of the stream? For certainly it was no longer there! No doubt, at the moment when I

had first started on this wrong path, I had failed to observe the absence of the stream. Evidently there had been a fork in the gallery, and I had taken one route, while the Hansbach, obeying the caprices of another slope, had led my companions into unknown depths!

How should I find them? My feet left no traces on the granite. I was lost, and I seemed to feel on my shoulders the whole weight of the ninety miles of rock above me! I was crushed.

At last, memories of my childhood brought with them the impulse to prayer, from which I rose in a calmer mood, and more ready to reflect on my situation intelligently. I had food for three days, and my flask was full; I must evidently go up and back, till I came to the fatal fork. There, I should find the lost stream.

I rose, and leaning on my iron-shod staff, made my way back, walking hopefully and unhesitatingly, knowing that there was no choice of routes. For half an hour there was no obstacle, and then I came to a place where there was no exit—solid rock in all directions!

I cannot describe my terror and despair. I was overwhelmed—my last hope crushed against that granite wall. Lost in a labyrinth which wound in every direction, I was doomed to the most terrible of deaths; and the whimsical thought came to me that if ever my fossilized remains were found ninety miles down, they would be the occasion of serious scientific controversy! I tried to speak aloud, but only hoarse sounds passed between my dry lips, and I stood panting.

In the midst of this anguish, a new terror invaded my spirit. My lamp had been injured by a fall. I had no means of repairing it, and the light was failing!

I watched the light due to the electric current gradually fading in the filament of the lamp. A procession of shadows passed along the walls of the gallery. I would not lower my eyes for fear of losing the last of the fleeting illumination. Finally, only a feeble glow remained; I followed it with my eyes to the last, and when it vanished completely, and I was left in the profound darkness of the earth's interior, a terrible cry broke from me.

What is anything we call darkness on earth to this utter privation of all light? I was absolutely, hopelessly blind. I lost my head; sprang up, holding out my hands to feel; rushed haphazard through the winding corridors, calling, shrieking, howling, wounded by the sharp rocks, falling and rising again, bleeding, constantly expecting to dash my head against some obstacle and perish! At last I fell exhausted on the ground, and lost consciousness.

When I regained my senses, I found my face wet with tears. I cannot say how long my swoon had lasted—I had no means of knowing. Never had solitude been like mine!

I had lost much blood, and was covered with it. How I regretted not being yet dead, and that the ordeal was still to come! I felt about to faint again—this time probably without return—when a loud noise smote on my ears, like the prolonged rumbling of thunder.

Whence could the sound come? From some explosion of subterranean gas? I lay and listened for a repetition of it, but silence reigned, and I could no longer hear the beating of my own heart.

Suddenly my ear, applied to the rock as I lay, appeared to catch the sound of *words* —vague, indistinct, remote. I shivered, and thought, "It is a hallucination!" But no—listening attentively, I did really hear a murmur of voices, though my brain was too feeble to grasp the meaning.

Dragging myself a few feet farther, I found I could hear more distinctly I caught low murmured words, one of which was "förlorad," spoken in a tone of distress.

Who was speaking? My uncle and Hans, evidently. But if I could hear them, they could hear me. "Help!" I cried with all my strength. "Help!"

I listened tensely, but no answer could be heard. Perhaps my voice was too feeble. "It must be they," I thought. "What other men are there ninety miles underground?"

I listened again. Placing my ear to the wall, I found the point at which the voices attained their maximum intensity. The word "förlorad" came again to my ear, and the roll of thunder which had aroused me.

"No," I said to myself, "it is not through the rock that the voices reach me; they must come by way of the gallery itself— some peculiar acoustic effect."

I listened again, and this time distinctly heard my own name, pronounced no doubt by my uncle, evidently talking with the guide, who had used the Danish word "förlorad", which means "lost".

Then I understood. I must speak along the gallery, which would conduct the sound; but there was no time to lose—if they left that particular spot, the acoustic effect would be done away with. So standing alongside the wall I spoke as distinctly as possible—"Uncle Lidenbrock!"

I waited in extreme anxiety. Sound does not travel very fast, and increased density in the air does not augment its speed, but only its intensity. Some seconds passed, which seemed like centuries, before I heard, "Axel, Axel, is it you?"

. . . . .

"Yes, yes!" I replied.

. . . . .

"My poor child, where are you?"

. . . . .

"Lost in the deepest darkness!"

. . . . .

"But your lamp?"

. . . . .

"Gone out."

. . . . .

"And the stream?"

. . . . .

"Disappeared."

. . . . .

"Axel, my poor dear boy, cheer up!"

. . . . .

"Wait a minute. I haven't the strength to talk—but talk to me."

"Take courage, we have hunted for you vainly, and at last, supposing you still on the track of the stream, we have come down it, firing shots as signals. Now, though our voices can reach each other by some acoustic effect, our hands cannot touch. But don't despair, Axel."

Meantime I was reflecting, and a ray of hope was returning to my heart. One thing was specially important. With my lips to the wall I said:

"Uncle!"

"Yes, my boy," came back in a few seconds.

"We must know how far apart we are."

"That is easy."

"You have your chronometer? Take it, and say my name, noting the exact second. Instantly I hear the sound I will repeat it, and you will again note the exact second at which the sound reaches your ear."

"Right; and half the time will be that taken by sound in travelling the distance between us," replied my uncle.

"Now, begin."

"Axel."

"Axel," I repeated as soon as I heard the word. Then I waited.

"Forty seconds," said my uncle. "So sound takes twenty seconds for the distance. At 1,020 feet a second, that makes 20,400 feet, or a little under four miles."

"Four miles!" I murmured.

"Well, that's quite a possible distance."

"But should I go up or down?"

"Down—I'll tell you why. We are in a great big space, with a number of corridors leading to it. The one you are in is sure to bring you to us, for all these great cracks seem to radiate from this spot. So get up and walk, drag yourself if necessary, slide down the steeper slopes, and never fear that you will find us at the end. Start, my boy, start!"

"Goodbye for the present then, Uncle; I shall not be able to speak to you on the way."

"No, but we shall meet."

These were the last words I heard. After one prayer to God, whose mercy had led me to the only spot at which the foregoing conversation would have been possible, I started, revolving in my mind what I had heard of the Whispering Gallery at St. Paul's Cathedral in London, and especially of the Ear of Dionysus, the quarry at Syracuse in Sicily, where a whisper in one part is distinctly heard at one distant spot, and there only.

Judging by these instances, there could be no obstacle between myself and my uncle, and I had only to follow the path traversed by the sound to find him.

The descent was steep; I dragged myself or slid, and finally found myself travelling with alarming rapidity, which in my exhausted condition I was unable to moderate. Suddenly the ground failed under my feet; I found myself falling down a vertical shaft, hit my head on a sharp rock, and lost consciousness.

When I came to myself, I was in semi-darkness, lying on thick rugs. My uncle was watching my face for signs of life. At my first sigh he took my hand; when I opened my eyes he uttered a cry of joy.

"He's alive! He's alive!" he cried.

"Yes," I answered feebly.

"My dear child, you are saved!" he exclaimed, straining me in his arms.

The Wonderful Tar Baby

Joel Chandler Harris

Illustrated by Harry Rowntree

Joel Chandler Harris (1848–1908) was a great collector of American Negro folk-stories. These tales which may have come with the Negro slaves from Africa and been handed down from father to son on the slave plantations of the southern states, are always tales of animals, fables of a sort. But they don't preach a moral like Aesop's fables. They are stories for the underdog—for the weak and helpless who, by using their wits manage to score off the strong. Thus Brer Rabbit (Brother Rabbit) is always engaged in a war of wits with his natural enemy, Brer Fox (Brother Fox).

Harris puts his collection of stories into the mouth of the shrewd old Negro, Uncle Remus, who tells the tales to his white master's children much as Harris may have heard them when a boy in Georgia. We have kept most of the original language because it is an authentic Southern Negro dialect, and once it has been mastered, the stories are extremely funny. Here is Brer Rabbit's most famous battle of wits with Brer Fox:

"DIDN'T the fox ever catch the rabbit, Uncle Remus?" asked the little boy.

"He come mighty nigh it, honey—Brer Fox did. One day Brer Fox went to work an' got 'im some tar, an' mix it wid some turpentine, an' fix up a contraption what he call a Tar Baby, an' he took dis 'ere Tar Baby an' he set 'er in de big road, an' den he lay off in de bushes for to see what de news was goin' to be. An' he didn't have to wait long, neither, 'cause by and by here come Brer Rabbit pacin' down de road— lippity-clippity, clippity-lippity—jest as saucy as a jay-bird. Brer Fox, he lay low. Brer Rabbit come prancin' 'long till he spy de Tar Baby, an' den he fetch up on his behin' legs like he was 'stonished. De Tar Baby, she sat dere, she did, an' Brer Fox, he lay low.

"'Mornin'!' says Brer Rabbit, says 'ee— 'nice wedder dis mornin',' says 'ee.

"Tar Baby ain't sayin' nothin', an' Brer Fox, he lay low.

"'How you doin'?' says Brer Rabbit, says 'ee.

"Brer Fox, he wink his eye slow, an' lay low, an' de Tar Baby, she ain't sayin' nothin'.

"'How you come on, den? Is you deaf?' says Brer Rabbit, says 'ee. 'Cause if you is, I can holler louder,' says 'ee.

"Tar Baby stay still, an' Brer Fox, he lay low.

"'You're stuck up, dat's what you is,' says Brer Rabbit, says 'ee, 'an I'm goin' to cure you, dat's what I'm a-goin' to do,' says 'ee.

"Brer Fox he sort of chuckle in his stomach, he did, but Tar Baby ain't sayin' nothin'.

"'I'm goin' to learn you how to talk to 'spectable folks if it's de las' act,' says Brer Rabbit, says 'ee. 'If you don't take off dat

'You look sorta stuck up,' says Brer Fox.

hat an' tell me howdy,* I'm goin' to bu'st you wide open,' says 'ee.

"Tar Baby stay still, an' Brer Fox, he lay low.

"Brer Rabbit keep on askin' 'er, an' de Tar Baby, she keep on sayin' nothin', till presently Brer Rabbit draw back wid 'is fist, he did, an' blip he took 'er side of de head. Right dere's where he broke his molasses jug.† His fist struck, an' he can't pull loose. De tar held 'im. But Tar Baby, she stay still, an' Brer Fox, he lay low.

" 'If you don't let me loose, I'll knock you again,' says Brer Rabbit, says 'ee, an' wid dat he fetch 'er a wipe wid de udder hand, an' *dat* stuck. Tar Baby, she ain't sayin' nothin', an' Brer Fox, he lay low.

" 'Turn me loose, 'fore I kick de stuffin' out of you,' says Brer Rabbit, says 'ee. But

de Tar Baby, she ain't sayin' nothin'. She just holds on, an' den Brer Rabbit lose de use of his feet in de same way. Brer Fox, he lay low. Den Brer Rabbit squall out dat if de Tar Baby don't turn 'im loose he butt 'er cranksided. An' den he butted an' his head got stuck. Den Brer Fox, he sauntered forth, lookin' just as innocent as one of your mammy's mockin'-birds.

" 'Howdy, Brer Rabbit,' says Brer Fox, says 'ee. 'You look sorta stuck up dis mornin',' says 'ee, an' den he rolled on de groun', an' laughed an' laughed till he couldn't laugh no more. 'I 'spect you'll take dinner wid me dis time, Brer Rabbit . . . I ain't goin' to take no 'scuse,' says Brer Fox, says 'ee."

Here Uncle Remus paused and drew a large sweet potato out of the ashes.

"Did the fox eat the rabbit?" asked the little boy to whom Uncle Remus was telling the story.

"Eat Brer Rabbit?" said Uncle Remus. "You wait an' hear where he's a-goin' to fetch up at. Brer Fox he feel mighty good, an' he roll on the ground an' laugh. Bimeby, he up an' say, says 'ee:

" 'Well, I 'spect I got you this time, Brer Rabbit,' says 'ee; 'maybe I ain't but I 'spect I is. You been runnin' roun' here saucing after me a mighty long time, but I 'spect you done come to de end of de road. You been cuttin' up your capers an' bouncin' roun' in dis neighbourhood until you come to b'lieve yourse'f de boss of de whole gang. An' den you're always somewheres where you got no business,' says Brer Fox, says 'ee. 'Who ask you for to come an' strike up acquaintance wid dis 'ere Tar Baby? An' who stuck you up dere where you is? Nobody in de roun' worl'. You jus' stuck an' jam yourse'f on dat Tar Baby widout waitin' for any invite,' says Brer Fox, says 'ee, 'an' dere you is, an' dere you'll stay, till I fixes up a brushwood pile an' fires her up, 'cause I'm goin' to barbecue‡ you dis day sure,' says Brer Fox, says 'ee.

* say how-do-you-do   † made a mistake   ‡ roast

360

"Den Brer Rabbit talk mighty 'umble:

" 'I don't care what you do wid me, Brer Fox,' says 'ee, 'but don't fling me in dat brier-patch,' says 'ee.

" 'Hit's so much trouble for to kindle a fire,' says Brer Fox, says 'ee, 'dat I 'spect I'll have to hang you,' says 'ee.

" 'Hang me jus' as high as you please, Brer Fox,' says Brer Rabbit, says 'ee, 'but do for de Lord's sake don't fling me in dat brier-patch,' says 'ee.

" 'I ain't got no string,' says Brer Fox, says 'ee, 'an' now I 'spect I'll have to drown you,' says 'ee.

" 'Drown me jus' as deep as you please, Brer Fox,' says Brer Rabbit, says 'ee, 'but do don't fling me in dat brier-patch,' says 'ee.

'I 'spect I got you this time, Brer Rabbit,' says 'ee.

" 'Dere ain't no water nigh,' says Brer Fox, says 'ee, 'an' now I 'spect I'll have to skin you,' says 'ee.

" 'Skin me, Brer Fox,' says Brer Rabbit, says 'ee, 'snatch out my eyeballs, tear out my ears by de roots, an' cut off my legs,' says 'ee, 'but do please, Brer Fox, don't fling me in dat brier-patch,' says 'ee.

"Course Brer Fox want to hurt Brer Rabbit bad as he can, so he catch him by de behin' legs an' slung 'im right in de middle of de brier-patch. Dere was a consider'ble flutter where Brer Rabbit struck de bushes, an' Brer Fox sort of hang roun' for to see what was goin' to happen.

"Bimeby he hear somebody call 'im an' 'way up de hill he see Brer Rabbit settin' cross-legged on a log, combing de pitch out of his hair wid a chip.

"Den Brer Fox know dat he bin tricked mighty bad.

"An' Brer Rabbit holler out:

" 'Bred an' born in a brier-patch, Brer Fox—bred an' born in a brier-patch!' an' wid dat he skip out jus' as lively as a cricket. . . ."

'Bred an' born in a brier-patch!'

361

He'll leap on your lap in the middle of your sewing.

362

The Rum Tum Tugger

The Rum Tum Tugger is a Curious Cat:
If you offer him pheasant he would rather have grouse.
If you put him in a house he would much prefer a flat,
If you put him in a flat then he'd rather have a house.
If you set him on a mouse then he only wants a rat,
If you set him on a rat then he'd rather chase a mouse.
Yes the Rum Tum Tugger is a Curious Cat—
    And there isn't any call for me to shout it:
        For he will do
        As he do do
            And there's no doing anything about it!

The Rum Tum Tugger is a terrible bore:
When you let him in, then he wants to be out;
He's always on the wrong side of every door,
And as soon as he's at home, then he'd like to get about.
He likes to lie in the bureau drawer,
But he makes such a fuss if he can't get out.
Yes the Rum Tum Tugger is a Curious Cat—
    And it isn't any use for you to doubt it:
        For he will do
        As he do do
            And there's no doing anything about it!

The Rum Tum Tugger is a curious beast:
His disobliging ways are a matter of habit.
If you offer him fish then he always wants a feast;
When there isn't any fish then he won't eat rabbit.
If you offer him cream then he sniffs and sneers,
For he only likes what he finds for himself;
So you'll catch him in it right up to the ears,
If you put it away on the larder shelf.
The Rum Tum Tugger is artful and knowing,
The Rum Tum Tugger doesn't care for a cuddle;
But he'll leap on your lap in the middle of your sewing,
For there's nothing he enjoys like a horrible muddle.
Yes the Rum Tum Tugger is a Curious Cat—
    And there isn't any need for me to spout it:
        For he will do
        As he do do
            And there's no doing anything about it!

T. S. ELIOT

Heroes

Aubrey de Selincourt

Illustrated by Trevor Parkin

Aubrey de Selincourt (1894–1962) was educated at Rugby and Oxford, and, after war service in Gallipoli and as a pilot in the Royal Flying Corps in France in the First World War (which ended for him as a prisoner in Germany) he became a schoolmaster and remained one for many years. He published about thirty books including a dozen children's novels, in which his love of the sea and knowledge of sailing are much to the fore. He had a cottage in the Isle of Wight and owned various sailing yachts in which he visited all the south coast ports. Like Arthur Ransome's, his stories are realistic and the adventures of his young characters are always wholly believable.

SAILING a boat is not a matter of mere knowledge. I mean, you can't learn it from a book, or even from practical experience. Not everybody, that is. You have to be born to it. Boats are queer things: they have whims, as if they were alive, and just won't do what some people tell them.

On the other hand, there are men they seem to take a pleasure in obeying. With such a one, any boat gets on terms at once, and does any mortal thing he asks of her. She answers his lightest touch—I almost said his lightest word.

Jesse was a man like that; so it was no wonder that Robin loved him. Robin's father used to say that Jesse could make a beer barrel sail to windward, if he wanted to.

Robin was eleven, and for longer than he could remember he had spent his holidays sailing in boats with his father—and with Jesse. He had a passionate wish to become a good seaman, to know everything that was to be known about the handling of boats: to be, in fact, like Jesse.

Jesse was a stocky man, with light hair and moustache, face burnt brown like a biscuit, and hands as strong as steel springs. The more gravely and quietly he spoke, the more his blue eyes laughed. He and Robin shared many a joke together—before the mast; for Jesse was skipper of his father's yacht.

In his youth—and that was long ago— Jesse had been an oyster-man. And in some past and miraculous age (as it seemed to Robin) he had been in big ships : barques, and such things. It was not only estuaries and summer seas that Jesse was acquainted with. Not by any means; he had lain out on a seventy-foot yard in blowing weather, fighting a sail a thousand miles from anywhere. There was nothing on the sea, or under it, that Jesse didn't know.

No wonder, indeed, that Robin loved him. Once Robin had been sailing alone in a little boat his father let him play in, and he had brought her back to her buoy against wind and tide, all sail shaking and with his heart in his mouth—for he knew Jesse was watching from the yacht near by. He got the buoy without mishap, and Jesse said to him later that he couldn't have done it better himself. It was the happiest day of Robin's life.

Sometimes on winter evenings Robin would go to Jesse's cottage a mile away, and in the little parlour, hot as an oven and filled with tobacco smoke, Jesse would teach him knots, useful or ornamental, with infinite patience—Turk's Head, bow-line on a bight, Matthew Walker, double carrick bend, and the delicate intricacy of a long splice. Whenever Robin mastered his lesson, Jesse was as pleased as he.

"We live and learn, Master Robin," he would say.

Now it happened that Robin's father, who liked experimenting with small boats, and seldom kept one long, had seen a little sixteen-footer which took his fancy in a yard at Burnham. He decided to buy her; and when he proposed, one fine summer morning when a smart westerly wind was blowing, that Robin should help him sail her home up river, Robin was naturally delighted.

It was better still when Robin's father added that they might take Jesse, too.

"I'd like his opinion of her," he said. "She's a funny little thing."

They went down to Burnham in the yacht's dinghy. It was a long pull, but with Jesse at the oars, and a fair wind and tide, they made light work of it. Robin was in the seventh heaven. To have his father and Jesse to himself was a thing that happened seldom. His father talked a good deal about the new boat as they went down the river, including Robin in a most satisfactory way in all his guesses and prognostications of her quality, so that Robin almost felt that *his* opinion, too, as well as Jesse's would be a matter of import. Jesse was mainly silent; but every now and then he and Robin would catch each other's eyes, and in Jesse's there would be a companionable twinkle which seemed to say, "We'll settle all that when we see her, won't we, Master Robin?"

They landed at the jetty in Batson's yard. Robin loved the yard and would gladly have spent hours watching the things that were going on in it, had there not been more urgent business to see to. For instance, he would have liked a peep into the great building shed, where he knew that a ten-tonner was being planked up, and amidst the noise of hammering and the delicious smell of teak shavings, men were working without hurry or fret, as if they had all time before them—and yet the vessel grew. Or he might have strayed into the store, and pleased his sight with the drums of manila and tarred Italian hemp, the loops of iron thimbles and shackles like beads on a string, the tins of paint, the parrel balls, fairleads, rigging screws, hanks of codline or marlin, canvas buckets, and a hundred other delightful objects which mere landsmen have never even heard of.

But this was no occasion for idling. There was a job to be done: *Ladybird* was to be sailed home.

Ladybird was lying on a buoy close in-shore, a little farther down the river, in a thick cluster of other small craft.

"She's all ready for you, sir," the foreman said to Robin's father. "If you like to leave your dinghy on the jetty, we'll put you off in the yard boat."

Five minutes later the three of them stepped aboard.

Ladybird was a centre-board boat, sloop-rigged and decked in as far as the mast. She was bright varnished, and looked fast and fragile, a pretty toy. Robin thought she was lovely.

"Of course," said Robin's father with his eye on Jesse, "she wasn't built for the Atlantic."

"No, sir," said Jesse gravely.

"But she's a jolly little thing."

This being a statement and not a question, called for no answer. Besides, Jesse was already busy with the halliards.

The mainsail was a biggish one, the boom projecting a good two feet beyond the counter. When Jesse had made the halliards fast, Robin's father looked at the sail a little doubtfully as it flickered and slatted in the fresh wind.

"There's a breeze," he said. "Perhaps we should put a reef in it."

Robin's heart jumped. "Oh *no* . . ." he said—but only to himself, not out loud. He looked at Jesse.

Jesse's eyes were full of quiet mirth. "She'll take the whole of it, sir," he said. "Maybe she won't sail under water more'n's comfortable."

Robin could have hugged him.

A moment afterwards the buoy was dropped overboard and *Ladybird* was off. She kicked up her heels and was away across the river like a young colt, all three on the weather gunwale to sit her up. Robin's father was at the tiller, his face alight with pleasure in his new toy. The wind was puffy and pretty fresh; even though it blew with the tide—for the ebb was not yet finished—it raised steep little waves which every now and then flung a drench of spray against Jesse's broad back, and made Robin, who was sitting by him, duck for cover. In the gusts *Ladybird* went over till the water lapped her gunwale, and Robin watched it wide-eyed and with a queer feeling in the pit of his stomach which was half fear, half delight.

"She takes a bit of holding," said Robin's father. "Ready about."

Ladybird spun round like a top and was off again on the other tack. The yachts in the anchorage lay as thick as peas in a pod. Again and again Robin's father took *Ladybird* so close under a yacht's stern that they could have touched her with their hands, or brought her with a wriggle and shake to clear a menacing bowsprit with only a yard to spare.

"Quick as an eel, she is," said Jesse.

Cloud shadows swept over the salterns; the river was flecked with white; the sweet warm wind blew merrily. Robin licked the salt off his lips and was happy.

The last boat in the anchorage lay under their lee. Beyond her the river stretched clear and empty. Once or twice as they swiftly approached the moored vessel, Robin's father peered under the straining mainsail—judging his distance, making sure he could pass to windward of her without mishap. For every sailing-man is a racing man at heart; if there is no other boat to race with, he competes with the elements, eager for his boat to do her best.

The tide was setting *Ladybird* to leeward. The moored yacht was very near. Robin saw Jesse put his hand on the jib sheet, ready for the call to tack. But Robin's father shook his head.

"She'll just do it," he said.

Robin took a quick look at Jesse for confirmation of his father's decision, but didn't find it. On the contrary, Jesse's face wore the peculiar wooden expression which, as Robin knew, meant his resigned refusal to take responsibility for whatever might be about to happen. Robin bit his lip, and prayed that after all his father might be right, and so prove himself as wise a skipper as Jesse himself. In his heart he knew that this could never be quite true; and perhaps this was why he wished so much that it might be so.

The wind headed them, and blew in a hard gust. With a muttered exclamation

Robin's father put the helm up just a trifle to get *Ladybird* sailing again. The bowsprit of the moored yacht speared at them, only a yard under their lee. The tide ran strong.

"Look out, sir," called Jesse.

But it was too late. Quite quietly, as it seemed, yet with a strange and awful suddenness, *Ladybird* lay flat over on her side. The water rushed over the gunwale in a green smooth wave, and Robin found himself gasping and spluttering and trying to keep himself afloat with desperate kicks. *Ladybird* had disappeared.

In two seconds Robin's father had hauled himself aboard the moored yacht by way of the bobstay and mooring chain. He threw Robin a line and helped him up.

"All right?" he said.

Robin nodded. His teeth were chattering—but he was all right.

"Good. Now, Jesse . . . quick, give me that line. . . ."

But Jesse was not there.

For a moment the two of them looked down into the water where *Ladybird* had sunk; then suddenly, quick as a flash, Robin's father dived overboard and swam with all his might down the tide. Robin, watching him, saw what his father had seen; two outstretched arms, and something pale between them, just below the surface of the water. They did not move or struggle, but seemed to undulate with the motion of the water, like weed.

It was Jesse . . . and he was drowning. Robin felt sick, overcome by a dreadful weakness. The spectacle before him became suddenly unreal, like a picture or a dream.

Robin's father reached Jesse, seized him by the collar of his jersey and dragged him up. As he did so, Robin's strength returned, and he yelled with all the power of his lungs: "Help! Help!"

But he need not have shouted; for others in the anchorage had seen the accident, and already three or four dinghies from various yachts had put off and were racing towards the two men in the water—already fifty yards down river on the fast-ebbing tide.

Robin saw his father scramble aboard the first of them, and willing arms hoist in Jesse's limp form after him. Then a man in the second dinghy raised a hand as if in answer to a request, and pulled towards the boat where Robin was waiting. The other, with Jesse and his father, made for the shore with all speed.

The man—he was a fisherman—pulled alongside, and looked up at Robin with a kindly grin.

"Come along, sonny," he said. "Your dad says you're to run home quick. I'll put you ashore."

"But Jesse...."

"The skipper'll be all right. Don't you fret about him."

"He's not ... dead?"

"Not on your life. Let 'em pump the water out of him and he'll be right as rain."

For all his relief, Robin was troubled.

"B-but ..." he stammered, "he's hurt ... I'm sure he's hurt. Something happened ... when we capsized ... because...."

"Now, now, my son," the fisherman cut him short; "you hop into the boat. We don't want you catching your death in them wet clothes, you know."

Robin obeyed. The fisherman put him ashore, and he made for home along the sea-wall at his best speed.

As he hurried on, half running, half walking, in his squelching shoes, Robin was surprised to find how little frightened he had been when the boat capsized. The experience had been strange, almost un-real, rather than frightening—as accidents usually are when they come swiftly, with-out warning. But the thought of Jesse was

different: it made him wretched. He could not rid his mind's eye of the sight of him just under the surface of the water—apparently so helpless, so resigned, making no fight. What had happened to him—to him who was so full of courage and resource, from whom no secret of the waters was hidden?

When Robin reached home—it took him the best part of an hour—his mother already knew of the disaster. There was an expression on her face that Robin was not familiar with, when she greeted him.

"Daddy has telephoned," she said. "Jesse is quite all right. Daddy himself got a change of clothes at the club and won't be back till late. He's got to see about get-ting *Ladybird* up again. But you're not to worry about Jesse."

"He was nearly drowned." Robin's voice was small and hollow.

"I know."

"But why. . . . Oh Mummy, *why* did it happen?"

"I suppose he can't swim." Robin's mother said.

"Of *course* he can swim!" Robin's face flushed and he spoke almost angrily. He could swim like a duck himself and had learnt when he was six. It was absurd to think for a moment that Jesse, of all people, could not do so simple a thing.

Suddenly, despite himself, Robin's lip began to tremble, and all dripping as he still was he flung his arms round his mother and held her tight.

Then with a little gulp: "I'd better go and change," he said.

Robin's father was not back to supper. At about eight o'clock, though it was nearly bed-time, Robin slipped out of the house and went down to Jesse's cottage on the edge of the salterns.

Jesse himself opened to his knock. Except that he was wearing a pair of old brown carpet slippers instead of the deck shoes or sea boots that Robin was accus-tomed to see him in, he looked no different. His eyes smiled as they always did, and it

"We shall never more, at any future time, delight our souls with talk of knightly deeds."
From "Morte d'Arthur"

The Queen became so fond of my company that she could not dine without me.
From "Some Adventures of Gulliver"

was with the same grave and kindly voice that he invited Robin to come in.

Robin hesitated. "Jesse," he said, "tell me . . . what happened?"

"What happened, Master Robin? Why, it's plain enough, I reckon. She fouled that yacht's bowsprit, as I knew she would, so's her sheet wouldn't run out, and the next puff of wind blew her over."

"No, no. . . ." Robin bit his lip. "Not that . . . I mean, about *you*."

Jesse looked at him with surprise as well as amusement in his eyes.

"Me, Master Robin?"

"Yes."

"I reckon I got a bellyful of salt water."

"I thought you were hurt . . . *weren't* you hurt . . . when we capsized?"

Jesse shook his head.

"You were nearly drowned." The tone of Robin's voice was almost accusing.

"That's it, Master Robin. But your Dad pulled me out. It's lucky for me he's such a grand swimmer—isn't it now?"

"Jesse. . . ."

"What is it, Master Robin?"

"Mummy said perhaps you couldn't swim—but you can, can't you?" He spoke with a sort of urgency, as if he were still catching at a hope. But once again Jesse shook his head.

There was a silence. They were still standing in the doorway of the cottage. The light was fading, the wind gone. Beyond the dark salterns the river gleamed. Robin looked up reproachfully into his old friend's face.

"But, Jesse," he muttered, "it's so *easy*. . . ."

Jesse laughed outright. "Be that as it may, Master Robin," he said, "I've never took to it. Come to think of it now, pretty well none of us chaps can swim. But tell me about yourself, Master Robin: are you none the worse for your ducking?"

"Oh no . . ." said Robin; "not a bit . . . of course not. . . ." They were absent words, for Robin was not thinking of his own ducking. Indeed at that moment he had

almost forgotten it. He was thinking of nothing but of the strange, the scarcely credible—yes, the bitter fact that Jesse couldn't swim. It was almost as if Jesse had let him down.

Rather awkwardly he said he must be going. "It's getting late," he mumbled, "and they'll wonder where I am."

Jesse wished him good-night and, standing in his doorway, watched the little figure hurrying away across the darkening field, until it disappeared.

When Robin got home he found his father on the verandah waiting for him.

"Hallo, Robin," he said. "Been to see Jesse? His wetting didn't do him much damage, did it?"

Robin shook his head, and took up his stand beside his father. For a moment both were silent, staring across the garden. At last Robin said: "Did you know Jesse couldn't swim, Daddy?"

"Yes. That's why I got into the water so double quick. Few sailors can swim. It seems odd to us; but perhaps their idea is, that if a man falls overboard at sea, being able to swim only prolongs the agony. All wrong, of course; but I expect that's the idea."

"I see," said Robin.

"But what a fellow he is," went on his father. "Knew I'd foul that bowsprit, of course. He always knows. I shouldn't have risked it."

"No," said Robin; and the thought of Jesse, and the expression on his face, just before the collision, came back to his mind with a warm rush. Of course, Jesse had known! There was nothing he *didn't* know—about boats. He looked up at his father puffing contentedly at his pipe, his face serene as if there had never been a fear of Jesse's drowning—as if he had never saved Jesse's life.

"Lucky for me," Jesse had said.

Suddenly he slipped his hand into his father's:

"You're a very good swimmer, aren't you, Daddy?" he said.

"Middling," his father answered.

"Jesse said you were a grand swimmer —and that it was lucky for him."

"Well, there's something in that," laughed his father.

"I shouldn't think," Robin went on, "many people could have got to Jesse so quickly. That's because you're so good at the crawl, isn't it?"

"It's a useful stroke for speed," his father agreed.

"I'd like to do the crawl properly," said Robin. "Like you. I think I'll start practising to-morrow."

"Good idea," said his father. "I'll come and watch."

"I wish you would," said Robin. "It'd be jolly useful—for life saving. Good-night, Daddy."

Poem

A wet sheet and a flowing sea,
*   A wind that follows fast*
And fills the white and rustling sail
*   And bends the gallant mast;*
And bends the gallant mast, my boys,
*   While like the eagle free*
Away the good ship flies, and leaves
*   Old England on the lee.*

O for a soft and gentle wind!
*   I heard a fair one cry;*
But give to me the snoring breeze
*   And white waves heaving high;*
And white waves heaving high, my lads,
*   The good ship tight and free—*
The world of waters is our home,
*   And merry men are we.*

There's tempest in yon hornéd moon,
*   And lightning in yon cloud;*
But hark the music, mariners!
*   The wind is piping loud;*
The wind is piping loud, my boys,
*   The lightning flashes free—*
While the hollow oak our palace is,
*   Our heritage the sea.*

ALLAN CUNNINGHAM

Tom Brown at Rugby

Thomas Hughes

Illustrated by Edmund J. Sullivan

Thomas Hughes (1822–1896) was a schoolboy at Rugby in the days of its great Victorian headmaster, Dr. Arnold; and his "Tom Brown's Schooldays", from which this piece is taken, captures the spirit of those days and remains "the greatest book in English of the schoolboy's life."

THE river Avon at Rugby is a slow and not very clear stream, in which chub, dace, roach, and other coarse fish are (or were) plentiful enough, together with a fair sprinkling of small jack, but no fish worth sixpence either for sport or food. It is, however, a capital river for bathing, as it has many nice small pools and several good reaches for swimming, all within about a mile of one another, and at an easy twenty minutes' walk from the school. This mile of water is rented, or used to be rented, for bathing purposes by the Trustees of the School, for the boys. The footpath to Brownsover crosses the river by "the Planks," a curious old single-plank bridge running for fifty or sixty yards into the flat meadows on each side of the river, —for in the winter there are frequent floods. Above the Planks were the bathing-places for the smaller boys; Sleath's, the first bathing-place, where all new boys had to begin, until they had proved to the bathing men (three steady individuals, who were paid to attend daily through the summer to prevent accidents) that they could swim pretty decently, when they were allowed to go on to Anstey's, about one hundred and fifty yards below. Here there was a hole about six feet deep and

twelve feet across, over which the puffing urchins struggled to the opposite side, and thought no small beer of themselves for having been out of their depths. Below the Planks came larger and deeper holes, the first of which was Wratislaw's, and the last Swift's, a famous hole, ten or twelve feet deep in parts, and thirty yards across, from which there was a fine swimming reach right down to the Mill. Swift's was reserved for the sixth and fifth forms, and had a spring board and two sets of steps: the others had one set of steps each, and were used indifferently by all the lower boys, though each house addicted itself more to one hole than to another. The Schoolhouse at this time affected Wratislaw's hole, and Tom and East, who had learnt to swim like fishes, were to be found there as regular as the clock through the summer, always twice, and often three times a day.

Now the boys either had, or fancied they had, a right also to fish at their pleasure over the whole of this part of the river, and would not understand that the right (if any) only extended to the Rugby side. As ill luck would have it, the gentleman who owned the opposite bank, after allowing it for some time without interference, had ordered his keepers not to let the boys fish on his side; the consequence of which had been, that there had been first wranglings and then fights between the keepers and boys; and so keen had the quarrel become, that the landlord and his keepers, after a ducking had been inflicted on one of the latter, and a fierce fight ensued thereon, had been up to the great school at calling-over to identify the delinquents, and it was all the Doctor himself and five or six masters could do to keep the peace. Not even his authority could prevent the hissing; and so strong was the feeling, that the four praeposters of the week walked up the school with their canes, shouting S-s-s-s-i-lenc-c-c-c-e at the top of their voices. However, the chief offenders for the time were flogged and kept in bounds, but the victorious party had brought a nice hornet's nest about their ears. The landlord was hissed at the School-gates as he rode past, and when he charged his horse at the mob of boys, and tried to thrash them with his whip, was driven back by cricket-bats and wickets, and pursued with pebbles and fives-balls; while the wretched keepers' lives were a burthen to them, from having to watch the waters so closely. The School-house boys of Tom's standing, one and all, as a protest against this tyranny and cutting short of their lawful amusements, took to fishing in all ways, and especially by means of night-lines. The little tackle-maker at the bottom of the town would soon have made his fortune had the rage lasted, and several of the barbers began to lay in fishing-tackle. The boys had this great advantage over their enemies, that they spent a large portion of the day in nature's garb by the river side, and so, when tired of swimming, would get out on the other side and fish, or set night-lines, till the keepers hove in sight, and then plunge in and swim back and mix with the other bathers, and the keepers were too wise to follow across the stream.

While things were in this state, one day, Tom and three or four others were bathing at Wratislaw's, and had, as a matter of course, been taking up and re-setting night-lines. They had all left the water and were sitting or standing about at their toilets, in all costumes from a shirt upwards, when they were aware of a man in a velveteen shooting-coat approaching from the other side. He was a new keeper, so they didn't recognize or notice him, till he pulled up right opposite, and began:

"I see'd some of you young gentlemen over this side a-fishing just now."

"Hullo, who are you? what business is that of yours, old Velveteens?"

"I'm the new under-keeper and master's told me to keep a sharp look-out on all o' you young chaps. And I tells 'ee I means business, and you'd better keep on your own side, or we shall fall out."

"Well, that's right, Velveteens—speak out, and let's know your mind at once."

"Look here, old boy," cried East, holding up a miserable coarse fish or two and a small jack, "would you like to smell 'em and see which bank they lived under?"

"I'll give you a bit of advice, keeper," shouted Tom, who was sitting in his shirt paddling with his feet in the river; "you'd better go down there to Swift's, where the big boys are; they're beggars at setting lines, and'll put you up to a wrinkle or two for catching the five pounders."

Tom was nearest to the keeper, and that officer, who was getting angry at the chaff, fixed his eyes on our hero, as if to take a note of him for future use. Tom returned his gaze with a steady stare, and then broke into a laugh, and struck into the middle of a favourite School-house song—

"As I and my companions
*   Were setting of a snare,*
The gamekeeper was watching us;
*   For him we did not care:*
For we can wrestle and fight, my boys,
*   And jump out anywhere.*
For it's my delight of a likely night,
*   In the season of the year."*

The chorus was taken up by the other boys with shouts of laughter, and the keeper turned away with a grunt, but evidently bent on mischief. The boys thought no more of the matter.

But now came on the may-fly season; the soft hazy summer weather lay sleepily along the rich meadows by Avon side, and the green and grey flies flickered with their graceful lazy up and down flight over the reeds and the water and the meadows, in myriads upon myriads. The may-flies must surely be the lotus-eaters of the ephemerae; the happiest, laziest, carelessest fly that dances and dreams out his few hours of sunshine life by English rivers.

Every little pitiful coarse fish in the Avon was on the alert for the flies, and gorging his wretched carcase with hundreds daily, the gluttonous rogue! and every lover of the gentle craft was out to avenge the poor may-flies.

So one fine Thursday afternoon, Tom having borrowed East's new rod, started by himself to the river. He fished for some time with small success: not a fish would rise at him; but as he prowled along the bank, he was presently aware of mighty ones feeding in a pool on the opposite side, under the shade of a huge willow tree.

The stream was deep here, but some fifty yards below was a shallow, for which he made off hot-foot; and forgetting landlords, keepers, solemn prohibitions of the Doctor, and everything else, pulled up his trousers, plunged across, and in three minutes was creeping along on all fours towards the clump of willows.

It isn't often that great chub or any other coarse fish, are in earnest about anything, but just then they were thoroughly bent on feeding, and in half an hour Master Tom had deposited three thumping fellows at the foot of the giant willow. As he was baiting for a fourth pounder, and just

"Oh, 'ee be up ther', be 'ee?"

going to throw in again, he became aware of a man coming up the bank not one hundred yards off. Another look told him that it was the under-keeper. Could he reach the shallow before him? No, not carrying his rod. Nothing for it but the tree; so Tom laid his bones to it, shinning up as fast as he could, and dragging up his rod after him. He had just time to reach and crouch along upon a huge branch some ten feet up, which stretched out over the river, when the keeper arrived at the clump.

Tom's heart beat fast as he came under the tree; two steps more and he would have passed, when as ill-luck would have it the gleam on the scales of the dead fish caught his eye, and he made a dead point at the foot of the tree. He picked up the fish one by one; his eye and touch told him that they had been alive and feeding within the hour. Tom crouched lower

373

along the branch, and heard the keeper beating the clump. "If I could only get the rod hidden," thought he, and began gently shifting it to get it alongside of him; "willow-trees don't throw out straight hickory shoots twelve feet long, with no leaves, worse luck."

Alas! the keeper catches the rustle, and then a sight of the rod, and then of Tom's hand and arm.

"Oh, 'ee be up ther', be 'ee?" says he, running under the tree. "Now you come down this minute."

"Tree'd at last," thinks Tom, making no answer, and keeping as close as possible, but working away at the rod which he takes to pieces: "I'm in for it, unless I can starve him out." And then he begins to meditate getting along the branch for a plunge, and scramble to the other side; but the small branches are so thick, and the opposite bank so difficult, that the keeper will have lots of time to get round by the ford before he can get out, so he gives that up. And now he hears the keeper beginning to scramble up the trunk. That will never do; so he scrambles himself back to where his branch joins the trunk, and stands with lifted rod.

"Hullo, Velveteens, mind your fingers if you come any higher."

The keeper stops and looks up, and then with a grin says, "Oh! be you, be it, young measter? Well, here's luck. Now I tells 'ee to come down at once, and 't'll be best for 'ee."

"Thank 'ee, Velveteens, I'm very comfortable," said Tom, shortening the rod in his hand, and preparing for battle.

"Werry well, please yourself," says the keeper, descending however to the ground again, and taking his seat on the bank; "I bean't in no hurry, so you may take your time. I'll larn 'ee to gee honest folk names afore I've done with 'ee."

"My luck as usual," thinks Tom: "what a fool I was to give him a black. If I'd called him 'keeper' now I might get off. The return match is all his way."

The keeper quietly proceeded to take out his pipe, fill, and light it, keeping an eye on Tom, who now sat disconsolately across the branch, looking at keeper—a pitiful sight for men and fishes. The more he thought of it the less he liked it. "It must be getting near second calling-over," thinks he. Keeper smokes on stolidly. "If he takes me up, I shall be flogged safe enough. I can't sit here all night. Wonder if he'll rise at silver."

"I say, keeper," said he meekly, "let me go for two bob?"

"Not for twenty neither," grunts his persecutor.

And so they sat on till long past second calling-over, and then sun came slanting in through the willow-branches, and telling of locking-up near at hand.

"I'm coming down, keeper," said Tom at last, with a sigh, fairly tired out. "Now what are you going to do?"

"Walk 'ee up to School, and give 'ee over to the Doctor, them's my orders," said Velveteens, knocking the ashes out of his fourth pipe, and standing up and shaking himself.

"Very good," said Tom; "but hands off, you know. I'll go with you quietly, so no collaring or that sort of thing."

Keeper looked at him a minute— "Werry good," said he at last; and so Tom descended, and wended his way drearily by the side of the keeper up to the School-house, where they arrived just at locking-up. As they passed the School-gates, the Tadpoles and several others who were standing there caught the state of things, and rushed out, crying "Rescue!" but Tom shook his head, so they only followed to the Doctor's gate, and went back sorely puzzled.

How changed and stern the Doctor seemed from the last time that Tom was up there, as the keeper told the story, not omitting to state how Tom had called him blackguard names. "Indeed, sir," broke in the culprit, "it was only Velveteens." The Doctor only asked one question.

"You know the rule about the banks, Brown?"

"Yes, sir."

"Then wait for me tomorrow, after first lesson."

"I thought so," muttered Tom.

"And about the rod, sir?" went on the keeper. "Master's told we as we might have all the rods—"

"Oh, please, sir," broke in Tom, "the rod isn't mine."

The Doctor looked puzzled; but the keeper, who was a good-hearted fellow, and melted at Tom's evident distress, gave up his claim. Tom was flogged next morning, and a few days afterwards met Velveteens, and presented him with half-a-crown for giving up the rod claim, and they became sworn friends; and I regret to say that Tom had many more fish from under the willow that may-fly season, and was never caught again by Velveteens.

It wasn't three weeks before Tom, and now East by his side, were again in the awful presence. This time, however, the Doctor was not so terrible. A few days before, they had been fagged at fives to fetch the balls that went off the Court. While standing watching the game, they saw five or six nearly new balls hit on the top of the School. "I say, Tom," said East, when they were dismissed, "couldn't we get those balls somehow?"

"Let's try, anyhow."

So they reconnoitred the walls carefully, borrowed a coal hammer from old Stumps, bought some big nails, and after one or two attempts, scaled the Schools, and possessed themselves of huge quantities of fives'-balls. The place pleased them so much that they spent all their spare time there, scratching and cutting their names on the top of every tower; and at last, having exhausted all other places, finished up with inscribing H. EAST, T. BROWN, on the minute-hand of the great clock; in the doing of which, they held the minute-hand and disturbed the clock's economy.

So next morning, when masters and boys came trooping down to prayers, and entered the quadrangle, the injured minute-hand was indicating three minutes to the hour. They all pulled up, and took their time. When the hour struck, doors were closed, and half the school late. Thomas being set to make inquiry, discovers their names on the minute-hand, and reports accordingly; and they are sent for, a knot of their friends making derisive and pantomimic allusions to what their fate will be as they walk off.

But the Doctor, after hearing their story, doesn't make much of it, and only gives them thirty lines of Homer to learn by heart, and a lecture on the likelihood of such exploits ending in broken bones.

They inscribed their names on the minute hand.

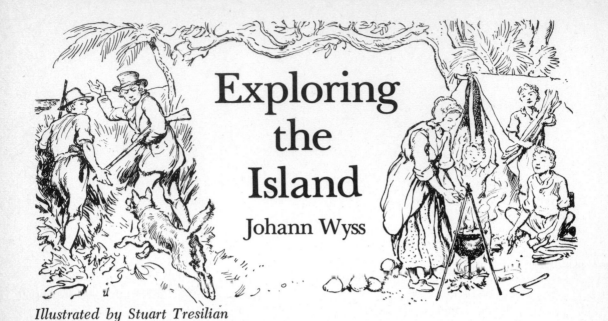

Exploring
the
Island

Johann Wyss

Illustrated by Stuart Tresilian

Johann Wyss (1781–1830), a Swiss author, wrote one of the very earliest books for young people about the life of a family shipwrecked on an island. He was also the first writer to imagine a house in a tree, since when, many a country child, with (or without) the help of an enterprising parent, has built one. "The Swiss Family Robinson" was a large family, and Father Robinson, who tells the tale, has a huge job on his hands to educate the children in the very varied animal and plant life with which the author has furnished the island. In such a setting, learning is an adventure, as you can see from this extract in which the narrator leaves the younger children with their mother and sets out with his eldest son on a voyage of exploration:

"IT IS impossible for me to take all of you," I said, "we know not yet what we are to set about, nor whither we are going. Your eldest brother, Fritz, and myself shall be better able to defend ourselves in any danger without you; besides that, with too many persons we could proceed but slowly. You will then all three remain with your mother in this place, which appears to be one of perfect safety, and you shall keep Flora to be your guard, while Fritz and I will take Turk with us. With such a dog to protect, and a gun well loaded, who shall dare treat us with disrespect? Make haste, Fritz, and tie up Flora, that she may not follow us; and have your eye on Turk, that he may be at hand to accompany us; and see the guns are ready."

"You need not be uneasy about their journey," said Ernest. "Like Robinson Crusoe, they will be sure enough to find some cocoa-nuts, which they will like much better than your miserable lobster; only think, a fine round nut, Jack, as big as my head, and with at least a teacupful of delicious sweet milk in it!"

"Oh! brother Fritz, pray do bring me some," cried little Francis.

We now prepared for our departure. We each took a bag for game, and a hatchet: I put a pair of pistols in the leather band round Fritz's waist, in addition to the gun and provided myself with the same articles, not forgetting a stock of biscuit and a flask of fresh river water. My wife now called us to breakfast, when all attacked the lobster; but its

376

flesh proved so hard that there was a great deal left when our meal was finished, and we packed it for our journey without further regret from any one.

Fritz urged me to set out before the excessive heat came on. "With all my heart," said I.

In about an hour we had completed the preparations for our departure. I had loaded the guns we left behind, and I now enjoined my wife to keep by day as near the boat as possible, which in case of danger was the best and most speedy means of escape. . . .

When we had walked about a hundred paces we heard a loud noise behind us, as if we were pursued, and perceiving a rustling motion in the grass, which was almost as tall as ourselves, I was a good deal alarmed, thinking that it might be made by some frightful serpent, a tiger, or other ferocious animal. But I was well satisfied with Fritz, who, instead of being frightened and running away, stood still and firm to face the danger, the only motion he made being to see that his piece was ready, and turning himself to front the spot whence the noise proceeded.

Our alarm was, however, short; for what was our joy on seeing rush out, not an enemy, but our faithful Turk, whom in the distress of the parting scene we had forgotten, and whom no doubt our anxious relatives had sent on to us! I received the poor creature with lively joy, and did not fail to commend both the bravery and discretion of my son, in not yielding to alarm, and for waiting till he saw the object before he resolved to fire. . . .

We next entered a forest to the right, and soon observed that some of the trees were of a singular kind. Fritz, whose sharp eye was continually on a journey of discovery, went up to examine them closely. "Oh, father, what odd trees, with wens growing all about their trunks!"

I had soon the surprise and satisfaction of assuring him that they were of the gourd-tree kind, the trunks of which bear fruit. Fritz, who had never heard of such a tree, could not conceive the meaning of what he saw, and asked me if the fruit was a sponge or a wen. "We will see," I replied, "if we cannot unravel the mystery. Try to get one of them down, and we will examine it minutely."

"I have got one," cried Fritz, "and it is exactly like a gourd, only the rind is thicker and harder."

"It, then, like the rind of that fruit, can be used for making various utensils," observed I; "plates, dishes, basins, flasks. We will name it the gourd-tree.

Fritz jumped for joy. "How happy my mother will be!" cried he in ecstasy; "she will no longer have the vexation of thinking, when she makes soup, that we shall all scald our fingers!"

We next proceeded to the manufacture of our plates and dishes. I taught my son how to divide the gourd with a bit of string, which would cut more equally than a knife: I tied the string round the middle of the gourd as tight as possible, striking it pretty hard with the handle of my knife, and I drew tighter and tighter till the gourd fell apart, forming two regular shaped bowls or vessels; while Fritz, who had used a knife for the same operation, had entirely spoiled his gourd by the irregular pressure of his instrument. . . .

Fritz was in the utmost astonishment at my success. "I cannot imagine, father," said he, "how this way of cutting the gourd could occur to you!"

"I have read the description of such a process," replied I, "in books of travels."

"And the flasks, father, in what manner are they made?"

"If a Negro wishes to have a flask or bottle with a neck, he binds a piece of string, linen, bark of a tree, or anything he can get, round the part nearest the stalk of a very young gourd; he draws this bandage so tight that the part at liberty soon forms itself to a round shape, while the part which is confined contracts, and remains ever after narrow. By this method it is that they obtain flasks or bottles of a perfect form."

Our conversation and our labour thus went on together. Fritz had completed some plates, and was not a little proud of the achievement. "Ah, how delighted my mother will be to eat from them!" cried he. "But how shall we convey them to her? They will not, I fear, bear travelling well."

"We must leave them here on the sand for the sun to dry them thoroughly; this will be accomplished by the time of our return this way, and we can then carry them with us; but care must be taken to fill them with sand, that they may not shrink or warp in so ardent a heat." My boy did not dislike this task; for he had no great fancy to the idea of carrying such a load on our journey of further discovery. Our service of porcelain was accordingly spread upon the ground, and for the present left to its fate.

While our labours had been going on, we had not neglected the great object of our pursuit—the making of every practicable search for our ship companions. But our endeavours, alas! were all in vain.

After a walk of about four leagues in all, we arrived at a spot where a slip of land reached far out into the sea, on which we observed a rising piece of ground or hill. On a moment's reflection we determined to ascend it, concluding we should obtain a clear view of all adjacent parts, which would save us the fatigue of farther rambles.

When at the top, we beheld a wild and solitary beauty, comprehending a vast extent of land and water. It was, however, in vain that we used our telescope in all directions; no trace of man appeared. The shore, rounded by a bay of some extent— the bank of which ended in a promontory on the farther side; the agreeable blue tint of its surface; the sea, gently agitated by waves in which the rays of the sun were reflected; the woods of varied hues and verdure, formed a picture of such magnificence, of such new and exquisite delight, that, if the recollection of our unfortunate companions, engulfed, perhaps, in this very ocean, had not intruded to depress our spirits, we should have yielded to the ecstasy the scene inspired.

In reality, from this moment we began to lose even the feeble hope we had entertained, and sadness stole into our hearts.

We descended the hill, and made our way to a wood of palms, which I had just pointed out to Fritz: our path was clothed with reeds, entwined with other plants, which greatly obstructed our march. We advanced slowly and cautiously, fearing at every step to receive a mortal bite from some serpent that might be concealed among them. We made Turk go before, to give us timely notice of anything dangerous. I also cut a reedstalk of uncommon length and thickness, for my defence against any enemy.

It was not without surprise that I perceived a gluey sap proceed from the divided end of the stalk. Prompted by curiosity I tasted this liquid, and found it sweet and of a pleasant flavour, so that not a doubt remained that we were passing through a plantation of sugar-canes. I again applied the cane to my lips, and sucked it for some moments, and felt singularly refreshed and strengthened. I determined not to tell Fritz immediately of the fortunate discovery I had made; preferring that he should find it out himself. As he was at some distance before me, I called out to him to cut a reed for

A great number of monkeys, their eyes fixed upon us, showed every mark of anger.

his defence. This he did, and, without any remark, used it simply for a stick, striking lustily with it on all sides to clear a passage. The motion occasioned the sap to run out abundantly upon his hand, and he stopped to examine so strange a circumstance. He lifted it up, and still a larger quantity escaped. He now tasted what was on his fingers. Oh! then came the exclamations—"Father, father, I have found some sugar!—some syrup! I have a sugar-cane in my hand! Run quickly, father!"

We were soon together, jointly partaking of the pleasure we had in store for his dear mother and his younger brothers. In the meantime Fritz kept sucking the juice of the single cane he had cut, till his relish for it was appeased. He persisted in cutting at least a dozen of the largest canes, tore off their leaves, tied them together, and, putting them under his arm, dragged them as well as he was able, through thick and thin, to the end of the plantation. We regained the wood of palms without accident; here we stretched our limbs in the shade, and finished our repast.

We were scarcely settled, when a great number of large monkeys, terrified by the sight of us and the barking of Turk, stole so nimbly and yet so quietly up the trees, that we scarcely perceived them till they had reached the topmost parts. From this height they fixed their eyes upon us, grinding their teeth, making horrible grimaces, and saluting us with screams of hostile import. Being now satisfied that the trees were palms, bearing cocoa-nuts, I conceived the hope of obtaining some of this fruit in a milky state through the monkeys. Fritz, on his part, prepared to shoot at them instantly. He threw his burdens on the ground, and it was with difficulty that I, by pulling his arm, could prevent him from firing.

"Ah, father, why did you not let me fire? Monkeys are such malicious, mischievous animals! Look how they deride us!"

"As long as an animal does no injury, or that his death can in no shape be useful in preserving our own lives, we have no right to destroy it, and still less to torture it for our amusement, or from a desire of revenge. But what will you say if I show you that we may find means to make living monkeys contribute to our service? See what I am going to do. But step aside, for fear of your head. If I succeed, the monkeys will furnish us with plenty of our much-desired cocoa-nuts."

I now began to throw some stones at the monkeys, and though I could not make them reach to half the height at which they had taken refuge, they showed every mark of anger. With their accustomed trick of imitation, they furiously tore off, nut by nut, all that grew upon the branches near them, to hurl them down upon us; so that it was with difficulty we avoided the blows; and, in a short time, a great number of cocoa-nuts lay on the ground round us. Fritz laughed heartily at the success of our stratagem; and, as

the shower of cocoa-nuts began to subside, we set about collecting them. We chose a place where we could repose at our ease, to feast on this rich harvest.

We opened the shells with a hatchet, but first enjoyed the sucking of the milk through the three small holes, where we found it easy to insert the point of a knife. The milk of the cocoa-nut has not a pleasant flavour; but it is excellent for quenching thirst. What we liked best was a kind of solid cream which adheres to the shell, and which we scraped off with our spoons. We mixed with it a little of the sap of our sugar-canes, and it made a delicious repast.

Our meals being finished, we prepared to leave the wood of palms. I tied together all the cocoa-nuts which had stalks, and threw them across my shoulder. Fritz resumed his bundle of sugar-canes. We divided the rest of the things between us and continued our way towards home.

"Sugar-canes! Sugar-canes!" exclaimed they all on our return; and, surrounding Fritz, made him give them full instructions on the art of sucking sugar-canes.

My wife also, who had always entertained a high respect for the article of sugar in her household management, was quite astonished, and asked us to inform her of all particulars. I gave her an account of our journey and our new acquisitions, which I exhibited one after the other for her inspection. No one of them afforded her more pleasure than the gourd dishes, because to persons of decent habits they were articles of sheer necessity.

Morte d'Arthur

Alfred, Lord Tennyson

*Illustrated by Robert Geary
and John Berry*

So all day long the noise of battle roll'd
Among the mountains by the winter sea;
Until King Arthur's table, man by man,
Had fallen in Lyonnesse about their Lord,
King Arthur: then, because his wound
    was deep,
The bold Sir Bedivere uplifted him,
Sir Bedivere, the last of all his knights,
And bore him to a chapel nigh the field,
A broken chancel with a broken cross,
That stood on a dark strait of barren land.
On one side lay the Ocean, and on one
Lay a great water, and the moon was full.
    Then spake King Arthur to Sir Bedivere:
"The sequel of today unsolders all
The goodliest fellowship of famous knights
Whereof this world holds record. Such a
    sleep
They sleep—the men I loved. I think
    that we
Shall never more, at any future time,
Delight our souls with talk of knightly
    deeds,
Walking about the gardens and the halls
Of Camelot, as in the days that were.
I perish by this people which I made,—
Tho' Merlin sware that I should come
    again
To rule once more—but let what will be,
    be,
I am so deeply smitten thro' the helm
That without help I cannot last till morn.
Thou therefore take my brand Excalibur,

Which was my pride: for thou remem-
    berest how
In those old days, one summer noon, an
    arm
Rose up from out the bosom of the lake,
Clothed in white samite, mystic,
    wonderful,
Holding the sword—and how I row'd
    across
And took it, and have worn it, like a king:
And, wheresoever I am sung or told
In aftertime, this also shall be known:
But now delay not: take Excalibur,
And fling him far into the middle mere:
Watch what thou seest, and lightly bring
    me word."
    To him replied the bold Sir Bedivere:
"It is not meet, Sir King, to leave thee thus,
Aidless, alone, and smitten thro' the helm.
A little thing may harm a wounded man.
Yet I thy hest will all perform at full,
Watch what I see, and lightly bring thee
    word."
    So saying, from the ruin'd shrine he stept
And in the moon athwart the place of
    tombs,
Where lay the mighty bones of ancient
    men,
Old knights, and over them the sea-wind
    sang
Shrill, chill, with flakes of foam. He,
    stepping down
By zig-zag paths, and juts of pointed rock,

381

Came on the shining levels of the lake.
   There drew he forth the brand
     Excalibur,
And o'er him, drawing it, the winter moon,
Brightening the skirts of a long cloud, ran
   forth
And sparkled keen with frost against the
   hilt:
For all the haft twinkled with diamond
   sparks,
Myriads of topaz-lights, and jacinth-work
Of subtlest jewellery. He gazed so long
That both his eyes were dazzled, as he
   stood,
This way and that dividing the swift mind,

In act to throw: but at the last it seem'd
Better to leave Excalibur conceal'd
There in the many-knotted waterflags,
That whistled stiff and dry about the
   marge.
So strode he back slow to the wounded
   King.
   Then spake King Arthur to Sir Bedivere:
"Hast thou perform'd my mission which I
   gave?
What is it thou hast seen? or what hast
   heard?"
   And answer made the bold Sir Bedivere:
"I heard the ripple washing in the reeds,
And the wild water lapping on the crag."
   To whom replied King Arthur, faint and
    pale:
"Thou hast betray'd thy nature and thy
   name,

Not rendering true answer, as beseem'd
Thy fealty, nor like a noble knight:
For surer sign had follow'd either hand,
Or voice, or else a motion of the mere.
This is a shameful thing for men to lie.
Yet now, I charge thee, quickly go again
As thou art lief and dear, and do the thing
I bad thee, watch, and lightly bring me
   word."
   Then went Sir Bedivere the second time
Across the ridge, and paced beside the
   mere,
Counting the dewy pebbles, fix'd in
   thought;
But when he saw the wonder of the hilt,
How curiously and strangely chased, he
   smote
His palms together, and he cried aloud,
   "And if indeed I cast the brand away,
Surely a precious thing, one worthy note,
Should thus be lost for ever from the earth,
Which might have pleased the eyes of
   many men.
What good should follow this, if this were
   done?
What harm, undone? deep harm to
   disobey,
Seeing obedience is the bond of rule.
Were it well to obey then, if a king demand
An act unprofitable, against himself?
The King is sick, and knows not what he
   does.
What record, or what relic of my lord
Should be to aftertime, but empty breath
And rumours of a doubt? but were this
   kept,
Stored in some treasure-house of mighty
   kings,
Some one might show it at a joust of arms,
Saying, 'King Arthur's sword, Excalibur,
Wrought by the lonely maiden of the Lake.
Nine years she wrought it, sitting in the
   deeps
Upon the hidden bases of the hills.'
So might some old man speak in the after-
   time.
To all the people, winning reverence.

waterflags = yellow flags or wild iris   lief = beloved

But now much honour and much fame were lost."

So spake he, clouded with his own conceit,
And hid Excalibur the second time,
And so strode back slow to the wounded King.
    Then spoke King Arthur, breathing heavily:
"What is it thou hast seen? or what hast heard?"
    And answer made the bold Sir Bedivere:
"I heard the water lapping on the crag,
And the long ripple washing in the reeds."
    To whom replied King Arthur, much in wrath:
"Ah, miserable and unkind, untrue,
Unknightly, traitor-hearted! Woe is me!
Authority forgets a dying king,
Laid widow'd of the power in his eye
That bow'd the will. I see thee what thou art,
For thou, the latest-left of all my knights,
In whom should meet the offices of all,
Thou wouldst betray me for the precious hilt;
Either from lust of gold, or like a girl
Valuing the giddy pleasure of the eyes.
Yet, for a man may fail in duty twice,
And the third time may prosper, get thee hence:
But, if thou spare to fling Excalibur,
I will arise and slay thee with my hands."
    Then quickly rose Sir Bedivere, and ran,
And, leaping down the ridges lightly, plunged
Among the bulrush-beds, and clutch'd the sword,
And strongly wheel'd and threw it. The great brand
Made lightnings in the splendour of the moon,
And flashing round and round, and whirl'd in an arch,
Shot like a streamer of the northern morn,
Seen where the moving isles of winter shock
By night, with noises of the northern sea.
So flash'd and fell the brand Excalibur:
But ere he dipt the surface, rose an arm
Clothed in white samite, mystic, wonderful,
And caught him by the hilt, and brandish'd him
Three times, and drew him under in the mere.
And lightly went the other to the King.

    Then spoke King Arthur, drawing thicker breath:
"Now see I by thine eyes that this is done.
Speak out; what is it thou hast heard, or seen?"
    And answer made the bold Sir Bedivere:
"Sir King, I closed mine eyelids, lest the gems
Should blind my purpose, for I never saw,
Nor shall see, here or elsewhere, till I die,
Not tho' I live three lives of mortal men,

So great a miracle as yonder hilt.
Then with both hands I flung him,
    wheeling him;
But when I look'd again, behold an arm,
Clothed in white samite, mystic,
    wonderful,
That caught him by the hilt, and
    brandish'd him
Three times, and drew him under in the
    mere."
    And answer made King Arthur,
        breathing hard:
"My end draws nigh; 'tis time that I were
    gone.
Make broad thy shoulders to receive my
    weight,
And bear me to the margin; yet I fear

My wound hath taken cold, and I shall
    die."
    So saying, from the pavement he half
        rose,
Slowly, with pain, reclining on his arm,
And looking wistfully with wide blue eyes
As in a picture. Him Sir Bedivere
Remorsefully regarded thro' his tears,
And would have spoken, but he found not
    words,
Then took with care, and kneeling on one
    knee,
O'er both his shoulders drew the languid
    hands,
And rising bore him thro' the place of
    tombs.

But, as he walk'd, King Arthur panted
    hard,
Like one that feels a nightmare on his bed
When all the house is mute. So sigh'd the
    King,
Muttering and murmuring at his ear,
    "Quick, quick!
I fear it is too late, and I shall die."
But the other swiftly strode from ridge to
    ridge,
Clothed with his breath, and looking, as he
    walk'd,
Larger than human on the frozen hills.
He heard the deep behind him, and a cry
Before. His own thought drove him, like
    a goad.
Dry clash'd his harness in the icy caves
And barren chasms, and all to left and
    right
The bare black cliff clang'd round him, as
    he based
His feet on juts of slippery crag that rang
Sharp-smitten with the dint of armèd
    heels—
And on a sudden, lo! the level lake,
And the long glories of the winter moon.
    Then saw they how there hove a dusky
        barge,
Dark as a funeral scarf from stem to
    stern,
Beneath them; and descending they were
    ware
That all the decks were dense with stately
    forms
Black-stoled, black-hooded, like a dream
    —by these
Three Queens with crowns of gold—and
    from them rose
A cry that shiver'd to the tingling stars,
And, as it were one voice an agony
Of lamentation, like a wind, that shrills
All night in a waste land, where no one
    comes,
Or hath come, since the making of the
    world.
    Then murmur'd Arthur, "Place me in the
        barge,"
And to the barge they came. There those
    three Queens

Put forth their hands, and took the King, and wept.
But she, that rose the tallest of them all
And fairest, laid his head upon her lap,
And loosed the shatter'd casque, and chafed his hands,
And call'd him by his name, complaining loud,
And dropping bitter tears against his brow
Striped with dark blood: for all his face was white
And colourless, and like the wither'd moon
Smote by the fresh beam of the springing east;
And all his greaves and cuisses dash'd with drops
Of onset; and the light and lustrous curls—
That made his forehead like a rising sun
High from the daïs-throne—were parch'd with dust;
Or, clotted into points and hanging loose,
Mix'd with the knightly growth that fringed his lips.
So like a shatter'd column lay the King;
Not like that Arthur who, with lance in rest,
From spur to plume a star of tournament,
Shot thro' the lists at Camelot, and charged
Before the eyes of ladies and of kings.
    Then loudly cried the bold Sir Bedivere,
"Ah! my Lord Arthur, whither shall I go?

Where shall I hide my forehead and my eyes?
For now I see the true old times are dead,
When every morning brought a noble chance,
And every chance brought out a noble knight.
Such times have been not since the light that led
The holy Elders with the gift of myrrh.
But now the whole ROUND TABLE is dissolved
Which was an image of the mighty world;
And I, the last, go forth companionless,
And the days darken round me, and the years,
Among new men, strange faces, other minds."
    And slowly answered Arthur from the barge:
"The old order changeth yielding place to new,
And God fulfils Himself in many ways,
Lest one good custom should corrupt the world.

Comfort thyself: what comfort is in me?
I have lived my life, and that which I have done
May He within Himself make pure! but thou,
If thou shouldst never see my face again,
Pray for my soul. More things are wrought by prayer

casque = helmet   greave = shin armour   cuisse = thigh armour

Than this world dreams of. Wherefore, let
thy voice
Rise like a fountain for me night and day.
For what are men better than sheep or
goats
That nourish a blind life within the brain,
If, knowing God, they lift not hands of
prayer
Both for themselves and those who call
them friend?
For so the whole round earth is every way
Bound by gold chains about the feet of
God.
But now farewell. I am going a long way
With these thou seest—if indeed I go—
(For all my mind is clouded with a doubt)
To the island-valley of Avilion;
Where falls not hail, or rain, or any snow,
Nor ever wind blows loudly; but it lies

Deep-meadow'd, happy, fair with orchard-
lawns
And bowery hollows crown'd with summer
sea,
Where I will heal me of my grievous
wound."
    So said he, and the barge with oar and
sail
Moved from the brink, like some full-
breasted swan
That, fluting a wild carol ere her death,
Ruffles her pure cold plume, and takes the
flood
With swarthy webs. Long stood Sir
Bedivere
Revolving many memories, till the hull
Look'd one black dot against the verge of
dawn,
And on the mere the wailing died away.

Some Adventures of Gulliver

Jonathan Swift

Illustrated by Robin Jacques and John Patience

The author of Gulliver's Travels, Jonathan Swift, Doctor of Divinity (1667–1745), was the son of an English couple living in Dublin. By profession a clergyman, he became well known as poet and pamphleteer, involving himself with the political and religious arguments of the day.

Dean Swift never wrote for children, but he wrote a book for adults which he intended to be a satire on the foibles of the human race. This is the famous story of the four voyages of Captain Lemuel Gulliver. Young readers gradually adopted this story (they had no real books of their own at the time) and it was read simply as an adventure story. Of Gulliver's adventures in Lilliput—where he was captured by the little people—you will certainly have already read. But, just to remind you, we include the passage in which he gains great honour among the Lilliputians by capturing for them the fleet of the miniature Empire of Blefuscu. Then we include extracts from the second voyage in which Gulliver is landed on the shores of Brobdingnag, the land of the giants, a particularly shocking experience after Lilliput. Notice how Swift never lets you forget how enormous and coarse everything in the land of giants must seem to a mere thumbling like Gulliver. He makes it wonderfully real—even as real as the much less fantastic adventures of Robinson Crusoe as described by Daniel Defoe.

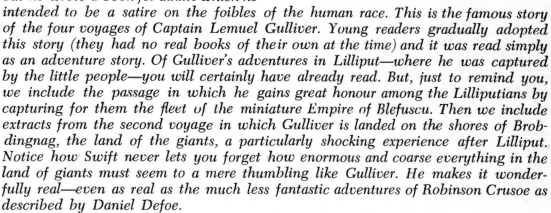

THE Empire of Blefuscu is an island situated to the north-north-east of Lilliput, from whence it is parted only by a channel of eight hundred yards wide. I had not yet seen it, and upon this notice of an intended invasion, I avoided appearing on that side of the coast for fear of being discovered by some of the enemies' ships, who had received no intelligence of me; all intercourse between the two Empires having been strictly forbidden during the war, upon pain of death: and an embargo laid by our Emperor upon all vessels whatsoever. I communicated to His Majesty a project I had formed of seizing the enemy's whole fleet; which, as our Scouts assured us, lay at anchor in the harbour ready to sail with the first fair wind. I consulted the most experienced seamen upon the depth of the channel, which they had often plumbed; who told me, that in the middle at high water it was seventy *glumgluffs* deep, which is about six foot of European measure: and the rest of it fifty *glumgluffs* at most. I walked to the north-east coast over against Blefuscu; where, lying down behind a hillock, I took out my small pocket perspective glass and viewed the enemy's fleet at anchor, consisting of about fifty men-of-war, and a great number of transports. I then came back to my house, and gave order (for which I had a warrant) for a great quantity of the strongest cable and bars of iron. The cable was about as thick as packthread, and the bars of the length and size of a knitting needle. I trebled the cable to make it stronger; and for the same reason I twisted three of the iron bars together, binding the extremities into a hook. Having thus fixed fifty hooks to as many cables, I went back to the north-east coast, and putting off my coat, shoes, and stockings, walked into the sea in my leathern jerkin, about half an hour before high water. I waded with what haste I could, and swam in the middle about thirty yards until I felt the ground; I arrived at the fleet in less than half an hour. The enemy was so frighted when they saw me, that they leaped out of their ships and swam to shore; where there could not be fewer than thirty thousand souls. I then took my tackling and, fastening a hook to the hole at the prow of each, I tied all the cords together at the end.

While I was thus employed the enemy discharged several thousand arrows, many of which stuck in my hands and face; and besides the excessive smart, gave me much disturbance in my work. My greatest apprehension was for my eyes, which I should have infallibly lost, if I had not suddenly thought of an expedient. I kept, among other little necessaries, a pair of spectacles in a private pocket, which, as I observed before, had escaped the Emperor's searchers. These I took out and fastened as strongly as I could upon my nose and, thus armed, went on boldly with my work in spite of the enemy's arrows; many of which struck against the glasses of my spectacles, but without any other effect further than a little to discompose them. I had now fastened all the hooks and, taking the knot in my hand, began to pull; but not a ship would stir, for they were all too fast held by their anchors; so that the boldest part of my enterprise remained. I therefore let go the cord, and leaving the hooks fixed to the ships, I resolutely cut with my knife the cables that fastened the anchors; receiving above two hundred shots in my face and hands. Then I took up the knotted end of the cables to which my hooks were tied; and with great ease drew fifty of the enemy's largest men-of-war after me.

The Blefuscudians, who had not the least imagination of what I intended, were at first confounded with astonishment. They had seen me cut the cables, and thought my design was only to let the ships run adrift, or fall foul on each other; but when they perceived the whole fleet moving in order, and saw me pulling at the end, they set up such a scream of grief and despair that it is almost impossible to describe or conceive. When I had got out of danger, I stopped a while to pick out the arrows that stuck in my hands and face, and rubbed on some of the same ointment that was given me at my first arrival, as I have formerly mentioned. I then took off my spectacles and, waiting about an hour until the tide was a little fallen, I waded through the middle with my cargo, and arrived safe at the royal port of Lilliput.

The Emperor and his whole court stood on the shore, expecting the issue of this great adventure. They saw the ships move forward in a large half-moon, but could not discern me, who was up to my breast in water. When I advanced to the middle of the channel, they were yet more in pain because I was under water to my neck. The Emperor concluded me to be drowned, and that the enemy's fleet was approaching in a hostile manner; but he was soon eased of his fears, for the channel growing shallower every step I made, I came in a short time within hearing and, holding up the end of the cable by which the fleet was fastened, I cried in a loud voice, *Long live the most puissant Emperor of Lilliput!* This great Prince received me at my landing with all possible encomiums, and created me a Nardac upon the spot, which is the highest title of honour among them.

[*After sailing away from Lilliput, Captain Gulliver is soon stepping ashore in another land where everything turns out to be on a huge scale. Here a blade of grass is as tall as a man and a wasp is as big as a partridge.*]

I fell into a high road, for so I took it to be, although it served to the inhabitants only as a footpath through a field of barley. Here I walked on for some time, but could see little on either side, it being now near harvest and the corn rising at least forty foot. I was an hour walking to the end of this field; which was fenced in with a hedge of at least one hundred and twenty foot high, and the trees so lofty that I could make no computation of their altitude. There was a stile to pass from this field into the next : it had four steps, and a stone to cross over when you came to the utmost. It was impossible for me to climb this stile, because every step was six foot high, and the upper stone above twenty. I was endeavouring to find some gap in the hedge, when I discovered one of the inhabitants in the next field advancing towards the stile. . . . He appeared as tall as an ordinary spire steeple; and took about ten yards at every stride, as near as I could guess. I was struck with the utmost fear and astonishment, and ran to hide myself in the corn, from whence I saw him at the top of the stile, looking back into the next field on the right hand; and heard him call in a voice many degrees louder than a speaking trumpet; but the noise was so high in the air, that at first I certainly thought it was thunder. Whereupon seven monsters like himself came towards him

with reaping hooks in their hands, each hook about the largeness of six scythes. These people were not so well clad as the first, whose servants or labourers they seemed to be. For, upon some words he spoke, they went to reap the corn in the field where I lay. I kept from them at as great a distance as I could, but was forced to move with extreme difficulty; for the stalks of the corn were sometimes not above a foot distant, so that I could hardly squeeze my body betwixt them. However, I made a shift to go forward till I came to a part of the field where the corn had been laid by the rain and wind. Here it was impossible for me to advance a step; for the stalks were so interwoven that I could not creep through, and the beards of the fallen ears so strong and pointed that they pierced through my clothes into my flesh. At the same time I heard the reapers not above an hundred yards behind me.

Being quite dispirited with toil, and wholly overcome by grief and despair, I lay down between two ridges, and heartily wished I might there end my days. I bemoaned my desolate widow, and fatherless children; I lamented my own folly and wilfulness in attempting a second voyage against the advice of all my friends and relations. In this terrible agitation of mind I could not forbear thinking of Lilliput, whose inhabitants looked upon me as the greatest prodigy that ever appeared in the world; where I was able to draw an imperial fleet in my hand, and perform those other actions which will be recorded for ever in the chronicles of that empire, while posterity shall hardly believe them, although attested by millions. I reflected what a mortification it must prove to me to appear as inconsiderable in this nation, as one single Lilliputian would be among us.

But this I conceived was to be the least of my misfortunes; for, as human creatures are observed to be more savage and cruel in proportion to their bulk, what could I expect but to be a morsel in the mouth of the first among these enormous bar-barians who should happen to seize me?

. . . Scared and confounded as I was, I could not forbear going on with these reflections; when one of the reapers approaching within ten yards of the ridge where I lay, made me apprehend that with the next step I should be squashed to death under his foot, or cut in two with his reap-ing hook. And therefore when he was again about to move, I screamed as loud as fear could make me. Whereupon the huge creature trod short, and looking round about under him for some time, at last espied me as I lay on the ground. He con-sidered a while with the caution of one who endeavours to lay hold on a small dangerous animal in such a manner that it shall not be able either to scratch or to bite him; as I myself have sometimes done with a weasel in England. At length he ventured to take me up behind by the middle between his forefinger and thumb, and brought me within three yards of his eyes, that he

might behold my shape more perfectly. I guessed his meaning; and my good fortune gave me so much presence of mind, that I resolved not to struggle in the least as he held me in the air above sixty foot from the ground; although he grievously pinched my sides, for fear I should slip through his fingers. All I ventured was to raise my eyes towards the sun, and place my hands together in a supplicating pos-ture, and to speak some words in an humble melancholy tone, suitable to the condition I then was in. For I appre-hended every moment that he would dash me against the ground, as we usually do any little hateful animal which we have a mind to destroy. But my good star would have it, that he appeared pleased with my voice and gestures, and began to look upon me as a curiosity; much wondering to hear me pronounce articulate words, although he could not understand them. In the meantime I was not able to forbear groan-ing and shedding tears, and turning my head towards my sides; letting him know, as well as I could, how cruelly I was hurt by the pressure of his thumb and finger. He seemed to apprehend my meaning; for lifting up the lappet of his coat, he put me gently into it, and immediately ran along with me to his master, who was a substan-tial farmer, and the same person I had first seen in the field.

The farmer having (as I supposed by their talk) received such an account of me as his servant could give him, took a piece of a small straw, about the size of a walk-ing staff, and therewith lifted up the lappets of my coat; which it seems he thought to be some kind of covering that Nature had given me. He blew my hairs aside to take a better view of my face. He called his hinds about him and asked them (as I afterwards learned) whether they had ever seen in the fields any little creature that resembled me. He then placed me softly on the ground upon all four; but I got immediately up, and walked slowly backwards and forwards, to let those people see I had no intent to run away. They all sat down in a circle about me, the better to observe my motions. I pulled off my hat, and made a low bow towards the farmer. I fell on my knees, and lifted up my hands and eyes, and spoke several words as loud as I could. I took a purse of gold out of my pocket, and humbly presented it to him. He received it on the palm of his hand, then applied it close to his eye, to see what it was, and afterwards turned it several times with the point of a pin (which he took out of his sleeve), but could make nothing of it. Whereupon I made a sign that he should place his hand on the ground; I then took the purse, and opening it, poured all the gold into his palm. There were six Spanish pieces of four pistoles each, besides twenty or thirty smaller coins. I saw him wet the tip of his little finger upon his tongue, and take up one of my largest pieces, and then another; but he seemed to be wholly ignorant what they were. He made me a sign to put them again into my purse, and the purse again into my pocket; which after offering to him several times, I thought it best to do.

The farmer by this time was convinced I must be a rational creature. He spoke often to me, but the sound of his voice pierced my ears like that of a water-mill; yet his words were articulate enough. I answered as loud as I could in several languages; and he often laid his ear within two yards of me, but all in vain, for we were wholly unintelligible to each other. He then sent his servants to their work, and taking his handkerchief out of his pocket, he doubled and spread it on his hand, which he placed flat on the ground with the palm upwards, making me a sign to step into it, as I could easily do, for it was not above a foot in thickness. I thought it my part to obey; and for fear of falling, laid myself at full length upon the handkerchief, with the remainder of which he lapped me up to the head for further security; and in this manner carried me home to his house. There he called his

wife, and shewed me to her; but she screamed and ran back as women in England do at the sight of a toad or a spider. However, when she had a while seen my behaviour, and how well I observed the signs her husband made, she was soon reconciled, and by degrees grew extremely tender of me.

[His captor's little daughter, a child of nine (who is herself about as tall as a cottage), becomes very fond of Gulliver, carrying him about in a little box, quilted inside with soft cloth and tied about her waist. And he needs her protection, for on one occasion a baby seizes him, shakes him like a rattle and puts his head in its mouth, and on another he is attacked by two rats and manages with difficulty to slay them with his sword—which is about as big as a needle compared with the rats. At length Gulliver is taken to the King and Queen of Brobdingnag to whom he is like a new toy, to be played with and admired.]

The Queen became so fond of my company that she could not dine without me. I had a table placed upon the same at which Her Majesty ate, just at her left elbow; and a chair to sit on. My little nurse stood upon a stool on the floor, near my table, to assist and take care of me. I had an entire set of silver dishes and plates, and other necessaries, which in proportion to those of the Queen, were not much bigger than what I have seen in a London toyshop, for the furniture of a baby house. These my little nurse kept in her pocket, in a silver box, and gave me at meals as I wanted them; always cleaning them herself.

No person dined with the Queen but the two Princesses Royal; the elder sixteen years old, and the younger at that time thirteen and a month. Her Majesty used to put a bit of meat upon one of my dishes, out of which I carved for myself; and her diversion was to see me eat in miniature. For the Queen (who had indeed but a weak stomach) took up at one mouthful, as

This malicious cub . . . let me drop into a large silver bowl of cream.

much as a dozen English farmers could eat at a meal, which to me was for some time a very nauseous sight. She would crunch the wing of a lark, bones and all, between her teeth, although it were nine times as large as that of a full-grown turkey; and put a bit of bread in her mouth, as big as two twelve-penny loaves. She drank out of a golden cup, above a hogshead at a draught. Her knives were twice as long as a scythe set straight upon the handle. The spoons, forks, and other instruments were all in the same proportion. I remember when my nurse carried me out of curiosity to see some of the tables at court, where ten or a dozen of these enormous knives and forks were lifted up together; I thought I had never till then beheld so terrible a sight. . . .

Nothing angered and mortified me so much as the Queen's Dwarf, who being of the lowest stature that was ever in that country (for I verily think he was not full thirty foot high), became so insolent at seeing a creature so much beneath him, that he would always affect to swagger and look big as he passed by me in the Queen's antechamber, while I was standing on some table talking with the Lords or Ladies of the Court; and he seldom failed of a smart word or two upon my littleness; against which I could only revenge myself by calling him Brother, challenging him to wrestle; and such repartees as are usual in the mouths of Court pages. One day at dinner this malicious little cub was so nettled with something I had said to him that, raising himself upon the frame of Her Majesty's chair, he took me up by the middle, as I was sitting down, not thinking any harm, and let me drop into a large silver bowl of cream; and then ran away as fast as he could. I fell over head and ears, and if I had not been a good swimmer it might have gone very hard with me; for my attendant in that instant happened to be at the other end of the room; and the Queen was in such a fright that she wanted

presence of mind to assist me. But my little nurse ran to my relief and took me out after I had swallowed above a quart of cream. I was put to bed; however, I received no other damage than the loss of a suit of clothes, which was utterly spoiled. The Dwarf was soundly whipped, and as a further punishment forced to drink up the bowl of cream, into which he had thrown me; neither was he ever restored to favour; for soon after, the Queen bestowed him to a lady of high quality; so that I saw him no more, to my very great satisfaction; for I could not tell to what extremities such a malicious urchin might have carried his resentment. . . .

I was frequently railed by the Queen upon account of my fearfulness; and she used to ask me whether the people of my country were as great cowards as myself. The occasion was this. The kingdom is much pestered with flies in summer; and these odious insects, each of them as big as a Dunstable lark, hardly gave me any rest while I sat at dinner, with their continual humming and buzzing about my ears. Sometimes they would fix upon my nose or forehead, where they stung me to the quick, smelling very offensively; and I could easily trace that viscous matter, which our naturalists tell us enables those creatures to walk with their feet upwards upon a ceiling. I had much ado to defend myself against these detestable animals, and could not forbear starting when they came on my face. It was the common practice of the Dwarf to catch a number of these insects in his hand, as schoolboys do among us, and let them out suddenly under my nose on purpose to frighten me, and divert the Queen. My remedy was to cut them in pieces with my knife as they flew in the air; wherein my dexterity was much admired.

I remember one morning when my nurse had set me in my box upon a window, as she usually did in fair days to give me air (for I durst not venture to let the box be hung on a nail out of the window, as we do with cages in England), after I had lifted up one of my sashes, and sat down at my table to eat a piece of sweetcake for my breakfast; above twenty wasps, allured by the smell, came flying into the room, humming louder than the drones of as many bagpipes. Some of them seized my cake, and carried it piecemeal away; others flew about my head and face, confounding me with the noise, and putting me in the utmost terror of their stings. However, I had the courage to rise and draw my hanger, and attack them in the air. I dispatched four of them, but the rest got away; and I presently shut my window. These insects were as large as partridges; I took out their stings, found them an inch and a half long, and as sharp as needles. I carefully preserved them all, and having since shewn them with some other curiosities in several parts of Europe; upon my return to England I gave three of them to Gresham College, and kept the fourth for myself.

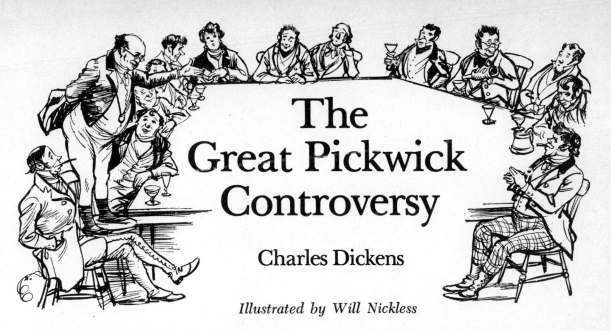

The Great Pickwick Controversy

Charles Dickens

Illustrated by Will Nickless

Here is another piece from Dickens, this time from "The Posthumous Papers of the Pickwick Club". Old Mr. Pickwick had so many diverting adventures that we sometimes forget how he started his travels as a member of an antiquarian society, for which he made at least one important discovery—which turns into an absurdity. The author is like a schoolboy devising a practical joke. Here we find Pickwick and his friend Tupman taking a little walk in the village of Cobham:

I T was at this moment that Mr. Pickwick made that immortal discovery, which has been the pride and boast of his friends, and the envy of every antiquarian in this or any other country. They had passed the door of their inn, and walked a little way down the village, before they recollected the precise spot in which it stood. As they turned back, Mr. Pickwick's eye fell upon a small broken stone, partially buried in the ground, in front of a cottage door. He paused.

"This is very strange," said Mr. Pickwick.

"What is strange?" inquired Mr. Tupman, staring eagerly at every object near him, but the right one. "God bless me, what's the matter?"

This last was an ejaculation of irrepressible astonishment, occasioned by seeing Mr. Pickwick, in his enthusiasm for discovery, fall on his knees before the little stone, and commence wiping the dust off it with his pocket-handkerchief.

"There is an inscription here," said Mr. Pickwick.

"Is it possible?" said Mr. Tupman.

"I can discern," continued Mr. Pickwick, rubbing away with all his might, and gazing intently through his spectacles: "I can discern a cross, a B, and then a T. This is important," continued Mr. Pickwick, starting up. "This is some very old inscription, existing perhaps long before the ancient alms-houses in this place. It must not be lost."

He tapped at the cottage door. A labouring man opened it.

"Do you know how this stone came here, my friend?" inquired the benevolent Mr. Pickwick.

"No, I doan't, sir," replied the man civilly. "It was here long afore I war born, or any on us."

Mr. Pickwick glanced triumphantly at his companion.

"You — you — are not particularly attached to it, I dare say," said Mr.

Pickwick, trembling with anxiety. "You wouldn't mind selling it, now?"

"Ah! but who'd buy it?" inquired the man, with an expression of face which he probably meant to be very cunning.

"I'll give you ten shillings for it, at once," said Mr. Pickwick, "if you would take it up for me."

The astonishment of the village may be easily imagined, when (the little stone having been raised with one wrench of a spade), Mr. Pickwick, by dint of great personal exertion, bore it with his own hands to the inn, and after having carefully washed it, deposited it on the table.

The exultation and joy of the Pickwickians knew no bounds, when their patience and assiduity, their washing and scraping, were crowned with success. The stone was uneven and broken, and the letters were straggling and irregular, but the following fragment of an inscription was clearly to be deciphered:

+
B I L S T
U M
P S H I
S. M.
A R K

Mr. Pickwick's eyes sparkled with delight, as he sat and gloated over the treasure he had discovered. He had attained one of the greatest objects of his ambition. In a county known to abound in remains of the early ages; in a village in which there still existed some memorials of the olden time, he—he, the Chairman of the Pickwick Club—had discovered a strange and curious inscription of un-questionable antiquity, which had wholly escaped the observation of the many learned men who had preceded him. He could hardly trust the evidence of his senses.

"This—this," said he, "determines me. We return to town, to-morrow."

"To-morrow!" exclaimed his admiring followers.

"To-morrow," said Mr. Pickwick. "This treasure must be at once deposited where it can be thoroughly investigated, and properly understood. I have another reason for this step. In a few days, an election is to take place for the borough of Eatanswill, at which Mr. Perker, a gentleman whom I lately met, is the agent of one of the candidates. We will behold, and minutely examine, a scene so interest-ing to every Englishman."

"We will," was the animated cry of three voices.

Mr. Pickwick looked round him. The attachment and fervour of his followers, lighted up a glow of enthusiasm within him. He was their leader, and he felt it.

"Let us celebrate this happy meeting with a convivial glass," said he. This proposition, like the other, was received with unanimous applause. Having him-self deposited the important stone in a small deal box, purchased from the land-lady for the purpose, he placed himself in an armchair at the head of the table; and the evening was devoted to festivity and conversation.

It was past eleven o'clock—a late hour for the little village of Cobham—when Mr. Pickwick retired to the bedroom which had been prepared for his reception. He threw open the lattice-window, and setting his light upon the table, fell into a train of meditation on the hurried events of the two preceding days.

The hour and the place were both favourable to contemplation; Mr. Pickwick was roused by the church-clock striking twelve. The first stroke of the hour sounded solemnly in his ear, but when the bell ceased the stillness seemed insupportable—he almost felt as if he had lost a companion. He was nervous and excited; and hastily undressing himself and placing his light in the chimney, got into bed.

The sun was shining brilliantly into his chamber when he awoke, and the morning was far advanced. The gloom which had oppressed him on the previous night, had disappeared with the dark shadows which shrouded the landscape, and his thoughts and feelings were as light and gay as the morning itself. After a hearty breakfast, the four gentlemen sallied forth to walk to Gravesend, followed by a man bearing the stone in its deal box. They reached that town about one o'clock (their luggage they had directed to be forwarded to the City, from Rochester), and being fortunate enough to secure places on the outside of a coach, arrived in London in sound health and spirits, on that same afternoon.

The next three or four days were occupied with the preparations which were necessary for their journey to the borough of Eatanswill. As any reference to that most important undertaking demands a separate chapter, we may devote the few lines which remain at the close of this, to narrate, with great brevity, the history of the antiquarian discovery.

It appears from the Transactions of the Club, then, that Mr. Pickwick lectured upon the discovery at a General Club Meeting, convened on the night succeeding their return, and entered into a variety of ingenious and erudite speculations on the meaning of the inscription. It also appears that a skilful artist executed a faithful delineation of the curiosity, which was engraven on stone, and presented to the Royal Antiquarian Society, and other learned bodies—that heartburnings and jealousies without number, were created by rival controversies which were penned upon the subject—and that Mr. Pickwick himself wrote a Pamphlet, containing ninety-six pages of very small print, and twenty-seven different readings of the inscription. That three old gentlemen cut off their eldest sons with a shilling a-piece for presuming to doubt the antiquity of the fragment—and that one enthusiastic individual cut himself off prematurely, in despair at being unable to fathom its meaning. That Mr. Pickwick was elected an honorary member of seventeen native and foreign societies, for making the discovery; that none of the seventeen could make anything of it; but that all the seventeen agreed it was very extraordinary.

Mr. Blotton, indeed—and the name will be doomed to the undying contempt of those who cultivate the mysterious and the sublime—Mr. Blotton, we say, with the doubt and cavilling peculiar to vulgar

minds, presumed to state a view of the case, as degrading as ridiculous. Mr. Blotton, with a mean desire to tarnish the lustre of the immortal name of Pickwick, actually undertook a journey to Cobham in person, and on his return, sarcastically observed in an oration at the club, that he had seen the man from whom the stone was purchased; that the man presumed the stone to be ancient, but solemnly denied the antiquity of the inscription—inasmuch as he represented it to have been rudely carved by himself in an idle mood, and to display letters intended to bear neither more nor less than the simple construction of "BILL STUMPS, HIS MARK"; and that Mr. Stumps, being little in the habit of original composition, and more accustomed to be guided by the sound of words than by the strict rules of orthography, had omitted the concluding "L" of his christian name.

The Pickwick Club (as might have been expected from so enlightened an Institution) received this statement with the contempt it deserved, expelled the presumptuous and ill-conditioned Blotton, and voted Mr. Pickwick a pair of gold spectacles, in token of their confidence and approbation; in return for which, Mr. Pickwick caused a portrait of himself to be painted, and hung up in the club room.

Mr. Blotton though ejected was not conquered. He also wrote a pamphlet, addressed to the seventeen learned societies, native and foreign, containing a repetition of the statement he had already made, and rather more than half intimating his opinion that the seventeen learned societies were so many "humbugs". Hereupon the virtuous indignation of the seventeen learned societies, native and foreign, being roused, several fresh pamphlets appeared; the foreign learned societies corresponded with the native learned societies; the native learned societies translated the pamphlets of the foreign learned societies into English; the foreign learned societies translated the pamphlets of the native learned societies into all sorts of languages; and thus commenced that celebrated scientific discussion so well known to all men, as the Pickwick controversy.

But this base attempt to injure Mr. Pickwick, recoiled upon the head of its calumnious author. The seventeen learned societies unanimously voted the presumptuous Blotton an ignorant meddler, and forthwith set to work upon more treatises than ever. And to this day the stone remains an illegible monument of Mr. Pickwick's greatness, and a lasting trophy to the littleness of his enemies.

The Solitude of Alexander Selkirk

(The seaman, whose life on a desert island gave
Defoe the theme of 'Robinson Crusoe')

I am monarch of all I survey;
My right there is none to dispute;
From the centre all round to the sea
I am lord of the fowl and the brute.
O Solitude! where are the charms
That sages have seen in thy face?
Better dwell in the midst of alarms,
Than reign in this horrible place.

I am out of humanity's reach,
I must finish my journey alone,
Never hear the sweet music of speech;
I start at the sound of my own.
The beasts that roam over the plain
My form with indifference see;
They are so unacquainted with man,
Their tameness is shocking to me.

Society, Friendship, and Love
Divinely bestow'd upon man,
Oh, had I the wings of a dove
How soon would I taste you again!
My sorrows I then mght assuage
In the ways of religion and truth,
Might learn from the wisdom of age,
And be cheer'd by the sallies of youth.

Ye winds that have made me your sport,
Convey to this desolate shore
Some cordial endearing report
Of a land I shall visit no more:
My friends, do they now and then send
A wish or a thought after me?
O tell me I yet have a friend,
Though a friend I am never to see.

How fleet is a glance of the mind!
Compared with the speed of its flight,
The tempest itself lags behind,
And the swift-wingéd arrows of light.
When I think of my own native land
In a moment I seem to be there;
But alas! recollection at hand
Soon hurries me back to despair.

But the sea-fowl is gone to her nest,
The beast is laid down in his lair;
Even here is a season of rest,
And I to my cabin repair.
There's mercy in every place,
And mercy, encouraging thought!
Gives even affliction a grace
And reconciles man to his lot.

WILLIAM COWPER

Acknowledgements

By arrangement with publishers, authors, artists and other owners of copyright, permission has been accorded to include certain copyright stories, poems and drawings in this book. The publishers have made every effort to trace copyright holders. If we have inadvertently omitted to acknowledge anyone we should be most grateful if this could be brought to our attention for correction at the first opportunity. Our thanks and acknowledgement for their help and courtesy are due to the following:

To G. Bell and Sons, Ltd., for "Peter Pan meets Wendy" from *The Story of Peter Pan*, retold from Barrie's play by Daniel O'Connor. To Ernest Benn, Ltd., for "The Deliverers of their Country" from *The Book of Dragons*, by E. Nesbit, with accompanying illustrations by Ronald Searle. To the Bodley Head and the author for "The Pool in the Forest" from *Brendon Chase* by "B. B." To Jonathan Cape, Ltd., and the author for "A Lesson in Tickling Trout" from *The Picts and the Martyrs*, by Arthur Ransome; for "Erich plays Detective" from *When I was a Little Boy*, by Erich Kästner, translated by Isabel and Florence McHugh and the drawing by Horst Lemke in the same book; to the publisher and Christopher Lofting for "The Rarest Animal of All" from *The Story of Dr. Dolittle* and for "The Great Bullfight" from *The Voyages of Dr. Dolittle*, both by Hugh Lofting, and for the accompanying drawings by the author; for "His First Flight" from *The Short Stories of Liam O'Flaherty* by Liam O'Flaherty. To Chatto and Windus, Ltd., and the author for "The Dark Child" from *The Spider's Palace*, by Richard Hughes; and to the same publishers and Laurence Whistler for a Rex Whistler illustration from that artist's edition of Hans Andersen's *Fairy Tales*. To James Clarke and Co. Ltd., for "The Prominent Man" from *The Golden Windows* by Laura E. Richards. To the author and Collins Publishers for "The Story of Cholmondeley" from *The New Noah*, by Gerald Durrell, copyright © Gerald Durrell 1955, and for an accompanying drawing by Ralph Thompson; for "Welcome back, Mary Poppins!" from *Mary Poppins opens the Door*, by P. L. Travers and for accompanying drawings by Mary Shepard. To Peter Davies, Ltd., for "The Raider" from *The Adventures of Sajo and the Beaver People*, by Grey Owl. To J. M. Dent and Sons, Ltd., and to Harcourt Brace Jovanovich Inc., for "Into the Unknown" from *The Borrowers Afield*, by Mary Norton; and to J. M. Dent and Sons, Ltd., and the author for "The Prize-giving" from *A Story-teller's Childhood*, by Patricia Lynch. To Eyre and Spottiswoode (Publishers), Ltd., and the author for "How the Trolls became Giants" from *The Death of the Dragon*, by J. B. Morton. To Faber and Faber, Ltd., and the author for "Susan goes to School" from *A Country Child*, by Alison Uttley; and for "The Rum Tum Tugger" from *Old Possum's Book of Practical Cats*, by T. S. Eliot. To George G. Harrap and Co., Ltd., for "Dick Whittington" and "What the Old Man does is always Right", with accompanying illustrations by Arthur Rackham, from *The Arthur Rackham Fairy Book*. To Sir Rupert Hart-Davis for "Jeremy at the Fair" from *Jeremy* by Sir Hugh Walpole. To William Heinemann, Ltd., for "Thomas dines in France" from *Alice and Thomas and Jane*, by Enid Bagnold; for translations of nine of Aesop's fables by V. S. Vernon Jones from *Aesop's Fables*, and for the accompanying illustrations by Arthur Rackham. To the Hutchinson Publishing Group Ltd., for "Don Quixote and the Windmills", retold by Majorie Hill and Audrey Walton. To Kaye and Ward Ltd., for "The Mermaid of Zennor" from *Folk Tales from the West* by Eileen Molony, copyright © Kaye and Ward Limited 1971. To the Literary Trustees of Walter de la Mare and the Society of Authors as their representatives, for "The Englishman", by Walter de la Mare. To Longmans, Green and Co., Ltd., and the Executrix of Sir Percy Fitzpatrick for "Lost in the Bushveld" from *Jock of the Bushveld*, by Sir Percy Fitzpatrick. To MacGibbon and Kee/Granada Publishing Ltd., and the author for "Theseus and the Minotaur" from *Men and Gods*, by Rex Warner. To The Macmillan Company of London and Basingstoke for three illustrations by Edmund J. Sullivan to "Tom Brown at Rugby" from *Tom Brown's Schooldays*; to the same publishers and the Executors of the Estate of Mrs Elsie Bambridge for "The Cat that walked by Himself" and an accompanying illustration by the author from *Just-So Stories*, by Rudyard Kipling. To Methuen and Co., Ltd., and McClelland and Stewart Ltd., for "A House for Eeyore" from *The House at Pooh Corner*, by A. A. Milne. To Methuen Children's Books Ltd., Text Copyright University Chest, Oxford, and Charles Scribner's Sons, New York, for "The Storming of Toad Hall" from *The Wind in the Willows*, by Kenneth Grahame. To Frederick Muller, Ltd., and the author for "Lily Rose and the Green Silk Petticoat" from *The Family at One End Street*, by Eve Garnett, and for the accompanying illustrations by the author. To John Murray (Publishers), Ltd., and the executors of Sir Arthur Conan Doyle for "Exploring the Lost World" from *The Lost World*, by Sir Arthur Conan Doyle. To Thomas Nelson and Sons, Ltd., and the author for "Salt" from *Old Peter's Russian Tales*, by Arthur Ransome. To the Oxford University Press and the author for "Robin Hood and the Potter" from *The Chronicles of Robin Hood*, by Rosemary Sutcliff; also for three illustrations by Robin Jacques from this illustrator's edition of *Gulliver's Travels*. To A. D. Peters and Co., Ltd., for "Kangaroos" from *The Wind on the Moon* by Eric Linklater. To the late Eden Phillpotts for "The Piebald Rat" from *The Human Boy*. To Putnam and Co., Ltd., for "The Three Magic Gifts" from *Tales from Ebony*, by Harcourt Williams. To the Executors of the Felix Salten Estate, and Simon and Schuster, Inc., for "A Narrow Escape" from *Bambi* by Felix Salten, and for the accompanying drawings by Kurt Wiese. To Charles Scribner's Sons, New York, for "My First Gun" from *Cowboy in the Making*, by Will James (copyright Charles Scribner's Sons), arranged from *Lone Cowboy*, by Will James, copyright 1930; renewed copyright 1958 Auguste Dufault. To Aubrey de Selincourt and Collins' Magazine for "Heroes". To the Estate of Ernest Shepard, E. P. Dutton Co., and Charles Scribner's Sons, for the illustrations accompanying the extracts from *The House at Pooh Corner* and *The Wind in the Willows*. To the Society of Authors as the literary representatives of the Estate of John Masefield and Macmillan Publishing Co., Inc., for "Sea-Fever". To the University of London Press, Ltd., and the author for "But that's not the end of the Story" from *A Book of Happy Tales*, by Margaret Baker, and for accompanying illustrations by Mary Baker.

The editor would like to acknowledge good counsel received from Roger Lancelyn Green's *Tellers of Tales* (Edmund Ward), which contains many out-of-the-way facts about children's writers; from May Lamberton Becker's *Choosing Books for Children* (Oxford University Press); from Geoffrey Trease's *Tales Out of School* (Heinemann); from Kathleen Line's useful survey of children's books in print, *Four to Fourteen* (Cambridge University Press), and from John Rowe Townsend's *Written for Children*.